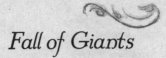

Fall of Giants

D1627195

FALL of GIANTS

Book One of The Century Trilogy
Circa 1914

PRAISE FOR THE NOVELS
OF KEN FOLLETT

Fall of Giants

"Follett at his finest . . . [a] sweeping epic that will thrill his fans for hours on end." —The Huffington Post

"Follett once again creates a world at once familiar and fantastic. . . . A guiltless pleasure, the book is impossible to put down. . . . Empires fall. Heroes rise. Love conquers. After going through a war with these characters, you're left hoping that Follett gets moving with the next giant installment." —*Time Out New York*

"Grand in scope, scale, and story." —The Associated Press

"Suspenseful, tightly constructed, sharply characterized, plot-driven." —*The Seattle Times*

World Without End

"[A] well-researched, beautifully detailed portrait of the late Middle Ages. . . . Follett's no-frills prose does its job, getting smoothly through more than a thousand pages of outlaws, war, death, sex, and politics to end with an edifice that is as well constructed and solid as Merthin's bridge. A." —*The Washington Post*

"Makes for giddy chutes-and-ladders reading . . . a breathless entertainment." —*Los Angeles Times*

"Juicy historical fiction." —*USA Today*

continued . . .

The Pillars of the Earth

"Enormous and brilliant ... crammed with characters un-
believably alive across the great gulf of centuries ... touches
all human emotion—love and hate, loyalty and treachery,
hope and despair. See for yourself. This is truly a novel to
get lost in."   *—Cosmopolitan*

"Wonderful ... will fascinate you, surround you."
                                                              —Chicago Sun-Times

"A towering tale ... a ripping read.... There's murder, ar-
son, treachery, torture, love, and lust."
                                                              —New York Daily News

"Ken Follett takes a giant step."*—San Francisco Chronicle*

"With this book, Follett risks all and comes out a clear
winner ... a historical novel of gripping readability, au-
thentic atmosphere, and memorable characterization. Beginning with a mystery that casts its shadow, the narrative is
a seesaw of tension, suspense, impeccable pacing ... action,
intrigue, violence, passion, greed, bravery, dedication, revenge, and love. A novel that entertains, instructs, and satis-
fies on a grand scale."   *—Publishers Weekly*

"An extraordinary epic buttressed by suspense ... a mysti-
fying puzzle involving the execution of an innocent man ...
the erection of a magnificent cathedral ... romance, rivalry,
and spectacle. A monumental masterpiece ... a towering
triumph from a major talent."   *—Booklist*

KEN FOLLETT

FALL *of* GIANTS

BOOK ONE OF THE CENTURY TRILOGY

A SIGNET BOOK

SIGNET
Published by New American Library, a division of
Penguin Group (USA) Inc., 375 Hudson Street,
New York, New York 10014, USA
Penguin Group (Canada), 90 Eglinton Avenue East, Suite 700, Toronto,
Ontario M4P 2Y3, Canada (a division of Pearson Penguin Canada Inc.)
Penguin Books Ltd., 80 Strand, London WC2R 0RL, England
Penguin Ireland, 25 St. Stephen's Green, Dublin 2,
Ireland (a division of Penguin Books Ltd.)
Penguin Group (Australia), 250 Camberwell Road, Camberwell, Victoria 3124,
Australia (a division of Pearson Australia Group Pty. Ltd.)
Penguin Books India Pvt. Ltd., 11 Community Centre, Panchsheel Park,
New Delhi - 110 017, India
Penguin Group (NZ), 67 Apollo Drive, Rosedale, Auckland 0632,
New Zealand (a division of Pearson New Zealand Ltd.)

Penguin Books (South Africa) (Pty.) Ltd., 24 Sturdee Avenue,
Rosebank, Johannesburg 2196, South Africa

Penguin Books Ltd., Registered Offices:
80 Strand, London WC2R 0RL, England

Published by Signet, an imprint of New American Library, a division of Penguin
Group (USA) Inc. Previously published in a Dutton edition.

Signet International Edition, June 2011
10 9 8 7 6 5 4 3 2 1

To the memory of my parents,

Martin and Veenie Follett

Cast of Characters

American

DEWAR FAMILY

Senator Cameron Dewar
Ursula Dewar, his wife
Gus Dewar, their son

VYALOV FAMILY

Josef Vyalov, businessman
Lena Vyalov, his wife
Olga Vyalov, their daughter

OTHERS

Rosa Hellman, journalist
Chuck Dixon, school friend of Gus's
Marga, nightclub singer
Nick Forman, thief
Ilya, thug
Theo, thug
Norman Niall, crooked accountant
Brian Hall, union leader

REAL HISTORICAL CHARACTERS

Woodrow Wilson, twenty-eighth president
William Jennings Bryan, secretary of state
Josephus Daniels, secretary of the navy

English and Scottish

FITZHERBERT FAMILY

Earl Fitzherbert, called Fitz

Princess Elizaveta, called Bea, his wife
Lady Maud Fitzherbert, his sister
Lady Hermia, called Aunt Herm, their poor aunt
Duchess of Sussex, their rich aunt
Gelert, Pyrenean mountain dog
Grout, Fitz's butler
Sanderson, Maud's maid

OTHERS

Mildred Perkins, Ethel Williams's lodger
Bernie Leckwith, secretary of the Aldgate branch of
    the Independent Labour Party
Bing Westhampton, Fitz's friend
Marquis of Lowther, "Lowthie," rejected suitor of
    Maud
Albert Solman, Fitz's man of business
Dr. Greenward, volunteer at the baby clinic
Lord "Johnny" Remarc, junior War Office minister
Colonel Hervey, aide to Sir John French
Lieutenant Murray, aide to Fitz
Mannie Litov, factory owner
Jock Reid, treasurer of the Aldgate Independent La-
    bour Party
Jayne McCulley, soldier's wife

REAL HISTORICAL CHARACTERS

King George V
Queen Mary
Mansfield Smith-Cumming, called "C," head of the
    Foreign Section of the Secret Service Bureau (later
    MI6)
Sir Edward Grey, M.P., foreign secretary
Sir William Tyrrell, private secretary to Grey
Frances Stevenson, mistress of Lloyd George
Winston Churchill, M.P.
H. H. Asquith, M.P., prime minister
Sir John French, commander of the British Expedition-
    ary Force

French

    Gini, a bar girl
    Colonel Dupuys, aide to General Galliéni
    General Lourceau, aide to General Joffre

REAL HISTORICAL CHARACTERS

    General Joffre, commander in chief of French forces
    General Galliéni, commander of the Paris garrison

German and Austrian

VON ULRICH FAMILY

    Otto von Ulrich, diplomat
    Susanne von Ulrich, his wife
    Walter von Ulrich, their son, military attaché at the
        German embassy in London
    Greta von Ulrich, their daughter
    Graf (Count) Robert von Ulrich, Walter's second
        cousin, military attaché at the Austrian embassy in
        London

OTHERS

    Gottfried von Kessel, cultural attaché at the German
        embassy in London
    Monika von der Helbard, Greta's best friend

REAL HISTORICAL CHARACTERS

    Prince Karl Lichnowsky, German ambassador to
        London
    Field Marshal Paul von Hindenburg
    General of Infantry Erich Ludendorff
    Theobald von Bethmann-Hollweg, German chancellor
    Arthur Zimmermann, German foreign minister

Russian

Peshkov family

Grigori Peshkov, metalworker
Lev Peshkov, horse wrangler

Putilov Machine Works

Konstantin, lathe operator, chairman of the Bolshevik
    discussion group
Isaak, captain of the football team
Varya, female laborer, Konstantin's mother
Serge Kanin, supervisor of the casting section
Count Maklakov, director

Others

Mikhail Pinsky, police officer
Ilya Kozlov, his sidekick
Nina, maid to Princess Bea
Prince Andrei, Bea's brother
Katerina, a peasant girl new to the city
Mishka, bar owner
Trofim, gangster
Fyodor, corrupt cop
Spirya, passenger on the *Angel Gabriel*
Yakov, passenger on the *Angel Gabriel*
Anton, clerk at the Russian embassy in London, also a
    spy for Germany
David, Jewish soldier
Sergeant Gavrik
Lieutenant Tomchak

Real historical characters

Vladimir Ilyich Lenin, leader of the Bolshevik Party
Leon Trotsky

Welsh

WILLIAMS FAMILY

David Williams, union organizer
Cara Williams, his wife
Ethel Williams, their daughter
Billy Williams, their son
Gramper, Cara's father

GRIFFITHS FAMILY

Len Griffiths, atheist and Marxist
Mrs. Griffiths
Tommy Griffiths, their son, Billy Williams's best friend

PONTI FAMILY

Mrs. Minnie Ponti
Giuseppe "Joey" Ponti, her son
Giovanni "Johnny" Ponti, his younger brother

MINERS

David Crampton, "Dai Crybaby"
Harry "Suet" Hewitt
John Jones the Shop
Dai Chops, the butcher's son
Pat Pope, Main Level onsetter
Micky Pope, Pat's son
Dai Ponies, horse wrangler
Bert Morgan

MINE MANAGEMENT

Perceval Jones, chairman of Celtic Minerals
Maldwyn Morgan, colliery manager
Rhys Price, colliery manager's deputy
Arthur "Spotty" Llewellyn, colliery clerk

STAFF AT TŷGWYN

Peel, butler
Mrs. Jevons, housekeeper
Morrison, footman

OTHERS

Dai Muck, sanitary worker
Mrs. Dai Ponies
Mrs. Roley Hughes
Mrs. Hywel Jones
Private George Barrow, B Company
Private Robin Mortimer, cashiered officer, B Company
Private Owen Bevin, B Company
Sergeant Elijah "Prophet" Jones, B Company
Second Lieutenant James Carlton-Smith, B Company
Captain Gwyn Evans, A Company
Second Lieutenant Roland Morgan, A Company

REAL HISTORICAL CHARACTERS

David Lloyd George, Liberal member of Parliament

PROLOGUE

INITIATION

CHAPTER ONE

June 22, 1911

On the day King George V was crowned at Westminster Abbey in London, Billy Williams went down the pit in Aberowen, South Wales. The twenty-second of June, 1911, was Billy's thirteenth birthday. He was woken by his father. Da's technique for waking people was more effective than it was kind. He patted Billy's cheek, in a regular rhythm, firmly and insistently. Billy was in a deep sleep, and for a second he tried to ignore it, but the patting went on relentlessly. Momentarily he felt angry; but then he remembered that he had to get up, he even wanted to get up, and he opened his eyes and sat upright with a jerk.

"Four o'clock," Da said; then he left the room, his boots banging on the wooden staircase as he went down.

Today Billy would begin his working life by becoming an apprentice collier, as most of the men in town had done at his age. He wished he felt more like a miner. But he was determined not to make a fool of himself. David Crampton had cried on his first day down the pit, and they still called him Dai Crybaby, even though he was twenty-five and the star of the town's rugby team.

It was the day after midsummer, and a bright early light came through the small window. Billy looked at his grandfather, lying beside him. Gramper's eyes were open. He was always awake, whenever Billy got up; he said old people did not sleep much.

Billy got out of bed. He was wearing only his underdrawers. In cold weather he wore his shirt to bed, but Britain was enjoying a hot summer, and the nights were mild. He pulled the pot from under the bed and took off the lid.

There was no change in the size of his penis, which he called his peter. It was still the childish stub it had always been. He had hoped it might have started to grow on the night before his birthday, or perhaps that he might see just one black hair sprouting somewhere near it, but he was disappointed. His best friend, Tommy Griffiths, who had been born on the same day, was different: he had a cracked voice and a dark fuzz on his upper lip, and his peter was like a man's. It was humiliating.

As Billy was using the pot, he looked out of the window. All he could see was the slag heap, a slate-gray mountain of tailings, waste from the coal mine, mostly shale and sandstone. This was how the world appeared on the second day of Creation, Billy thought, before God said: "Let the earth bring forth grass." A gentle breeze wafted fine black dust off the slag onto the rows of houses.

Inside the room there was even less to look at. This was the back bedroom, a narrow space just big enough for the single bed, a chest of drawers, and Gramper's old trunk. On the wall was an embroidered sampler that read:

BELIEVE ON THE
LORD JESUS CHRIST
AND THOU SHALT
BE SAVED

There was no mirror.

One door led to the top of the stairs, the other to the front bedroom, which could be accessed only through this one. It was larger and had space for two beds. Da and Mam slept there, and Billy's sisters had, too, years ago. The eldest, Ethel, had now left home, and the other three had died, one from measles, one from whooping cough, and one from diphtheria. There had been an older brother, too, who had shared Billy's bed before Gramper came. Wesley had been his name, and he had been killed underground by a runaway dram, one of the wheeled tubs that carried coal.

Billy pulled on his shirt. It was the one he had worn to school yesterday. Today was Thursday, and he changed his shirt only on Sunday. However, he did have a new pair of trousers, his first long ones, made of the thick water-repellent cotton called moleskin. They were the symbol of entry into the world of men, and he pulled them on proudly, enjoying the heavy masculine feel of the fabric. He put on a thick leather belt and the boots he had inherited from Wesley; then he went downstairs.

Most of the ground floor was taken up by the living room, fifteen feet square, with a table in the middle and a fireplace to one side, and a homemade rug on the stone floor. Da was sitting at the table reading an old copy of the *Daily Mail*, a pair of spectacles perched on the bridge of his long, sharp nose. Mam was making tea. She put down the steaming kettle, kissed Billy's forehead, and said: "How's my little man on his birthday?"

Billy did not reply. The "little" was wounding, because he was little, and the "man" was just as hurtful because he was not a man. He went into the scullery at the back of the house. He dipped a tin bowl into the water barrel, washed his face and hands, and poured the water away in the shallow stone sink. The scullery had a copper with a fire grate underneath, but it was used only on bath night, which was Saturday.

They had been promised running water soon, and some of the miners' houses already had it. It seemed a miracle to Billy that people could get a cup of cold clear water just by turning the tap, and not have to carry a bucket to the standpipe out in the street. But indoor water had not yet come to Wellington Row, where the Williamses lived.

He returned to the living room and sat at the table. Mam put a big cup of milky tea in front of him, already sugared. She cut two thick slices off a loaf of homemade bread and got a slab of dripping from the pantry under the stairs. Billy put his hands together, closed his eyes, and said: "Thank you, Lord, for this food. Amen." Then he drank some tea and spread dripping on his bread.

Da's pale blue eyes looked over the top of the paper. "Put salt on your bread," he said. "You'll sweat underground."

Billy's father was a miners' agent, employed by the South Wales Miners' Federation, which was the strongest trade union in Britain, as he said whenever he got the chance. He was known as Dai Union. A lot of men were called Dai, pronounced "die," short for David, or Dafydd in Welsh. Billy had learned in school that David was popular in Wales because it was the name of the country's patron saint, like Patrick in Ireland. All the Dais were distinguished one from another not by their surnames—almost everyone in town was Jones, Williams, Evans, or Morgan—but by a nickname. Real names were rarely used when there was a humorous alternative. Billy was William Williams, so they called him Billy Twice. Women were sometimes given their husband's nickname, so that Mam was Mrs. Dai Union.

Gramper came down while Billy was eating his second slice. Despite the warm weather he wore a jacket and waistcoat. When he had washed his hands he sat opposite Billy. "Don't look so nervous," he said. "I went down the pit when I was ten. And *my* father was carried to the pit on his father's back at the age of five, and worked from six in the morning until seven in the evening. He never saw daylight from October to March."

"I'm not nervous," Billy said. This was untrue. He was scared stiff.

However, Gramper was kindly, and he did not press the point. Billy liked Gramper. Mam treated Billy like a baby, and Da was stern and sarcastic, but Gramper was tolerant and talked to Billy as to an adult.

"Listen to this," said Da. He would never buy the *Mail,* a right-wing rag, but he sometimes brought home someone else's copy and read the paper aloud in a scornful voice, mocking the stupidity and dishonesty of the ruling class. "'Lady Diana Manners has been criticized for wearing the same dress to two different balls. The younger daughter of the Duke of Rutland won "best lady's costume" at the Savoy Ball for her off-the-shoulder boned bodice with full hooped skirt, receiving a prize of two hundred and fifty guineas.'" He lowered the paper and said: "That's at least five years' wages for you, Billy boy." He resumed: "'But she drew the frowns of the cognoscenti by wearing the same dress to Lord Winterton and F. E. Smith's party at Claridge's Hotel. One can have too much of a good thing, people said.'" He looked up from the paper. "You'd better change that frock, Mam," he said. "You don't want to draw the frowns of the cognoscenti."

Mam was not amused. She was wearing an old brown

wool dress with patched elbows and stains under the armpits. "If I had two hundred and fifty guineas, I'd look better than Lady Diana Muck," she said, not without bitterness.

"It's true," Gramper said. "Cara was always the pretty one—just like her mother." Mam's name was Cara. Gramper turned to Billy. "Your grandmother was Italian. Her name was Maria Ferrone." Billy knew this, but Gramper liked to retell familiar stories. "That's where your mother gets her glossy black hair and lovely dark eyes—and your sister. Your gran was the most beautiful girl in Cardiff—and I got her!" Suddenly he looked sad. "Those were the days," he said quietly.

Da frowned with disapproval—such talk suggested the lusts of the flesh—but Mam was cheered by her father's compliments, and she smiled as she put his breakfast in front of him. "Oh, aye," she said. "Me and my sisters were considered beauties. We'd show those dukes what a pretty girl is, if we had the money for silk and lace."

Billy was surprised. He had never thought of his mother as beautiful or otherwise, though when she dressed for the chapel social on Saturday evening she did look striking, especially in a hat. He supposed she might once have been a pretty girl, but it was hard to imagine.

"Mind you," said Gramper, "your gran's family were clever, too. My brother-in-law was a miner, but he got out of the industry and opened a café in Tenby. Now there's a life for you—sea breezes, and nothing to do all day but make coffee and count your money."

Da read another item. "'As part of the preparations for the coronation, Buckingham Palace has produced a book of instructions two hundred and twelve pages long.'" He looked over the paper. "Mention that down the pit today, Billy. The men will be relieved to know that nothing has been left to chance."

Billy was not very interested in royalty. What he liked was the adventure stories the *Mail* often printed about tough rugby-playing public-school men catching sneaky German spies. According to the paper, such spies infested every town in Britain, although there did not seem to be any in Aberowen, disappointingly.

Billy stood up. "Going down the street," he announced. He left the house by the front door. "Going down the street" was a family euphemism: it meant going to the toilets, which stood halfway down Wellington Row. A low brick hut with a corrugated iron roof was built over a deep hole in the earth. The hut was divided into two compartments, one for men and one for women. Each compartment had a double seat, so that people went to the toilet two by two. No one knew why the builders had chosen this arrangement, but everyone made the best of it. Men looked straight ahead and said nothing, but—as Billy could often hear—women chatted companionably. The smell was suffocating, even when you experienced it every day of your life. Billy always tried to breathe as little as possible while he was inside, and came out gasping for air. The hole was shoveled out periodically by a man called Dai Muck.

When Billy returned to the house he was delighted to see his sister Ethel sitting at the table. "Happy birthday, Billy!" she cried. "I had to come and give you a kiss before you go down the pit."

Ethel was eighteen, and Billy had no trouble seeing *her* as beautiful. Her mahogany-colored hair was irrepressibly curly, and her dark eyes twinkled with mischief. Perhaps Mam had looked like this once. Ethel wore the plain black dress and white cotton cap of a housemaid, an outfit that flattered her.

Billy worshipped Ethel. As well as pretty, she was funny and clever and brave, sometimes even standing up to Da. She told Billy things no one else would explain, such as the monthly episode women called the curse, and what was the crime of public indecency that had caused the Anglican vicar to leave town in such a hurry. She had been top of the class all the way through school, and her essay "My Town or Village" had taken first prize in a contest run by the *South Wales Echo*. She had won a copy of *Cassell's Atlas of the World*.

She kissed Billy's cheek. "I told Mrs. Jevons the housekeeper that we were running out of boot polish and I'd better get some more from the town." Ethel lived and worked at Tŷ Gwyn, the vast home of Earl Fitzherbert, a mile away up the mountain. She handed Billy something wrapped in a clean rag. "I stole a piece of cake for you."

"Oh, thanks, Eth!" said Billy. He loved cake.

Mam said: "Shall I put it in your snap?"

"Aye, please."

Mam got a tin box from the cupboard and put the cake inside. She cut two more slabs of bread, spread them with dripping, sprinkled salt, and put them in the tin. All the miners had a "snap" tin. If they took food underground wrapped in a rag, the mice would eat it before the mid-morning break. Mam said: "When you bring me home your wages, you can have a slice of boiled bacon in your snap."

Billy's earnings would not be much, at first, but all the same they would make a difference to the family. He wondered how much Mam would allow him for pocket money and whether he would ever be able to save enough for a bicycle, which he wanted more than anything else in the world.

Ethel sat at the table. Da said to her: "How are things at the big house?"

"Nice and quiet," she said. "The earl and princess are in London for the coronation." She looked at the clock on the mantelpiece. "They'll be getting up soon—they need to be at the abbey early. *She* won't like it—she's not used to early hours—but she can't be late for the king." The earl's wife, Bea, was a Russian princess, and very grand.

Da said: "They'll want to get seats near the front, so they can see the show."

"Oh, no, you can't sit anywhere you like," Ethel said. "They've had six thousand mahogany chairs made special, with the names of the guests on the back in gold writing."

Gramper said: "Well, there's a waste! What will they do with them after?"

"I don't know. Perhaps everyone will take them home as souvenirs."

Da said dryly: "Tell them to send a spare one to us. There's only five of us here, and already your mam's got to stand."

When Da was being facetious there might be real anger underneath. Ethel leaped to her feet. "Oh, sorry, Mam. I didn't think."

"Stay where you are. I'm too busy to sit down," said Mam.

The clock struck five. Da said: "Best get there early, Billy boy. Start as you mean to go on."

Billy got to his feet reluctantly and picked up his snap.

Ethel kissed him again, and Gramper shook his hand. Da gave him two six-inch nails, rusty and a bit bent. "Put those in your trousers pocket."

"What for?" said Billy.

"You'll see," Da said with a smile.

Mam handed Billy a quart bottle with a screw top, full of cold tea with milk and sugar. She said: "Now, Billy, remember that Jesus is always with you, even down the pit."

"Aye, Mam."

He could see a tear in her eye, and he turned away quickly, because it made him feel weepy, too. He took his cap from the peg. "Bye, then," he said, as if he was only going to school; and he stepped out of the front door.

The summer had been hot and sunny so far, but today was overcast, and it even looked as if it might rain. Tommy was leaning against the wall of the house, waiting. "Aye, aye, Billy," he said.

"Aye, aye, Tommy."

They walked down the street side by side.

Aberowen had once been a small market town, serving hill farmers round about, Billy had learned in school. From the top of Wellington Row you could see the old commercial center, with the open pens of the cattle market, the wool exchange building, and the Anglican church, all on one side of the Owen River, which was little more than a stream. Now a railway line cut through the town like a wound, terminating at the pithead. The miners' houses had spread up the slopes of the valley, hundreds of gray stone homes with roofs of darker gray Welsh slate. They were built in long serpentine rows that followed the contours of the mountainsides, the rows crossed by shorter streets that plunged headlong to the valley bottom.

"Who do you think you'll be working with?" said Tommy.

Billy shrugged. New boys were assigned to one of the colliery manager's deputies. "No way to know."

"I hope they put me in the stables." Tommy liked horses. About fifty ponies lived in the mine. They pulled the drams that the colliers filled, drawing them along railway tracks. "What sort of work do you want to do?"

Billy hoped he would not be given a task too heavy for his childish physique, but he was not willing to admit that. "Greasing drams," he said.

"Why?"

"It seems easy."

They passed the school where yesterday they had been pupils. It was a Victorian building with pointed windows like a church. It had been built by the Fitzherbert family, as the headmaster never tired of reminding the pupils. The earl still appointed the teachers and decided the curriculum. On the walls were paintings of heroic military victories, and the greatness of Britain was a constant theme. In the Scripture lesson with which every day began, strict Anglican doctrines were taught, even though nearly all the children were from Nonconformist families. There was a school management committee, of which Da was a member, but it had no power except to advise. Da said the earl treated the school as his personal property.

In their final year Billy and Tommy had been taught the principles of mining, while the girls learned to sew and cook. Billy had been surprised to discover that the ground beneath him consisted of layers of different kinds of earth, like a stack of sandwiches. A coal seam—a phrase he had heard all his life without really understanding it—was one such layer. He had also been told that coal was made of dead leaves and other vegetable matter, accumulated over thousands of years and compressed by the weight of earth above it. Tommy, whose father was an atheist, said this proved the Bible was not true; but Billy's da said that was only one interpretation.

The school was empty at this hour, its playground deserted. Billy felt proud that he had left school behind, although part of him wished he could go back there instead of down the pit.

As they approached the pithead, the streets began to fill with miners, each with his snap tin and bottle of tea. They all dressed the same, in old suits that they would take off once they reached their workplace. Some mines were cold but Aberowen was a hot pit, and the men worked in underwear and boots, or in the coarse linen shorts they called bannickers. Everyone wore a padded cap, all the time, because tunnel roofs were low and it was easy to bang your head.

Over the houses Billy could see the winding gear, a tower topped by two great wheels rotating in opposite directions, drawing the cables that raised and lowered the cage. Similar pithead structures loomed over most towns in the South Wales valleys, the way church spires dominated farming villages.

Other buildings were scattered around the pithead as if dropped by accident: the lamp room, the colliery office, the smithy, the stores. Railway lines snaked between the buildings. On the waste ground were broken drams, old cracked timbers, feed sacks, and piles of rusty disused machinery, all covered with a layer of coal dust. Da always said there would be fewer accidents if miners kept things tidy.

Billy and Tommy went to the colliery office. In the front room was Arthur "Spotty" Llewellyn, a clerk not much older than they were. His white shirt had a dirty collar and cuffs. They were expected—their fathers had previously arranged for them to start work today. Spotty wrote their names in a ledger, then took them into the colliery manager's office. "Young Tommy Griffiths and young Billy Williams, Mr. Morgan," he said.

Maldwyn Morgan was a tall man in a black suit. There was no coal dust on his cuffs. His pink cheeks were free of stubble, which meant he must shave every day. His engineering diploma hung in a frame on the wall, and his bowler hat—the other badge of his status—was displayed on the coat stand by the door.

To Billy's surprise, he was not alone. Next to him stood an even more formidable figure: Perceval Jones, chairman of Celtic Minerals, the company that owned and operated the Aberowen coal mine and several others. A small, aggressive man, he was called Napoleon by the miners. He wore morning dress, a black tailcoat and striped gray trousers, and he had not taken off his tall black top hat.

Jones looked at the boys with distaste. "Griffiths," he said. "Your father's a revolutionary socialist."

"Yes, Mr. Jones," said Tommy.

"And an atheist."

"Yes, Mr. Jones."

He turned his gaze on Billy. "And your father's an official of the South Wales Miners' Federation."

"Yes, Mr. Jones."

"I don't like socialists. Atheists are doomed to eternal damnation. And trade unionists are the worst of the lot."

He glared at them, but he had not asked a question, so Billy said nothing.

"I don't want troublemakers," Jones went on. "In the Rhondda Valley they've been on strike for forty-three weeks because of people like your fathers stirring them up."

Billy knew that the strike in the Rhondda had not been caused by troublemakers, but by the owners of the Ely Pit at Penygraig, who had locked out their miners. But he kept his mouth shut.

"Are you troublemakers?" Jones pointed a bony finger at Billy, making Billy shake. "Did your father tell you to stand up for your rights when you're working for me?"

Billy tried to think, though it was difficult when Jones looked so threatening. Da had not said much this morning, but last night he had given some advice. "Please, sir, he told me: 'Don't cheek the bosses. That's my job.'"

Behind him, Spotty Llewellyn sniggered.

Perceval Jones was not amused. "Insolent savage," he said. "But if I turn you away, I'll have the whole of this valley on strike."

Billy had not thought of that. Was he so important? No—but the miners might strike for the principle that the children of their officials must not suffer. He had been at work less than five minutes, and already the union was protecting him.

"Get them out of here," said Jones.

Morgan nodded. "Take them outside, Llewellyn," he said to Spotty. "Rhys Price can look after them."

Billy groaned inwardly. Rhys Price was one of the more unpopular deputy managers. He had set his cap at Ethel, a year ago, and she had turned him down flat. She had done the same to half the single men in Aberowen, but Price had taken it hard.

Spotty jerked his head. "Out," he said, and he followed them. "Wait outside for Mr. Price."

Billy and Tommy left the building and leaned on the wall by the door. "I'd like to punch Napoleon's fat belly," said Tommy. "Talk about a capitalist bastard."

"Yeah," said Billy, though he had had no such thought.

Rhys Price showed up a minute later. Like all the deputies, he wore a low round-crowned hat called a billycock, more expensive than a miner's cap but cheaper than a bowler. In the pockets of his waistcoat he had a notebook and a pencil, and he carried a yardstick. Price had dark stubble on his cheeks and a gap in his front teeth. Billy knew him to be clever but sly.

"Good morning, Mr. Price," Billy said.

Price looked suspicious. "What business have you got saying good morning to me, Billy Twice?"

"Mr. Morgan said we are to go down the pit with you."

"Did he, now?" Price had a way of darting looks to the left and right, and sometimes behind, as if he expected trouble from an unknown quarter. "We'll see about that." He looked up at the winding wheel, as if seeking an explanation there. "I haven't got time to deal with boys." He went into the office.

"I hope he gets someone else to take us down," Billy said. "He hates my family because my sister wouldn't walk out with him."

"Your sister thinks she's too good for the men of Aberowen," said Tommy, obviously repeating something he had heard.

"She *is* too good for them," Billy said stoutly.

Price came out. "All right, this way," he said, and headed off at a rapid walk.

The boys followed him into the lamp room. The lamp man handed Billy a shiny brass safety lamp, and he hooked it onto his belt as the men did.

He had learned about miners' lamps in school. Among the dangers of coal mining was methane, the inflammable gas that seeped out of coal seams. The men called it firedamp, and it was the cause of all underground explosions. Welsh pits were notoriously gassy. The lamp was ingeniously designed so that its flame would not ignite firedamp. In fact the flame would change its shape, becoming longer, thereby giving a warning—for firedamp had no smell.

If the lamp went out, the miner could not relight it himself. Carrying matches was forbidden underground, and the lamp was locked to discourage the breaking of the rule. An extinguished lamp had to be taken to a lighting station, usually at the pit bottom near the shaft. This might be a walk of a mile or more, but it was worth it to avoid the risk of an underground explosion.

In school the boys had been told that the safety lamp was one of the ways in which mine owners showed their care and concern for their employees—"as if," Da said, "there was no benefit to the bosses in preventing explosions and stoppage of work and damage to tunnels."

After picking up their lamps, the men stood in line for the cage. Cleverly placed alongside the queue was a notice board. Handwritten or crudely printed signs advertised cricket practice, a darts match, a lost penknife, a recital by the Aberowen Male Voice Choir, and a lecture on Karl Marx's theory of historical materialism at the Free Library. But deputies did not have to wait, and Price pushed his way to the front, with the boys tagging along.

Like most pits, Aberowen had two shafts, with fans placed to force air down one and up the other. The owners often gave the shafts whimsical names, and here they were Pyramus and Thisbe. This one, Pyramus, was the up shaft, and Billy could feel the draft of warm air coming from the pit.

Last year Billy and Tommy had decided they wanted to look down the shaft. On Easter Monday, when the men were not working, they had dodged the watchman and sneaked across the waste ground to the pithead, then climbed the guard fence. The shaft mouth was not completely enclosed by the cage housing, and they had lain on their bellies and looked over the rim. They had stared with dreadful fascination into that terrible hole, and Billy had felt his stomach turn. The blackness seemed infinite. He experienced a thrill that was half joy because he did not have to go down, half terror because one day he would. He had thrown a stone in, and they had listened as it bounced against the wooden cage-conductor and the brick lining of the shaft. It seemed a horrifically long time before they heard the faint, distant splash as it hit the pool of water at the bottom.

Now, a year later, he was about to follow the course of that stone.

He told himself not to be a coward. He had to behave like a man, even if he did not feel like one. The worst thing of all would be to disgrace himself. He was more afraid of that than of dying.

He could see the sliding grille that closed off the shaft. Beyond it was empty space, for the cage was on its way up.

On the far side of the shaft he could see the winding engine that turned the great wheels high above. Jets of steam escaped from the mechanism. The cables slapped their guides with a whiplash sound. There was an odor of hot oil.

With a clash of iron, the empty cage appeared behind the gate. The banksman, in charge of the cage at the top end, slid the gate back. Rhys Price stepped into the empty cage and the two boys followed. Thirteen miners got in behind them—the cage held sixteen in total. The banksman slammed the gate shut.

There was a pause. Billy felt vulnerable. The floor beneath his feet was solid, but he might without much difficulty have squeezed through the widely spaced bars of the sides. The cage was suspended from a steel rope, but even that was not completely safe: everyone knew that the winding cable at Tirpentwys had snapped one day in 1902, and the cage had plummeted to the pit bottom, killing eight men.

He nodded to the miner beside him. It was Harry "Suet" Hewitt, a pudding-faced boy only three years older, though a foot taller. Billy remembered Harry in school: he had been stuck in Standard Three with the ten-year-olds, failing the exam every year, until he was old enough to start work.

A bell rang, signifying that the onsetter at the pit bottom had closed his gate. The banksman pulled a lever and a different bell rang. The steam engine hissed; then there was another bang.

The cage fell into empty space.

Billy knew that it went into free fall, then braked in time for a soft landing; but no theoretical foreknowledge could have prepared him for the sensation of dropping unhindered into the bowels of the earth. His feet left the floor. He screamed in terror. He could not help himself.

All the men laughed. They knew it was his first time and had been waiting for his reaction, he realized. Too late, he saw that they were all holding the bars of the cage to prevent themselves floating up. But the knowledge did nothing to calm his fear. He managed to stop screaming only by clamping his teeth together.

At last the brake engaged. The speed of the fall slowed, and Billy's feet touched the floor. He grabbed a bar and tried to stop shaking. After a minute the fear was replaced by a sense of injury so strong that tears threatened. He looked into the laughing face of Suet and shouted over the noise: "Shut your great gob, Hewitt, you shitbrain."

Suet's face changed in an instant and he looked furious, but the other men laughed all the more. Billy would have to say sorry to Jesus for swearing, but he felt a bit less of a fool.

He looked at Tommy, who was white-faced. Had Tommy screamed? Billy was afraid to ask in case the answer might be no.

The cage stopped, the gate was thrown back, and Billy and Tommy walked shakily out into the mine.

It was gloomy. The miners' lamps gave less light than the paraffin lights on the walls at home. The pit was as dark as a night with no moon. Perhaps they did not need to see well to hew coal, Billy thought. He splashed through a puddle, and looking down he saw water and mud everywhere, gleaming with the faint reflections of lamp flames. There was a strange taste in his mouth: the air was thick with coal dust. Was it possible that men breathed this all day? That must be why miners coughed and spat constantly.

Four men were waiting to enter the cage and go up to the surface. Each carried a leather case, and Billy realized they were the firemen. Every morning, before the miners started, the firemen tested for gas. If the concentration of methane was unacceptably high, they would order the men not to work until the ventilation fans cleared the gas.

In the immediate neighborhood Billy could see a row of stalls for ponies and an open door leading to a brightly lit room with a desk, presumably an office for deputies. The men dispersed, walking away along four tunnels that radiated from the pit bottom. Tunnels were called headings, and they led to the districts where the coal was won.

Price took them to a shed and undid a padlock. The place was a tool store. He selected two shovels, gave them to the boys, and locked up again.

They went to the stables. A man wearing only shorts and boots was shoveling soiled straw out of a stall, pitching it into a coal dram. Sweat ran down his muscular back. Price said to him: "Do you want a boy to help you?"

The man turned around, and Billy recognized Dai Ponies, an elder of the Bethesda Chapel. Dai gave no sign of recognizing Billy. "I don't want the little one," he said.

"Right," said Price. "The other is Tommy Griffiths. He's yours."

Tommy looked pleased. He had got his wish. Even though he would only be mucking out stalls, he was working in the stables.

Price said: "Come on, Billy Twice," and he walked into one of the headings.

Billy shouldered his shovel and followed. He felt more anxious now that Tommy was no longer with him. He wished he had been set to mucking out stalls alongside his friend. "What will I be doing, Mr. Price?" he said.

"You can guess, can't you?" said Price. "Why do you think I gave you a fucking shovel?"

Billy was shocked by the casual use of the forbidden word. He could not guess what he would be doing, but he asked no more questions.

The tunnel was round, its roof reinforced by curved steel supports. A two-inch pipe ran along its crown, presumably carrying water. Every night the headings were sprinkled in an attempt to reduce the dust. It was not merely a danger to men's lungs—if that were all, Celtic Minerals probably would not have cared—but it constituted a fire hazard. However, the sprinkler system was inadequate. Da had argued that a pipe of six inches' diameter was needed, but Perceval Jones had refused to spend the money.

After about a quarter of a mile they turned into a cross tunnel that sloped upward. This was an older, smaller passage, with timber props rather than steel rings. Price had to duck his head where the roof sagged. At intervals of about thirty yards they passed the entrances to workplaces where the miners were already hewing the coal.

Billy heard a rumbling sound, and Price said: "Into the manhole."

"What?" Billy looked at the ground. A manhole was a feature of town pavements, and he could see nothing on the floor but the railway tracks that carried the drams. He looked up to see a pony trotting toward him, coming fast down the slope, drawing a train of drams.

"In the manhole!" Price shouted.

Still Billy did not understand what was required of him, but he could see that the tunnel was hardly wider than the

JUNE 22, 1911 ✦ 19

drams, and he would be crushed. Then Price seemed to step into the wall and disappear.

Billy dropped his shovel, turned, and ran back the way he had come. He tried to get ahead of the pony, but it was moving surprisingly fast. Then he saw a niche cut into the wall, the full height of the tunnel, and he realized that he had seen such niches, without remarking them, every twenty-five yards or so. This must be what Price meant by a manhole. He threw himself in, and the train rumbled past.

When it had gone he stepped out, breathing hard.

Price pretended to be angry, but he was smiling. "You'll have to be more alert than that," he said. "Otherwise you'll get killed down here—like your brother."

Most men enjoyed exposing and mocking the ignorance of boys, Billy found. He was determined to be different when he grew up.

He picked up his shovel. It was undamaged. "Lucky for you," Price commented. "If the dram had broken it, you would have had to pay for a new one."

They went on and soon entered an exhausted district where the workplaces were deserted. There was less water underfoot, and the ground was covered with a thick layer of coal dust. They took several turnings and Billy lost his sense of direction.

They came to a place where the tunnel was blocked by a dirty old dram. "This area has to be cleaned up," Price said. It was the first time he had bothered to explain anything, and Billy had a feeling he was lying. "Your job is to shovel the muck into the dram."

Billy looked around. The dust was a foot thick to the limit of the light cast by his lamp, and he guessed it went a lot farther. He could shovel for a week without making much impression. And what was the point? The district was worked out. But he asked no questions. This was probably some kind of test.

"I'll come back in a bit and see how you're getting on," Price said, and he retraced his steps, leaving Billy alone.

Billy had not expected this. He had assumed he would be working with older men and learning from them. But he could only do what he was told.

He unhooked the lamp from his belt and looked around

for somewhere to put it. There was nothing he could use as a shelf. He put the lamp on the floor, but it was almost useless there. Then he remembered the nails Da had given him. So this was what they were for. He took one from his pocket. Using the blade of his shovel, he hammered it into a timber prop, then hung up his lamp. That was better.

The dram was chest high to a man but shoulder height to Billy, and when he started work he found that half the dust slipped off his shovel before he could get it over the lip. He developed an action that turned the blade to prevent this happening. In a few minutes he was bathed in sweat, and he realized what the second nail was for. He hammered it into another timber and hung up his shirt and trousers.

After a while he felt that someone was watching him. Out of the corner of his eye he saw a dim figure standing as still as a statue. "Oh, God!" he shrieked, and he turned around to face it.

It was Price. "I forgot to check your lamp," he said. He took Billy's lamp off the nail and did something to it. "Not so good," he said. "I'll leave you mine." He hung up the other lamp and disappeared.

He was a creepy character, but at least he seemed to have Billy's safety in mind.

Billy resumed work. Before long his arms and legs began to ache. He was used to shoveling, he told himself: Da kept a pig in the waste ground behind the house, and it was Billy's job to muck out the sty once a week. But that took about a quarter of an hour. Could he possibly keep this up all day?

Under the dust was a floor of rock and clay. After a while he had cleared an area four feet square, the width of the tunnel. The muck hardly covered the bottom of the dram, but he felt exhausted.

He tried to pull the dram forward so that he would not have to walk so far with his shovelful, but its wheels seemed to have locked with disuse.

He had no watch, and it was difficult to know how much time had passed. He began to work more slowly, conserving his strength.

Then his light went out.

The flame flickered first, and he looked anxiously at the lamp hanging on the nail, but he knew that the flame would lengthen if there was firedamp. This was not what he was seeing, so he felt reassured. Then the flame went out altogether.

He had never known darkness like this. He saw nothing, not even patches of gray, not even different shades of black. He lifted his shovel to face level and held it an inch from his nose, but he could not see it. This was what it must be like to be blind.

He stood still. What was he to do? He was supposed to take the lamp to the lighting station, but he could not have found his way back through the tunnels even if he had been able to see. In this blackness he might blunder about for hours. He had no idea how many miles the disused workings extended, and he did not want the men to have to send a search party for him.

He would just have to wait for Price. The deputy had said he would come back "in a bit." That could mean a few minutes, or an hour or more. And Billy suspected it would be later rather than sooner. Price had surely intended this. A safety lamp could not blow out, and anyway there was little wind here. Price had taken Billy's lamp and substituted one that was low on oil.

He felt a surge of self-pity, and tears came to his eyes. What had he done to deserve this? Then he pulled himself together. It was another test, like the cage. He would show them he was tough enough.

He should carry on working, even in the dark, he decided. Moving for the first time since the light went out, he put his shovel to the ground and ran it forward, trying to pick up dust. When he lifted it he thought, by its weight, that there was a load on the blade. He turned and walked two paces, then hefted it, trying to throw the muck into the dram, but he misjudged the height. The shovel clanged against the side of the dram and felt suddenly lighter as its load fell to the ground.

He would adjust. He tried again, lifting the shovel higher. When he had unloaded the blade he let it fall, and felt the wooden shaft bang against the lip of the dram. That was better.

As the work took him farther from the dram, he continued to miss occasionally, until he began to count his paces aloud. He got into a rhythm, and although his muscles hurt he was able to carry on.

As the work became automatic, his mind was free to wander, which was not so good. He wondered how far the tunnel extended ahead of him and how long it had been disused. He thought of the earth above his head, extending for half a mile, and the weight being held up by these old timber props. He recalled his brother, Wesley, and the other men who had died in this mine. But their spirits were not here, of course. Wesley was with Jesus. The others might be, too. If not they were in a different place.

He began to feel frightened and decided it was a mistake to think about spirits. He was hungry. Was it time for his snap? He had no idea, but he thought he might as well eat it. He made his way to the place where he had hung his clothes, fumbled on the ground below, and found his flask and tin.

He sat with his back against the wall and took a long drink of cold, sweet tea. As he was eating his bread-and-dripping, he heard a faint noise. He hoped it might be the creaking of Rhys Price's boots, but that was wishful thinking. He knew that squeak: it was rats.

He was not afraid. There were plenty of rats in the ditches that ran along every street in Aberowen. But they seemed bolder in the dark, and a moment later one ran over his bare legs. Transferring his food to his left hand, he picked up his shovel and lashed out. It did not even scare them, and he felt the tiny claws on his skin again. This time one tried to run up his arm. Obviously they could smell the food. The squeaking increased, and he wondered how many there were.

He stood up and crammed the last of his bread into his mouth. He drank some more tea, then ate his cake. It was delicious, full of dried fruit and almonds; but a rat ran up his leg, and he was forced to gobble the cake.

They seemed to know the food was gone, for the squeaking gradually died down and then stopped altogether.

Eating gave Billy renewed energy for a while, and he went back to work, but he had a burning ache in his back. He kept going more slowly, stopping for frequent rests.

To cheer himself up, he told himself it might be later than he thought. Perhaps it was noon already. Someone would come to fetch him at the end of the shift. The lamp man checked the numbers, so they always knew if a man had not come back up. But Price had taken Billy's lamp and substituted a different one. Could he be planning to leave Billy down here overnight?

It would never work. Da would raise the roof. The bosses were afraid of Da—Perceval Jones had more or less admitted it. Sooner or later, someone was sure to look for Billy.

But when he got hungry again he felt sure many hours must have passed. He started to get scared, and this time he could not shake it off. It was the darkness that unnerved him. He could have borne the waiting if he had been able to see. In the complete blackness he felt he was losing his mind. He had no sense of direction, and every time he walked back from the dram he wondered if he was about to crash into the tunnel side. Earlier he had worried about crying like a child. Now he had to stop himself screaming.

Then he recalled what Mam had said to him: "Jesus is always with you, even down the pit." At the time he had thought she was just telling him to behave well. But she had been wiser than that. Of course Jesus was with him. Jesus was everywhere. The darkness did not matter, nor the passage of time. Billy had someone taking care of him.

To remind him of that, he sang a hymn. He disliked his voice, which was still a treble, but there was no one to hear him, so he sang as loud as he could. When he had sung all the verses, and the scary feeling began to return, he imagined Jesus standing just the other side of the dram, watching, with a look of grave compassion on his bearded face.

Billy sang another hymn. He shoveled and paced to the time of the music. Most of the hymns went with a swing. Every now and then he suffered again the fear that he might have been forgotten, the shift might have ended and he might be alone down there; then he would just remember the robed figure standing with him in the dark.

He knew plenty of hymns. He had been going to the Bethesda Chapel three times every Sunday since he was old enough to sit quietly. Hymn books were expensive, and not all the congregation could read, so everyone learned the words.

When he had sung twelve hymns, he reckoned an hour had passed. Surely it must be the end of the shift? But he sang another twelve. After that it was hard to keep track. He sang his favorites twice. He worked slower and slower.

He was singing "Up from the Grave He Arose" at the top of his voice when he saw a light. The work had become so automatic that he did not stop, but picked up another shovelful and carried it to the dram, still singing, while the light grew stronger. When the hymn came to an end he leaned on his shovel. Rhys Price stood watching him, lamp at his belt, with a strange look on his shadowed face.

Billy would not let himself feel relief. He was not going to show Price how he felt. He put on his shirt and trousers, then took the unlit lamp from the nail and hung it on his belt.

Price said: "What happened to your lamp?"

"You know what happened," Billy said, and his voice sounded strangely grown-up.

Price turned away and walked back along the tunnel.

Billy hesitated. He looked the opposite way. Just the other side of the dram he glimpsed a bearded face and a pale robe, but the figure disappeared like a thought. "Thank you," Billy said to the empty tunnel.

As he followed Price, his legs ached so badly that he felt he might fall down, but he hardly cared if he did. He could see again, and the shift was over. Soon he would be home and he could lie down.

They reached the pit bottom and got into the cage with a crowd of black-faced miners. Tommy Griffiths was not among them, but Suet Hewitt was. As they waited for the signal from above, Billy noticed they were looking at him with sly grins.

Hewitt said: "How did you get on, then, on your first day, Billy Twice?"

"Fine, thank you," Billy said.

Hewitt's expression was malicious: no doubt he was remembering that Billy had called him shitbrain. He said: "No problems?"

Billy hesitated. Obviously they knew something. He wanted them to know that he had not succumbed to fear. "My lamp went out," he said, and he just about managed to keep his voice steady. He looked at Price, but decided it would be more manly not to accuse him. "It was a bit difficult shoveling in the dark all day," he finished. That was too understated—they might think his ordeal had been nothing much—but it was better than admitting to fear.

An older man spoke. It was John Jones the Shop, so called because his wife ran a little general store in their parlor. "All day?" he said.

Billy said: "Aye."

John Jones looked at Price and said: "You bastard, it's only supposed to be for an hour."

Billy's suspicion was confirmed. They all knew what had happened, and it sounded as if they did something similar to all new boys. But Price had made it worse than usual.

Suet Hewitt was grinning. "Weren't you scared, Billy boy, on your own in the dark?"

He thought about his answer. They were all looking at him, waiting to hear what he would say. Their sly smiles had gone, and they seemed a bit ashamed. He decided to tell the truth. "I was scared, yes, but I wasn't on my own."

Hewitt was baffled. "Not on your own?"

"No, of course not," Billy said. "Jesus was with me."

Hewitt laughed loudly, but no one else did. His guffaw resounded in the silence and stopped suddenly.

The hush lasted several seconds. Then there was a clang of metal and a jerk, and the cage lifted. Harry turned away.

After that, they called him Billy-with-Jesus.

PART ONE

THE DARKENING SKY

CHAPTER TWO

January 1914

Earl Fitzherbert, age twenty-eight, known to his family and friends as Fitz, was the ninth-richest man in Britain.

He had done nothing to earn his huge income. He had simply inherited thousands of acres of land in Wales and Yorkshire. The farms made little money, but there was coal beneath them, and by licensing mineral rights Fitz's grandfather had become enormously wealthy.

Clearly God intended the Fitzherberts to rule over their fellow men, and to live in appropriate style; but Fitz felt he had not done much to justify God's faith in him.

His father, the previous earl, had been different. A naval officer, he had been made admiral after the bombardment of Alexandria in 1882, had become the British ambassador to St. Petersburg, and finally had been a minister in the government of Lord Salisbury. The Conservatives lost the general election of 1906, and Fitz's father died a few weeks later—his end hastened, Fitz felt sure, by seeing irresponsible Liberals such as David Lloyd George and Winston Churchill take over His Majesty's government.

Fitz had taken his seat in the House of Lords, the upper chamber of the British Parliament, as a Conservative peer. He spoke good French and he could get by in Russian, and he would have liked one day to be his country's foreign secretary. Regrettably, the Liberals had continued to win elections, so he had had no chance yet of becoming a government minister.

His military career had been equally undistinguished. He had attended the army's officer training academy at Sandhurst, and had spent three years with the Welsh Rifles, ending as a captain. On marriage he had given up full-time soldiering, but had become honorary colonel of the South Wales Territorials. Unfortunately an honorary colonel never won medals.

However, he did have something to be proud of, he thought as the train steamed up through the South Wales valleys. In two weeks' time, the king was coming to stay at Fitz's country house. King George V and Fitz's father had been shipmates in their youth. Recently the king had expressed a wish to know what the younger men were thinking, and Fitz had organized a discreet house party for His Majesty to meet some of them. Now Fitz and his wife, Bea, were on their way to the house to get everything ready.

Fitz cherished traditions. Nothing known to mankind was superior to the comfortable order of monarchy, aristocracy, merchant, and peasant. But now, looking out of the train window, he saw a threat to the British way of life greater than any the country had faced for a hundred years. Covering the once-green hillsides, like a gray-black leaf blight on a rhododendron bush, were the terraced houses of the coal miners. In those grimy hovels there was talk of republicanism, atheism, and revolt. It was only a century or so since the French nobility had been driven in carts to the guillotine, and the same would happen here if some of those muscular black-faced miners had their way.

Fitz would gladly have given up his earnings from coal, he told himself, if Britain could go back to a simpler era. The royal family was a strong bulwark against insurrection. But Fitz felt nervous about the visit, as well as proud. So much could go wrong. With royalty, an oversight might be seen as a sign of carelessness, and therefore disrespectful. Every detail of the weekend would be reported, by the visitors' servants, to other servants and thence to those servants' employers, so that every woman in London society would quickly know if the king were given a hard pillow, a bad potato, or the wrong brand of champagne.

Fitz's Rolls-Royce Silver Ghost was waiting at Aberowen railway station. With Bea at his side he was driven a mile to Tŷ Gwyn, his country house. A light but persistent drizzle was falling, as it so often did in Wales.

"Tŷ Gwyn" was Welsh for White House, but the name had become ironic. Like everything else in this part of the world, the building was covered with a layer of coal dust, and its once-white stone blocks were now a dark gray color that smeared the skirts of ladies who carelessly brushed against its walls.

Nevertheless it was a magnificent building, and it filled Fitz with pride as the car purred up the drive. The largest private house in Wales, Tŷ Gwyn had two hundred rooms. Once when he was a boy he and his sister, Maud, had counted the windows and found 523. It had been built by his grandfather, and there was a pleasing order to the three-story design. The ground-floor windows were tall, letting plenty of light into the grand reception rooms. Upstairs were dozens of guest rooms, and in the attic countless small servants' bedrooms, revealed by long rows of dormer windows in the steep roofs.

The fifty acres of gardens were Fitz's joy. He supervised the gardeners personally, making decisions about planting and pruning and potting. "A house fit for a king to visit," he said as the car stopped at the grand portico. Bea did not reply. Traveling made her bad-tempered.

Getting out of the car, Fitz was greeted by Gelert, his Pyrenean mountain dog—a bear-sized creature that licked his hand, then raced joyously around the courtyard in celebration.

In his dressing room Fitz took off his traveling clothes and changed into a suit of soft brown tweed. Then he went through the communicating door into Bea's rooms.

The Russian maid, Nina, was unpinning the elaborate hat Bea had worn for the journey. Fitz caught sight of Bea's face in the dressing-table mirror, and his heart skipped a beat. He was taken back four years, to the St. Petersburg ballroom where he had first seen that impossibly pretty face framed by blond curls that could not quite be tamed. Then as now she had worn a sulky look that he found strangely alluring. In a heartbeat he had decided that she of all women was the one he wanted to marry.

Nina was middle-aged and her hand was unsteady—Bea

often made her servants nervous. As Fitz watched, a pin pricked Bea's scalp, and she cried out.

Nina went pale. "I'm terribly sorry, Your Highness," she said in Russian.

Bea snatched up a hatpin from the dressing table. "See how you like it!" she cried, and jabbed the maid's arm.

Nina burst into tears and ran from the room.

"Let me help you," Fitz said to his wife in a soothing tone.

She was not to be mollified. "I'll do it myself."

Fitz went to the window. A dozen or so gardeners were at work trimming bushes, edging lawns, and raking gravel. Several shrubs were in flower: pink viburnum, yellow winter jasmine, witch hazel, and scented winter honeysuckle. Beyond the garden was the soft green curve of the mountainside.

He had to be patient with Bea, and remind himself that she was a foreigner, isolated in a strange country, away from her family and all that was familiar. It had been easy in the early months of their marriage, when he was still intoxicated by how she looked and smelled and the touch of her soft skin. Now it took an effort. "Why don't you rest?" he said. "I'll see Peel and Mrs. Jevons and find out how their plans are progressing." Peel was the butler and Mrs. Jevons the housekeeper. It was Bea's job to organize the staff, but Fitz was nervous enough about the king's visit to welcome an excuse to get involved. "I'll report back to you later, when you're refreshed." He took out his cigar case.

"Don't smoke in here," she said.

He took that for assent and went to the door. Pausing on his way out, he said: "Look, you won't behave like that in front of the king and queen, will you? Striking the servants, I mean."

"I didn't strike her. I stuck a pin in her as a lesson."

Russians did that sort of thing. When Fitz's father had complained about the laziness of the servants at the British embassy in St. Petersburg, his Russian friends had told him he did not beat them enough.

Fitz said to Bea: "It would embarrass the monarch to have to witness such a thing. As I've told you before, it's not done in England."

"When I was a girl, I was made to watch three peasants being hanged," she said. "My mother didn't like it, but my grandfather insisted. He said: 'This is to teach you to punish your servants. If you do not slap them or flog them for small offenses of carelessness and laziness, they will eventually commit larger sins and end up on the scaffold.' He taught me that indulgence to the lower classes is cruel, in the long run."

Fitz began to lose patience. Bea looked back to a childhood of limitless wealth and self-indulgence, surrounded by troops of obedient servants and thousands of happy peasants. If her ruthless, capable grandfather had still been alive, that life might have continued; but the family fortune had been frittered away by Bea's father, a drunk, and her weak brother, Andrei, who was always selling the timber without replanting the woods. "Times have changed," Fitz said. "I'm asking you—I'm ordering you—not to embarrass me in front of my king. I hope I have left no room for doubt in your mind." He went out and closed the door.

He walked along the wide corridor, feeling irritated and a bit sad. When they were first married, such spats had left him bewildered and regretful; now he was becoming inured to them. Were all marriages like that? He did not know.

A tall footman polishing a doorknob straightened up and stood with his back to the wall and his eyes cast down, as Tŷ Gwyn servants were trained to do when the earl went by. In some great houses the staff had to face the wall, but Fitz thought that was too feudal. Fitz recognized this man, having seen him play cricket in a match between Tŷ Gwyn staff and Aberowen miners. He was a good left-handed batsman. "Morrison," said Fitz, remembering his name. "Tell Peel and Mrs. Jevons to come to the library."

"Very good, my lord."

Fitz walked down the grand staircase. He had married Bea because he had been enchanted by her, but he had had a rational motive, too. He dreamed of founding a great Anglo-Russian dynasty that would rule vast tracts of the earth, much as the Habsburg dynasty had ruled parts of Europe for centuries.

But for that he needed an heir. Bea's mood meant she would not welcome him to her bed tonight. He could insist, but that was never very satisfactory. It was a couple of weeks since the last time. He did not wish for a wife who was vulgarly eager about that sort of thing but, on the other hand, two weeks was a long time.

His sister, Maud, was still single at twenty-three. Besides, any child of hers would probably be brought up a rabid socialist who would fritter away the family fortune printing revolutionary tracts.

He had been married three years, and he was beginning to worry. Bea had been pregnant just once, last year, but she had suffered a miscarriage at three months. It had happened just after a quarrel. Fitz had canceled a planned trip to St. Petersburg, and Bea had become terribly emotional, crying that she wanted to go home. Fitz had put his foot down—a man could not let his wife dictate to him, after all—but then, when she miscarried, he felt guiltily convinced it was his fault. If only she could get pregnant again he would make absolutely sure nothing was allowed to upset her until the baby was born.

Putting that worry to the back of his mind, he went into the library and sat down at the leather-inlaid desk to make a list.

A minute or two later, Peel came in with a housemaid. The butler was the younger son of a farmer, and there was an outdoor look about his freckled face and salt-and-pepper hair, but he had been a servant at Tŷ Gwyn all his working life. "Mrs. Jevons have been took poorly, my lord," he said. Fitz had long ago given up trying to correct the grammar of Welsh servants. "Stomach," Peel added lugubriously.

"Spare me the details." Fitz looked at the housemaid, a pretty girl of about twenty. Her face was vaguely familiar. "Who's this?"

The girl spoke for herself. "Ethel Williams, my lord. I'm Mrs. Jevons's assistant." She had the lilting accent of the South Wales valleys.

"Well, Williams, you look too young to do a housekeeper's job."

"If your lordship pleases, Mrs. Jevons said you would probably bring down the housekeeper from Mayfair, but she hopes I might give satisfaction in the meantime."

Was there a twinkle in her eye when she talked of giving satisfaction? Although she spoke with appropriate deference, she had a cheeky look. "Very well," said Fitz.

Williams had a thick notebook in one hand and two pencils in the other. "I visited Mrs. Jevons in her room, and she was well enough to go through everything with me."

"Why have you got two pencils?"

"In case one breaks," she said, and she grinned.

Housemaids were not supposed to grin at the earl, but Fitz could not help smiling back. "All right," he said. "Tell me what you've got written down in your book."

"Three subjects," she said. "Guests, staff, and supplies."

"Very good."

"From your lordship's letter, we understand there will be twenty guests. Most will bring one or two personal staff, say an average of two, therefore an extra forty in servants' accommodation. All arriving on the Saturday and leaving on the Monday."

"Correct." Fitz felt a mixture of pleasure and apprehension very like his emotions before making his first speech in the House of Lords: he was thrilled to be doing this and, at the same time, worried about doing it well.

Williams went on: "Obviously Their Majesties will be in the Egyptian Apartment."

Fitz nodded. This was the largest suite of rooms. Its wallpaper had decorative motifs from Egyptian temples.

"Mrs. Jevons suggested which other rooms should be opened up, and I've wrote it down by here."

The phrase "by here" was a local expression, pronounced like the Bayeux Tapestry. It was a redundancy, meaning exactly the same as "here." Fitz said: "Show me."

She came around the desk and placed her open book in front of him. House servants were obliged to bathe once a week, so she did not smell as bad as the working class generally did. In fact her warm body had a flowery fragrance. Perhaps she had been stealing Bea's scented soap. He read her list. "Fine," he said. "The princess can allocate guests to rooms—she may have strong opinions."

Williams turned the page. "This is a list of extra staff needed: six girls in the kitchen, for peeling vegetables and washing up; two men with clean hands to help serve at table; three extra chambermaids; and three boys for boots and candles."

"Do you know where we're going to get them?"

"Oh, yes, my lord, I've got a list of local people who've worked here before, and if that's not sufficient we'll ask them to recommend others."

"No socialists, mind," Fitz said anxiously. "They might

try to talk to the king about the evils of capitalism." You never knew with the Welsh.

"Of course, my lord."

"What about supplies?"

She turned another page. "This is what we need, based on previous house parties."

Fitz looked at the list: a hundred loaves of bread, twenty dozen eggs, ten gallons of cream, a hundred pounds of bacon, fifty stone of potatoes . . . He began to feel bored. "Shouldn't we leave this until the princess has decided the menus?"

"It's all got to come up from Cardiff," Williams replied. "The shops in Aberowen can't cope with orders of this size. And even the Cardiff suppliers need notice, to be sure they have sufficient quantities on the day."

She was right. He was glad she was in charge. She had the ability to plan ahead—a rare quality, he found. "I could do with someone like you in my regiment," he said.

"I can't wear khaki. It doesn't suit my complexion," she replied saucily.

The butler looked indignant. "Now, now, Williams, none of your cheek."

"I beg your pardon, Mr. Peel."

Fitz felt it was his own fault for speaking facetiously to her. Anyway, he did not mind her impudence. In fact he rather liked her.

Peel said: "Cook have come up with some suggestions for the menus, my lord." He handed Fitz a slightly grubby sheet of paper covered with the cook's careful, childish handwriting. "Unfortunately we're too early for spring lamb, but we can get plenty of fresh fish sent up from Cardiff on ice."

"This looks very like what we had at our shooting party in November," Fitz said. "On the other hand, we don't want to attempt anything new on this occasion—better to stick with tried and tested dishes."

"Exactly, my lord."

"Now, the wines." He stood up. "Let's go down to the cellar."

Peel looked surprised. The earl did not often descend to the basement.

There was a thought at the back of Fitz's mind that he

did not want to acknowledge. He hesitated, then said: "Williams, you come as well, to take notes."

The butler held the door, and Fitz left the library and went down the back stairs. The kitchen and servants' hall were in a semibasement. Etiquette was different here, and the skivvies and boot boys curtsied or touched their forelocks as he passed.

The wine cellar was in a subbasement. Peel opened the door and said: "With your permission, I'll lead the way." Fitz nodded. Peel struck a match and lit a candle lamp on the wall, then went down the steps. At the bottom he lit another lamp.

Fitz had a modest cellar, about twelve thousand bottles, much of it laid down by his father and grandfather. Champagne, port, and hock predominated, with lesser quantities of claret and white burgundy. Fitz was not an aficionado of wine, but he loved the cellar because it reminded him of his father. "A wine cellar requires order, forethought, and good taste," the old man used to say. "These are the virtues that made Britain great."

Fitz would serve the very best to the king, of course, but that required a judgment. The champagne would be Perrier-Jouët, the most expensive, but which vintage? Mature champagne, twenty or thirty years old, was less fizzy and had more flavor, but there was something cheerfully delicious about younger vintages. He took a bottle from a rack at random. It was filthy with dust and cobwebs. He used the white linen handkerchief from the breast pocket of his jacket to wipe the label. He still could not see the date in the dim candlelight. He showed the bottle to Peel, who had put on a pair of glasses.

"Eighteen fifty-seven," said the butler.

"My goodness, I remember this," Fitz said. "The first vintage I ever tasted, and probably the greatest." He felt conscious of the maid's presence, leaning close to him and peering at the bottle that was many years older than she. To his consternation, her nearness made him slightly out of breath.

"I'm afraid the fifty-seven may be past its best," said Peel. "May I suggest the eighteen ninety-two?"

Fitz looked at another bottle, hesitated, and made a decision. "I can't read in this light," he said. "Fetch me a magnifying glass, Peel, would you?"

Peel went up the stone steps.

Fitz looked at Williams. He was about to do something foolish, but he could not stop. "What a pretty girl you are," he said.

"Thank you, my lord."

She had dark curls escaping from under the maid's cap. He touched her hair. He knew he would regret this. "Have you ever heard of droit du seigneur?" He heard the throaty tone in his own voice.

"I'm Welsh, not French," she said, with the impudent lift of her chin that he was already seeing as characteristic.

He moved his hand from her hair to the back of her neck, and looked into her eyes. She returned his gaze with bold confidence. But did her expression mean that she wanted him to go further—or that she was ready to make a humiliating scene?

He heard heavy footsteps on the cellar stairs. Peel was back. Fitz stepped away from the maid.

She surprised Fitz by giggling. "You look so guilty!" she said. "Like a schoolboy."

Peel appeared in the dim candlelight, proffering a silver tray on which there was an ivory-handled magnifying glass.

Fitz tried to breathe normally. He took the glass and returned to his examination of the wine bottles. He was careful not to meet Williams's eye.

My God, he thought, what an extraordinary girl.

{ II }

Ethel Williams felt full of energy. Nothing bothered her; she could handle every problem, cope with any setback. When she looked in a mirror she could see that her skin glowed and her eyes sparkled. After chapel on Sunday her father had commented on it, with his usual sarcastic humor. "You're cheerful," he had said. "Have you come into money?"

She found herself running, not walking, along the endless corridors of Tŷ Gwyn. Every day she filled more pages of her notebook with shopping lists, staff timetables, schedules for clearing tables and laying them again, and calculations: numbers of pillowcases, vases, napkins, candles, spoons . . .

This was her big chance. Despite her youth, she was acting housekeeper, at the time of a royal visit. Mrs. Jevons showed no sign of rising from her sickbed, so Ethel bore the full responsibility of preparing Tŷ Gwyn for the king and queen. She had always felt she could excel, if only she were given the chance; but in the rigid hierarchy of the servants' hall there were few opportunities to show that you were better than the rest. Suddenly such an opening had appeared, and she was determined to use it. After this, perhaps the ailing Mrs. Jevons would be given a less demanding job, and Ethel would be made housekeeper, at double her present wages, with a bedroom to herself and her own sitting room in the servants' quarters.

But she was not there yet. The earl was obviously happy with the job she was doing, and he had decided not to summon the housekeeper from London, which Ethel took as a great compliment; but, she thought apprehensively, there was yet time for that tiny slip, that fatal error, that would spoil everything: the dirty dinner plate, the overflowing sewer, the dead mouse in the bathtub. And then the earl would be angry.

On the morning of the Saturday when the king and queen were due to arrive, she visited every guest room, making sure the fires were lit and the pillows were plumped. Each room had at least one vase of flowers, brought that morning from the hothouse. There was Tŷ Gwyn–headed writing paper at every desk. Towels, soap, and water were provided for washing. The old earl had not liked modern plumbing, and Fitz had not yet got around to installing running water in all rooms. There were only three water closets, in a house with a hundred bedrooms, so most rooms also needed chamber pots. Potpourri was provided, made by Mrs. Jevons to her own recipe, to take away the smell.

The royal party was due at teatime. The earl would meet them at Aberowen railway station. There would undoubtedly be a crowd there, hoping for a glimpse of royalty, but at this point the king and queen would not meet the people. Fitz would bring them to the house in his Rolls-Royce, a large closed car. The king's equerry, Sir Alan Tite, and the rest of the royal traveling staff would follow, with the luggage, in an assortment of horse-drawn vehicles. In front of Tŷ Gwyn a battalion from the Welsh Rifles was already assembling either side of the drive to provide a guard of honor.

The royal couple would show themselves to their subjects on Monday morning. They planned a progress around nearby villages in an open carriage, and a stop at Aberowen town hall to meet the mayor and councilors, before going to the railway station.

The other guests began to arrive at midday. Peel stood in the hall and assigned maids to guide them to their rooms and footmen to carry their bags. The first were Fitz's uncle and aunt, the Duke and Duchess of Sussex. The duke was a cousin of the king and had been invited to make the monarch feel more comfortable. The duchess was Fitz's aunt, and like most of the family she was deeply interested in politics. At their London house she held a salon that was frequented by cabinet ministers.

The duchess informed Ethel that King George V was a bit obsessed with clocks and hated to see different clocks in the same house telling different times. Ethel cursed silently: Tŷ Gwyn had more than a hundred clocks. She borrowed Mrs. Jevons's pocket watch and began to go around the house setting them all.

In the small dining room she came across the earl. He was standing at the window, looking distraught. Ethel studied him for a moment. He was the handsomest man she had ever seen. His pale face, lit by the soft winter sunlight, might have been carved in white marble. He had a square chin, high cheekbones, and a straight nose. His hair was dark but he had green eyes, an unusual combination. He had no beard or mustache or even side-whiskers. With a face like that, Ethel thought, why cover it with hair?

He caught her eye. "I've just been told that the king likes a bowl of oranges in his room!" he said. "There's not a single orange in the damn house."

Ethel frowned. None of the grocers in Aberowen would have oranges this early in the season—their customers could not afford such luxuries. The same would apply to every other town in the South Wales valleys. "If I might use the telephone, I could speak to one or two greengrocers in Cardiff," she said. "They might have oranges at this time of year."

"But how will we get them here?"

"I'll ask the shop to put a basket on the train." She looked at the clock she had been adjusting. "With luck the oranges will come at the same time as the king."

"That's it," he said. "That's what we'll do." He gave her a direct look. "You're astonishing," he said. "I'm not sure I've ever met a girl quite like you."

She stared back at him. Several times in the last two weeks he had spoken like this, overly familiar and a bit intense, and it gave Ethel a strange feeling, a sort of uneasy exhilaration, as if something dangerously exciting were about to happen. It was like the moment in a fairy tale when the prince enters the enchanted castle.

The spell was broken by the sound of wheels on the drive outside, then a familiar voice. "Peel! How delightful to see you."

Fitz looked out of the window. His expression was comical. "Oh, no," he said. "My sister!"

"Welcome home, Lady Maud," said Peel's voice. "Though we were not expecting you."

"The earl forgot to invite me, but I came anyway."

Ethel smothered a smile. Fitz loved his feisty sister, but he found her difficult to deal with. Her political opinions were alarmingly liberal: she was a suffragette, a militant campaigner for votes for women. Ethel thought Maud was wonderful—just the kind of independent-minded woman she herself would have liked to be.

Fitz strode out of the room, and Ethel followed him into the hall, an imposing room decorated in the Gothic style beloved of Victorians such as Fitz's father: dark paneling, heavily patterned wallpaper, and carved oak chairs like medieval thrones. Maud was coming through the door. "Fitz, darling, how are you?" she said.

Maud was tall like her brother, and they looked similar, but the sculpted features that made the earl seem like the statue of a god were not so flattering on a woman, and Maud was striking rather than pretty. Contrary to the popular image of feminists as frumpy, she was fashionably dressed, wearing a hobble skirt over button boots, a navy-blue coat with an oversize belt and deep cuffs, and a hat with a tall feather pinned to its front like a regimental flag.

She was accompanied by Aunt Herm. Lady Hermia was

Fitz's other aunt. Unlike her sister, who had married a rich duke, Herm had wedded a thriftless baron who died young and broke. Ten years ago, after Fitz and Maud's parents had both died within a few months, Aunt Herm had moved in to mother the thirteen-year-old Maud. She continued to act as Maud's somewhat ineffectual chaperone.

Fitz said to Maud: "What are you doing here?"

Aunt Herm murmured: "I told you he wouldn't like it, dear."

"I couldn't be absent when the king came to stay," Maud said. "It would have been disrespectful."

Fitz's tone was fondly exasperated. "I don't want you talking to the king about women's rights."

Ethel did not think he needed to worry. Despite Maud's radical politics, she knew how to flatter and flirt with powerful men, and even Fitz's Conservative friends liked her.

"Take my coat, please, Morrison," Maud said. She undid the buttons and turned to allow the footman to remove it. "Hello, Williams. How are you?" she said to Ethel.

"Welcome home, my lady," Ethel said. "Would you like the Gardenia Suite?"

"Thank you. I love that view."

"Will you have some lunch while I'm getting the room ready?"

"Yes, please. I'm starving."

"We're serving it club style today, because guests are arriving at different times." Club style meant that guests were served whenever they came into the dining room, as in a gentlemen's club or a restaurant, instead of all at the same time. It was a modest lunch today: hot mulligatawny soup, cold meats and smoked fish, stuffed trout, lamb cutlets, and a few desserts and cheeses.

Ethel held the door and followed Maud and Herm into the large dining room. Already at lunch were the von Ulrich cousins. Walter von Ulrich, the younger one, was handsome and charming, and seemed delighted to be at Tŷ Gwyn. Robert was fussy: he had straightened the painting of Cardiff Castle on his wall, asked for more pillows, and discovered that the inkwell on his writing desk was dry—an oversight that made Ethel wonder fretfully what else she might have forgotten.

They stood up when the ladies walked in. Maud went

straight up to Walter and said: "You haven't changed since you were eighteen! Do you remember me?"

His face lit up. "I do, although you *have* changed since you were thirteen."

They shook hands and then Maud kissed him on both cheeks, as if he were family. "I had the most agonizing schoolgirl passion for you at that age," she said with startling candor.

Walter smiled. "I was rather taken with you, too."

"But you always acted as if I was a terrible young pest!"

"I had to hide my feelings from Fitz, who protected you like a guard dog."

Aunt Herm coughed, indicating her disapproval of this instant intimacy. Maud said: "Aunt, this is Herr Walter von Ulrich, an old school friend of Fitz's who used to come here in the holidays. Now he's a diplomat at the German embassy in London."

Walter said: "May I present my cousin the Graf Robert von Ulrich." *Graf* was German for count, Ethel knew. "He is a military attaché at the Austrian embassy."

They were actually second cousins, Peel had explained gravely to Ethel: their grandfathers had been brothers, the younger of whom had married a German heiress and left Vienna for Berlin, which was how come Walter was German whereas Robert was Austrian. Peel liked to get such things right.

Everyone sat down. Ethel held a chair for Aunt Herm. "Would you like some mulligatawny soup, Lady Hermia?" she asked.

"Yes, please, Williams."

Ethel nodded to a footman, who went to the sideboard where the soup was being kept hot in an urn. Seeing that the new arrivals were comfortable, Ethel quietly left to arrange their rooms. As the door was closing behind her, she heard Walter von Ulrich say: "I remember how fond you were of music, Lady Maud. We were just discussing the Russian ballet. What do you think of Diaghilev?"

Not many men asked a woman for her opinion. Maud would like that. As Ethel hurried down the stairs to find a couple of maids to do the rooms, she thought: That German is quite a charmer.

{ III }

The Sculpture Hall at Tŷ Gwyn was an anteroom to the dining room. The guests gathered there before dinner. Fitz was not much interested in art—it had all been collected by his grandfather—but the sculptures gave people something to talk about while they were waiting for their dinner.

As he chatted to his aunt the duchess, Fitz looked around anxiously at the men in white tie and tails and the women in low-cut gowns and tiaras. Protocol demanded that every other guest had to be in the room before the king and queen entered. Where was Maud? Surely she would not cause an incident! No, there she was, in a purple silk dress, wearing their mother's diamonds, talking animatedly to Walter von Ulrich.

Fitz and Maud had always been close. Their father had been a distant hero, their mother his unhappy acolyte; the two children had got the affection they needed from each other. After both parents died they had clung together, sharing their grief. Fitz had been eighteen then, and had tried to protect his little sister from the cruel world. She, in turn, had worshipped him. In adulthood, she had become independent-minded, whereas he continued to believe that as head of the family he had authority over her. However, their affection for each other had proved strong enough to survive their differences—so far.

Now she was drawing Walter's attention to a bronze cupid. Unlike Fitz, she understood such things. Fitz prayed she would talk about art all evening and keep off women's rights. George V hated liberals; everyone knew that. Monarchs were usually conservative, but events had sharpened this king's antipathy. He had come to the throne in the middle of a political crisis. Against his will he had been forced, by Liberal prime minister H. H. Asquith—strongly backed by public opinion—to curb the power of the House of Lords. This humiliation still rankled. His Majesty knew that Fitz, as a Conservative peer in the House of Lords, had fought to the last ditch against the so-called reform. All the same, if he were harangued by Maud tonight, he would never forgive Fitz.

Walter was a junior diplomat, but his father was one of

the kaiser's oldest friends. Robert, too, was well-connected: he was close to the archduke Franz Ferdinand, the heir to the throne of the Austro-Hungarian Empire. Another guest who moved in exalted circles was the tall young American now talking to the duchess. His name was Gus Dewar, and his father, a senator, was intimate adviser to U.S. president Woodrow Wilson. Fitz felt he had done well in assembling such a group of young men, the ruling elite of the future. He hoped the king was pleased.

Gus Dewar was amiable but awkward. He stooped, as if he would have preferred to be shorter and less conspicuous. He seemed unsure of himself, but he was pleasantly courteous to everyone. "The American people are concerned with domestic issues more than foreign policy," he was saying to the duchess. "But President Wilson is a liberal, and as such he is bound to sympathize with democracies such as France and Britain more than with authoritarian monarchies such as Austria and Germany."

At that moment the double doors opened, the room fell silent, and the king and queen walked in. Princess Bea curtsied, Fitz bowed, and everyone else followed suit. There were a few moments of mildly embarrassed silence, for no one was allowed to speak until one of the royal couple had said something. At last the king said to Bea: "I stayed at this house twenty years ago, you know," and people began to relax.

The king was a neat man, Fitz reflected as the four of them made small talk. His beard and mustache were carefully barbered. His hair was receding, but he had enough left on top to comb with a parting as straight as a ruler. Close-fitting evening clothes suited his slim figure: unlike his father, Edward VII, he was not a gourmet. He relaxed with hobbies that required precision: he liked to collect postage stamps, sticking them meticulously into albums, a pastime that drew mockery from disrespectful London intellectuals.

The queen was a more formidable figure, with graying curls and a severe line to her mouth. She had a magnificent bosom, shown off to great advantage by the extremely low neckline that was currently de rigueur. She was the daughter of a German prince. Originally she had been engaged to George's older brother, Albert, but he had died of pneumonia before the wedding. When George became heir to the throne, he also took over his brother's fiancée, an arrangement that was regarded by some people as a bit medieval.

Bea was in her element. She was enticingly dressed in pink silk, and her fair curls were perfectly arranged to look slightly disordered, as if she had suddenly broken away from an illicit kiss. She talked animatedly to the king. Sensing that mindless chatter would not charm George V, she was telling him how Peter the Great had created the Russian navy, and he was nodding interestedly.

Peel appeared in the dining room door, an expectant look on his freckled face. He caught Fitz's eye and gave an emphatic nod. Fitz said to the queen: "Would you care to go in to dinner, Your Majesty?"

She gave him her arm. Behind them, the king stood arm in arm with Bea, and the rest of the party formed up in pairs according to precedence. When everyone was ready, they walked into the dining room in procession.

"How pretty," the queen murmured when she saw the table.

"Thank you," said Fitz, and breathed a silent sigh of relief. Bea had done a wonderful job. Three chandeliers hung low over the long table. Their reflections twinkled in the crystal glasses at each place. All the cutlery was gold, as were the salt and pepper containers and even the small boxes of matches for smokers. The white tablecloth was strewn with hothouse roses and, in a final dramatic touch, Bea had trailed delicate ferns from the chandeliers down to the pyramids of grapes on golden platters.

Everyone sat down, the bishop said grace, and Fitz relaxed. A party that began well almost always continued successfully. Wine and food made people less disposed to find fault.

The menu began with hors d'oeuvres *Russes*, a nod to Bea's home country: little blinis with caviar and cream, triangles of toast and smoked fish, crackers with soused herring, all washed down with the Perrier-Jouët 1892 champagne, which was as mellow and delicious as Peel had promised. Fitz kept an eye on Peel, and Peel watched the king. As soon as His Majesty put down his cutlery, Peel took away his plate, and that was the signal for the foot-

men to clear all the rest. Any guest who happened to be
still tucking into the dish had to abandon it in deference.

Soup followed, a pot-au-feu, served with a fine dry ol-
oroso sherry from Sanlúcar de Barrameda. The fish was
sole, accompanied by a mature Meursault Charmes like a
mouthful of gold. With the medallions of Welsh lamb Fitz
had chosen the Château Lafite 1875—the 1870 was still not
ready to drink. The red wine continued to be served with
the parfait of goose liver that followed and with the final
meat course, quails with grapes baked in pastry.

No one ate all this. The men took what they fancied and
ignored the rest. The women picked at one or two dishes.
Many plates went back to the kitchen untouched.

There was salad, a dessert, a savory, fruit, and petits
fours. Finally, Princess Bea raised a discreet eyebrow to
the queen, who replied with an almost imperceptible nod.
They both got up, everyone else stood, and the ladies left
the room.

The men sat down again, the footmen brought boxes of
cigars, and Peel placed a decanter of Ferreira 1847 port at
the king's right hand. Fitz drew thankfully on a cigar. Things
had gone well. The king was famously unsociable, feeling
comfortable only with old shipmates from his happy navy
days. But this evening he had been charming and nothing
had gone wrong. Even the oranges had arrived.

Fitz had spoken earlier with Sir Alan Tite, the king's
equerry, a retired army officer with old-fashioned side-
whiskers. They had agreed that tomorrow the king would
have an hour or so alone with each of the men around the
table, all of whom had inside knowledge of one government
or another. This evening, Fitz was to break the ice with some
general political conversation. He cleared his throat and addressed Walter von Ulrich. "Walter, you and I have been
friends for fifteen years—we were together at Eton." He
turned to Robert. "And I've known your cousin since the
three of us shared an apartment in Vienna when we were
students." Robert smiled and nodded. Fitz liked them both:
Robert was a traditionalist, like Fitz; Walter, though not
so conservative, was very clever. "Now we find the world
talking about war between our countries," Fitz went on. "Is
there really a chance of such a tragedy?"

Walter answered: "If talking about war can make it happen, then yes, we will fight, for everyone is getting ready for it. But is there a real reason? I don't see it."

Gus Dewar raised a tentative hand. Fitz liked Dewar, despite his liberal politics. Americans were supposed to be brash, but this one was well-mannered and a bit shy. He was also startlingly well-informed. Now he said: "Britain and Germany have many reasons to quarrel."

Walter turned to him. "Would you give me an example?"

Gus blew out cigar smoke. "Naval rivalry."

Walter nodded. "My kaiser does not believe there is a God-given law that the German navy should remain smaller than the British forever."

Fitz glanced nervously at the king. He loved the Royal Navy and might easily be offended. On the other hand, Kaiser Wilhelm was his cousin. George's father and Willy's mother had been brother and sister, both children of Queen Victoria. Fitz was relieved to see that His Majesty was smiling indulgently.

Walter went on: "This has caused friction in the past, but for two years now we have been in agreement, informally, about the relative size of our navies."

Dewar said: "How about economic rivalry?"

"It is true that Germany is daily growing more prosperous, and may soon catch up with Britain and the United States in economic production. But why should this be a problem? Germany is one of Britain's biggest customers. The more we have to spend, the more we buy. Our economic strength is good for British manufacturers!"

Dewar tried again. "It's said that Germany wants more colonies."

Fitz glanced at the king again, wondering if he minded the conversation being dominated by these two; but His Majesty appeared fascinated.

Walter said: "There have been wars over colonies, notably in your home country, Mr. Dewar. But nowadays we seem able to decide such squabbles without firing our guns. Three years ago Germany, Great Britain, and France quarreled about Morocco, but the argument was settled without war. More recently, Britain and Germany have reached agreement about the thorny issue of the Baghdad Railway. If we simply carry on as we are, we will not go to war."

Dewar said: "Would you forgive me if I used the term *German militarism*?"

That was a bit strong, and Fitz winced. Walter colored, but he spoke smoothly. "I appreciate your frankness. The German Empire is dominated by Prussians, who play something of the role of the English in Your Majesty's United Kingdom."

It was daring to compare Britain with Germany, and England with Prussia. Walter was right on the edge of what was permissible in a polite conversation, Fitz thought uneasily.

Walter went on: "The Prussians have a strong military tradition, but do not go to war for no reason."

Dewar said skeptically: "So Germany is not aggressive."

"On the contrary," said Walter. "I put it to you that Germany is the *only* major power on mainland Europe that is *not* aggressive."

There was a murmur of surprise around the table, and Fitz saw the king raise his eyebrows. Dewar sat back, startled, and said: "How do you figure that?"

Walter's perfect manners and amiable tone took the edge off his provocative words. "First, consider Austria," he went on. "My Viennese cousin Robert will not deny that the Austro-Hungarian Empire would like to extend its borders to the southeast."

"Not without reason," Robert protested. "That part of the world, which the British call the Balkans, has been part of the Ottoman domain for hundreds of years; but Ottoman rule has crumbled, and now the Balkans are unstable. The Austrian emperor believes it is his holy duty to maintain order and the Christian religion there."

"Quite so," said Walter. "But Russia, too, wants territory in the Balkans."

Fitz felt it was his job to defend the Russian government, perhaps because of Bea. "They, too, have good reasons," he said. "Half their foreign trade crosses the Black Sea, and passes from there through the straits to the Mediterranean Sea. Russia cannot allow any other great power to dominate the straits by acquiring territory in the eastern Balkans. It would be like a noose around the neck of the Russian economy."

"Exactly so," said Walter. "Turning to the western end of

Europe, France has ambitions to take from Germany the territories of Alsace and Lorraine."

At this point the French guest, Jean-Pierre Charlois, bridled. "Stolen from France forty-three years ago!"

"I will not argue about that," Walter said. "Let us say that Alsace-Lorraine was joined to the German Empire in 1871, after the defeat of France in the Franco-Prussian War. Whether stolen or not, you allow, Monsieur le Comte, that France wants those lands back."

"Naturally." The Frenchman sat back and sipped his port.

Walter said: "Even Italy would like to take, from Austria, the territories of Trentino—"

"Where most people speak Italian!" cried Signor Falli.

"—plus much of the Dalmatian coast—"

"Full of Venetian lions, Catholic churches, and Roman columns!"

"—and Tyrol, a province with a long history of self-government, where most people speak German."

"Strategic necessity."

"Of course."

Fitz realized how clever Walter had been. Not rude, but discreetly provocative, he had stung the representatives of each nation into confirming, in more or less belligerent language, their territorial ambitions.

Now Walter said: "But what new territory is Germany asking for?" He looked around the table, but no one spoke. "None," he said triumphantly. "And the only other major country in Europe that can say the same is Britain!"

Gus Dewar passed the port and said in his American drawl: "I guess that's right."

Walter said: "So why, my old friend Fitz, should we ever go to war?"

{ IV }

On Sunday morning before breakfast Lady Maud sent for Ethel.

Ethel had to suppress an exasperated sigh. She was terribly busy. It was early, but the staff were already hard at work. Before the guests got up all the fireplaces had to be cleaned, the fires relit, and the scuttles filled with coal. The principal rooms—dining room, morning room, library, smoking room, and the smaller public rooms—had to be cleaned and tidied. Ethel was checking the flowers in the billiard room, replacing those that were fading, when she was summoned. Much as she liked Fitz's radical sister, she hoped Maud did not have some elaborate commission for her.

When Ethel had come to work at Tŷ Gwyn, at the age of thirteen, the Fitzherbert family and their guests were hardly real to her: they seemed like people in a story, or strange tribes in the Bible, Hittites perhaps, and they terrified her. She was frightened that she would do something wrong and lose her job, but also deeply curious to see these strange creatures close up.

One day a kitchen maid had told her to go upstairs to the billiard room and bring down the tantalus. She had been too nervous to ask what a tantalus was. She had gone to the room and looked around, hoping it would be something obvious like a tray of dirty dishes, but she could see nothing that belonged downstairs. She had been in tears when Maud walked in.

Maud was then a gangly fifteen-year-old, a woman in girl's clothes, unhappy and rebellious. It was not until later that she made sense of her life by turning her discontent into a crusade. But even at fifteen she had had the quick compassion that made her sensitive to injustice and oppression.

She had asked Ethel what was the matter. The tantalus turned out to be a silver container with decanters of brandy and whisky. It tantalized, because it had a locking mechanism to prevent servants stealing sips, she explained. Ethel thanked her emotionally. It was the first of many kindnesses and, over the years, Ethel had come to worship the older girl.

Ethel went up to Maud's room, tapped on the door, and walked in. The Gardenia Suite had elaborate flowery wallpaper of a kind that had gone out of fashion at the turn of the century. However, its bay window overlooked the most charming part of Fitz's garden, the West Walk, a long straight path through flower beds to a summerhouse.

Maud was pulling on boots, Ethel saw with displeasure. "I'm going for a walk—you must be my chaperone," she said. "Help me with my hat and tell me the gossip."

Ethel could hardly spare the time, but she was intrigued as well as bothered. Who was Maud going to walk with; where was her normal chaperone, Aunt Herm; and why was she putting on such a charming hat just to go into the garden? Could there be a man in the picture?

As she pinned the hat to Maud's dark hair, Ethel said: "There's a scandal below stairs this morning." Maud collected gossip the way the king collected stamps. "Morrison didn't get to bed until four o'clock. He's one of the footmen—tall with a blond mustache."

"I know Morrison. And I know where he spent the night." Maud hesitated.

Ethel waited a moment, then said: "Aren't you going to tell me?"

"You'll be shocked."

Ethel grinned. "All the better."

"He spent the night with Robert von Ulrich." Maud glanced at Ethel in the dressing-table mirror. "Are you horrified?"

Ethel was fascinated. "Well, I never! I knew Morrison wasn't much of a ladies' man, but I didn't think he might be one of *those,* if you see what I mean."

"Well, Robert is certainly one of *those,* and I saw him catch Morrison's eye several times during dinner."

"In front of the king, too! How do you know about Robert?"

"Walter told me."

"What a thing for a gentleman to say to a lady! People tell you everything. What's the gossip in London?"

"They're all talking about Mr. Lloyd George."

David Lloyd George was the chancellor of the Exchequer, in charge of the country's finances. A Welshman, he was a fiery left-wing orator. Ethel's da said Lloyd George should have been in the Labour Party. During the coal strike of 1912 he had even talked about nationalizing the mines. "What are they saying about him?" Ethel asked.

"He has a mistress."

"No!" This time Ethel was really shocked. "But he was brought up a Baptist!"

Maud laughed. "Would it be less outrageous if he were Anglican?"

"Yes!" Ethel refrained from adding *obviously.* "Who is she?"

"Frances Stevenson. She started as his daughter's governess, but she's a clever woman—she has a degree in classics—and now she's his private secretary."

"That's terrible."

"He calls her Pussy."

Ethel almost blushed. She did not know what to say to that. Maud stood up, and Ethel helped her with her coat. Ethel asked: "What about his wife, Margaret?"

"She stays here in Wales with their four children."

"Five, it was, only one died. Poor woman."

Maud was ready. They went along the corridor and down the grand staircase. Walter von Ulrich was waiting in the hall, wrapped in a long dark coat. He had a small mustache and soft hazel eyes. He looked dashing in a buttoned-up, German sort of way, the kind of man who would bow, click his heels, and then give you a little wink, Ethel thought. So this was why Maud did not want Lady Hermia as her chaperone.

Maud said to Walter: "Williams came to work here when I was a girl, and we've been friends ever since."

Ethel liked Maud, but it was going too far to say they were friends. Maud was kind, and Ethel admired her, but they were still mistress and servant. Maud was really saying that Ethel could be trusted.

Walter addressed Ethel with the elaborate politeness such people employed when speaking to their inferiors. "I'm pleased to make your acquaintance, Williams. How do you do?"

"Thank you, sir. I'll get my coat."

She ran downstairs. She did not really want to be going for a walk while the king was there—she would have preferred to be on hand to supervise the housemaids—but she could not refuse.

In the kitchen Princess Bea's maid, Nina, was making tea Russian style for her mistress. Ethel spoke to a chambermaid. "Herr Walter is up," she said. "You can do the Gray Room." As soon as the guests appeared, the maids needed to go into the bedrooms to clean, make the beds, empty the chamber pots, and put out fresh water for washing. She saw Peel, the butler, counting plates. "Any movement upstairs?" she asked him.

"Nineteen, twenty," he said. "Mr. Dewar has rung for hot water for shaving, and Signor Falli asked for coffee."

"Lady Maud wants me to go outside with her."

"That's inconvenient," Peel said crossly. "You're needed in the house."

Ethel knew that. She said sarcastically: "What shall I do, Mr. Peel, tell her to go and get knotted?"

"None of your sauce. Be back as quick as you can."

When she went back upstairs the earl's dog, Gelert, was standing at the front door, panting eagerly, having divined that a walk was in prospect. They all went out and crossed the East Lawn to the woods.

Walter said to Ethel: "I suppose Lady Maud has taught you to be a suffragette."

"It was the other way around," Maud told him. "Williams was the first person to introduce me to liberal ideas."

Ethel said: "I learned it all from my father."

Ethel knew they did not really want to talk to her. Etiquette did not permit them to be alone, but they wanted the next best thing. She called to Gelert, then ran ahead, playing with the dog, giving them the privacy they were probably longing for. Glancing back, she saw that they were holding hands.

Maud was a fast worker, Ethel thought. From what she had said yesterday, she had not seen Walter for ten years. Even then there had been no acknowledged romance, just an unspoken attraction. Something must have happened last night. Perhaps they had sat up late talking. Maud flirted with everyone—it was how she got information out of them—but clearly this was more serious.

A moment later, Ethel heard Walter sing a snatch of a tune. Maud joined in; then they stopped and laughed. Maud loved music, and could play the piano quite well, unlike Fitz, who was tone-deaf. It seemed Walter was also musical. His voice was a pleasant light baritone that would have been much appreciated, Ethel thought, in the Bethesda Chapel.

Her mind wandered to her work. She had not seen polished pairs of shoes outside any of the bedroom doors. She needed to chase the boot boys and hurry them up. She wondered fretfully what the time was. If this went on much longer she might have to insist on returning to the house.

She glanced back, but this time she could not see Walter or Maud. Had they stopped, or gone off in a different direction? She stood still for a minute or two, but she could not wait out there all morning, so she retraced her steps through the trees.

A moment later she saw them. They were locked in an embrace, kissing passionately. Walter's hands were on Maud's behind and he was pressing her to him. Their mouths were open, and Ethel heard Maud groan.

She stared at them. She wondered whether a man would ever kiss her that way. Spotty Llewellyn had kissed her on the beach during a chapel outing, but it had not been with mouths open and bodies pressed together, and it certainly had not made Ethel moan. Little Dai Chops, the son of the butcher, had put his hand up her skirt in the Palace Cinema in Cardiff, but she had pushed it away after a few seconds. She had really liked Llewellyn Davies, a schoolteacher's son, who had talked to her about the Liberal government, and told her she had breasts like warm baby birds in a nest; but he had gone away to college and never written. With them she had been intrigued, and curious to do more, but never passionate. She envied Maud.

Then Maud opened her eyes, caught a glimpse of Ethel, and broke the embrace.

Gelert whined suddenly and walked around in a circle with his tail between his legs. What was the matter with him?

A moment later Ethel felt a tremor in the ground, as if an express train were passing, even though the railway line ended a mile away.

Maud frowned and opened her mouth to speak; then there was a crack like a clap of thunder.

"What on earth was that?" said Maud.

Ethel knew.

She screamed, and began to run.

{ V }

Billy Williams and Tommy Griffiths were having a break.

They were working a seam called the Four-Foot Coal, only six hundred yards deep, not as far down as the Main Level. The seam was divided into five districts, all named after British racecourses, and they were in Ascot, the one nearest to the upcast shaft. Both boys were working as butties, assistants to older miners. The collier used his mandrel, a straight-bladed pick, to hew the coal away from the coal face, and his butty shoveled it into a wheeled dram. They had started work at six o'clock in the morning, as always, and now after a couple of hours they were taking a rest, sitting on the damp ground with their backs to the side of the tunnel, letting the soft breath of the ventilation system cool their skin, drinking long drafts of lukewarm sweet tea from their flasks.

They had been born on the same day in 1898, and were six months away from their sixteenth birthday. The difference in their physical development, so embarrassing to Billy when he was thirteen, had vanished. Now they were both young men, broad-shouldered and strong-armed, and they shaved once a week though they did not really need to. They were dressed only in their shorts and boots, and their bodies were black with a mixture of perspiration and coal dust. In the dim lamplight they gleamed like ebony statues of pagan gods. The effect was spoiled only by their caps.

The work was hard, but they were used to it. They did not complain of aching backs and stiff joints, as older men did. They had energy to spare, and on days off they found equally strenuous things to do, playing rugby or digging flower beds or even bare-knuckle boxing in the barn behind the Two Crowns pub.

Billy had not forgotten his initiation three years ago—indeed, he still burned with indignation when he thought of it. He had vowed then that he would never mistreat new boys. Only today he had warned little Bert Morgan: "Don't be surprised if the men play a trick on you. They may leave you in the dark for an hour or something stupid like that. Little things please little minds." The older men in the cage had glared at him, but he met their eyes: he knew he was in the right, and so did they.

Mam had been even angrier than Billy. "Tell me," she had said to Da, standing in the middle of the living room with her hands on her hips and her dark eyes flashing righteousness, "how is the Lord's purpose served by torturing little boys?"

"You wouldn't understand—you're a woman," Da had replied, an uncharacteristically weak response from him.

Billy believed that the world in general, and the Aberowen pit in particular, would be better places if all men led God-fearing lives. Tommy, whose father was an atheist and a disciple of Karl Marx, believed that the capitalist system would soon destroy itself, with a little help from a revolutionary working class. The two boys argued fiercely but continued best friends.

"It's not like you to work on a Sunday," Tommy said.

That was true. The mine was doing extra shifts to cope with the demand for coal but, in deference to religion, Celtic Minerals made the Sunday shifts optional. However, Billy was working despite his devotion to the Sabbath. "I think the Lord wants me to have a bicycle," he said.

Tommy laughed, but Billy was not joking. The Bethesda Chapel had opened a sister church in a small village ten miles away, and Billy was one of the Aberowen congregation who had volunteered to go across the mountain every other Sunday to encourage the new chapel. If he had a bicycle he could go there on weeknights as well, and help start a Bible class or a prayer meeting. He had discussed this plan with the elders, and they had agreed that the Lord would bless Billy's working on the Sabbath day for a few weeks.

Billy was about to explain this when the ground beneath him shook, there was a bang like the crack of doom, and his flask was blown out of his hand by a terrific wind.

His heart seemed to stop. Suddenly he remembered that he was half a mile underground, with millions of tons of earth and rock over his head, held up only by a few timber props.

"What the bloody hell was that?" said Tommy in a scared voice.

Billy jumped to his feet, shaking with fright. He lifted

his lamp and looked both ways along the tunnel. He saw no flames, no fall of rock, and no more dust than was normal. When the reverberations died away, there was no noise.

"It was an explosion," he said, his voice unsteady. This was what every miner dreaded every day. A sudden release of firedamp could be produced by a fall of rock, or just by a collier hacking through to a fault in the seam. If no one noticed the warning signs—or if the concentration simply built up too quickly—the inflammable gas could be ignited by a spark from a pony's hoof, or from the electric bell of a cage, or by a stupid miner lighting his pipe against all regulations.

Tommy said: "But where?"

"It must be down on the Main Level—that's why we escaped."

"Jesus Christ, help us."

"He will," said Billy, and his terror began to ebb. "Especially if we help ourselves." There was no sign of the two colliers for whom the boys had been working—they had gone to spend their break in the Goodwood district. Billy and Tommy had to make their own decisions. "We'd better go to the shaft."

They pulled on their clothes, hooked their lamps to their belts, and ran to the upcast shaft, called Pyramus. The landing onsetter, in charge of the elevator, was Dai Chops. "The cage isn't coming!" he said with panic in his voice. "I've been ringing and ringing!"

The man's fear was infectious, and Billy had to fight down his own panic. After a moment he said: "What about the telephone?" The onsetter communicated with his counterpart on the surface by signals on an electric bell, but recently phones had been installed on both levels, connected with the office of the colliery manager, Maldwyn Morgan.

"No answer," said Dai.

"I'll try again." The phone was fixed to the wall beside the cage. Billy picked it up and turned the handle. "Come on, come on!"

A quavery voice answered. "Yes?" It was Arthur Llewellyn, the manager's clerk.

"Spotty, this is Billy Williams," Billy shouted into the mouthpiece. "Where's Mr. Morgan?"

"Not here. What was that bang?"

"It was an explosion underground, you clot! Where's the boss?"

"He have gone to Merthyr," Spotty said plaintively.

"Why's he gone—never mind, forget that. Here's what you got to do. Spotty, are you listening to me?"

"Aye." The voice seemed stronger.

"First of all, send someone to the Methodist chapel and tell Dai Crybaby to assemble his rescue team."

"Right."

"Then phone the hospital and get them to send the ambulance to the pithead."

"Is someone injured?"

"Bound to be, after a bang like that! Third, get all the men in the coal-cleaning shed to run out fire hoses."

"Fire?"

"The dust will be burning. Fourth, call the police station and tell Geraint there have been an explosion. He'll phone Cardiff." Billy could not think of anything else. "All right?"

"All right, Billy."

Billy put the earpiece back on the hook. He was not sure how effective his instructions would be, but speaking to Spotty had focused his mind. "There will be men injured on the Main Level," he said to Dai Chops and Tommy. "We must get down there."

Dai said: "We can't. The cage isn't here."

"There's a ladder in the shaft wall, isn't there?"

"It's two hundred yards down!"

"Well, if I was a sissy I wouldn't be a collier, now, would I?" His words were brave, but all the same he was scared. The shaft ladder was seldom used, and it might not have been well-maintained. One slip, or a broken rung, could cause him to fall to his death.

Dai opened the gate with a clang. The shaft was lined with brick, damp and moldy. A narrow shelf ran horizontally around the lining, outside the wooden cage housing. An iron ladder was fixed by brackets cemented into the brickwork. There was nothing reassuring about its thin side rails and narrow treads. Billy hesitated, regretting his impulsive bravado. But to back out now would be too humiliating. He took a deep breath and said a silent prayer, then stepped onto the shelf.

He edged around until he reached the ladder. He wiped

his hands on his trousers, grasped the side rails, and put his feet on the treads.

He went down. The iron was rough to his touch, and rust flaked off on his hands. In places the brackets were loose, and the ladder shifted unnervingly under his feet. The lamp hooked to his belt was bright enough to illuminate the treads below him, but not to show the bottom of the shaft. He did not know whether that was better or worse.

Unfortunately, the descent gave him time to think. He remembered all the ways miners could die. To be killed by the explosion itself was a mercifully quick end for the luckiest. The burning of the methane produced suffocating carbon dioxide, which the miners called afterdamp. Many were trapped by falls of rock, and might bleed to death before rescue came. Some died of thirst, with their workmates just a few yards away trying desperately to tunnel through the debris.

Suddenly he wanted to go back, to climb upward to safety instead of down into destruction and chaos—but he could not, with Tommy immediately above him, following him down.

"Are you with me, Tommy?" he called.

Tommy's voice came from just above his head. "Aye!"

That strengthened Billy's nerve. He went down faster, his confidence returning. Soon he saw light, and a moment later he heard voices. As he approached the Main Level he smelled smoke.

Now he heard an eerie racket, screaming and banging, which he struggled to identify. It threatened to undermine his courage. He got a grip on himself: there had to be a rational explanation. A moment later he realized he was hearing the terrified whinnying of the ponies, and the sound of them kicking the wooden sides of their stalls, desperate to escape. Comprehension did not make the noise less disturbing: he felt the same way they did.

He reached the Main Level, sidled around the brick ledge, opened the gate from inside, and stepped gratefully onto muddy ground. The dim underground light was further reduced by traces of smoke, but he could see the main tunnels.

The pit bottom onsetter was Patrick O'Connor, a middle-aged man who had lost a hand in a roof collapse. A

Catholic, he was inevitably known as Pat Pope. He stared with incredulity. "Billy-with-Jesus!" he said. "Where the bloody hell have you come from?"

"From the Four-Foot Coal," Billy answered. "We heard the bang."

Tommy followed Billy out of the shaft and said: "What's happened, Pat?"

"Far as I can make out, the explosion must have been at the other end of this level, near Thisbe," said Pat. "The deputy and everyone else have gone to see." He spoke calmly, but there was desperation in his look.

Billy went to the phone and turned the handle. A moment later he heard his father's voice. "Williams here. Who's that?"

Billy did not pause to wonder why a union official was answering the colliery manager's phone—anything could happen in an emergency. "Da, it's me, Billy."

"God in His mercy be thanked, you're all right," said his father, with a break in his voice; then he became his usual brisk self. "Tell me what you know, boy."

"Me and Tommy were in the Four-Foot Coal. We've climbed down Pyramus to the Main Level. The explosion was over toward Thisbe, we think. There's a bit of smoke, not much. But the cage isn't working."

"The winding mechanism have been damaged by the upward blast," Da said in a calm voice. "But we're working on it and we'll have it fixed in a few minutes. Get as many men as you can to the pit bottom so we can start bringing them up as soon as the cage is fixed."

"I'll tell them."

"The Thisbe shaft is completely out of action, so make sure no one tries to escape that way—they could get trapped by the fire."

"Right."

"There's breathing apparatus outside the deputies' office."

Billy knew that. It was a recent innovation, demanded by the union and made compulsory by the Coal Mines Act of 1911. "The air's not bad at the moment," he said.

"Where you are, perhaps, but it may be worse farther in."

"Right." Billy put the earpiece back on the hook.

He repeated to Tommy and Pat what his father had said. Pat pointed to a row of new lockers. "The key should be in the office."

Billy ran to the deputies' office, but he could see no keys. He guessed they were on someone's belt. He looked again at the row of lockers, each labeled: "Breathing Apparatus." They were made of tin. "Got a crowbar, Pat?" he said.

The onsetter had a tool kit for minor repairs. Pat handed him a stout screwdriver. Billy swiftly broke open the first locker.

It was empty.

Billy stared, unbelieving.

Pat said: "They tricked us!"

Tommy said: "Bastard capitalists."

Billy opened another locker. It, too, was empty. He broke open the others with angry savagery, wanting to expose the dishonesty of Celtic Minerals and Perceval Jones.

Tommy said: "We'll manage without."

Tommy was impatient to get going, but Billy was trying to think clearly. His eye fell on the fire dram. It was the management's pathetic excuse for a fire engine: a coal dram filled with water, with a hand pump strapped to it. It was not completely useless: Billy had seen it operate after what the miners called a "flash," when a small quantity of firedamp close to the roof of the tunnel would ignite, briefly, and they would all throw themselves to the floor. The flash would sometimes light the coal dust on the tunnel walls, which then had to be sprayed.

"We'll take the fire dram," he shouted to Tommy.

It was already on rails, and the two of them were able to push it along. Billy thought briefly of harnessing a pony to it, then decided it would take too long, especially as the beasts were all in a panic.

Pat Pope said: "My boy Micky is working in Marigold district, but I can't go and look for him. I've got to stay here." There was desperation in his face, but in an emergency the onsetter had to stay by the shaft—it was an inflexible rule.

"I'll keep an eye open for him," Billy promised.

"Thank you, Billy boy."

The two lads pushed the dram along the main road. Drams had no brakes: their drivers slowed them by sticking a stout piece of wood into the spokes. Many deaths and countless injuries were caused by runaway drams. "Not too fast," Billy said.

They were a quarter of a mile into the tunnel when the temperature rose and the smoke thickened. Soon they heard voices. Following the sound they turned into a branch tunnel. This part of the seam was currently being worked. On either side Billy could see, at regular intervals, the entrances to miners' workplaces, usually called gates, but sometimes just holes. As the noise grew, they stopped pushing the dram and looked ahead.

The tunnel was on fire. Flames licked up from walls and floor. A handful of men stood at the edge of the conflagration, silhouetted against the glow like souls in hell. One held a blanket and was batting it ineffectually at a blazing stack of timber. Others were shouting; no one was listening. In the distance, dimly visible, was a train of drams. The smoke had a strange whiff of roast meat, and Billy realized with a sick feeling that it must come from the pony that had been pulling the drams.

Billy spoke to one of the men. "What's happening?"

"There's men trapped in their gates—but we can't get to them."

Billy saw that the man was Rhys Price. No wonder nothing was being done. "We've brought the fire dram," he said.

Another man turned to him, and he was relieved to see John Jones the Shop, a more sensible character. "Good man!" said Jones. "Let's have the hose on this bloody lot."

Billy ran out the hose while Tommy connected the pump. Billy aimed the jet at the ceiling of the tunnel, so that the water would run down the walls. He soon realized that the mine's ventilation system, blowing down Thisbe and up Pyramus, was forcing the flames and smoke toward him. As soon as he got the chance he would tell the people on the surface to reverse the fans. Reversible fans were now mandatory—another requirement of the 1911 act.

Despite the difficulty, the fire began to die back, and Billy was able to go forward slowly. After a few minutes the nearest gate was clear of flame. Immediately two miners ran out, gasping the relatively good air of the tunnel. Billy recognized the Ponti brothers, Giuseppe and Giovanni, known as Joey and Johnny.

Some of the men ran into the gate. John Jones came out carrying the limp form of Dai Ponies, the horse wrangler. Billy could not tell whether he was dead or just unconscious. He said: "Take him to Pyramus, not Thisbe."

Price butted in: "Who are you to be giving orders, Billy-with-Jesus?"

Billy was not going to waste time arguing with Price. He addressed Jones. "I spoke on the phone to the surface. Thisbe is badly damaged but the cage should soon be operating in Pyramus. I was told to tell everyone to head for Pyramus."

"Right, I'll spread the word," said Jones, and he went off.

Billy and Tommy continued to fight the fire, clearing farther gates, freeing more trapped men. Some were bleeding, many were scorched, and a few had been hurt by falling rock. Those who could walk carried the dead and the seriously injured in a grim procession.

Too soon, their water was gone. "We'll push the dram back and fill it from the pond at the bottom of the shaft," Billy said.

Together they hurried back. The cage was still not working, and there were now a dozen or so rescued miners waiting, and several bodies on the ground, some groaning in agony, others ominously still. While Tommy filled the dram with muddy water, Billy picked up the phone. Once again his father answered. "The winding gear will be operating in five minutes," he said. "How is it down there?"

"We've got some dead and injured out of the gates. Send down drams full of water as soon as you can."

"What about you?"

"I'm all right. Listen, Da, you should reverse the ventilation. Blow down Pyramus and up Thisbe. That will drive the smoke and afterdamp away from the rescuers."

"Can't be done," said his father.

"But it's the law—pit ventilation *must* be reversible!"

"Perceval Jones told the inspectors a sob story, and they gave him another year to modify the blowers."

Billy would have cursed if anyone other than his father had been on the line. "How about turning on the sprinklers—can you do that?"

"Aye, we can," said Da. "Why didn't I think of that?" He spoke to someone else.

Billy replaced the earpiece. He helped Tommy refill the dram, taking turns with the hand pump. It took as long to fill as it had to empty. The flow of men from the afflicted district slowed while the fire raged unchecked. At last the tub was full and they started back.

The sprinklers came on, but when Billy and Tommy reached the fire, they found that the flow of water from the narrow overhead pipe was too slight to put out the flames. However, Jones the Shop had now got the men organized. He was keeping the uninjured survivors with him, for rescue work, and sending the walking wounded to the shaft. As soon as Billy and Tommy had connected the hose, he seized it and ordered another man to pump. "You two go back and get another dram of water!" he said. "That way we can keep on hosing."

"Right," said Billy, but before he turned to go something caught his eye. A figure came running through the flames with his clothes on fire. "Good God!" Billy said, horrified. As he watched, the runner stumbled and fell.

Billy shouted at Jones: "Hose me!" Without waiting for acknowledgment, he ran into the tunnel. He felt a jet of water strike his back. The heat was terrible. His face hurt and his clothes smoldered. He grabbed the prone miner under the shoulders and pulled, running backward. He could not see the face but he could tell it was a boy of his own age.

Jones kept the hose on Billy, soaking his hair, his back, and his legs, but the front of him was dry, and he could smell his skin scorching. He screamed in pain but managed to keep hold of the unconscious body. A second later he was out of the fire. He turned and let Jones spray his front. The water on his face was blessed relief: though he still hurt, it was bearable.

Jones sprayed the boy on the floor. Billy turned him over and saw that it was Michael O'Connor, known as Micky Pope, the son of Pat. Pat had asked Billy to look out for him. Billy said: "Dear Jesus, have mercy on Pat."

He bent down and picked Micky up. The body was limp and lifeless. "I'll take him to the shaft," Billy said.

"Aye," said Jones. He was staring at Billy with an odd expression. "You do that, Billy boy."

Tommy went with Billy. Billy felt light-headed, but he was able to carry Micky. On the main road they encountered a rescue team with a pony pulling a small train of drams filled with water. They must have come from the surface, which meant the cage was operating and the rescue was now being properly managed, Billy reasoned wearily.

He was right. As he reached the shaft, the cage arrived again and disgorged more rescuers in protective clothing and more drams of water. When the newcomers had dispersed, heading for the fire, the wounded began to board the cage, carrying the dead and unconscious.

When Pat Pope had sent the cage up, Billy went to him, holding Micky in his arms.

Pat stared at Billy with a terrified look, shaking his head in negation, as if he could deny the news.

"I'm sorry, Pat," said Billy.

Pat would not look at the body. "No," he said. "Not my Micky."

"I pulled him out of the fire, Pat," said Billy. "But I was too bloody late, that's all." Then he began to cry.

{ VI }

The dinner had been a great success in every way. Bea had been in a sparkling mood: she would have liked a royal party every week. Fitz had gone to her bed, and as he expected she had welcomed him. He stayed until morning, slipping away only just before Nina arrived with the tea.

He was afraid the debate amongst the men might have been too controversial for a royal dinner, but he need not have worried. The king thanked him at breakfast, saying: "Fascinating discussion, very illuminating, just what I wanted." Fitz had glowed with pride.

Thinking it over as he smoked his after-breakfast cigar, Fitz realized that the thought of war did not horrify him. He had spoken of it as a tragedy, in an automatic way, but it would not be entirely a bad thing. War would unite the nation against a common enemy, and dampen the fires of unrest. There would be no more strikes, and talk of republicanism would be seen as unpatriotic. Women might even stop demanding the vote. And in a personal way he found himself strangely drawn to the prospect. War would be his chance to be useful, to prove his courage, to serve his country, to do something in return for the wealth and privilege that had been lavished on him all his life.

The news from the pit, coming at midmorning, took the sparkle off the party. Only one of the guests actually went into Aberowen—Gus Dewar, the American. Nevertheless, they all had the feeling, unusual for them, of being far from the center of attention. Lunch was a subdued affair, and the afternoon's entertainments were canceled. Fitz feared the king would be displeased with him, even though he had nothing to do with the operation of the mine. He was not a director or shareholder of Celtic Minerals. He merely licensed the mining rights to the company, which paid him a royalty per ton. So he felt sure that no reasonable person could possibly blame him for what had happened. Still, the nobility could not be seen to indulge in frivolous pursuits while men were trapped underground, especially when the king and queen were visiting. That meant that reading and smoking were just about the only acceptable pursuits. The royal couple were sure to be bored.

Fitz was angered. Men died all the time: soldiers were killed in battle, sailors went down with their ships, railway trains crashed, hotels full of sleeping guests burned to the ground. Why did a pit disaster have to happen just when he was entertaining the king?

Shortly before dinner Perceval Jones, mayor of Aberowen and chairman of Celtic Minerals, came to the house to brief the earl, and Fitz asked Sir Alan Tite whether the king might like to hear the report. His Majesty would, came the reply, and Fitz was relieved: at least the monarch had something to do.

The male guests gathered in the small drawing room, an informal space with soft chairs and potted palms and a piano. Jones was wearing the black tailcoat he had undoubtedly put on for church this morning. A short, pompous man, he looked like a strutting bird in a double-breasted gray waistcoat.

The king was in evening dress. "Good of you to come," he said briskly.

Jones said: "I had the honor of shaking Your Majesty's hand in 1911, when you came to Cardiff for the investiture of the Prince of Wales."

"I'm glad to renew our acquaintanceship, though sorry it should happen in such distressing circumstances," the king replied. "Tell me what happened in plain words, just as if you were explaining it to one of your fellow directors, over a drink at your club."

That was clever, Fitz thought; it set just the right tone—though no one offered Jones a drink, and the king did not invite him to sit down.

"So kind of Your Majesty." Jones spoke with a Cardiff accent, harsher than the lilt of the valleys. "There were two hundred and twenty men down the pit when the explosion occurred, fewer than normal as this is a special Sunday shift."

"You know the exact figure?" the king asked.

"Oh, yes, sir. We note the name of each man going down."

"Forgive the interruption. Please carry on."

"Both shafts were damaged, but firefighting teams brought the blaze under control, with the help of our sprinkler system, and evacuated the men." He looked at his watch. "As of two hours ago, two hundred and fifteen had been brought up."

"It sounds as if you have dealt with the emergency very efficiently, Jones."

"Thank you very much, Your Majesty."

"Are all the two hundred and fifteen alive?"

"No, sir. Eight are dead. Another fifty have injuries sufficiently serious to require a doctor."

"Dear me," said the king. "How very sad."

As Jones was explaining the steps being taken to locate and rescue the remaining five men, Peel slipped into the room and approached Fitz. The butler was in evening clothes, ready to serve dinner. Speaking very low, he said: "Just in case it's of interest, my lord . . ."

Fitz whispered: "Well?"

"The maid Williams just came back from the pithead. Her brother was something of a hero, apparently. Whether the king might like to hear the story from her own lips . . . ?"

Fitz thought for a moment. Williams would be upset, and might say the wrong thing. On the other hand, the king would probably like to speak to someone directly affected. He decided to take a chance. "Your Majesty," he said. "One of my servants has just returned from the pithead, and may have more up-to-date news. Her brother was underground when the gas exploded. Would you care to question her?"

"Yes, indeed," said the king. "Send her in, please."

A few moments later Ethel Williams entered. Her uniform was smudged with coal dust, but she had washed her face. She curtsied, and the king said: "What is the latest news?"

"Please, Your Majesty, there are five men trapped in Carnation district by a fall of rock. The rescue team are digging through the debris but the fire is still burning."

Fitz noticed that the king's manners with Ethel were subtly different. He had hardly looked at Perceval Jones, and had tapped a finger restlessly on the arm of his chair while listening; but he gave Ethel a direct look, and seemed more interested in her. In a softer voice, he asked: "What does your brother say?"

"The explosion of firedamp set light to the coal dust, and that's what's burning. The fire trapped many of the men in their workplaces, and some suffocated. My brother and the others couldn't rescue them because they had no breathing apparatus."

"That's not so," Jones said.

"I think it is," Gus Dewar contradicted him. As always, the American was a bit diffident in his manner, but he made an effort to speak insistently. "I spoke to some of the men coming up. They said the lockers marked 'Breathing Apparatus' turned out to be empty." He seemed to be suppressing anger.

Ethel Williams said: "And they couldn't put out the flames because there was insufficient water kept underground." Her eyes flashed with fury in a way that Fitz found alluring, and his heart skipped a beat.

"There's a fire engine!" Jones protested.

Gus Dewar spoke again. "A coal dram filled with water, and a hand pump."

Ethel Williams went on: "They should have been able to reverse the flow of ventilation, but Mr. Jones has not modified the machinery in accordance with the law."

Jones looked indignant. "It wasn't possible—"

Fitz interrupted. "All right, Jones. This isn't a public inquiry. His Majesty just wants to get people's impressions."

"Quite so," said the king. "But there is one subject on which you might be able to advise me, Jones."

"I should be honored—"

"I was planning to visit Aberowen and some of the surrounding villages tomorrow morning, and indeed to call upon your good self at the town hall. But in these circumstances a parade seems inappropriate."

Sir Alan, sitting behind the king's left shoulder, shook his head and murmured: "Quite impossible."

"On the other hand," the king went on, "it seems wrong to go away without any acknowledgment of the disaster. People might think us indifferent."

Fitz guessed there was a clash between the king and his staff. They probably wanted to cancel the visit, imagining that was the least risky course; whereas the king felt the need to make some gesture.

There was a silence while Perceval considered the question. When he spoke, he said only: "It's a difficult choice."

Ethel Williams said: "May I make a suggestion?"

Peel was aghast. "Williams!" he hissed. "Speak only when spoken to!"

Fitz was startled by her impertinence in the presence of the king. He tried to keep his voice calm as he said: "Perhaps later, Williams."

But the king smiled. To Fitz's relief, he seemed quite taken with Ethel. "We might as well hear what this young person has to propose," he said.

That was all Ethel needed. Without further ado she said: "You and the queen should visit the bereaved families. No parade, just one carriage with black horses. It would mean a lot to them. And everybody would think you were wonderful." She bit her lip and subsided into silence.

That last sentence was a breach of etiquette, Fitz thought anxiously; the king did not need to make people think he was wonderful.

Sir Alan was horrified. "Never been done before," he said in alarm.

But the king seemed intrigued by the idea. "Visit the bereaved . . ." he said musingly. He turned to his equerry. "By Jove, I think that's capital, Alan. Commiserate with my people in their suffering. No cavalcade, just one carriage." He turned back to the maid. "Very good, Williams," he said. "Thank you for speaking up."

Fitz breathed a sigh of relief.

{ VII }

In the end there was more than one carriage, of course. The king and queen went in the first with Sir Alan and a lady-in-waiting; Fitz and Bea followed in a second with the bishop; and a pony-and-trap with assorted servants brought up the rear. Perceval Jones had wanted to be one of the party, but Fitz had squashed that idea. As Ethel had pointed out, the bereaved might have tried to take him by the throat.

It was a windy day, and a cold rain lashed the horses as they trotted down the long drive of Tŷ Gwyn. Ethel was in the third vehicle. Because of her father's job she was familiar with every mining family in Aberowen. She was the only person at Tŷ Gwyn who knew the names of all the dead and injured. She had given directions to the drivers, and it would be her job to remind the equerry who was who. She had her fingers crossed. This was her idea, and if it went wrong she would be blamed.

As they drove out of the grand iron gates, she was struck, as always, by the sudden transition. Inside the grounds all was order, charm, and beauty; outside was the ugliness of the real world. A row of agricultural laborers' cottages stood beside the road, tiny houses of two rooms, with odd bits of lumber and junk in front and a couple of dirty children playing in the ditch. Soon afterward the miners' terraces began, superior to the farm cottages but still ungainly and monotonous to an eye such as Ethel's, spoiled by the perfect proportions of Tŷ Gwyn's windows and doorways and roofs. The people out here had cheap clothes that quickly became shapeless and worn, and were colored with dyes that faded, so that all the men were in grayish suits and all the women brownish dresses. Ethel's maid's outfit was envied for its warm wool skirt and crisp cotton blouse, for all that some of the girls liked to say they would never lower themselves to be servants. But the biggest difference was in the people themselves. Out here they had blemished skin, dirty hair, and black fingernails. The men coughed, the women sniffed, and the children all had runny noses. The poor shambled and limped along roads where the rich strode confidently.

The carriages drove down the mountainside to Mafeking Terrace. Most of the inhabitants were lining the pavements, waiting, but there were no flags, and they did not cheer, just bowed and curtsied, as the cavalcade pulled up outside number 19.

Ethel jumped down and spoke quietly to Sir Alan. "Sian Evans, five children, lost her husband, David Evans, an underground horse wrangler." David Evans, known as Dai Ponies, had been familiar to Ethel as an elder of the Bethesda Chapel.

Sir Alan nodded, and Ethel stepped smartly back while he murmured in the ear of the king. Ethel caught Fitz's eye, and he gave her a nod of approval. She felt a glow. She was assisting the king—and the earl was pleased with her.

The king and queen went to the front door. Its paint was peeling, but the step was polished. I never thought I'd see this, Ethel thought, the king knocking on the door of a collier's house. The king wore a tailcoat and a tall black hat; Ethel had strongly advised Sir Alan that the people of Aberowen would not wish to see their monarch in the kind of tweed suit that they themselves might wear.

The door was opened by the widow in her Sunday best, complete with hat. Fitz had suggested that the king should surprise people, but Ethel had argued against that, and Sir Alan had agreed with her. On a surprise visit to a distraught family the royal couple might have been confronted with drunken men, half-naked women, and fighting children. Better to forewarn everyone.

"Good morning. I'm the king," said the king, raising his hat politely. "Are you Mrs. David Evans?"

She looked blank for a moment. She was more used to being called Mrs. Dai Ponies.

"I have come to say how very sorry I am about your husband, David," said the king.

Mrs. Dai Ponies seemed too nervous to feel any emotion. "Thank you very much," she said stiffly.

It was too formal, Ethel saw. The king was as uncomfortable as the widow. Neither was able to say how they really felt.

Then the queen touched Mrs. Dai's arm. "It must be very hard for you, my dear," she said.

"Yes, ma'am, it is," said the widow in a whisper, and then she burst into tears.

Ethel wiped a tear from her own cheek.

The king was embarrassed, but to his credit, he stood his ground, murmuring: "Very sad, very sad."

Mrs. Evans sobbed uncontrollably, but she seemed rooted to the spot, and did not turn her face away. There was nothing gracious about grief, Ethel saw: Mrs. Dai's face was blotched red, her open mouth showed that she had lost half her teeth, and her sobs were hoarse with desperation.

"There, there," said the queen. She pressed her handkerchief into Mrs. Dai's hand. "Take this."

Mrs. Dai was not yet thirty, but her big hands were knotted and lumpy with arthritis like an old woman's. She wiped her face with the queen's handkerchief. Her sobs subsided. "He was a good man, ma'am," she said. "Never raised a hand to me."

The queen did not know what to say about a man whose virtue was that he did not beat his wife.

"He was even kind to his ponies," Mrs. Dai added.

"I'm sure he was," said the queen, back on familiar ground.

A toddler emerged from the depths of the house and clung to its mother's skirt. The king tried again. "I believe you have five children," he said.

"Oh, sir, what are they going to do with no da?"

"It's very sad," the king repeated.

Sir Alan coughed, and the king said: "We're going on to see some other people in the same sad position as yourself."

"Oh, sir, it was kind of you to come. I can't tell you how much it means to me. Thank you, thank you."

The king turned away.

The queen said: "I will pray for you tonight, Mrs. Evans." Then she followed the king.

As they were getting into their carriage, Fitz gave Mrs. Dai an envelope. Inside, Ethel knew, were five gold sovereigns and a note, handwritten on blue crested Tŷ Gwyn paper, saying: "Earl Fitzherbert wishes you to have this token of his deep sympathy."

That, too, had been Ethel's idea.

{ VIII }

One week after the explosion Billy went to chapel with his da, mam, and gramper.

The Bethesda Chapel was a square whitewashed room with no pictures on the walls. The chairs were arranged in neat rows on four sides of a plain table. On the table stood a loaf of white bread on a Woolworth's china plate and a jug of cheap sherry—the symbolic bread and wine. The service was not called Communion or mass, but simply the breaking of the bread.

By eleven o'clock the congregation of a hundred or so worshippers were in their seats, the men in their best suits, the women in hats, the children scrubbed and fidgeting in the back rows. There was no set ritual: the men would do as the Holy Spirit moved them—extemporize a prayer, announce a hymn, read a passage from the Bible, or give a short sermon. The women would remain silent, of course.

In practice there was a pattern. The first prayer was always spoken by one of the elders, who would then break the loaf and hand the plate to the nearest person. Each member of the congregation, excluding the children, would take a small piece and eat it. Next the wine was passed around, and everyone drank from the jug, the women taking tiny sips, some of the men enjoying a good mouthful. After that they all sat in silence until someone was moved to speak.

When Billy had asked his father at what age he should begin taking a vocal part in the service, Da had said: "There's no rule. We follow where the Holy Spirit leads." Billy had taken him at his word. If the first line of a hymn came into his mind, at some point during the hour, he took that as a nudge from the Holy Spirit, and he would stand up and announce the hymn. He was precocious in doing so at his age, he knew, but the congregation accepted that. The story of how Jesus had appeared to him during his underground initiation had been retold in half the chapels in the South Wales coalfield, and Billy was seen as special.

This morning every prayer begged for consolation for the bereaved, especially Mrs. Dai Ponies, who was sitting there in a veil, her eldest son beside her looking scared. Da asked God for the greatness of heart to forgive the wicked-

ness of the mine owners in flouting laws about breathing
equipment and reversible ventilation. Billy felt something
was missing. It was too simple just to ask for healing. He
wanted help in understanding how the explosion fitted into
God's plan.

He had never yet extemporized a prayer. Many of the
men prayed with fine-sounding phrases and quotations
from the Scriptures, almost as if they were sermonizing.
Billy himself suspected God was not so easily impressed.
He always felt most moved by simple prayers that seemed
heartfelt.

Toward the end of the service, words and sentences began to take shape in his mind, and he felt a strong impulse
to give voice to them. Taking that for the guidance of the
Holy Spirit, he eventually stood up.

With his eyes shut tight he said: "Oh, God, we have
asked Thee this morning to bring comfort to those who
have lost a husband, a father, a son, especially our sister in
the Lord Mrs. Evans, and we pray that the bereaved will
open their hearts to receive Thy benison."

This had been said by others. Billy paused, then went on:
"And now, Lord, we ask for one more gift: the blessing of
understanding. We need to know, Lord, why this explosion
have took place down the pit. All things are in Thy power,
so why didst Thou allow firedamp to fill the Main Level,
and why didst Thou permit it to catch alight? How come,
Lord, that men are set over us, directors of Celtic Minerals,
who in their greed for money become careless of the lives
of Thy people? How can the deaths of good men, and the
mangling of the bodies Thou didst create, serve Thy holy
purpose?"

He paused again. He knew it was wrong to make demands of God, as if negotiating with the management, so
he added: "We know that the suffering of the people of Aberowen must play a part in Thy eternal plan." He thought
he should probably leave it there, but he could not refrain
from adding: "But, Lord, we can't see how, so please explain it to us."

He finished: "In the name of the Lord Jesus Christ."

The congregation said: "Amen."

{ IX }

That afternoon the people of Aberowen were invited to view the gardens at Tŷ Gwyn. It meant a lot of work for Ethel.

A notice had gone up in the pubs on Saturday night, and the message was read in churches and chapels after services on Sunday morning. The gardens had been made especially lovely for the king, despite the winter season, and now Earl Fitzherbert wished to share their beauty with his neighbors, the invitation said. The earl would be wearing a black tie, and he would be glad to see his visitors wearing a similar token of respect for the dead. Although it would obviously be inappropriate to have a party, nevertheless refreshments would be offered.

Ethel had ordered three marquees to be pitched on the East Lawn. In one were half a dozen 108-gallon butts of pale ale brought by train from the Crown Brewery in Pontyclun. For teetotallers, of whom there were many in Aberowen, the next tent had trestle tables bearing giant tea urns and hundreds of cups and saucers. In the third, smaller tent, sherry was offered to the town's diminutive middle class, including the Anglican vicar, both doctors, and the colliery manager, Maldwyn Morgan, who was already being referred to as Gone-to-Merthyr Morgan.

By good luck it was a sunny day, cold but dry, with a few harmless-looking white clouds high in a blue sky. Four thousand people came—very nearly the entire population of the town—and almost everyone wore a black tie, ribbon, or armband. They strolled around the shrubbery, peered through the windows into the house, and churned up the lawns.

Princess Bea stayed in her room: this was not her kind of social event. All upper-class people were selfish, in Ethel's experience, but Bea had made an art of it. All her energy was focused on pleasing herself and getting her own way. Even when giving a party—something she did well—her motive was mainly to provide a showcase for her own beauty and charm.

Fitz held court in the Victorian-Gothic splendor of the Great Hall, with his huge dog lying on the floor beside him like a fur rug. He wore the brown tweed suit that made him seem more approachable, albeit with a stiff collar and black tie. He looked handsomer than ever, Ethel thought. She brought the relatives of the dead and injured to see him in groups of three or four, so that he was able to commiserate with every Aberowen resident who had suffered. He spoke to them with his usual charm, and sent each one away feeling special.

Ethel was now the housekeeper. After the king's visit, Princess Bea had insisted that Mrs. Jevons retire permanently: she had no time for tired old servants. In Ethel she had seen someone who would work hard to fulfill her wishes, and had promoted her despite her youth. So Ethel had achieved her ambition. She had taken over the housekeeper's little room off the servants' hall, and had hung up a photograph of her parents, in their Sunday best, taken outside the Bethesda Chapel the day it had opened.

When Fitz came to the end of the list, Ethel asked permission to spend a few minutes with her family.

"Of course," said the earl. "Take as much time as you like. You've been absolutely marvelous. I don't know how I would have managed without you. The king was grateful for your help, too. How do you remember all those names?"

She smiled. She was not sure why it gave her such a thrill to be praised by him. "Most of these people have been to our house, sometime or other, to see my father about compensation for an injury, or a dispute with an overseer, or a worry about some safety measure down the pit."

"Well, I think you're remarkable," he said, and he gave the irresistible smile that occasionally came over his face and made him seem almost like the boy next door. "Give my respects to your father."

She went out and ran across the lawn, feeling on top of the world. She found Da, Mam, Billy, and Gramper in the tea tent. Da looked distinguished in his black Sunday suit and a white shirt with a stiff collar. Billy had a nasty burn on his cheek. Ethel said: "How are you feeling, Billy boy?"

"Not bad. It looks horrible, but the doctor says it's better without a bandage."

"Everybody's talking about how brave you were."

"It wasn't enough to save Micky Pope, though."

There was nothing to say to that, but Ethel touched her brother's arm in sympathy.

Mam said proudly: "Billy led us in prayer this morning at Bethesda."

"Well done, Billy! I'm sorry I missed it." Ethel had not gone to chapel—there was too much to do in the house. "What did you pray about?"

"I asked the Lord to help us understand why He allowed the explosion down the pit." Billy cast a nervous glance at Da, who was not smiling.

Da said severely: "Billy might have done better to ask God to strengthen his faith, so that he can believe *without* understanding."

Clearly they had already argued about this. Ethel did not have the patience for theological disputes that made no difference to anything in the end. She tried to brighten the mood. "Earl Fitzherbert asked me to give you his respects, Da," she said. "Wasn't that nice of him?"

Da did not melt. "I was sorry to see you taking part in that farce on Monday," he said sternly.

"Monday?" she said incredulously. "When the king visited the families?"

"I saw you whispering the names to that flunky."

"That was Sir Alan Tite."

"I don't care what he calls himself. I know a lickspittle when I see one."

Ethel was shocked. How could Da be scornful of her great moment? She felt like crying. "I thought you'd be proud of me, helping the king!"

"How dare the king offer sympathy to our folk? What does a king know of hardship and danger?"

Ethel fought back tears. "But, Da, it meant so much to people that he went to see them!"

"It distracted everyone's attention from the dangerous and illegal actions of Celtic Minerals."

"But they need comfort." Why could he not see this?

"The king softened them up. Last Sunday afternoon this town was ready to revolt. By Monday evening all they could talk about was the queen giving her handkerchief to Mrs. Dai Ponies."

Ethel went swiftly from heartbreak to anger. "I'm sorry you feel that way," she said coldly.

"Nothing to be sorry for—"

"I'm sorry because you are wrong," she said, firmly overriding him.

Da was taken aback. It was rare for him to be told he was wrong by anyone, let alone a girl.

Mam said: "Now, Eth—"

"People have feelings, Da," she said recklessly. "That's what you always forget."

Da was speechless.

Mam said: "That's enough, now!"

Ethel looked at Billy. Through a mist of tears she saw his expression of awestruck admiration. That encouraged her. She sniffed and wiped her eyes with the back of her hand and said: "You and your union, and your safety regulations and your Scriptures—I know they're important, Da, but you can't do away with people's feelings. I hope that one day socialism will make the world a better place for working people, but in the meantime they need consolation."

Da found his voice at last. "I think we've heard enough from you," he said. "Being with the king has gone to your head. You're a slip of a girl, and you've no business lecturing your elders."

She was crying too much to argue further. "I'm sorry, Da," she said. After a heavy silence she added: "I'd better get back to work." The earl had told her to take all the time she liked, but she wanted to be alone. She turned away from her father's glare and walked back to the big house. She kept her eyes downcast, hoping the crowds would not notice her tears.

She did not want to meet anyone so she slipped into the Gardenia Suite. Lady Maud had returned to London, so the room was empty and the bed was stripped. Ethel threw herself down on the mattress and cried.

She had been feeling so proud. How could Da undermine everything she had done? Did he want her to do a *bad* job? She worked for the nobility. So did every coal miner in Aberowen. Even though Celtic Minerals employed them, it was the earl's coal they were digging, and he was paid the same per ton as the miner who dug it out of the earth—a fact her father never tired of pointing out. If it was all right to be a good collier, efficient and productive, what was wrong with being a good housekeeper?

She heard the door open. Quickly she jumped to her feet. It was the earl. "What on earth is the matter?" he said kindly. "I heard you from outside the door."

"I'm very sorry, my lord. I shouldn't have come in here."

"That's all right." There was genuine concern on his impossibly handsome face. "Why are you crying?"

"I was so proud to have helped the king," she said woefully. "But my father says it was a farce, all done just to stop people feeling angry with Celtic Minerals." She burst into fresh tears.

"What nonsense," he said. "Anyone could tell that the king's concern was genuine. And the queen's." He took the white linen handkerchief from the breast pocket of his jacket. She expected him to hand it to her, but instead he wiped the tears from her cheeks with a gentle touch. "I was proud of you last Monday, even if your father wasn't."

"You're so kind."

"There, there," he said, and he bent down and kissed her lips.

She was dumbfounded. It was the last thing in the world she had expected. When he straightened up she stared at him uncomprehendingly.

He gazed back at her. "You are absolutely enchanting," he said in a low voice; then he kissed her again.

This time she pushed him away. "My lord, what are you doing?" she said in a shocked whisper.

"I don't know."

"But what can you be thinking of?"

"I'm not thinking at all."

She stared up at his chiseled face. The green eyes studied her intently, as if trying to read her mind. She realized that she adored him. Suddenly she was flooded with excitement and desire.

"I can't help myself," he said.

She sighed happily. "Kiss me again, then," she said.

CHAPTER THREE

February 1914

At half past ten the looking glass in the hall of Earl Fitzherbert's Mayfair house showed a tall man immaculately dressed in the daytime clothing of an upper-class Englishman. He wore an upright collar, disliking the fashion for soft collars, and his silver tie was fastened with a pearl. Some of his friends thought it was undignified to dress well. "I say, Fitz, you look like a damn tailor, about to open his shop in the morning," the young Marquis of Lowther had said to him once. But Lowthie was a scruff, with crumbs on his waistcoat and cigar ash on the cuffs of his shirt, and he wanted everyone else to look as bad. Fitz hated to be grubby; it suited him to be spruce.

He put on a gray top hat. With his walking stick in his right hand and a new pair of gray suede gloves in his left, he went out of the house and turned south. In Berkeley Square a blond girl of about fourteen winked at him and said: "Suck you for a shilling?"

He crossed Piccadilly and entered Green Park. A few snowdrops clustered around the roots of the trees. He passed Buckingham Palace and entered an unattractive neighborhood near Victoria Station. He had to ask a policeman for directions to Ashley Gardens. The street turned out to be behind the Roman Catholic cathedral. Really, Fitz thought, if one is going to ask members of the nobility to call, one should have one's office in a respectable quarter.

He had been summoned by an old friend of his father's

named Mansfield Smith-Cumming. A retired naval officer, Smith-Cumming was now doing something vague in the War Office. He had sent Fitz a rather short note. "I should be grateful for a word on a matter of national importance. Can you call on me tomorrow morning at, say, eleven o'clock?" The note was typewritten and signed, in green ink, with the single letter "C."

In truth Fitz was pleased that someone in the government wanted to talk to him. He had a horror of being thought of as an ornament, a wealthy aristocrat with no function other than to decorate social events. He hoped he was going to be asked for his advice, perhaps about his old regiment, the Welsh Rifles. Or there might be some task he could perform in connection with the South Wales Territorials, of which he was honorary colonel. Anyway, just being summoned to the War Office made him feel he was not completely superfluous.

If this really was the War Office. The address turned out to be a modern block of apartments. A doorman directed Fitz to an elevator. Smith-Cumming's flat seemed to be part home, part office, but a briskly efficient young man with a military air told Fitz that "C" would see him right away.

C did not have a military air. Podgy and balding, he had a nose like Mr. Punch and wore a monocle. His office was cluttered with miscellaneous objects: model aircraft, a telescope, a compass, and a painting of peasants facing a firing squad. Fitz's father had always referred to Smith-Cumming as "the seasick sea captain" and his naval career had not been brilliant. What was he doing here? "What exactly is this department?" Fitz asked as he sat down.

"This is the Foreign Section of the Secret Service Bureau," said C.

"I didn't know we had a Secret Service Bureau."

"If people knew, it wouldn't be secret."

"I see." Fitz felt a twinge of excitement. It was flattering to be given confidential information.

"Perhaps you'd be kind enough not to mention it to anyone."

Fitz was being given an order, albeit politely phrased. "Of course," he said. He was pleased to feel a member of an inner circle. Did this mean that C might ask him to work for the War Office?

"Congratulations on the success of your royal house party. I believe you put together an impressive group of well-connected young men for His Majesty to meet."

"Thank you. It was a quiet social occasion, strictly speaking, but I'm afraid word gets around."

"And now you're taking your wife to Russia."

"The princess is Russian. She wants to visit her brother. It's a long-postponed trip."

"And Gus Dewar is going with you."

C seemed to know everything. "He's on a world tour," Fitz said. "Our plans coincided."

C sat back in his chair and said conversationally: "Do you know why Admiral Alexeev was put in charge of the Russian army in the war against Japan, even though he knew nothing about fighting on land?"

Having spent time in Russia as a boy, Fitz had followed the progress of the Russo-Japanese War of 1904–1905, but he did not know this story. "Tell me."

"Well, it seems the grand duke Alexis was involved in a punch-up in a brothel in Marseilles and got arrested by the French police. Alexeev came to the rescue and told the gendarmes that it was he, not the grand duke, who had misbehaved. The similarity of their names made the story plausible and the grand duke was let out of jail. Alexeev's reward was command of the army."

"No wonder they lost."

"All the same, the Russians deploy the largest army the world has ever known—six million men, by some calculations, assuming they call up all their reserves. No matter how incompetent their leadership, it's a formidable force. But how effective would they be in, say, a European war?"

"I haven't been back since my marriage," Fitz said. "I'm not sure."

"Nor are we. That's where you come in. I would like you to make some inquiries while you're there."

Fitz was surprised. "But surely our embassy should do that."

"Of course." C shrugged. "But diplomats are always more interested in politics than military matters."

"Still, there must be a military attaché."

"An outsider such as yourself can offer a fresh perspective—in much the same way as your group at Tŷ Gwyn gave the king something he could not have got from the Foreign Office. But if you feel you can't . . ."

"I'm not refusing," Fitz said hastily. On the contrary, he was pleased to be asked to do a job for his country. "I'm just surprised that things should be done this way."

"We are a newish department with few resources. My best informants are intelligent travelers with enough military background to understand what they're looking at."

"Very well."

"I'd be interested to know whether you felt the Russian officer class has moved on since 1905. Have they modernized, or are they still attached to old ideas? You'll meet all the top men in St. Petersburg—your wife is related to half of them."

Fitz was thinking about the last time Russia went to war. "The main reason they lost against Japan was that the Russian railways were inadequate to supply their army."

"But since then they have been trying to improve their rail network—using money borrowed from France, their ally."

"Have they made much progress, I wonder?"

"That's the key question. You'll be traveling by rail. Do the trains run on time? Keep your eyes open. Are the lines still mostly single-track, or double? The German generals have a contingency plan for war that is based on a calculation of how long it will take to mobilize the Russian army. If there is a war, much will hang on the accuracy of that timetable."

Fitz was as excited as a schoolboy, but he forced himself to speak with gravity. "I'll find out all I can."

"Thank you." C looked at his watch.

Fitz stood up and they shook hands.

"When are you going, exactly?" C asked.

"We leave tomorrow," said Fitz. "Good-bye."

{ II }

Grigori Peshkov watched his younger brother, Lev, taking money off the tall American. Lev's attractive face wore an expression of boyish eagerness, as if his main aim was to show off his skill. Grigori suffered a familiar pang of anxiety. One day, he feared, Lev's charm would not be enough to keep him out of trouble.

"This is a memory test," Lev said in English. He had learned the words by rote. "Take any card." He had to raise his voice over the racket of the factory: heavy machinery clanking, steam hissing, people yelling instructions and questions.

The visitor's name was Gus Dewar. He wore a jacket, waistcoat, and trousers all in the same fine gray woollen cloth. Grigori was especially interested in him because he came from Buffalo.

Dewar was an amiable young man. With a shrug, he took a card from Lev's pack and looked at it.

Lev said: "Put it on the bench, facedown."

Dewar put the card on the rough wooden workbench.

Lev took a ruble note from his pocket and placed it on the card. "Now you put a dollar down." This could be done only with rich visitors.

Grigori knew that Lev had already switched the playing card. In his hand, concealed by the ruble note, there had been a different card. The skill—which Lev had practiced for hours—lay in picking up the first card, and concealing it in the palm of the hand, immediately after putting down the ruble note and the new card.

"Are you sure you can afford to lose a dollar, Mr. Dewar?" said Lev.

Dewar smiled, as the marks always did at that point. "I think so," he said.

"Do you remember your card?" Lev did not really speak English. He could say these phrases in German, French, and Italian, too.

"Five of spades," said Dewar.

"Wrong."

"I'm pretty sure."

"Turn it over."

Dewar turned over the card. It was the queen of clubs.

Lev scooped up the dollar bill and his original ruble.

Grigori held his breath. This was the dangerous moment. Would the American complain that he had been robbed, and accuse Lev?

Dewar grinned ruefully and said: "You got me."

"I know another game," Lev said.

It was enough: Lev was about to push his luck. Although he was twenty years old, Grigori still had to protect him. "Don't play against my brother," Grigori said to Dewar in Russian. "He always wins."

Dewar smiled and replied hesitantly in the same tongue. "That's good advice."

Dewar was the first of a small group of visitors touring the Putilov Machine Works. It was the largest factory in St. Petersburg, employing thirty thousand men, women, and children. Grigori's job was to show them his own small but important section. The factory made locomotives and other large steel artifacts. Grigori was foreman of the shop that made train wheels.

Grigori was itching to speak to Dewar about Buffalo. But before he could ask a question the supervisor of the casting section, Kanin, appeared. A qualified engineer, he was tall and thin with receding hair.

With him was a second visitor. Grigori knew from his clothes that this must be the British lord. He was dressed like a Russian nobleman, in a tailcoat and a top hat. Perhaps this was the clothing worn by the ruling class all over the world.

The lord's name, Grigori had been told, was Earl Fitzherbert. He was the handsomest man Grigori had ever seen, with black hair and intense green eyes. The women in the wheel shop stared as if at a god.

Kanin spoke to Fitzherbert in Russian. "We are now producing two new locomotives every week here," he said proudly.

"Amazing," said the English lord.

Grigori understood why these foreigners were so interested. He read the newspapers, and he went to lectures and discussion groups organized by the St. Petersburg Bolshevik Committee. The locomotives made here were essential to Russia's ability to defend itself. The visitors might pretend to be idly curious, but they were collecting military intelligence.

Kanin introduced Grigori. "Peshkov here is the factory's chess champion." Kanin was management, but he was all right.

Fitzherbert was charming. He spoke to Varya, a woman of about fifty with her gray hair in a head scarf. "Very kind of you to show us your workplace," he said, cheerfully speaking fluent Russian with a heavy accent.

Varya, a formidable figure, muscular and big-bosomed, giggled like a schoolgirl.

The demonstration was ready. Grigori had placed steel ingots in the hopper and fired up the furnace, and the metal was now molten. But there was one more visitor to come: the earl's wife, who was said to be Russian—hence his knowledge of the language, which was unusual in a foreigner.

Grigori wanted to question Dewar about Buffalo, but before he had a chance, the earl's wife came into the wheel shop. Her floor-length skirt was like a broom pushing a line of dirt and swarf in front of her. She wore a short coat over her dress, and she was followed by a manservant carrying a fur cloak, a maid with a bag, and one of the directors of the factory, Count Maklakov, a young man dressed like Fitzherbert. Maklakov was obviously very taken with his guest, smiling and talking in a low voice and taking her arm unnecessarily. She was extraordinarily pretty, with fair curls and a coquettish tilt to her head.

Grigori recognized her immediately. She was Princess Bea.

His heart lurched and he felt nauseated. He fiercely repressed the ugly memory that rose out of the distant past. Then, as in any emergency, he checked on his brother. Would Lev remember? He had been only six years old at the time. Lev was looking with curiosity at the princess, as if trying to place her. Then, as Grigori watched, Lev's face changed and he remembered. He went pale and looked ill; then suddenly he reddened with anger.

By that time Grigori was at Lev's side. "Stay calm," he murmured. "Don't say anything. Remember, we're going to America—nothing must interfere with that!"

Lev made a disgusted noise.

"Go back to the stables," Grigori said. Lev was a pony driver, working with the many horses used in the factory.

Lev glared a moment longer at the oblivious princess. Then he turned and walked away, and the moment of danger passed.

Grigori began the demonstration. He nodded to Isaak, a man of his own age, who was captain of the factory football team. Isaak opened up the mold. Then he and Varya picked up a polished wooden template of a flanged train wheel. This in itself was a work of great skill, with spokes that were elliptical in cross-section and tapered by one in twenty from hub to rim. The wheel was for a big 4-6-4 locomotive, and the template was almost as tall as the people lifting it.

They pressed it into a deep tray filled with damp sandy molding mixture. Isaak swung the cast-iron chill on top of that, to form the tread and the flange, and then finally the top of the mold.

They opened up the assemblage and Grigori inspected the hole made by the template. There were no visible irregularities. He sprayed the molding sand with a black oily liquid; then they closed the flask again. "Please stand well back now," he said to the visitors. Isaak moved the spout of the hopper to the funnel on top of the mold. Then Grigori pulled the lever that tilted the hopper.

Molten steel poured slowly into the mold. Steam from the wet sand hissed out of vents. Grigori knew by experience when to raise the hopper and stop the flow. "The next step is to perfect the shape of the wheel," he said. "Because the hot metal takes so long to cool, I have here a wheel that was cast earlier."

It was already set up on a lathe, and Grigori nodded to Konstantin, the lathe operator, who was Varya's son. A thin, gangling intellectual with wild black hair, Konstantin was chairman of the Bolshevik discussion group and Grigori's closest friend. He started the electric motor, turning the wheel at high speed, and began to shape it with a file.

"Please keep well away from the lathe," Grigori said to the visitors, raising his voice over the whine of the machine. "If you touch it, you may lose a finger." He held up his left hand. "As I did, here in this factory, at the age of twelve." His third finger, the ring finger, was an ugly stump. He caught a glance of irritation from Count Maklakov, who did not enjoy being reminded of the human cost of his profits. The look he got from Princess Bea mingled disgust with fascination, and he wondered whether she was weirdly interested in squalor and suffering. It was unusual for a lady to tour a factory.

He made a sign to Konstantin, who stopped the lathe. "Next, the dimensions of the wheel are checked with calipers." He held up the tool used. "Train wheels must be exactly sized. If the diameter varies by more than one-sixteenth of an inch—which is about the width of the lead in a pencil—the wheel must be melted down and remade."

Fitzherbert said in broken Russian: "How many wheels can you make per day?"

"Six or seven on average, allowing for rejects."

The American, Dewar, asked: "What hours do you work?"

"Six in the morning until seven in the evening, Monday through Saturday. On Sunday we are allowed to go to church."

A boy of about eight came racing into the wheel shop, pursued by a shouting woman—presumably his mother. Grigori made a grab for him, to keep him away from the furnace. The boy dodged and cannoned into Princess Bea, his close-cropped head striking her in the ribs with an audible thump. She gasped, hurt. The boy stopped, apparently dazed. Furious, the princess drew back her arm and slapped his face so hard that he rocked on his feet, and Grigori thought he was going to fall over. The American said something abrupt in English, sounding surprised and indignant. In the next instant the mother swept the boy up in her strong arms and turned away.

Kanin, the supervisor, looked scared, knowing he might be blamed. He said to the princess: "Most High Excellency, are you hurt?"

Princess Bea was visibly enraged, but she took a deep breath and said: "It's nothing."

Her husband and the count went to her, looking concerned. Only Dewar stood back, his face a mask of disapproval and revulsion. He had been shocked by the slap, Grigori guessed, and he wondered whether all Americans were equally soft-hearted. A slap was nothing: Grigori and his brother had been flogged with canes as children in this factory.

The visitors began to move away. Grigori was afraid he might lose his chance of questioning the tourist from Buffalo. Boldly, he touched Dewar's sleeve. A Russian nobleman would have reacted with indignation, and shoved him away or struck him for insolence, but the American merely turned to him with a polite smile.

"You are from Buffalo, New York, sir?" said Grigori.

"That's right."

"My brother and I are saving to go to America. We will live in Buffalo."

"Why that city?"

"Here in St. Petersburg is a family who get the necessary papers—for a fee, of course—and promise us jobs with their relatives in Buffalo."

"Who are these people?"

"Vyalov is the name." The Vyalovs were a criminal gang, though they had lawful businesses, too. They were not the most trustworthy people in the world, so Grigori wanted their claims independently verified. "Sir, is the Vyalov family of Buffalo, New York, really an important rich family?"

"Yes," said Dewar. "Josef Vyalov employs several hundred people in his hotels and bars."

"Thank you." Grigori was relieved. "That is very good to know."

{ III }

Grigori's earliest memory was of the day the tsar came to Bulovnir. He was six.

The people of the village had talked of little else for days. Everyone got up at dawn, even though it was obvious the tsar would have his breakfast before setting out, so he could not possibly get there before midmorning. Grigori's father carried the table out of their one-room dwelling and set it beside the road. On it he placed a loaf of bread, a bunch of flowers, and a small container of salt, explaining to his elder son that these were the traditional Russian symbols of welcome. Most of the other villagers did the same. Grigori's grandmother had put on a new yellow head scarf.

It was a dry day in early autumn, before the onset of the hard winter cold. The peasants sat on their haunches to wait. The village elders walked up and down in their best clothes, looking important, but they were waiting just like everyone else. Grigori soon got bored and started to play in the dirt beside the house. His brother, Lev, was only a year old, and still being nursed by their mother.

Noon passed, but no one wanted to go indoors and make dinner for fear they might miss the tsar. Grigori tried to eat some of the loaf on the table and got his head smacked, but his mother brought him a bowl of cold porridge.

Grigori was not sure who or what the tsar was. He was frequently mentioned in church as loving all the peasants and watching over them while they slept, so he was clearly on a level with St. Peter and Jesus and the angel Gabriel. Grigori wondered if he would have wings or a crown of thorns, or just an embroidered coat like a village elder. Anyway, it was obvious that people were blessed just by seeing him, like the crowds that followed Jesus.

It was late afternoon when a cloud of dust appeared in the distance. Grigori could feel vibrations in the ground beneath his felt boots, and soon he heard the drumming of hooves. The villagers got down on their knees. Grigori knelt beside his grandmother. The elders lay facedown in the road with their foreheads in the dirt, as they did when Prince Andrei and Princess Bea came.

Outriders appeared, followed by a closed carriage drawn by four horses. The horses were huge, the biggest Grigori had ever seen, and they were being driven at speed, their flanks shining with sweat, their mouths foaming around their bits. The elders realized they were not going to stop and scrambled out of the way before they were trampled. Grigori screamed in fear, but his cry was inaudible. As the carriage passed, his father shouted: "Long live the tsar, father of his people!"

By the time he finished, the carriage was already leaving the village behind. Grigori had not been able to see the passengers because of the dust. He realized he had missed seeing the tsar, and therefore would receive no blessing, and he burst into tears.

His mother took the loaf from the table, broke off an end, and gave it to him to eat, and he felt better.

{ IV }

When the shift at the Putilov Machine Works finished at seven o'clock, Lev usually went off to play cards with his pals or drink with his easygoing girlfriends. Grigori often went to a meeting of some kind: a lecture on atheism, a socialist discussion group, a magic-lantern show about foreign lands, a poetry reading. But tonight he had nothing to do. He would go home, make a stew for supper, leave some in the pot for Lev to eat later, and go to bed early.

The factory was on the southern outskirts of St. Petersburg, its sprawl of chimneys and sheds covering a large site on the shore of the Baltic Sea. Many of the workers lived at the factory, some in barracks and some lying down to sleep beside their machines. That was why there were so many children running around.

Grigori was among those who had a home outside the factory. In a socialist society, he knew, houses for workers would be planned at the same time as factories, but haphazard Russian capitalism left thousands of people with nowhere to live. Grigori was well-paid, but he lived in a single room half an hour's walk from the factory. In Buffalo, he knew, factory hands had electricity and running water in their homes. He had been told that some had their own telephones, but that seemed ridiculous, like saying the streets were paved with gold.

Seeing Princess Bea had taken him back to his childhood. As he wound his way through the icy streets, he refused to allow himself to dwell on the unbearable memory she brought to mind. All the same he thought about the wooden hut where he had lived then, and he saw again the holy corner where the icons were hung, and opposite it the sleeping corner where he lay down at night, usually with a goat or calf beside him. What he remembered most distinctly was something he had hardly noticed at the time: the smell. It came from the stove, the animals, the black smoke of the kerosene lamp, and the homemade tobacco his father smoked rolled into newspaper cigarettes. The windows were shut tight with rags stuffed around the frames to keep the cold out, so the atmosphere was dense. He could smell it now in his imagination, and it made him nostalgic for the days before the nightmare, the last time in his life when he had felt secure.

Not far from the factory he came upon a sight that made him stop. In the pool of light thrown by a streetlamp two policemen, in black uniforms with green facings, were questioning a young woman. Her homespun coat, and the way she tied the head scarf with a knot at the back of the neck, suggested a peasant newly arrived in the city. At first glance he took her to be about sixteen—the age he had been when he and Lev were orphaned.

The stocky policeman said something and patted the girl's face. She flinched, and the other cop laughed. Grigori remembered being ill-treated by everyone in authority as a sixteen-year-old orphan, and his heart went out to this vulnerable girl. Against his better judgment, he approached the little group. Just to have something to say, he said: "If you're looking for the Putilov works, I can show you the way."

The stocky policeman laughed and said: "Get rid of him, Ilya."

His sidekick had a small head and a mean face. "Get lost, scum," he said.

Grigori was not afraid. He was tall and strong, his muscles hardened by constant heavy work. He had been in street fights ever since he was a boy and he had not lost one for many years. Lev was the same. Nevertheless, it was better not to annoy the police. "I'm a foreman at the works," he said to the girl. "If you're looking for a job, I can help you."

The girl shot him a grateful look.

"A foreman is nothing," said the stocky cop. As he spoke he looked directly at Grigori for the first time. In the yellow light from the kerosene streetlamp Grigori now recognized the round face with the look of stupid belligerence. The man was Mikhail Pinsky, the local precinct captain. Grigori's heart sank. It was madness to pick a fight with the precinct captain—but he had gone too far now to turn back.

The girl spoke, and her voice told Grigori that she was nearer to twenty than sixteen. "Thank you. I'll go with you, sir," she said to Grigori. She was pretty, he saw, with delicately molded features and a wide, sensual mouth.

Grigori looked around. Unfortunately, there was no one else about: he had left the factory a few minutes after the seven o'clock rush. He knew he should back down, but he could not abandon this girl. "I'll take you to the factory office," he said, though in fact it was now closed.

"She's coming with me—aren't you, Katerina?" Pinsky said, and he pawed her, squeezing her breasts through the thin coat and thrusting a hand between her legs.

She jumped back a pace and said: "Keep your filthy hands off."

With surprising speed and accuracy Pinsky punched her in the mouth.

She cried out, and blood spurted from her lips.

Grigori was angered. Throwing caution to the wind he stepped forward, put a hand to Pinsky's shoulder, and shoved hard. Pinsky staggered sideways and fell to one knee. Grigori turned to Katerina, who was crying. "Run like hell!" he said; then he felt an agonizing blow to the back of his head. The second policeman, Ilya, had deployed his nightstick faster than Grigori expected. The pain was excruciating, and he fell to his knees, but he did not black out.

Katerina turned and ran, but she did not get far. Pinsky reached out and grabbed her foot, and she fell full-length.

Grigori turned and saw the nightstick coming at him again. He dodged the blow and scrambled to his feet. Ilya swung and missed again. Grigori aimed a blow at the side of the man's head and punched with all his force. Ilya fell to the ground.

Grigori turned to see Pinsky standing over Katerina, kicking her repeatedly with his heavy boots.

A motorcar approached from the direction of the factory. As it passed, its driver braked hard, and it squealed to a stop under the streetlamp.

Two long strides brought Grigori to a position just behind Pinsky. He put both arms around the police captain, gripped him in a bear hug, and lifted him off the ground. Pinsky kicked his legs and waved his arms to no avail.

The car door opened and, to Grigori's surprise, the American from Buffalo got out. "What is happening?" he said. His youthful face, lit by the streetlight, showed outrage as he addressed the wriggling Pinsky. "Why do you kick a helpless woman?"

This was great good luck, Grigori thought. Only foreigners would object to a policeman kicking a peasant.

The long, thin figure of Kanin, the supervisor, unfolded out of the car behind Dewar. "Let the policeman go, Peshkov," he said to Grigori.

Grigori set Pinsky on the ground and released him. He spun around, and Grigori got ready to dodge a blow, but

Pinsky restrained himself. In a voice full of poison he said: "I'll remember you, *Peshkov*." Grigori groaned: the man knew his name.

Katerina got to her knees, moaning. Dewar gallantly helped her to her feet, saying: "Are you badly hurt, miss?"

Kanin looked embarrassed. No Russian would address a peasant so courteously.

Ilya got up, looking dazed.

From within the car came the voice of Princess Bea, speaking English, sounding annoyed and impatient.

Grigori addressed Dewar. "With your permission, Excellency, I will take this woman to a nearby doctor."

Dewar looked at Katerina. "Is that your wish?"

"Yes, sir," she said through bloody lips.

"Very well," he said.

Grigori took her arm and led her away before anyone could suggest otherwise.

At the corner he glanced back. The two cops stood arguing with Dewar and Kanin under the streetlamp.

Still holding Katerina's arm, he hurried her along, even though she was limping. They needed to put distance between themselves and Pinsky.

As soon as they had turned the corner, she said: "I have no money for a doctor."

"I could give you a loan," he said, with a pang of guilt: his money was for passage to America, not to soothe the bruises of pretty girls.

She gave him a calculating look. "I don't really want a doctor," she said. "What I need is a job. Could you take me to the factory office?"

She had guts, he thought admiringly. She had just been beaten up by a policeman, and all she could think about was getting a job. "The office is closed. I just said that to confuse the cops. But I can take you there in the morning."

"I have nowhere to sleep." She gave him a guarded look that he did not quite understand. Was she offering herself? Many peasant girls who came to the city ended up doing that. But perhaps her look meant the opposite, that she wanted a bed but was not prepared to pay with sexual favors.

"In the house where I live there's a room shared by a number of women," he said. "They sleep three or more to a bed, and they can always find space for another one."

"How far is it?"

He pointed ahead to a street that ran alongside a railway embankment. "Just here."

She nodded assent, and a few moments later they entered the house.

He had a back room on the first floor. The narrow bed that he shared with Lev stood against one wall. There was a fireplace with a hob, and a table and two chairs next to the window that overlooked the railway. An upended packing case served as a nightstand, with a jug and bowl for washing.

Katerina inspected the place with a long look that took everything in; then she said: "You have all this to yourself?"

"No—I'm not rich! I share with my brother. He'll be here later."

She looked thoughtful. Perhaps she was afraid she might be expected to have sex with both of them. To reassure her, Grigori said: "Shall I introduce you to the women in the house?"

"Plenty of time for that." She sat in one of the two chairs. "Let me rest a while."

"Of course." The fire was laid, ready to be lit: he always built it in the morning before going to work. He put a match to the kindling.

There was a thunderous noise, and Katerina looked frightened. "It's just a train," Grigori said. "We're right next to the railway."

He poured water from the jug into the bowl, then set the bowl on the hob to warm. He sat opposite Katerina and looked at her. She had straight fair hair and pale skin. At first he had judged her to be quite pretty, but now he saw that she was really beautiful, with an oriental cast to her bone structure that suggested Siberian ancestry. There was strength of character in her face, too: her wide mouth was sexy, but also determined, and there seemed to be iron purpose in her blue-green eyes.

Her lips were swelling up from Pinsky's punch. "How do you feel?" Grigori asked.

She ran her hands over her shoulders, ribs, hips, and thighs. "Bruised all over," she said. "But you pulled that animal off me before he could do any serious damage."

She was not going to feel sorry for herself. He liked

that. He said: "When the water's warm, I'll wash away the blood."

He kept food in a tin box. He took out a knuckle of ham and dropped it in the saucepan, then added water from the jug. He rinsed a turnip and began to slice it into the pan. He caught Katerina's eye and saw a look of surprise. She said: "Did your father cook?"

"No," said Grigori, and in a blink he was transported back to the age of eleven. The nightmare memories of Princess Bea could no longer be resisted. He put the pan down heavily on the table, then sat on the edge of the bed and buried his head in his hands, overwhelmed by grief. "No," he repeated, "my father didn't cook."

{ V }

They came to the village at dawn: the local land captain and six cavalrymen. As soon as Ma heard the trotting hoofbeats, she picked up Lev. He was a heavy burden at age six, but Ma was broad-shouldered and strong-armed. She grabbed Grigori's hand and ran out of the house. The horsemen were being led by the village elders, who must have met them at the outskirts. Because there was only one door, Grigori's family had no chance of concealment, and as soon as they appeared the soldiers spurred their mounts.

Ma pounded around the side of the house, scattering chickens and scaring the goat so that it broke its tether and bolted, too. She ran across the waste ground at the back toward the trees. They might have escaped, but Grigori suddenly realized that his grandmother was not with them. He stopped and pulled his hand free. "We forgot Gran!" he squealed.

"She can't run!" Ma yelled back.

Grigori knew that. Gran could hardly walk. But all the same he felt they must not leave her behind.

"Grishka, come on!" Ma shouted, and she ran ahead, still carrying Lev, who was now shrieking with fear. Grigori followed, but the delay had been fatal. The horsemen came closer, one approaching on either side. The path to the woods was cut off. In desperation Ma ran into the pond, but her feet sank into the mud, she slowed down, and at last she fell into the water.

The soldiers hooted with laughter.

They tied Ma's hands and marched her back. "Make sure the boys come, too," said the land captain. "Prince's orders."

Grigori's father had been taken away a week ago, along with two other men. Yesterday, Prince Andrei's household carpenters had built a scaffold in the north meadow. Now, as Grigori followed his mother into the meadow, he saw three men standing on the scaffold, bound hand and foot, with ropes around their necks. Beside the scaffold stood a priest.

Ma screamed: "No!" She began to struggle with the rope that bound her hands. A cavalryman drew a rifle from the holster fixed to his saddle and, reversing it, hit her in the face with its wooden stock. She stopped struggling and began to sob.

Grigori knew what this meant: his father was going to die here. He had seen horse thieves hanged by the village elders, though that had seemed different because the victims were men he did not know. He was seized by a terror that turned his entire body numb and feeble.

Perhaps something would happen to prevent the execution. The tsar might intervene, if he truly watched over his people. Or perhaps an angel. Grigori's face felt wet and he realized he was crying.

He and his mother were forced to stand right in front of the scaffold. The other villagers gathered around. Like Ma, the wives of the other two men had to be dragged there, screaming and crying, their hands bound, their children holding on to their skirts and howling in terror.

On the dirt track beyond the field gate stood a closed carriage, its matching chestnut horses cropping the roadside grass. When everyone was present, a black-bearded figure emerged from the carriage in a long dark coat: Prince Andrei. He turned and gave his hand to his little sister, Princess Bea, with furs around her shoulders against the morning cold. The princess was beautiful, Grigori could not help noticing, with pale skin and fair hair, just as he imagined angels to look, even though she was obviously a devil.

The prince addressed the villagers. "This meadow belongs to Princess Bea," he said. "No one may graze cattle here without her permission. To do so is to steal the princess's grass."

There was a murmur of resentment from the crowd. They did not believe in this kind of ownership, despite what they were told every Sunday in church. They adhered to an older, peasant morality, according to which the land was for those who worked it.

The prince pointed to the three men on the scaffold. "These fools broke the law—not once, but repeatedly." His voice was shrill with outrage, like a child whose toy has been snatched. "Worse, they told others that the princess had no right to stop them, and that fields the landowner is not using should be available to poor peasants." Grigori had heard his father say such things often. "As a result, men from other villages have started grazing cattle on land that belongs to the nobility. Instead of repenting their sins, these three have turned their neighbors into sinners, too! That is why they have been sentenced to death." He nodded to the priest.

The priest climbed the makeshift steps and spoke quietly to each man in turn. The first nodded expressionlessly. The second wept and began to pray aloud. The third, Grigori's father, spat in the priest's face. No one was shocked: the villagers had a low opinion of the clergy, and Grigori had heard his father say that they told the police everything they heard in the confessional.

The priest descended the steps, and Prince Andrei nodded to one of his servants, who was standing by with a sledgehammer. Grigori noticed for the first time that the three condemned men were standing on a crudely hinged wooden platform supported only by a single prop, and he realized with terror that the sledgehammer was to knock away the prop.

Now, he thought, this is when an angel should appear.

The villagers moaned. The wives began to scream, and this time the soldiers did not stop them. Little Lev was hysterical. He probably did not understand what was about to happen, Grigori thought, but he was scared by their mother's shrieks.

Pa showed no emotion. His face was stony. He looked

into the distance and awaited his fate. Grigori wanted to be that strong. He struggled to maintain his self-control, even though he needed to howl like Lev. He could not hold back the tears, but he bit his lip and remained as silent as his father.

The servant hefted his sledgehammer, touched it to the prop to get his range, swung backward, and struck. The prop flew through the air. The hinged platform came down with a bang. The three men dropped, then jerked, their fall arrested by the ropes around their necks.

Grigori was unable to look away. He stared at his father. Pa did not die instantly. He opened his mouth, trying to breathe, or to shout, but could not do either. His face turned red and he struggled with the ropes that bound him. It seemed to go on for a long time. His face became redder.

Then his skin turned a bluish color and his movements became weaker. At last he was still.

Ma stopped screaming and began to sob.

The priest prayed aloud, but the villagers ignored him and, one by one, they turned away from the sight of the three dead men.

The prince and the princess got back into their carriage, and after a moment, the coachman cracked his whip and drove away.

{ VI }

Grigori was calm again by the time he finished telling the story. He dragged his sleeve across his face to dry his tears, then turned his attention back to Katerina. She had listened to him in compassionate silence, but she was not shocked. She must have seen similar sights herself: hanging, flogging, and mutilation were normal punishments in the villages.

Grigori put the bowl of warm water on the table and found a clean towel. Katerina tilted her head back, and Grigori hung the kerosene lamp from a hook on the wall so that he could see better.

There was a cut on her forehead and a bruise on her cheek, and her lips were puffy. Even so, staring at her close up took Grigori's breath away. She looked back at him with a candid, fearless gaze that he found enchanting.

He dipped a corner of the towel in warm water.

"Be gentle," she said.

"Of course." He began by wiping her forehead. Her injury there was only a graze, he saw when he had dabbed away the blood.

"That feels better," she said.

She watched his face while he worked. He washed her cheeks and her throat, then said: "I've left the painful part until last."

"It will be all right," she said. "You have such a light touch." All the same, she winced when his towel touched her swollen lips.

"Sorry," he said.

"Keep going."

The abrasions were already healing, he saw as he cleaned them. She had the even white teeth of a young girl. He wiped the corners of her wide mouth. As he bent closer, he could feel her warm breath on his face.

When he had finished he felt a sense of disappointment, as if he had been waiting for something that had not happened.

He sat back and rinsed the towel in the water, which was now dark with her blood.

"Thank you," she said. "You have very good hands."

His heart was racing. He had bathed people's wounds before, but he had never experienced this dizzy sensation. He felt he might be about to do something foolish.

He opened the window and emptied the bowl, making a pink splash on the snow in the yard.

The mad thought crossed his mind that Katerina might be a dream. He turned, half expecting her chair to be empty. But there she was, looking back at him with those blue-green eyes, and he realized he wanted her never to go away.

It occurred to him that he might be in love.

He had never thought that before. He was usually too busy looking after Lev to chase women. He was not a virgin: he had had sex with three different women. It had always been a joyless experience, perhaps because he had not much cared for any of them.

But now, he thought shakily, he wanted, more than anything else in the world, to lie down with Katerina on the narrow bed against the wall and kiss her hurt face and tell her—

And tell her that he loved her.

Don't be stupid, he said to himself. You met her an hour ago. What she wants from you is not love, but a loan and a job and a place to sleep.

He closed the window with a slam.

She said: "So you cook for your brother, and you have gentle hands, and yet you can knock a policeman to the ground with one punch."

He did not know what to say.

"You told me how your father died," she went on. "But your mother died, too, when you were young—didn't she?"

"How did you know?"

Katerina shrugged. "Because you had to become a mother."

{ VII }

She died on January 9, 1905, by the old Russian calendar. It was a Sunday, and in the days and years that followed it came to be known as Bloody Sunday.

Grigori was sixteen and Lev eleven. Like Ma, both boys worked at the Putilov factory. Grigori was an apprentice foundryman, Lev a sweep. That January all three of them were on strike, along with more than a hundred thousand other St. Petersburg factory workers, for an eight-hour day and the right to form trade unions. On the morning of the ninth they put on their best clothes and went out, holding hands and tramping through a fresh fall of snow, to a church near the Putilov factory. After the service they joined the thousands of workers marching from all points of the city toward the Winter Palace.

"Why do we have to march?" young Lev whined. He would have preferred to play soccer in an alleyway.

"Because of your father," said Ma. "Because princes and princesses are murdering brutes. Because we have to overthrow the tsar and all his kind. Because I will not rest until Russia is a republic."

It was a perfect St. Petersburg day, cold but dry, and Grigori's face was warmed by the sun just as his heart was warmed by the feeling of comradeship in a just cause.

Their leader, Father Gapon, was like an Old Testament prophet, with his long beard, his biblical language, and the light of glory in his eye. He was no revolutionary: his self-help clubs, approved by the government, started all meetings with the Lord's Prayer and ended with the national anthem. "I can see now what the tsar intended Gapon to be," Grigori said to Katerina nine years later, in his room overlooking the railway line. "A safety valve, designed to take the pressure for reform and release it harmlessly in tea drinking and country dancing. But it didn't work."

Wearing a long white robe and carrying a crucifix, Gapon led the procession along the Narva highway. Grigori, Lev, and Ma were right beside him: he encouraged families to march at the front, saying that the soldiers would never fire on infants. Behind them two neighbors carried a large portrait of the tsar. Gapon told them that the tsar was the father of his people. He would listen to their cries, overrule his hard-hearted ministers, and grant the workers' reasonable demands. "The Lord Jesus said: 'Suffer the little children to come unto me,' and the tsar says the same," Gapon cried, and Grigori believed him.

They had approached the Narva Gate, a massive triumphal arch, and Grigori remembered looking up at the statue of a chariot with six gigantic horses; then a squadron of cavalry charged the marchers, almost as if the copper horses atop the monument had come thunderously alive.

Some demonstrators fled; some fell to the hammer blows of the hooves. Grigori froze in place, terrified, as did Ma and Lev.

The soldiers did not draw weapons, and seemed intent simply on scaring people away; but there were too many workers, and a few minutes later the cavalry wheeled their horses and rode off.

The march resumed in a different spirit. Grigori sensed that the day might not end peacefully. He thought about the forces ranged against them: the nobility, the ministers, and the army. How far would they go to keep the people from speaking to their tsar?

His answer came almost immediately. Looking over the

heads in front of him he saw a line of infantry and realized, with a shudder of dread, that they were in firing position.

The march slowed as people comprehended what they faced. Father Gapon, who was within touching distance of Grigori, turned and shouted to his followers: "The tsar will never allow his armies to shoot at his beloved people!"

There was a deafening rattle, like a hailstorm on a tin roof: the soldiers had fired a salvo. The acrid smell of gunpowder stung Grigori's nostrils, and fear clutched at his heart.

The priest shouted: "Don't worry—they're firing into the air!"

Another volley rang out, but no bullets seemed to land. All the same, Grigori's bowels clenched in terror.

Then there was a third salvo, and this time the bullets did not fly harmlessly up. Grigori heard screams and saw people fall. He stared around in confusion for a moment; then Ma shoved him violently, shouting: "Lie down!" He fell flat. At the same time Ma threw Lev to the ground and dropped on top of him.

We're going to die, Grigori thought, and his heart thudded louder than the guns.

The shooting continued relentlessly, a nightmare noise that could not be shut out. As people fled in panic, Grigori was trodden on by heavy boots, but Ma protected his head and Lev's. They lay there trembling while the shooting and screaming went on above them.

Then the firing stopped. Ma moved, and Grigori raised his head to look around. People were hurrying away in all directions, shouting to one another, but the screaming died down. "Get up, come on," said Ma, and they scrambled to their feet and hurried away from the road, jumping over still bodies and running around the bleeding wounded. They reached a side street and slowed down. Lev whispered to Grigori: "I've wet myself! Don't tell Ma!"

Ma's blood was up. "We WILL speak to the tsar!" she cried, and people stopped to look at her broad peasant face and intense gaze. She was deep-chested, and her voice boomed out across the street. "They cannot prevent us—we must go to the Winter Palace!" Some people cheered, and others nodded agreement. Lev started to cry.

Listening to the story, nine years later, Katerina said:

"Why did she do that? She should have taken her children home to safety!"

"She used to say she did not want her sons to live as she had," Grigori replied. "I think she felt it would be better for us all to die than to give up the hope of a better life."

Katerina looked thoughtful. "I suppose that's brave."

"It's more than bravery," Grigori said stoutly. "It's heroism."

"What happened next?"

They had walked into the city center, along with thousands of others. As the sun rose higher over the snowy city, Grigori unbuttoned his coat and unwound his scarf. It was a long walk for Lev's short legs, but the boy was too shocked and scared to complain.

At last they reached Nevsky Prospekt, the broad boulevard that ran through the heart of the city. It was already thronged with people. Streetcars and omnibuses drove up and down, and horse cabs dashed dangerously in all directions—in those days, Grigori recalled, there had been no motor taxis.

They ran into Konstantin, a lathe operator from the Putilov works. He told Ma, ominously, that demonstrators had been killed in other parts of the city. But she did not break her pace, and the rest of the crowd seemed equally resolute. They moved steadily past shops selling German pianos, hats made in Paris, and special silver bowls to hold hothouse roses. In the jewelry stores there a nobleman could spend more on a bauble for his mistress than a factory worker would earn in a lifetime, Grigori had been told. They passed the Soleil Cinema, which Grigori longed to visit. Vendors were doing good business, selling tea from samovars and colored balloons for children.

At the end of the street they came to three great St. Petersburg landmarks standing side by side on the bank of the frozen Neva River: the equestrian statue of Peter the Great, always called *The Bronze Horseman;* the Admiralty building with its spire; and the Winter Palace. When he had first seen the palace, at the age of twelve, he had refused to believe that such a large building could be a place for people to actually live. It seemed inconceivable, like something in a story, a magic sword or a cloak of invisibility.

The square in front of the palace was white with snow.

On the far side, ranged in front of the dark red building, were cavalry, riflemen in long coats, and cannon. The crowds massed around the edges of the square, keeping their distance, fearful of the military; but newcomers kept pouring in from the surrounding streets, like the waters of the tributaries emptying into the Neva, and Grigori was constantly pushed forward. Not all those present were workers, Grigori noted with surprise: many wore the warm coats of the middle classes on their way home from church, some looked like students, and a few even wore school uniforms.

Ma prudently moved them away from the guns and into the Alexandrovskii Garden, a park in front of the long yellow-and-white Admiralty building. Other people had the same idea, and the crowd there became animated. The man who normally gave deer sled rides to middle-class children had gone home. Everyone there was talking of massacres: all over the city, marchers had been mown down by gunfire and hacked to death by Cossack sabres. Grigori spoke to a boy his own age and told him what had happened at the Narva Gate. As the demonstrators learned what had happened to others, they grew angrier.

Grigori stared up at the long façade of the Winter Palace, with its hundreds of windows. Where was the tsar?

"He was not at the Winter Palace that morning, as we found out later," Grigori told Katerina, and he could hear in his own voice the bitter resentment of a disappointed believer. "He was not even in town. The father of his people had gone to his palace at Tsarskoye Selo, to spend the weekend taking country walks and playing dominoes. But we did not know that then, and we called to him, begging him to show himself to his loyal subjects."

The crowd grew; the calls for the tsar became more insistent; some of the demonstrators started to jeer at the soldiers. Everyone was becoming tense and angry. Suddenly a detachment of guards charged into the gardens, ordering everyone out. Grigori watched, fearful and incredulous, as they lashed out indiscriminately with whips, some using the flat sides of their sabres. He looked at Ma for guidance. She said: "We can't give up now!" Grigori did not know what, exactly, they all expected the tsar to do: he just felt sure, as everyone did, that their monarch would somehow redress their grievances if only he knew about them.

The other demonstrators were as resolute as Ma and, although those who were attacked by guards cowered away, no one left the area.

Then the soldiers took up firing positions.

Near the front, several people fell to their knees, took off their caps, and crossed themselves. "Kneel down!" said Ma, and the three of them knelt, as did more of the people around them, until most of the crowd had assumed the position of prayer.

A silence descended that made Grigori scared. He stared at the rifles pointed at him, and the riflemen stared back expressionlessly, like statues.

Then Grigori heard a bugle call.

It was a signal. The soldiers fired their weapons. All around Grigori, people screamed and fell. A boy who had climbed a statue for a better view cried out and tumbled to the ground. A child fell out of a tree like a shot bird.

Grigori saw Ma go facedown. Thinking she was avoiding the gunfire, he did the same. Then, looking at her as they both lay on the ground, he saw the blood, bright red on the snow around her head.

"No!" he shouted. "No!"

Lev screamed.

Grigori grabbed Ma's shoulders and pulled her up. Her body was limp. He stared at her face. At first he was bewildered by the sight that met his eyes. What was he seeing? Where her forehead and her eyes should have been there was just a mass of unrecognizable pulp.

It was Lev who grasped the truth. "She's dead!" he screamed. "Ma's dead. My mother is dead!"

The firing stopped. All around, people were running, limping, or crawling away. Grigori tried to think. What should he do? He must take Ma away from here, he decided. He put his arms under her and picked her up. She was not light, but he was strong.

He turned around, looking for the way home. His vision was strangely blurred, and he realized he was weeping. "Come on," he said to Lev. "Stop screaming. We have to go."

At the edge of the square they were stopped by an old man, the skin of his face creased around watery eyes. He wore the blue tunic of a factory worker. "You're young," he said to Grigori. There was anguish and rage in his voice. "Never forget this," he said. "Never forget the murders committed here today by the tsar."

Grigori nodded. "I won't forget, sir," he said.

"May you live long," said the old man. "Long enough to take revenge on the bloodstained tsar for the evil he has done this day."

{ VIII }

"I carried her for about a mile. Then I got tired, so I boarded a streetcar, still holding her," Grigori told Katerina.

She stared at him. Her beautiful, bruised face was pale with horror. "You carried your dead mother home on a streetcar?"

He shrugged. "At the time I had no idea I was doing anything strange. Or, rather, everything that happened that day was so strange that nothing I did seemed odd."

"What about the people riding the car?"

"The conductor said nothing. I suppose he was too shocked to throw me off, and he didn't ask me for the fare—which I would not have been able to pay, of course."

"So you just sat down?"

"I sat there, with her body in my arms, and Lev beside me, crying. The passengers just stared at us. I didn't care what they thought. I was concentrating on what I had to do, which was to get her home."

"And so you became the head of your family, at the age of sixteen."

Grigori nodded. Although the memories were painful, he felt the most intense pleasure from her concentrated attention. Her eyes were fixed on him, and she listened with her mouth open and a look on her lovely face of mingled fascination and horror.

"What I remember most about that time is that no one helped us," he said, and he was revisited by the panicky feeling that he was alone in a hostile world. The memory never failed to fill his soul with rage. It's over now, he told himself; I've got a home and a job, and my brother has grown up strong and handsome. The bad times are over. But nevertheless he wanted to take someone by the neck—a soldier, a policeman, a government minister, or the tsar himself—and squeeze until there was no life left. He closed his eyes, shuddering, until the feeling passed.

"As soon as the funeral was over, the landlord threw us out, saying we would not be able to pay; and he took our furniture—for back rent, he said, although Ma was never behind with payments. I went to the church and told the priest we had nowhere to sleep."

Katerina laughed harshly. "I can guess what happened there."

He was surprised. "Can you?"

"The priest offered you a bed—his bed. That's what happened to me."

"Something like that," Grigori said. "He gave me a few kopeks and sent me to buy hot potatoes. The shop wasn't where he said, but instead of searching for it I hurried back to the church, because I didn't like the look of him. Sure enough, when I went into the vestry he was taking Lev's trousers down."

She nodded. "Priests have been doing that sort of thing to me since I was twelve."

Grigori was shocked. He had assumed that that particular priest was uniquely evil. Katerina obviously believed that depravity was the norm. "Are they all like that?" he said angrily.

"Most of them, in my experience."

He shook his head in disgust. "And you know what amazed me the most? When I caught him, he wasn't even ashamed! He just looked annoyed, as if I had interrupted him while he was meditating on the Bible."

"What did you do?"

"I told Lev to do up his trousers, and we left. The priest asked for his kopeks back, but I told him they were alms for the poor. I used them to pay for a bed in a lodging house that night."

"And then?"

"Eventually I got a good enough job, by lying about my age, and I found a room, and I learned, day by day, how to be independent."

"And now you're happy?"

"Certainly not. My mother intended us to have a better

life, and I'm going to make sure of it. We're leaving Russia. I've saved up almost enough money. I'm going to America, and when I get there I'll send money back for a ticket for Lev. They have no tsar in America—no emperor or king of any kind. The army can't just shoot anyone they like. The people rule the country!"

She was skeptical. "Do you really believe that?"

"It's true!"

There was a tap at the window. Katerina was startled—they were on the second floor—but Grigori knew it was Lev. Late at night, when the door of the house was locked, Lev had to cross the railway line to the backyard, climb onto the washhouse roof, and come in through the window.

Grigori opened up and Lev climbed in. He was dressed smartly, in a jacket with mother-of-pearl buttons and a cap with a velvet band. His waistcoat sported a brass watch chain. His hair was cut in the fashionable "Polish" style with a parting at the side, instead of down the middle as the peasants wore it. Katerina looked surprised, and Grigori guessed she had not expected his brother to be so dashing.

Normally Grigori was pleased to see Lev, and relieved if he was sober and in one piece. Now he wished he could have had longer alone with Katerina.

He introduced them, and Lev's eyes gleamed with interest as he shook her hand. She wiped tears from her cheeks. "Grigori was telling me about the death of your mother," she explained.

"He has been mother and father to me for nine years," Lev said. He tilted his head and sniffed the air. "And he makes good stew."

Grigori got out bowls and spoons, and put a loaf of black bread on the table. Katerina explained to Lev about the fight with the policeman Pinsky. The way she told the story made Grigori seem braver than he felt, but he was happy to be a hero in her eyes.

Lev was enchanted by Katerina. He leaned forward, listening as if he had never heard anything so fascinating, smiling and nodding, looking amazed or disgusted, according to what she was saying.

Grigori spooned the stew into bowls and pulled the packing case up to the table for use as a third chair. The food was good: he had added an onion to the pot, and the ham bone gave a hint of meaty richness to the turnips. The atmosphere lightened as Lev talked of inconsequential matters, odd incidents at the factory and funny things people said. He kept Katerina laughing.

When they had finished, Lev asked Katerina how she came to be in the city.

"My father died and my mother remarried," she said. "Unfortunately, my stepfather seemed to like me better than my mother." She tossed her head, and Grigori could not tell whether she was ashamed or defiant. "At any rate, that's what my mother believed, and she threw me out."

Grigori said: "Half the population of St. Petersburg have come here from a village. Soon there will be no one left to till the soil."

Lev said: "What was your journey like?"

It was a familiar tale of third-class railway tickets and lifts begged on carts, but Grigori was mesmerized by her face as she talked.

Once again Lev listened with rapt attention, making amusing comments, asking the occasional question.

Soon, Grigori noticed, Katerina had turned in her seat and was talking exclusively to Lev.

Almost, Grigori thought, as if I was not even here.

CHAPTER FOUR

March 1914

"So," Billy said to his father, "all the books of the Bible were originally written in various languages and then translated into English."

"Aye," said Da. "And the Roman Catholic Church tried to ban translations—they didn't want people like us reading the Bible for ourselves and arguing with the priests."

Da was a bit un-Christian when he spoke of Catholics. He seemed to hate Catholicism more than atheism. But he loved an argument. "Well, then," said Billy, "where are the originals?"

"What originals?"

"The original books of the Bible, written in Hebrew and Greek. Where are they kept?"

They were sitting on opposite sides of the square table in the kitchen of the house in Wellington Row. It was midafternoon. Billy was home from the pit and had washed his hands and face, but still wore his work clothes. Da had hung up his suit jacket, and sat in his waistcoat and shirtsleeves, with a collar and tie—he would be going out again after dinner, to a union meeting. Mam was heating the stew on the fire. Gramper sat with them, listening to the discussion with a faint smile, as if he had heard it all before.

"Well, we don't have the actual originals," Da said. "They wore out, centuries ago. We have copies."

"Where are the copies, then?"

"All different places—monasteries, museums . . ."

"They should be kept in one place."

"But there's more than one copy of each book—and some are better than others."

"How can one copy be better than another? Surely they're not different."

"Yes. Over the years, human error crept in."

This startled Billy. "Well, how do we know which is right?"

"That's a study called textual scholarship—comparing the different versions and coming up with an agreed text."

Billy was shocked. "You mean there isn't an indisputable book that is the actual Word of God? Men argue about it and make a judgment?"

"Yes."

"Well, how do we know they're right?"

Da smiled knowingly, a sure sign that his back was to the wall. "We believe that if they work in prayerful humility, God will guide their labors."

"But what if they don't?"

Mam put four bowls on the table. "Don't argue with your father," she said. She cut four thick slices off a loaf of bread.

Gramper said: "Leave him be, Cara, my girl. Let the boy ask his questions."

Da said: "We have faith in God's power to ensure that His Word comes to us as He would wish."

"You're completely illogical!"

Mam interrupted again. "Don't speak to your father like that! You're still a boy—you don't know anything."

Billy ignored her. "Why didn't God guide the labors of the copiers, and stop them making mistakes, if He really wanted us to know His Word?"

Da said: "Some things are not given to us to understand."

That answer was the least convincing of all, and Billy ignored it. "If the copiers could make mistakes, obviously the textual scholars could, too."

"We must have faith, Billy."

"Faith in the Word of God, yes—not faith in a lot of professors of Greek!"

Mam sat at the table and pushed her graying hair out of her eyes. "So you are right, and everyone else is wrong, as usual, I suppose?"

This frequently used ploy always stung him, because it seemed justified. It was not possible that he was wiser than everyone else. "It's not me," he protested. "It's logic!"

"Oh, you and your old logic," said his mother. "Eat your dinner."

The door opened and Mrs. Dai Ponies walked in. This was normal in Wellington Row: only strangers knocked. Mrs. Dai wore a pinafore and a man's boots on her feet: whatever she had to say was so urgent that she had not even put on a hat before leaving her house. Visibly agitated, she brandished a sheet of paper. "I'm being thrown out!" she said. "What am I supposed to do?"

Da stood up and gave her his chair. "Sit down by here and catch your breath, Mrs. Dai Ponies," he said calmly. "Let me have a read of that letter, now." He took it from her red, knotted hand and laid it flat on the table.

Billy could see that it was typed on the letterhead of Celtic Minerals.

"'Dear Mrs. Evans,'" Da read aloud. "'The house at the above address is now required for a working miner.'" Celtic Minerals had built most of the houses in Aberowen. Over the years, some had been sold to their occupiers, including the one the Williams family lived in; but most were still rented to miners. "'In accordance with the terms of your lease, I—'" Da paused, and Billy could see he was shocked. "'I hereby give you two weeks' notice to quit!'" he finished.

Mam said: "Notice to quit—and her husband buried not six weeks ago!"

Mrs. Dai cried: "Where am I to go, with five children?"

Billy was shocked, too. How could the company do this to a woman whose husband had been killed in their pit?

"It's signed 'Perceval Jones, Chairman of the Board,' at the bottom," Da finished.

Billy said: "What lease? I didn't know miners had leases."

Da said to him: "There's no written lease, but the law says there's an implied contract. We've already fought that battle and lost." He turned to Mrs. Dai. "The house goes with the job, in theory, but widows are usually allowed to stay on. Sometimes they leave anyway, and go to live elsewhere, perhaps with their parents. Often they remarry, to another miner, and he takes over the lease. Usually they have at least one boy who becomes a miner when he's old enough. It's not really in the company's interest to throw widows out."

"So why do they want to get rid of me and my children?" wailed Mrs. Dai.

Gramper said: "Perceval Jones is in a hurry. He must think the price of coal is going up. That'll be why he started the Sunday shift."

Da nodded. "They want higher production, that's for sure, whatever the reason. But they're not going to get it by evicting widows." He stood up. "Not if I can help it."

{ II }

Eight women were being evicted, all widows of men who had died in the explosion. They had received identical letters from Perceval Jones, as Da established that afternoon when he visited each woman in turn, taking Billy with him. Their reactions varied from the hysterics of Mrs. Hywel Jones, who could not stop crying, to the grim fatalism of Mrs. Roley Hughes, who said this country needed a guillotine like they had in Paris for men like Perceval Jones.

Billy was boiling with outrage. Was it not enough that these women had lost their men to the pit? Must they be homeless as well as husbandless? "Can the company do this, Da?" he said as he and his father walked down the mean gray terraces to the pithead.

"Only if we let them, boy. The working class are more numerous than the ruling class, and stronger. They depend on us for everything. We provide their food and build their houses and make their clothes, and without us they die. They can't do *anything* unless we let them. Always remember that."

They went into the manager's office, stuffing their caps into their pockets. "Good afternoon, Mr. Williams," said Spotty Llewellyn nervously. "If you would just wait a minute, I'll ask if Mr. Morgan can see you."

"Don't be daft, boy—of course he'll see me," said Da, and without waiting he walked into the inner office. Billy followed.

Maldwyn Morgan was perusing a ledger, but Billy had a feeling he was only pretending. He looked up, his pink cheeks closely shaved as always. "Come in, Williams," he said unnecessarily. Unlike many men, he was not afraid of Da. Morgan was Aberowen-born, the son of a schoolmaster, and had studied engineering. He and Da were similar, Billy realized: intelligent, self-righteous, and stubborn.

"You know what I've come about, Mr. Morgan," said Da.

"I can guess, but tell me anyway."

"I want you to withdraw these eviction notices."

"The company needs the houses for miners."

"There will be trouble."

"Are you threatening me?"

"Don't get on your high horse," Da said mildly. "These women lost their husbands in your pit. Don't you feel responsible for them?"

Morgan tilted up his chin defensively. "The public inquiry found that the explosion was not caused by the company's negligence."

Billy wanted to ask him how an intelligent man could say such a thing and not feel ashamed of himself.

Da said: "The inquiry found a list of violations as long as the train to Paddington—electrical equipment not shielded, no breathing apparatus, no proper fire engine—"

"But the violations did not cause the explosion, or the deaths of miners."

"The violations could not be *proved* to have caused the explosion or the deaths."

Morgan shifted uncomfortably in his chair. "You didn't come here to argue about the inquiry."

"I came here to get you to see reason. As we speak, the news of these letters is going around the town." Da gestured at the window, and Billy saw that the winter sun was going down behind the mountain. "Men are rehearsing with choirs, drinking in pubs, going to prayer meetings, playing chess—and they're all talking about the eviction of the widows. And you can bet your boots they're angry."

"I have to ask you again: are you trying to intimidate the company?"

Billy wanted to throttle the man, but Da sighed. "Look

here, Maldwyn. We've known each other since school days. Be reasonable, now. You know there are men in the union who will be more aggressive than me." Da was talking about Tommy Griffiths's father. Len Griffiths believed in revolution, and he always hoped the next dispute would be the spark that lit the conflagration. He also wanted Da's job. He could be relied upon to propose drastic measures.

Morgan said: "Are you telling me you're calling a strike?"

"I'm telling you the men will be angry. What they will do I can't predict. But I don't want trouble and you don't want trouble. We're talking about eight houses out of, what, eight hundred? I've come here to ask you, is it worth it?"

"The company has made its decision," Morgan said, and Billy felt intuitively that Morgan did not agree with the company.

"Ask the board of directors to reconsider. What harm could that do?"

Billy was impatient with Da's mild words. Surely he should raise his voice, and point his finger, and accuse Morgan of the ruthless cruelty of which the company was obviously guilty? That was what Len Griffiths would have done.

Morgan was unmoved. "I'm here to carry out the board's decisions, not question them."

"So the evictions have already been approved by the board," Da said.

Morgan looked flustered. "I didn't say that."

But he had implied it, Billy thought, thanks to Da's clever questioning. Maybe mildness was not such a bad idea.

Da changed tack. "What if I could find you eight houses where the occupiers are prepared to take in new miners as lodgers?"

"These men have families."

Da said slowly and deliberately: "We *could* work out a compromise, *if* you were willing."

"The company must have the power to manage its own affairs."

"Regardless of the consequences to others?"

"This is our coal mine. The company surveyed the land, negotiated with the earl, dug the pit, and bought the machinery, and it built the houses for the miners to live in. We paid for all this and we own it, and we won't be told what to do with it by anyone else."

Da put his cap on. "You didn't put the coal in the earth, though, did you, Maldwyn?" he said. "God did that."

{ III }

Da tried to book the assembly rooms of the town hall for a gathering at seven thirty the following night, but the space was already taken by the Aberowen Amateur Dramatic Club, who were rehearsing *Henry IV, Part One,* so Da decided the miners would meet at Bethesda Chapel. Billy and Da, with Len and Tommy Griffiths and a few other active union members, went around the town announcing the meeting orally and pinning up handwritten notices in pubs and chapels.

By a quarter past seven the next evening, the chapel was packed. The widows sat in a row at the front, and everyone else stood. Billy was at the side near the front, where he could see the men's faces. Tommy Griffiths stood beside him.

Billy was proud of his da for his boldness, his cleverness, and the fact that he had put his cap back on before leaving Morgan's office. All the same he wished Da had been more aggressive. He should have talked to Morgan the way he talked to the congregation of Bethesda, predicting hellfire and brimstone for those who refused to see the plain truth.

At exactly seven thirty, Da called for quiet. In his authoritative preaching voice he read out the letter from Perceval Jones to Mrs. Dai Ponies. "The identical letter have been sent to eight widows of men killed in the explosion down the pit six weeks ago."

Several men called out: "Shame!"

"It is our rule that men speak when called upon by the chairman of the meeting, and not otherwise, so that each may be heard in his turn, and I will thank you for observing the rule, even on an occasion such as this when feelings run high."

Someone called out: "It's a bloody disgrace!"

"Now, now, Griff Pritchard, no swearing, please. This is a chapel and, besides, there are ladies present."

Two or three of the men said: "Hear, hear." They pronounced the word to rhyme with "fur."

Griff Pritchard, who had been in the Two Crowns since the shift ended that afternoon, said: "Sorry, Mr. Williams."

"I held a meeting yesterday with the colliery manager, and asked him formally to withdraw the eviction notices, but he refused. He implied that the board of directors had made the decision, and it was not in his power to change it, or even question it. I pressed him to discuss alternatives, but he said the company had the right to manage its affairs without interference. That is all the information I have for you." That was a bit low-key, Billy thought. He wanted Da to call for revolution. But Da just pointed to a man who had his hand up. "John Jones the Shop."

"I've lived in number twenty-three Gordon Terrace all my life," said Jones. "I was born there and I'm still there. But my father died when I was eleven. Very hard it was, too, for my mam, but she was allowed to stay. When I was thirteen I went down the pit, and now I pay the rent. That's how it's always been. No one said anything about throwing us out."

"Thank you, John Jones. Have you got a motion to propose?"

"No, I'm just saying."

"I have a motion," said a new voice. "Strike!"

There was a chorus of agreement.

Billy's father said: "Dai Crybaby."

"Here's how I see it," said the captain of the town's rugby team. "We can't let the company get away with this. If they're allowed to evict widows, none of us can feel that our families have any security. A man could work all his life for Celtic Minerals and die on the job, and two weeks later his family could be out on the street. Dai Union have been to the office and tried to talk sense to Gone-to-Merthyr Morgan, but it haven't done no good, so we got no alternative but to strike."

"Thank you, Dai," said Da. "Should I take that as a formal motion for strike action?"

"Aye."

Billy was surprised that Da had accepted that so quickly. He knew his father wanted to avoid a strike.

"Vote!" someone shouted.

Da said: "Before I put the proposal to a vote, we need to decide when the strike should take place."

Ah, Billy thought, he's not accepting it.

Da went on: "We might consider starting on Monday. Between now and then, while we work on, the threat of a strike might make the directors see sense—and we could get what we want without any loss of earnings."

Da was arguing for postponement as the next best thing, Billy realized.

But Len Griffiths had come to the same conclusion. "May I speak, Mr. Chairman?" he said. Tommy's father had a bald dome with a fringe of black hair, and a black mustache. He stepped forward and stood next to Da, facing the crowd, so that it looked as if the two of them had equal authority. The men went quiet. Len, like Da and Dai Crybaby, was among a handful of people they always heard in respectful silence. "I ask, is it wise to give the company four days' grace? Suppose they don't change their minds— which seems a strong possibility, given how stubborn they have been so far. Then we'll get to Monday with nothing achieved, and the widows will have that much less time left." He raised his voice slightly for rhetorical effect. "I say, comrades: don't give an inch!"

There was a cheer, and Billy joined in.

"Thank you, Len," said Da. "I have two motions on the table, then: Strike tomorrow, or strike Monday. Who else would like to speak?"

Billy watched his father manage the meeting. The next man called was Giuseppe "Joey" Ponti, top soloist with the Aberowen Male Voice Choir, older brother of Billy's schoolmate Johnny. Despite his Italian name, he had been born in Aberowen and spoke with the same accent as every other man in the room. He, too, argued for an immediate strike.

Da then said: "In fairness, may I have a speaker in favor of striking on Monday?"

Billy wondered why Da did not throw his personal authority into the balance. If he argued for Monday he might change their minds. But then, if he failed, he would be in an awkward position, leading a strike that he had argued against. Da was not completely free to say what he felt, Billy realized.

The discussion ranged widely. Coal stocks were high, so the management could hold out; but demand was high, too, and they would want to sell while they could. Spring was coming, so miners' families would soon be able to manage without their ration of free coal. The miners' case was well grounded in long-established practice, but the letter of the law was on the management's side.

Da let the discussion run on, and some of the speeches became tedious. Billy wondered what his father's motivation was, and guessed he was hoping that heads would cool. But in the end he had to put it to the vote.

"First, all those in favor of no strike at all."

A few men raised their hands.

"Next, those in favor of a strike starting Monday."

There was a strong vote for this, but Billy was not sure if it was enough to win. It would depend upon how many men abstained.

"Finally, those in favor of a strike starting tomorrow."

There was a cheer, and a forest of arms waved in the air. There could be no doubt about the result.

"The motion to strike tomorrow is passed," Da said. No one proposed a count.

The meeting broke up. As they went out, Tommy said brightly: "Day off, tomorrow, then."

"Aye," said Billy. "And no money to spend."

{ IV }

The first time Fitz went with a prostitute, he had tried to kiss her—not because he wanted to, but he assumed it was the done thing. "I don't kiss," she had said abruptly in her Cockney accent, and after that he had never tried it again. Bing Westhampton said a lot of prostitutes refused to kiss, which was odd, considering what other intimacies they permitted. Perhaps that trivial prohibition preserved a remnant of their dignity.

Girls of Fitz's social class were not supposed to kiss anyone before marriage. They did, of course, but only in rare moments of brief privacy, in a suddenly deserted side room at a ball, or behind a rhododendron bush in a country garden. There was never time for passion to develop.

The only woman Fitz had kissed properly was his wife, Bea. She gave him her body as a cook might present a special cake, fragrant and sugared and beautifully decorated for his enjoyment. She let him do anything, but made no demands. She offered her lips for him to kiss, and opened her mouth to his tongue, but he never felt she was hungry for his touch.

Ethel kissed as if she had one minute left to live.

They stood in the Gardenia Suite, beside the bed covered with its dust sheet, wrapped in each other's arms. She sucked his tongue and bit his lips and licked his throat, and at the same time she stroked his hair, clutched the back of his neck, and thrust her hands under his waistcoat so that she could rub her palms against his chest. When at last they broke apart, out of breath, she put her hands on either side of his face, holding his head still, staring at him, and said: "You are so beautiful."

He sat on the edge of the bed, holding her hands, and she stood in front of him. He knew that some men regularly seduced their servants, but he did not. When he was fifteen he had fallen in love with a parlor maid at the London house: his mother had guessed it within a few days and sacked the girl immediately. His father had smiled and said: "Good choice, though." Since then he had not touched an employee. But he could not resist Ethel.

She said: "Why have you come back? You were expected to stay in London all of May."

"I wanted to see you." He could tell that she found it hard to believe him. "I kept thinking about you, all day, every day, and I just had to come back."

She bent down and kissed him again. Holding the kiss, he slowly fell back on the bed, pulling her with him until she was lying on top of him. She was so slim that she weighed no more than a child. Her hair escaped from its pins and he buried his fingers in her glossy curls.

After a while she rolled off and lay beside him, panting. He leaned on his elbow and looked at her. She had said he was beautiful, but right now she was the prettiest thing he had ever seen. Her cheeks were flushed, her hair was mussed, and her red lips were moist and parted. Her dark eyes gazed at him with adoration.

He put his hand on her hip, then stroked her thigh. She covered his hand with her own, holding it still, as if afraid he was going too far. She said: "Why do they call you Fitz? Your name is Edward, isn't it?"

She was talking in an attempt to let their passion cool, he felt sure. "It started at school," he said. "All the boys had nicknames. Then Walter von Ulrich came home with me one vacation, and Maud picked it up from him."

"Before that, what did your parents call you?"

"Teddy."

"Teddy," she said, trying it on her tongue. "I like it better than Fitz."

He started to stroke her thigh again, and this time she let him. Kissing her, he slowly pulled up the long skirt of her black housekeeper's dress. She wore calf-length stockings, and he stroked her bare knees. Above the knee she had long cotton underdrawers. He touched her legs through the cotton, then moved his hand to the fork of her thighs. When he touched her there, she groaned and thrust upward against his hand.

"Take them off," he whispered.

"No!"

He found the drawstring at the waist. It was tied in a bow. He undid the knot with a tug.

She put her hand over his again. "Stop."

"I just want to touch you there."

"I want it more than you do," she said. "But, no."

He knelt up on the bed. "We won't do anything you don't want," he said. "I promise." Then he took the waist of her drawers in both hands and ripped the material apart. She gasped with shock, but she did not protest. He lay down again and explored her with his hand. She parted her legs immediately. Her eyes were closed and she was breathing hard, as if she had been running. He guessed that no one had done this to her before, and a faint voice told him he should not take advantage of her innocence, but he was too far gone in desire to listen.

He unbuttoned his trousers and lay on top of her.

"No," she said.

"Please."

"What if I fall for a baby?"

"I'll withdraw before the end."

"Promise?"

"I promise," he said, and he slid inside her.

He felt an obstruction. She was a virgin. His conscience spoke again, and this time its voice was not so faint. He stopped. But now it was she who was too far gone. She grasped his hips and pulled him into her, raising herself slightly at the same time. He felt something break, and she gave a sharp cry of pain; then the obstruction was gone. As he moved in and out, she matched his rhythm eagerly. She opened her eyes and looked at his face. "Oh, Teddy, Teddy," she said, and he saw that she loved him. The thought moved him almost to tears, and at the same time excited him beyond control, and his climax came unexpectedly soon. In desperate haste he withdrew, and spilled his seed on her thigh with a groan of passion mingled with disappointment. She put her hand behind his head and pulled his face to hers, kissing him wildly; then she closed her eyes and gave a small cry that sounded like surprise and pleasure; and then it was over.

I hope I pulled out in time, he thought.

{ V }

Ethel went about her work as usual, but all the time she felt as if she had a secret diamond in her pocket that she could touch from time to time, feeling its slick surfaces and its sharp edges when no one was looking.

In her more sober moments she worried about what this love meant and where it was going, and now and again she was horrified by the thought of what her God-fearing socialist father would think if he found out. But most of the time she just felt as if she was dropping through the air with no way to arrest her fall. She loved the way he walked, the way he smelled, his clothes, his careful good manners, his air of authority. She also loved the way he occasionally looked bewildered. And when he came out of his wife's room with that hurt look on his face, she could cry. She was in love and out of control.

Most days she spoke to him at least once, and they usually managed a few moments alone and a long, yearning kiss. Just kissing him made her wet, and she sometimes had to wash her drawers in the middle of the day. He took other liberties, too, whenever there was a chance, touching her body all over, which made her more excited. Twice more they had been able to meet in the Gardenia Suite and lie on the bed.

One thing puzzled Ethel: both times they had lain together, Fitz had bitten her, quite hard, once on her inner thigh and once on her breast. It had caused her to give a cry of pain, hastily muffled. The cry seemed to inflame him more. And, although it hurt, at the same time she, too, was aroused by the bite, or at least by the thought that his desire for her was so overwhelming that he was driven to express it that way. She had no idea whether this was normal, and no one she could ask.

But her main worry was that one day Fitz would fail to withdraw at the crucial moment. The tension was so high that it was almost a relief when he and Princess Bea had to go back to London.

Before he went she persuaded him to feed the children of the striking miners. "Not the parents, because you can't be seen to take sides," she said. "Just the little boys and girls. The strike has been on for two weeks now, and they're on starvation rations. It wouldn't cost you much. There would be about five hundred of them, I'd guess. They'd love you for it, Teddy."

"We could put up a marquee on the lawn," he said, lying on the bed in the Gardenia Suite with his trousers unbuttoned and his head in her lap.

"And we can make the food here in the kitchens," Ethel said enthusiastically. "A stew with meat and potatoes in it, and all the bread they can eat."

"And a suet pudding with currants in it, eh?"

Did he love her? she wondered. At that moment, she felt he would have done anything she asked: given her jewels, taken her to Paris, bought her parents a nice house. She did not want any of those things—but what *did* she want? She did not know, and she refused to let her happiness be blighted by unanswerable questions about the future.

A few days later she stood on the East Lawn at midday on a Saturday, watching the children of Aberowen tuck into their first free dinner. Fitz did not know that this was better food than they got when their fathers were working. Suet pudding with currants, indeed! The parents were not allowed in, but most of the mothers stood outside the gates, watching their lucky offspring. Glancing that way, she saw someone waving at her, and she walked down the drive.

The group at the gate was mostly women: men did not look after children, even during a strike. They gathered around Ethel, looking agitated.

"What's happened?" she said.

Mrs. Dai Ponies answered her. "Everyone have been evicted!"

"Everyone?" Ethel said, not understanding. "Who?"

"All the miners who rent their houses from Celtic Minerals."

"Good grief!" Ethel was horrified. "God save us all." Shock was followed by puzzlement. "But why? How does that help the company? They'll have no miners left."

"These men," said Mrs. Dai. "Once they get into a fight, all they care about is winning. They won't give in, whatever the cost. They're all the same. Not that I wouldn't have my Dai back, if I could."

"This is awful." How could the company find enough blacklegs to keep the pit going? she wondered. If they closed the mine, the town would die. There would be no customers left for the shops, no children to go to the schools, no patients for the doctors . . . Her father, too, would have no work. No one had expected Perceval Jones to be so obstinate.

Mrs. Dai said: "I wonder what the king would say, if he knew."

Ethel wondered, too. The king had seemed to show real compassion. But he probably did not know the widows had been evicted.

And then she was struck by a thought. "Perhaps you should tell him," she said.

Mrs. Dai laughed. "I will, next time I sees him."

"You could write him a letter."

"Don't talk daft, now, Eth."

"I mean it. You should do it." She looked around the group. "A letter signed by widows the king visited, telling him you are being thrown out of your homes and the town is on strike. He'd have to take notice, surely?"

Mrs. Dai looked scared. "I wouldn't like to get into trouble."

Mrs. Minnie Ponti, a thin blond woman of strong opinions, said to her: "You have no husband and no home and nowhere to go—how much more trouble could you be in?"

"That's true enough. But I wouldn't know what to say. Do you put 'Dear King,' or 'Dear George the Fifth,' or what?"

Ethel said: "You put: 'Sir, with my humble duty.' I know all that rubbish, from working here. Let's do it now. Come into the servants' hall."

"Will it be all right?"

"I'm the housekeeper now, Mrs. Dai. I'm the one who says what's all right."

The women followed her up the drive and around the back of the house to the kitchen. They sat around the servants' dining table, and the cook made a pot of tea. Ethel had a stock of plain writing paper that she used for correspondence with tradesmen.

"'Sir, with our humble duty,'" she said, writing. "What next?"

Mrs. Dai Ponies said: "'Forgive our cheek in writing to Your Majesty.'"

"No," Ethel said decisively. "Don't apologize. He's our king—we're entitled to petition him. Let's say: 'We are the widows Your Majesty visited in Aberowen after the pit explosion.'"

"Very good," said Mrs. Ponti.

Ethel went on: "'We were honored by your visit and comforted by your kind condolences, and the gracious sympathy of Her Majesty the queen.'"

Mrs. Dai said: "You've got the gift for this, like your father."

Mrs. Ponti said: "That's enough soft soap, though."

"All right. Now then. 'We are asking for your help as our king. Because our husbands are dead, we are being evicted from our homes.'"

"By Celtic Minerals," put in Mrs. Ponti.

"'By Celtic Minerals. The whole pit have gone on strike for us but now they are being evicted, too.'"

"Don't make it too long," said Mrs. Dai. "He might be too busy to read it."

"All right, then. Let's finish with: 'Is this the kind of thing that should be allowed in your kingdom?' "

Mrs. Ponti said: "It's a bit tame."

"No, it's good," said Mrs. Dai. "It appeals to his sense of right and wrong."

Ethel said: " 'We have the honor to be, sir, Your Majesty's most humble and obedient servants.' "

"Do we have to have that?" said Mrs. Ponti. "I'm not a servant. No offense, Ethel."

"It's the normal thing. The earl puts it when he writes a letter to *The Times.*"

"All right, then."

Ethel passed the letter around the table. "Put your addresses next to your signatures."

Mrs. Ponti said: "My writing's awful. You sign my name."

Ethel was about to protest; then it occurred to her that Mrs. Ponti might be illiterate, so she did not argue, but simply wrote: "Mrs. Minnie Ponti, 19 Wellington Row."

She addressed the envelope:

> *His Majesty the King*
> *Buckingham Palace*
> *London*

She sealed the letter and stuck on a stamp. "There we are, then," she said. The women gave her a round of applause.

She posted the letter the same day.

No reply was ever received.

{ VI }

The last Saturday in March was a gray day in South Wales. Low clouds hid the mountaintops and a tireless drizzle fell on Aberowen. Ethel and most of the servants at Tŷ Gwyn left their posts—the earl and princess were away in London—and walked into town.

Policemen had been sent from London to enforce the evictions, and they stood on every street, their heavy raincoats dripping. The Widows' Strike was national news, and reporters from Cardiff and London had come up on the first morning train, smoking cigarettes and writing in notebooks. There was even a big camera on a tripod.

Ethel stood with her family outside their house and watched. Da was employed by the union, not by Celtic Minerals, and he owned their house; but most of their neighbors were being thrown out. During the course of the morning, they brought their possessions out onto the streets: beds, tables and chairs, cooking pots and chamber pots, a framed picture, a clock, an orange box of crockery and cutlery, a few clothes wrapped in newspaper and tied with string. A small pile of near-worthless goods stood like a sacrificial offering outside each door.

Da's face was a mask of suppressed rage. Billy looked as if he wanted to have a fight with someone. Gramper kept shaking his head and saying: "I never seen the like, not in all my seventy years." Mam just looked grim.

Ethel cried and could not stop.

Some of the miners had got other jobs, but it was not easy: a miner could not adapt readily to the work of a shop assistant or a bus conductor, and employers knew this and turned them away when they saw the coal dust under their fingernails. Half a dozen had become merchant sailors, signing on as stokers and getting a pay advance to give to their wives before they left. A few were going to Cardiff or Swansea, hoping for jobs in the steelworks. Many were moving in with relatives in neighboring towns. The rest were simply crowding into another Aberowen house with a non-mining family until the strike was settled.

"The king never replied to the widows' letter," Ethel said to Da.

"You handled it wrong," he said bluntly. "Look at your Mrs. Pankhurst. I don't believe in votes for women, but she knows how to get noticed."

"What should I have done, got myself arrested?"

"You don't need to go that far. If I'd known what you were doing, I'd have told you to send a copy of the letter to the *Western Mail.*"

"I never thought of that." Ethel was disheartened to think that she could have done something to prevent these evictions, and had failed.

"The newspaper would have asked the palace whether they had received the letter, and it would have been hard for the king to say he was just going to ignore it."

"Oh, dammo, I wish I'd asked your advice."

"Don't swear," her mother said.

"Sorry, Mam."

The London policemen looked on in bewilderment, not understanding the foolish pride and stubbornness that had led to this. Perceval Jones was nowhere to be seen. A reporter from the *Daily Mail* asked Da for an interview, but the newspaper was hostile to workers, and Da refused.

There were not enough handcarts in town, so people took it in turns to move their goods. The process took hours, but by midafternoon the last pile of possessions had gone, and the keys had been left sticking out of the locks on the front doors. The policemen went back to London.

Ethel stayed in the street for a while. The windows of the empty houses looked blankly back at her, and the rainwater ran down the street pointlessly. She looked across the wet gray slates of the roofs, downhill to the scattered pithead buildings in the valley bottom. She could see a cat walking along a railway line, but otherwise there was no movement. No smoke came from the engine room, and the great twin wheels of the winding gear stood on top of their tower, motionless and redundant in the soft relentless rain.

CHAPTER FIVE

April 1914

The German embassy was a grand mansion in Carlton House Terrace, one of London's most elegant streets. It looked across a leafy garden to the pillared portico of the Athenaeum, the club for gentleman intellectuals. At the back, its stables opened on the Mall, the broad avenue that ran from Trafalgar Square to Buckingham Palace.

Walter von Ulrich did not live there—yet. Only the ambassador himself, Prince Lichnowsky, had that privilege. Walter, a mere military attaché, lived in a bachelor apartment ten minutes' walk away in Piccadilly. However, he hoped that one day he might inhabit the ambassador's grand private apartment within the embassy. Walter was not a prince, but his father was a close friend of Kaiser Wilhelm II. Walter spoke English like an Old Etonian, which he was. He had spent two years in the army and three years at the war academy before joining the Foreign Service. He was twenty-eight years old, and a rising star.

He was not attracted only by the prestige and glory of being an ambassador. He felt passionately that there was no higher calling than to serve his country. His father felt the same.

They disagreed about everything else.

They stood in the hall of the embassy and looked at each other. They were the same height, but Otto was heavier, and bald, and his mustache was the old-fashioned soup-strainer type, whereas Walter had a modern toothbrush.

Today they were identically dressed in black velvet suits with knee breeches, silk stockings, and buckled shoes. Both wore swords and cocked hats. Amazingly, this was the normal costume for presentation at Britain's royal court. "We look as if we should be on the stage," Walter said. "Ridiculous outfits."

"Not at all," said his father. "It's a splendid old custom."

Otto von Ulrich had spent much of his life in the German army. A young officer in the Franco-Prussian War, he had led his company across a pontoon bridge at the Battle of Sedan. Later, Otto had been one of the friends the young Kaiser Wilhelm had turned to after he broke with Bismarck, the Iron Chancellor. Now Otto had a roving brief, visiting European capitals like a bee landing on flowers, sipping the nectar of diplomatic intelligence and taking it all back to the hive. He believed in the monarchy and the Prussian military tradition.

Walter was just as patriotic, but he thought Germany had to become modern and egalitarian. Like his father, he was proud of his country's achievements in science and technology, and of the hardworking and efficient German people; but he thought they had a lot to learn—democracy from the liberal Americans, diplomacy from the sly British, and the art of gracious living from the stylish French.

Father and son left the embassy and went down a broad flight of steps to the Mall. Walter was to be presented to King George V, a ritual that was considered a privilege even though it brought with it no particular benefits. Junior diplomats such as he were not normally so honored, but his father had no compunction about pulling strings to advance Walter's career.

"Machine guns make all handheld weapons obsolete," Walter said, continuing an argument they had begun earlier. Weapons were his specialty, and he felt strongly that the German army should have the latest in firepower.

Otto thought differently. "They jam, they overheat, and they miss. A man with a rifle takes careful aim. But give him a machine gun and he'll wield it like a garden hose."

"When your house is on fire, you don't throw water on it in cupfuls, no matter how accurate. You *want* a hose."

Otto wagged his finger. "You've never been in battle— you have no idea what it's like. Listen to me. I know."

This was how their arguments often ended.

Walter felt his father's generation was arrogant. He understood how they had got that way. They had won a war, they had created the German Empire out of Prussia and a group of smaller independent monarchies, and then they had made Germany one of the world's most prosperous countries. Of course they thought they were wonderful. But it made them incautious.

A few hundred yards along the Mall, Walter and Otto turned into St. James's Palace. This sixteenth-century brick pile was older and less impressive than neighboring Buckingham Palace. They gave their names to a doorman who was dressed as they were.

Walter was mildly anxious. It was so easy to make a mistake of etiquette—and there were no minor errors when you were dealing with royalty.

Otto spoke to the doorman in English. "Is Señor Diaz here?"

"Yes, sir, he arrived a few moments ago."

Walter frowned. Juan Carlos Diego Diaz was a representative of the Mexican government. "Why are you interested in Diaz?" he said in German as they walked on through a series of rooms decorated with wall displays of swords and guns.

"The British Royal Navy is converting its ships from coal power to oil."

Walter nodded. Most advanced nations were doing the same. Oil was cheaper, cleaner, and easier to deal with—you just pumped it in, instead of employing armies of black-faced stokers. "And the British get oil from Mexico."

"They have bought the Mexican oil wells in order to secure supplies for their navy."

"But if we interfere in Mexico, what would the Americans think?"

Otto tapped the side of his nose. "Listen and learn. And, whatever you do, don't say anything."

The men about to be presented were waiting in an anteroom. Most had on the same velvet court dress, though one or two were in the comic-opera costumes of nineteenth-century generals, and one—presumably a Scot—wore full-dress uniform with a kilt. Walter and Otto strolled around the room, nodding to familiar faces on the diplomatic circuit, until they came to Diaz, a thickset man with a mustache that curled up at the tips.

After the usual pleasantries Otto said: "You must be glad that President Wilson has lifted the ban on arms sales to Mexico."

"Arms sales to the rebels," said Diaz, as if correcting him.

The American president, always inclined to take a moral stand, had refused to recognize General Huerta, who had come to power after the assassination of his predecessor. Calling Huerta a murderer, Wilson was backing a rebel group, the Constitutionalists.

Otto said: "If arms may be sold to the rebels, surely they may be sold to the government?"

Diaz looked startled. "Are you telling me that Germany would be willing to do that?"

"What do you need?"

"You must already know that we are desperate for rifles and ammunition."

"We could talk further about it."

Walter was as startled as Diaz. This would cause trouble. He said: "But, Father, the United States—"

"One moment!" His father held up a hand to silence him.

Diaz said: "By all means let us talk further. But tell me: what other subjects might come up?" He had guessed that Germany would want something in return.

The door to the throne room opened, and a footman came out carrying a list. The presentation was about to start. But Otto continued unhurriedly: "In time of war, a sovereign country is entitled to withhold strategic supplies."

Diaz said: "You're talking about oil." It was the only strategic supply Mexico had.

Otto nodded.

Diaz said: "So you would give us guns—"

"Sell, not give," Otto murmured.

"You would sell us guns now, in exchange for a promise that we would withhold oil from the British in the event of war." Diaz was clearly not used to the elaborate waltz of normal diplomatic conversation.

"It might be worth discussing." In the language of diplomacy that was a yes.

The footman called out: "Monsieur Honoré de Picard de la Fontaine!" and the presentations began.

Otto gave Diaz a direct look. "What I'd like to know from you is how such a proposal might be received in Mexico City."

"I believe President Huerta would be interested."

"So, if the German minister to Mexico, Admiral Paul von Hintze, were to make a formal approach to your president, he would not receive a rebuff?"

Walter could tell that his father was determined to get an unequivocal answer to this. He did not want the German government to risk the embarrassment of having such an offer flung back in their faces.

In Walter's anxious view, embarrassment was not the greatest danger to Germany in this diplomatic ploy. It risked making an enemy of the United States. But it was frustratingly difficult to point this out in the presence of Diaz.

Answering the question, Diaz said: "He would not be rebuffed."

"You're sure?" Otto insisted.

"I guarantee it."

Walter said: "Father, may I have a word—"

But the footman cried: "Herr Walter von Ulrich!"

Walter hesitated, and his father said: "Your turn. Go on!"

Walter turned away and stepped into the Throne Room.

The British liked to overawe their guests. The high coffered ceiling had diamond-patterned coving, the red plush walls were hung with enormous portraits, and at the far end the throne was overhung by a high canopy with dark velvet drapes. In front of the throne stood the king in a naval uniform. Walter was pleased to see the familiar face of Sir Alan Tite at the king's side—no doubt whispering names in the royal ear.

Walter approached and bowed. The king said: "Good to see you again, von Ulrich."

Walter had rehearsed what he would say. "I hope Your Majesty found the discussions at Tŷ Gwyn interesting."

"Very! Although the party was dreadfully overshadowed, of course."

"By the pit disaster. Indeed, so tragic."

"I look forward to our next meeting."

Walter understood this was his dismissal. He walked backward, bowing repeatedly in the required manner, until he reached the doorway.

His father was waiting for him in the next room.

"That was quick!" Walter said.

"On the contrary, it took longer than normal," said Otto. "Usually the king says: 'I'm glad to see you in London,' and that's the end of the conversation."

They left the palace together. "Admirable people, the British, in many ways, but soft," said Otto as they walked up St. James's Street to Piccadilly. "The king is ruled by his ministers, the ministers are subject to Parliament, and members of Parliament are chosen by the ordinary men. What sort of way is that to run a country?"

Walter did not rise to that provocation. He believed that Germany's political system was out-of-date, with its weak parliament that could not stand up to the kaiser or the generals; but he had had that argument with his father many times, and besides, he was still worried by the conversation with the Mexican envoy. "What you said to Diaz was risky," he said. "President Wilson won't like us selling rifles to Huerta."

"What does it matter what Wilson thinks?"

"The danger is that we will make a friend of a weak nation, Mexico, by making an enemy of a strong nation, the United States."

"There's not going to be a war in America."

Walter supposed that was true, but all the same he was uneasy. He did not like the idea of his country being at odds with the United States.

In his apartment they took off their antiquated costumes and dressed in tweed suits with soft-collared shirts and brown trilby hats. Back in Piccadilly they boarded a motorized omnibus heading east.

Otto had been impressed by Walter's invitation to meet the king at Tŷ Gwyn in January. "Earl Fitzherbert is a good connection," he had said. "If the Conservative Party comes to power, he may be a minister, perhaps foreign secretary one day. You must keep up the friendship."

Walter had been inspired. "I should visit his charity clinic, and make a small donation."

"Excellent idea."

"Perhaps you would like to come with me?"

His father had taken the bait. "Even better."

Walter had an ulterior motive, but his father was all unsuspecting.

The bus took them past the theaters of the Strand, the newspaper offices of Fleet Street, and the banks of the financial district. Then the streets became narrower and dirtier. Top hats and bowlers were replaced by cloth caps. Horse-drawn vehicles predominated, and motorcars were few. This was the East End.

They got off at Aldgate. Otto looked around disdainfully. "I didn't know you were taking me to the slums," he said.

"We're going to a clinic for the poor," Walter replied. "Where would you expect it to be?"

"Does Earl Fitzherbert himself come here?"

"I suspect he just pays for it." Walter knew perfectly well that Fitz had never been there in his life. "But he will of course hear about our visit."

They zigzagged through backstreets to a nonconformist chapel. A hand-painted wooden sign read: "Calvary Gospel Hall." Pinned to the board was a sheet of paper with the words:

Baby Clinic
Free of Charge
Today and
every Wednesday

Walter opened the door and they went in.

Otto made a disgusted noise, then took out a handkerchief and held it to his nose. Walter had been there before, so he had been expecting the smell, but even so it was startlingly unpleasant. The hall was full of ragged women and half-naked children, all filthy dirty. The women sat on benches and the children played on the floor. At the far end of the room were two doors, each with a temporary label, one saying "Doctor" and the other "Patroness."

Near the door sat Fitz's aunt Herm, listing names in a book. Walter introduced his father. "Lady Hermia Fitzherbert, my father, Herr Otto von Ulrich."

At the other end of the room, the door marked "Doctor" opened and a ragged woman came out carrying a tiny baby and a medicine bottle. A nurse looked out and said: "Next, please."

Lady Hermia consulted her list and called: "Mrs. Blatsky and Rosie!"

An older woman and a girl went into the doctor's surgery.

Walter said: "Wait here a moment, please, Father, and I'll fetch the boss."

He hurried to the far end, stepping around the toddlers on the floor. He tapped on the door marked "Patroness," and walked in.

The room was little more than a cupboard, and indeed there was a mop and bucket in a corner. Lady Maud Fitzherbert sat at a small table writing in a ledger. She wore a simple dove-gray dress and a broad-brimmed hat. She looked up, and the smile that lit up her face when she saw Walter was bright enough to bring tears to his eyes. She leaped out of her chair and threw her arms around him.

He had been looking forward to this all day. He kissed her mouth, which opened to him immediately. He had kissed several women, but she was the only one he had ever known to press her body against him this way. He felt embarrassed, fearing that she would feel his erection, and he arched his body away; but she only pressed more closely, as if she really wanted to feel it, so he gave in to the pleasure.

Maud was passionate about everything: poverty, women's rights, music—and Walter. He felt amazed and privileged that she had fallen in love with him.

She broke the kiss, panting. "Aunt Herm will become suspicious," she said.

Walter nodded. "My father is outside."

Maud patted her hair and smoothed her dress. "All right."

Walter opened the door and they went back into the hall. Otto was chatting amiably to Hermia: he liked respectable old ladies.

"Lady Maud Fitzherbert, may I present my father, Herr Otto von Ulrich."

Otto bowed over her hand. He had learned not to click his heels: the English thought it comical.

Walter watched them size each other up. Maud smiled as if amused, and Walter guessed she was wondering if this was what *he* would look like in years to come. Otto took in Maud's expensive cashmere dress and the fashionable hat with approval. So far, so good.

Otto did not know that they were in love. Walter's plan was that his father would get to know Maud first. Otto approved of wealthy women doing charitable work, and insisted that Walter's mother and his sister visit poor families at Zumwald, their country estate in East Prussia. He would find out what a wonderful and exceptional woman Maud was; then his defenses would be down by the time he learned that Walter wanted to marry her.

It was a little foolish, Walter knew, to be so nervous. He was twenty-eight years old: he had a right to choose the woman he loved. But eight years ago he had fallen in love with another woman. Tilde had been passionate and intelligent, like Maud, but she was seventeen and a Catholic. The von Ulrichs were Protestants. Both sets of parents had been angrily hostile to the romance, and Tilde had been unable to defy her father. Now Walter had fallen in love with an unsuitable woman for the second time. It was going to be difficult for his father to accept a feminist and a foreigner. But Walter was older and craftier now, and Maud was stronger and more independent than Tilde had been.

All the same, he was terrified. He had never felt like this about a woman, not even Tilde. He wanted to marry Maud and spend his life with her; in fact he could not imagine being without her. And he did not want his father to make trouble about it.

Maud was on her best behavior. "It is very kind of you to visit us, Herr von Ulrich," she said. "You must be tremendously busy. For a trusted confidant of a monarch, as you are to your kaiser, I imagine work has no end."

Otto was flattered, as she had intended. "I'm afraid this is true," he said. "However your brother, the earl, is such a long-standing friend of Walter's that I was very keen to come."

"Let me introduce you to our doctor." Maud led the way across the room and knocked at the surgery door. Walter was curious: he had never met the doctor. "May we come in?" she called.

They stepped into what must normally have been the pastor's office, furnished with a small desk and a shelf of ledgers and hymn books. The doctor, a handsome young man with black eyebrows and a sensual mouth, was examining Rosie Blatsky's hand. Walter felt a twinge of jealousy: Maud spent whole days with this attractive fellow.

Maud said: "Dr. Greenward, we have a most distinguished visitor. May I present Herr von Ulrich?"

Otto said stiffly: "How do you do?"

"The doctor works here for no fee," Maud said. "We're most grateful to him."

Greenward nodded curtly. Walter wondered what was causing the evident tension between his father and the doctor.

The doctor returned his attention to his patient. There was an angry-looking cut across her palm, and the hand and wrist were swollen. He looked at the mother and said: "How did she do this?"

The child answered. "My mother doesn't speak English," she said. "I cut my hand at work."

"And your father?"

"My father's dead."

Maud said quietly: "The clinic is for fatherless families, though in practice we never turn anyone away."

Greenward said to Rosie: "How old are you?"

"Eleven."

Walter murmured: "I thought children were not allowed to work under thirteen."

"There are loopholes in the law," Maud replied.

Greenward said: "What work do you do?"

"I clean up at Mannie Litov's garment factory. There was a blade in the sweepings."

"Whenever you cut yourself, you must wash the wound and put on a clean bandage. Then you have to change the bandage every day so that it doesn't get too dirty." Greenward's manner was brisk, but not unkind.

The mother barked a question at the daughter in heavily accented Russian. Walter could not understand her, but he got the gist of the child's reply, which was a translation of what the doctor had said.

The doctor turned to his nurse. "Clean the hand and bandage it, please." To Rosie he said: "I'm going to give you some ointment. If your arm swells more you must come back and see me next week. Do you understand?"

"Yes, sir."

"If you let the infection get worse, you may lose your hand."

Tears came to Rosie's eyes.

Greenward said: "I'm sorry to frighten you, but I want you to understand how important it is to keep your hand clean."

As the nurse prepared a bowl of what was presumably antiseptic fluid, Walter said: "May I express my admiration and respect for your work here, Doctor."

"Thank you. I'm happy to give my time, but we need to buy medical supplies. Any help you can offer will be much appreciated."

Maud said: "We must leave the doctor to get on—there are at least twenty patients waiting."

The visitors left the surgery. Walter was bursting with pride. Maud had more than compassion. When told of young children working in sweatshops, many aristocratic ladies could wipe away a tear with an embroidered handkerchief; but Maud had the determination and the nerve to give real help.

And, he thought, she loves me!

Maud said: "May I offer you some refreshment, Herr von Ulrich? My office is cramped, but I do have a bottle of my brother's best sherry."

"Most kind, but we must be going."

That was a bit quick, Walter thought. Maud's charm had stopped working on Otto. He had a nasty feeling that something had gone wrong.

Otto took out his pocketbook and extracted a banknote. "Please accept a modest contribution to your excellent work here, Lady Maud."

"How generous!" she said.

Walter gave her a similar note. "Perhaps I may be allowed to donate something, too."

"I appreciate anything you can offer me," she said. Walter hoped he was the only one to notice the sly look she gave him as she said it.

Otto said: "Please be sure to give my respects to Earl Fitzherbert."

They took their leave. Walter felt worried about his father's reaction. "Isn't Lady Maud wonderful?" he said breezily as they walked back toward Aldgate. "Fitz pays for everything, of course, but Maud does all the work."

"Disgraceful," Otto said. "Absolutely disgraceful."

Walter had sensed he was grumpy, but this astonished him. "What on earth do you mean? You approve of well-born ladies doing something to help the poor!"

"Visiting sick peasants with a few groceries in a basket is one thing," Otto said. "But I am appalled to see the sister of an earl in a place like that with a Jew doctor!"

"Oh, God," Walter groaned. Of course; Dr. Greenward was Jewish. His parents had probably been Germans called Grunwald. Walter had not met the doctor before today, and anyway might not have noticed or cared about his race. But Otto, like most men of his generation, thought such things important. Walter said: "Father, the man is working for nothing—Lady Maud cannot afford to refuse the help of a perfectly good doctor just because he's Jewish."

Otto was not listening. "Fatherless families—where did she get that phrase?" he said with disgust. "The spawn of prostitutes is what she means."

Walter felt heartsick. His plan had gone horribly wrong. "Don't you see how brave she is?" he said miserably.

"Certainly not," said Otto. "If she were my sister, I'd give her a good thrashing."

{ II }

There was a crisis in the White House.

In the small hours of the morning of April 21, Gus Dewar was in the West Wing. This new building provided badly needed office space, leaving the original White House free to be used as a residence. Gus was sitting in the president's study near the Oval Office, a small, drab room lit by a dim bulb. On the desk was the battered Underwood portable typewriter used by Woodrow Wilson to write his speeches and press releases.

Gus was more interested in the phone. If it rang, he had to decide whether to wake the president.

A telephone operator could not make such a decision. On the other hand, the president's senior advisers needed their sleep. Gus was the lowliest of Wilson's advisers, or the highest of his clerks, depending on point of view. Either way, it had fallen to him to sit all night by the phone to decide whether to disturb the president's slumbers—or those of the first lady, Ellen Wilson, who was suffering from a mysterious illness. Gus was nervous that he might say or do the wrong thing. Suddenly all his expensive education seemed superfluous: even at Harvard there had never been a class in when to wake the president. He was hoping the phone would never ring.

Gus was there because of a letter he had written. He had described to his father the royal party at Tŷ Gwyn, and the after-dinner discussion about the danger of war in Europe. Senator Dewar had found the letter so interesting and amusing that he had shown it to his friend Woodrow Wilson, who had said: "I'd like to have that boy in my office." Gus had been taking a year off between Harvard, where he had studied international law, and his first job at a Washington law firm. He had been halfway through a world tour, but he had eagerly cut short his travels and rushed home to serve his president.

Nothing fascinated Gus so much as the relationships between nations—the friendships and hatreds, the alliances and the wars. As a teenager he had attended sessions of the Senate Committee on Foreign Relations—his father was a member—and he had found it more fascinating than a play at the theater. "This is how countries create peace and prosperity—or war, devastation, and famine," his father had said. "If you want to change the world, then foreign relations is the field in which you can do the most good—or evil."

And now Gus was in the middle of his first international crisis.

An overzealous Mexican government official had arrested eight American sailors in the port of Tampico. The men had already been released, the official had apologized, and the trivial incident might have ended there. But the squadron commander, Admiral Mayo, had demanded a twenty-one-gun salute. President Huerta had refused. Piling on the pressure, Wilson had threatened to occupy Veracruz, Mexico's biggest port.

And so America was on the brink of war. Gus greatly admired the high-principled Woodrow Wilson. The president was not content with the cynical view that one Mexican bandit was pretty much like another. Huerta was a reactionary who had killed his predecessor, and Wilson was looking for a pretext to unseat him. Gus was thrilled that a world leader would say it was not acceptable for men to achieve power through murder. Would there come a day when that principle was accepted by all nations?

The crisis had been cranked up a notch by the Germans. A German ship called the *Ypiranga* was approaching Veracruz with a cargo of rifles and ammunition for Huerta's government.

Tension had been high all day, but now Gus was struggling to stay awake. On the desk in front of him, illuminated by a green-shaded lamp, was a typewritten report from army intelligence on the strength of the rebels in Mexico. Intelligence was one of the army's smaller departments, with only two officers and two clerks, and the report was scrappy. Gus's mind kept wandering to Caroline Wigmore.

When he arrived in Washington he had called to see Professor Wigmore, one of his Harvard teachers who had moved to Georgetown University. Wigmore had not been at home, but his young second wife was there. Gus had met Caroline several times at campus events, and had been strongly drawn to her quietly thoughtful demeanor and her quick intelligence. "He said he needed to order new shirts," she said, but Gus could see the strain on her face, and then she added: "But I know he's gone to his mistress." Gus had wiped her tears with his handkerchief and she had kissed his lips and said: "I wish I were married to someone trustworthy."

Caroline had turned out to be surprisingly passionate. Although she would not allow sexual intercourse, they did everything else. She had shuddering orgasms when he did no more than stroke her.

Their affair had been going on for only a month, but already Gus knew that he wanted her to divorce Wigmore and marry him. But she would not hear of it, even though she had no children. She said it would ruin Gus's career, and she was probably right. It could not be done discreetly, for the scandal would be too juicy—the attractive wife leaving a well-known professor and rapidly marrying a wealthy younger man. Gus knew exactly what his mother would say about such a marriage: "It's understandable, if the professor was unfaithful, but one can't meet the woman socially, of course." The president would be embarrassed, and so would the kind of people a lawyer wanted for clients. It would certainly put paid to any hopes Gus might have had of following his father into the Senate.

Gus told himself he did not care. He loved Caroline and he would rescue her from her husband. He had plenty of money, and when his father died he would be a millionaire. He would find some other career. Perhaps he might become a journalist, reporting from foreign capitals.

All the same he felt a stabbing pain of regret. He had just got a job in the White House, something young men dreamed of. It would be agonizingly hard to give that up, along with all it might lead to.

The phone rang, and Gus was startled by its sudden jangling in the quiet of the West Wing at night. "Oh, my God," he said, staring at it. "Oh, my God, this is it." He hesitated several seconds, then at last picked up the handset. He heard the fruity voice of Secretary of State William Jennings Bryan. "I have Josephus Daniels on the line with me, Gus." Daniels was secretary of the navy. "And the president's secretary is listening on an extension."

"Yes, Mr. Secretary, sir," said Gus. He made his voice calm, but his heart was racing.

"Wake the president, please," said Secretary Bryan.

"Yes, sir."

Gus went through the Oval Office and out into the Rose Garden in the cool night air. He ran across to the old building. A guard let him in. He hurried up the main staircase and across the hall to the bedroom door. He took a deep breath and knocked hard, hurting his knuckles.

After a moment he heard Wilson's voice. "Who is it?"

"Gus Dewar here, Mr. President," he called. "Secretary Bryan and Secretary Daniels are on the telephone."

"Just a minute."

President Wilson came out of the bedroom putting on his rimless glasses, looking vulnerable in pajamas and a dressing gown. He was tall, though not as tall as Gus. At fifty-seven he had dark gray hair. He thought he was ugly, and he was not far wrong. He had a beak of a nose and sticking-out ears, but the thrust of his big chin gave his face a determined look that accurately reflected the strength of character that Gus respected. When he spoke, he showed bad teeth.

"Good morning, Gus," he said amiably. "What's the excitement?"

"They didn't tell me."

"Well, you'd better listen in on the extension next door."

Gus hurried into the next room and picked up the phone.

He heard Bryan's sonorous tones. "The *Ypiranga* is due to dock at ten this morning."

Gus felt a thrill of apprehension. Surely the Mexican president would cave in now? Otherwise there would be bloodshed.

Bryan read a cable from the American consul in Veracruz. "'Steamer *Ypiranga*, owned by Hamburg-Amerika line, will arrive tomorrow from Germany with two hundred machine guns and fifteen million cartridges; will go to pier four and start discharging at ten thirty.'"

"Do you realize what this means, Mr. Bryan?" said Wilson, and Gus thought his voice sounded querulous. "Daniels, are you there, Daniels? What do you think?"

Daniels replied: "The munitions should not be permitted to reach Huerta." Gus was surprised at this tough line from the peace-loving navy secretary. "I can wire Admiral Fletcher to prevent it and take the customs house."

There was a long pause. Gus was gripping the phone so hard that his hand hurt. At last the president spoke. "Daniels, send this order to Admiral Fletcher: Take Veracruz at once."

"Yes, Mr. President," said the navy secretary.

And America was at war.

{ III }

Gus did not go to bed that night or the following day.

Shortly after eight thirty, Secretary Daniels brought the news that an American warship had blocked the path of the *Ypiranga*. The German ship, an unarmed freighter, switched its engines to reverse and left the scene. American marines would go ashore at Veracruz later that morning, Daniels said.

Gus was dismayed by the rapidly developing crisis but thrilled to be at the heart of things.

Woodrow Wilson did not shrink from war. His favorite play was Shakespeare's *Henry V,* and he liked to quote the line "If it be a sin to covet honour, I am the most offending soul alive."

News came in by wireless and cable, and it was Gus's job to take the messages in to the president. At midday the marines took control of the Veracruz customs house.

Shortly afterward, he was told that there was someone to see him—a Mrs. Wigmore.

Gus frowned worriedly. This was indiscreet. Something must be wrong.

He hurried to the lobby. Caroline looked distraught. Although she wore a neat tweed coat and a plain hat, her hair was untidy and her eyes red with crying. Gus was shocked and distressed to see her in this state. "My darling!" he said in a low voice. "What on earth has happened?"

"This is the end," she said. "I can never see you again. I'm so sorry." She began to cry.

Gus wanted to hug her, but he could not do so there. He had no office of his own. He looked around. The guard at the door was staring at them. There was nowhere they could be private. It was maddening. "Come outside," he said, taking her arm. "We'll walk."

She shook her head. "No. I'll be all right. Stay here."

"What has upset you?"

She would not meet his eye, and looked at the floor. "I must be faithful to my husband. I have obligations."

"Let me be your husband."

She raised her face, and her yearning look broke his heart. "Oh, how I wish I could."

"But you can!"

"I have a husband already."

"He is not faithful to you—why should you be to him?"

She ignored that. "He's accepted a chair at Berkeley. We're moving to California."

"Don't go."

"I've made up my mind."

"Obviously," Gus said flatly. He felt as if he had been knocked down. His chest hurt and he found it hard to breathe. "California," he said. "Hell."

She saw his acceptance of the inevitable, and she began to recover her composure. "This is our last meeting," she said.

"No!"

"Please listen to me. There's something I want to tell you, and this is my only chance."

"All right."

"A month ago I was ready to kill myself. Don't look at me like that—it's true. I thought I was so worthless that no one would care if I died. Then you appeared on my doorstep. You were so affectionate, so courteous, so thoughtful, that you made me think it was worth staying alive. You cherished me." The tears were streaming down her cheeks, but she kept on. "And you were so happy when I kissed you. If I could give someone that much joy, I couldn't be completely useless, I realized; and that thought kept me going. You saved my life, Gus. May God bless you."

He almost felt angry. "What does that leave me with?"

"Memories," she said. "I hope you will treasure them as I will treasure mine."

She turned away. Gus followed her to the door, but she did not look back. She went out, and he let her go.

When she was out of sight he headed automatically for the Oval Office, then changed direction: his mind was in too much of a turmoil for him to be with the president. He went into the men's room for a moment's peace. Fortunately there was no one else there. He washed his face, then looked in the mirror. He saw a thin man with a big head: he was shaped like a lollipop. He had light brown hair and brown eyes, and was not very handsome, but women usually liked him, and Caroline loved him.

Or she had, at least, for a little while.

He should not have let her go. How could he have watched her walk away like that? He should have persuaded her to postpone her decision, think about it, talk to him some more. Perhaps they could have thought of alternatives. But in his heart he knew there were no alternatives. She had already been through all that in her mind, he guessed. She must have lain awake nights, with her husband sleeping beside her, going over and over the situation. She had made up her mind before coming here.

He needed to return to his post. America was at war. But how could he put this out of his mind? When he could not see her, he spent all day looking forward to the next time he could. Now he could not stop thinking about life without her. It already seemed a strange prospect. What would he do?

A clerk came into the men's room, and Gus dried his hands on a towel and returned to his station in the study next to the Oval Office.

A few moments later, a messenger brought him a cable from the American consul in Veracruz. Gus looked at it and said: "Oh, no!" It read: FOUR OF OUR MEN KILLED COMMA TWENTY WOUNDED COMMA FIRING ALL AROUND THE CONSULATE STOP.

Four men killed, Gus thought with horror: four good American men with mothers and fathers, and wives or girl-friends. The news seemed to put his sadness in perspective. At least, he thought, Caroline and I are alive.

He tapped on the door of the Oval Office and handed the cable to Wilson. The president read it and went pale.

Gus looked keenly at him. How did he feel, knowing they were dead because of the decision he had made in the middle of the night?

This was not supposed to happen. The Mexicans wanted freedom from tyrannical governments, didn't they? They should have welcomed the Americans as liberators. What had gone wrong?

Bryan and Daniels showed up a few minutes later, followed by the secretary of war, Lindley Garrison, a man normally more belligerent than Wilson, and Robert Lansing, the State Department counselor. They gathered in the Oval Office to wait for more news.

The president was wired tighter than a violin string. Pale, restless, and twitchy, he paced the floor. It was a pity, Gus thought, that Wilson did not smoke—it might have calmed him.

We all knew there might be violence, Gus thought, but somehow the reality is more shocking than we anticipated.

More details came in sporadically, and Gus handed the messages to Wilson. The news was all bad. Mexican troops had resisted, firing on the marines from their fort. The troops were supported by citizens, who took potshots at Americans from their upstairs windows. In retaliation the USS *Prairie,* anchored offshore, turned its three-inch guns on the city and shelled it.

Casualties mounted: six Americans killed, eight, twelve— and more wounded. But it was a hopelessly unequal contest, and more than a hundred Mexicans died.

The president seemed baffled. "We don't want to fight the Mexicans," he said. "We want to serve them, if we can. We want to serve mankind."

For the second time in a day, Gus felt knocked off his feet. The president and his advisers had had nothing but good intentions. How had things gone so wrong? Was it really so difficult to do good in international affairs?

A message came from the State Department. The German ambassador, Count Johann von Bernstorff, had been instructed by the kaiser to call on the secretary of state, and wished to know whether nine o'clock tomorrow morning would be convenient. Unofficially, his staff indicated that the ambassador would be lodging a formal protest against the halting of the *Ypiranga.*

"A protest?" said Wilson. "What the dickens are they talking about?"

Gus saw immediately that the Germans had international law on their side. "Sir, there had been no declaration of war, nor of a blockade, so, strictly speaking, the Germans are correct."

"What?" Wilson turned to Lansing. "Is that right?"

"We'll double-check, of course," said the State Department counselor. "But I'm pretty sure Gus is right. What we did was contrary to international law."

"So what does that mean?"

"It means we'll have to apologize."

"Never!" said Wilson angrily.

But they did.

{ IV }

Maud Fitzherbert was surprised to find herself in love with Walter von Ulrich. On the other hand, she would have been surprised to find herself in love with any man. She rarely met one she even liked. Plenty had been attracted to her, especially during her first season as a debutante, but most had quickly been repelled by her feminism. Others had planned to take her in hand—like the scruffy Marquis of Lowther, who had told Fitz that she would see the error of her ways when she met a truly masterful man. Poor Lowthie, he had been shown the error of his.

Walter thought she was wonderful the way she was. Whatever she did, he marveled. If she espoused extreme points of view, he was impressed by her arguments; when she shocked society by helping unmarried mothers and their children, he admired her courage; and he loved the way she looked in daring fashions.

Maud was bored by wealthy upper-class Englishmen who thought the way society was currently arranged was pretty satisfactory. Walter was different. Coming as he did from a conservative German family, he was surprisingly radical. From where she sat, in the back row of seats in her brother's box at the opera, she could see Walter in the stalls, with a small group from the German embassy. He did not look like a rebel, with his carefully brushed hair, his trim mustache, and his perfectly fitting evening clothes. Even sitting down, he was upright and straight-shouldered. He looked at the stage with intense concentration as Don Giovanni, accused of trying to rape a simple country girl, brazenly pretended to have caught his servant, Leporello, committing the crime.

In fact, she mused, *rebel* was not the right word for Walter. Although unusually open-minded, Walter was sometimes conventional. He was proud of the great musical tradition of German-speaking people, and got cross with blasé London audiences for arriving late, chatting to their friends during the performance, and leaving early. He would be irritated at Fitz, now, for making comments about the soprano's figure to his pal Bing Westhampton, and at Bea for talking to the Duchess of Sussex about Madame Lucille's shop in Hanover Square, where they bought their gowns. She even knew what Walter would say: "They listen to the music only when they have run out of gossip!"

Maud felt the same, but they were in a minority. For most of London's high society, the opera was just one more opportunity to show off clothes and jewels. However, even they fell silent toward the end of act 1, as Don Giovanni threatened to kill Leporello, and the orchestra played a thunderstorm on drums and double basses. Then, with characteristic insouciance, Don Giovanni released Leporello and walked jauntily away, defying them all to stop him; and the curtain came down.

Walter stood up immediately, looking toward the box, and waved. Fitz waved back. "That's von Ulrich," he said to Bing. "All those Germans are pleased with themselves because they embarrassed the Americans in Mexico."

Bing was an impish, curly-haired Lothario distantly related to the royal family. He knew little of world affairs, being mainly interested in gambling and drinking in the capital cities of Europe. He frowned and said in puzzlement: "What do the Germans care about Mexico?"

"Good question," Fitz said. "If they think they can win colonies in South America, they're deceiving themselves—the United States will never allow it."

Maud left the box and went down the grand staircase, nodding and smiling to acquaintances. She knew something like half the people there: London society was a surprisingly small set. On the red-carpeted landing she encountered a group surrounding the slight, dapper figure of David Lloyd George, the chancellor of the Exchequer. "Good evening, Lady Maud," he said with the twinkle that appeared in his bright blue eyes whenever he spoke to an attractive woman. "I hear your royal house party went well." He had the nasal accent of North Wales, less musical than the South Wales lilt. "But what a tragedy in the Aberowen pit."

"The bereaved families were much comforted by the king's condolences," Maud said. Among the group was an attractive woman in her twenties. Maud said: "Good evening, Miss Stevenson. How nice to see you again." Lloyd George's political secretary and mistress was a rebel, and Maud felt drawn to her. In addition, a man was always grateful to people who were polite to his mistress.

Lloyd George spoke to the group. "That German ship delivered the guns to Mexico after all. It simply went to another port and quietly unloaded. So nineteen American troops died for nothing. It's a terrible humiliation for Woodrow Wilson."

Maud smiled and touched Lloyd George's arm. "Would you explain something to me, Chancellor?"

"If I can, my dear," he said indulgently. Most men were pleased to be asked to explain things, especially to attractive young women, Maud found.

She said: "Why does anyone care what happens in Mexico?"

"Oil, dear lady," Lloyd George replied. "Oil."

Someone else spoke to him, and he turned away.

Maud spotted Walter. They met at the foot of the staircase. He bowed over her gloved hand, and she had to resist the temptation to touch his fair hair. Her love for Walter had awakened within her a sleeping lion of physical desire, a beast that was both stimulated and tormented by their stolen kisses and furtive fumbles.

"How are you enjoying the opera, Lady Maud?" he said formally, but his hazel eyes said, *I wish we were alone.*

"Very much—the Don has a wonderful voice."

"For me the conductor goes a little too fast."

He was the only person she had ever met who took music as seriously as she did. "I disagree," she said. "It's a comedy, so the melodies need to bounce along."

"But not just a comedy."

"That's true."

"Perhaps he will slow down when things turn nasty in act two."

"You seem to have won some kind of diplomatic coup in Mexico," she said, changing the subject.

"My father is . . ." He searched for words, something that was unusual for him. "Cock-a-hoop," he said after a pause.

"And you are not?"

He frowned. "I worry that the American president may want to get his own back one day."

At that moment Fitz walked past and said: "Hello, von Ulrich. Come and join us in our box. We've got a spare seat."

"With pleasure!" said Walter.

Maud was delighted. Fitz was just being hospitable: he did not know his sister was in love with Walter. She would have to bring him up-to-date soon. She was not sure how he would take the news. Their countries were at odds, and although Fitz regarded Walter as a friend, that was a long step from welcoming him as a brother-in-law.

She and Walter walked up the stairs and along the corridor. The back row in Fitz's box had only two seats with a poor view. Without discussion, Maud and Walter took those seats.

A few minutes later the house lights went down. In the half dark, Maud could almost imagine herself alone with Walter. The second act began with the duet between the Don and Leporello. Maud liked the way Mozart made masters and servants sing together, showing the complex and intimate relationships between upper and lower orders. Many dramas dealt only with the upper classes, and portrayed servants as part of the furniture—as many people wished they were.

Bea and the duchess returned to the box during the trio "Ah! Taci, ingiusto core." Everyone seemed to have exhausted the available topics of conversation, for they talked less and listened more. No one spoke to Maud or Walter, or even turned to look at them, and Maud wondered excitedly whether she might take advantage of the situation. Feeling daring, she reached out and furtively took Walter's hand. He smiled, and stroked her fingers with the ball of his thumb. She wished she could kiss him, but that would be foolhardy.

When Zerlina sang her aria "Vedrai, carino" in sentimental three-eight time, an irresistible impulse tempted Maud, and as Zerlina pressed Masetto's hand to her heart, Maud laid Walter's hand on her breast. He gave an involuntary gasp, but no one noticed because Masetto was making similar noises, having just been beaten up by the Don.

She turned his hand so that he could feel her nipple with his palm. He loved her breasts, and touched them whenever he could, which was seldom. She wished it were oftener: she loved it. This was another discovery. Other people had stroked them—a doctor, an Anglican priest, an older girl at dancing class, a man in a crowd—and she had been disturbed and at the same time flattered at the thought that she could arouse people's lust, but she had never enjoyed it until now. She glanced at Walter's face and saw that he was staring at the stage, but there was a glint of perspiration on his forehead. She wondered if she was wrong to excite him in this way, when she could not give him satisfaction; but he made no move to withdraw his hand, so she concluded that he liked what she was doing. So did she. But, as always, she wanted more.

What had changed her? She had never been like this. It was him, of course, and the connection she felt with him, an intimacy so intense that she felt she could say anything, do whatever she liked, suppress nothing. What made him so different from every other man who had ever taken a fancy to her? A man such as Lowthie, or even Bing, expected a woman to act like a well-behaved child: to listen respectfully when he was being ponderous, to laugh appreciatively at his wit, to obey when he was masterful, and to give him a kiss whenever he asked. Walter treated her as a grown-up. He did not flirt, or condescend, or show off, and he listened at least as much as he talked.

The music turned sinister as the statue came to life, and the Commendatore stalked into the Don's dining room to a discord that Maud recognized as a diminished seventh. This was the dramatic high point of the opera, and Maud was almost certain no one would look around. Perhaps she could give Walter satisfaction after all, she thought; and the idea made her breathless.

As the trombones blared over the deep bass voice of the Commendatore, she placed her hand on Walter's thigh. She could feel the warmth of his skin through the fine wool of his dress trousers. Still he did not look at her, but she could see that his mouth was open and he was breathing heavily. She slid her hand up his thigh and, as the Don bravely took the Commendatore's hand, she found Walter's stiff penis and grasped it.

She was excited and, at the same time, curious. She had never done this before. She explored it through the fabric of his trousers. It was bigger than she expected and harder, too, more like a piece of wood than a part of the body. How strange, she thought, that such a remarkable physical change should occur just because of a woman's touch. When she was aroused it showed in tiny changes: that almost imperceptible feeling of puffiness, and the dampness inside. For men it was like raising a flag.

She knew what boys did, for she had spied on Fitz when he was fifteen; and now she imitated the action she had seen him perform, the up-and-down movement of the hand, while the Commendatore called upon the Don to repent, and the Don repeatedly refused. Walter was panting, now, but no one could hear because the orchestra was so loud. She was overjoyed that she could please him so much. She watched the backs of the heads of the others in the box, terrified that one of them might look around, but she was too caught up in what she was doing to stop. Walter covered her hand with his own, teaching her how to do it, gripping harder on the downstroke and releasing the pressure on the up, and she imitated what he did. As the Don was dragged into the flames, Walter jerked in his seat. She felt a kind of spasm in his penis—once, twice, and a third time—and then, as the Don died of fright, Walter seemed to slump, exhausted.

Maud suddenly knew that what she had done was completely mad. She quickly withdrew her hand. She flushed with shame. She found she was panting, and tried to breathe normally.

The final ensemble began onstage, and Maud relaxed. She did not know what had possessed her, but she had got away with it. The release of tension made her want to laugh. She suppressed a giggle.

She caught Walter's eye. He was looking at her with adoration. She felt a glow of pleasure. He leaned over and put his lips to her ear. "Thank you," he murmured.

She sighed and said: "It was a pleasure."

CHAPTER SIX

June 1914

At the beginning of June Grigori Peshkov at last
had enough money for a ticket to New York.
The Vyalov family in St. Petersburg sold him
both the ticket and the papers necessary for
immigration into the United States, including
a letter from Mr. Josef Vyalov in Buffalo promising to give
Grigori a job.

Grigori kissed the ticket. He could hardly wait to leave.
It was like a dream, and he was afraid he might wake up
before the boat sailed. Now that departure was so close, he
longed even more for the moment when he would stand
on deck and look back to watch Russia disappear over the
horizon and out of his life forever.

On the evening before his departure, his friends organized a party.

It was held at Mishka's, a bar near the Putilov Machine
Works. There were a dozen workmates, most of the members of the Bolshevik Discussion Group on Socialism and
Atheism, and the girls from the house where Grigori and
Lev lived. They were all on strike—half the factories in St.
Petersburg were on strike—so no one had much money,
but they clubbed together and bought a barrel of beer and
some herrings. It was a warm summer evening, and they sat
on benches in a patch of waste ground next to the bar.

Grigori was not a great party lover. He would have preferred to spend the evening playing chess. Alcohol made
people stupid, and flirting with other men's wives and girl-

friends just seemed pointless. His wild-haired friend Konstantin, the chairman of the discussion group, had a row about the strike with aggressive Isaak, the footballer, and they ended up in a shouting match. Big Varya, Konstantin's mother, drank most of a bottle of vodka, punched her husband, and passed out. Lev brought a crowd of friends—men Grigori had never met, and girls he did not want to meet— and they drank all the beer without paying for anything.

Grigori spent the evening staring mournfully at Katerina. She was in a good mood—she loved parties. Her long skirt whirled and her blue-green eyes flashed as she moved around, teasing the men and charming the women, that wide, generous mouth always smiling. Her clothes were old and patched, but she had a wonderful body, the kind of figure Russian men loved, with a full bust and broad hips. Grigori had fallen in love with her on the day he had met her, and he was still in love four months later. But she preferred his brother.

Why? It had nothing to do with looks. The two brothers were so alike that people sometimes mistook one for the other. They were the same height and weight, and could wear each other's clothes. But Lev had charm by the ton. He was unreliable and selfish, and he lived on the edge of the law, but women adored him. Grigori was honest and dependable, a hard worker and a serious thinker, and he was single.

It would be different in the United States. Everything would be different there. American landowners were not allowed to hang their peasants. American police had to put people on trial before punishing them. The government could not even jail socialists. There were no noblemen: everyone was equal, even Jews.

Could it be real? Sometimes America seemed too much of a fantasy, like the stories people told of South Seas islands where beautiful maidens gave their bodies to anyone who asked. But it must be true: thousands of immigrants had written letters home. At the factory a group of revolutionary socialists had started a series of lectures on American democracy, but the police had closed them down.

He felt guilty about leaving his brother behind, but it was the best way. "Look after yourself," he said to Lev toward the end of the evening. "I won't be here to get you out of trouble anymore."

"I'll be fine," Lev said carelessly. "You look after yourself,"

"I'll send you the money for your ticket. It won't take long on American wages."

"I'll be waiting."

"Don't move house—we could lose touch."

"I'm not going anywhere, big brother."

They had not discussed whether Katerina, too, would eventually come to America. Grigori had left it to Lev to raise the subject, but he had not. Grigori did not know whether to hope or dread that Lev would want to bring her.

Lev took Katerina's arm and said: "We have to go now."

Grigori was surprised. "Where are you off to at this time of night?"

"I'm meeting Trofim."

Trofim was a minor member of the Vyalov family. "Why do you have to see him tonight?"

Lev winked. "Never mind. We'll be back before morning—in plenty of time to take you to Gutuyevsky Island." This was where the transatlantic steamers docked.

"All right," said Grigori. "Don't do anything dangerous," he added, knowing it was pointless.

Lev waved gaily and disappeared.

It was almost midnight. Grigori said his good-byes. Several of his friends wept, but he did not know whether it was from sorrow or just booze. He walked back to the house with some of the girls, and they all kissed him in the hall. Then he went to his room.

His secondhand cardboard suitcase stood on the table. Though small, it was half-empty. He was taking shirts, underwear, and his chess set. He had only one pair of boots. He had not accumulated much in the nine years since his mother died.

Before going to bed, he looked in the cupboard where Lev kept his revolver, a Belgian-made Nagant M1895. He saw, with a sinking feeling, that the gun was not in its usual place.

He unlatched the window so that he would not have to get out of bed to open it when Lev came in.

Lying awake, listening to the familiar thunder of passing trains, he wondered what it would be like, four thousand miles from here. He had lived with Lev all his life, and he had been a substitute mother and father. From tomorrow, he would not know when Lev was out all night and carrying a gun. Would it be a relief, or would he worry more?

As always, Grigori woke at five. His ship sailed at eight, and the dock was an hour's walk. He had plenty of time.

Lev had not come home.

Grigori washed his hands and face. Looking in a broken shard of mirror, he trimmed his mustache and beard with a pair of kitchen scissors. Then he put his best suit on. He would leave his other suit behind for Lev.

He was heating a pan of porridge on the fire when he heard a loud knocking at the door of the house.

It was sure to be bad news. Friends stood outside and shouted; only the authorities knocked. Grigori put on his cap, then stepped into the hall and looked down the staircase. The landlady was admitting two men in the black-and-green uniforms of the police. Looking more carefully, Grigori recognized the podgy moon-shaped face of Mikhail Pinsky and the small ratlike head of his sidekick, Ilya Kozlov.

He thought fast. Obviously someone in the house was suspected of a crime. The likeliest culprit was Lev. Whether it was Lev or another boarder, everyone in the building would be interrogated. The two cops would remember the incident back in February when Grigori had rescued Katerina from them, and they would seize the opportunity of arresting Grigori.

And Grigori would miss his ship.

The dreadful thought paralyzed him. To miss the ship! After all the saving and waiting and longing for this day. No, he thought; no, I won't let it happen.

He ducked back into his room as the two policemen started up the stairs. It would be no use to plead with them—quite the reverse: if Pinsky discovered that Grigori was about to emigrate, he would take even more pleasure in keeping him incarcerated. Grigori would not even have a chance to cash his ticket and get the money back. All those years of saving would be wasted.

He had to flee.

He scanned the tiny room frantically. It had one door and one window. He would have to go out the way Lev came in at night. He looked out: the backyard was empty. The St. Petersburg police were brutal, but no one had ever

accused them of being smart, and it had not occurred to
Pinsky and Kozlov to cover the rear of the house. Perhaps
they knew there was no exit from the yard except across
the railway—but a railway line was not much of a barrier
to a desperate man.

Grigori heard shouts and cries from the girls' room next
door: the police had gone there first.

He patted the breast of his jacket. His ticket, papers, and
money were in his pocket. All the rest of his worldly possessions were already packed in the cardboard suitcase.

Picking up his suitcase, he leaned as far as he could out
of the window. He held the case out and threw it. It landed
flat and seemed undamaged.

The door of his room burst open.

Grigori put his legs through the window, sat on the sill
for a split second, then jumped to the roof of the washhouse. His feet slipped on the tiles and he sat down hard.
He slid down the sloping roof to the gutter. He heard a
shout behind him but he did not look back. He jumped
from the washhouse roof to the ground and landed unhurt.

He picked up his suitcase and ran.

A shot rang out, scaring him into running faster. Most
policemen could not hit the Winter Palace from three
yards, but accidents sometimes happened. He scrambled up
the railway embankment, conscious that as he climbed to
the level of the window he was becoming an easier target.
He heard the distinctive thud-and-gasp of a railway engine
and looked to his right to see a goods train approaching
fast. There was another shot, and he sensed a thump somewhere, but he felt no pain, and guessed the slug had hit his
suitcase. He reached the top of the embankment, knowing his body was now outlined against the clear morning
sky. The train was a few yards away. The driver sounded his
klaxon loud and long. A third shot rang out. Grigori threw
himself across the line just ahead of the train.

The locomotive howled past him, steel wheels clashing
with steel rails, steam trailing as the klaxon faded. Grigori
scrambled to his feet. Now he was shielded from gunfire
by a train of open trucks loaded with coal. He ran across
the remaining tracks. As the last of the coal wagons passed,
he descended the far embankment and walked through the
yard of a small factory into the street.

He looked at his suitcase. There was a bullet hole in one edge. It had been a near miss.

He walked briskly, catching his breath, and asked himself what he should do next. Now that he was safe—at least for the moment—he began to worry about his brother. He needed to know whether Lev was in trouble, and if so what kind.

He decided to start in the last place he had seen Lev, which was Mishka's Bar.

As he headed for the bar, he felt nervous about being spotted. It would be bad luck, but it was not impossible: Pinsky might be roaming the streets. He pulled his cap down over his forehead, not really believing it would disguise his identity. He came across some workers heading for the docks and attached himself to the group, but with his suitcase he did not look as if he belonged.

However, he reached Mishka's without incident. The bar was furnished with homemade wooden benches and tables. It smelled of last night's beer and tobacco smoke. In the morning Mishka served bread and tea to people who had nowhere at home to make breakfast, but business was slow because of the strike, and the place was almost empty.

Grigori intended to ask Mishka if he knew where Lev had been headed when he left, but before he could do so he saw Katerina. She looked as if she had been up all night. Her blue-green eyes were bloodshot, her fair hair was awry, and her skirt was crumpled and stained. She was visibly distressed, with shaking hands and tear streaks on her grimy cheeks. Yet that made her more beautiful to Grigori, and he longed to take her in his arms and comfort her. Since he could not, he would do the next best thing, and come to her aid. "What's happened?" he said. "What's the matter?"

"Thank God you're here," she said. "The police are after Lev."

Grigori groaned. So his brother *was* in trouble—today of all days. "What has he done?" Grigori did not bother to consider the possibility that Lev was innocent.

"There was a mess-up last night. We were supposed to unload some cigarettes from a barge." They would be stolen cigarettes, Grigori assumed. Katerina went on: "Lev paid for them. Then the bargeman said it wasn't enough money, and there was an argument. Someone started shooting. Lev fired back; then we ran away."

"Thank heaven neither of you got hurt!"

"Now we don't have the cigarettes or the money."

"What a mess." Grigori looked at the clock over the bar. It was a quarter past six. He still had plenty of time. "Let's sit down. Do you want some tea?" He beckoned to Mishka and asked for two glasses of tea.

"Thank you," said Katerina. "Lev thinks one of the wounded must have talked to the police. Now they're after him."

"And you?"

"I'm all right—no one knows my name."

Grigori nodded. "So what we have to do is keep Lev out of the hands of the police. He'll have to lie low for a week or so, then slip out of St. Petersburg."

"He hasn't got any money."

"Of course not." Lev never had any money for essentials, though he could always buy drinks, place a bet, and entertain girls. "I can give him something." Grigori would have to dip into the money he had saved for the journey. "Where is he?"

"He said he would meet you at the ship."

Mishka brought their tea. Grigori was hungry—he had left his porridge on the fire—and he asked for some soup.

Katerina said: "How much can you give Lev?"

She was looking earnestly at him, and that always made him feel he would do anything she asked. He looked away. "Whatever he needs," he said.

"You're so good."

Grigori shrugged. "He's my brother."

"Thank you."

It pleased Grigori when Katerina was grateful, but it embarrassed him, too. The soup came and he began to eat, glad of the diversion. The food made him feel more optimistic. Lev was always in and out of trouble. He would slip out of this difficulty as he had many times before. It did not mean Grigori had to miss his sailing.

Katerina watched him, sipping her tea. She had lost the frantic look. Lev puts you in danger, Grigori thought, and I come to the rescue, yet you prefer him.

Lev was probably at the dock now, skulking in the

shadow of a derrick, nervously looking out for policemen as he waited. Grigori needed to get going. But he might never see Katerina again, and he could hardly bear the thought of saying good-bye to her forever.

He finished his soup and looked at the clock. It was almost seven. He was cutting things too fine. "I have to go," he said reluctantly.

Katerina walked with him to the door. "Don't be too hard on Lev," she said.

"Was I ever?"

She put her hands on his shoulders, stood on tiptoe, and kissed him briefly on the lips. "Good luck," she said.

Grigori walked away.

He went quickly through the streets of southwest St. Petersburg, an industrial quarter of warehouses, factories, storage yards, and overcrowded slums. The shameful impulse to weep left him after a few minutes. He walked on the shady side, kept his cap low and his head down, and avoided wide-open areas. If Pinsky had circulated a description of Lev, an alert policeman might easily arrest Grigori.

But he reached the docks without being spotted. His ship, the *Angel Gabriel,* was a small, rusty vessel that took both cargo and passengers. Right now it was being loaded with stoutly nailed wooden packing cases marked with the name of the city's largest fur trader. As he watched, the last box went into the hold and the crew fastened the hatch.

A family of Jews were showing their tickets at the head of the gangplank. All Jews wanted to go to America, in Grigori's experience. They had even more reason than he did. In Russia there were laws forbidding them to own land, to enter the civil service, to be army officers, and countless other prohibitions. They could not live where they liked, and there were quotas limiting the number who could go to universities. It was a miracle any of them made a living. And if they did prosper, against the odds, it would not be long before they were set upon by a crowd—usually egged on by policemen such as Pinsky—and beaten up, their families terrified, their windows smashed, their property set on fire. The surprise was that any of them stayed.

The ship's hooter sounded for "All aboard."

He could not see his brother. What had gone wrong? Had Lev changed plans again? Or had he been arrested already?

A small boy tugged at Grigori's sleeve. "A man wants to talk to you," the boy said.

"What man?"

"He looks like you."

Thank God, thought Grigori. "Where is he?"

"Behind the planks."

There was a stack of timber on the dock. Grigori hurried around it and found Lev hiding behind it, nervously smoking a cigarette. He was fidgety and pale—a rare sight, for he usually remained cheerful even in adversity.

"I'm in trouble," Lev said.

"Again."

"Those bargemen are liars!"

"And thieves, probably."

"Don't get sarcastic with me. There isn't time."

"No, you're right. We need to get you out of town until the fuss dies down."

Lev shook his head in negation, blowing out smoke at the same time. "One of the bargemen died. I'm wanted for murder."

"Oh, hell." Grigori sat down on a shelf of timber and buried his head in his hands. "Murder," he said.

"Trofim was badly wounded and the police got him to talk. He fingered me."

"How do you know all this?"

"I saw Fyodor half an hour ago." Fyodor was a corrupt policeman of Lev's acquaintance.

"This is bad news."

"There's worse. Pinsky has vowed to get me—as revenge on you."

Grigori nodded. "That's what I was afraid of."

"What am I going to do?"

"You'll have to go to Moscow. St. Petersburg won't be safe for you for a long time, maybe forever."

"I don't know that Moscow is far enough, now that the police have telegraph machines."

He was right, Grigori realized.

The ship's hooter sounded again. Soon the gangplanks would be withdrawn. "We only have a minute left," said Grigori. "What are you going to do?"

Lev said: "I could go to America."

Grigori stared at him.

Lev said: "You could give me your ticket."

Grigori did not want even to think about it.

But Lev went on with remorseless logic. "I could use your passport and papers for entering the United States—no one would know the difference."

Grigori saw his dream fading, like the ending of a motion picture at the Soleil Cinema in Nevsky Prospekt, when the house lights came up to show the drab colors and dirty floors of the real world. "Give you my ticket," he repeated, desperately postponing the moment of decision.

"You'd be saving my life," Lev said.

Grigori knew he had to do it, and the realization was like a pain in his heart.

He took the papers from the pocket of his best suit and gave them to Lev. He handed over all the money he had saved for the journey. Then he gave his brother the cardboard suitcase with the bullet hole.

"I'll send you the money for another ticket," Lev said fervently. Grigori made no reply, but his skepticism must have shown on his face, for Lev protested: "I really will. I swear it. I'll save up."

"All right," Grigori said.

They embraced. Lev said: "You always took care of me."

"Yes, I did."

Lev turned and ran for the ship.

The sailors were untying the ropes. They were about to pull up the gangplank, but Lev shouted and they waited a few seconds more for him.

He ran up onto the deck.

He turned, leaned on the rail, and waved to Grigori.

Grigori could not bring himself to wave back. He turned and walked away.

The ship hooted, but he did not look back.

His right arm felt strangely light without the burden of the suitcase. He walked through the docks, looking down at the deep black water, and the odd thought occurred to him that he could throw himself in. He shook himself: he was not prey to such foolish ideas. All the same he was depressed and bitter. Life never dealt him a winning hand.

He was unable to cheer himself up as he retraced his steps through the industrial district. He walked along with his eyes cast down, not even bothering to keep an eye open for the police: it hardly mattered if they arrested him now.

What was he going to do? He felt he could not summon the energy for anything. They would give him back his job at the factory, when the strike was over: he was a good worker and they knew it. He should probably go there now, and find out whether there had been any progress in the dispute—but he could not be bothered.

After an hour he found himself approaching Mishka's. He intended to go straight past but, glancing inside, he saw Katerina, sitting where he had left her two hours ago, with a cold glass of tea in front of her. He had to tell her what had happened.

He went inside. The place was empty except for Mishka, who was sweeping the floor.

Katerina stood up, looking scared. "Why are you here?" she said. "Did you miss your boat?"

"Not exactly." He could not think how to break the news.

"What, then?" she said. "Is Lev dead?"

"No, he's all right. But he's wanted for murder."

She stared at him. "Where is he?"

"He had to go away."

"Where?"

There was no gentle way to put it. "He asked me to give him my ticket."

"Your ticket?"

"And passport. He's gone to America."

"No!" she screamed.

Grigori just nodded.

"No!" she yelled again. "He wouldn't leave me! Don't you say that! Never say it!"

"Try to stay calm."

She slapped Grigori's face. She was only a girl, and he hardly flinched. "Swine!" she screeched. "You've sent him away!"

"I did it to save his life."

"Bastard! Dog! I hate you! I hate your stupid face!"

"Nothing you say could make me feel any worse," Grigori said, but she was not listening. Ignoring her curses, he walked away, her voice fading as he went out through the door.

The screaming stopped, and he heard footsteps running

along the street after him. "Stop!" she cried. "Stop, please, Grigori. Don't turn your back on me. I'm so sorry."

He turned.

"Grigori, you have to look after me now that Lev's gone."

He shook his head. "You don't need me. The men of this city will form a queue to look after you."

"No, they won't," she said. "There's something you don't know."

Grigori thought: What now?

She said: "Lev didn't want me to tell you."

"Go on."

"I'm expecting a baby," she said, and she began to weep.

Grigori stood still, taking it in. Lev's baby, of course. And Lev knew. Yet he had gone to America. "A baby," Grigori said.

She nodded, crying.

His brother's child. His nephew or niece. His family.

He put his arms around her and drew her to him. She was shaking with sobs. She buried her face in his jacket. He stroked her hair. "All right," he said. "Don't worry. You'll be okay. So will your baby." He sighed. "I will take care of you both."

{ II }

Traveling on the *Angel Gabriel* was grim, even for a boy from the slums of St. Petersburg. There was only one class, steerage, and the passengers were treated as so much more cargo. The ship was dirty and unsanitary, especially when there were huge waves and people were seasick. It was impossible to complain because none of the crew spoke Russian. Lev was not sure what nationality they were, but he failed to get through to them with either his smattering of English or his even fewer words of German. Someone said they were Dutch. Lev had never heard of Dutch people.

Nevertheless the mood among the passengers was high optimism. Lev felt he had burst the walls of the tsar's prison and escaped, and now he was free. He was on his way to America, where there were no noblemen. When the sea was calm, passengers sat on the deck and told the stories they had heard about America: the hot water coming out of taps, the good-quality leather boots worn even by workers, and most of all the freedom to practice any religion, join any political group, state your opinion in public, and not be afraid of the police.

On the evening of the tenth day Lev was playing cards. He was dealer, but he was losing. Everyone was losing except Spirya, an innocent-looking boy of Lev's age who was also traveling alone. "Spirya wins every night," said another player, Yakov. The truth was that Spirya won when Lev was dealing.

They were steaming slowly through a fog. The sea was calm, and there was no sound but the low bass of the engines. Lev had not been able to find out when they would arrive. People gave different answers. The most knowledgeable said it depended on the weather. The crew were inscrutable as always.

As night fell, Lev threw in his hand. "I'm cleaned out," he said. In fact he had plenty more money inside his shirt, but he could see that the others were running low, all except Spirya. "That's it," he said. "When we get to America, I'm just going to have to catch the eye of a rich old woman and live like a pet dog in her marble palace."

The others laughed. "But why would anyone want you for a pet?" said Yakov.

"Old ladies get cold at night," he said. "She would need my heating appliance."

The game ended in good humor, and the players drifted away.

Spirya went aft and leaned on the rail, watching the wake disappear into the fog. Lev joined him. "My half comes to seven rubles even," Lev said.

Spirya took paper currency from his pocket and gave it to Lev, shielding the transaction with his body so that no one else could see money changing hands.

Lev pocketed the notes and filled his pipe.

Spirya said: "Tell me something, Grigori." Lev was using his brother's papers, so he had to tell people his name was Grigori. "What would you do if I refused to give you your share?"

This kind of talk was dangerous. Lev slowly put his

tobacco away and put the unlit pipe back into his jacket pocket. Then he grabbed Spirya by the lapels and pushed him up against the rail so that he was bent backward and leaning out to sea. Spirya was taller than Lev but not as tough, by a long way. "I would break your stupid neck," Lev said. "Then I would take back all the money you've made with me." He pushed Spirya farther over. "Then I would throw you in the damn sea."

Spirya was terrified. "All right!" he said. "Let me go!"

Lev released his grip.

"Jesus!" Spirya gasped. "I only asked a question."

Lev lit his pipe. "And I gave you the answer," he said. "Don't forget it."

Spirya walked away.

When the fog lifted they were in sight of land. It was night, but Lev could see the lights of a city. Where were they? Some said Canada, some said Ireland, but no one knew.

The lights came nearer, and the ship slowed. They were going to make landfall. Lev heard someone say they had arrived in America already! Ten days seemed quick. But what did he know? He stood at the rail with his brother's cardboard suitcase. His heart beat faster.

The suitcase reminded him that Grigori should have been the one arriving in America now. Lev had not forgotten his vow to Grigori, to send him the price of a ticket. That was one promise he ought to keep. Grigori had probably saved his life—again. I'm lucky, Lev thought, to have such a brother.

He was making money on the ship, but not fast enough. Seven rubles went nowhere. He needed a big score. But America was the land of opportunity. He would make his fortune there.

Lev had been intrigued to find a bullet hole in the suitcase, and a slug embedded in a box containing a chess set. He had sold the chess set to one of the Jews for five kopeks. He wondered how Grigori had come to be shot at that day.

He was missing Katerina. He loved to walk around with a girl like that on his arm, knowing that every man envied him. But there would be plenty of girls here in America.

He wondered if Grigori knew about Katerina's baby yet. Lev suffered a pang of regret: would he ever see his son or daughter? He told himself not to worry about leaving Katerina to raise the child alone. She would find someone else to look after her. She was a survivor.

It was after midnight when at last the ship docked. The quay was dimly lit and there was no one in sight. The passengers disembarked with their bags and boxes and trunks. An officer from the *Angel Gabriel* directed them into a shed where there were a few benches. "You must wait here until the immigration people come for you in the morning," he said, demonstrating that he did, after all, speak a little Russian.

It was a bit of an anticlimax for people who had saved up for years to come here. The women sat on the benches and the children went to sleep while the men smoked and waited for morning. After a while they heard the ship's engines, and Lev went outside and saw it moving slowly away from its mooring. Perhaps the crates of furs had to be unloaded elsewhere.

He tried to recall what Grigori had told him, in casual conversation, about the first steps in the new country. Immigrants had to pass a medical inspection—a tense moment, for unfit people were sent back, their money wasted and their hopes dashed. Sometimes the immigration officers changed people's names, to make them easier for Americans to pronounce. Outside the docks, a representative of the Vyalov family would be waiting to take them by train to Buffalo. There they would get jobs in hotels and factories owned by Josef Vyalov. Lev wondered how far Buffalo was from New York. Would it take an hour to get there, or a week? He wished he had listened more carefully to Grigori.

The sun rose over miles of crowded docks, and Lev's excitement returned. Old-fashioned masts and rigging clustered side by side with steam funnels. There were grand dockside buildings and tumbledown sheds, tall derricks and squat capstans, ladders and ropes and carts. To landward, Lev could see serried ranks of railway trucks full of coal, hundreds of them—no, thousands—fading into the distance beyond the limit of his vision. He was disappointed that he could not see the famous Liberty statue with its torch: it must be out of sight around a headland, he guessed.

Dockworkers arrived, first in small groups, then in

crowds. Ships departed and others arrived. A dozen women began to unload sacks of potatoes from a small vessel in front of the shed. Lev wondered when the immigration police would come.

Spirya came up to him. He seemed to have forgiven the way Lev had threatened him. "They've forgotten about us," he said.

"Looks that way," Lev said, puzzled.

"Shall we take a walk around—see if we can find someone who speaks Russian?"

"Good idea."

Spirya spoke to one of the older men. "We're going to see if we can find out what's happening."

The man looked nervous. "Maybe we should stay here as we were told."

They ignored him and walked over to the potato women. Lev gave them his best grin and said: "Does anyone speak Russian?" One of the younger women smiled back, but no one answered the question. Lev felt frustrated: his winning ways were useless with people who could not understand what he was saying.

Lev and Spirya walked in the direction from which most of the workers had come. No one took any notice of them. They came to a big set of gates, walked through, and found themselves in a busy street of shops and offices. The road was crowded with motorcars, electric trams, horses, and handcarts. Every few yards Lev spoke to someone, but no one responded.

Lev was mystified. What kind of place allowed anyone to walk off a ship and into the city without permission?

Then he spotted a building that intrigued him. It was a bit like a hotel, except that two poorly dressed men in sailors' caps were sitting on the steps, smoking. "Look at that place," he said.

"What about it?"

"I think it's a seamen's mission, like the one in St. Petersburg."

"We're not sailors."

"But there might be people there who speak foreign languages."

They went inside. A gray-haired woman behind a counter spoke to them.

Lev said in his own tongue: "We don't speak American."

She replied with a single word in the same language: "Russian?"

Lev nodded.

She made a beckoning sign with her finger, and Lev's hopes rose.

They followed her along a corridor to a small office with a window overlooking the water. Behind the desk was a man who looked, to Lev, like a Russian Jew, although he could not have said why he thought that. Lev said to him: "Do you speak Russian?"

"I am Russian," the man said. "Can I help you?"

Lev could have hugged him. Instead he looked the man in the eye and gave him a warm smile. "Someone was supposed to meet us off the ship and take us to Buffalo, but he didn't show up," he said, making his voice friendly but concerned. "There are about three hundred of us . . ." To gain sympathy he added: "Including women and children. Do you think you could help us find our contact?"

"Buffalo?" the man said. "Where do you think you are?"

"New York, of course."

"This is Cardiff."

Lev had never heard of Cardiff, but at least now he understood the problem. "That stupid captain set us down in the wrong port," he said. "How do we get to Buffalo from here?"

The man pointed out of the window, across the sea, and Lev had a sick feeling that he knew what was coming.

"It's that way," the man said. "About three thousand miles."

{ III }

Lev inquired the price of a ticket from Cardiff to New York. When converted to rubles it was ten times the amount of money he had inside his shirt.

He suppressed his rage. They had all been cheated by the Vyalov family, or the ship's captain—or both, most probably, since it would be easier to work the scam between them. All Grigori's hard-earned money had been stolen by those lying pigs. If he could have got the captain of the *Angel Gabriel* by the throat, he would have squeezed the life out of the man, and laughed when he died.

But there was no point in dreams of vengeance. The thing was not to give in. He would find a job, learn to speak English, and get into a high-stakes card game. It would take time. He would have to be patient. He must learn to be a bit more like Grigori.

That first night they all slept on the floor of the synagogue. Lev tagged along with the rest. The Cardiff Jews did not know, or perhaps did not care, that some of the passengers were Christian.

For the first time in his life he saw the advantage of being Jewish. In Russia Jews were so persecuted that Lev had always wondered why more of them did not abandon their religion, change their clothes, and mix in with everyone else. It would have saved a lot of lives. But now he realized that, as a Jew, you could go anywhere in the world and always find someone to treat you like family.

It turned out that this was not the first group of Russian immigrants to buy tickets to New York and end up somewhere else. It had happened before, in Cardiff and other British ports; and, as so many Russian migrants were Jewish, the elders of the synagogue had a routine. Next day the stranded travelers were given a hot breakfast and got their money changed to British pounds, shillings, and pence; then they were taken to boardinghouses where they were able to rent cheap rooms.

Like every city in the world, Cardiff had thousands of stables. Lev studied enough words to say he was an experienced worker with horses, then went around the city asking for a job. It did not take people long to see that he was good with the animals, but even well-disposed employers wanted to ask a few questions, and he could not understand or answer.

In desperation he learned more rapidly, and after a few days he could understand prices and ask for bread or beer. However, employers were asking complicated questions, presumably about where he had worked before and whether he had ever been in trouble with the police.

He returned to the seamen's mission and explained his problem to the Russian in the little office. He was given an address in Butetown, the neighborhood nearest the docks, and told to ask for Filip Kowal, pronounced "cole," known as Kowal the Pole. Kowal turned out to be a ganger who hired out foreign labor cheap and spoke a smattering of most European languages. He told Lev to be on the fore-court of the city's main railway station, with his suitcase, on the following Monday morning at ten o'clock.

Lev was so glad that he did not even ask what the job was.

He showed up along with a couple of hundred men, mostly Russian, but including Germans, Poles, Slavs, and one dark-skinned African. He was pleased to see Spirya and Yakov there, too.

They were herded onto a train, their tickets paid for by Kowal, and they steamed north through pretty mountain country. Between the green hillsides, the industrial towns lay pooled like dark water in the valleys. A feature of every town was at least one tower with a pair of giant wheels on top, and Lev learned that the main business of the region was coal mining. Several of the men with him were min-ers; some had other crafts such as metalworking; and many were unskilled laborers.

After an hour they got off the train. As they filed out of the station Lev realized this was no ordinary job. A crowd of several hundred men, all dressed in the caps and rough clothes of workers, stood waiting for them in the square. At first the men were ominously silent; then one of them shouted something, and the others quickly joined in. Lev had no idea what they were saying but there was no doubt it was hostile. There were also twenty or thirty policemen present, standing at the front of the crowd, keeping the men behind an imaginary line.

Spirya said in a frightened voice: "Who are these people?"

Lev said: "Short, muscular men with hard faces and clean hands—I'd say they are coal miners on strike."

"They look as if they want to kill us. What the hell is going on?"

"We're strikebreakers," Lev said grimly.

"God save us."

Kowal the Pole shouted: "Follow me!" in several lan-guages, and they all marched up the main street. The crowd continued to shout, and men shook their fists, but no one broke the line. Lev had never before felt grateful to policemen. "This is awful," he said.

Yakov said: "Now you know what it's like to be a Jew."

They left the shouting miners behind and walked uphill through streets of row houses. Lev noticed that many of the houses appeared empty. People still stared as they went by, but the insults stopped. Kowal started to allocate houses to the men. Lev and Spirya were astonished to be given a house to themselves. Before leaving, Kowal pointed out the pithead—the tower with twin wheels—and told them to be there tomorrow morning at six. Those who were miners would be digging coal; the others would be maintaining tunnels and equipment or, in Lev's case, looking after ponies.

Lev gazed around his new home. It was no palace, but it was clean and dry. It had one big room downstairs and two up—a bedroom for each of them! Lev had never had a room to himself. There was no furniture, but they were used to sleeping on the floor, and in June they did not even need blankets.

Lev had no wish to leave, but eventually they became hungry. There was no food in the house, so, reluctantly, they went out to get their dinner. With trepidation they entered the first pub they came to, but the dozen or so customers glared angrily at them, and when Lev said in English: "Two pints of half-and-half, please," the bartender ignored him.

They walked downhill into the town center and found a café. Here at least the clientele did not appear to be spoiling for a fight. But they sat at a table for half an hour and watched the waitress serve everyone who came in after them. Then they left.

It was going to be difficult living here, Lev suspected. But it would not be for long. As soon as he had enough money he would go to America. Nevertheless, while he was here he had to eat.

They went into a bakery. This time Lev was determined to get what he wanted. He pointed to a rack of loaves and said in English: "One bread, please."

The baker pretended not to understand.

Lev reached across the counter and grabbed the loaf he wanted. Now, he thought, let him try to take it back.

"Hey!" cried the baker, but he stayed on his side of the counter.

Lev smiled and said: "How much, please?"

"Penny farthing," the baker said sulkily.

Lev put the coins on the counter. "Thank you very much," he said.

He broke the loaf and gave half to Spirya; then they walked down the street eating. They came to the railway station, but the crowd had dispersed. On the forecourt, a news vendor was calling his wares. His papers were selling fast, and Lev wondered if something important had happened.

A large car came along the road, going fast, and they had to jump out of the way. Looking at the passenger in the back, Lev was astonished to recognize Princess Bea.

"Good God!" he said. In a flash, he was transported back to Bulovnir, and the nightmare sight of his father dying on the gallows while this woman looked on. The terror he had felt then was unlike anything he had ever known. Nothing would ever scare him like that, not street fights nor policemen's nightsticks nor guns pointed at him.

The car pulled up at the station entrance. Hatred, disgust, and nausea overwhelmed Lev as Princess Bea got out. The bread in his mouth seemed like gravel and he spat it out.

Spirya said: "What's the matter?"

Lev pulled himself together. "That woman is a Russian princess," he said. "She had my father hanged fourteen years ago."

"Bitch. What on earth is she doing here?"

"She married an English lord. They must live nearby. Perhaps it's his coal mine."

The chauffeur and a maid busied themselves with luggage. Lev heard Bea speak to the maid in Russian, and the maid replied in the same tongue. They all went into the station; then the maid came back out and bought a newspaper.

Lev approached her. Taking off his cap, he gave a deep bow and said in Russian: "You must be the princess Bea."

She laughed merrily. "Don't be a fool. I'm her maid, Nina. Who are you?"

Lev introduced himself and Spirya and explained how they came to be there, and why they could not buy dinner.

"I'll be back tonight," Nina said. "We're only going to Cardiff. Come to the kitchen door of Tŷ Gwyn, and I'll give you some cold meat. Just follow the road north out of town until you come to a palace."

"Thank you, beautiful lady."

"I'm old enough to be your mother," she said, but she simpered just the same. "I'd better take the princess her paper."

"What's the big story?"

"Oh, foreign news," she said dismissively. "There's been an assassination. The princess is terribly upset. The archduke Franz Ferdinand of Austria was killed at a place called Sarajevo."

"That's frightening, to a princess."

"Yes," Nina said. "Still, I don't suppose it will make any difference to the likes of you and me."

"No," said Lev. "I don't suppose it will."

CHAPTER SEVEN

Early July 1914

The Church of St. James in Piccadilly had the most expensively dressed congregation in the world. It was the favorite place of worship for London's elite. In theory, ostentation was frowned upon; but a woman had to wear a hat, and these days it was almost impossible to buy one that did not have ostrich feathers, ribbons, bows, and silk flowers. From the back of the nave Walter von Ulrich looked at a jungle of extravagant shapes and colors. The men, by contrast, all looked the same, with their black coats and white stand-up collars, holding their top hats in their laps.

Most of these people did not understand what had happened in Sarajevo seven days ago, he thought sourly; some of them did not even know where Bosnia was. They were shocked by the murder of the archduke, but they could not work out what it meant for the rest of the world. They were vaguely bewildered.

Walter was not bewildered. He knew exactly what the assassination portended. It created a serious threat to the security of Germany, and it was up to people such as Walter to protect and defend their country in this moment of danger.

Today his first task was to find out what the Russian tsar was thinking. This was what everyone wanted to know: the German ambassador, Walter's father, the foreign minister in Berlin, and the kaiser himself. And Walter, like the good intelligence officer he was, had a source of information.

He scanned the congregation, trying to identify his man among the backs of heads, fearing he might not be there. Anton was a clerk at the Russian embassy. They met in Anglican churches because Anton could be sure there would be no one from his embassy there: most Russians belonged to the Orthodox Church, and those who did not were never employed in the diplomatic service.

Anton was in charge of the cable office at the Russian embassy, so he saw every incoming and outgoing telegram. His information was priceless. But he was difficult to manage, and caused Walter much anxiety. Espionage frightened Anton, and when he got scared he would fail to show up—often at moments of international tension, like this one, when Walter needed him most.

Walter was distracted by spotting Maud. He recognized the long, graceful neck rising out of a fashionable man-style wing collar, and his heart missed a beat. He kissed that neck whenever he got the chance.

When he thought about the danger of war, his mind went first to Maud, then to his country. He felt ashamed of this selfishness, but he could not do anything about it. His greatest fear was that she would be taken from him; the threat to the fatherland came second. For Germany's sake he was willing to die—but not to live without the woman he loved.

A head in the third row from the back turned, and Walter met the eye of Anton. The man had thinning brown hair and a patchy beard. Relieved, Walter walked to the south aisle, as if looking for a place, and after a moment's hesitation sat down.

Anton's soul was full of bitterness. Five years ago, a nephew whom he had loved had been accused, by the tsar's secret police, of revolutionary activities, and had been imprisoned in the Fortress of Peter and Paul, across the river from the Winter Palace in the heart of St. Petersburg. The boy had been a theology student, and quite innocent of subversion; but before he could be released he had contracted pneumonia and died. Anton had been wreaking his quiet, deadly revenge against the tsar's government ever since.

It was a pity the church was so well-lit. The architect, Christopher Wren, had put in long rows of huge round-arched windows. For this kind of work, a gloomy Gothic twilight would have been better. Still, Anton had chosen his position well, at the end of a row, with a child next to him and a massive wooden pillar behind.

"Good place to sit," Walter murmured.

"We can still be observed from the gallery," Anton fretted.

Walter shook his head. "They will all be looking toward the front."

Anton was a middle-aged bachelor. A small man, he was neat to the point of fussiness: the tie knotted tightly, every button done up on the jacket, the shoes gleaming. His well-worn suit was shiny from years of brushing and pressing. Walter thought this was a reaction against the grubbiness of espionage. After all, the man was there to betray his country. And I'm here to encourage him, Walter thought grimly.

Walter said nothing more during the hush before the service, but as soon as the first hymn started he said in a low voice: "What's the mood in St. Petersburg?"

"Russia does not want war," Anton said.

"Good."

"The tsar fears that war will lead to revolution." When Anton mentioned the tsar he looked as if he was going to spit. "Half St. Petersburg is on strike already. Of course, it does not occur to him that his own stupid brutality is what makes people want a revolution."

"Indeed." Walter always had to adjust for the fact that Anton's opinions were distorted by hate, but in this case the spy was not entirely wrong. Walter did not hate the tsar, but feared him. He had at his disposal the largest army in the world. Every discussion of Germany's security had to take that army into account. Germany was like a man whose next-door neighbor keeps a giant bear on a chain in the front garden. "What will the tsar do?"

"It depends on Austria."

Walter suppressed an impatient retort. Everyone was waiting to see what the Austrian emperor would do. He had to do *something*, because the assassinated archduke had been heir to his throne. Walter was hoping to learn about Austrian intentions from his cousin Robert later that day. That branch of the family was Catholic, like all the Austrian elite, and Robert would be at mass in Westminster Cathedral right now, but Walter would see him for lunch. Meanwhile Walter needed to know more about the Russians.

He had to wait for another hymn. He tried to be patient. He looked up and studied the extravagant gilding of Wren's barrel vaults.

The congregation broke into "Rock of Ages." "Suppose there is fighting in the Balkans," Walter murmured to Anton. "Will the Russians stay out of it?"

"No. The tsar cannot stand aside if Serbia is attacked."

Walter felt a chill. This was exactly the kind of escalation he was afraid of. "It would be madness to go to war over this!"

"True. But the Russians can't let Austria control the Balkan region—they have to protect the Black Sea route."

There was no arguing with that. Most of Russia's exports—grain from the southern cornfields and oil from the wells around Baku—were shipped to the world from Black Sea ports.

Anton went on: "On the other hand, the tsar is also urging everyone to tread carefully."

"In short, he can't make up his mind."

"If you call it a mind."

Walter nodded. The tsar was not an intelligent man. His dream was to return Russia to the golden age of the seventeenth century, and he was stupid enough to think that was possible. It was as if King George V were to try to recreate the Merrie England of Robin Hood. Since the tsar was barely rational, it was maddeningly difficult to predict what he would do.

During the last hymn Walter's gaze wandered to Maud, sitting two rows in front on the other side. He watched her profile fondly as she sang with gusto.

Anton's ambivalent report was unnerving. Walter felt more worried than he had been an hour ago. He said: "From now on, I need to see you every day."

Anton looked panicky. "Not possible!" he said. "Too risky."

"But the picture is changing hour by hour."

"Next Sunday morning, Smith Square."

That was the trouble with idealistic spies, Walter thought with frustration: you had no leverage. On the other hand, men who spied for money were never trustworthy. They would tell you what you wanted to hear in the hope of getting a bonus. With Anton, if he said the tsar was dithering, Walter could be confident that the tsar had not made a decision.

"Meet me once in the middle of the week, then," Walter pleaded as the hymn came to an end.

Anton did not reply. Instead of sitting down, he slipped away and left the church. "Damn," Walter said quietly, and the child in the next seat stared at him with disapproval.

When the service was over he stood in the paved church-yard greeting acquaintances until Maud emerged with Fitz and Bea. Maud looked supernaturally graceful in a stylish gray figured velvet dress with a darker gray crepe overdress. It was not a very feminine color, perhaps, but it heightened her sculptured beauty and seemed to make her skin glow. Walter shook hands all round, wishing desperately for a few minutes alone with her. He exchanged pleasantries with Bea, a confection in candy-pink and cream lace, and agreed with a solemn Fitz that the assassination was a "bad business." Then the Fitzherberts moved away, and Walter feared he had missed his chance; but, at the last moment, Maud murmured: "I'll be at the duchess's house for tea."

Walter smiled at her elegant back. He had seen Maud yesterday and he would see her tomorrow, yet he had been terrified that he might not get another chance to see her today. Was he really incapable of passing twenty-four hours without her? He did not think of himself as a weak man, but she had cast a spell over him. However, he had no wish to escape.

It was her independent spirit that he found so attractive. Most women of his generation seemed content to play the passive role that society gave them, dressing beautifully and organizing parties and obeying their husbands. Walter was bored by the doormat type. Maud was more like some of the women he had met in the United States, during a stint at the German embassy in Washington. They were elegant and charming but not subservient. To be loved by a woman like that was unbearably exciting.

He walked with a jaunty step along Piccadilly and stopped at a newsstand. Reading British papers was never pleasant: most were viciously anti-German, especially the rabid *Daily Mail*. They had the British believing they were surrounded by German spies. How Walter wished it were true! He had a dozen or so agents in coast towns, making notes of comings and goings at the docks, as the British had in German ports, but nothing like the thousands reported by hysterical newspaper editors.

He bought a copy of the *People*. The trouble in the Balkans was not big news here: the British were more worried about Ireland. A minority of Protestants had ruled the roost there for hundreds of years, with scant regard for the Catholic majority. If Ireland won independence the boot would be on the other foot. Both sides were heavily armed, and civil war threatened.

A single paragraph at the bottom of the front page referred to the "Austro-Servian Crisis." As usual, the newspapers had no idea what was really going on.

As Walter turned into the Ritz Hotel, Robert jumped out of a motor taxi. He was wearing a black waistcoat and a black tie in mourning for the archduke. Robert had been one of Franz Ferdinand's set—progressive thinkers by the standards of the Viennese court, albeit conservative by any other measure. He had liked and respected the murdered man and his family, Walter knew.

They left their top hats in the cloakroom and went into the dining room together. Walter felt protective toward Robert. Since they were boys he had known that his cousin was different. People called such men effeminate, but that was too crude: Robert was not a woman in a man's body. However, he had a lot of feminine traits, and this led Walter to treat him with a kind of understated chivalry.

He looked like Walter, with the same regular features and hazel eyes, but his hair was longer and his mustache waxed and curled. "How are things with Lady M?" he said as they sat down. Walter had confided in him: Robert knew all about forbidden love.

"She's wonderful, but my father can't get over her working in a slum clinic with a Jewish doctor."

"Oh, dear—that's harsh," Robert said. "His objection might be understandable if she herself were a Jew."

"I've been hoping he would warm to her gradually, meeting her socially now and again, and realizing that she is friendly with the most powerful men in the land; but it's not working."

"Unfortunately, the crisis in the Balkans is only going to increase tension in"—Robert smiled—"forgive me, international relations."

Walter forced a laugh. "We will work it out, whatever happens."

Robert said nothing, but looked as if he was not so confident.

Over Welsh lamb and potatoes with parsley sauce, Walter gave Robert the inconclusive information he had gleaned from Anton.

Robert had news of his own. "We have established that the assassins got their guns and bombs from Serbia."

"Oh, hell," said Walter.

Robert let his anger show. "The arms were supplied by the head of Serbian military intelligence. The murderers were given target practice in a park in Belgrade."

Walter said: "Intelligence officers sometimes act unilaterally."

"Often. And the secrecy of their work means they may get away with it."

"So this does not prove that the Serbian government organized the assassination. And, when you think logically about it, a small nation such as Serbia, trying desperately to preserve its independence, would be mad to provoke its powerful neighbor."

"It is even possible that Serbian intelligence acted in direct opposition to the wishes of the government," Robert conceded. But then he said firmly: "That makes absolutely no difference at all. Austria must take action against Serbia."

This was what Walter feared. The affair could no longer be regarded merely as a crime, to be dealt with by the police and the courts. It had escalated, and now an empire had to punish a small nation. Emperor Franz Joseph of Austria had been a great man in his time, conservative and devoutly religious but a strong leader. However, he was now eighty-four, and age had not made him any less authoritarian and narrow-minded. Such men thought they knew everything just because they were old. Walter's father was the same.

My fate is in the hands of two monarchs, Walter thought, the tsar and the emperor. One is foolish, the other geriatric; yet they control the destiny of Maud and me and countless millions more Europeans. What an argument against monarchy!

He thought hard while they ate dessert. When the coffee came he said optimistically: "I assume your aim will be to teach Serbia a sharp lesson without involving any other country."

Robert swiftly dashed his hopes. "On the contrary," he said. "My emperor has written a personal letter to your kaiser."

Walter was startled. He had heard nothing of this. "When?"

"It was delivered yesterday."

Like all diplomats, Walter hated it when monarchs talked directly to each other, instead of through their ministers. Anything could happen then. "What did he say?"

"That Serbia must be eliminated as a political power."

"No!" This was worse than Walter had feared. Shocked, he said: "Does he mean it?"

"Everything depends on the reply."

Walter frowned. Emperor Franz Joseph was asking for backing from Kaiser Wilhelm—that was the real point of the letter. The two countries were allies, so the kaiser was obliged to sound supportive, but his emphasis might be enthusiastic or reluctant, encouraging or cautious.

"I trust Germany will back Austria, whatever my emperor decides to do," Robert said severely.

"You can't possibly want Germany to attack Serbia!" Walter protested.

Robert was offended. "We want a reassurance that Germany will fulfill her obligations as our ally."

Walter controlled his impatience. "The problem with that way of thinking is that it raises the stakes. Like Russia making supportive noises about Serbia, it encourages aggression. What we ought to do is calm everyone down."

"I'm not sure I agree," Robert said stiffly. "Austria has suffered a terrible blow. The emperor cannot be seen to take it lightly. He who defies the giant must be crushed."

"Let's try to keep this in proportion."

Robert raised his voice. "The heir to the throne has been murdered!" A diner at the next table glanced up and frowned to hear German spoken in angry tones. Robert softened his speech but not his expression. "Don't talk to me about proportion."

Walter tried to suppress his own feelings. It would be stupid and dangerous for Germany to get involved in this squabble, but telling Robert that would serve no purpose. It was Walter's job to glean information, not have an argument. "I quite understand," he said. "Is your view shared by everyone in Vienna?"

"In Vienna, yes," said Robert. "Tisza is opposed." István Tisza was the prime minister of Hungary, but subordinate to the Austrian emperor. "His alternative proposal is diplomatic encirclement of Serbia."

"Less dramatic, perhaps, but also less risky," Walter observed carefully.

"Too weak."

Walter called for the bill. He was deeply unsettled by what he had heard. However, he did not want any ill feeling between himself and Robert. They trusted and helped each other, and he did not want that to change. On the pavement outside, he shook Robert's hand and clasped his elbow in a gesture of firm comradeship. "Whatever happens, we must stick together, cousin," he said. "We are allies, and always will be." He left it to Robert to decide whether he was talking about the two of them or their countries. They parted friends.

He walked briskly across Green Park. Londoners were enjoying the sunshine, but there was a cloud of gloom over Walter's head. He had hoped that Germany and Russia would stay out of the Balkan crisis, but what he had learned so far today ominously suggested the opposite. Reaching Buckingham Palace, he turned left and walked along the Mall to the back entrance of the German embassy.

His father had an office in the embassy: he spent about one week in three there. There was a painting of Kaiser Wilhelm on the wall and a framed photograph of Walter in lieutenant's uniform on the desk. Otto held in his hand a piece of pottery. He collected English ceramics, and loved to go hunting for unusual items. Looking more closely, Walter saw that this was a creamware fruit bowl, the edges delicately pierced and molded to mimic basketwork. Knowing his father's taste, he guessed it was eighteenth century.

With Otto was Gottfried von Kessel, a cultural attaché whom Walter disliked. Gottfried had thick dark hair combed with a side parting, and wore spectacles with thick lenses. He was the same age as Walter and also had a father in the diplomatic service, but despite having that much in common, they were not friends. Walter thought Gottfried was a toady.

He nodded to Gottfried and sat down. "The Austrian emperor has written to our kaiser."

"We know that," Gottfried said quickly.

Walter ignored him. Gottfried was always trying to start a pissing contest. "No doubt the kaiser's reply will be amicable," he said to his father. "But a lot may depend upon nuance."

"His Majesty has not yet confided in me."

"But he will."

Otto nodded. "It is the kind of thing he sometimes asks me about."

"And if he urges caution, he might persuade the Austrians to be less belligerent."

Gottfried said: "Why should he do that?"

"To avoid Germany's being dragged into a war over such a worthless piece of territory as Serbia!"

"What are you afraid of?" Gottfried said scornfully. "The Serbian army?"

"I am afraid of the Russian army, and so should you be," Walter replied. "It is the largest in history—"

"I know that," said Gottfried.

Walter ignored the interruption. "In theory, the tsar can put six million men into the field within a few weeks—"

"I know—"

"—and that is more than the total population of Serbia."

"I know."

Walter sighed. "You seem to know everything, von Kessel. Do you know where the assassins got their guns and bombs?"

"From Slav nationalists, I presume."

"Any *particular* Slav nationalists, do you presume?"

"Who knows?"

"The Austrians know, I gather. They believe the arms came from the head of Serbian intelligence."

Otto grunted in surprise. "That *would* make the Austrians vengeful."

Gottfried said: "Austria is still ruled by its emperor. In the end, the decision for war can be made only by him."

Walter nodded. "Not that a Habsburg emperor has ever needed much of an excuse to be ruthless and brutal."

"What other way is there to rule an empire?"

Walter did not rise to the bait. "Other than the Hungarian prime minister, who does not carry much weight, there seems to be no one urging caution. That role must fall to us." Walter stood up. He had reported his findings, and he did not want to stay any longer in the same room as the irritating Gottfried. "If you will excuse me, Father, I'll go to tea at the Duchess of Sussex's house and see what else is being said around town."

Gottfried said: "The English don't pay calls on Sundays."

"I have an invitation," Walter replied, and went out before he lost his temper.

He threaded his way through Mayfair to Park Lane, where the Duke of Sussex had his palace. The duke played no role in the British government, but the duchess held a political salon. When Walter had arrived in London in December Fitz had introduced him to the duchess, who had made sure he was invited everywhere.

He entered her drawing room, bowed, shook her plump hand, and said: "Everyone in London wants to know what will happen in Serbia, so, even though it is Sunday, I have come here to ask you, Your Grace."

"There will be no war," she said, showing no awareness that he was joking. "Sit down and have a cup of tea. Of course it is tragic about the poor archduke and his wife, and no doubt the culprits will be punished, but how silly to think that great nations such as Germany and Britain would go to war over Serbia."

Walter wished he could feel so confident. He took a chair near Maud, who smiled happily, and Lady Hermia, who nodded. There were a dozen people in the room, including the first lord of the Admiralty, Winston Churchill. The decor was grandly out-of-date: too much heavy carved furniture, rich fabrics of a dozen different patterns, and every surface covered with ornaments, framed photographs, and vases of dried grasses. A footman handed Walter a cup of tea and offered milk and sugar.

Walter was happy to be near Maud but, as always, he wanted more, and he immediately began to wonder whether there was any way they could contrive to be alone, even if only for a minute or two.

The duchess said: "The problem, of course, is the weakness of the Turks."

The pompous old bat was right, Walter thought. The Ottoman Empire was in decline, held back from modernization by a conservative Muslim priesthood. For centuries the Turkish sultan had kept order in the Balkan peninsula, from the Mediterranean coast of Greece as far north as Hungary, but now, decade by decade, it was pulling back. The nearest Great Powers, Austria and Russia, were trying to fill the vacuum. Between Austria and the Black Sea were Bosnia, Serbia, and Bulgaria in a line. Five years ago Austria had taken control of Bosnia. Now Austria was in a quarrel with Serbia, the middle one. The Russians looked at the map and saw that Bulgaria was the next domino, and that the Austrians could end up controlling the west coast of the Black Sea, threatening Russia's international trade.

Meanwhile the subject peoples of the Austrian Empire were starting to think they might rule themselves—which was why the Bosnian nationalist Gavrilo Princip had shot Archduke Franz Ferdinand in Sarajevo.

Walter said: "It's a tragedy for Serbia. I should think their prime minister is ready to throw himself into the Danube."

Maud said: "You mean the Volga."

Walter looked at her, glad of the excuse to drink in her appearance. She had changed her clothes, and was wearing a royal blue tea gown over a pale pink lace blouse and a pink felt hat with a blue pompom. "I most certainly do not, Lady Maud," he said.

She said: "The Volga runs through Belgrade, which is the capital of Serbia."

Walter was about to protest again; then he hesitated. She knew perfectly well that the Volga hardly came within a thousand miles of Belgrade. What was she up to? "I am reluctant to contradict someone as well-informed as you, Lady Maud," he said. "All the same—"

"We will look it up," she said. "My uncle, the duke, has one of the greatest libraries in London." She stood. "Come with me, and I shall prove you wrong."

This was bold behavior for a well-bred young woman, and the duchess pursed her lips.

Walter mimed a helpless shrug and followed Maud to the door.

For a moment, Lady Hermia looked as if she might go, too, but she was comfortably sunk in deep velvet upholstery, with a cup and saucer in her hand and a plate in her lap, and it was too much effort to move. "Don't be long," she said quietly, and ate some more cake. Then they were out of the room.

Maud preceded Walter across the hall, where a couple of footmen stood like sentries. She stopped in front of a door and waited for Walter to open it. They went inside.

The big room was silent. They were alone. Maud threw herself into Walter's arms. He hugged her hard, pressing her body against his. She turned her face up. "I love you," she said, and kissed him hungrily.

After a minute she broke away, breathless. Walter looked at her adoringly. "You're outrageous," he said. "Saying the Volga runs through Belgrade!"

"It worked, didn't it?"

He shook his head in admiration. "I would never have thought of it. You're so clever."

"We need an atlas," she said. "In case anyone comes in."

Walter scanned the shelves. This was the library of a collector rather than a reader. All the books were in fine bindings, most looking as if they had never been opened. A few reference books lurked in a corner, and he pulled out an atlas and found a map of the Balkans.

"This crisis," Maud said anxiously. "In the long run . . . it's not going to split us up, is it?"

"Not if I can help it," Walter said.

He drew her behind a bookcase, so that they could not be seen immediately by someone coming in, and kissed her again. She was deliciously needy today, rubbing her hands over his shoulders and arms and back as she kissed him. She broke the kiss to whisper: "Lift my skirt."

He swallowed. He had daydreamed of this. He grasped the material and drew it up.

"And the petticoats," she said. He took a bunch of fabric in each hand. "Don't crease it," she said. He tried to raise the garments without crushing the silk, but everything slipped through his hands. Impatient, she bent down, grasped skirt and petticoats by the hems, and lifted everything to her waist. "Feel me," she said, looking him in the eye.

He was nervous that someone would come in, but too overwhelmed with love and desire to restrain himself. He put his right hand on the fork of her thighs—and gasped with shock: she was naked there. The realization that she must have planned to give him this pleasure inflamed him further. He stroked her gently, but she thrust her hips forward against his hand, and he pressed harder. "That's right," she said. He closed his eyes, but she said: "Look at me, my darling—please, look at me while you're doing it," and he opened them again. Her face was flushed and she was breathing hard through open lips. She gripped his hand and guided him, as he had guided her in the opera box. She whispered: "Put your finger in." She leaned against his shoulder. He could feel the heat of her breath through his clothes. She thrust against him again and again. Then she made a small sound in the back of her throat, like the muted cry of someone dreaming; and at last she slumped against him.

He heard the door open, and then Lady Hermia's voice. "Come along, Maud, dear. We must take our leave."

Walter withdrew his hand and Maud hastily smoothed her skirt. In a shaky voice she said: "I'm afraid I was wrong, Aunt Herm, and Herr von Ulrich was right—it's the Danube, not the Volga, that runs through Belgrade. We've just found it in the atlas."

They bent over the book as Lady Hermia came around the end of the bookcase. "I never doubted it," she said. "Men are generally right about these things, and Herr von Ulrich is a diplomat, who has to know a great many facts with which women do not need to trouble themselves. You shouldn't argue, Maud."

"I expect you're right," said Maud with breathtaking insincerity.

They all left the library and crossed the hall. Walter opened the door to the drawing room. Lady Hermia went in first. As Maud followed, she met his eye. He raised his right hand, put the tip of his finger into his mouth, and sucked it.

{ II }

This could not go on, Walter thought as he made his way back to the embassy. It was like being a schoolboy. Maud was twenty-three years old and he was twenty-eight, yet they had to resort to absurd subterfuges in order to spend five minutes alone together. It was time they got married.

He would have to ask Fitz's permission. Maud's father was dead, so her brother was the head of the family. Fitz would undoubtedly have preferred her to marry an Englishman. However, he would probably come around: he must be worrying that he might never get his feisty sister married off.

No, the major problem was Otto. He wanted Walter to marry a well-behaved Prussian maiden who would be happy to spend the rest of her life breeding heirs. And when Otto wanted something he did all he could to get it, crushing opposition remorselessly—which was what had made him a good army officer. It would never occur to him that his son had a right to choose his own bride, without interference or pressure. Walter would have preferred to have his father's encouragement and support: he certainly did not look forward to the inevitable stand-up confrontation. However, his love was a force more powerful by far than filial deference.

It was Sunday evening, but London was not quiet. Although Parliament was not sitting, and the mandarins of Whitehall had gone to their suburban homes, politics continued in the palaces of Mayfair, the gentlemen's clubs of St. James's, and the embassies. On the streets Walter recognized several members of Parliament, a couple of junior ministers from Britain's Foreign Office, and some European diplomats. He wondered whether Britain's bird-watching foreign secretary, Sir Edward Grey, had stayed in town this weekend instead of going to his beloved country cottage in Hampshire.

Walter found his father at his desk, reading decoded telegrams. "This may not be the best time to tell you my news," Walter began.

Otto grunted and carried on reading.

Walter plunged on. "I'm in love with Lady Maud."

Otto looked up. "Fitzherbert's sister? I suspected as much. You have my profound sympathy."

"Be serious, please, Father."

"No, you be serious." Otto threw down the papers he was reading. "Maud Fitzherbert is a feminist, a suffragette, and a social maverick. She's not a fit wife for anyone, let alone a German diplomat from a good family. So let's hear no more of it."

Hot words came to Walter's lips, but he clenched his teeth and kept his temper. "She's a wonderful woman, and I love her, so you'd better speak politely of her, whatever your opinions."

"I'll say what I think," Otto said carelessly. "She's dreadful." He looked down at his telegrams.

Walter's eye fell on the creamware fruit bowl his father had bought. "No," he said. He picked up the bowl. "You will not say what you think."

"Be careful with that."

Walter had his father's full attention now. "I feel protective of Lady Maud, the way you feel protective of this trinket."

"Trinket? Let me tell you, it's worth—"

"Except, of course, that love is stronger than the collector's greed." Walter tossed the delicate object into the air and caught it one-handed. His father let out an anguished cry of inarticulate protest. Walter went on heedlessly: "So when you speak insultingly of her, I feel as you do when you think I'm going to drop this—only more so."

"Insolent pup—"

Walter raised his voice over his father's. "And if you continue to trample all over my sensibilities, I will crush this stupid piece of pottery beneath my heel."

"All right, you've made your point. Put it down, for God's sake."

Walter took that for acquiescence, and replaced the ornament on a side table.

Otto said maliciously: "But there is something else you need to take into account . . . if I may mention it without treading on your *sensibilities.*"

"All right."

"She is English."

"For God's sake!" Walter cried. "Wellborn Germans

have been marrying English aristocrats for years. Prince Albert of Saxe-Coburg and Gotha married Queen Victoria—his grandson is now king of England. And the queen of England was born a Württemberg princess!"

Otto raised his voice. "Things have changed! The English are determined to keep us a second-rate power. They befriend our adversaries, Russia and France. You would be marrying an enemy of your fatherland."

Walter knew this was how the old guard thought, but it was irrational. "We should not be enemies," he said in exasperation. "There's no reason for it."

"They will never allow us to compete on equal terms."

"That's just not true!" Walter heard himself shouting, and tried to be calmer. "The English believe in free trade—they allow us to sell our manufactures throughout the British Empire."

"Read that, then." Otto threw across the desk the telegram he had been reading. "His Majesty the kaiser has asked for my comments."

Walter picked it up. It was a draft reply to the Austrian emperor's personal letter. Walter read it with mounting alarm. It ended: "The Emperor Franz Joseph may, however, rest assured that His Majesty will faithfully stand by Austria-Hungary, as is required by the obligations of his alliance and of his ancient friendship."

Walter was horrified. "But this gives Austria carte blanche!" he said. "They can do anything they like and we will support them!"

"There are some qualifications."

"Not many. Has this been sent?"

"No, but it has been agreed. It will be sent tomorrow."

"Can we stop it?"

"No, and I would not want to."

"But it commits us to support Austria in a war against Serbia."

"No bad thing."

"We don't want war!" Walter protested. "We need science, and manufacturing, and commerce. Germany must modernize and become liberal and grow. We want peace and prosperity." And, he added silently, we want a world in which a man can marry the woman he loves without being accused of treason.

"Listen to me," Otto said. "We have powerful enemies on both sides, France to the west and Russia to the east—and they are hand in glove. We can't fight a war on two fronts."

Walter knew this. "That's why we have the Schlieffen Plan," he said. "If we are forced to go to war, we first invade France with an overwhelming force, achieve victory within a few weeks, and then, with the west secure, we turn east to face Russia."

"Our only hope," Otto said. "But when that plan was adopted by the German army nine years ago, our intelligence told us it would take the Russian army forty days to mobilize. That gave us almost six weeks in which to conquer France. Ever since then, the Russians have been improving their railways—with money loaned by France!" Otto banged the desk, as if he could squash France under his fist. "As the Russians' mobilization time gets shorter, so the Schlieffen Plan becomes more risky. Which means"—he pointed his finger dramatically at Walter—"the sooner we have this war, the better for Germany!"

"No!" Why could the old man not see how dangerous this thinking was? "It means we should be seeking peaceful solutions to petty disputes."

"Peaceful solutions?" Otto shook his head knowingly. "You're a young idealist. You think there is an answer to every question."

"You actually want war," Walter said incredulously. "You really do."

"No one wants war," said Otto. "But sometimes it's better than the alternative."

{ III }

Maud had inherited a pittance from her father—three hundred pounds a year, barely enough to buy gowns for the season. Fitz got the title, the lands, the houses, and nearly all the money. That was the English system. But it was not what angered Maud. Money meant little to her: she did not really need her three hundred. Fitz paid for anything she wanted without question: he thought it ungentlemanly to be careful with money.

Her great resentment was that she had had no education. When she was seventeen, she had announced that
she was going to university—whereupon everyone had
laughed at her. It turned out that you had to come from a
good school, and pass examinations, before they would let
you in. Maud had never been to school, and even though
she could discuss politics with the great men of the land, a
succession of governesses and tutors had completely failed
to equip her to pass any sort of exam. She had cried and
raged for days, and even now thinking about it could still
put her in a foul mood. This was what made her a suffragette: she knew girls would never get a decent education until women had the vote.

She had often wondered why women married. They
contracted themselves to a lifetime of slavery and, she
had asked, what did they get in return? Now, however, she
knew the answer. She had never felt anything as intensely
as her love for Walter. And the things they did to express
that love gave her the most exquisite pleasure. To be able
to touch each other that way anytime you liked would be
heaven. She would have enslaved herself three times over,
if that were the price.

But slavery was not the price, at least not with Walter.
She had asked him whether he thought a wife should obey
her husband in all things, and he had answered: "Certainly
not. I don't see that obedience comes into it. Two adults
who love each other should be able to make decisions together, without one having to obey the other."

She spent a lot of time thinking about their life together.
For a few years he would probably be posted from one em-
bassy to another, and they would travel the world: Paris,
Rome, Budapest, perhaps even farther afield to Addis
Ababa, Tokyo, Buenos Aires. She thought of the story of
Ruth in the Bible: "Whither thou goest, I will go." Their
sons would be taught to treat women as equals, and their
daughters would grow up independent and strong-willed.
Perhaps they would eventually settle in a town house in
Berlin, so that their children could go to good German
schools. At some point, no doubt, Walter would inherit
Zumwald, his father's country house in East Prussia. When
they were old, and their children were adults, they would
spend more time in the country, walking hand in hand

around the estate, reading side by side in the evenings, and reflecting on how the world had changed since they were young.

Maud had trouble thinking about anything else. She sat in her office at the Calvary Gospel Hall, staring at a price list of medical supplies, and remembered how Walter had sucked his fingertip at the door to the duchess's drawing room. People were beginning to notice her absentmindedness: Dr. Greenward had asked if she was feeling all right, and Aunt Herm had told her to wake up.

She tried again to concentrate on the order form, and this time she was interrupted by a tap at the door. Aunt Herm looked in and said: "Someone to see you." She seemed a bit awestruck, and handed Maud a card.

General Otto von Ulrich
ATTACHÉ
EMBASSY OF THE EMPIRE OF GERMANY
CARLTON HOUSE TERRACE, LONDON

"Walter's father!" said Maud. "What on earth . . . ?"

"What shall I say?" whispered Aunt Herm.

"Ask him if he would like tea or sherry, and show him in."

Von Ulrich was formally dressed in a black frock coat with satin lapels, a white piqué waistcoat, and striped trousers. His red face was perspiring in the summer heat. He was rounder than Walter, and not as handsome, but they had the same straight-backed, chin-up military stance.

Maud summoned her habitual insouciance. "My dear Herr von Ulrich, is this a formal visit?"

"I want to talk to you about my son," he said. His English was almost as good as Walter's, though he had an accent where Walter did not.

"It's kind of you to come to the point so quickly," Maud replied with a touch of sarcasm that went right over his head. "Please sit down. Lady Hermia will order some refreshment."

"Walter comes from an old aristocratic family."

"As do I," said Maud.

"We are traditional, conservative, devoutly religious . . . perhaps a little old-fashioned."

"Just like my family," Maud said.

This was not going the way Otto had planned. "We are Prussians," he said with a touch of exasperation.

"Ah," said Maud as if trumped. "Whereas we, of course, are Anglo-Saxons."

She was fencing with him, as if this were nothing more than a battle of wits, but underneath she was frightened. Why was he here? What was his aim? She felt it could not be benign. He was against her. He would try to come between her and Walter, she felt bleakly certain.

Anyway, he was not to be put off by facetiousness. "Germany and Great Britain are at odds. Britain makes friends with our enemies, Russia and France. This makes Britain our adversary."

"I'm sorry to hear that you think that way. Many do not."

"The truth is not arrived at by majority vote." Again she heard a note of asperity in his voice. He was used to being heard uncritically, especially by women.

Dr. Greenward's nurse brought in tea on a tray and poured. Otto remained silent until she left. Then he said: "We may go to war in the next few weeks. If we do not fight over Serbia, there will be some other casus belli. Sooner or later, Britain and Germany must do battle for mastery of Europe."

"I'm sorry you feel so pessimistic."

"Many others think the same."

"But the truth is not arrived at by majority vote."

Otto looked annoyed. He evidently expected her to sit and listen to his pomposity in silence. He did not like to be mocked. He said angrily: "You should pay attention to me. I'm telling you something that affects you. Most Germans regard Britain as their enemy. If Walter were to marry an Englishwoman, think of the consequences."

"I have, of course. Walter and I have talked at length about this."

"First, he would suffer my disapproval. I could not welcome an English daughter-in-law into my family."

"Walter feels that your love for your son would help you get over your revulsion for me, in the end. Is there really no chance of that?"

"Second," he said, ignoring her question, "he would be regarded as disloyal to the kaiser. Men of his own class would no longer be his friends. He and his wife would not be received in the best houses."

Maud was becoming angry. "I find that hard to credit. Surely not *all* Germans are so narrow-minded?"

He appeared not to notice her rudeness. "Third, and finally, Walter's career is with the foreign ministry. He will distinguish himself. I sent him to schools and universities in different countries. He speaks perfect English and passable Russian. Despite his immature idealistic views, he is well thought of by his superiors, and the kaiser has spoken kindly to him more than once. He could be foreign minister one day."

"He's brilliant," Maud said.

"But if he marries you, his career is over."

"That's ridiculous," she said, shocked.

"My dear young lady, is it not obvious? A man who is married to one of the enemy cannot be trusted."

"We have talked about this. His loyalty would naturally lie with Germany. I love him enough to accept that."

"He might be too concerned about his wife's family to give total loyalty to his own country. Even if he ruthlessly ignored the connection, men would still ask the question."

"You're exaggerating," she said, but she was beginning to lose confidence.

"He certainly could not work in any area that required secrecy. Men would not speak of confidential matters in his presence. He would be finished."

"He doesn't have to be in military intelligence. He can switch to other areas of diplomacy."

"All diplomacy requires secrecy. And then there is my own position."

Maud was surprised by this. She and Walter had not considered Otto's career.

"I am a close confidant of the kaiser's. Would he continue to place absolute trust in me if my son were married to an enemy alien?"

"He ought to."

"He would, perhaps, if I took firm, positive action, and disowned my son."

Maud gasped. "You would not do that."

Otto raised his voice. "I would be obliged to!"

She shook her head. "You would have a choice," she said desperately. "A man always has a choice."

"I will not sacrifice everything I have earned—my position, my career, the respect of my countrymen—for a *girl*," he said contemptuously.

Maud felt as if she had been slapped.

Otto went on: "But Walter will, of course."

"What are you saying?"

"If Walter were to marry you he would lose his family, his country, and his career. But he will do it. He has declared his love for you without fully thinking through the consequences, and sooner or later he will understand what a catastrophic mistake he has made. But he undoubtedly considers himself unofficially engaged to you, and he will not back out of a commitment. He is too much of a gentleman. 'Go ahead, disown me,' he will say to me. He would consider himself a coward otherwise."

"That's true," Maud said. She felt bewildered. This horrible old man saw the truth more clearly than she did.

Otto went on: "So *you* must break off the engagement."

She felt stabbed. "No!"

"It is the only way to save him. You must give him up."

Maud opened her mouth to object again, but Otto was right, and she could not think of anything to say.

Otto leaned forward and spoke with pressing intensity. "Will you break with him?"

Tears ran down Maud's face. She knew what she had to do. She could not ruin Walter's life, even out of love. "Yes," she sobbed. Her dignity was gone, and she did not care; the pain was too much. "Yes, I will break with him."

"Do you promise?"

"Yes, I promise."

Otto stood up. "Thank you for your courtesy in listening to me." He bowed. "I bid you good afternoon." He went out.

Maud buried her face in her hands.

CHAPTER EIGHT

Mid-July 1914

There was a cheval glass in Ethel's new bedroom at Tŷ Gwyn. It was old, the woodwork cracked and the glass misted, but she could see herself full-length. She considered it a great luxury.

She looked at herself in her underwear. She seemed to have become more voluptuous since falling in love. She had put on a little weight around her waist and hips, and her breasts seemed fuller, perhaps because Fitz stroked and squeezed them so much. When she thought about him, her nipples hurt.

Fitz had arrived that morning, with Princess Bea and Lady Maud, and had whispered that he would meet her in the Gardenia Suite after lunch. Ethel had put Maud in the Pink Room, making up an excuse about repairs to the floorboards in Maud's usual apartment.

Now Ethel had come to her room to wash and put on clean underwear. She loved preparing herself for him like this, anticipating how he would touch her body and kiss her mouth, hearing in advance the way he would groan with desire and pleasure, thinking of the smell of his skin and the voluptuous texture of his clothes.

She opened a drawer to take out fresh stockings, and her eye fell on a pile of clean strips of white cotton, the rags she used when menstruating. It occurred to her that she had not washed them since she had moved into this room. Suddenly there was a tiny seed of pure dread in her mind. She sat down heavily on the narrow bed. It was now the middle

of July. Mrs. Jevons had left at the beginning of May. That
was ten weeks ago. In that time Ethel should have used
the rags not once but twice. "Oh, no," she said aloud. "Oh,
please, no!"

She forced herself to think calmly and worked it out
again. The king's visit had taken place in January. Ethel
had been made housekeeper immediately afterward, but
Mrs. Jevons had been too ill to move then. Fitz had gone
to Russia in February, and had come back in March, which
was when they had first made love properly. In April Mrs.
Jevons had rallied, and Fitz's man of business, Albert Solman, had come down from London to explain her pension
to her. She had left at the beginning of May, and that was
when Ethel had moved into this room and put that frightening little pile of white cotton strips into the drawer. It
was ten weeks ago. Ethel could not make the arithmetic
come out any differently.

How many times had they met in the Gardenia Suite?
At least eight. Each time, Fitz withdrew before the end, but
sometimes he left it a bit late, and she felt the first of his
spasms while he was still inside her. She had been deliri-
ously happy to be with him that way, and in her ecstasy she
had closed her eyes to the risk. Now she had been caught.

"Oh, God forgive me," she said aloud.

Her friend Dilys Pugh had fallen for a baby. Dilys was
the same age as Ethel. She had been working as a housemaid for Perceval Jones's wife and walking out with
Johnny Bevan. Ethel recalled how Dilys's breasts had got
larger around the time she realized that you could, in fact,
get pregnant from doing it standing up. They were married
now.

What was going to happen to Ethel? She could not
marry the father of her child. Apart from anything else, he
was already married.

It was time to go and meet him. There would be no rolling on the bed today. They would have to talk about the
future. She put on her housekeeper's black silk dress.

What would he say? He had no children: would he be
pleased, or horrified? Would he cherish his love child, or be
embarrassed by it? Would he love Ethel more for conceiv-
ing, or would he hate her?

She left her attic room and went along the narrow corridor and down the back stairs to the west wing. The familiar wallpaper with its pattern of gardenias quickened her desire, in the same way that the sight of her knickers aroused Fitz.

He was already there, standing by the window, looking over the sunlit garden, smoking a cigar; and when she saw him, she was struck again by how beautiful he was. She threw her arms around his neck. His brown tweed suit was soft to the touch because, she had discovered, it was made of cashmere. "Oh, Teddy, my lovely, I'm so happy to see you," she said. She liked being the only person who called him Teddy.

"And I to see you," he said, but he did not immediately stroke her breasts.

She kissed his ear. "I got something to say to you," she said solemnly.

"And I have something to tell you! May I go first?"

She was about to say no, but he detached himself from her embrace and took a step back, and suddenly her heart filled with foreboding. "What?" she said. "What is it?"

"Bea is expecting a baby." He drew on his cigar and blew out smoke like a sigh.

At first she could make no sense of his words. "What?" she said in a bewildered tone.

"The princess Bea, my wife, is pregnant. She is going to have a baby."

"You mean you've been at it with her at the same time as with me?" Ethel said angrily.

He looked startled. It seemed he had not expected her to resent that. "I must!" he protested. "I need an heir."

"But you said you loved me!"

"I do, and in a way I always will."

"No, Teddy!" she cried. "Don't say it like that—please don't!"

"Keep your voice down!"

"Keep my voice down? You're throwing me over! What is it to me now if people know?"

"It's everything to me."

Ethel was distraught. "Teddy, please, I love you."

"But it's over now. I have to be a good husband and a father to my child. You must understand."

"Understand, hell!" she raged. "How can you say it so

easily? I've seen you show more emotion over a dog that had to be shot!"

"It's not true," he said, and there was a catch in his voice.

"I gave myself to you, in this room, on that bed by there."

"And I shan't—" He stopped. His face, frozen until now in an expression of rigid self-control, suddenly showed anguish. He turned away, hiding from her gaze. "I shan't ever forget that," he whispered.

She moved closer to him, and saw tears on his cheeks, and her anger evaporated. "Oh, Teddy, I'm so sorry," she said.

He tried to pull himself together. "I care for you very much, but I must do my duty," he said. The words were cold, but his voice was tormented.

"Oh, God." She tried to stop crying. She had not told him her news yet. She wiped her eyes with her sleeve, sniffed, and swallowed. "Duty?" she said. "You don't know the half."

"What are you talking about?"

"I'm pregnant, too."

"Oh, my good God." He put his cigar to his lips, mechanically, then lowered it again without puffing on it. "But I always withdrew!"

"Not soon enough, then."

"How long have you known?"

"I just realized. I looked in my drawer and saw my clean rags." He winced. Evidently he did not like talk of menstruation. Well, he would have to put up with it. "I worked out that I haven't had the curse since I moved into Mrs. Jevons's old room, and that's ten weeks ago."

"Two cycles. That makes it definite. That's what Bea said. Oh, hell." He touched the cigar to his lips, found that it had gone out, and dropped it on the floor with a grunt of irritation.

A wry thought occurred to her. "You might have two heirs."

"Don't be ridiculous," he said sharply. "A bastard doesn't inherit."

"Oh," she said. She had not seriously intended to make a claim for her child. On the other hand, she had not until now thought of it as a bastard. "Poor little thing," she said. "My baby, the bastard."

He looked guilty. "I'm sorry," he said. "I didn't mean that. Forgive me."

She could see that his better nature was at war with his selfish instincts. She touched his arm. "Poor Fitz."

"God forbid that Bea should find out about this," he said.

She felt mortally wounded. Why should his main concern be the other woman? Bea would be all right: she was rich and married, and carrying the loved and honored child of the Fitzherbert clan.

Fitz went on: "The shock might be too much for her."

Ethel recalled a rumor that Bea had suffered a miscarriage last year. All the female servants had discussed it. According to Nina, the Russian maid, the princess blamed the miscarriage on Fitz, who had upset her by canceling a planned trip to Russia.

Ethel felt terribly rejected. "So your main concern is that the news of our baby might upset your wife."

He stared at her. "I don't want her to miscarry—it's important!"

He had no idea how callous he was being. "Damn you," Ethel said.

"What do you expect? The child Bea is carrying is one I have been hoping and praying for. Yours is not wanted by you, me, or anyone else."

"That's not how I see it," she said in a small voice, and she began to cry again.

"I've got to think about this," he said. "I need to be alone." He took her by the shoulders. "We'll talk again tomorrow. In the meantime, tell no one. Do you understand?"

She nodded.

"Promise me."

"I promise."

"Good girl," he said, and he left the room.

Ethel bent down and picked up the dead cigar.

{ II }

She told no one, but she was unable to pretend that everything was all right, so she feigned illness and went to bed. As she lay alone, hour after hour, grief slowly gave way to anxiety. How would she and her baby live?

She would lose her job here at Tŷ Gwyn—that was automatic, even if her baby had not been the earl's. That alone hurt. She had been so proud of herself when she was made housekeeper. Gramper was fond of saying that pride comes before a fall. He was right in this case.

She was not sure she could return to her parents' house: the disgrace would kill her father. She was almost as upset about that as she was about her own shame. It would wound him more than her, in a way; he was so rigid about this sort of thing.

Anyway, she did not want to live as an unmarried mother in Aberowen. There were two already: Maisie Owen and Gladys Pritchard. They were sad figures with no proper place in the town's social order. They were single, but no man was interested in them; they were mothers, but they lived with their parents as if they were still children; they were not welcome in any church, pub, shop, or club. How could she, Ethel Williams, who had always considered herself a cut above the rest, sink to the lowest level of all?

She had to leave Aberowen, then. She was not sorry. She would be glad to turn her back on the rows of grim houses, the prim little chapels, and the endless quarrels between miners and management. But where would she go? And would she be able to see Fitz?

As darkness fell she lay awake looking through the window at the stars, and at last she made a plan. She would start a new life in a new place. She would wear a wedding ring and tell a story about a dead husband. She would find someone to mind the baby, get a job of some kind, and earn money. She would send her child to school. It would be a girl, she felt, and she would be clever, a writer or a doctor, or perhaps a campaigner like Mrs. Pankhurst, championing women's rights and getting arrested outside Buckingham Palace.

She had thought she would not sleep, but emotion had drained her, and she drifted off around midnight and fell into a heavy, dreamless slumber.

The rising sun woke her. She sat upright, looking forward to the new day as always; then she remembered that her old life was over, ruined, and she was in the middle of a tragedy. She almost succumbed to grief again, but fought against it. She could not afford the luxury of tears. She had to start a new life.

She got dressed and went down to the servants' hall, where she announced that she was fully recovered from yesterday's malady and fit to do her normal work.

Lady Maud sent for her before breakfast. Ethel made up a coffee tray and took it to the Pink Room. Maud was at her dressing table in a purple silk negligee. She had been crying. Ethel had troubles of her own, but all the same her sympathy quickened. "What's the matter, my lady?"

"Oh, Williams, I've had to give him up."

Ethel assumed she meant Walter von Ulrich. "But why?"

"His father came to see me. I hadn't really faced the fact that Britain and Germany are enemies, and marriage to me would ruin Walter's career—and possibly his father's, too."

"But everyone says there's not going to be a war—Serbia's not important enough."

"If not now, it will be later; and even if it never happens, the threat is enough." There was a frill of pink lace around the dressing table, and Maud was picking at it nervously, tearing the expensive lace. It was going to take hours to mend, Ethel thought. Maud went on: "No one in the German foreign ministry would trust Walter with secrets if he were married to an Englishwoman."

Ethel poured the coffee and handed Maud a cup. "Herr von Ulrich will give up his job if he really loves you."

"But I don't want him to!" Maud stopped tearing the lace and drank some coffee. "I can't be the person that ended his career. What kind of basis is that for marriage?"

He could have another career, Ethel thought; and if he really loved you, he would. Then she thought of the man *she* loved, and how quickly his passion had cooled when it became inconvenient. I'll keep my opinions to myself, she thought; I don't know a bloody thing. She asked: "What did Walter say?"

"I haven't seen him. I wrote him a letter. I stopped going to all the places where I usually meet him. Then he started to call at the house, and it became embarrassing to keep telling the servants I was not at home, so I came down here with Fitz."

"Why won't you talk to him?"

"Because I know what will happen. He will take me in his arms and kiss me, and I'll give in."

I know that feeling, Ethel thought.

Maud sighed. "You're quiet this morning, Williams. You've probably got worries of your own. Are things very hard with this strike?"

"Yes, my lady. The whole town is on short rations."

"Are you still feeding the miners' children?"

"Every day."

"Good. My brother is very generous."

"Yes, my lady." When it suits him, she thought.

"Well, you'd better get on with your work. Thank you for the coffee. I expect I'm boring you with my problems."

Impulsively, Ethel seized Maud's hand. "Please don't say that. You've always been good to me. I'm very sorry about Walter, and I hope you will always tell me your troubles."

"What a kind thing to say." Fresh tears came to Maud's eyes. "Thank you very much, Williams." She squeezed Ethel's hand, then released it.

Ethel picked up the tray and left. When she reached the kitchen, Peel, the butler, said: "Have you done something wrong?"

Little do you know, she thought. "Why do you ask?"

"His lordship wants to see you in the library at half past ten."

So it was to be a formal talk, Ethel thought. Perhaps that was better. They would be separated by a desk, and she would not be tempted to throw herself into his arms. That would help her keep back the tears. She would need to be cool and unemotional. The entire course of the rest of her life would be set by this discussion.

She went about her household duties. She was going to miss Tŷ Gwyn. In the years she had worked there she had come to love the gracious old furniture. She had picked up the names of the pieces, and learned to recognize a torchère, a buffet, an armoire, or a canterbury. As she dusted and polished she noticed the marquetry, the swags and scrolls, the feet shaped like lions' paws clasping balls. Occasionally, someone like Peel would say: "That's French—Louis Quinze," and she had realized that every room was decorated and furnished consistently in a style, baroque or neoclassical or Gothic. She would never live with such furniture again.

After an hour she made her way to the library. The books had been collected by Fitz's ancestors. Nowadays the room was not much used: Bea read only French novels, and Fitz did not read at all. Houseguests sometimes came here for peace and quiet, or to use the ivory chess set on the center table. This morning the blinds were pulled halfway down, on Ethel's instructions, to shade the room from the July sun and keep it cool. Consequently the room was gloomy.

Fitz sat in a green leather armchair. To Ethel's surprise, Albert Solman was there, too, in a black suit and a stiff-collared shirt. A lawyer by training, Solman was what Edwardian gentlemen called a man of business. He managed Fitz's money, checking his income from coal royalties and rents, paying the bills, and issuing cash for staff wages. He also dealt with leases and other contracts, and occasionally brought lawsuits against people who tried to cheat Fitz. Ethel had met him before and did not like him. She thought he was a know-all. Perhaps all lawyers were; she did not know: he was the only one she had ever met.

Fitz stood up, looking embarrassed. "I have taken Mr. Solman into my confidence," he said.

"Why?" said Ethel. She had had to promise to tell no one. Fitz's telling this lawyer seemed like a betrayal.

Fitz looked ashamed of himself—a rare sight. "Solman will tell you what I propose," he said.

"Why?" Ethel said again.

Fitz gave her a pleading look, as if to beg her not to make this any worse for him.

But she felt unsympathetic. It was not easy for her—why should it be easy for him? "What is it that you're frightened to tell me yourself?" she said, challenging him.

He had lost all his arrogant confidence. "I will leave him to explain," he said; and to her astonishment he left the room.

When the door closed behind him she stared at Solman, thinking: How can I talk about my baby's future with this stranger?

Solman smiled at her. "So, you've been naughty, have you?"

That stung her. "Did you say that to the earl?"

"Of course not!"

"Because he did the same thing, you know. It takes two people to make a baby."

"All right, there's no need to go into all that."

"Just don't speak as if I did this all on my own."

"Very well."

Ethel took a seat, then looked at him again. "You may sit down, if you wish," she said, just as if she were the lady of the house condescending to the butler.

He reddened. He did not know whether to sit, and look as if he had been waiting for permission, or remain standing, like a servant. In the end he paced up and down. "His lordship has instructed me to make you an offer," he said. Pacing did not really work, so he stopped and stood in front of her. "It is a generous offer, and I advise you to accept it."

Ethel said nothing. Fitz's callousness had one useful effect: it made her realize she was in a negotiation. This was familiar territory to her. Her father was always in negotiations, arguing and dealing with the mine management, always trying to get higher wages, shorter hours, and better safety precautions. One of his maxims was "Never speak unless you have to." So she remained silent.

Solman looked at her expectantly. When he gathered that she was not going to respond, he looked put out. He resumed: "His lordship is willing to give you a pension of twenty-four pounds a year, paid monthly in advance. I think that's very good of him. Don't you?"

The lousy rotten miser, Ethel thought. How could he be so mean to me? Twenty-four pounds was a housemaid's wage. It was half what Ethel was getting as housekeeper, and she would be losing her room and board.

Why did men think they could get away with this? Probably because they usually could. A woman had no rights. It took two people to make a baby, but only one was obliged to look after it. How had women let themselves get into such a weak position? It made her angry.

Still she did not speak.

Solman pulled up a chair and sat close to her. "Now, you must look on the bright side. You'll have ten shillings a week—"

"Not quite," she said quickly.

"Well, say we make it twenty-six pounds a year—that's ten shillings a week. What do you say?"

Ethel said nothing.

"You can find a nice little room in Cardiff for two or three shillings, and you can spend the rest on yourself." He patted her knee. "And, who knows, you may find another generous man to make life a little easier for you . . . eh? You're a very attractive girl, you know."

She pretended not to take his meaning. The idea of being the lover of a creepy lawyer such as Solman disgusted her. Did he really think he could take the place of Fitz? She did not respond to his innuendo. "Are there conditions?" she said coldly.

"Conditions?"

"Attached to the earl's offer."

Solman coughed. "The usual ones, of course."

"The usual? So you've done this before."

"Not for Earl Fitzherbert," he said quickly.

"But for someone else."

"Let us stick to the business at hand, please."

"You may go on."

"You must not put the earl's name on the child's birth certificate, or in any other way reveal to anyone that he is the father."

"And in your experience, Mr. Solman, do women usually accept these conditions of yours?"

"Yes."

Of course they do, she thought bitterly. What choice have they got? They are not entitled to anything, so they take what they can get. Of course they accept the conditions. "Are there any more?"

"After you leave Tŷ Gwyn, you must not attempt in any way to get in touch with his lordship."

So, Ethel thought, he doesn't want to see me or his child. Disappointment surged up inside her like a wave of weakness: if she had not been sitting down she might have fallen. She clenched her jaw to stop the tears. When she had herself under control, she said: "Anything else?"

"I believe that's all."

Ethel stood up.

Solman said: "You must contact me about where the monthly payments should be made." He took out a small silver box and extracted a card.

"No," she said when he offered it to her.

"But you will need to get in touch with me—"

"No, I won't," she said again.

"What do you mean?"

"The offer is not acceptable."

"Now, don't be foolish, Miss Williams—"

"I'll say it again, Mr. Solman, so there can be no doubt in your mind. The offer is not acceptable. My answer is no. I got nothing more to say to you. Good day." She went out and banged the door.

She returned to her room, locked her door, and cried her heart out.

How could Fitz be so cruel? Did he really never want to see her again? Or his baby? Did he think that everything that had happened between them could be wiped out by twenty-four pounds a year?

Did he really not love her any longer? Had he ever loved her? Was she a fool?

She had thought he loved her. She had felt sure that meant *something*. Perhaps he had been playacting all the time, and had deceived her—but she did not think so. A woman could tell when a man was faking.

So what was he doing now? He must be suppressing his feelings. Perhaps he was a man of shallow emotions. That was possible. He might have loved her, genuinely, but with a love that was easily forgotten when it became inconvenient. Such weakness of character might have escaped her notice in the throes of passion.

At least his hard-heartedness made it easier for her to bargain. She had no need to think of his feelings. She could concentrate on trying to get the best for herself and the baby. She must always think how Da would have handled things. A woman was not quite powerless, despite the law.

Fitz would be worried now, she guessed. He must have expected her to take the offer, or at worst hold out for a higher price; then he would have felt his secret was safe. Now he would be baffled as well as anxious.

She had not given Solman a chance to ask what she *did* want. Let them flounder around in the dark for a while. Fitz would begin to fear that Ethel intended to get revenge by telling Princess Bea about the baby.

She looked out of the window at the clock on the roof of the stable. It was a few minutes before twelve. On the front lawn, the staff would be getting ready to serve dinner to the miners' children. Princess Bea usually liked to see the housekeeper at about twelve. She often had complaints: she did not like the flowers in the hall, the footmen's uniforms were not pressed, the paintwork on the landing was flaking. In her turn the housekeeper had questions to ask about allocating rooms to guests, renewing china and glassware, hiring and firing maids and kitchen girls. Fitz usually came into the morning room at about half past twelve for a glass of sherry before lunch.

Then Ethel would turn the thumbscrews.

{ III }

Fitz watched the miners' children queuing up for their lunch—or "dinner," as they called it. Their faces were dirty, their hair was unkempt, and their clothes were ragged, but they looked happy. Children were amazing. These were among the poorest in the land, and their fathers were locked in a bitter dispute, but the children showed no sign of it.

Ever since marrying Bea he had longed for a child. She had miscarried once, and he was terrified she might do so again. Last time she had thrown a tantrum simply because he had canceled their trip to Russia. If she found out that he had made their housekeeper pregnant, her rage would be uncontrollable.

And the dreadful secret was in the hands of a servant girl.

He was tortured by worry. It was a terrible punishment for his sin. In other circumstances he might have taken some joy in having a child with Ethel. He could have put mother and baby into a little house in Chelsea and visited them once a week. He felt another stab of regret and longing at the poignancy of that daydream. He did not want to treat Ethel harshly. Her love had been sweet to him: her yearning kisses, her eager touch, the heat of her young passion. Even while he was telling her the bad news, he had wished he could run his hands over her lithe body and feel her kissing his neck in that hungry way that he found so exhilarating. But he had to harden his heart.

As well as being the most exciting woman he had ever kissed, she was intelligent and well-informed and funny. Her father always talked about current affairs, she had told him. And the housekeeper at Tŷ Gwyn was entitled to read the earl's newspapers after the butler had finished with them—a below-stairs rule that he had not known about. Ethel asked him unexpected questions that he could not always answer, such as "Who ruled Hungary before the Austrians?" He was going to miss that, he thought sadly.

But she would not behave the way a discarded mistress was supposed to. Solman had been shaken by his conversation with her. Fitz had asked him: "What *does* she want?" but Solman did not know. Fitz harbored a dreadful suspicion that Ethel might tell Bea the whole story, just out of some twisted moral desire to let the truth come out. God help me keep her away from my wife, he prayed.

He was surprised to see the small round form of Perceval Jones, strutting across the lawn in green plus fours and walking boots. "Good morning, my lord," said the mayor, doffing his brown felt hat.

"Morning, Jones." As chairman of Celtic Minerals, Jones was the source of a great deal of Fitz's wealth, but all the same he did not like the man.

"The news is not good," Jones said.

"You mean from Vienna? I understand the Austrian emperor is still working on the wording of his ultimatum to Serbia."

"No, I mean from Ireland. The Ulstermen won't accept home rule, you know. It will make them a minority under a Roman Catholic government. The army is already mutinous."

Fitz frowned. He did not like to hear talk of mutiny in the British army. He said stiffly: "No matter what the newspapers may say, I don't believe that British officers will disobey the orders of their sovereign government."

"They already have!" said Jones. "What about the Curragh Mutiny?"

"No one disobeyed orders."

"Fifty-seven officers resigned when ordered to march on the Ulster Volunteers. You may not call that mutiny, my lord, but everyone else does."

Fitz grunted. Jones was unfortunately right. The truth

was that English officers would not attack their fellow men in the defense of a mob of Irish Catholics. "Ireland should never have been promised independence," he said.

"I agree with you there," said Jones. "But I really came to talk to you about this." He indicated the children, seated on benches at trestle tables, eating boiled cod with cabbage. "I wish you'd put an end to it."

Fitz did not like to be told what to do by his social inferiors. "I don't care to let the children of Aberowen starve, even if it's the fault of their fathers."

"You're just prolonging the strike."

The fact that Fitz received a royalty on every ton of coal did not mean, in his view, that he was obliged to take the side of the mine owners against the men. Offended, he said: "The strike is your concern, not mine."

"You take the money quick enough."

Fitz was outraged. "I have no more to say to you." He turned away.

Jones was instantly contrite. "I beg your pardon, my lord, do forgive me—an overhasty remark, most ill-judged, but the matter is extremely tiresome."

It was hard for Fitz to refuse an apology. He was not mollified, but all the same he turned back and spoke to Jones courteously. "All right, but I shall continue to give the children dinner."

"You see, my lord, a coal miner may be stubborn on his own account, and suffer a good deal of hardship through foolish pride; but what breaks him, in the end, is to see his children go hungry."

"You're working the pit anyway."

"With third-rate foreign labor. Most of the men are not trained miners, and their output is small. Mainly we're using them to maintain the tunnels and keep the horses alive. We're not bringing up much coal."

"For the life of me I can't think why you evicted those wretched widows from their homes. There were only eight of them, and after all, they had lost their husbands in the damn pit."

"It's a dangerous principle. The house goes with the collier. Once we depart from that, we'll end up as nothing better than slum landlords."

Perhaps you should not have built slums, then, Fitz

thought, but he held his tongue. He did not want to prolong the conversation with this pompous little tyrant. He looked at his watch. It was half past twelve: time for a glass of sherry. "It's no good, Jones," he said. "I shan't fight your battles for you. Good day." He walked briskly to the house.

Jones was the least of his worries. What was he going to do about Ethel? He had to make sure Bea was not upset. Apart from the danger to the unborn baby, he felt the pregnancy might be a new start for their marriage. The child might bring them together and re-create the warmth and intimacy they had had when they were first together. But that hope would be dashed if Bea learned he had been dallying with the housekeeper. She would be incandescent.

He was grateful for the cool of the hall, with its flagstones underfoot and hammer-beam ceiling. His father had chosen this feudal decor. The only book Papa had ever read, apart from the Bible, was Gibbon's *Decline and Fall of the Roman Empire*. He believed that the even greater British Empire would go the same way unless noblemen fought to preserve its institutions, especially the Royal Navy, the Church of England, and the Conservative Party.

He was right, Fitz had no doubt.

A glass of dry sherry was just the thing before lunch. It perked him up and sharpened his appetite. With a pleasant feeling of anticipation, he entered the morning room. There he was horrified to see Ethel talking to Bea. He stopped in the doorway and stared in consternation. What was she saying? Was he too late? "What's going on here?" he said sharply.

Bea looked at him in surprise and said coolly: "I am discussing pillowcases with my housekeeper. Did you expect something more dramatic?" Her Russian accent rolled the letter *r* in "dramatic."

For a moment he did not know what to say. He realized he was staring at his wife and his mistress. The thought of how intimate he had been with both these women was unsettling. "I don't know, I'm sure," he muttered, and he sat down at a writing desk with his back to them.

The two women carried on with their conversation. It was indeed about pillowcases: how long they lasted, how worn ones could be patched and used by servants, and whether it was best to buy them embroidered or get plain ones and have the housemaids do the embroidery. But Fitz was still shaken. The little tableau, mistress and servant in quiet conversation, reminded him of how terrifyingly easy it would be for Ethel to tell Bea the truth. This could not go on. He had to take action.

He took a sheet of blue crested writing paper from the drawer, dipped a pen in the inkwell, and wrote: "Meet me after lunch." He blotted the note and slipped it into a matching envelope.

After a couple of minutes, Bea dismissed Ethel. As she was leaving, Fitz spoke without turning his head. "Come here, please, Williams."

She came to his side. He noticed the light fragrance of scented soap—she had admitted stealing it from Bea. Despite his anger, he was uncomfortably aware of the closeness of her slim, strong thighs under the black silk of the housekeeper's dress. Without looking at her he handed her the envelope. "Send someone to the veterinary surgery in town to get a bottle of these dog pills. They're for kennel cough."

"Very good, my lord." She went out.

He would resolve the situation in a couple of hours' time.

He poured his sherry. He offered a glass to Bea but she declined. The wine warmed his stomach and eased his tension. He sat next to his wife, and she gave him a friendly smile. "How do you feel?" he said.

"Revolting, in the mornings," she said. "But that passes. I'm fine now."

His thoughts quickly returned to Ethel. She had him over a barrel. She had said nothing, but implicitly she was threatening to tell Bea everything. It was surprisingly crafty of her. He fretted impotently. He would have liked to settle the matter even sooner than this afternoon.

They had lunch in the small dining room, sitting at a square-legged oak table that might have come from a medieval monastery. Bea told him she had discovered there were some Russians in Aberowen. "More than a hundred, Nina tells me."

With an effort, Fitz put Ethel from his mind. "They will be among the strikebreakers brought in by Perceval Jones."

"Apparently they are being ostracized. They can't get service in the shops and cafés."

"I must get Reverend Jenkins to preach a sermon on loving your neighbor, even if he is a strikebreaker."

"Can't you just order the shopkeepers to serve them?"

Fitz smiled. "No, my dear, not in this country."

"Well, I feel sorry for them and I would like to do something for them."

He was pleased. "That's a kindly impulse. What do you have in mind?"

"I believe there is a Russian Orthodox church in Cardiff. I will get a priest up here to perform a service for them one Sunday."

Fitz frowned. Bea had converted to the Church of England when they married, but he knew that she hankered for the church of her childhood, and he saw it as a sign that she was unhappy in her adopted country. But he did not want to cross her. "Very well," he said.

"Then we could give them dinner in the servants' hall."

"It's a nice thought, my dear, but they might be a rough crowd."

"We'll feed only those who come to the service. That way we will exclude the Jews and the worst of the troublemakers."

"Shrewd. Of course, the townspeople may not like you for it."

"But that is of no concern to me or you."

He nodded. "Very well. Jones has been complaining that I am supporting the strike by feeding the children. If you entertain the strikebreakers, at least no one can say that we're taking sides."

"Thank you," she said.

The pregnancy had already improved their relationship, Fitz thought.

He had two glasses of hock with his lunch, but his anxiety came back when he left the dining room and made his way to the Gardenia Suite. Ethel held his fate in her hands. She had all of a woman's soft, emotional nature, but nevertheless she would not be told what to do. He could not control her, and that scared him.

But she was not there. He looked at his watch. It was a quarter past two. He had said "after lunch." Ethel would have known when coffee had been served and she should have been waiting for him. He had not specified the location, but surely she could work that out.

He began to feel apprehensive.

After five minutes he was tempted to leave. No one kept him waiting like this. But he did not want to leave the issue unresolved for another day, or even another hour, so he stayed.

She came in at half past two.

He said angrily: "What are you trying to do to me?"

She ignored the question. "What the hell were you thinking of, to make me talk to a lawyer from London?"

"I thought it would be less emotional."

"Don't be bloody daft." Fitz was shocked. No one had talked to him like this since he was a schoolboy. She went on: "I'm having your baby. How can it be unemotional?"

She was right: he had been foolish, and her words stung, but at the same time he could not help loving the music of her accent—the word "unemotional" having a different note for each of its five syllables, so that it sounded like a melody. "I'm sorry," he said. "I'll pay you double—"

"Don't make it worse, Teddy," she said, but her tone was softer. "Don't bargain with me, as if this was a matter of the right price."

He pointed an accusing finger. "You are not to speak to my wife, do you hear me? I won't have it!"

"Don't give me orders, Teddy. I've got no reason to obey you."

"How dare you speak to me like that?"

"Shut up and listen, and I'll tell you."

He was infuriated by her tone, but he remembered that he could not afford to antagonize her. "Go on, then," he said.

"You've behaved to me in a very unloving way."

He knew that was true, and he felt a stab of guilt. He was wretchedly sorry to have hurt her. But he tried not to show it.

She went on: "I still love you too much to want to spoil your happiness."

He felt even worse.

"I don't want to hurt you," she said. She swallowed and turned away, and he saw tears in her eyes. He began to speak, but she held up her hand to silence him. "You are asking me to leave my job and my home, so you must help me start a new life."

"Of course," he said. "If that's what you wish." Talking in more practical terms helped them both suppress their feelings.

"I'm going to London."

"Good idea." He could not help being pleased: no one in Aberowen would know she had a baby, let alone whose it was.

"You're going to buy me a little house. Nothing fancy—a working-class neighborhood will suit me very well. But I want six rooms, so that I can live on the ground floor and take in a lodger. The rent will pay for repairs and maintenance. I will still have to work."

"You've thought about this carefully."

"You're wondering how much it will cost, I expect, but you don't want to ask me, because a gentleman doesn't like to ask the price of things."

It was true.

"I looked in the newspaper," she said. "A house like that is about three hundred pounds. Probably cheaper than paying me two pounds a month for the rest of my life."

Three hundred pounds was nothing to Fitz. Bea could spend that much on clothes in one afternoon at the Maison Paquin in Paris. He said: "But you would promise to keep the secret?"

"And I promise to love and care for your child, and raise her—or him—to be happy and healthy and well-educated, even though you don't show any sign of being concerned about that."

He felt indignant, but she was right. He had hardly given a thought to the child. "I'm sorry," he said. "I'm too worried about Bea."

"I know," she said, her tone softening as it always did when he allowed his anxiety to show.

"When will you leave?"

"Tomorrow morning. I'm in just as much of a hurry as you. I'll get the train to London, and start looking for a house right away. When I've found the right place, I'll write to Solman."

"You'll have to stay in lodgings while you look for a house." He took his wallet from the inside pocket of his jacket and handed her two white five-pound notes.

She smiled. "You have no idea how much things cost, do

you, Teddy?" She gave back one of the notes. "Five pounds is plenty."

He looked offended. "I don't want you to feel that I'm short-changing you."

Her manner changed, and he caught a glimpse of underlying rage. "Oh, you are, Teddy, you are," she said sourly. "But not in money."

"We both did it," he said defensively, glancing at the bed.

"But only one of us is going to have a baby."

"Well, let's not argue. I'll tell Solman to do what you have suggested."

She held out her hand. "Good-bye, Teddy. I know you'll keep your word." Her voice was even, but he could tell that she was struggling to maintain her composure.

He shook hands, even though it seemed odd for two people who had made passionate love. "I will," he said.

"Please leave now, quickly," she said, and she turned aside.

He hesitated a moment longer, then left the room.

As he walked away, he was surprised and ashamed to feel unmanly tears come to his eyes. "Good-bye, Ethel," he whispered to the empty corridor. "May God bless and keep you."

{ IV }

She went to the luggage store in the attic and stole a small suitcase, old and battered. No one would ever miss it. It had belonged to Fitz's father, and had his crest stamped in the leather: the gilding had worn off long ago, but the impression could still be made out. She packed stockings and underwear and some of the princess's scented soap.

Lying in bed that night, she decided she did not want to go to London after all. She was too frightened to go through this alone. She wanted to be with her family. She needed to ask her mother questions about pregnancy. She should be in a familiar place when the baby came. Her child would need its grandparents and its uncle Billy.

In the morning she put on her own clothing, left her housekeeper's dress hanging from its nail, and crept out of Tŷ Gwyn early. At the end of the drive she looked back at the house, its stones black with coal dust, its long rows of windows reflecting the rising sun, and she thought how much she had learned since she first came here to work as a thirteen-year-old fresh from school. Now she knew how the elite lived. They had strange food, prepared in complicated ways, and they wasted more than they ate. They all spoke with the same strangled accent, even some of the foreigners. She had handled rich women's beautiful underwear, fine cotton and slippery silk, hand-sewn and embroidered and trimmed with lace, twelve of everything piled in their chests of drawers. She could look at a sideboard and tell at a glance in what century it had been made. Most of all, she thought bitterly, she had learned that love is not to be trusted.

She walked down the mountainside into Aberowen and made her way to Wellington Row. The door of her parents' house was unlocked, as always. She went inside. The main room, the kitchen, was smaller than the Vase Room at Tŷ Gwyn, used only for arranging flowers.

Mam was kneading dough for bread, but when she saw the suitcase she stopped and said: "What's gone wrong?"

"I've come home," Ethel said. She put down the case and sat at the square kitchen table. She felt too ashamed to say what had happened.

However, Mam guessed. "You've been sacked!"

Ethel could not look at her mother. "Aye. I'm sorry, Mam."

Mam wiped her hands on a rag. "What have you done?" she said angrily. "Out with it, now!"

Ethel sighed. Why was she holding back? "I fell for a baby," she said.

"Oh, no—you wicked girl!"

Ethel fought back tears. She had hoped for sympathy, not condemnation. "I am a wicked girl," she said. She took off her hat, trying to keep her composure.

"It have all gone to your head—working at the big house, and meeting the king and queen. It have made you forget how you were raised."

"I expect you're right."

"It will kill your father."

"He doesn't have to give birth," Ethel said sarcastically. "I expect he'll be all right."

"Don't be cheeky. It's going to break his heart."

"Where is he?"

"Gone to another strike meeting. Think of his position in the town: elder of the chapel, miners' agent, secretary of the Independent Labour Party—how will he hold up his head at meetings, with everyone thinking his daughter's a slut?"

Ethel's control failed. "I'm very sorry to cause him shame," she said, and she began to cry.

Mam's expression changed. "Oh, well," she said. "It's the oldest story in the world." She came around the table and pressed Ethel's head to her breast. "Never mind, never mind," she said, just as she had when Ethel was a child and grazed her knees.

After a while, Ethel's sobs eased.

Mam released her and said: "We'd better have a cup of tea." There was a kettle kept permanently on the hob. She put tea leaves into a pot and poured boiling water in, then stirred the mixture with a wooden spoon. "When's the baby due?"

"February."

"Oh, my goodness." Mam turned from the fire to look at Ethel. "I'm going to be a grandmother!"

They both laughed. Mam set out cups and poured the tea. Ethel drank some and felt better. "Did you have easy births, or difficult?" she asked.

"There are no easy births, but mine were better than most, my mother said. I've had a bad back ever since Billy, all the same."

Billy came downstairs, saying: "Who's talking about me?" He could sleep late, Ethel realized, because he was on strike. Every time she saw him he seemed taller and broader. "Hello, Eth," he said, and kissed her with a bristly mustache. "Why the suitcase?" He sat down, and Mam poured him tea.

"I've done something stupid, Billy," said Ethel. "I'm having a baby."

He stared at her, too shocked to speak. Then he blushed, no doubt thinking of what she had done to get pregnant. He looked down, embarrassed. Then he drank some tea. At last he said: "Who's the father?"

"No one you know." She had thought about this and

worked out a story of sorts. "He was a valet who came to Tŷ Gwyn with one of the guests, but he's gone in the army now."

"But he'll stand by you."

"I don't even know where he is."

"I'll find the beggar."

Ethel put a hand on his arm. "Don't get angry, my lovely. If I need your help, I'll ask for it."

Billy evidently did not know what to say. Threatening revenge was clearly no good, but he had no other response. He looked bewildered. He was still only sixteen.

Ethel remembered him as a baby. She had been only five years old when he arrived, but she had been completely fascinated by him, his perfection and his vulnerability. Soon I'll have a beautiful, helpless infant, she thought; and she did not know whether to feel happy or terrified.

Billy said: "Da's going to have something to say about it, I expect."

"That's what I'm worried about," said Ethel. "I wish there was something I could do to make it right for him."

Gramper came down. "Sacked, is it?" he said when he saw the suitcase. "Too cheeky, were you?"

Mam said: "Don't be cruel, now, Papa. She's expecting a baby."

"Oh, jowch," he said. "One of the toffs up there at the big house, was it? The earl himself, I wouldn't be surprised."

"Don't talk daft, Gramper," said Ethel, dismayed that he had guessed the truth so quickly.

Billy said: "It was a valet who came with a houseguest. Gone in the army now, he is. She doesn't want us to go after him."

"Oh, aye?" said Gramper. Ethel could tell he was not convinced, but he did not persist. Instead he said: "It's the Italian in you, my girl. Your grandmother was hot-blooded. She would have got into trouble if I hadn't married her. As it was she didn't want to wait for the wedding. In fact—"

Mam interrupted: "Papa! Not in front of the children."

"What's going to shock them, after this?" he said. "I'm too old for fairy tales. Young women want to lie with young men, and they want it so badly they'll do it, married or not. Anyone who pretends otherwise is a fool—and that includes your husband, Cara, my girl."

"You be careful what you say," Mam said.

"Aye, all right," said Gramper, and he subsided into silence and drank his tea.

A minute later Da came in. Mam looked at him in surprise. "You're back early!" she said.

He heard the displeasure in her voice. "You make it sound as if I'm not welcome."

She got up from the table, making a space for him. "I'll brew a fresh pot of tea."

Da did not sit down. "The meeting was canceled." His eye fell on Ethel's suitcase. "What's this?"

They all looked at Ethel. She saw fear on Mam's face, defiance on Billy's, and a kind of resignation on Gramper's. It was up to her to answer the question. "I've got something to tell you, Da," she said. "You're going to be cross about it, and all I can say is that I'm sorry."

His face darkened. "What have you done?"

"I've left my job at Tŷ Gwyn."

"That's nothing to be sorry for. I never liked you bowing and scraping to those parasites."

"I left for a reason."

He moved closer and stood over her. "Good or bad?"

"I'm in trouble."

He looked thunderous. "I hope you don't mean what girls sometimes mean when they say that."

She stared down at the table and nodded.

"Have you—" He paused, searching for appropriate words. "Have you been overtaken in moral transgression?"

"Aye."

"You wicked girl!"

It was what Mam had said. Ethel cringed away from him, although she did not really expect him to strike her.

"Look at me!" he said.

She looked up at him through a blur of tears.

"So you are telling me you have committed the sin of fornication."

"I'm sorry, Da."

"Who with?" he shouted.

"A valet."

"What's his name?"

"Teddy." It came out before she could think.

"Teddy what?"

"It doesn't matter."

"Doesn't matter? What on earth do you mean?"

"He came to the house on a visit with his master. By the time I found out my condition, he'd gone in the army. I've lost touch with him."

"On a visit? Lost touch?" Da's voice rose to an enraged roar. "You mean you're not even engaged to him? You committed this sin . . ." He spluttered, hardly able to get the disgusting words out. "You committed this foul sin *casually*?"

Mam said: "Don't get angry, now, Da."

"Don't get angry? When else should a man get angry?"

Gramper tried to calm him. "Take it easy, now, Dai boy. It does no good to shout."

"I'm sorry to have to remind you, Gramper, that this is my house, and I will be the judge of what does no good."

"Aye, all right," said Gramper pacifically. "Have it your way."

Mam was not ready to give in. "Don't say anything you might regret, now, Da."

These attempts to calm Da's wrath were only making him angrier. "I will not be ruled by women or old men!" he shouted. He pointed his finger at Ethel. "And I will not have a fornicator in my house! Get out!"

Mam began to cry. "No, please don't say that!"

"Out!" he shouted. "And never come back!"

Mam said: "But your grandchild!"

Billy spoke. "Will you be ruled by the Word of God, Da? Jesus said: 'I came not to call the righteous, but sinners to repentance.' Gospel of Luke, chapter five, verse thirty-two."

Da rounded on him. "Let me tell you something, you ignorant boy. My grandparents were never married. No one knows who my grandfather was. My grandmother sank as low as a woman can go."

Mam gasped. Ethel was shocked, and she could see that Billy was flabbergasted. Gramper seemed as if he already knew.

"Oh, yes," Da said, lowering his voice. "My father was brought up in a house of ill fame, if you know what that is; a place where sailors went, down the docks in Cardiff. Then one day, when his mother was in a drunken stupor, God led his childish footsteps into a chapel Sunday school, where he met Jesus. In the same place he learned to read and write and, eventually, to bring up his own children in the paths of righteousness."

Mam said softly: "You never told me this, David." She seldom called him by his Christian name.

"I hoped never to think of it again." Da's face was twisted into a mask of shame and rage. He leaned on the table and stared Ethel in the eye, and his voice sank to a whisper. "When I courted your mother, we held hands, and I kissed her cheek every evening until the wedding day." He banged his fist on the table, making the cups shake. "By the grace of our Lord Jesus Christ, my family dragged itself up out of the stinking gutter." His voice rose again to a shout. "We are not going back there! Never! Never! Never!"

There was a long moment of stunned silence.

Da looked at Mam. "Get Ethel out of here," he said.

Ethel stood up. "My case is packed and I've got some money. I'll get the train to London." She looked hard at her father. "I won't drag the family into the gutter."

Billy picked up her suitcase.

Da said: "Where are you going to, boy?"

"I'll walk her to the station," Billy said, looking frightened.

"Let her carry her own case."

Billy stooped to put it down, then changed his mind. An obstinate look came over his face. "I'll walk her to the station," he repeated.

"You'll do what you're told!" Da shouted.

Billy still looked scared, but now he was defiant, too. "What are you going to do, Da—throw me out of the house and all?"

"I'll put you across my knee and thrash you," Da said. "You're not too old."

Billy was white-faced, but he looked Da in the eye. "Yes, I am," he said. "I am too old." He shifted the case to his left hand and clenched his right fist.

Da took a step forward. "I'll teach you to make a fist at me, boy."

"No!" Mam screamed. She stood between them and pushed at Da's chest. "That's enough! I will not have a fight in my kitchen." She pointed her finger at Da's face. "David Williams, you keep your hands to yourself. Remember that you're an elder of Bethesda Chapel. What would people think?"

That calmed him.

Mam turned to Ethel. "You'd better go. Billy will go with you. Quick, now."

Da sat down at the table.

Ethel kissed her mother. "Good-bye, Mam."

"Write me a letter," Mam said.

Da said: "Don't you dare write to anyone in this house! The letters will be burned unopened!"

Mam turned away, weeping. Ethel went out and Billy followed.

They walked down the steep streets to the town center. Ethel kept her eyes on the ground, not wanting to speak to people she knew and be asked where she was off to.

At the station she bought a ticket to Paddington.

"Well," said Billy, as they stood on the platform, "two shocks in one day. First you, then Da."

"He have kept that bottled up inside him all these years," Ethel said. "No wonder he's so strict. I can almost forgive him for throwing me out."

"I can't," said Billy. "Our faith is about redemption and mercy, not about bottling things up and punishing people."

A train from Cardiff came in, and Ethel saw Walter von Ulrich get off. He touched his hat to her, which was nice of him: gentlemen did not do that to servants, normally. Lady Maud had said she had thrown him over. Perhaps he had come to win her back. She silently wished him luck.

"Do you want me to buy you a newspaper?" Billy said.

"No, thank you, my lovely," she said. "I don't think I could concentrate on it."

Waiting for her train she said: "Do you remember our code?" In childhood they had devised a simple way to write notes that their parents could not understand.

For a moment Billy looked puzzled; then his face cleared. "Oh, aye."

"I'll write to you in code, so Da can't read it."

"Right," he said. "And send the letter via Tommy Griffiths."

The train puffed into the station in clouds of steam. Billy hugged Ethel. She could see he was trying not to cry.

"Look after yourself," she said. "And take care of our mam."

"Aye," he said, and wiped his eyes with his sleeve. "We'll be all right. You be careful up there in London, now."

"I will."

Ethel boarded the train and sat by the window. A minute later it pulled out. As it picked up speed, she watched the pithead winding gear recede into the distance, and wondered if she would ever see Aberowen again.

{ V }

Maud had breakfast late with Princess Bea in the small dining room at Tŷ Gwyn. The princess was in high spirits. Normally she complained a lot about living in Britain—although Maud recalled, from her time as a child in the British embassy, that life in Russia was much more uncomfortable: the houses cold, the people surly, services unreliable, and government disorganized. But Bea had no complaints today. She was happy that she had at last conceived.

She even spoke generously of Fitz. "He saved my family, you know," she said to Maud. "He paid off the mortgages on our estate. But until now there has been no one to inherit it—my brother has no children. It would seem such a tragedy if all Andrei's land and Fitz's went to some distant cousin."

Maud could not see this as a tragedy. The distant cousin in question might well be a son of hers. But she had never expected to inherit a fortune and she gave little thought to such things.

Maud was not good company this morning, she realized as she drank coffee and toyed with toast. In fact she was miserable. She felt oppressed by the wallpaper, a Victorian riot of foliage that covered the ceiling as well as the walls, even though she had lived with it all her life.

She had not told her family about her romance with Walter, so now she could not tell them that it was over, and that meant she had no one to sympathize with her. Only the sparky little housekeeper, Williams, knew the story, and she seemed to have disappeared.

Maud read *The Times*'s report of Lloyd George's speech last night at the Mansion House dinner. He had been optimistic about the Balkan crisis, saying it could be resolved peacefully. She hoped he was right. Even though she had given Walter up, she was still horrified by the thought that he might have to put on a uniform and be killed or maimed in a war.

She read a short report in *The Times* datelined Vienna and headed THE SERVIAN SCARE. She asked Bea if Russia would defend Serbia against the Austrians. "I hope not!" Bea said, alarmed. "I don't want my brother to go to war."

Maud could remember having breakfast here in the small dining room with Fitz and Walter in the school holidays, when she was twelve and they were seventeen. The boys had had enormous appetites, she recalled, consuming eggs and sausages and great piles of buttered toast every morning before going off to ride horses or swim in the lake. Walter had been such a glamorous figure, handsome and foreign. He had treated her as courteously as if she were his age, which was flattering to a young girl—and, she could now see, a subtle way of flirting.

While she was reminiscing, the butler, Peel, came in and shocked her by saying to Bea: "Herr von Ulrich is here, Your Highness."

Walter could not possibly be here, Maud thought bewilderedly. Could it be Robert? Equally unlikely.

A moment later, Walter walked in.

Maud was too stupefied to speak. Bea said: "What a pleasant surprise, Herr von Ulrich."

Walter was wearing a lightweight summer suit of pale blue-gray tweed. His blue satin tie was the same color as his eyes. Maud wished she had put on something other than the plain cream-colored peg-top dress that had seemed perfectly adequate for breakfast with her sister-in-law.

"Forgive this intrusion, Princess," Walter said to Bea. "I had to visit our consulate in Cardiff—a tiresome business about German sailors who got into trouble with the local police."

That was rubbish. Walter was a military attaché: his job did not involve getting sailors out of jail.

"Good morning, Lady Maud," he said, shaking her hand. "What a delightful surprise to find you here."

More rubbish, she thought. He was here to see her. She had left London so that he could not badger her, but deep in her heart she could not help being pleased by his persistence in following her all this way. Flustered, she just said: "Hello, how are you?"

Bea said: "Do have some coffee, Herr von Ulrich. The earl is out riding, but he'll be back soon." She naturally assumed Walter was there to see Fitz.

"How kind you are." Walter sat down.

"Will you stay for lunch?"

"I would love to. Then I must catch a train back to London."

Bea stood up. "I should speak to the cook."

Walter jumped to his feet and pulled out her chair.

"Talk to Lady Maud," Bea said as she left the room. "Cheer her up. She's worried about the international situation."

Walter raised his eyebrows at the note of mockery in Bea's voice. "All sensible people are worried about the international situation," he said.

Maud felt awkward. Desperate for something to say, she pointed to *The Times*. "Do you think it's true that Serbia has called up seventy thousand reservists?"

"I doubt if they have seventy thousand reservists," Walter said gravely. "But they are trying to raise the stakes. They hope that the danger of a wider war will make Austria cautious."

"Why is it taking the Austrians so long to send their demands to the Serbian government?"

"Officially, they want to get the harvest in before doing anything which might require them to call men to the army. Unofficially, they know that the president of France and his foreign minister happen to be in Russia, which makes it dangerously easy for the two allies to agree on a concerted response. There will be no Austrian note until President Poincaré leaves St. Petersburg."

He was such a clear thinker, Maud reflected. She loved that about him.

His reserve failed him suddenly. His mask of formal courtesy fell away, and his face looked anguished. Abruptly, he said: "Please come back to me."

She opened her mouth to speak, but her throat seemed choked with emotion, and no words came out.

He said miserably: "I know you threw me over for my own sake, but it won't work. I love you too much."

Maud found words. "But your father . . ."

"He must work out his own destiny. I cannot obey him, not in this." His voice sank to a whisper. "I cannot bear to lose you."

"He might be right: perhaps a German diplomat can't have an English wife, at least not now."

"Then I'll follow another career. But I could never find another you."

Her resolve melted and her eyes flooded.

He reached across the table and took her hand. "May I speak to your brother?"

She bunched up her white linen napkin and blotted her tears. "Don't talk to Fitz yet," she said. "Wait a few days, until the Serbian crisis blows over."

"That may take more than a few days."

"In that case, we'll think again."

"I shall do as you wish, of course."

"I love you, Walter. Whatever happens, I want to be your wife."

He kissed her hand. "Thank you," he said solemnly. "You have made me very happy."

{ VI }

A strained silence descended on the house in Wellington Row. Mam made dinner, and Da and Billy and Gramper ate it, but no one said much. Billy was eaten up with a rage he could not express. In the afternoon he climbed the mountainside and walked for miles on his own.

Next morning he found his mind returning again and again to the story of Jesus and the woman taken in adultery. Sitting in the kitchen in his Sunday clothes, waiting to go with his parents and Gramper to the Bethesda Chapel for the service of the breaking of bread, he opened his Bible at the Gospel According to John and found chapter 8. He read the story over and over. It seemed to be about exactly the kind of crisis that had struck his family.

He continued to think of it in chapel. He looked around the room at his friends and neighbors: Mrs. Dai Ponies, John Jones the Shop, Mrs. Ponti and her two big sons, Suet Hewitt . . . They all knew that Ethel had left Tŷ Gwyn yesterday and bought a train ticket to Paddington; and although they did not know why, they could guess. In their minds, they were already judging her. But Jesus was not.

During the hymns and extempore prayers, he decided that the Holy Spirit was leading him to read those verses out. Toward the end of the hour he stood up and opened his Bible.

There was a little murmur of surprise. He was a bit young to be leading the congregation. Still, there was no age limit: the Holy Spirit could move anyone.

"A few verses from John's Gospel," he said. There was a slight shake in his voice, and he tried to steady it.

"'They say unto him: Master, this woman was taken in adultery, in the very act.'"

Bethesda Chapel went suddenly quiet: no one fidgeted, whispered, or coughed.

Billy read on: "'Now Moses in the Law commanded us that such should be stoned, but what sayest thou? This they said, tempting him, that they might have to accuse him. But Jesus stooped down, and with his finger wrote on the ground, as if he heard them not. So when they continued asking him, he lifted himself up, and said unto them'—"

Here Billy paused and looked up.

With careful emphasis he said: "'He that is without sin among you, let him first cast a stone at her.'"

Every face in the room stared back at him. No one moved.

Billy resumed: "'And again he stooped down, and wrote on the ground. And they which heard it, being convicted by their own conscience, went out one by one, beginning at the eldest, even unto the last: and Jesus was left alone, and the woman standing in the midst. When Jesus had lifted himself, and saw none but the woman, he said unto her: Woman, where are those thine accusers? Hath no man condemned thee? She said: No man, Lord.'"

Billy looked up from the book. He did not need to read the last verse: he knew it by heart. He looked at his father's stony face and spoke very slowly. "'And Jesus said unto her: Neither do I condemn thee. Go, and sin no more.'"

After a long moment he closed the Bible with a clap that sounded like thunder in the silence. "This is the Word of God," he said.

He did not sit down. Instead he walked to the exit. The congregation stared, rapt. He opened the big wooden door and walked out.

He never went back.

CHAPTER NINE

Late July 1914

Walter von Ulrich could not play ragtime. He could play the tunes, which were simple. He could play the distinctive chords, which often used the interval of the flatted seventh. And he could play both together—but it did not sound like ragtime. The rhythm eluded him. His effort was more like something you might hear from a band in a Berlin park. For one who could play Beethoven sonatas effortlessly, this was frustrating.

Maud had tried to teach him, that Saturday morning at Tŷ Gwyn, at the upright Bechstein among the potted palms in the small drawing room, with the summer sun coming through the tall windows. They had sat hip to hip on the piano stool, their arms interlaced, and Maud had laughed at his efforts. It had been a moment of golden happiness.

His mood had darkened when she explained how his father had talked her into breaking with Walter. If he had seen his father on the evening when he returned to London, there would have been an explosion. But Otto had left for Vienna, and Walter had had to swallow his rage. He had not seen his father since.

He had agreed to Maud's proposal that they should keep their engagement secret until the Balkan crisis was over. It was still going on, though things had calmed down. Almost four weeks had passed since the assassination in Sarajevo, but the Austrian emperor still had not sent to the Serbians the note he had been mulling so long. The delay encouraged Walter to hope that tempers had cooled and moderate counsels had prevailed in Vienna.

Sitting at the baby grand piano in the compact drawing room of his bachelor flat in Piccadilly, he reflected that there was much the Austrians could do, short of war, to punish Serbia and soothe their wounded pride. For example, they could force the Serbian government to close anti-Austrian newspapers, and purge nationalists from the Serbian army and civil service. The Serbians could submit to that: it would be humiliating, but better than a war they could not win.

Then the leaders of the great European countries could relax and concentrate on their domestic problems. The Russians could crush their general strike, the English could pacify the mutinous Irish Protestants, and the French could enjoy the murder trial of Madame Caillaux, who had shot the editor of *Le Figaro* for printing her husband's love letters.

And Walter could marry Maud.

That was his focus now. The more he thought about the difficulties, the more determined he became to overcome them. Having looked, for a few days, at the joyless prospect of life without her, he was even more sure that he wanted to marry her, regardless of the price they might both have to pay. As he avidly followed the diplomatic game being played on the chessboard of Europe, he scrutinized every move to assess its effect first on him and Maud, and only second on Germany and the world.

He was going to see her tonight, at dinner and at the Duchess of Sussex's ball. He was already dressed in white tie and tails. It was time to leave. But as he closed the lid of the piano, the doorbell rang, and his manservant announced Count Robert von Ulrich.

Robert looked surly. It was a familiar expression. Robert had been a troubled and unhappy young man when they were students together in Vienna. His feelings drew him irresistibly toward a group whom he had been brought up to regard as decadent. Then, when he came home after an evening with men like himself, he wore that look, guilty but defiant. In time he had discovered that homosexuality, like adultery, was officially condemned but—in sophisticated circles, at least—unofficially tolerated; and he had become reconciled to who he was. Today he wore that face for some other reason.

"I've just seen the text of the emperor's note," Robert said immediately.

Walter's heart leaped in hope. This might be the peaceful resolution he was waiting for. "What does it say?"

Robert handed him a sheet of paper. "I copied out the main part."

"Has it been delivered to the Serbian government?"

"Yes, at six o'clock Belgrade time."

There were ten demands. The first three followed the lines Walter had anticipated, he saw with relief: Serbia had to suppress liberal newspapers, break up the secret society called the Black Hand, and clamp down on nationalist propaganda. Perhaps the moderates in Vienna had won the argument after all, he thought gratefully.

Point four seemed reasonable at first—the Austrians demanded a purge of nationalists in the Serbian civil service—but there was a sting in the tail: the Austrians would supply the names. "That seems a bit strong," Walter said anxiously. "The Serbian government can't just sack everyone the Austrians tell them to."

Robert shrugged. "They will have to."

"I suppose so." For the sake of peace, Walter hoped they would.

But there was worse to come.

Point five demanded that Austria assist the Serbian government in crushing subversion, and point six, Walter read with dismay, insisted that Austrian officials take part in Serbia's judicial inquiry into the assassination. "But Serbia can't agree to this!" Walter protested. "It would amount to giving up their sovereignty."

Robert's face darkened further. "Hardly," he said peevishly.

"No country in the world could agree to it."

"Serbia will. It must, or be destroyed."

"In a war?"

"If necessary."

"Which could engulf all of Europe!"

Robert wagged his finger. "Not if other governments are sensible."

Unlike yours, Walter thought, but he bit back the retort

and read on. The remaining points were arrogantly expressed, but the Serbs could probably live with them: arrest of conspirators, prevention of smuggling of weapons into Austrian territory, and a clampdown on anti-Austrian pronouncements by Serbian officials.

But there was a forty-eight-hour deadline for reply.

"My God, this is harsh," said Walter.

"People who defy the Austrian emperor must expect harshness."

"I know, I know, but he hasn't even given them room to save face."

"Why should he?"

Walter let his exasperation show. "For goodness' sake, does he *want* war?"

"The emperor's family, the Habsburg dynasty, has governed vast areas of Europe for hundreds of years. Emperor Franz Joseph knows that God intends him to rule over inferior Slavic peoples. This is his destiny."

"God spare us from men of destiny," Walter muttered. "Has my embassy seen this?"

"They will any minute now."

Walter wondered how others would react. Would they accept this, as Robert had, or be outraged like Walter? Would there be an international howl of protest or just a helpless diplomatic shrug? He would find out this evening. He looked at the clock on the mantelpiece. "I'm late for dinner. Are you going to the Duchess of Sussex's ball later?"

"Yes. I'll see you there."

They left the building and parted company in Piccadilly. Walter headed for Fitz's house, where he was to dine. He felt breathless, as if he had been knocked down. The war he dreaded had come dangerously closer.

He arrived with just enough time to bow to Princess Bea, in a lavender gown festooned with silk bows, and shake hands with Fitz, impossibly handsome in a wing collar and a white bow tie; then dinner was announced. He was glad to find himself assigned to escort Maud through to the dining room. She wore a dark red dress of some soft material that clung to her body the way Walter wanted to. As he held her chair, he said: "What a very attractive gown."

"Paul Poiret," she said, naming a designer so famous

that even Walter had heard of him. She lowered her voice a little. "I thought you might like it."

The remark was only mildly intimate, but all the same it gave him a thrill, rapidly followed by a shiver of fear at the thought that he could yet lose this enchanting woman.

Fitz's house was not quite a palace. Its long dining room, at the corner of the street, looked over two thoroughfares. Electric chandeliers burned despite the bright summer evening outside, and reflected lights glittered in the crystal glasses and silver cutlery marshaled at each place. Looking around the table at the other female guests, Walter marveled anew at the indecent amount of bosom revealed by upper-class Englishwomen at dinner.

Such observations were adolescent. It was time he got married.

As soon as he sat down, Maud slipped off a shoe and pushed her stockinged toe up the leg of his trousers. He smiled at her, but she saw immediately that he was distracted. "What's the matter?" she said.

"Start a conversation about the Austrian ultimatum," he murmured. "Say you've heard it has been delivered."

Maud addressed Fitz, at the head of the table. "I believe the Austrian emperor's note has at last been handed in at Belgrade," she said. "Have you heard anything, Fitz?"

Fitz put down his soup spoon. "The same as you. But no one knows what is in it."

Walter said: "I believe it is very harsh. The Austrians insist on taking a role in the Serbian judicial process."

"Taking a role!" said Fitz. "But if the Serbian prime minister agreed to that, he'd have to resign."

Walter nodded. Fitz foresaw the same consequences as he did. "It is almost as if the Austrians want war." He was perilously close to speaking disloyally about one of Germany's allies, but he felt anxious enough not to care. He caught Maud's eye. She was pale and silent. She, too, had immediately seen the threat.

"One has sympathy for Franz Joseph, of course," Fitz said. "Nationalist subversion can destabilize an empire if it is not firmly dealt with." Walter guessed he was thinking of Irish independence campaigners and South African Boers threatening the British Empire. "But you don't need a sledgehammer to crack a nut," Fitz finished.

Footmen took away the soup bowls and poured a different wine. Walter drank nothing. It was going to be a long evening, and he needed a clear head.

Maud said quietly: "I happened to see Prime Minister Asquith today. He said there could be a real Armageddon." She looked scared. "I'm afraid I did not believe him—but now I see he might have been right."

Fitz said: "It's what we're all afraid of."

Walter was impressed as always by Maud's connections. She hobnobbed casually with the most powerful men in London. Walter recalled that as a girl of eleven or twelve, when her father was a minister in a Conservative government, she would solemnly question his cabinet colleagues when they visited Tŷ Gwyn; and even then such men would listen to her attentively and answer her patiently.

She went on: "On the bright side, if there is a war Asquith thinks Britain need not be involved."

Walter's heart lifted. If Britain stayed out, the war need not separate him from Maud.

But Fitz looked disapproving. "Really?" he said. "Even if . . ." He looked at Walter. "Forgive me, von Ulrich—even if France is overrun by Germany?"

Maud replied: "We will be spectators, Asquith says."

"As I have long feared," Fitz said pompously, "the government does not understand the balance of power in Europe." As a Conservative, he mistrusted the Liberal government, and personally he hated Asquith, who had enfeebled the House of Lords; but, most important, he was not totally horrified by the prospect of war. In some ways, Walter feared, he might relish the thought, just as Otto did. And he certainly thought war preferable to any weakening of British power.

Walter said: "Are you quite sure, my dear Fitz, that a German victory over France *would* upset the balance of power?" This line of discussion was rather sensitive for a dinner party, but the issue was too important to be brushed under Fitz's expensive carpet.

Fitz said: "With all due respect to your honored country, and to His Majesty Kaiser Wilhelm, I fear Britain could not permit German control of France."

That was the trouble, Walter thought, trying hard not to show the anger and frustration he felt at these glib words.

A German attack on Russia's ally France would, in reality, be defensive—but the English talked as if Germany was trying to dominate Europe. Forcing a genial smile, he said: "We defeated France forty-three years ago, in the conflict you call the Franco-Prussian War. Great Britain was a spectator then. And you did not suffer by our victory."

Maud added: "That's what Asquith said."

"There's a difference," Fitz said. "In 1871, France was defeated by Prussia and a group of minor German kingdoms. After the war, that coalition became one country, the modern Germany—and I'm sure you will agree, von Ulrich, my old friend, that Germany today is a more formidable presence than old Prussia."

Men like Fitz were so dangerous, Walter thought. With faultless good manners they would lead the world to destruction. He struggled to keep the tone of his reply light. "You're right, of course—but perhaps formidable is not the same as hostile."

"That's the question, isn't it?"

At the other end of the table, Bea coughed reproachfully. No doubt she thought this topic too contentious for polite conversation. She said brightly: "Are you looking forward to the duchess's ball, Herr von Ulrich?"

Walter felt reproved. "I feel sure the ball will be absolutely splendid," he gushed, and was rewarded with a grateful nod from Bea.

Aunt Herm put in: "You're such a good dancer!"

Walter smiled warmly at the old woman. "Perhaps you will grant me the honor of the first dance, Lady Hermia?"

She was flattered. "Oh, my goodness, I'm too old for dancing. Besides, you youngsters have steps that didn't even exist when I was a debutante."

"The latest craze is the czardas. It's a Hungarian folk dance. Perhaps I should teach you it."

Fitz said: "Would that constitute a diplomatic incident, do you think?" It was not very funny, but everyone laughed, and the conversation turned to other trivial but safe subjects.

After dinner the party boarded carriages to drive the four hundred yards to Sussex House, the duke's palace in Park Lane.

Night had fallen, and light blazed from every window:

the duchess had at last given in and installed electricity. Walter climbed the grand staircase and entered the first of three grand reception rooms. The orchestra was playing the most popular tune of recent years, "Alexander's Ragtime Band." His left hand twitched: the syncopation was the crucial element.

He kept his promise and danced with Aunt Herm. He hoped she would have lots of partners: he wanted her to get tired and doze off in a side room, so that Maud would be left unchaperoned. He kept remembering what he and Maud had done in the library of this house a few weeks ago. His hands itched to touch her through that clinging dress.

But first he had work to do. He bowed to Aunt Herm, took a glass of pink champagne from a footman, and began to circulate. He moved through the Small Ballroom, the Salon, and the Large Ballroom, talking to the political and diplomatic guests. Every ambassador in London had been invited, and many had come, including Walter's boss, Prince Lichnowsky. Numerous members of Parliament were there. Most were Conservative, like the duchess, but there were some Liberals, including several government ministers. Robert was deep in conversation with Lord Remarc, a junior minister in the War Office. No Labour M.P.s were to be seen: the duchess considered herself an openminded woman, but there were limits.

Walter learned that the Austrians had sent copies of their ultimatum to all the major embassies in Vienna. It would be cabled to London and translated overnight, and by morning everyone would know its contents. Most people were shocked by its demands, but no one knew what to do about it.

By one o'clock in the morning he had learned all he could, and he went to find Maud. He walked down the stairs and into the garden, where supper was laid out in a striped marquee. So much food was served in English high society! He found Maud toying with some grapes. Aunt Herm was happily nowhere to be seen.

Walter put his worries aside. "How can you English eat so much?" he said to Maud playfully. "Most of these people have had a hearty breakfast, a lunch of five or six courses, tea with sandwiches and cakes, and a dinner of at least eight courses. Do they now really need soup, stuffed quails, lobster, peaches, and ice cream?"

She laughed. "You think we're vulgar, don't you?"

He did not, but he teased her by pretending to. "Well, what culture do the English have?" He took her arm and, as if moving aimlessly, walked her out of the tent into the garden. The trees were decked with fairy lights that gave little illumination. On the winding paths between shrubs, a few other couples walked and talked, some holding hands discreetly in the gloom. Walter saw Robert with Lord Remarc again, and wondered if they, too, had found romance. "English composers?" he said, still teasing Maud. "Gilbert and Sullivan. Painters? While the French Impressionists were changing the way the world sees itself, the English were painting rosy-cheeked children playing with puppies. Opera? All Italian, when it's not German. Ballet? Russian."

"And yet we rule half the world," she said with a mocking smile.

He took her in his arms. "And you can play ragtime."

"It's easy, once you get the rhythm."

"That's the part I find difficult."

"You need lessons."

He put his mouth to her ear and murmured: "Teach me, please?" The murmur turned to a groan as she kissed him, and after that they did not speak for some time.

{ II }

That was in the small hours of Friday, July 24. On the following evening, when Walter attended another dinner and another ball, the rumor on everyone's lips was that the Serbians would concede every Austrian demand, except only for a request for clarification on points five and six. Surely, Walter thought elatedly, the Austrians could not reject such a cringing response? Unless, of course, they were determined to have a war regardless.

On his way home at daybreak on Saturday he stopped at the embassy to write a note about what he had learned during the evening. He was at his desk when the ambassador himself, Prince Lichnowsky, appeared in immaculate morning dress, carrying a gray top hat. Startled, Walter jumped to his feet, bowed, and said: "Good morning, Your Highness."

"You're here very early, von Ulrich," said the ambassador. Then, noting Walter's evening dress, he said: "Or rather, very late." He was handsome in a craggy way, with a big curved nose over his mustache.

"I was just writing you a short note on last night's gossip. Is there anything I can do for Your Highness?"

"I've been summoned by Sir Edward Grey. You can come with me and make notes, if you've got a different coat."

Walter was elated. The British foreign secretary was one of the most powerful men on earth. Walter had met him, of course, in the small world of London diplomacy, but had never exchanged more than a few words with him. Now, at Lichnowsky's characteristically casual invitation, Walter was to be present at an informal meeting of two men who were deciding the fate of Europe. Gottfried von Kessel would be sick with envy, he thought.

He reproved himself for being petty. This could be a critical meeting. Unlike the Austrian emperor, Grey might not want war. Would this be about preventing it? Grey was hard to predict. Which way would he jump? If he was against war, Walter would seize any chance to help him.

He kept a frock coat on a hook behind his door for just such emergencies as this. He pulled off his evening tailcoat and buttoned the daytime coat over his white waistcoat. He picked up a notebook and left the building with the ambassador.

The two men walked across St. James's Park in the cool of the early morning. Walter told his boss the rumor about the Serbian reply. The ambassador had a rumor of his own to report. "Albert Ballin dined with Winston Churchill last night," he said. Ballin, a German shipping magnate, was close to the kaiser, despite being Jewish. Churchill was in charge of the Royal Navy. "I'd love to know what was said," Lichnowsky finished.

He obviously feared the kaiser was bypassing him and sending messages to the British via Ballin. "I'll try to find out," said Walter, pleased at the opportunity.

They entered the Foreign Office, a neoclassical building that made Walter think of a wedding cake. They were shown to the foreign secretary's opulent room overlooking the park. The British are the richest people on earth, the building seemed to say, and we can do anything we like to the rest of you.

Sir Edward Grey was a thin man with a face like a skull. He disliked foreigners and almost never traveled abroad: in British eyes, that made him the perfect foreign secretary. "Thank you so much for coming," he said politely. He was alone but for an aide with a notebook. As soon as they were seated he got down to business. "We must do what we can to calm the situation in the Balkans."

Walter's hopes rose. That sounded pacific. Grey did not want war.

Lichnowsky nodded. The prince was part of the peace faction in the German government. He had sent a sharp telegram to Berlin urging that Austria be restrained. He disagreed with Walter's father and others who believed that war now was better, for Germany, than war later when Russia and France might be stronger.

Grey went on: "Whatever the Austrians do, it must not be so threatening to Russia as to provoke a military response from the tsar."

Exactly, Walter thought excitedly.

Lichnowsky obviously shared his view. "If I may say so, Foreign Secretary, you have hit the nail on the head."

Grey was oblivious to compliments. "My suggestion is that you and we, that is to say Germany and Britain, should together ask the Austrians to extend their deadline." He glanced reflexively at the clock on the wall: it was a little after six a.m. "They have demanded an answer by six tonight, Belgrade time. They could hardly refuse to give the Serbians another day."

Walter was disappointed. He had been hoping Grey had a plan to save the world. This postponement was such a small thing. It might make no difference. And in Walter's view the Austrians were so belligerent they easily *could* refuse the request, petty though it was. However, no one asked his opinion, and in this stratospherically elevated company he was not going to speak unless spoken to.

"A splendid idea," said Lichnowsky. "I will pass it to Berlin with my endorsement."

"Thank you," said Grey. "But, failing that, I have another proposal."

So, Walter thought, Grey was not really confident the Austrians would give Serbia more time.

Grey went on: "I propose that Britain, Germany, Italy,

and France should together act as mediators, meeting at a four-power conference to produce a solution that would satisfy Austria without menacing Russia."

That was more like it, Walter thought.

"Austria would not agree in advance to be bound by the conference decision, of course," Grey continued. "But that's not necessary. We could ask the Austrian emperor at least to take no further action until he hears what the conference has to say."

Walter was delighted. It would be hard for Austria to refuse a plan that came from its allies as well as its rivals.

Lichnowsky looked pleased, too. "I will recommend this to Berlin most strongly."

Grey said: "It's good of you to come to see me so early in the morning."

Lichnowsky took that as dismissal and stood up. "Not at all," he said. "Will you get down to Hampshire today?"

Grey's hobbies were fly-fishing and bird-watching, and he was happiest at his cottage on the river Itchen in Hampshire.

"Tonight, I hope," said Grey. "This is wonderful fishing weather."

"I trust you will have a restful Sunday," said Lichnowsky, and they left.

Walking back across the park, Lichnowsky said: "The English are amazing. Europe is on the brink of war, and the foreign secretary is going fishing."

Walter felt elated. Grey might seem to lack a sense of urgency, but he was the first person to come up with a workable solution. Walter was grateful. I'll invite him to my wedding, he thought, and thank him in my speech.

When they got back to the embassy he was startled to find his father there.

Otto beckoned Walter into his office. Gottfried von Kessel was standing by the desk. Walter was bursting to confront his father about Maud, but he was not going to speak of such things in front of von Kessel, so he said: "When did you get here?"

"A few minutes ago. I came overnight on the boat train from Paris. What were you doing with the ambassador?"

"We were summoned to see Sir Edward Grey." Walter was gratified to see a look of envy cross von Kessel's face.

Otto said: "And what did he have to say?"

"He proposed a four-power conference to mediate between Austria and Serbia."

Von Kessel said: "Waste of time."

Walter ignored him and asked his father: "What do you think?"

Otto narrowed his eyes. "Interesting," he said. "Grey is crafty."

Walter could not hide his enthusiasm. "Do you think the Austrian emperor might agree?"

"Absolutely not."

Von Kessel snickered.

Walter was crushed. "But why?"

Otto said: "Suppose the conference proposes a solution and Austria rejects it?"

"Grey mentioned that. He said Austria would not be obliged to accept the conference recommendation."

Otto shook his head. "Of course not—but what then? If Germany is part of a conference that makes a peace proposal, and Austria rejects our proposal, how could we then back the Austrians when they go to war?"

"We could not."

"So Grey's purpose in making this suggestion is to drive a wedge between Austria and Germany."

"Oh." Walter felt foolish. He had seen none of this. His optimism was punctured. Dismally, he said: "So we won't support Grey's peace plan?"

"Not a chance," said his father.

{ III }

Sir Edward Grey's proposal came to nothing, and Walter and Maud watched, hour by hour, as the world lurched closer to disaster.

The next day was Sunday, and Walter met with Anton. Once again everyone was desperate to know what the Russians would do. The Serbians had given in to almost every Austrian demand, only asking for more time to discuss the two harshest clauses; but the Austrians had announced that this was unacceptable, and Serbia had begun to mobilize its little army. There would be fighting, but would Russia join in?

Walter went to the church of St. Martin-in-the-Fields, which was not in the fields but in Trafalgar Square, the busiest traffic junction in London. The church was an eighteenth-century building in the Palladian style, and Walter reflected that his meetings with Anton were giving him an education in the history of English architecture as well as information about Russian intentions.

He mounted the steps and passed through the great pillars into the nave. He looked around anxiously: at the best of times he was afraid Anton might not show up, and this would be the worst possible moment for the man to get cold feet. The interior was brightly lit by a big Venetian window at the east end, and he spotted Anton immediately. Relieved, he sat next to the vengeful spy a few seconds before the service began.

As always, they talked during the hymns. "The Council of Ministers met on Friday," Anton said.

Walter knew that. "What did they decide?"

"Nothing. They only make recommendations. The tsar decides."

Walter knew that, too. He controlled his impatience. "Excuse me. What did they *recommend*?"

"To permit four Russian military districts to prepare for mobilization."

"No!" Walter's cry was involuntary, and the hymn singers nearby turned and stared at him. This was the first preliminary to war. Calming himself with an effort, Walter said: "Did the tsar agree?"

"He ratified the decision yesterday."

Despairingly, Walter said: "Which districts?"

"Moscow, Kazan, Odessa, and Kiev."

During the prayers, Walter pictured a map of Russia. Moscow and Kazan were in the middle of that vast country, a thousand miles and more from its European borders, but Odessa and Kiev were in the southwest, near the Balkans. In the next hymn he said: "They are mobilizing against Austria."

"It's not mobilization—it's preparation for mobilization."

"I understand that," said Walter patiently. "But yesterday we were talking about Austria attacking Serbia, a minor Balkan conflict. Today we're talking about Austria and Russia, and a major European war."

The hymn ended, and Walter waited impatiently for the next one. He had been brought up by a devout Protestant mother, and he always suffered a twinge of conscience about using church services as a cover for his clandestine work. He said a brief prayer for forgiveness.

When the congregation began to sing again, Walter said: "Why are they in such a hurry to make these warlike preparations?"

Anton shrugged. "The generals say to the tsar: 'Every day you delay gives the enemy an advantage.' It's always the same."

"Don't they see that the preparations make the war more likely?"

"Soldiers want to win wars, not avoid them."

The hymn ended and the service came to a close. As Anton stood up, Walter held his arm. "I have to see you more often," he said.

Anton looked panicky. "We've been through that—"

"I don't care. Europe is on the brink of war. You say the Russians are *preparing* to mobilize in *some* districts. What if they authorize other districts to prepare? What other steps will they take? When does preparation turn into the real thing? I have to have daily reports. Hourly would be better."

"I can't take the risk." Anton tried to withdraw his arm.

Walter tightened his grip. "Meet me at Westminster Abbey every morning before you go to your embassy. Poet's Corner, in the south transept. The church is so big that no one will notice us."

"Absolutely not."

Walter sighed. He would have to threaten, which he did not like doing, not least because it risked the complete withdrawal of the spy. But he had to take the chance. "If you aren't there tomorrow, I'll come to your embassy and ask for you."

Anton went pale. "You can't do that! They will kill me!"

"I must have the information! I'm trying to prevent a war."

"I hope there *is* a war," the little clerk said savagely. His voice dropped to a hiss. "I hope my country is flattened and destroyed by the German army." Walter stared at him, astonished. "I hope the tsar is killed, brutally murdered, and all his family with him. And I hope they all go to hell, as they deserve."

He turned on his heel and scurried out of the church into the hubbub of Trafalgar Square.

{ IV }

Princess Bea was "at home" on Tuesday afternoons at tea-time. This was when her friends called to discuss the parties they had been to and show off their daytime clothes. Maud was obliged to attend, as was Aunt Herm, both being poor relations who lived on Fitz's generosity. Maud found the conversation particularly stultifying today, when all she wanted to talk about was whether there would be a war.

The morning room at the Mayfair house was modern. Bea was attentive to decorating trends. Matching bamboo chairs and sofas were arranged in small conversational groups, with plenty of space between for people to move around. The up-holstery had a quiet mauve pattern and the carpet was light brown. The walls were not papered, but painted a restful beige. There was no Victorian clutter of framed photographs, ornaments, cushions, and vases. One did not need to show off one's prosperity, fashionable people said, by cramming one's rooms full of stuff. Maud agreed.

Bea was talking to the Duchess of Sussex, gossiping about the prime minister's mistress, Venetia Stanley. Bea ought to be worried, Maud thought; if Russia joins in the war, her brother, Prince Andrei, will have to fight. But Bea appeared carefree. In fact she looked particularly bonny today. Perhaps she had a lover. It was not uncommon in the highest social circles, where many marriages were arranged. Some people disapproved of adulterers—the duchess would cross such a woman off her invitation list for all eternity—but others turned a blind eye. However, Maud did not really think Bea was the type.

Fitz came in for tea, having escaped from the House of Lords for an hour, and Walter was right behind him. They both looked elegant in their gray suits and double-breasted waistcoats. Involuntarily, in her imagination Maud saw them in army uniforms. If the war spread, both might have to fight—almost certainly on opposite sides. They would be officers, but neither would slyly wangle a safe job at head-quarters: they would want to lead their men from the front. The two men she loved might end up shooting at each other. She shuddered. It did not bear thinking about.

Maud avoided Walter's eye. She had a feeling that the more intuitive women in Bea's circle had noticed how much time she spent talking to him. She did not mind their suspicions—they would learn the truth soon enough—but she did not want rumors to reach Fitz before he had been officially told. He would be mightily offended. So she was trying not to let her feelings show.

Fitz sat beside her. Casting about for a topic of conver-sation that did not involve Walter, she thought of Tŷ Gwyn, and asked: "Whatever happened to your Welsh house-keeper, Williams? She disappeared, and when I asked the other servants, they went all vague."

"I had to get rid of her," Fitz said.

"Oh!" Maud was surprised. "Somehow I had the im-pression you liked her."

"Not especially." He seemed embarrassed.

"What did she do to displease you?"

"She suffered the consequences of unchastity."

"Fitz, don't be pompous!" Maud laughed. "Do you mean she got pregnant?"

"Keep your voice down, please. You know what the duchess is like."

"Poor Williams. Who's the father?"

"My dear, do you imagine I asked?"

"No, of course not. I hope he's going to 'stand by her,' as they say."

"I have no idea. She's a servant, for goodness' sake."

"You're not normally callous about your servants."

"One mustn't reward immorality."

"I liked Williams. She was more intelligent and interest-ing than most of these society women."

"Don't be absurd."

Maud gave up. For some reason, Fitz was pretending he did not care about Williams. But he never liked explaining himself, and it was useless to press him.

Walter came over, balancing a cup and saucer and a

plate with cake in one hand. He smiled at Maud, but spoke to Fitz. "You know Churchill, don't you?"

"Little Winston?" said Fitz. "I certainly do. He started out in my party, but switched to the Liberals. I think his heart is still with us Conservatives."

"Last Friday he had dinner with Albert Ballin. I'd love to know what Ballin had to say."

"I can enlighten you—Winston has been telling everyone. If there is a war, Ballin said that if Britain will stay out of it, Germany will promise to leave France intact afterward, taking no extra territory—by contrast with last time, when they helped themselves to Alsace and Lorraine."

"Ah," said Walter with satisfaction. "Thank you. I've been trying to find that out for days."

"Your embassy doesn't know?"

"This message was intended to bypass normal diplomatic channels, obviously."

Maud was intrigued. It seemed like a hopeful formula for keeping Britain out of any European war. Perhaps Fitz and Walter would not have to shoot at each other, after all. She said: "How did Winston respond?"

"Noncommittally," said Fitz. "He reported the conversation to the cabinet, but it was not discussed."

Maud was about to ask indignantly why not when Robert von Ulrich appeared, looking aghast, as if he had just learned of the death of a loved one. "What on earth is the matter with Robert?" Maud said as he bowed to Bea.

He turned to speak to everyone in the room. "Austria has declared war on Serbia," he announced.

For a moment Maud felt as if the world had stopped. No one moved and no one spoke. She stared at Robert's mouth under that curled mustache and willed him to unsay the words. Then the clock on the mantelpiece struck, and a buzz of consternation rose from the men and women in the room.

Tears welled up in Maud's eyes. Walter offered her a neatly folded white linen handkerchief. She said to Robert: "You will have to fight."

"I certainly will," Robert said. He said it briskly, as if stating the obvious, but he looked scared.

Fitz stood up. "I'd better get back to the Lords and find out what's going on."

Several others took their leave. In the general hubbub, Walter spoke quietly to Maud. "Albert Ballin's proposal has suddenly become ten times more important."

Maud thought so, too. "Is there anything we can do?"

"I need to know what the British government really thinks of it."

"I'll try to find out." She was glad of a chance to do something.

"I have to get back to the embassy."

Maud watched Walter go, wishing she could kiss him good-bye. Most of the guests went at the same time, and Maud slipped upstairs to her room.

She took off her dress and lay down. The thought of Walter going to war made her weep helplessly. After a while she cried herself to sleep.

When she woke up, it was time to go out. She was invited to Lady Glenconner's musical soiree. She was tempted to stay home; then it struck her that there might be a government minister or two at the Glenconners' house. She might learn something useful to Walter. She got up and dressed.

She and Aunt Herm took Fitz's carriage through Hyde Park to Queen Anne's Gate, where the Glenconners lived. Among the guests was Maud's friend Johnny Remarc, a War Office minister; but, more important, Sir Edward Grey was there. She made up her mind to speak to him about Albert Ballin.

The music began before she had a chance, and she sat down to listen. Campbell McInnes was singing selections from Handel—a German composer who had lived most of his life in London, Maud thought wryly.

She watched Sir Edward covertly during the recital. She did not like him much: he belonged to a political group called the Liberal Imperialists, more traditional and conservative than most of the party. However, she felt a pang of sympathy for him. He was never very jolly, but tonight his cadaverous face looked ashen, as if he had the weight of the world on his shoulders—which he did, of course.

McInnes sang well, and Maud thought with regret how much Walter would have enjoyed this, had he not been too busy to come.

As soon as the music finished, she buttonholed the foreign secretary. "Mr. Churchill tells me he gave you an interesting message from Albert Ballin," she said. She saw Grey's face stiffen, but she plowed on. "If we stay out of any European war, the Germans promise not to grab any French territory."

"Something like that," Grey said coldly.

Clearly she had raised a distasteful topic. Etiquette demanded that she abandon it instantly. But this was not just a diplomatic maneuver: it was about whether Fitz and Walter would have to go to war. She pressed on. "I understood that our main concern was that the balance of power in Europe should not be disturbed, and I imagined that Herr Ballin's proposal might satisfy us. Was I wrong?"

"You most certainly were," he said. "It is an infamous proposal." He was almost emotional.

Maud was downcast. How could he dismiss it? It offered a glimpse of hope! She said: "Will you explain, to a mere woman who does not grasp these matters as quickly as you, why you say that so definitely?"

"To do as Ballin suggested would be to pave the way for France to be invaded by Germany. We would be complicit. It would be a squalid betrayal of a friend."

"Ah," she said. "I think I see. It is as if someone said: 'I'm going to burgle your neighbor, but if you stand back and don't interfere, I promise not to burn his house down, too.' Is that it?"

Grey warmed up a little. "A good analogy," he said with a skeletal smile. "I shall use it myself."

"Thank you," said Maud. She felt dreadfully disappointed, and she knew it was showing on her face, but she could not help it. She said gloomily: "Unfortunately, this leaves us perilously close to war."

"I'm afraid it does," said the foreign secretary.

{ V }

Like most parliaments around the world, the British had two chambers. Fitz belonged to the House of Lords, which included the higher aristocracy, the bishops, and the senior judges. The House of Commons was made up of elected representatives known as members of Parliament, or M.P.s.

Both chambers met in the Palace of Westminster, a purpose-built Victorian Gothic building with a clock tower. The clock was called Big Ben, although Fitz was fond of pointing out that that was actually the name of the great bell.

As Big Ben struck twelve noon on Wednesday, July 29, Fitz and Walter ordered a prelunch sherry on the terrace beside the smelly river Thames. Fitz looked at the palace with satisfaction, as always: it was extraordinarily large, rich, and solid, like the empire that was ruled from its corridors and chambers. The building looked as if it might last a thousand years—but would the empire survive? Fitz trembled when he thought of the threats to it: rabble-rousing trade unionists, striking coal miners, the kaiser, the Labour Party, the Irish, militant feminists—even his own sister.

However, he did not give utterance to such solemn thoughts, especially as his guest was a foreigner. "This place is like a club," he said lightheartedly. "It has bars, dining rooms, and a jolly good library; and only the right sort of people are allowed in." Just then a Labour M.P. walked past with a Liberal peer, and Fitz added: "Although sometimes the riffraff sneak past the doorman."

Walter was bursting with news. "Have you heard?" he said. "The kaiser has done a complete volte-face."

Fitz had not heard. "In what way?"

"He says the Serbian reply leaves no further reason for war, and the Austrians must halt at Belgrade."

Fitz was suspicious of peace plans. His main concern was that Britain should maintain its position as the most powerful nation in the world. He was afraid the Liberal government might let that position slip, out of some foolish belief that all nations were equally sovereign. Sir Edward Grey was fairly sound, but he could be ousted by the left wing of the party—led by Lloyd George, in all likelihood—and then anything could happen.

"Halt at Belgrade," he said musingly. The capital was on the border: to capture it, the Austrian army would have to venture only a mile inside Serbian territory. The Russians might be persuaded to regard that as a local police action that did not threaten them. "I wonder."

Fitz did not want war, but there was a part of him that secretly relished the prospect. It would be his chance to prove his courage. His father had won distinction in naval actions, but Fitz had never seen combat. There were certain things one had to do before one could really call oneself a man, and fighting for king and country was among them.

They were approached by a messenger wearing court dress—velvet knee breeches and white silk stockings. "Good afternoon, Earl Fitzherbert," he said. "Your guests have arrived and gone straight to the dining room, my lord."

When he had gone Walter said: "Why do you make them dress like that?"

"Tradition," said Fitz.

They drained their glasses and went inside. The corridor had a thick red carpet and walls with linenfold paneling. They walked to the Peers' Dining Room. Maud and Aunt Herm were already seated.

This lunch had been Maud's idea: Walter had never been inside the palace, she said. As Walter bowed, and Maud smiled warmly at him, a stray thought crossed Fitz's mind: could there be a little tendresse between them? No, it was ridiculous. Maud might do anything, of course, but Walter was much too sensible to contemplate an Anglo-German marriage at this time of tension. Besides, they were like brother and sister.

As they sat down, Maud said: "I was at your baby clinic this morning, Fitz."

He raised his eyebrows. "Is it *my* clinic?"

"You pay for it."

"My recollection is that you told me there ought to be a clinic in the East End for mothers and children who had no man to support them, and I said indeed there should, and the next thing I knew the bills were coming to me."

"You're so generous."

Fitz did not mind. A man in his position had to give to charity, and it was useful to have Maud do all the work. He did not broadcast the fact that most of the mothers were not married and never had been: he did not want his aunt the duchess to be offended.

"You'll never guess who came in this morning," Maud went on. "Williams, the housekeeper from Tŷ Gwyn." Fitz went cold. Maud added cheerfully: "We were talking about her only last night!"

Fitz tried to keep a look of stony indifference on his

face. Maud, like most women, was quite good at reading him. He did not want her to suspect the true depth of his involvement with Ethel: it was too embarrassing.

He knew Ethel was in London. She had found a house in Aldgate, and Fitz had instructed Solman to buy it in her name. Fitz feared the embarrassment of meeting Ethel on the street, but it was Maud who had run into her.

Why had she gone to the clinic? He hoped she was all right. "I trust she's not ill," he said, trying to make it sound no more than a courteous inquiry.

"Nothing serious," Maud said.

Fitz knew that pregnant women suffered minor ailments. Bea had had a little bleeding and had been worried, but Professor Rathbone had said it often happened at about three months and usually meant nothing, though she should not overexert herself—not that there was much danger of Bea's doing that.

Walter said: "I remember Williams—curly hair and a cheeky smile. Who is her husband?"

Maud answered: "A valet who visited Tŷ Gwyn with his master some months ago. His name is Teddy Williams."

Fitz felt a slight flush. So she was calling her fictional husband Teddy! He wished Maud had not met her. He wanted to forget Ethel. But she would not go away. To conceal his embarrassment he made a show of looking around for a waiter.

He told himself not to be so sensitive. Ethel was a servant girl and he was an earl. Men of high rank had always taken their pleasures where they found them. This kind of thing had been going on for hundreds of years, probably thousands. It was foolish to get sentimental about it.

He changed the subject by repeating, for the benefit of the ladies, Walter's news about the kaiser.

"I heard that, too," said Maud. "Goodness, I hope the Austrians will listen," she added fervently.

Fitz raised an eyebrow at her. "Why so passionate?"

"I don't want you to be shot at!" she said. "And I don't want Walter to be our enemy." There was a catch in her voice. Women were so emotional.

Walter said: "Do you happen to know, Lady Maud, how the kaiser's suggestion has been received by Asquith and Grey?"

Maud pulled herself together. "Grey says that in combination with his proposal of a four-power conference, it could prevent war."

"Excellent!" said Walter. "That was what I was hoping for." He was boyishly eager, and the look on his face reminded Fitz of their school days. Walter had looked like that when he won the Music Prize at Speech Day.

Aunt Herm said: "Did you see that that dreadful Madame Caillaux was found not guilty?"

Fitz was astonished. "Not guilty? But she shot the man! She went to a shop, bought a gun, loaded it, drove to the offices of *Le Figaro*, asked to see the editor, and shot him dead—how could she not be guilty?"

Aunt Herm replied: "She said: 'These guns go off by themselves.' Honestly!"

Maud laughed.

"The jury must have liked her," said Fitz. He was annoyed with Maud for laughing. Capricious juries were a threat to orderly society. It did not do to take murder lightly. "How very French," he said with disgust.

"I admire Madame Caillaux," Maud said.

Fitz grunted disapprovingly. "How can you say that about a murderess?"

"I think more people should shoot newspaper editors," Maud said gaily. "It might improve the press."

{ VI }

Walter was still full of hope the next day, Thursday, when he went to see Robert.

The kaiser was hesitating on the brink, despite pressure from men such as Otto. The war minister, Erich von Falkenhayn, had demanded a declaration *Zustand drohender Kriegsgefahr,* a preliminary that would light the fuse for war—but the kaiser had refused, believing that a general conflict might be avoided if the Austrians would halt at Belgrade. And when the Russian tsar had ordered his army to mobilize, Wilhelm had sent a personal telegram begging him to reconsider.

The two monarchs were cousins. The kaiser's mother and

the tsar's mother-in-law had been sisters, both daughters of Queen Victoria. The kaiser and the tsar communicated in English, and called each other "Nicky" and "Willy." Tsar Nicholas had been touched by his cousin Willy's cable, and had countermanded his mobilization order.

If they could both just stand firm, then the future might be bright for Walter and Maud and millions of other people who just wanted to live in peace.

The Austrian embassy was one of the more imposing houses in prestigious Belgrave Square. Walter was shown to Robert's office. They always shared news. There was no reason not to: their two nations were close allies. "The kaiser seems determined to make his 'halt at Belgrade' plan work," Walter said as he sat down. "Then all remaining issues can be worked out."

Robert did not share his optimism. "It's not going to succeed," he said.

"But why should it not?"

"We're not willing to halt at Belgrade."

"For God's sake!" said Walter. "Are you sure?"

"It will be discussed by ministers in Vienna tomorrow morning, but I'm afraid the result is a foregone conclusion. We can't halt at Belgrade without reassurances from Russia."

"Reassurances?" Walter said indignantly. "You have to stop fighting and *then* talk about the problems. You can't demand assurances first!"

"I'm afraid we don't see it that way," Robert said stiffly.

"But we are your allies. How can you reject our peace plan?"

"Easily. Think about it. What can you do? If Russia mobilizes, you're threatened, so you have to mobilize, too."

Walter was about to protest, but he saw that Robert was right. The Russian army, when mobilized, was too big a threat.

Robert went on remorselessly. "You have to fight on our side, whether you want to or not." He made an apologétic face. "Forgive me if I sound arrogant. I'm just stating the reality."

"Hell," said Walter. He felt like crying. He had been holding on to hope, but Robert's grim words had shattered him. "This is going the wrong way, isn't it?" he said. "Those who want peace are going to lose the contest."

Robert's voice changed, and suddenly he looked sad. "I've known that from the start," he said. "Austria must attack."

Until now Robert had been sounding eager, not sad. Why the change? Probing, Walter said: "You may have to leave London."

"You, too."

Walter nodded. If Britain joined in the war, all Austrian and German embassy staff would have to go home at short notice. He lowered his voice. "Is there . . . someone you will especially miss?"

Robert nodded, and there were tears in his eyes.

Walter hazarded a guess. "Lord Remarc?"

Robert laughed mirthlessly. "Is it so obvious?"

"Only to someone who knows you."

"Johnny and I thought we were being so discreet." Robert shook his head miserably. "At least you can marry Maud."

"I wish I could."

"Why not?"

"A marriage between a German and an Englishwoman, when the two nations are at war? She would be shunned by everyone she knows. So would I. For myself I would hardly care, but I could never impose such a fate on her."

"Do it secretly."

"In London?"

"Get married in Chelsea. No one would know you there."

"Don't you have to be a resident?"

"You have to produce an envelope with your name and a local address. I live in Chelsea—I can give you a letter addressed to Mr. von Ulrich." He rummaged in a drawer of his desk. "Here you are. A bill from my tailor, addressed to Von Ulrich, Esquire. They think Von is my first name."

"There may not be time."

"You can get a special license."

"Oh, my God," Walter said. He felt stunned. "You're right, of course. I can."

"You have to go to the town hall."

"Yes."

"Shall I show you the way?"

Walter thought for a long moment, then said: "Yes, please."

{ VII }

"The generals won," said Anton, standing in front of the tomb of Edward the Confessor in Westminster Abbey on Friday, July 31. "The tsar gave in yesterday afternoon. The Russians are mobilizing."

It was a death sentence. Walter felt a cold chill around his heart.

"It is the beginning of the end," Anton went on, and Walter saw in his eyes the glitter of revenge. "The Russians think they are strong, because their army is the largest in the world. But they have weak leadership. It will be Armageddon."

It was the second time this week that Walter had heard that word. But this time he knew it was justified. In a few weeks' time the Russian army of six million men—six *million*—would be massed on the borders of Germany and Hungary. No leader in Europe could ignore such a threat. Germany would have to mobilize: the kaiser no longer had any choice.

There was nothing more Walter could do. In Berlin the General Staff were pressing for German mobilization and the chancellor, Theobald von Bethmann-Hollweg, had promised a decision by noon today. This news meant there was only one decision he could possibly make.

Walter had to inform Berlin immediately. He took an abrupt leave of Anton and went out of the great church. He walked as fast as he could through the little street called Storey's Gate, jogged along the eastern edge of St. James's Park, and ran up the steps by the Duke of York's memorial and into the German embassy.

The ambassador's door was open. Prince Lichnowsky sat at his desk, and Otto stood beside him. Gottfried von Kessel was using the telephone. There were a dozen other people in the room, with clerks hurrying in and out.

Walter was breathing hard. Panting, he spoke to his father. "What's happening?"

"Berlin has received a cable from our embassy in St. Petersburg that just says: 'First day of mobilization 31 July.' Berlin is trying to confirm the report."

"What is von Kessel doing?"

"Keeping the phone line to Berlin open so that we hear instantly."

Walter took a deep breath and stepped forward. "Your Highness," he said to Prince Lichnowsky.

"Yes?"

"I can confirm the Russian mobilization. My source told me less than an hour ago."

"Right." Lichnowsky reached for the phone and von Kessel gave it to him.

Walter looked at his watch. It was ten minutes to eleven—in Berlin, just short of the noon deadline.

Lichnowsky said into the phone: "Russian mobilization has been confirmed by a reliable source here."

He listened for a few moments. The room went quiet. No one moved. "Yes," Lichnowsky said at last. "I understand. Very well."

He hung up with a click that sounded like a thunderclap. "The chancellor has decided," he said; and then he repeated the words Walter had been dreading. "*Zustand drohender Kriegsgefahr.* Prepare for imminent war."

CHAPTER TEN

August 1–3, 1914

Maud was frantic with worry. On Saturday morning she sat in the breakfast room at the Mayfair house, eating nothing. The summer sun shone in through the tall windows. The decor was supposed to be restful—Persian rugs, eau-de-Nil paintwork, mid-blue curtains—but nothing could calm her. War was coming and no one seemed able to stop it: not the kaiser, not the tsar, not Sir Edward Grey.

Bea came in, wearing a filmy summer dress and a lace shawl. Grout, the butler, poured her coffee with gloved hands, and she took a peach from a bowl.

Maud looked at the newspaper but was unable to read beyond the headlines. She was too anxious to concentrate. She tossed the newspaper aside. Grout picked it up and folded it neatly. "Don't you worry, my lady," he said. "We'll give the Germans a bashing if we have to."

She glared at him but said nothing. It was foolish to argue with servants—they always ended up agreeing out of deference.

Aunt Herm tactfully got rid of him. "I'm sure you're right, Grout," she said. "Bring some more hot rolls, would you?"

Fitz came in. He asked Bea how she was feeling, and she shrugged. Maud sensed that something in their relationship had changed, but she was too distracted to think about that. She immediately asked Fitz: "What happened last night?" She knew he had been in conference with leading Conservatives at a country house called Wargrave.

"F.E. arrived with a message from Winston." F. E. Smith, a Conservative M.P., was close friends with the Liberal Winston Churchill. "He proposed a Liberal-Conservative coalition government."

Maud was shocked. She usually knew what was happening in Liberal circles, but Prime Minister Asquith had kept this secret. "That's outrageous!" she said. "It makes war *more* likely."

With irritating calmness, Fitz took some sausages from the hot buffet on the sideboard. "The left wing of the Liberal Party are little better than pacifists. I imagine that Asquith is afraid they will attempt to tie his hands. But he doesn't have enough support in his own party to overrule them. Who can he turn to for help? Only the Conservatives. Hence the proposal of a coalition."

That was what Maud feared. "What did Bonar Law say to the offer?" Andrew Bonar Law was the Conservative leader.

"He turned it down."

"Thank God."

"And I supported him."

"Why? Don't you want Bonar Law to have a seat in the government?"

"I'm hoping for more. If Asquith wants war, and Lloyd George leads a left-wing rebellion, the Liberals could be too divided to rule. Then what happens? We Conservatives have to take over—and Bonar Law becomes prime minister."

Furiously, Maud said: "You see how everything seems to conspire toward war? Asquith wants a coalition with the Conservatives because they are more aggressive. If Lloyd George leads a rebellion against Asquith, the Conservatives will take over anyway. Everyone is jockeying for position instead of struggling for peace!"

"What about you?" Fitz said. "Did you go to Halkyn House last night?" The home of the Earl of Beauchamp was the headquarters of the peace faction.

Maud brightened. There was a ray of hope. "Asquith has called a cabinet meeting this morning." This was unusual on a Saturday. "Morley and Burns want a declaration that Britain will in no circumstance fight Germany."

Fitz shook his head. "They can't prejudge the issue like that. Grey would resign."

"Grey is always threatening to resign, but never does."

"Still, you can't risk a split in the cabinet now, with my lot waiting in the wings, panting to take over."

Maud knew Fitz was right. She could have screamed with frustration.

Bea dropped her knife and made a strange noise.

Fitz said: "Are you all right, my dear?"

She stood up, holding her stomach. Her face was pale. "Excuse me," she said, and she rushed out of the room.

Maud stood up, concerned. "I'd better go to her."

"I'll go," said Fitz, surprising her. "You finish your breakfast."

Maud's curiosity would not let her leave it at that. As Fitz went to the door, she said: "Is Bea suffering from morning sickness?"

Fitz paused in the doorway. "Don't tell anyone," he said.

"Congratulations. I'm very happy for you."

"Thanks."

"But the child . . ." Maud's voice caught in her throat.

"Oh!" said Aunt Herm, cottoning on. "How lovely!"

Maud went on with an effort. "Will the child be born into a world at war?"

"Oh, dear me," said Aunt Herm. "I didn't think of that."

Fitz shrugged. "A newborn will not know the difference."

Maud felt tears come. "When is the baby due?"

"January," said Fitz. "Why are you so upset?"

"Fitz," Maud said, and she was weeping helplessly now. "Fitz, will you still be alive?"

{ II }

Saturday morning at the German embassy was frenzied. Walter was in the ambassador's room, fielding phone calls, bringing in telegrams, and taking notes. It would have been the most exciting time of his life, had he not been so worried about his future with Maud. But he could not enjoy the thrill of being a player in a great international power game, because he was tortured by the fear that he and the woman he loved would become enemies in war.

There were no more friendly messages between Willy

and Nicky. Yesterday afternoon the German government had sent a cold ultimatum to the Russians, giving them twelve hours to halt the mobilization of their monstrous army.

The deadline had passed with no reply from St. Petersburg.

Yet Walter still believed the war could be confined to eastern Europe, so that Germany and Britain might remain friends. Ambassador Lichnowsky shared his optimism. Even Asquith had said that France and Britain could be spectators. After all, neither country was much involved in the future of Serbia and the Balkan region.

France was the key. Berlin had sent a second ultimatum yesterday afternoon, this one to Paris, asking the French to declare themselves neutral. It was a slender hope, though Walter clung to it desperately. The ultimatum expired at noon. Meanwhile, Chief of Staff Joseph Joffre had demanded immediate mobilization of the French army, and the cabinet was meeting this morning to decide. As in every country, Walter thought gloomily, army officers were pressing their political masters to take the first steps to war.

It was frustratingly difficult to guess which way the French would jump.

At a quarter to eleven, with seventy-five minutes to go before time ran out for France, Lichnowsky received a surprise visitor: Sir William Tyrrell. A key official with long experience in foreign affairs, he was private secretary to Sir Edward Grey. Walter showed him into the ambassador's room immediately. Lichnowsky motioned for Walter to stay.

Tyrrell spoke German. "The foreign secretary has asked me to let you know that a council of ministers taking place just now may result in his being able to make a statement to you."

This was obviously a rehearsed speech, and Tyrrell's German was perfectly fluent, but all the same his meaning escaped Walter. He glanced at Lichnowsky and saw that he, too, was baffled.

Tyrrell went on: "A statement that may, perhaps, prove helpful in preventing the great catastrophe."

That was hopeful but vague. Walter wanted to say, *Get to the point!*

Lichnowsky replied with the same strained diplomatic formality. "What indication can you give me of the subject of the statement, Sir William?"

For God's sake, Walter thought, we're talking about life and death here!

The civil servant spoke with careful precision. "It may be that, if Germany were to refrain from attacking France, then both France and Great Britain might consider whether they were truly obliged to intervene in the conflict in eastern Europe."

Walter was so shocked that he dropped his pencil. France and Britain staying out of the war—this was what he wanted! He stared at Lichnowsky. The ambassador, too, looked startled and delighted. "This is very hopeful," he said.

Tyrrell held up a cautionary hand. "Please understand that I make no promises."

Fine, Walter thought, but you didn't come here for a casual chat.

Lichnowsky said: "Then let me say quite simply that a proposal to confine the war to the east would be examined with great interest by His Majesty Kaiser Wilhelm and the German government."

"Thank you." Tyrrell stood up. "I shall report back to Sir Edward accordingly."

Walter showed Tyrrell out. He was elated. If France and Britain could be kept out of the war, there would be nothing to stop him marrying Maud. Was this a pipe dream?

He returned to the ambassador's room. Before they had a chance to discuss Tyrrell's statement, the phone rang. Walter picked it up and heard a familiar English voice say: "This is Grey. May I speak to His Excellency?"

"Of course, sir." Walter handed the phone to the ambassador. "Sir Edward Grey."

"Lichnowsky here. Good morning . . . Yes, Sir William has just left . . ."

Walter stared at the ambassador, listening avidly to his half of the conversation and trying to read his face.

"A most interesting suggestion . . . Permit me to make our position clear. Germany has no quarrel with either France or Great Britain."

It sounded as if Grey was going over the same ground as Tyrrell. Clearly the English were very serious about this.

Lichnowsky said: "The Russian mobilization is a threat that clearly cannot be ignored, but it is a threat to our eastern border, and that of our ally Austria-Hungary. We have asked France for a guarantee of neutrality. If France can give us that—or, alternatively, if Britain can guarantee French neutrality—there will be no reason for war in western Europe . . . Thank you, Foreign Secretary. Perfect—I will call on you at half past three this afternoon." He hung up.

He looked at Walter. They both smiled triumphantly. "Well," said Lichnowsky, "I didn't expect that!"

{ III }

Maud was at Sussex House, where a group of influential Conservative M.P.s and peers had gathered in the duchess's morning room for tea, when Fitz came in boiling with rage. "Asquith and Grey are crumbling!" he said. He pointed to a silver cake stand. "Crumbling like that dashed scone. They're going to betray our friends. I feel ashamed to be British."

Maud had feared this. Fitz was no compromiser. He believed that Britain should issue orders and the world should obey. The idea that the government might have to negotiate with others as equals was abhorrent to him. And there were distressingly many who agreed.

The duchess said: "Calm down, Fitz, dear, and tell us all what's happened."

Fitz said: "Asquith sent a letter this morning to Douglas." Maud presumed he meant General Sir Charles Douglas, chief of the Imperial General Staff. "Our prime minister wanted to put it on record that the government had never promised to send British troops to France in the event of a war with Germany!"

Maud, as the only Liberal present, felt obliged to defend the government. "But it's true, Fitz. Asquith is only making it clear that all our options are open."

"Then what on earth was the point of all the talks we've held with the French military?"

"To explore possibilities! To make contingency plans!

Talks are not contracts—especially in international politics."

"Friends are friends. Britain is a world leader. A woman
doesn't necessarily understand these things, but people expect us to stand by our neighbors. As gentlemen, we abhor
the least hint of deceit, and we should do the same as a
country."

That was the kind of talk that might yet get Britain em-
broiled in a war, Maud thought with a shiver of panic. She
just could not get her brother to understand the danger.
Their love for each other had always been stronger than
their political differences, but now they were so angry that
they might quarrel gravely. And when Fitz fell out with
someone, he never made it up. Yet he was the one who
would have to fight and perhaps die, shot or bayoneted or
blown to pieces—Fitz, and Walter, too. Why could Fitz not
see that? It made her want to scream.

While she struggled to find adequate words, one of the
other guests spoke. Maud recognized him as the foreign
editor of *The Times*, a man called Steed. "I can tell you
that there is a dirty German-Jewish international financial
attempt to bully my paper into advocating neutrality," he
said.

The duchess pursed her lips: she disliked the language
of the gutter press.

"What makes you say so?" Maud said coldly to Steed.

"Lord Rothschild spoke to our financial editor yesterday," the journalist said. "Wants us to moderate the anti-
German tone of our articles in the interests of peace."

Maud knew Natty Rothschild, who was a Liberal. She
said: "And what does Lord Northcliffe think of Rothschild's
request?" Northcliffe was the proprietor of *The Times*.

Steed grinned. "He ordered us to print an even stiffer
leading article today." He picked up a copy of the paper
from a side table and waved it. "'Peace is not our strongest
interest,'" he quoted.

Maud could not think of anything more contemptible
than deliberately encouraging war. She could see that even
Fitz was disgusted by the journalist's frivolous attitude. She
was about to say something when Fitz, with his unfailing
courtesy even to brutes, changed the subject. "I've just seen
the French ambassador, Paul Cambon, coming out of the

Foreign Office," he said. "He was as white as that table-cloth. He said: *'Ils vont nous lacher.'* 'They're going to let us down.' He had been with Grey."

The duchess asked: "Do you know what Grey had said, to upset Monsieur Cambon so?"

"Yes, Cambon told me. Apparently, the Germans are willing to leave France alone, if France promises to stay out of the war—and if the French refuse that offer, the British will not feel obliged to help defend France."

Maud felt sorry for the French ambassador, but her heart leaped with hope at the suggestion that Britain might stay out of the war.

"But France must refuse that offer," the duchess said. "She has a treaty with Russia, according to which each must come to the other's aid in war."

"Exactly!" said Fitz angrily. "What is the point of international alliances if they are to be broken at the moment of crisis?"

"Nonsense," Maud said, knowing she was being rude but not caring. "International alliances are broken whenever convenient. That isn't the issue."

"And what is, pray?" Fitz said frostily.

"I think Asquith and Grey are simply trying to frighten the French with a dose of reality. France cannot defeat Germany without our help. If they think they might have to go it alone, perhaps the French will become peacemakers, and pressure their Russian allies to back off from war with Germany."

"And what about Serbia?"

Maud said: "Even at this stage, it's not too late for Russia and Austria to sit down at a table and work out a solution for the Balkans that both can live with."

There was a silence that lasted for a few seconds; then Fitz said: "I doubt very much that anything like that will happen."

"But surely," said Maud, and even as she spoke she could hear the desperation in her own voice, "surely we must keep hope alive?"

{ IV }

Maud sat in her room and could not summon the energy to change her clothes for dinner. Her maid had laid out a gown and some jewelry, but Maud just stared at them.

She went to parties almost every night during the London season, because much of the politics and diplomacy that fascinated her was done at social occasions. But tonight she felt she could not do it—could not be glamorous and charming, could not entice powerful men to tell her what they were thinking, could not play the game of changing their minds without their even suspecting that they were being persuaded.

Walter was going to war. He would put on a uniform and carry a gun, and enemy troops would fire shells and mortars and machine-gun rounds at him and try to kill him, or wound him so badly that he was no longer able to stand up. She found it hard to think about anything else, and she was constantly on the edge of tears. She had even had harsh words with her beloved brother.

There was a tap at the door. Grout stood outside. "Herr von Ulrich is here, my lady," he said.

Maud was shocked. She had not been expecting Walter. Why had he come?

Noticing her surprise, Grout added: "When I said my master was not at home, he asked for you."

"Thank you," said Maud, and she pushed past Grout and headed down the stairs.

Grout called after her: "Herr von Ulrich is in the drawing room. I will ask Lady Hermia to join you." Even Grout knew that Maud was not supposed to be left alone with a young man. But Aunt Herm did not move fast, and it would be several minutes before she arrived.

Maud rushed into the drawing room and threw herself into Walter's arms. "What are we going to do?" she wailed. "Walter, what are we going to do?"

He hugged her hard, then gazed at her gravely. His face was gray and drawn. He looked as if he had been told of a death. He said: "France has not replied to the German ultimatum."

"Have they said nothing at all?" she cried.

"Our ambassador in Paris insisted on a response. The message from Premier Viviani was: 'France will have regard to her own interests.' They will not promise neutrality."

"But there may still be time—"

"No. They have decided to mobilize. Joffre won the argument—as the military have in every country. The telegrams were sent at four o'clock this afternoon, Paris time."

"There must be something you can do!"

"Germany has run out of choices," he said. "We cannot fight Russia with a hostile France at our backs, armed and eager to win back Alsace-Lorraine. So we must attack France. The Schlieffen Plan has already been set in motion. In Berlin, the crowds are singing the 'Kaiserhymne' in the streets."

"You'll have to join your regiment," she said, and she could not hold back the tears.

"Of course."

She wiped her face. Her handkerchief was too small, a stupid scrap of embroidered lawn. She used her sleeve instead. "When?" she said. "When will you have to leave London?"

"Not for a few days." He was fighting back tears himself, she saw. He said: "Is there any chance at all that Britain can be kept out of the war? Then at least I wouldn't be fighting against your country."

"I don't know," she said. "Tomorrow will tell." She pulled him close. "Please hold me tight." She rested her head on his shoulder and closed her eyes.

{ V }

Fitz was angered to see an antiwar demonstration in Trafalgar Square on Sunday afternoon. Keir Hardie, the Labour M.P., was speaking, dressed in a tweed suit—like a gamekeeper, Fitz thought. He stood on the plinth of Nelson's Column, shouting hoarsely in his Scots accent, desecrating the memory of the hero who died for Britain at the Battle of Trafalgar.

Hardie said that the coming war would be the greatest catastrophe the world had ever seen. He represented a mining constituency—Merthyr, near Aberowen. He was the illegitimate son of a maidservant, and had been a coal miner until he went into politics. What did he know about war?

Fitz stalked off in disgust and went to the duchess's for tea. In the grand hall he came upon Maud deep in conversation with Walter. The crisis was driving him away from both of them, to his profound regret. He loved his sister and he was fond of Walter, but Maud was a Liberal and Walter a German, and in times like these it was hard even to speak to them. However, he did his best to seem amiable as he said to Maud: "I hear this morning's cabinet was stormy."

She nodded. "Churchill mobilized the fleet last night without asking anyone. John Burns resigned this morning in protest."

"I can't pretend to be sorry." Burns was an old radical, the most fervently antiwar cabinet minister. "So the rest must have endorsed Winston's action."

"Reluctantly."

"We must be grateful for small mercies." It was appalling, Fitz felt, that at this time of national danger the government should be in the hands of these leftist ditherers.

Maud said: "But they refused Grey's request for a commitment to defend France."

"Still acting like cowards, then," Fitz said. He knew he was being rude to his sister, but he felt too bitter to hold back.

"Not quite," Maud said evenly. "They agreed to prevent the German navy passing through the English Channel to attack France."

Fitz brightened a little. "Well, that's something."

Walter put in: "The German government has responded by saying we have no intention of sending ships into the English Channel."

Fitz said to Maud: "You see what happens when you stand firm?"

"Don't be so smug, Fitz," she said. "If we do go to war it will be because people such as you have not tried hard enough to prevent it."

"Oh, really?" He was offended. "Well, let me tell you something. I spoke to Sir Edward Grey last night at

Brooks's Club. He has asked both the French and the Germans to respect the neutrality of Belgium. The French agreed immediately." Fitz looked challengingly at Walter. "The Germans have not responded."

"It's true." Walter gave an apologetic shrug. "My dear Fitz, you as a soldier will see that we couldn't answer that question, one way or the other, without giving away our war plans."

"I do see, but in the light of that, I want to know why my sister thinks I am a warmonger and you are a peacemaker."

Maud avoided the question. "Lloyd George thinks Britain should intervene only if the German army violates Belgian territory *substantially*. He may suggest it at tonight's cabinet."

Fitz knew what that meant. Furiously he said: "So we will give Germany permission to attack France via the southern corner of Belgium?"

"I suppose that is exactly what it means."

"I knew it," Fitz said. "The traitors. They're planning to wriggle out of their duty. They will do anything to avoid war!"

"I wish you were right," said Maud.

{ VI }

Maud had to go to the House of Commons on Monday afternoon to hear Sir Edward Grey address members of Parliament. The speech would be a turning point, everyone agreed. Aunt Herm went with her. For once, Maud was glad of an old lady's reassuring company.

Maud's fate would be decided this afternoon, as well as the fate of thousands of men of fighting age. Depending on what Grey said, and how Parliament reacted, women all over Europe could become widows, their children orphans.

Maud had stopped being angry—worn-out with it, perhaps. Now she was just frightened. War or peace, marriage or loneliness, life or death: her destiny.

It was a holiday, so the city's huge population of bank clerks, civil servants, lawyers, stockbrokers, and merchants all had the day off. Most of them seemed to have gathered near the great departments of government in Westminster, hoping to be the first to hear news. The chauffeur steered Fitz's seven-passenger Cadillac limousine slowly through the vast crowds in Trafalgar Square, Whitehall, and Parliament Square. The weather was cloudy but warm, and the more fashionable young men wore straw boaters. Maud glimpsed a placard for the *Evening Standard* that read: ON THE BRINK OF CATASTROPHE.

The crowd cheered as the car drew up outside the Palace of Westminster; then there was a little groan of disappointment when it disgorged nothing more interesting than two ladies. The onlookers wanted to see their heroes, men such as Lloyd George and Keir Hardie.

The palace epitomized the Victorian mania for decoration, Maud thought. The stone was elaborately carved, there was linenfold paneling everywhere, the floor tiles were multicolored, the glass was stained, and the carpets were patterned.

Although it was a holiday, the House was sitting and the place was crowded with members and peers, most of them in the parliamentary uniform of black morning coat and black silk top hat. Only the Labour members defied the dress code by wearing tweeds or lounge suits.

The peace faction was still a majority in cabinet, Maud knew. Lloyd George had won his point last night, and the government would stand aside if Germany committed a merely technical violation of Belgian territory.

Helpfully, the Italians had declared neutrality, saying their treaty with Austria obliged them to join only in a defensive war, whereas Austria's action in Serbia was clearly aggressive. So far, Maud thought, Italy was the only country to have shown common sense.

Fitz and Walter were waiting in the octagonal Central Lobby. Maud immediately said: "I haven't heard what happened at this morning's cabinet—have you?"

"Three more resignations," Fitz said. "Morley, Simon, and Beauchamp."

All three were antiwar. Maud was discouraged, and also puzzled. "Not Lloyd George?"

"No."

"Strange." Maud felt a chill of foreboding. Was there a split in the peace faction? "What is Lloyd George up to?"

Walter said: "I don't know, but I can guess." He looked solemn. "Last night, Germany demanded free passage through Belgium for our troops."

Maud gasped.

Walter went on: "The Belgian cabinet sat from nine o'clock yesterday evening until four this morning, then rejected the demand and said they would fight."

This was dreadful.

Fitz said: "So Lloyd George was wrong—the German army is not going to commit a merely technical violation."

Walter said nothing, but spread his hands in a gesture of helplessness.

Maud feared that the brutal German ultimatum, and the Belgian government's foolhardy defiance, might have undermined the peace faction in the cabinet. Belgium and Germany looked too much like David and Goliath. Lloyd George had a nose for public opinion: had he sensed that the mood was about to change?

"We must take our places," said Fitz.

Full of apprehension, Maud passed through a small door and climbed a long staircase to emerge in the Strangers' Gallery overlooking the chamber of the House of Commons. Here sat the sovereign government of the British Empire. In this room, matters of life and death were decided for the 444 million people who lived under some form of British rule. Every time she came here Maud was struck by how small it was, with less room than the average London church.

Government and opposition faced each other on tiered rows of benches, separated by a gap that—according to legend—was two sword lengths, so that opponents could not fight. For most debates the chamber was almost empty, with no more than a dozen or so members sprawled comfortably on the green leather upholstery. Today, however, the benches were packed, and M.P.s who could not find seats were standing at the entrance. Only the front rows were vacant, those places being reserved by tradition for cabinet ministers, on the government side, and opposition leaders on the other.

It was significant, Maud thought, that today's debate was to take place in this chamber, not in the House of Lords. In fact many of the peers were, like Fitz, here in the gallery, watching. The House of Commons had the authority that came from being elected by the people— even though not many more than half of adult men, and no women, had the vote. Much of Asquith's time as prime minister had been spent fighting the Lords, especially over Lloyd George's plan to give all old people a small pension. The battles had been fierce but, each time, the Commons had won. The underlying reason, Maud believed, was that the English aristocracy were terrified that the French revolution would be repeated here, so in the end they always accepted a compromise.

The front-benchers came in, and Maud was immediately struck by the atmosphere among the Liberals. The prime minister, Asquith, was smiling at something said by the Quaker Joseph Pease, and Lloyd George was talking to Sir Edward Grey. "Oh, God," Maud muttered.

Walter, sitting next to her, said: "What?"

"Look at them," she said. "They're all pals together. They've made up their differences."

"You can't tell that just by looking."

"Yes, I can."

The speaker entered in an old-fashioned wig and sat on the raised throne. He called on the foreign secretary, and Grey stood up, his gaunt face pale and careworn.

He had no skill as a speaker. He was wordy and ponderous. Nevertheless, the members squeezed along the benches, and the visitors in the packed gallery listened in attentive silence, waiting patiently for the important part.

He spoke for three-quarters of an hour before mentioning Belgium. Then, at last, he revealed the details of the German ultimatum that Walter had told Maud about an hour earlier. The M.P.s were electrified. Maud saw that, as she had feared, this changed everything. Both sides of the Liberal Party—the right-wing imperialists and the left-wing defenders of the rights of small nations—were outraged.

Grey quoted Gladstone, asking "whether, under the circumstances of the case, this country, endowed as it is with influence and power, would quietly stand by and witness the perpetration of the direst crime that ever stained the pages of history, and thus become participators in the sin?"

This was rubbish, Maud thought. An invasion of Belgium would not be the direst crime in history—what about the Cawnpore Massacre? What about the slave trade? Britain did not intervene every time a country was invaded. It was ludicrous to say that such inaction made the British people participants in the sin.

But few present saw things her way. Members on both sides cheered. Maud stared in consternation at the government front bench. All the ministers who had been fervently against war yesterday were now nodding agreement: young Herbert Samuel; Lewis "Lulu" Harcourt; the Quaker Joseph Pease, who was president of the Peace Society; and, worst of all, Lloyd George himself. The fact that Lloyd George was supporting Grey meant that the political battle was over, Maud realized in despair. The German threat to Belgium had united the opposing factions.

Grey could not play on his audience's emotions, as Lloyd George did, nor could he sound like an Old Testament prophet, as Churchill did; but today he did not need such skills, Maud reflected: the facts were doing all the work. She turned to Walter and said in a fierce whisper: "Why? Why has Germany done this?"

His face twisted in an agonized expression, but he answered with his usual calm logic. "South of Belgium, the border between Germany and France is heavily fortified. If we attacked there, we would win, but it would take too long—Russia would have time to mobilize and attack us from behind. The only way for us to be sure of a quick victory is to go through Belgium."

"But it also ensures that Britain will go to war against you!"

Walter nodded. "But the British army is small. You rely on your navy, and this is not a sea war. Our generals think Britain will make little difference."

"Do you agree?"

"I believe it's never smart to make an enemy of a rich and powerful neighbor. But I lost that argument."

And that was what had happened repeatedly over the last two weeks, Maud thought despairingly. In every country, those who were against war had been overruled. The Austrians had attacked Serbia when they might have held back; the Russians had mobilized instead of negotiating; the Germans had refused to attend an international conference to settle the issue; the French had been offered the chance to remain neutral and had spurned it; and now the British were about to join in when they might easily have remained on the sidelines.

Grey had reached his peroration. "I have put the vital facts before the House, and if, as seems not improbable, we are forced, and rapidly forced, to take our stand upon these issues, then I believe, when the country realizes what is at stake, what the real issues are, the magnitude of the impending dangers in the west of Europe, which I have endeavored to describe to the House, we shall be supported throughout, not only by the House of Commons, but by the determination, the resolution, the courage, and the endurance of the whole country."

He sat down to cheers from all sides. There had been no vote, and Grey had not even proposed anything; but it was clear from the reaction that the M.P.s were ready for war.

The leader of the opposition, Andrew Bonar Law, got up to say that the government could rely on the support of the Conservatives. Maud was not surprised: they were always more warlike than the Liberals. But she was amazed, as was everyone else, when the Irish Nationalist leader said the same thing. Maud felt as if she was living in a madhouse. Was she the only person in the world who wanted peace?

Only the Labour Party leader dissented. "I think he is wrong," said Ramsay MacDonald, speaking of Grey. "I think the government which he represents and for which he speaks is wrong. I think the verdict of history will be that they are wrong."

But no one was listening. Some M.P.s were already leaving the chamber. The gallery was also emptying. Fitz stood up, and the rest of his group followed suit. Maud went along listlessly. Down in the chamber, MacDonald was saying: "If the right honorable gentleman had come here today and told us that our country is in danger, I do not care what party he appealed to, or to what class he appealed, we would be with him . . . What is the use of talking about coming to the aid of Belgium, when, as a matter of fact, you are engaging in a whole European war?" Maud passed out of the gallery and heard no more.

This was the worst day of her life. Her country was going to fight an unnecessary war; her brother and the man she loved were going to risk their lives; and she was going to be separated from her fiancé, perhaps forever. All hope was lost and she was in total despair.

They went down the stairs, Fitz leading the way. "Most interesting, Fitz dear," said Aunt Herm politely, as if she had been taken to an art exhibition that had turned out better than expected.

Walter grasped Maud's arm and held her back. She let three or four other people get ahead of them, so that Fitz was out of earshot. But she was not prepared for what came next.

"Marry me," Walter said quietly.

Her heart raced. "What?" she whispered. "How?"

"Marry me, please, tomorrow."

"It can't be done—"

"I have a special license." He tapped the breast pocket of his coat. "I went to Chelsea Register Office on Friday."

Her mind was in a whirl. All she could think of to say was: "We agreed to wait." As soon as it was out, she wanted to take it back.

But he was already speaking. "We have waited. The crisis is over. Your country and mine will be at war tomorrow or the day after. I will have to leave Britain. I want to marry you before I go."

"We don't know what's going to happen!" she said.

"Indeed we don't. But, however the future turns out, I want you to be my wife."

"But—" Maud stopped speaking. Why was she voicing objections? He was right. No one knew what was going to happen, but that made no difference now. She wanted to be his wife, and no future that she could imagine would change that.

Before she could say more they reached the foot of the stairs and emerged into the Central Lobby, where a crowd was abuzz with excited conversation. Maud desperately wanted to ask Walter more questions, but Fitz gallantly insisted on escorting her and Aunt Herm out, because of the crowds. In Parliament Square Fitz handed the two women into the car. The chauffeur activated the automatic crank, the engine rumbled, and the car pulled smoothly away, leaving Fitz and Walter standing on the pavement, with the crowd of bystanders waiting to hear their fate.

{ VII }

Maud wanted to be Walter's wife. It was the only thing she was sure of. She held on to that thought while questions and speculations buzzed around her head. Should she fall in with Walter's plan, or would it be better to wait? If she agreed to marry him tomorrow, whom would she tell? Where would they go after the ceremony? Would they live together? If so, where?

That evening before dinner her maid brought her an envelope on a silver tray. It contained a single sheet of heavy cream-colored paper covered with Walter's precise, upright handwriting in blue ink.

> Six o'clock p.m.
>
> My dearest love,
>
> At half past three tomorrow I will wait for you in a car across the road from Fitz's house. I will bring with me the requisite two witnesses. The registrar is booked for four o'clock. I have a suite at the Hyde Hotel. I have checked in already, so that we can go to our room without delaying in the lobby. We are to be Mr. and Mrs. Woolridge. Wear a veil.
>
> I love you, Maud.
>
> Your betrothed,
> W.

With a shaky hand, she put the sheet of paper down on the polished mahogany top of her dressing table. Her breath was coming fast. She stared at the floral wallpaper and tried to think calmly.

He had chosen the time well: midafternoon was a quiet moment when Maud might be able to slip out of the house unnoticed. Aunt Herm took a nap after lunch, and Fitz would be at the House of Lords.

Fitz must not know in advance, for he would try to stop her. He might simply lock her in her room. He could even get her committed to a lunatic asylum. A wealthy upper-class man could have a female relative put away without much difficulty. All Fitz would have to do was to find two doctors willing to agree with him that she must be mad to want to marry a German.

She would not tell *anyone*.

The false name and the veil indicated that Walter meant to be clandestine. The Hyde was a discreet hotel in Knightsbridge, where they were unlikely to meet anyone they knew. She shivered with a thrill of anticipation when she thought of spending the night with Walter.

But what would they do the next day? A marriage could not be secret forever. Walter would be leaving Britain in two or three days. Would she go with him? She was afraid she would blight his career. How could he be trusted to fight for his country if he was married to an Englishwoman? And if he did fight, he would be away from home—so what was the point of her going to Germany?

Despite all the unknowns, she was full of delicious excitement. "Mrs. Woolridge," she said to the bedroom, and she hugged herself with joy.

CHAPTER ELEVEN

August 4, 1914

At sunrise Maud got up and sat at her dressing table to write a letter. She had a stack of Fitz's blue paper in her drawer, and the silver inkwell was filled every day. *My darling,* she began; then she stopped to think.

She caught sight of herself in the oval mirror. Her hair was tousled and her nightdress rumpled. A frown creased her forehead and turned down the corners of her mouth. She picked a fragment of some green vegetable from between her teeth. If he could see me now, she thought, he might not want to marry me. Then she realized that if she went along with his plan he would see her exactly like this tomorrow morning. It was a strange thought, scary and thrilling at the same time.

She wrote:

> Yes, with all my heart, I want to marry you. But what is your plan? Where would we live?

She had been thinking about this half the night. The obstacles seemed immense.

> If you stay in Britain they will put you in a prison camp. If we go to Germany I will never see you because you will be away from home, with the army.

Their relatives might create more trouble than the authorities.

When are we to tell our families about the marriage? Not beforehand, please, because Fitz will find a way to stop us. Even afterwards there will be difficulties with him and with your father. Tell me what you are thinking.

I love you dearly.

She sealed the envelope and addressed it to his flat, which was a quarter of a mile away. She rang the bell and a few minutes later her maid tapped on the door. Sanderson was a plump girl with a big smile. Maud said: "If Mr. Ulrich is out, go to the German embassy in Carlton House Terrace. Either way, wait for his reply. Is that clear?"

"Yes, my lady."

"No need to tell any of the other servants what you're doing."

A worried look came over Sanderson's young face. Many maids were party to their mistresses' intrigues, but Maud had never had secret romances, and Sanderson was not used to deception. "What shall I say when Mr. Grout asks me where I'm going?"

Maud thought for a moment. "Tell him you have to buy me certain feminine articles." Embarrassment would curb Grout's curiosity.

"Yes, my lady."

Sanderson left and Maud got dressed.

She was not sure how she was going to maintain a semblance of normality in front of her family. Fitz might not notice her mood—men rarely did—but Aunt Herm was not completely oblivious.

She went downstairs at breakfast time, although she was too tense to feel hungry. Aunt Herm was eating a kipper and the smell made Maud feel rather ill. She sipped coffee.

Fitz appeared a minute later. He took a kipper from the sideboard and opened *The Times*. What do I normally do? Maud asked herself. I talk about politics. Then I must do that now. "Did anything happen last night?" she said.

"I saw Winston after cabinet," Fitz replied. "We are asking the German government to withdraw its ultimatum to Belgium." He gave a contemptuous emphasis to the word *asking*.

Maud did not dare to feel hope. "Does that mean we have not completely given up working for peace?"

"We might as well," he said scornfully. "Whatever the Germans may be thinking, they're not likely to change their minds because of a polite request."

"A drowning man may clutch at a straw."

"We're not clutching at straws. We're going through the ritual preliminaries to a declaration of war."

He was right, she thought dismally. All governments would want to say that they had not wanted war, but had been forced into it. Fitz showed no awareness of the danger to himself, no sign that this diplomatic fencing might result in a mortal wound to himself. She longed to protect him and at the same time she wanted to strangle him for his foolish obstinacy.

To distract herself she looked through *The Manchester Guardian*. It contained a full-page advertisement placed by the Neutrality League with the slogan "Britons, do your duty and keep your country out of a wicked and stupid war." Maud was glad to know there were still people who thought as she did. But they had no chance of prevailing.

Sanderson came in with an envelope on a silver tray. With a shock, Maud recognized Walter's handwriting. She was aghast. What was the maid thinking of? Did she not realize that if the original note was a secret, the reply must be, too?

She could not read Walter's note in front of Fitz. Heart racing, she took it with pretended carelessness and dropped it beside her plate, then asked Grout for more coffee.

She looked at her newspaper to hide her panic. Fitz did not censor her mail but, as the head of the family, he had the right to read any letter addressed to a female relative living in his house. No respectable woman would object.

She had to finish breakfast as fast as possible and take the note away unopened. She tried to eat a piece of toast, forcing the crumbs down her dry throat.

Fitz looked up from *The Times*. "Aren't you going to read your letter?" he said. And then, to her horror, he added: "That looks like von Ulrich's handwriting."

She had no choice. She slit the envelope with a clean butter knife and tried to fix her face in a neutral expression.

Nine o'clock a.m.

My dear love,

All of us at the embassy have been told to pack our bags, pay our bills, and be ready to leave Britain at a few hours' notice.

You and I should tell no one of our plan. After tonight I will return to Germany and you will remain here, living with your brother. Everyone agrees this war cannot last more than a few weeks or, at most, months. As soon as it is over, if we are both still alive, we will tell the world our happy tidings and start our new life together.

And in case we do not survive the war, oh, please, let us have one night of happiness as husband and wife.

I love you.
W.

P.S. Germany invaded Belgium an hour ago.

Maud's mind was in a whirl. Married secretly! No one would know. Walter's superiors would still trust him, not knowing about his marriage to an enemy, and he could fight as his honor demanded, and even work in secret intelligence. Men would continue to court Maud, thinking her single, but she could deal with that: she had been giving suitors the brush-off for years. They would live apart until the end of the war, which would come in a few months at most.

Fitz interrupted her thoughts. "What does he say?"

Maud's mind went blank. She could not tell Fitz any of this. How was she to answer his question? She looked down at the sheet of heavy cream-colored paper and the upright handwriting, and her eye fell on the P.S. "He says Germany invaded Belgium at eight o'clock this morning."

Fitz put down his fork. "That's it, then." For once even he looked shocked.

Aunt Herm said: "Little Belgium! I think those Germans are the most frightful bullies." Then she looked confused and said: "Except Herr von Ulrich, of course. He's charming."

Fitz said: "So much for the British government's polite request."

"It's madness," said Maud desolately. "Thousands of men are going to be killed in a war no one wants."

"I should have thought you might have supported the war," Fitz said argumentatively. "After all, we will be defending France, which is the only other real democracy in Europe. And our enemies will be Germany and Austria, whose elected parliaments are virtually powerless."

"But our ally will be Russia," Maud said bitterly. "So we will be fighting to preserve the most brutal and backward monarchy in Europe."

"I see your point."

"Everyone at the embassy has been told to pack," she said. "We may not see Walter again." She casually put the letter down.

It did not work. Fitz said: "May I see?"

Maud froze. She could not possibly show it to him. Not only would he lock her up: if he read the sentence about *one night of happiness,* he might take a gun and shoot Walter.

"May I?" Fitz repeated, holding out his hand.

"Of course," she said. She hesitated another second, then reached for the letter. At the last moment she was inspired, and she knocked over her cup, spilling coffee on the sheet of paper. "Oh, dash it," she said, noting with relief that the coffee had caused the blue ink to run and the words had already become illegible.

Grout stepped forward and began to clear up the mess. Pretending to be helpful, Maud picked up the letter and folded it, ensuring that any writing that might so far have escaped the coffee was now soaked. "I'm sorry, Fitz," she said. "But in fact there was no further information."

"Never mind," he said, and went back to his newspaper.

Maud put her hands in her lap to hide their shaking.

{ II }

That was only the beginning.

It was going to be difficult for Maud to get out of the house alone. Like all upper-class ladies, she was not supposed to go anywhere unescorted. Men pretended this was because they were so concerned to protect their women, but in truth it was a means of control. No doubt it would remain until women won the vote.

Maud had spent half her life finding ways to flout this rule. She would have to sneak out without being seen. This was quite difficult. Although only four family members lived in Fitz's Mayfair mansion, there were at least a dozen servants in the house at any time.

And then she had to stay out all night without anyone's knowledge.

She put her plan into place carefully.

"I have a headache," she said at the end of lunch. "Bea, will you forgive me if I don't come down to dinner tonight?"

"Of course," said Bea. "Is there anything I can do? Shall I send for Professor Rathbone?"

"No, thank you, it's nothing serious." A headache that was not serious was the usual euphemism for a menstrual period, and everyone accepted this without further comment.

So far, so good.

She went up to her room and rang for her maid. "I'm going to bed, Sanderson," she said, beginning a speech she had worked out carefully. "I'll probably stay there for the rest of the day. Please tell the other servants that I'm not to be disturbed for any reason. I may ring for a dinner tray, but I doubt it: I feel as if I could sleep the clock round."

That should ensure that her absence was not noticed for the rest of the day.

"Are you sick, my lady?" Sanderson asked, looking concerned. Some ladies took to their beds frequently, but it was rare for Maud.

"It's the normal female affliction, just worse than usual."

Sanderson did not believe her, Maud could tell. Already today the maid had been sent out with a secret message, something that had never happened before. Sanderson knew something unusual was going on. But maids were not permitted to cross-examine their mistresses. Sanderson would just have to wonder.

"And don't wake me in the morning," Maud added. She did not know what time she would get back, or how she would sneak unobserved into the house.

Sanderson left. It was a quarter past three. Maud undressed quickly, then looked in her wardrobe.

She was not used to getting her own clothes out—normally Sanderson did it. Her black walking dress had a hat with a veil, but she could not wear black for her wedding.

She looked at the clock above the fireplace: twenty past three. There was no time to dither.

She chose a stylish French outfit. She put on a tight-fitting white lace blouse with a high collar, to emphasize her long neck. Over it she wore a dress of a sky blue so pale it was almost white. In the latest daring fashion it ended an inch or two above her ankles. She added a broad-brimmed straw hat in dark blue with a veil the same color, and a gay blue parasol with a white lining. She had a blue velvet drawstring bag that matched the outfit. Into it she put a comb, a small vial of perfume, and a clean pair of drawers.

The clock struck half past three. Walter would be outside now, waiting. She felt her heart beating hard.

She pulled down the veil and examined herself in a full-length mirror. It was not quite a wedding dress, but it would look just right, she imagined, in a register office. She had never been to a civil wedding so she was not sure.

She took the key from the lock and stood by the closed door, listening. She did not want to meet anyone who might question her. It might not matter if she were seen by a footman or a boot boy, who would not care what she did, but all the maids would know by now that she was supposed to be unwell, and if she ran into one of the family her deception would be exposed instantly. She hardly cared about the embarrassment, but she was afraid they would try to stop her.

She was about to open the door when she heard heavy footsteps and caught a whiff of smoke. It must be Fitz, still finishing his after-lunch cigar, leaving for the House of Lords or perhaps White's Club. She waited impatiently.

After a few moments of silence she looked out. The broad corridor was deserted. She stepped out, closed the door, locked it, and dropped the key into her velvet bag. Now anyone trying the door would assume she was asleep inside.

She walked silently along the carpeted corridor to the top of the stairs and looked down. There was no one in the hall below. She went quickly down the steps. As she reached the half landing she heard a noise and froze. The door to the basement swung open and Grout emerged.

Maud held her breath. She looked down at the bald dome of Grout's head as he crossed the hall carrying two decanters of port. He had his back to the stairs, and he entered the dining room without looking up.

As the door closed behind him, she ran down the last flight, throwing caution to the wind. She opened the front door, stepped out, and slammed it behind her. Too late, she wished she had thought to close it quietly.

The quiet Mayfair street baked in the August sun. She looked up and down and saw a horse-drawn fishmonger's cart, a nanny with a perambulator, and a cabbie changing the wheel of a motor taxi. A hundred yards along, on the opposite side of the road, stood a white car with a blue canvas canopy. Maud liked cars, and she recognized this as a Benz 10/30 belonging to Walter's cousin Robert.

As she crossed the road, Walter got out, and her heart filled with joy. He was wearing a light gray morning suit with a white carnation. He met her eye and she saw, from his expression, that until this moment he had not been sure she would come. The thought brought a tear to her eye.

Now, though, his face lit up with delight. How strange and wonderful it was, she thought, to be able to bring such happiness to another person.

She glanced anxiously back to the house. Grout was in the doorway, looking up and down the road with a puzzled frown. He had heard the door slam, she guessed. She turned her face resolutely forward, and the thought that came into her head was: Free at last!

Walter kissed her hand. She wanted to kiss him properly, but her veil was in the way. Besides, it was inappropriate before the wedding. There was no need to throw *all* the proprieties out of the window.

Robert was at the wheel, she saw. He touched his gray top hat to her. Walter trusted him. He would be one of the witnesses.

Walter opened the door and Maud got into the backseat. Someone was already there, and Maud recognized the housekeeper from Tŷ Gwyn. "Williams!" she cried.

Williams smiled. "You'd better call me Ethel now," she said. "I'm to be a witness at your wedding."

"Of course—I'm sorry." Impulsively, Maud hugged her. "Thank you for coming."

The car pulled away.

Maud leaned forward and spoke to Walter. "How did you find Ethel?"

"You told me she had come to your clinic. I got her address from Dr. Greenward. I knew you trusted her because you chose her to chaperone us at Tŷ Gwyn."

Ethel handed Maud a small posy of flowers. "Your bouquet."

They were roses, coral pink—the flower of passion. Did Walter know the language of flowers? "Who chose them?"

"It was my suggestion," said Ethel. "And Walter liked it when I explained the meaning." Ethel blushed.

Ethel knew how passionate they were because she had seen them kiss, Maud realized. "They're perfect," she said.

Ethel was wearing a pale pink dress that looked new and a hat decorated with more pink roses. Walter must have paid for that. How thoughtful he was.

They drove down Park Lane and headed for Chelsea. I'm getting married, Maud thought. In the past, whenever she had imagined her wedding, she had assumed it would be like those of all her friends, a long day of tedious ceremony. This was a better way to do things. There had been no planning, no guest list, and no caterer. There would be no hymns, no speeches, and no drunk relations trying to kiss her: just the bride and groom and two people they liked and trusted.

She thrust from her mind all thoughts about the future. Europe was at war, and anything might happen. She was just going to enjoy the day—and night.

They drove down King's Road and suddenly she felt nervous. She took Ethel's hand for courage. She had a nightmare vision of Fitz following behind in his Cadillac, shouting: "Stop that woman!" She glanced back. Of course neither Fitz nor his car was in sight.

They pulled up outside the classical façade of the Chelsea town hall. Robert took Maud's arm and led her up the steps to the entrance, and Walter followed with Ethel. Passersby stopped to watch: everyone loved a wedding.

Inside, the building was extravagantly decorated in the Victorian manner, with colored floor tiles and plaster moldings on the walls. It felt like the right sort of place to get married.

They had to wait in the lobby: another wedding had taken place at half past three and had not yet finished. The four of them stood in a little circle and no one could think of anything to say. Maud inhaled the scent of her roses, and the perfume went to her head, making her feel as if she had gulped a glass of champagne.

After a few minutes the earlier wedding party emerged, the bride wearing an everyday dress and the groom in the uniform of an army sergeant. Perhaps they, too, had made a sudden decision because of the war.

Maud and her party went in. The registrar sat at a plain table, wearing a morning coat and a silver tie. He had a carnation in his buttonhole, which was a nice touch, Maud thought. Beside him was a clerk in a lounge suit. They gave their names as Mr. von Ulrich and Miss Maud Fitzherbert. Maud raised her veil.

The registrar said: "Miss Fitzherbert, can you provide evidence of identity?"

She did not know what he was talking about.

Seeing her blank look, he said: "Your birth certificate, perhaps?"

She did not have her birth certificate. She had not known it was required, and even if she had she would not have been able to get hold of it, for Fitz kept it in the safe, along with other family documents such as his will. Panic seized her.

Then Walter said: "I think this will serve." He took from his pocket a stamped and franked envelope addressed to Miss Maud Fitzherbert at the street address of the baby clinic. He must have picked it up when he went to see Dr. Greenward. How clever of him.

The registrar handed the envelope back without comment. He said: "It is my duty to remind you of the solemn and binding nature of the vows you are about to take."

Maud felt mildly offended at the suggestion that she might not know what she was doing; then she realized that was something he had to say to everyone.

Walter stood more upright. This is it, Maud thought; no turning back. She felt quite sure she wanted to marry Walter—but, more than that, she was acutely aware that she had reached the age of twenty-three without meeting anyone else she would remotely have considered as a husband. Every other man she had ever met had treated her and all women like overgrown children. Only Walter was different. It was him or no one.

The registrar was speaking words for Walter to repeat. "I do solemnly declare that I know not of any lawful impediment why I, Walter von Ulrich, may not be joined in matrimony to Maud Elizabeth Fitzherbert." Walter pronounced his own name the English way, "Wall-ter," rather than the correct German "Val-ter."

Maud watched his face as he spoke. His voice was firm and clear.

In his turn he watched her solemnly as she made her declaration. She loved his seriousness. Most men, even quite clever ones, became silly when they talked to women. Walter spoke to her just as intelligently as he spoke to Robert or Fitz, and—even more unusually—he listened to her answers.

Next came the vows. Walter looked her in the eye as he took her for his wife, and this time she heard a little shake of emotion in his voice. That was the other thing she loved: she knew she could undermine his seriousness. She could make him tremble with love or happiness or desire.

She made the same vow. "I call upon these persons here present to witness that I, Maud Elizabeth Fitzherbert, do take thee, Walter von Ulrich, to be my lawful wedded husband." There was no unsteadiness in her voice, and she felt a little embarrassed that she was not visibly moved—but that was not her style. She preferred to appear cool even when she was not. Walter understood that, and he more than anyone knew about the storms of unseen passion that blew through her heart.

"Do you have a ring?" said the registrar. Maud had not even thought about it—but Walter had. He drew a plain gold wedding band from his waistcoat pocket, took her hand, and slipped it onto her finger. He must have guessed the size, but it was a near fit, perhaps just one size too big. As their marriage was to be secret, she would not be wearing it for a while after today.

"I now pronounce you man and wife," said the registrar. "You may kiss the bride."

Walter kissed her lips softly. She put her arm around his waist and drew him closer. "I love you," she whispered.

The registrar said: "And now for the marriage certificate. Perhaps you would like to sit down . . . Mrs. Ulrich."

Walter smiled, Robert giggled, and Ethel gave a little cheer. Maud guessed the registrar enjoyed being the first person to call the bride by her married name. They all sat down, and the registrar's clerk began to fill out the certificate. Walter gave his father's occupation as army officer and his place of birth as Danzig. Maud put her father down as George Fitzherbert, farmer—there was, in fact, a small flock of sheep at Tŷ Gwyn, so the description was not actually false—and her place of birth as London. Robert and Ethel signed as witnesses.

Suddenly it was over, and they were walking out of the room and through the lobby—where another pretty bride was waiting with a nervous groom to make a lifelong commitment. As they walked arm in arm down the steps to the car parked at the curb, Ethel threw a handful of confetti over them. Among the bystanders, Maud noticed a middle-class woman of her own age carrying a parcel from a shop. The woman looked hard at Walter, then turned her gaze on Maud, and what Maud saw in her eyes was envy. Yes, Maud thought, I'm a lucky girl.

Walter and Maud sat in the back of the car, and Robert and Ethel rode up front. As they drove away, Walter took Maud's hand and kissed it. They looked into each other's eyes and laughed. Maud had seen couples do that, and had always thought it was stupid and sentimental, but now it seemed the most natural thing in the world.

In a few minutes they arrived at the Hyde Hotel. Maud dropped her veil. Walter took her arm and they walked through the lobby to the stairs. Robert said: "I'll order the champagne."

Walter had taken the best suite and filled it with flowers. There must have been a hundred coral-pink roses. Tears came to Maud's eyes, and Ethel gasped in awe. On a sideboard was a big bowl of fruit and a box of chocolates. The afternoon sun shone through large windows onto chairs and sofas upholstered in gay fabrics.

"Let's make ourselves comfortable!" Walter said jovially.

While Maud and Ethel were inspecting the suite, Robert came in, followed by a waiter with champagne and glasses on a tray. Walter popped the cork and poured. When they each had a glass, Robert said: "I would like to propose a toast." He cleared his throat, and Maud realized with amusement that he was going to make a speech.

"My cousin Walter is an unusual man," he began. "He has always seemed older than me, although in fact we are the same age. When we were students together in Vienna, he never got drunk. If a group of us went out in the evening, to visit certain houses in the city, he would stay home and study. I thought perhaps he was the type of man who does not love women." Robert gave a wry smile. "In fact it was I who was made that way—but that's another story, as the English say. Walter loves his family and his work, and he loves Germany, but he has never loved a woman—until now. He has changed." Robert grinned mischievously. "He buys new ties. He asks me questions—when do you kiss a girl, should men wear cologne, what colors flatter him—as if I knew anything about what women like. And—most terrible of all, in my view . . ." Robert paused dramatically. "He plays ragtime!"

The others laughed. Robert raised his glass. "Let us toast the woman who has wrought such changes—the bride!"

They drank and then, to Maud's surprise, Ethel spoke. "It falls to me to propose the toast to the groom," she said as if she had been making speeches all her life. How had a servant from Wales acquired such confidence? Then Maud remembered that her father was a preacher and a political activist, so she had an example to follow.

"Lady Maud is different from every other woman of her class I have ever met," Ethel began. "When I started work as a maid at Tŷ Gwyn, she was the only member of the family who even noticed me. Here in London, when young unmarried women have babies, most respectable ladies grumble about moral decay—but Maud offers them real practical help. In the East End of London, she is regarded as a saint. However, she has her faults, and they are grave."

Maud thought: What now?

"She is too serious to attract a normal man," Ethel went on. "All the most eligible men in London have been drawn to her by her striking good looks and vivacious personality, only to be frightened away by her brains and her tough political realism. Some time ago I realized it would take a rare man to win her. He would have to be clever, but open-minded; strictly moral, but not orthodox; strong, but not domineering." Ethel smiled. "I thought it was impossible. And then, January, he came up the hill from Aberowen in the station taxi and walked into Tŷ Gwyn, and the wait was over." She raised her glass. "To the groom!"

They all drank again; then Ethel took Robert's arm. "Now you can take me to the Ritz for dinner, Robert," she said.

Walter seemed surprised. "I assumed we would all have dinner together here," he said.

Ethel gave him an arch look. "Don't be daft, man," she said. She walked to the door, drawing Robert with her.

"Good night," Robert said, though it was only six o'clock. The two of them went out and closed the door.

Maud laughed. Walter said: "That housekeeper is extremely intelligent."

"She understands me," Maud said. She went to the door and turned the key. "Now," she said. "The bedroom."

"Would you prefer to undress in private?" Walter said, looking worried.

"Not really," Maud said. "Wouldn't you like to watch?"

He swallowed, and when he spoke he sounded a little hoarse. "Yes, please," he said. "I would." He held the bedroom door open and she passed through.

Despite her show of boldness, she felt nervous as she sat on the edge of the bed and took off her shoes. No one had seen her naked since she was eight years old. She did not know whether her body was beautiful because she had never seen anyone else's. By comparison with the nudes in museums, she had small breasts and wide hips. And there was a growth of hair between her legs that paintings never showed. Would Walter think her body was ugly?

He took off his coat and waistcoat and hung them up in a matter-of-fact way. She supposed they would get used to this one day. Everyone did it all the time. But somehow it felt strange, more intimidating than exciting.

She pulled down her stockings and took off her hat. She had nothing else superfluous. The next step was the big one. She stood up.

Walter stopped undoing his tie.

Quickly, Maud unfastened her dress and let it fall to the

floor. Then she dropped her petticoat and pulled her lace blouse over her head. She stood in front of him in her underwear and watched his face.

"You are so beautiful," he said in a half whisper.

She smiled. He always said the right thing.

He took her in his arms and kissed her. She began to feel less nervous, almost relaxed. She savored the touch of his mouth on hers, the gentle lips and the bristles of the mustache. She stroked his cheek, squeezed his earlobe between her fingertips, and ran her hand around the column of his neck, feeling everything with heightened awareness, thinking: All this is mine now.

"Let's lie down," he said.

"No," she said. "Not yet." She stepped away from him. "Wait." She took off her chemise, revealing that she was wearing one of the newfangled brassieres. She reached behind her back, unfastened the clasp, and threw it to the floor. She looked at him defiantly, daring him not to like her breasts.

He said: "They are beautiful—may I kiss them?"

"You may do anything you like," she said, feeling deliciously wanton.

He bent his head to her chest and kissed one, then the other, letting his lips brush delicately across her nipples, which stood up suddenly as if the air had turned cold. She had a sudden yen to do the same to him, and wondered if he would think it odd.

He might have kissed her breasts forever. She pushed him away gently. "Take off the rest of your clothes," she said. "Quickly."

He pulled off shoes, socks, tie, shirt, undershirt, and trousers; then he hesitated. "I feel shy," he said, laughing. "I don't know why."

"I'll go first," she said. She untied the string of her drawers and pulled them off. When she looked up he was naked, too, and she saw with a shock that his penis was sticking up from the thatch of fair hair at his groin. She remembered grasping it through his clothes at the opera, and now she wanted to touch it again.

He said: "May we now lie down?"

He sounded so correct that she laughed. A hurt look crossed his face, and she was immediately apologetic. "I love you," she said, and his expression cleared. "Please let us lie down." She was so excited she felt she might burst.

At first they lay side by side, kissing and touching. "I love you," she said again. "How soon will you get bored with my saying that?"

"Never," he said gallantly.

She believed him.

After a while he said: "Now?" and she nodded.

She parted her legs. He lay on top of her, resting his weight on his elbows. She was taut with anticipation. Shifting his weight to his left arm, he reached between her thighs, and she felt his fingers opening her moist lips, then something larger. He pushed, and suddenly she felt a pain. She cried out.

"I'm sorry!" he said. "I hurt you. I'm so terribly sorry."

"Just wait a moment," she said. The pain was not very bad. She was more shocked than anything else. "Try again," she said. "Just gently."

She felt the head of his penis touch her lips again, and she knew that it would not go inside: it was too big, or the hole was too small, or both. But she let him push, hoping for the best. It hurt, but this time she gritted her teeth and stopped herself from crying out. Her stoicism did no good. After a few moments he stopped. "It won't go in," he said.

"What's wrong?" she said miserably. "I thought this was supposed to happen naturally."

"I don't understand it," he said. "I have no experience."

"And I certainly have none." She reached down and grasped his penis. She loved the feel of it in her hand, stiff but silky. She tried to maneuver it inside her, raising her hips to make it easier; but after a moment he pulled away, saying: "Ah! Sorry! It hurts me, too."

"Do you think you're bigger than usual?" she said tentatively.

"No. When I was in the army I saw many men naked. Some fellows have extra-large ones, and they are very proud, but I am average, and anyway I never heard even one of them complain of this difficulty."

Maud nodded. The only other penis she had ever seen was Fitz's, and as far as she could remember, it was about the same size as Walter's. "Perhaps I'm too small."

He shook his head. "When I was sixteen, I went to stay

in Robert's family castle in Hungary. There was a maid there who was very ... vivacious. We did not have sexual intercourse, but we did experiment. I touched her the way I touched you in the library at Sussex House. I hope I am not making you angry by telling you this."

She kissed his chin. "Not in the least."

"She was not very different from you in that area."

"Then what is wrong?"

He sighed and rolled off her. He put his arm under her head and pulled her to him, kissing her forehead. "I have heard that newly married couples may have difficulties. Sometimes the man is so nervous that he does not become erect. I have also heard of men who become overexcited and ejaculate even before intercourse takes place. I think we must be patient and love each other and see what happens."

"But we have only one night!" Maud began to cry.

Walter patted her and said: "There, there," but it did no good. She felt a complete failure. I believed I was so clever, she thought, escaping from my brother and marrying Walter secretly, and now it has all turned into a disaster. She was disappointed for herself but even more for Walter. How terrible for him to wait until the age of twenty-eight, then marry a woman who could not satisfy him!

She wished she could talk to someone about this, another woman—but who? The thought of discussing it with Aunt Herm was ludicrous. Some women shared secrets with their maids, but Maud had never had that kind of relationship with Sanderson. Perhaps she could talk to Ethel. Now that she came to think of it, it was Ethel who had told her it was normal to have hair between your legs. But Ethel had gone off with Robert.

Walter sat upright. "Let us order supper, and perhaps a bottle of wine," he said. "We will sit down together as man and wife, and talk of this and that for a while. Then, later, we will try again."

Maud had no appetite and could not imagine having a conversation about "this and that," but she did not have a better idea, so she consented. Miserably, she put her clothes back on. Walter dressed quickly, went to the next room, and rang the bell for a waiter. She heard him ordering cold meats, smoked fish, salads, and a bottle of hock.

She sat by an open window and looked down at the street below. A newspaper placard said BRITISH ULTIMATUM TO GERMANY. Walter might be killed in this war. She did not want him to die a virgin.

Walter called her when the food had arrived and she joined him in the next room. The waiter had spread a white cloth and laid out smoked salmon, sliced ham, lettuce, tomatoes, cucumber, and sliced white bread. She did not feel hungry, but sipped the white wine he poured, and nibbled some salmon to show she was willing.

In the end, they did talk of this and that. Walter reminisced about his childhood, his mother, and his time at Eton. Maud spoke about house parties at Tŷ Gwyn when her father was alive. The most powerful men in the land were guests, and her mother would have to arrange the allocation of bedrooms so that men could be near their mistresses.

At first, Maud found herself consciously making conversation, as if they were two people who hardly knew each other; but soon they relaxed into their normal intimacy, and she just said whatever came into her mind. The waiter cleared away the supper and they moved to the couch, where they continued to talk, holding hands. They speculated about the sex lives of other people: their parents, Fitz, Robert, Ethel, even the duchess. Maud was fascinated to learn about men such as Robert: where they met, how they recognized one another, and what they did. They kissed each other just as men kissed women, Walter told her, and they did what she had done to him at the opera, and other things . . . He said he was not sure of the details, but she thought he did know and just felt embarrassed to say.

She was surprised when the clock on the mantelpiece struck midnight. "Let's go to bed," she said. "I want to lie in your arms, even if things don't happen the way they're supposed to."

"All right." He stood up. "Do you mind if I do something first? There is a telephone in the lobby for the use of guests. I'd like to phone the embassy."

"Of course."

He went out. Maud went to the bathroom along the corridor, then returned to the suite. She took off her clothes and got into bed naked. She almost felt she did not care what happened now. They loved each other, and they were together, and if that was all it would be enough.

Walter returned a few minutes later. His face was grim and she knew immediately that the news was bad. "Britain has declared war on Germany," he said.

"Oh, Walter, I'm so sorry!"

"The note was received at the embassy an hour ago. Young Nicolson brought it round from the Foreign Office and got Prince Lichnowsky out of bed."

They had known it was almost certain to happen, but even so the reality struck Maud like a blow. She could see that Walter was upset, too.

He took off his clothes automatically, as if he had been undressing in front of her for years. "We leave tomorrow," he said. He took off his underpants, and she saw that his penis in its normal state was small and wrinkled. "I must be at Liverpool Street station, with my bags packed, by ten o'clock." He turned off the electric light and got into bed with her.

They lay side by side, not touching, and for an awful moment Maud thought he was going to go to sleep like that; then he turned to her and took her in his arms and kissed her mouth. Despite everything she was flooded with desire for him; indeed, it was almost as if their troubles had made her love him more urgently and desperately. She felt his penis grow and harden against her soft belly. After a moment he got on top of her. As before, he leaned on his left arm and touched her with his right hand. As before, she felt the hard penis pressing her lips. As before, it hurt—but only for a moment. This time, it slipped inside her.

There was another moment of resistance; then she lost her virginity; and suddenly he was all the way in and they were locked together in the oldest embrace of all.

"Oh, thank heaven," she said; then relief gave way to delight, and she began to move in happy rhythm with him; and, at last, they made love.

PART TWO

THE WAR
of
GIANTS

CHAPTER TWELVE

Early to Late August 1914

Katerina was distraught. When the mobilization posters went up all over St. Petersburg, she sat in Grigori's room at the boardinghouse weeping, running her fingers distractedly through her long fair hair, and saying: "What am I going to do? What am I going to do?"

It made him long to take her in his arms and kiss her tears away and promise never to leave her side. But he could not make such a promise and, anyway, she loved his brother.

Grigori had done his military service and was therefore a reservist, theoretically ready for battle. In fact most of his training had consisted of marching and building roads. Nevertheless he expected to be among the first summoned.

It made him fume with rage. The war was as stupid and pointless as everything else Tsar Nicholas did. There had been a murder in Bosnia, and a month later Russia was at war with Germany! Thousands of working-class men and peasants would be killed on both sides, and nothing would be achieved. It proved, to Grigori and everyone he knew, that the Russian nobility were too stupid to govern.

Even if he survived, the war would ruin his plans. He was saving for another ticket to America. With his wages from the Putilov factory he might do it in two or three years, but on army pay it would take forever. How many more years must he suffer the injustice and brutality of tsarist rule?

He was even more worried about Katerina. What would she do if he had to go to war? She was sharing a room with three other girls at the boardinghouse, and working at the Putilov factory, packing rifle cartridges into cardboard boxes. But she would have to stop work when the baby was born, at least for a while. Without Grigori, how would she support herself and the child? She would be desperate, and he knew what country girls did in St. Petersburg when they were desperate for money. God forbid that she should sell her body on the streets.

However, he was not called up on the first day, or the first week. According to the newspapers, two and a half million reservists had been mobilized on the last day of July, but that was just a story. It was impossible for so many men to be marshaled, issued with uniforms, and put on trains to the front all in one day, or indeed one month. They were called in groups, some sooner, some later.

As the first hot days of August went by, Grigori began to think he might have been left out. It was a tantalizing possibility. The army was one of the worst-managed institutions in a hopelessly disorganized country, and there would probably be thousands of men who were overlooked through sheer incompetence.

Katerina had got into the habit of coming to his room early every morning, while he was making breakfast. It was the highlight of his day. He was always washed and dressed by then, but she appeared wearing the shift she slept in, her hair bewitchingly tousled, yawning. The garment was too small for her, now that she was putting on weight. He calculated that she must be four and a half months pregnant. Her breasts and hips were larger, and there was a small but noticeable bulge in her belly. Her voluptuousness was a delightful torture. Grigori tried not to stare at her body.

One morning she came in while he was scrambling two hen's eggs in a pan over the fire. He no longer made do with porridge for breakfast: his brother's unborn child needed good food to grow strong and healthy. Most days Grigori had something nourishing to share with Katerina: ham, or herrings, or her favorite, sausage.

Katerina was always hungry. She sat at the table, cut a thick slice of black bread from the loaf, and began to eat, too impatient to wait. With her mouth full she said: "When a soldier is killed, who gets his back pay?"

Grigori recalled giving the name and address of his next of kin. "In my case, Lev," he said.

"I wonder if he's in America yet."

"He must be. It doesn't take eight weeks to get there."

"I hope he's found a job."

"You don't need to worry. He'll be all right. Everyone likes him." Grigori suffered a pang of angry resentment at his brother. It should have been Lev here in Russia looking after Katerina and her unborn baby, and worrying about the draft, while Grigori started the new life he had saved and planned for. But Lev had snatched that opportunity. And still Katerina fretted about the man who had abandoned her, not the one who had stayed.

She said: "I'm sure he's doing well in America, but still I wish we'd had a letter from him."

Grigori shaved a heel of hard cheese over the eggs and added salt. He wondered sadly whether they would ever hear from America. Lev had never been sentimental, and he might have decided to shuck off his past, like a lizard crawling out of its old skin. But Grigori did not voice this thought, out of kindness to Katerina, who was still hoping Lev would send for her.

She said: "Do you think you will fight?"

"Not if I can help it. What are we fighting for?"

"For Serbia, they say."

Grigori spooned the eggs onto two plates and sat at the table. "The issue is whether Serbia will be tyrannized by the Austrian emperor or the Russian tsar. I doubt if the Serbs care one way or the other, and I certainly don't." He began to eat.

"For the tsar, then."

"I would fight for you, for Lev, for myself, or for your baby . . . but for the tsar? No."

Katerina ate her egg rapidly and wiped the plate with a fresh slice of bread. "What names do you like for a boy?"

"My father's name was Sergei, and his father was Tikhon."

"I like Mikhail," she said. "The same as the archangel."

"So do most people. That's why the name is so common."

"Perhaps I should call him Lev. Or even Grigori."

Grigori was touched by this. He would be thrilled to

have a nephew named after him. But he did not like to make demands on her. "Lev would be nice," he said.

The factory whistle blew—a sound that could be heard all over the Narva district—and Grigori stood up to go.

"I'll wash the plates," Katerina said. Her job did not begin until seven, an hour later than Grigori's.

She turned her cheek up and Grigori kissed her. It was only a brief kiss, and he did not allow his lips to linger, but all the same he relished the soft smoothness of her skin and the warm, sleepy smell of her neck.

Then he put on his cap and went out.

The summer weather was warm and humid, despite the early hour. Grigori began to perspire as he walked briskly through the streets.

In the two months since Lev had left, Grigori and Katerina had settled into an uneasy friendship. She relied on him, and he looked after her, but it was not what either of them wanted. Grigori wanted love, not friendship. Katerina wanted Lev, not Grigori. But Grigori found a kind of fulfillment in making sure she ate well. It was the only way he had of expressing his love. It could hardly be a long-term arrangement, but right now it was difficult to think long-term. He still planned to escape from Russia and find his way to the promised land of America.

At the factory gate new mobilization posters had been stuck up, and men crowded around, those unable to read begging others to read aloud. Grigori found himself standing next to Isaak, the football captain. They were the same age and had been reservists together. Grigori scanned the notices, looking for the name of their unit.

Today it was there.

He looked again, but there was no mistake: Narva Regiment.

He looked down the list of names and found his own.

He had not really believed it could happen. But he had been fooling himself. He was twenty-five, fit and strong, perfect soldier material. Of course he was going to war.

What would happen to Katerina? And her baby?

Isaak cursed aloud. His name was also on the list.

A voice behind them said: "No need to worry."

They turned to see the long, thin shape of Kanin, the amiable supervisor of the casting section, an engineer in his thirties. "No need to worry?" said Grigori skeptically. "Katerina is having Lev's baby and there's no one to look after her. What am I going to do?"

"I've been to see the man in charge of mobilization for this district," Kanin said. "He promised me exemption for any of my workers. Only the troublemakers have to go."

Grigori's heart leaped with hope again. It sounded too good to be true.

Isaak said: "What do we have to do?"

"Just don't go to the barracks. You'll be all right. It's fixed."

Isaak was an aggressive character—no doubt that was why he made such a good sportsman—and he was not satisfied with Kanin's answer. "Fixed how?" he demanded.

"The army gives the police a list of men who fail to show, and the police have to round them up. Your name simply won't be on the list."

Isaak grunted with dissatisfaction. Grigori shared his dislike of such semiofficial arrangements—there was too much room for things to go wrong—but dealing with the government was always like this. Kanin had either bribed an official or performed some other favor. It was pointless to be churlish about it. "That's great," Grigori said to Kanin. "Thank you."

"Don't thank me," Kanin said mildly. "I did it for myself—and for Russia. We need skilled men like you two to make trains, not stop German bullets—an illiterate peasant can do that. The government hasn't worked this out yet, but they will in time, and then they'll thank me."

Grigori and Isaak passed through the gates. "We might as well trust him," Grigori said. "What have we got to lose?" They stood in line to check themselves in by each dropping a numbered metal square into a box. "It's good news," he said.

Isaak was not convinced. "I just wish I could feel surer," he said.

They headed for the wheel shop. Grigori put his worries out of his mind and prepared himself for the day's work. The Putilov plant was making more trains than ever. The army had to assume that locomotives and wagons would be destroyed by shelling, so they would be needing replacements as soon as the fighting started. The pressure was on Grigori's team to produce wheels faster.

He began to roll up his sleeves as he stepped into the wheel shop. It was a small shed, and the furnace made it hot in winter, a baking oven now at the height of summer. Metal screeched and rang as lathes shaped and polished it.

He saw Konstantin standing by his lathe, and his friend's stance made him frown. Konstantin's face telegraphed a warning: something was wrong. Isaak saw it, too. Reacting faster than Grigori, he stopped, grabbed Grigori's arm, and said: "What—?"

He did not finish the question.

A figure in a black-and-green uniform stepped from behind the furnace and hit Grigori in the face with a sledgehammer.

He tried to dodge the blow, but his reaction was a moment too slow and, although he ducked, the wooden head of the big hammer struck him high on the cheekbone and knocked him to the ground. An agonizing pain shot through his head and he cried out loud.

It took several moments for his vision to clear. At last he looked up and saw the stout figure of Mikhail Pinsky, the local police captain.

He should have expected this. He had got off too lightly after that fight back in February. Policemen never forgot such things.

He also saw Isaak fighting with Pinsky's sidekick, Ilya Kozlov, and two other cops.

Grigori remained on the ground. He was not going to fight back if he could help it. Let Pinsky take his revenge; then perhaps he would be satisfied.

In the next second he failed to keep that resolution.

Pinsky raised the sledgehammer. In a flash of redundant insight Grigori recognized the tool as his own, used for tapping templates into the molding sand. Then it came down at his head.

He lurched to the right but Pinsky slanted his swing, and the heavy oak tool landed on Grigori's left shoulder. He roared with pain and anger. While Pinsky was recovering his balance, Grigori leaped to his feet. His left arm was limp and useless, but there was nothing amiss with his right, and he drew back his fist to hit Pinsky, regardless of the consequences.

He never struck the blow. Two figures he had not noticed materialized on either side of him in black-and-green uniforms, and his arms were grabbed and held firmly. He tried to shake off his captors but failed. Through a mist of rage he saw Pinsky draw back the hammer and strike. The blow hit him in the chest, and he felt ribs crack. The next blow was lower, and pounded his belly. He convulsed and vomited his breakfast. Then another blow struck the side of his head. He blacked out for a moment, and came around to find himself hanging limply in the grip of the two policemen. Isaak was similarly pinned by two others.

"Feeling calmer now?" said Pinsky.

Grigori spat blood. His body was a mass of pain and he could not think straight. What was going on? Pinsky hated him, but something must have happened to trigger this. And it was bold of Pinsky to act right here in the middle of the factory, surrounded by workers who had no reason to like the police. For some reason he must have been feeling sure of himself.

Pinsky hefted the sledgehammer and looked thoughtful, as if considering one more blow. Grigori braced himself and fought the temptation to beg for mercy. Then Pinsky said: "What is your name?"

Grigori tried to speak. At first nothing but blood came out of his mouth. At last he managed to say: "Grigori Sergeivich Peshkov."

Pinsky hit him in the stomach again. Grigori groaned and vomited blood. "Liar," said Pinsky. "What is your name?" He lifted the sledgehammer again.

Konstantin stepped from his lathe and came forward. "Officer, this man is Grigori Peshkov!" he protested. "All of us have known him for years!"

"Don't lie to me," Pinsky said. He lifted the hammer. "Or you'll get a taste of this."

Konstantin's mother, Varya, intervened. "It's no lie, Mikhail Mikhailovich," she said. Her use of the patronymic indicated that she knew Pinsky. "He is who he says he is." She stood with her arms folded over her large bosom as if defying the policeman to doubt her.

"Then explain this," said Pinsky, and he pulled from his pocket a sheet of paper. "Grigori Sergeivich Peshkov left St. Petersburg two months ago aboard the *Angel Gabriel*."

Kanin, the supervisor, appeared and said: "What's going on here? Why is no one working?"

Pinsky pointed to Grigori. "This man is Lev Peshkov, Grigori's brother—wanted for the murder of a police officer!"

They all began to shout at once. Kanin held up his hand for quiet and said: "Officer, I know Grigori and Lev Peshkov, and have seen both men almost every day for several years. They look alike, as brothers generally do, but I can assure you that this is Grigori. And you are holding up the work of this section."

"If this is Grigori," said Pinsky with the air of one who plays a trump card, "then who left on the *Angel Gabriel*?"

As soon as he had asked the question, the answer became obvious. After a moment it dawned on Pinsky, too, and he looked foolish.

Grigori said: "My passport and ticket were stolen."

Pinsky began to bluster. "Why did you not report this to the police?"

"What was the point? Lev had left the country. You could not bring him back, nor my property."

"That makes you an accomplice in his escape."

Kanin intervened again. "Captain Pinsky, you began by accusing this man of murder. Perhaps that was a good enough reason to stop production in the wheel shop. But you have admitted that you were in error, and now you allege only that he failed to report the theft of some documents. Meanwhile, your country is at war, and you are delaying the manufacture of locomotives desperately needed by the Russian army. Unless you wish your name to be mentioned in our next report to the army high command, I suggest you finish your business here quickly."

Pinsky looked at Grigori. "What reserve unit are you in?"

Without thinking, Grigori replied: "Narva Regiment."

"Hah!" said Pinsky. "They were called up today." He looked at Isaak. "You, too, I'll bet."

Isaak said nothing.

"Release them," Pinsky said.

Grigori staggered when they let go of his arms, but he managed to stay upright.

"You'd better make sure you show up at the depot as ordered," Pinsky said to Grigori and Isaak. "Otherwise I'll be after you." He turned on his heel and exited with what little dignity he had left. His men followed him.

Grigori sat down heavily on a stool. He had a blinding

headache, a pain in his ribs, and a bruised ache in his belly. He needed to curl up in a corner and pass out. The thought that kept him conscious was a scorching desire to destroy Pinsky and the entire system of which he was part. One of these days, he kept thinking, we will wipe out Pinsky and the tsar and everything they stand for.

Kanin said: "The army won't pursue you two—I've made sure of that—but I'm afraid I can't do anything about the police."

Grigori nodded grimly. It was as he had feared. Pinsky's most savage blow, worse than any he had struck with the sledgehammer, would be to make sure that Grigori and Isaak joined the army.

Kanin said: "I'll be sorry to lose you. You've been a good worker." He seemed genuinely moved, but he was impotent. He paused a moment longer, threw up his hands in a gesture of helplessness, and left the shop.

Varya appeared in front of Grigori with a bowl of water and a clean rag. She washed the blood from his face. She was a bulky woman but her broad hands had a gentle touch. "You should go to the factory barracks," she said. "Find an empty bed and lie down for an hour."

"No," Grigori said. "I'm going home."

Varya shrugged and moved to Isaak, who was not so badly injured.

With an effort, Grigori stood up. The factory spun around him for a while, and Konstantin held his arm when he staggered; but eventually he felt able to stand alone.

Konstantin picked up his cap from the floor and gave it to him.

He felt unsteady when he began to walk, but he waved away offers of support, and after a few steps he regained his normal stride. His head cleared with the effort, but the pain in his ribs forced him to tread carefully. He made his slow way through the maze of benches and lathes, furnaces and presses, to the outside of the building, and then to the factory gate.

There he met Katerina coming in.

"Grigori!" she said. "You've been called up—I saw the poster!" Then she noticed his damaged face. "What happened?"

"An encounter with your favorite police captain."

"That pig Pinsky. You're hurt!"

"The bruises will heal."

"I'll take you home."

Grigori was surprised. This was a switch of roles. Katerina had never before offered to take care of him. "I can make it on my own," he said.

"I'll come with you all the same."

She took his arm and they walked through the narrow streets against the tide of thousands of workers swarming to the factory. Grigori's body hurt and he felt ill, but all the same it was a joy to him to be walking arm in arm with Katerina as the sun rose over the dilapidated houses and the dirty streets.

However, the familiar walk tired him more than he expected, and when at last they got home he sat heavily on the bed and then, after a moment, lay down.

"I've got a bottle of vodka hidden in the girls' room," Katerina said.

"No, thanks, but I'd like some tea."

He did not have a samovar, but she made tea in a saucepan and gave him a cup with a lump of sugar. When he had drunk it, he felt a little better. He said: "The worst of it is, I could have avoided the draft—but Pinsky swore he would make sure I didn't."

She sat on the bed beside him and took from her pocket a pamphlet. "One of the girls gave me this."

Grigori glanced at it. It appeared dull and official, like a government publication. Its title was "Aid to Soldiers' Families."

Katerina said: "If you're the wife of a soldier you're entitled to a monthly allowance from the army. It's not just for the poor—everyone gets it."

Grigori vaguely remembered hearing about this. He had not taken much notice, as it did not apply to him.

Katerina went on: "There's more. You get cheap home fuel, cheap railway tickets, and help with children's schooling."

"That's good," Grigori said. He wanted to sleep. "Unusual for the army to be so sensible."

"But you have to be married."

Grigori became more alert. Surely she could not possibly be thinking . . . "Why are you telling me this?" he said.

"As it is I won't get anything."

Grigori lifted himself on one elbow and looked at her. Suddenly his heart was racing.

She said: "If I was married to a soldier I'd be better off. So would my baby."

"But . . . you love Lev."

"I know." She began to cry. "But Lev is in America and he doesn't care enough even to write and ask how I am."

"So . . . what do you want to do?" Grigori knew the answer, but he had to hear it.

"I want to get married," she said.

"Just so that you can get the soldier's wife's allowance."

She nodded, and with that nod she extinguished in him a faint, foolish hope that had flared briefly. "It would mean so much," she said. "To have a little money when the baby comes—especially as you'll be away with the army."

"I understand," he said with a heavy heart.

"Can we get married?" she said. "Please?"

"Yes," he said. "Of course."

{ II }

Five couples were married at the same time in the Church of the Blessed Virgin. The priest read the service fast, and Grigori observed with irritation that he did not look anyone in the eye. The man would hardly have noticed if one of the brides had been a gorilla.

Grigori did not much care. Whenever he passed a church, he remembered the priest who had tried to have some kind of sex with eleven-year-old Lev. Grigori's contempt for Christianity had later been reinforced by lectures on atheism at Konstantin's Bolshevik discussion group.

Grigori and Katerina were getting married at short notice, as were the other four couples. All the men were in uniform. Mobilization had caused a rush to matrimony, and the church was struggling to keep up. Grigori hated the uniform as a symbol of servitude.

He had told no one about the marriage. He did not feel it was a reason for celebration. Katerina had made it clear that it was a purely practical measure, a way for her to get an allowance. As such it was a very good idea, and Grigori would be less anxious, when he was away with the army, knowing that she had financial security. All the same he could not help feeling there was something horribly farcical about the wedding.

Katerina was not so shy, and all the girls from the boardinghouse were in the congregation, as well as several workers from the Putilov plant.

Afterward there was a party in the girls' room at the boardinghouse, with beer and vodka and a violinist who played folk tunes they all knew. When people started to get drunk, Grigori slipped out and went to his own room. He took off his boots and lay on the bed in his uniform trousers and shirt. He blew out the candle but he could see by the light from the street. He still ached from Pinsky's beating: his left arm hurt when he tried to use it and his cracked ribs gave him a stabbing pain every time he turned over in bed.

Tomorrow he would be on a train west. The shooting would start any day now. He was scared: only a mad person would feel otherwise. But he was smart and determined and he would try his best to stay alive, which was what he had done ever since his mother died.

He was still awake when Katerina came in. "You left the party early," she complained.

"I didn't want to get drunk."

She pulled up the skirt of her dress.

He was astonished. He stared at her body, outlined by the light from the streetlamps, the long curves of her thighs and the fair curls. He was aroused and confused. "What are you doing?" he said.

"Coming to bed, of course."

"Not here."

She kicked off her shoes. "What are you talking about? We're married."

"Just so that you can collect your allowance."

"Still, you deserve something in return." She lay on the bed and kissed his mouth with the smell of vodka on her breath.

He could not help the desire that rose within him, making him flush with passion and shame. All the same he managed to say a choked: "No."

She took his hand and pulled it to her breast. Against his will he caressed her, gently squeezing the soft flesh, his fingertips finding her nipple through the coarse fabric of her dress. "You see?" she said. "You want to."

The note of triumph angered him. "Of course I want to," he said. "I've loved you since the day I first saw you. But you love Lev."

"Oh, why do you always think about Lev?"

"It's a habit I got into when he was small and vulnerable."

"Well, he's a big man now, and he doesn't care two ko-peks for you, or for me. He took your passport, your ticket, and your money, and left us with nothing except his baby."

She was right: Lev had always been selfish. "But you don't love your family because they're kind and consider-ate. You love them because they're your family."

"Oh, give yourself a treat," she said with irritation. "You're joining the army tomorrow. You don't want to die regretting that you didn't fuck me when you had the chance."

He was powerfully tempted. Even though she was half drunk, her body was warm and inviting beside him. Was he not entitled to one night of bliss?

She ran her hand up his leg and grasped his stiff penis. "Come on, you've married me. You might as well take what you're entitled to."

And that was the problem, he thought. She did not love him. She was offering herself in payment for what he had done. It was prostitution. He felt insulted to the point of anger, and the fact that he longed to give in only made the feeling worse.

She began to rub his penis up and down. Furious and inflamed, he pushed her away. The shove was rougher than he really intended, and she fell off the bed.

She cried out in surprise and pain.

He had not meant it to happen, but he was too angry to apologize.

For several long moments she lay on the floor, weeping and cursing at the same time. He resisted the temptation to help her. She struggled to her feet, staggering from the vodka. "You pig!" she said. "How can you be so cruel?" She straightened her dress, covering her beautiful legs. "What sort of wedding night is this for a girl—to be kicked out of her husband's bed?"

Grigori was stung by her words, but he lay still and said nothing.

"I never thought you could be so hard-hearted," she raved. "Go to hell! Go to hell!" She picked up her shoes, flung open the door, and stormed out of the room.

Grigori felt utterly miserable. On his last day as a civilian he had quarreled with the woman he adored. If he died in battle now, he would die unhappy. What a rotten world, he thought; what a lousy life.

He went to the door to close it. As he did so, he heard Katerina in the next room, speaking with forced gaiety. "Grigori can't get it up—too drunk!" she said. "Give me some more vodka and let's have another dance!"

He slammed the door and threw himself on the bed.

{ III }

Eventually he fell into a troubled sleep. Next morning he woke early. He washed and put on his uniform and ate some bread.

When he put his head around the door of the girls' room, he saw them all fast asleep, the floor littered with bottles, the air foul with stale tobacco smoke and spilled beer. He stared for a long minute at Katerina, sleeping with her mouth open. Then he left the house, not knowing if he would ever see her again, telling himself he did not care.

But his spirits lifted with the excitement and confusion of reporting to his regiment, being issued a gun and ammunition, finding the right train, and meeting his new comrades. He stopped thinking about Katerina and turned his mind to the future.

He boarded a train with Isaak and several hundred other reservists in their new gray-green uniform breeches and tunics. Like the rest of them, he carried a Russian-made Mosin-Nagant rifle, as tall as himself with its long spiked bayonet. The huge bruise that the sledgehammer had left, covering most of one side of his face, made the other men think he was some kind of thug, and they treated him with wary respect. The train steamed out of St. Petersburg and chuffed steadily through fields and forests.

The setting sun was generally ahead and to the right, so they were going southwest, toward Germany. That seemed obvious to Grigori, though when he said it his fellow soldiers were surprised and impressed: most of them did not know in which direction Germany lay.

This was only the second time he had been on a train, and he was reminded vividly of the first. When he was eleven his mother had brought him and little Lev to St. Petersburg. His father had been hanged a few days earlier, and Grigori's young head was full of fear and grief, but like any boy he had been thrilled by the ride: the oiled smell of the mighty locomotive, the huge wheels, the camaraderie of the peasants in the third-class carriage, and the intoxicating speed with which the countryside sped by. Some of that exhilaration came back to him now, and he could not help feeling that he was on an adventure that could be exciting as well as terrible.

This time, however, he was traveling in a cattle truck, as were all but the officers. The wagon contained about forty men: pale-skinned, sly-eyed St. Petersburg factory workers; long-bearded, slow-talking peasants who looked at everything with wondering curiosity; and half a dozen dark-eyed, dark-haired Jews.

One of the Jews sat next to Grigori and introduced himself as David. His father manufactured iron buckets in the backyard of their house, he said, and he went from village to village selling them. There were a lot of Jews in the army, he explained, because they found it more difficult to get exemption from military service.

They were all under the orders of a Sergeant Gavrik, a regular soldier who looked anxious, barked orders, and used a great deal of profanity. He pretended to think all the men were peasants, and called them cowfuckers. He was about Grigori's age, too young to have been in the Japanese war of 1904–1905, and Grigori guessed that underneath the bluster he was scared.

Every few hours the train stopped at a country station and the men got out. Sometimes they were given soup and beer, sometimes just water. In between stops they sat on the floor of the wagon. Gavrik made sure they knew how to clean their rifles and reminded them of the different military ranks and how officers should be addressed. Lieutenants and captains were "Your Honor," but superior officers required a variety of honorifics all the way up to "Most High Radiance" for those who were also aristocrats.

By the second day, Grigori calculated they must be in the territory of Russian Poland.

He asked the sergeant which part of the army they were in. Grigori knew they were the Narva Regiment, but no one had told them how they fitted into the overall picture. Gavrik said: "None of your fucking business. Just go where you're sent and do as you're told." Grigori guessed he did not know the answer.

After a day and a half the train stopped at a town called Ostrolenka. Grigori had never heard of it, but he could see that it was the end of the railway line, and he guessed it must be near the German border. Here hundreds of railway wagons were being unloaded. Men and horses sweated and heaved to maneuver huge guns off the trains. Thousands of troops milled around as bad-tempered officers attempted to muster them in platoons and companies. At the same time tons of supplies had to be transferred to horse-drawn carts: sides of meat, sacks of flour, barrels of beer, crates of bullets, artillery shells in packing cases, and tons of oats for all the horses.

At one point Grigori saw the loathed face of Prince Andrei. He wore a gorgeous uniform—Grigori was not sufficiently familiar with badges and stripes to identify the regiment or rank—and rode on a tall chestnut horse. Behind him walked a corporal carrying a canary in a cage. I could shoot him now, Grigori thought, and avenge my father. It was a stupid idea, of course, but he stroked the trigger of his rifle as the prince and his caged bird disappeared into the crowd.

The weather was hot and dry. That night Grigori slept on the ground with the rest of the men from his wagon. He realized that they constituted a platoon, and would be together for the foreseeable future. The next morning they met their officer, an unnervingly young second lieutenant called Tomchak. He led them out of Ostrolenka on a road that headed northwest.

Lieutenant Tomchak told Grigori they were in 13 Corps, commanded by General Klyuev, which was part of the Second Army under General Samsonov. When Grigori relayed this information to the other men, they were spooked, because the number thirteen was unlucky, and Sergeant Gavrik said: "I told you it was none of your business, Peshkov, you cocksucking homo."

They were not far out of town when the metaled road ran out and became a sand track through a forest. The supply carts got stuck, and the drivers soon found out that a single horse could not pull a loaded army wagon through sand. All the horses had to be unhitched and reharnessed two to a cart, and every second wagon had to be abandoned at the roadside.

They marched all day and slept under the stars again. Each night when he went to bed Grigori said to himself: Another day, and I'm still alive to take care of Katerina and the baby.

That evening Tomchak received no orders, so they sat under the trees all the next morning. Grigori was glad: his legs ached from yesterday's march, and his feet hurt in the new boots. The peasants were used to walking all day, and they laughed at the weakness of the city dwellers.

At midday a runner brought orders commanding them to set out at eight a.m., four hours earlier.

There was no provision for supplying the marching men with water, so they had to drink from wells and streams they came across on the way. They soon learned to drink their fill at every opportunity, and keep their standard-issue water bottles topped up. There was no means of cooking, either, and the only food they got was the dry biscuits called hardtack. Every few miles they would be called upon to help pull a wheeled cannon out of a swamp or sandpit.

They marched until sundown and slept under the trees again.

Halfway through the third day they emerged from a wood to see a fine farmhouse set amid fields of ripening oats and wheat. It was a two-story building with a steeply pitched roof. In the yard was a concrete wellhead, and there was a low stone structure that seemed to be a pigsty, except that it was clean. The place looked like the home of a prosperous land captain, or perhaps the younger son of a nobleman. It was locked up and deserted.

A mile farther on, to everyone's astonishment, the road passed through an entire village of such places, all abandoned. The realization began to dawn on Grigori that he had crossed the border into Germany, and these luxurious houses were the homes of German farmers who had fled, with their families and livestock, to escape the oncoming Russian army. But where were the hovels of the poor peasants? What had been done with the filth of the pigs and cows? Why were there no tumbledown wooden cowsheds with patched walls and holes in the roofs?

The soldiers were jubilant. "They're running away from us!" said a peasant. "They're scared of us Russians. We'll take Germany without firing a shot!"

Grigori knew, from Konstantin's discussion group, that the German plan was to conquer France first and then deal with Russia. The Germans were not surrendering; they were choosing the best time to fight. Even so, it would be surprising if they were to give up this prime territory without a struggle.

"What part of Germany is this, Your Honor?" he asked Tomchak.

"They call it East Prussia."

"Is it the wealthiest part of Germany?"

"I don't think so," said the lieutenant. "I see no palaces."

"Are ordinary people in Germany rich enough to live in homes such as these?"

"I suppose they are."

Evidently Tomchak, who looked as if he was barely out of school, did not know much more than Grigori.

Grigori walked on, but he felt demoralized. He had thought himself a well-informed man, but he had had no idea that the Germans lived so well.

It was Isaak who voiced his doubts. "Our army is already having trouble feeding us, even though not a single shot has yet been fired," he said quietly. "How can we possibly fight against people who are so well organized that they keep their pigs in stone houses?"

{ IV }

Walter was elated by events in Europe. There was every prospect of a short war and a quick victory for Germany. He could be reunited with Maud by Christmas.

Unless he died, of course. But, if that happened, he would die happy.

He shuddered with joy whenever he remembered the night they had spent together. They had not wasted precious moments sleeping. They had made love three times. The initial, heartbreaking difficulty had in the end only intensified their euphoria. In between lovemaking they had lain side by side, talking and idly caressing each other. It was a conversation unlike any other. Anything Walter could say to himself, he could say to Maud. Never had he felt so close to another person.

Around dawn they had eaten all the fruit in the bowl and all the chocolates in the box. Then, at last, they had had to leave: Maud to sneak back into Fitz's house, pretending to the servants that she had been out for an early walk; Walter to his flat, to change his clothes, pack a bag, and leave his valet instructions to ship the rest of his possessions home to Berlin.

In the cab on the short ride from Knightsbridge to Mayfair they had held hands tightly and said little. Walter had stopped the driver around the corner from Fitz's house. Maud had kissed him once more, her tongue finding his in desperate passion; then she had gone, leaving him wondering if he would ever see her again.

The war had begun well. The German army was storming through Belgium. Farther south the French—led by sentiment rather than strategy—had invaded Lorraine, only to be mown down by German artillery. Now they were in full retreat.

Japan had sided with the French and British allies, which unfortunately freed up Russian soldiers in the far east to be switched to the European battlefield. But the Americans had confirmed their neutrality, to Walter's great relief. How small the world had become, he reflected: Japan was about as far east as you could go, and America as far west. This war encircled the globe.

According to German intelligence, the French had sent a stream of telegrams to St. Petersburg, begging the tsar to attack, in the hope that the Germans might be distracted. And the Russians had moved faster than anyone expected. Their First Army had astonished the world by marching across the German border a mere twelve days after mobilization began. Meanwhile the Second Army invaded farther south, from the railhead at Ostrolenka, on a trajectory that would close the teeth of the pincers near a town called Tannenberg. Both armies were unopposed.

The uncharacteristic German torpor that allowed this to happen soon came to an end. The commander in chief in the region, General Prittwitz, known as *der Dicke*, the Fat One, was smartly fired by the high command and replaced by the duo of Paul von Hindenburg, summoned out of retirement, and Erich Ludendorff, one of the few senior military men without an aristocratic "von" to his name. At forty-nine, Ludendorff was also among the younger generals. Walter admired him for having risen so high purely on merit, and was pleased to be his intelligence liaison.

On the way from Belgium to Prussia they stopped briefly on Sunday, August 23, in Berlin, where Walter had a few moments with his mother on the station platform. Her sharp nose was reddened by a summer cold. She hugged him hard, shaking with emotion. "You are safe," she said.

"Yes, Mother, I'm safe."

"I'm terribly worried about Zumwald. The Russians are so close!" Zumwald was the von Ulrichs' country estate in the east.

"I'm sure it will be all right."

She was not so easily fobbed off. "I have spoken to the kaiserin." She knew the kaiser's wife well. "Several other ladies have done the same."

"You should not bother the royal family," Walter reproved her. "They already have so many worries."

She sniffed. "We cannot abandon our estates to the Russian army!"

Walter sympathized. He, too, hated the thought of primitive Russian peasants and their barbaric knout-wielding lords overrunning the well-kept pastures and orchards of the von Ulrich inheritance. Those hardworking German farmers, with their muscular wives and scrubbed children and fat cattle, deserved to be protected. Was that not what the war was about? And he planned to take Maud to Zumwald one day, and show the place off to his wife. "Ludendorff is going to stop the Russian advance, Mother," he said. He hoped it was true.

Before she could respond the whistle blew, and Walter kissed her and boarded the train.

Walter felt the sting of personal responsibility for the German reverses on the eastern front. He was one of the intelligence experts who had forecast that the Russians could not attack so soon after ordering mobilization. He was mortified with shame whenever he thought of it. But he suspected he had not been entirely wrong, and the Russians were sending ill-prepared troops forward with inadequate supplies.

This suspicion was reinforced, when he arrived in East Prussia later that Sunday with Ludendorff's entourage, by reports that the Russian First Army, in the north, had halted. They were only a few miles inside German territory, and military logic dictated that they should press forward. What were they waiting for? Walter guessed they were running out of food.

But the southern arm of the pincer was still advancing, and Ludendorff's priority was to stop it.

The following morning, Monday, August 24, Walter brought Ludendorff two priceless reports. Both were Russian wireless messages, intercepted and translated by German intelligence.

The first, sent at five thirty that morning by General Rennenkampf, gave marching orders for the Russian First Army. At last Rennenkampf was on the move again—but instead of turning south to close the pincers by meeting up with the Second Army, he was inexplicably heading west on a line that did not threaten any German forces.

The second message had been sent half an hour later by General Samsonov, the commander of the Russian Second Army. He ordered his 13 and 15 Corps to go after the German XX Corps, which he believed to be in retreat.

"This is astonishing!" said Ludendorff. "How did we get this information?" He looked suspicious, as if Walter might have been deceiving him. Walter had a feeling Ludendorff mistrusted him as a member of the old military aristocracy. "Do we know their codes?" Ludendorff demanded.

"They don't use codes," Walter told him.

"They send orders in clear? For heaven's sake, why?"

"Russian soldiers aren't sufficiently educated to deal with codes," Walter explained. "Our prewar intelligence estimates suggested that there are hardly enough literate men to operate the wireless transmitters."

"Then why don't they use field telephones? A phone call can't be intercepted."

"I think they have probably run out of telephone wire."

Ludendorff had a downturned mouth and a thrusting chin, and he always looked as if he were frowning aggressively. "This couldn't be a trick, could it?"

Walter shook his head. "The idea is inconceivable, sir. The Russians are barely able to organize normal communications. The use of phony wireless signals to deceive the enemy is as far beyond them as flying to the moon."

Ludendorff bent his balding head over the map on the table in front of him. He was a tireless worker, but he was often afflicted by terrible doubts, and Walter guessed he was driven by fear of failure. Ludendorff put his finger on the map. "Samsonov's 13 and 15 Corps form the center of the Russian line," he said. "If they move forward . . ."

Walter saw immediately what Ludendorff was thinking: the Russians could be drawn into an envelope trap, surrounded on three sides.

Ludendorff said: "On our right we have von François and his I Corps. At our center, Scholtz and the XX Corps, who have fallen back but are not on the run, contrary to what the Russians seem to think. And on our left, but fifty kilometers to the north, we have Mackensen and the XVII Corps. Mackensen is keeping an eye on the northern arm of the Russian pincer, but if those Russians are heading the wrong way, perhaps we can ignore them, for the moment, and turn Mackensen south."

"A classic maneuver," Walter said. It was simple, but he himself had not seen it until Ludendorff pointed it out. That, he thought admiringly, was why Ludendorff was the general.

Ludendorff said: "But it will work only if Rennenkampf and the Russian First Army continue in the wrong direction."

"You saw the intercept, sir. The Russian orders have gone out."

"Let's hope Rennenkampf doesn't change his mind."

{ V }

Grigori's battalion had no food, but a wagonload of spades had arrived, so they dug a trench. The men dug in shifts, relieving one another after half an hour, so it did not take long. The result was not very neat, but it would serve.

Earlier that day, Grigori and Isaak and their comrades had overrun a deserted German position, and Grigori had noticed that their trenches had a kind of zigzag at regular intervals, so that you could not see very far along. Lieutenant Tomchak said the zigzag was called a traverse, but he did not know what it was for. He did not order his men to copy the German design. But Grigori felt sure it must have a purpose.

Grigori had not yet fired his rifle. He had heard shooting, rifles and machine guns and artillery, and his unit had taken a good deal of German territory, but so far he had shot at no one, and no one had shot at him. Everywhere 13 Corps went, they found that the Germans had just left.

There was no logic to this. Everything in war was confusion, he was realizing. No one was quite sure where they were or where the enemy was. Two men from Grigori's platoon had been killed, but not by Germans: one had accidentally shot himself in the thigh with his own rifle and bled to death astonishingly quickly, and the other had been trampled by a runaway horse and never recovered consciousness.

They had not seen a cook wagon for days. They had finished their emergency rations, and even the hardtack had run out. None of them had eaten since yesterday morning. After digging the trench, they slept hungry. Fortunately it was summer, so at least they were not cold.

The shooting began at dawn the next day.

It started some distance away to Grigori's left, but he could see clouds of shrapnel burst in the air, and loose earth erupt suddenly where shells landed. He knew he ought to be scared, but he was not. He was hungry, thirsty, tired, aching, and bored, but he was not frightened. He wondered if the Germans felt the same.

There was heavy gunfire on his right, too, some miles to the north, but here it was quiet. "Like the eye of the storm," said David, the Jewish bucket salesman.

Soon enough, orders came to advance. Wearily, they

climbed out of their trench and walked forward. "I suppose we should be grateful," Grigori said.

"For what?" Isaak demanded.

"Marching is better than fighting. We've got blisters, but we're alive."

In the afternoon they approached a town that Lieutenant Tomchak said was called Allenstein. They assembled in marching order on the outskirts, and entered the center in formation.

To their surprise, Allenstein was full of well-dressed German citizens going about their normal Thursday afternoon business, posting letters and buying groceries and walking babies in perambulators. Grigori's unit halted in a small park where the men sat in the shade of tall trees. Tomchak went into a nearby barbershop and came out shaved and with his hair cut. Isaak went to buy vodka, but returned saying the army had posted sentries outside all the wine shops with orders to keep soldiers out.

At last a horse and cart appeared with a barrel of freshwater. The men lined up to fill their canteens. As the afternoon cooled into evening, more carts arrived with loaves of bread, bought or requisitioned from the town's bakers. Night fell, and they slept under the trees.

At dawn there was no breakfast. Leaving a battalion behind to hold the town, Grigori and the rest of 13 Corps were marched out of Allenstein, heading southwest on the road to Tannenberg.

Although they had seen no action, Grigori noticed a change of mood among the officers. They cantered up and down the line and conferred in fretful huddles. Voices were raised in argument, with a major pointing one way and a captain gesturing in the opposite direction. Grigori continued to hear heavy artillery to the north and south, though it seemed to be moving eastward while 13 Corps went west. "Whose artillery is that?" said Sergeant Gavrik. "Ours or theirs? And why is it moving east when we're going west?" The fact that he used no profanity suggested to Grigori that he was seriously worried.

A few kilometers out of Allenstein, a battalion was left to guard the rear, which surprised Grigori, since he assumed the enemy was ahead, not behind. The 13 Corps was being stretched thin, he thought with a frown.

Around the middle of the day, his battalion was detached from the main march. While their comrades continued southwest, they were directed southeast, on a broad path through a forest.

There, at last, Grigori encountered the enemy.

They stopped for a rest by a stream, and the men filled their bottles. Grigori walked off into the trees to answer a call of nature. He was standing behind a thick pine trunk when he heard a noise off to his left and was astonished to see, a few meters away, a German officer, complete with spiked helmet, on a fine black horse. The German was looking through a telescope toward the place where the battalion had stopped. Grigori wondered what he was looking at: the man could not see far through the trees. Perhaps he was trying to make out whether the uniforms were Russian or German. He sat as motionless as a monument in a St. Petersburg square, but his horse was not so still, and it shifted and repeated the noise that had alerted Grigori.

Grigori carefully buttoned his trousers, picked up his rifle, and backed away, keeping the tree between himself and the German.

Suddenly the man moved. Grigori suffered a moment of fear, thinking he had been seen; but the German expertly turned his horse and headed west, breaking into a trot.

Grigori ran back to Sergeant Gavrik. "I saw a German!" he said.

"Where?"

Grigori pointed. "Over there—I was taking a leak."

"Are you sure it was a German?"

"He had a spiked helmet."

"What was he doing?"

"Sitting on his horse, looking at us through a telescope."

"A scout!" said Gavrik. "Did you shoot at him?"

Only then did Grigori remember that he was supposed to kill German soldiers, not run away from them. "I thought I should tell you," he said feebly.

"You great fairy, why do you think we gave you a fucking gun?" Gavrik yelled.

Grigori looked at the loaded rifle in his hand, with its vicious-looking bayonet. Of course he should have fired it. What was he thinking? "I'm sorry," he said.

"Now that you've let him get away, the enemy know where we are!"

Grigori was humiliated. This situation had never been mentioned during his time as a reservist, but he should have been able to work it out himself.

"Which way did he go?" Gavrik demanded.

At least Grigori could answer that. "West."

Gavrik turned and walked quickly to Lieutenant Tomchak, who was leaning against a tree, smoking. A moment later Tomchak threw down his cigarette and ran to Major Bobrov, a handsome older officer with flowing silver hair.

After that everything happened quickly. They had no artillery, but the machine-gun section unloaded its weapons. The six hundred men of the battalion were spread out in a ragged north-south line a thousand yards long. A few men were chosen to go ahead. Then the rest moved slowly west, toward the afternoon sun slanting through the leaves.

Minutes later the first shell landed. It made a screaming noise in the air, then crashed through the forest canopy, and finally hit the ground some distance behind Grigori and exploded with a deep bang that shook the ground.

"That scout gave them the range," said Tomchak. "They're firing at where we were. Good thing we moved."

But the Germans were logical, too, and they appeared to discover their mistake, for the next shell landed slightly in front of the advancing Russian line.

The men around Grigori became jumpy. They looked around them constantly, held their rifles at the ready, and cursed one another at the least provocation. David kept looking up as if he might be able to see a shell coming and dodge it. Isaak wore an aggressive expression, as he did on the football pitch when the other side started to play dirty. The knowledge that someone was trying his best to kill you was overwhelmingly oppressive, Grigori found. He felt as if he had received dreadfully bad news but could not quite remember what it was. He had a foolish fantasy of digging a hole in the ground and hiding in it.

He wondered what the gunners could see. Was there an observer stationed on a hill, raking the woods with powerful German binoculars? You couldn't see one man in a forest, but perhaps you could see six hundred moving through the trees in a group.

Someone had decided the range was right, for in the next few seconds several shells landed, some of them dead on target. To both sides of Grigori there were deafening bangs, fountains of earth gushed up, men screamed, and parts of bodies flew through the air. Grigori shook with terror. There was nothing you could do, no way to protect yourself: either the shell got you or it missed. He quickened his pace, as if moving faster might help. The other men must have had the same thought because, without an order, they all broke into a jog-trot.

Grigori gripped his rifle with sweaty hands and tried not to panic. More shells fell, behind him and in front, to left and right. He ran faster.

The artillery fire became so heavy that he could no longer distinguish individual shells: there was just one continuous noise like a hundred express trains. Then the battalion seemed to get inside the gunners' range, for the shells began to land behind them. Soon the shelling petered out. A few moments later, Grigori realized why. Ahead of him a machine gun opened up, and he knew with a sickening feeling of dread that he was close to the enemy line.

Machine-gun rounds sprayed the forest, tearing up the foliage and splintering the pines. Grigori heard a scream beside him and saw Tomchak fall. Kneeling beside the lieutenant, he saw blood on his face and on the breast of his tunic. With horror, he saw that one eye had been destroyed. Tomchak tried to move, then screamed in pain. Grigori said: "What do I do? What do I do?" He could have bandaged a flesh wound, but how could he help a man who had been shot through the eye?

He felt a blow to his head and looked up to see Gavrik run past him, shouting: "Keep moving, Peshkov, you stupid cunt!"

He stared at Tomchak a moment longer. It seemed to him the officer was no longer breathing. He could not be sure, but all the same he stood up and ran forward.

The firing intensified. Grigori's fear turned to anger. The enemy's bullets produced a feeling of outrage. In the back of his mind he knew it was irrational, but he could not help it. Suddenly he wanted to kill those bastards. A couple of hundred yards ahead, across a clearing, he saw gray uniforms and spiked helmets. He dropped to one knee behind a tree, peeped around the trunk, raised his rifle, sighted on a German, and for the first time pulled the trigger.

Nothing happened, and he remembered the safety catch.

It was not possible to release the catch on a Mosin-Nagant while it was shouldered. He lowered the gun, sat on the ground behind the tree, and cradled the stock in the crook of his elbow, then turned the large knurled knob that unlocked the bolt.

He looked about him. His comrades had stopped running and taken cover as he had. Some were firing, some reloading, some writhing in the agony of wounds, some lying in the stillness of death.

Grigori peered around the trunk, shouldered his weapon, and squinted along the barrel. He saw a rifle poking out of a bush and a spiked helmet above it. His heart was filled with hatred, and he pulled the trigger five times fast. The rifle he was aiming at was hastily withdrawn, but did not fall, and Grigori guessed he had missed. He felt disappointed and frustrated.

The Mosin-Nagant held only five rounds. He opened his ammunition pack and reloaded. Now he wanted to kill Germans as fast as he could.

Looking around the tree again, he spotted a German running across a gap in the woods. He emptied his magazine, but the man kept running and disappeared behind a clump of saplings.

It was no good just shooting, Grigori decided. Hitting the enemy was difficult—much more difficult in a real fight than in the small amount of target practice he had had in training. He would have to try harder.

As he was reloading again, he heard a machine gun open up, and the vegetation around him was sprayed. He pressed his back against the tree and drew in his legs, making himself a smaller target. His hearing told him the gun must be a couple of hundred yards to his left.

When it paused he heard Gavrik shout: "Target that machine gun, you dumb pricks! Shoot them while they're reloading!" Grigori poked his head out and looked for the nest. He spotted the tripod standing between two large trees. He aimed his rifle, then paused. No good just shooting, he reminded himself. He breathed evenly, steadied the heavy barrel, and got a pointed helmet in his sight. He lowered the barrel slightly so that he could see the man's chest. The uniform tunic was open at the neck: the man was hot from his exertions.

Grigori pulled the trigger.

He missed. The German appeared not to have noticed the shot. Grigori had no idea where the bullet might have gone.

He fired again, emptying the magazine to no effect. It was maddening. Those pigs were trying to kill him and he was incapable of hitting even one of them. Perhaps he was too far away. Or perhaps he was just a lousy shot.

The machine gun opened up again, and everyone froze.

Major Bobrov appeared, crawling on hands and knees across the forest floor. "You men!" he yelled. "On my command, rush that machine gun!"

You must be mad, Grigori thought. Well, I'm not.

Sergeant Gavrik repeated the order. "Prepare to rush the machine-gun nest! Wait for the command!"

Bobrov stood upright and ran, crouching, along the line. Grigori heard him shout the same order a bit farther away. You're wasting your breath, Grigori thought. Do you imagine we're all suicidal?

The machine gun's chatter stopped, and the major stood up, exposing himself recklessly. He had lost his hat, and his silver hair made a highly visible target. "Go!" he screamed.

Gavrik repeated the order. "Go, go, go!"

Bobrov and Gavrik both led by example, running through the trees toward the machine-gun nest. Suddenly Grigori found himself doing the same, crashing through bushes and jumping over deadfalls, running in a half crouch, trying not to drop his unwieldy rifle. The machine gun remained silent but the Germans fired with everything else they had, and the effect of dozens of rifles shooting at the same time seemed almost as bad, but Grigori ran on as if it were the only thing he could do. He could see the machine-gun team desperately reloading, their hands fumbling the magazine, their faces white with fear. Some of the Russians were firing, but Grigori did not have that much presence of mind—he just ran. He was still some distance from the machine gun when he saw three Germans hiding behind a bush. They looked terribly young, and stared at him with frightened faces. He charged them with his bayoneted rifle held in front of him like a medieval lance. He heard some-one screaming and realized it was himself. The three young soldiers ran away.

He went after them, but he was weak from hunger, and they easily outran him. After a hundred yards he stopped, exhausted. All around him the Germans were fleeing and the Russians giving chase. The machine-gun crew had abandoned their weapon. Grigori supposed he should be shooting, but for the moment he did not have the energy to raise his rifle.

Major Bobrov reappeared, running along the Russian line. "Forward!" he shouted. "Don't let them get away—kill them all, or they'll come back to shoot you another day! Go!"

Wearily, Grigori started to run. Then the picture changed. There was a commotion to his left: firing, shout-ing, cursing. Suddenly Russian soldiers appeared from that direction, running for their lives. Bobrov, standing next to Grigori, said: "What the hell?"

Grigori realized they were being attacked from the side.

Bobrov shouted: "Stand firm! Take cover and shoot!"

No one was listening. The newcomers poured through the woods in a panic, and Grigori's comrades began to join the stampede, turning right and running northward.

"Hold position, you men!" Bobrov yelled. He drew his pistol. "Hold position, I say!" He aimed at the crowd of Russian troops streaming past him. "I warn you, I will shoot deserters!" There was a crack, and blood stained his hair. He fell down. Grigori did not know whether he had been felled by a stray German bullet or one from his own side.

Grigori turned and ran with the rest.

There was firing on all sides now. Grigori did not know who was shooting whom. The Russians spread out through the woods, and gradually he seemed to be leaving the noise of battle behind. He kept running as long as he could, then at last collapsed on a carpet of leaves, unable to move. He lay there for a long time, feeling paralyzed. He still had his rifle, which surprised him: he did not know why he had not dropped it.

Eventually he rose sluggishly to his feet. For some time his right ear had been painful. He touched it, and cried out in pain. His fingers came away sticky with blood. Gingerly, he felt his ear again. To his horror he found that most of it had gone. He had been wounded without knowing it. At some point a bullet had taken away the top half of his ear.

He checked his rifle. The magazine was empty. He reloaded, though he was not sure why: he seemed incapable of hitting anyone. He set the safety knob.

The Russians had been caught in an ambush, he guessed. They had been lured forward until they were surrounded; then the Germans had closed the trap.

What should he do? There was no one in sight, so he could not ask an officer for orders. But he could not stay where he was. The corps was in retreat, that was certain, so he supposed he should head back. If there was any of the Russian force left, it was presumably to the east.

He turned so that the setting sun was at his back, and began to walk. He moved as quietly as he could through the forest, not knowing where the Germans might be. He wondered if the entire Second Army had been defeated and fled. He could starve to death in the forest.

After an hour he stopped to drink from a stream. He considered bathing his wound, and decided it might be best to leave it alone. When he had drunk his fill, he rested, squatting on the ground, eyes closed. Soon it would be dark. Fortunately the weather was dry, and he could sleep on the ground.

He was in a half doze when he heard a noise. Looking up, he was shocked to see a German officer on horseback moving slowly through the trees ten yards away. The man had passed without noticing Grigori crouching by the stream.

Stealthily, Grigori picked up his rifle and turned the safety knob. Kneeling, he shouldered it and took careful aim at the middle of the German's back. The man was now fifteen yards away, point-blank range for a rifle.

At the last moment the German was alerted by a sixth sense, and he turned in the saddle.

Grigori squeezed the trigger.

The bang was deafening in the quiet of the forest. The horse leaped forward. The officer fell sideways and hit the ground, but one foot remained caught in a stirrup. The horse dragged him through the undergrowth for a hundred yards, then slowed down and stopped.

Grigori listened carefully in case the sound of the shot had attracted anyone else. He heard nothing but a mild evening breeze riffling the leaves.

He walked toward the horse. As he got closer he shouldered his rifle and pointed it at the officer, but his caution was unnecessary. The man lay still, face upward, his eyes wide-open, his pointed helmet lying beside him. He had cropped blond hair and rather beautiful green eyes. It might have been the man Grigori had seen earlier: he could not be sure. Lev would have known—he would have remembered the horse.

Grigori opened the saddlebags. One contained maps and a telescope. The other held a sausage and a hunk of black bread. Grigori was starving. He bit off a piece of the sausage. It was strongly flavored with pepper, herbs, and garlic. The pepper made his cheeks hot and sweaty. He chewed rapidly, swallowed, then stuffed some of the bread into his mouth. The food was so good he could have wept. He stood there, leaning against the side of the big horse, eating as fast as he could, while the man he had killed stared up at him with dead green eyes.

{ VI }

Walter said to Ludendorff: "We estimate thirty thousand Russian dead, General." He was trying not to show his elation too obviously, but the German victory was overwhelming, and he could not get the smile off his face.

Ludendorff was coolly controlled. "Prisoners?"

"At the latest count about ninety-two thousand, sir."

It was an amazing statistic, but Ludendorff took it in his stride. "Any generals?"

"General Samsonov shot himself. We have his body. Martos, commander of the Russian 15 Corps, has been taken prisoner. We have captured five hundred artillery guns."

"In summary," said Ludendorff, at last looking up from his field desk, "the Russian Second Army has been wiped out. It no longer exists."

Walter could not help grinning. "Yes, sir."

Ludendorff did not return the smile. He waved the sheet of paper he had been studying. "Which makes this news all the more ironic."

"Sir?"

"They're sending us reinforcements."

Walter was astounded. "What? I beg your pardon, General—reinforcements?"

"I am as surprised as you. Three corps and a cavalry division."

"From where?"

"From France—where we need every last man if the Schlieffen Plan is to work."

Walter recalled that Ludendorff had worked on the details of the Schlieffen Plan, with his customary energy and meticulousness, and he knew what was needed in France, down to the last man, horse, and bullet. "But what has brought this about?" Walter said.

"I don't know, but I can guess." Ludendorff's tone became bitter. "It's political. Princesses and countesses in Berlin have been crying and sobbing to the kaiserin about their family estates being overrun by the Russians. The high command has bowed under the pressure."

Walter felt himself blush. His own mother was one of those who had pestered the kaiserin. For women to become worried and beg for protection was understandable, but for the army to give in to their pleas, and risk derailing the entire war strategy, was unforgivable. "Isn't this exactly what the Allies want?" he said indignantly. "The French persuaded the Russians to invade with a half-ready army, in the hope that we would panic and rush reinforcements to the eastern front, thereby weakening our army in France!"

"Exactly. The French are on the run—outnumbered, outgunned, defeated. Their only hope was that we might be distracted. And their wish has been granted."

"So," said Walter despairingly, "despite our great victory in the east, the Russians have achieved the strategic advantage their allies needed in the west!"

"Yes," said Ludendorff. "Exactly."

CHAPTER THIRTEEN

September to December 1914

The sound of a woman crying woke Fitz.

At first he thought it was Bea. Then he remembered that his wife was in London and he was in Paris. The woman in bed beside him was not a twenty-three-year-old pregnant princess, but a nineteen-year-old French bar girl with the face of an angel.

He raised himself on his elbow and looked at her. She had blond eyelashes that lay on her cheeks like butterflies on petals. Now they were wet with tears. *"J'ai peur,"* she sobbed. "I'm frightened."

He stroked her hair. *"Calme-toi,"* he said. "Relax." He had learned more French from women such as Gini than he ever had at school. Gini was short for Ginette, but even that sounded like a made-up name. She had probably been christened something prosaic such as Françoise.

It was a fine morning, and a warm breeze came through the open window of Gini's room. Fitz heard no gunfire, no stamp of marching boots on the cobblestones. "Paris has not yet fallen," he murmured in a reassuring tone.

It was the wrong thing to say, for it brought forth fresh sobs.

Fitz looked at his wristwatch. It was half past eight. He had to be back at his hotel by ten o'clock without fail.

Gini said: "If the Germans come, will you take care of me?"

"Of course, *chérie,*" he said, suppressing a guilty pang. He would if he could, but she would not be his top priority.

"Will they come?" she asked in a small voice.

Fitz wished he knew. The German army was twice as numerous as predicted by French intelligence. It had stormed across northeast France, winning every battle. Now the avalanche had reached a line north of Paris—exactly how far north, Fitz would find out in the next couple of hours.

"Some say the city will not be defended," Gini sobbed. "Is it true?"

Fitz did not know that either. If Paris resisted, it would be mauled by German artillery. Its splendid buildings would be wrecked, its broad boulevards cratered, its bistros and boutiques turned to rubble. It was tempting to think the city *should* surrender, and escape all that. "It might be better for you," he said to Gini with false heartiness. "You will make love to a fat Prussian general who will call you his *Liebling*."

"I don't want a Prussian." Her voice sank to a whisper. "I love you."

Perhaps she did, he thought; or perhaps she just saw him as a ticket out of here. Everyone who could was leaving town, but it was not easy. Most private cars had been commandeered. Railway trains were liable to be requisitioned at any moment, their civilian passengers thrown out and stranded in the middle of nowhere. A taxi to Bordeaux cost fifteen hundred francs, the price of a small house.

"It may not happen," he told her. "The Germans must be exhausted by now. They've been marching and fighting for a month. They can't keep it up forever."

He half believed this. The French had fought hard in retreat. The soldiers were worn-out, starving and demoralized, but few had been taken prisoner and they had lost only a handful of guns. The unflappable commander in chief, General Joffre, had held the Allied forces together and withdrawn to a line southeast of Paris, where he was regrouping. He had also ruthlessly sacked senior French officers who did not come up to scratch: two army commanders, seven corps commanders, and dozens of others had been mercilessly dismissed.

The Germans did not know this. Fitz had seen decrypted German messages that suggested overconfidence. The German high command had actually removed troops from France and sent them as reinforcements to East Prussia.

Fitz thought that might be a mistake. The French were not finished yet.

He was not so sure about the British.

The British Expeditionary Force was small—five and a half divisions, by contrast with the seventy French divisions in the field. They had fought bravely at Mons, making Fitz proud; but in five days they had lost fifteen thousand of their one hundred thousand men, and had gone into retreat.

The Welsh Rifles were part of the British force, but Fitz was not with them. At first he had been disappointed to be posted to Paris as a liaison officer: he yearned to be fighting with his regiment. He felt sure the generals were treating him as an amateur who had to be sent someplace where he could not do much harm. But he knew Paris and spoke French, so he could hardly deny that he was well-qualified.

As it turned out, the job was more important than he had thought. Relations between the French commanders and their British opposite numbers were dangerously bad. The British Expeditionary Force was commanded by a touchy fusspot whose name, slightly confusingly, was Sir John French. He had taken offense, early on, by what he saw as a lack of consultation by General Joffre, and had gone into a sulk. Fitz struggled to maintain a flow of information and intelligence between the two Allied commanders despite the atmosphere of hostility.

All this was embarrassing and a bit shameful, and Fitz as a representative of the British was mortified by the ill-disguised scorn of French officers. But it had got dramatically worse a week ago. Sir John had told Joffre that his troops required two days' rest. The next day he had changed his requirement to ten days. The French had been horrified, and Fitz had felt deeply ashamed of his own country.

He had remonstrated with Colonel Hervey, a sycophantic aide to Sir John, but his complaint had met with indignation and denial. In the end Fitz had spoken by phone to Lord Remarc, a junior minister in the War Office. They had been schoolboys at Eton together, and Remarc was one of Maud's gossipy friends. Fitz had not felt good about going behind the backs of his superior officers this way, but the struggle for Paris was so finely balanced that he felt he had to act. Patriotism was not so simple, he had learned.

The effect of his complaint had been explosive. Prime

Minister Asquith had sent the new minister of war, Lord Kitchener, hotfoot to Paris, and Sir John had been carpeted by his boss the day before yesterday. Fitz had high hopes that he would shortly be replaced. Failing that, at least he might be jerked out of his lethargy.

Fitz would soon find out.

He turned away from Gini and put his feet on the floor.

"Are you leaving?" she said.

He stood up. "I have work to do."

She kicked off the sheet. Fitz looked at her perfect breasts. Catching his eye, she smiled through her tears and parted her legs invitingly.

He resisted temptation. "Make some coffee, *chérie*," he said.

She put on a pale-green silk wrap and heated water while Fitz got dressed. Last night he had dined at the British embassy in his regimental mess kit, but after dinner he had shed the conspicuous scarlet military jacket and substituted a short tuxedo to go slumming.

She gave him strong coffee in a big cup like a bowl. "I will wait for you tonight at Albert's Club," she said. The nightclubs were officially closed, as were theaters and cinemas. Even the Folies Bergère was dark. Cafés closed at eight, and restaurants at nine thirty. But it was not so easy to shut down the nightlife of a great city, and enterprising types such as Albert had been quick to open illicit joints where they could sell champagne at extortionate prices.

"I'll try to get there by midnight," he said. The coffee was bitter but it washed away the last traces of sleepiness. He gave Gini a gold British sovereign. It was a generous payment for one night, and in such times gold was greatly preferred to paper money.

When he kissed her good-bye, she clung to him. "You will be there tonight, won't you?" she said.

He felt sorry for her. Her world was collapsing and she did not know what to do. He would have liked to take her under his wing and promise to look after her, but he could not. He had a pregnant wife, and if Bea was upset she could lose the baby. Even if he had been a single man, to have encumbered himself with a French tart would have made him a laughingstock. Anyway, Gini was only one of millions. Everyone was frightened, except those who were dead. "I'll do my best," he said, and extracted himself from her embrace.

His blue Cadillac was parked at the curb. A small Union Jack flew from the bonnet. There were few private cars on the streets, and most had a flag, usually a tricolor or a red cross, to show they were being used for essential war work.

Getting the car there from London had taken ruthless use of Fitz's connections and a small fortune in bribes, but he was glad he had taken the trouble. He needed to move daily between British and French headquarters, and it was a relief not to have to beg the loan of a car or a horse from the hard-pressed armies.

He pressed the automatic crank, and the engine turned over and fired. The streets were mostly empty of traffic. Even the buses had been commandeered for supplying the army at the front. He had to stop for a huge flock of sheep crossing town, presumably on their way to the Gare de l'Est to be sent by train to feed the troops.

He was intrigued to see a small crowd gathered around a poster freshly pasted to the wall of the Palais Bourbon. He pulled up and joined the people reading it.

ARMY OF PARIS
CITIZENS OF PARIS

Fitz's eye went to the foot of the notice and he saw that it was signed by General Galliéni, the military governor of the city. Galliéni, a crusty old soldier, had been brought out of retirement. He was famous for holding meetings at which no one was allowed to sit down: he believed people reached decisions faster that way.

The body of his message was characteristically terse.

The members of the Government of the Republic have left Paris to give new impetus to the national defense.

Fitz was dismayed. The government had fled! There had been rumors for the last few days that ministers would decamp to Bordeaux, but the politicians had hesitated, not wanting to abandon the capital. However, now they had gone. It was a very bad sign.

The rest of the announcement was defiant.

I have been entrusted with the duty of defending Paris against the invader.

So, Fitz thought, Paris will not surrender after all. The city will fight. Good! That was certainly in British interests. If the capital had to fall, at least the enemy should be made to pay heavily for their conquest.

This duty I shall carry out to the last extremity.

Fitz could not help smiling. Thank God for old soldiers.

The people around seemed to have mixed feelings. Some comments were admiring. Galliéni was a fighter, someone said with satisfaction; he would not let Paris be taken. Others were more realistic. The government has left us, a woman said; that means the Germans will be here to-day or tomorrow. A man with a briefcase said he had sent his wife and children to his brother's house in the country. A well-dressed woman said she had thirty kilos of dried beans in the kitchen cupboard.

Fitz just felt that the British contribution to the war effort, and his part in it, had become even more important.

With a strong sense of doom, he drove on to the Ritz.

He entered the lobby of his favorite hotel and went into a phone booth. There he called the British embassy and left a message for the ambassador, telling him about Galliéni's notice, just in case the news had not yet reached the rue du Faubourg St.-Honoré.

When he came out of the booth he ran into Sir John's aide Colonel Hervey.

Hervey looked at Fitz's tuxedo and said: "Major Fitz-herbert! Why the devil are you dressed like that?"

"Good morning, Colonel," said Fitz, deliberately not answering the question. It was obvious that he had been out all night.

"It's nine o'clock in the bloody morning! Don't you know we're at war?"

This was another question that did not require an answer. Coolly Fitz said: "Is there something I can do for you, sir?"

Hervey was a bully who hated people he could not intimidate. "Less of your insolence, Major," he said. "We've got enough to do, with interfering bloody visitors from London."

Fitz raised an eyebrow. "Lord Kitchener *is* the minister of war."

"The politicians should leave us to do our job. But someone with friends in high places has stirred them up." He looked as if he suspected Fitz, but did not have the courage to say so.

"You can hardly have been surprised at the War Office being concerned," Fitz said. "Ten days' rest, with the Germans at the gates!"

"The men are exhausted!"

"In ten days the war might be over. What are we here for, if not to save Paris?"

"Kitchener took Sir John away from his headquarters on a crucial day of battle," Hervey blustered.

"Sir John wasn't in much of a hurry to get back to his troops, I noticed," Fitz rejoined. "I saw him dining here at the Ritz that evening." He knew he was being insolent but he could not help himself.

"Get out of my sight," said Hervey.

Fitz turned on his heel and went upstairs.

He was not as insouciant as he had pretended. Nothing would make him kowtow to idiots such as Hervey, but it was important to him to have a successful military career. He hated the thought that people might say he was not the man his father was. Hervey was not much use to the army because he spent all his time and energy patronizing his favorites and undermining his rivals, but by the same token he could ruin the careers of men who concentrated on other things, such as winning the war.

Fitz brooded as he bathed, shaved, and dressed in the khaki uniform of a major in the Welsh Rifles. Knowing that he might get nothing to eat until dinner, he ordered an omelette sent up to his suite with more coffee.

At ten o'clock sharp his working day began, and he put the malign Hervey out of his mind. Lieutenant Murray, a keen young Scot, arrived from British headquarters, bringing into Fitz's suite the dust of the road and the morning's aerial reconnaissance report.

Fitz rapidly translated the document into French and wrote it out in his clear, swooping script on pale blue Ritz paper. Every morning British planes overflew German positions and noted the direction in which enemy forces were moving. It was Fitz's job to get the information to General Galliéni as quickly as possible.

Going out through the lobby he was called by the head porter to take a phone call.

The voice that said: "Fitz, is that you?" was distant and distorted, but to his astonishment it was, unmistakably, that of his sister, Maud.

"How the devil did you manage this?" he said. Only the government and the military could phone Paris from London.

"I'm in Johnny Remarc's room at the War Office."

"I'm glad to hear your voice," Fitz said. "How are you?"

"Everyone's terribly worried here," she said. "At first the papers printed nothing but good news. Only people who knew their geography understood that after each gallant French victory the Germans seemed to be another fifty miles inside France. But on Sunday *The Times* published a special edition. Isn't that odd? The everyday paper is full of lies, so when they tell the truth they have to bring out a special edition."

She was trying to be witty and cynical, but Fitz could hear the fear and anger underneath. "What did the special edition say?"

"It spoke of our 'retreating and broken army.' Asquith is furious. Now everyone expects Paris to fall any day." Her façade cracked, and there was a sob in her voice as she said: "Fitz, are you going to be all right?"

He could not lie to her. "I don't know. The government has moved to Bordeaux. Sir John French has been told off, but he's still here."

"Sir John has complained to the War Office that Kitchener went to Paris in the uniform of a field marshal, which was a breach of etiquette because he is now a government minister and therefore a civilian."

"Good God. At a time like this he's thinking about etiquette! Why hasn't he been sacked?"

"Johnny says it would look like an admission of failure."

"What will it look like if Paris falls to the Germans?"

"Oh, Fitz!" Maud began to cry. "What about the baby Bea is expecting—your child?"

"How is Bea?" Fitz said, remembering guiltily where he had spent the night.

Maud sniffed and swallowed. More calmly, she said: "Bea looks bonny, and she no longer suffers from that tiresome morning sickness."

"Tell her I miss her."

There was a burst of interference, and another voice came on the line for a few seconds, then disappeared. That meant they might get cut off any second. When Maud spoke again, her voice was plaintive. "Fitz, when will it end?"

"Within the next few days," Fitz said. "One way or the other."

"Please look after yourself!"

"Of course."

The line went dead.

Fitz cradled the phone, tipped the head porter, and went out into the Place Vendôme.

He got into his car and drove off. Maud had upset him by speaking of Bea's pregnancy. Fitz was willing to die for his country, and hoped he would die bravely, but he wanted to see his baby. He had not yet been a parent and he was eager to meet his child, to watch him learn and grow, to help him become an adult. He did not want his son or daughter raised without a father.

He drove across the river Seine to the complex of army buildings known as Les Invalides. Galliéni had made his headquarters in a nearby school called the Lycée Victor-Duruy, set back behind trees. The entrance was closely guarded by sentries in bright blue tunics and red trousers with red caps, so much smarter than the mud-colored British khaki. The French had not yet grasped that accurate modern rifles meant that today's soldier wanted to disappear into the landscape.

Fitz was well known to the guards and walked straight in. It was a girls' school, with paintings of pets and flowers, and Latin verbs conjugated on blackboards that had been pushed out of the way. The rifles of the sentries and the boots of the officers seemed to offend against the gentility of what had gone before.

Fitz went straight to the staff room. As soon as he walked in he sensed an atmosphere of excitement. On the wall was a large map of central France on which the positions of the armies had been marked with pins. Galliéni was tall, thin, and upright despite the prostate cancer that had caused him to retire in February. Now back in uniform, he stared aggressively at the map through his pince-nez glasses.

Fitz saluted, then shook hands, French style, with his opposite number, Colonel Dupuys, and asked in a whisper what was going on.

"We're tracking von Kluck," said Dupuys.

Galliéni had a squadron of nine old aircraft that he was using to monitor the movements of the invading army. General von Kluck was in command of the First Army, the nearest German force to Paris.

"What have you got?" Fitz asked.

"Two reports." Dupuys pointed at the map. "Our aerial reconnaissance indicates that von Kluck is moving southeast, toward the river Marne."

This confirmed what the British had reported. On that trajectory, the First Army would pass to the east of Paris. And, since von Kluck commanded the German right wing, that meant their entire force would bypass the city. Would Paris escape after all?

Dupuys went on: "And we have a report from a cavalry scout that suggests the same."

Fitz nodded thoughtfully. "German military theory is to destroy the enemy's army first, and take possession of cities later."

"But don't you see?" said Dupuys excitedly. "They are exposing their flank!"

Fitz had not thought of that. His mind had been on the fate of Paris. Now he realized that Dupuys was right, and this was the reason for the air of exhilaration. If the intelligence was right, von Kluck had made a classic military error. The flank of an army was more vulnerable than its head. A flank attack was like a stab in the back.

Why had von Kluck made such a mistake? He must believe the French to be so weak that they were incapable of counterattack.

In which case, he was wrong.

Fitz addressed the general. "I think this will interest you greatly, sir," he said, and handed over his envelope. "It's our aerial reconnaissance report of this morning."

"Aha!" said Galliéni eagerly.

Fitz stepped up to the map. "If I may, General?"

The general nodded permission. The British were not popular, but all intelligence was welcome.

Consulting the English-language original, Fitz said: "Our people put von Kluck's army here." He stuck a new pin in the map. "And moving in this direction." It confirmed what the French already believed.

For a moment, the room was silent.

"It's true, then," said Dupuys quietly. "They have exposed their flank."

General Galliéni's eyes glittered behind his pince-nez. "So," he said, "this is our moment to attack."

{ II }

Fitz was at his most pessimistic at three o'clock in the morning, lying next to Gini's slim body, when sex was over and he found himself missing his wife. Then he thought dispiritedly that von Kluck must surely realize his mistake and reverse course.

But next morning, Friday, September 4, to the delight of the French defenders, von Kluck continued southeast. That was enough for General Joffre. He gave orders for the French Sixth Army to move out from Paris the following morning and strike at von Kluck's rearguard.

But the British continued to retreat.

Fitz was in despair that evening when he met Gini at Albert's. "This is our last chance," he explained to her over a champagne cocktail that did nothing to cheer him up. "If we can seriously rattle the Germans now, when they are exhausted and their supply lines are fully stretched, we may bring their advance to a halt. But if this counterattack fails, Paris will fall."

She was sitting on a barstool, and she crossed her long legs with a whisper of silk stockings. "But why are you so gloomy?"

"Because, at a time like this, the British are retreating. If Paris falls now, we will never live down the shame of it."

"General Joffre must confront Sir John and demand that the British fight! You must speak to Joffre yourself!"

"He doesn't give audience to British majors. Besides, he would probably think it was some kind of trick by Sir John. And I would be in deep trouble, not that I care about that."

"Then speak to one of his advisers."

"Same problem. I can't walk into French army headquarters and announce that the British are betraying them."

"But you could have a quiet word in the ear of General Lourceau, without anyone knowing about it."

"How?"

"He is sitting over there."

Fitz followed her gaze and saw a Frenchman of about sixty in civilian clothes sitting at a table with a young woman in a red dress.

"He is very amiable," Gini added.

"You know him?"

"We were friends for a while, but he preferred Lizette."

Fitz hesitated. Once again he was contemplating going behind the backs of his superiors. But this was no time for niceties. Paris was at stake. He had to do whatever he could.

"Introduce me," he said.

"Give me a minute." Gini slid elegantly off her stool and walked across the club, swaying slightly to the ragtime piano, until she came to the general's table. She kissed him on the lips, smiled at his companion, and sat down. After a few moments' earnest conversation she beckoned to Fitz.

Lourceau stood up and the two men shook hands. "I'm honored to meet you, sir," Fitz said.

"This is not the place for serious conversation," the general said. "But Gini assures me that what you have to say to me is terribly urgent."

"It most certainly is," Fitz said, and he sat down.

{ III }

Next day Fitz went to the British camp at Melun, twenty-five miles southeast of Paris, and learned to his dismay that the Expeditionary Force was still retreating.

Perhaps his message had not got through to Joffre. Or perhaps it had, and Joffre simply felt there was nothing he could do.

Fitz entered Vaux-le-Pénil, the magnificent Louis XV château Sir John was using as headquarters, and ran into Colonel Hervey in the hall. "May I ask, sir, why we are retreating when our allies are launching a counterattack?" he said as politely as he could.

"No, you may not ask," said Hervey.

Fitz persisted, suppressing his anger. "The French feel they and the Germans are evenly balanced, and even our small force may tip the scales."

Hervey laughed scornfully. "I'm sure they do." He spoke as if the French had no right to demand the help of their allies.

Fitz felt himself losing self-control. "Paris could be lost because of our timidity!"

"Do not dare to use such a word, Major."

"We were sent here to save France. This may be the decisive battle." Fitz could not help raising his voice. "If Paris is lost, and France with it, how will we explain, back home, that we were *resting* at the time?"

Instead of replying, Hervey stared over Fitz's shoulder. Fitz turned to see a heavy, slow-moving figure in French uniform: a black tunic that was unbuttoned over the large waist, ill-fitting red breeches, tight leggings, and the red-and-gold cap of a general pulled low over the forehead. Colorless eyes glanced at Fitz and Hervey from under salt-and-pepper eyebrows. Fitz recognized General Joffre.

When the general had lumbered past, followed by his entourage, Hervey said: "Are you responsible for this?"

Fitz was too proud to lie. "Possibly," he said.

"You haven't heard the last of it," Hervey said, and he turned and hurried after Joffre.

Sir John received Joffre in a small room with only a few officers present, and Fitz was not among them. He waited in the officers' mess, wondering what Joffre was saying and whether he could persuade Sir John to end the shameful British retreat and join in the assault.

He learned the answer two hours later from Lieutenant Murray. "They say Joffre tried everything," Murray reported. "He begged, he wept, and he insinuated that British honor was in danger of being forever besmirched. And he won his point. Tomorrow we turn north."

Fitz grinned broadly. "Hallelujah," he said.

A minute later Colonel Hervey approached. Fitz stood up politely.

"You've gone too far," Hervey said. "General Lourceau told me what you did. He thought he was paying you a compliment."

"I shan't deny it," Fitz said. "The outcome suggests that it was the right thing."

"You listen to me, Fitzherbert," Hervey said, lowering his voice. "You're fucking finished. You've been disloyal to a superior officer. There's a black mark against your name that will never be erased. You won't get a promotion, even if the war goes on for a year. Major you are and major you will always be."

"Thank you for your frankness, Colonel," said Fitz. "But I joined the army to win battles, not promotions."

{ IV }

Sir John's advance on Sunday was embarrassingly cautious, Fitz felt, but to his relief it was enough to force von Kluck to meet the threat by sending troops he could not easily spare. Now the German was fighting on two fronts, west and south, every commander's nightmare.

Fitz woke up on Monday morning, after a night on a blanket on the château floor, feeling optimistic. He had breakfast in the officers' mess, then waited impatiently for the spotter planes to return from their morning sortie. War was either a mad dash or futile inactivity. In the grounds of the château was a church said to date from the year 1000, and he went to look at it, but he had never really understood what people saw in old churches.

The reconnaissance debriefing took place in the magnificent salon overlooking the park and the river. The officers sat on camp chairs at a cheap board table with lavish eighteenth-century decor all around them. Sir John had a jutting chin and a mouth that seemed, underneath the white walrus mustache, to be permanently twisted into an expression of injured pride.

The aviators reported that there was open country ahead of the British force, because the German columns were marching away north.

Fitz was elated. The Allied counterattack had been unexpected, and the Germans had been caught napping, it seemed. Of course they would regroup soon, but for now they seemed to be in trouble.

He waited for Sir John to order a rapid advance but, disappointingly, the commander simply confirmed the limited objectives set earlier.

Fitz wrote his report in French, then got into his car. He drove the twenty-five miles to Paris as fast as he could against the flow of trucks, cars, and horse-drawn vehicles leaving the city, crammed with people and piled high with luggage, heading south to escape the Germans.

In Paris he was delayed by a formation of dark-skinned Algerian troops marching across the city from one railway station to another. Their officers rode mules and wore bright red cloaks. As they passed, women gave them flowers and fruit, and café proprietors brought them cold drinks.

When they had passed, Fitz drove on to Les Invalides and took his report into the school.

Once again, the British reconnaissance confirmed the French reports. Some German forces were retreating. "We must press the attack!" said the old general. "Where are the British?"

Fitz went to the map and pointed to the British position and the marching objectives given by Sir John for the end of the day.

"It's not enough!" said Galliéni angrily. "You must be more aggressive! We need you to attack, so that von Kluck will be too busy with you to reinforce his flank. When will you cross the river Marne?"

Fitz could not say. He felt ashamed. He agreed with every caustic word Galliéni uttered, but he could not admit it, so he merely said: "I will emphasize this to Sir John most strongly, General."

But Galliéni was already figuring out how to compensate for British lassitude. "We will send the 7th Division of the 4 Corps to reinforce Manoury's army on the Ourcq River this afternoon," he said decisively.

Immediately his staff began to write out orders.

Then Colonel Dupuys said: "General, we don't have enough trains to get them all there by this evening."

"Then use cars," said Galliéni.

"Cars?" Dupuys looked baffled. "Where would we get that many cars?"

"Hire taxis!"

Everyone in the room stared at him. Had the general gone off his head?

"Telephone the chief of police," said Galliéni. "Tell him to order his men to stop every taxi in the city, kick out the passengers, and direct the drivers here. We will fill them with soldiers and send them to the battlefield."

Fitz grinned when he realized Galliéni was serious. This was the kind of attitude he liked. Let's do whatever it takes, just so long as we win.

Dupuys shrugged and picked up a telephone. "Please get the chief of police on the phone immediately," he said.

Fitz thought: I have to see this.

He went outside and lit a cigar. He did not have long to wait. After a few minutes a red Renault taxi came across the Alexander III Bridge, drove around the large ornamental lawn, and parked in front of the main building. It was followed by two more, then a dozen, then a hundred.

In a couple of hours several hundred identical red taxis were parked at Les Invalides. Fitz had never seen anything like it.

The cabbies leaned against their cars, smoking pipes and talking animatedly, waiting for instructions. Every driver had a different theory as to why they were there.

Eventually Dupuys came out of the school and across the street with a megaphone in one hand and a sheaf of army requisition slips in the other. He climbed on the bonnet of a taxi, and the drivers fell quiet.

"The military commander of Paris requires five hundred taxis to go from here to Blagny," he shouted through the megaphone.

The drivers stared at him in incredulous silence.

"There each car will pick up five soldiers and drive them to Nanteuil."

Nanteuil was thirty miles east and very close to the front line. The drivers began to understand. They looked at one another, nodding and grinning. Fitz guessed they were pleased to be part of the war effort, especially in such an unusual way.

"Please take one of these forms before you leave and fill it out in order to claim payment on your return."

There was a buzz of reaction. They were going to get paid! That clinched their support.

"When five hundred cars have left, I will give instructions for the next five hundred. *Vive Paris! Vive la France!*"

The drivers broke into wild cheering. They mobbed Dupuys for the forms. Fitz, delighted, helped distribute the papers.

Soon the little cars began to leave, turning around in front of the great building and heading across the bridge in the sunshine, sounding their horns in enthusiasm, a long bright red lifeline to the forces on the battlefront.

{ V }

The British took three days to march twenty-five miles. Fitz was mortified. Their advance had been largely unopposed: if they had moved faster, they might have struck a decisive blow.

However, on the morning of Wednesday, September 9, he found Galliéni's men in an optimistic mood. Von Kluck was retreating. "The Germans are scared!" said Colonel Dupuys.

Fitz did not believe the Germans were scared, and the map offered a more plausible explanation. The British, slow and timid though they were, had marched into a gap that had appeared between the German First and Second armies, a gap made when von Kluck pulled his forces westward to face the attack from Paris. "We've found a weak point, and we're driving a wedge into it," Fitz said, and there was a tremor of hope in his voice.

He told himself to calm down. The Germans had won every battle so far. On the other hand, their supply lines were stretched, their men were exhausted, and their numbers had been reduced by the need to send reinforcements to East Prussia. By contrast the French in this zone had received heavy reinforcements and had virtually no supply lines to worry about, being on home ground.

Fitz's hopes went into reverse when the British halted five miles north of the river Marne. What was Sir John stopping for? He had encountered hardly any opposition!

But the Germans seemed not to notice the timidity of the Brits, for they continued to retreat, and hopes rose again in the lycée.

As the shadows of the trees lengthened outside the school windows, and the last reports of the day came in, a sense of suppressed jubilation began to permeate Galliéni's staff. By the end of the day the Germans were on the run.

Fitz could hardly believe it. The despair of a week ago had turned to hope. He sat on a chair that was too small for him and stared at the map on the wall. Seven days ago the German line had seemed like a springboard for the launch of their final attack; now it looked like a wall at which they had been turned back.

When the sun went down behind the Eiffel Tower, the Allies had not won a victory, exactly, but for the first time in weeks the German advance had ground to a halt.

Dupuys embraced Fitz, then kissed him on both cheeks; and for once Fitz did not mind at all.

"We have stopped them," said Galliéni, and to Fitz's surprise, tears gleamed behind the old general's pince-nez. "We have stopped them."

{ VI }

Soon after the Battle of the Marne, both sides began to dig trenches.

The heat of September turned into the cold, depressing rain of October. The stalemate at the eastern end of the line spread irresistibly west, like a paralysis creeping through the body of a dying man.

The decisive battle of the autumn was over the Belgian town of Ypres, at the westernmost end of the line, twenty miles from the sea. The Germans attacked fiercely in an all-out attempt to turn the flank of the British force. The fighting raged for four weeks. Unlike all previous battles this one was static, with both sides hiding in trenches from each other's artillery and coming out only for suicidal sorties against the enemy's machine guns. In the end the British were saved by reinforcements, including a corps of brown-faced Indians shivering in their tropical uniforms. When it was over, seventy-five thousand British soldiers had died, and the Expeditionary Force was broken; but the Allies had completed a defensive barricade from the Swiss border to the English Channel, and the invading Germans had been stopped.

On December 24 Fitz was at British headquarters in the town of St.-Omer, not far from Calais, in a gloomy frame of mind. He remembered how glibly he and others had told the men they would be home for Christmas. Now it looked as if the war could go on for a year or even more. The opposing armies sat in their trenches day after day, eating bad food, getting dysentery and trench foot and lice, and desultorily killing the rats that thrived on the dead bodies littering no-man's-land. It had once seemed very clear to Fitz why Britain had to go to war, but he could no longer remember the reasons.

That day the rain stopped and the weather turned cold. Sir John sent a message to all units warning that the enemy was contemplating a Christmas attack. This was entirely imaginary, Fitz knew: there was no supporting intelligence. The truth was that Sir John did not want the men to relax their vigilance on Christmas Day.

Every soldier was to receive a gift from Princess Mary, the seventeen-year-old daughter of the king and queen. It was an embossed brass box containing tobacco and cigarettes, a picture of the princess, and a Christmas card from the king. There were different gifts for nonsmokers, Sikhs, and nurses, all of whom would get chocolate or candy instead of tobacco. Fitz helped distribute the boxes to the Welsh Rifles. At the end of the day, too late to return to the relative comfort of St.-Omer, he found himself at the headquarters of the Fourth Battalion, a damp dugout a quarter of a mile behind the front line, reading a Sherlock Holmes story and smoking the small, thin cigars he had taken to. They were not as good as his panatelas, but these days he hardly ever got time to smoke a big cigar. He was with Murray, who had been promoted to captain after Ypres. Fitz had not been promoted: Hervey was keeping his promise.

Soon after nightfall he was surprised to hear scattered rifle fire. It turned out that the men had seen lights and thought the enemy were trying a sneak attack. In fact the lights were colored lanterns with which the Germans were decorating their parapet.

Murray, who had been on the front line for a while, talked about the Indian troops defending the next sector. "Poor sods arrived in their summer uniforms, because someone told them the war would be over before the weather turned cold," he said. "But I'll tell you something, Fitz: your darkie soldier is an ingenious blighter. You know we've been asking the War Office to give us trench mortars like the ones the Germans have, that lob a grenade over the parapet? Well, the Indians have made their own out of odd pieces of cast-iron pipe. Looks like a bit of bodged plumbing in a pub toilet, but it works!"

In the morning there was a freezing fog and the ground underfoot was hard. Fitz and Murray gave out the princess's gifts at first light. Some of the men were huddled around braziers, trying to get warm, but they said they were grateful for the frost, which was better than the mud, especially for those suffering from trench foot. Some spoke to one another in Welsh, Fitz noticed, although they always used English with officers.

The German line, four hundred yards away, was hidden by a morning mist the same color as the German uniforms, a faded silver-blue called field gray. Fitz heard faint music: the Germans were singing carols. Fitz was not very musical, but he thought he recognized "Silent Night."

He returned to the dugout for a grim breakfast of stale bread and tinned ham with the other officers. Afterward he stepped outside to smoke. He had never been quite so miserable in all his life. He thought of the breakfast that was being served at that moment in Tŷ Gwyn: hot sausages, fresh eggs, deviled kidneys, smoky kippers, buttered toast, and fragrant coffee with cream in it. He longed for clean underwear, a crisply ironed shirt, and a soft wool suit. He wanted to sit by the blazing coal fire in the morning room with nothing better to do than read the stupid jokes in *Punch* magazine.

Murray followed him out of the dugout and said: "You're wanted on the telephone, Major. It's headquarters."

Fitz was surprised. Someone had gone to a lot of trouble to locate him. He hoped it was not on account of some quarrel that had flared up between the French and the British while he had been handing out Christmas presents. With a worried frown he ducked inside and picked up the field telephone. "Fitzherbert."

"Good morning, Major," said a voice he did not recognize. "Captain Davies here. You don't know me, but I've been asked to pass you a message from home."

From home? Fitz hoped it was not bad news. "Very kind of you, Captain," he said. "What does the message say?"

"Your wife has given birth to a bouncing baby boy, sir. Mother and son are both doing fine."

"Oh!" Fitz sat down suddenly on a box. The baby was not due yet—it must be a week or two early. Premature babies were vulnerable. But the message said he was in good health. And so was Bea.

Fitz had a son, and the earldom had an heir.

"Are you there, Major?" said Captain Davies.

"Yes, yes," said Fitz. "Just a bit shocked. It's early."

"As it's Christmas, sir, we thought the news might cheer you up."

"It does, I can tell you!"

"May I be the first to offer my congratulations."

"Most kind," Fitz said. "Thank you." But Captain Davies had already hung up.

After a moment Fitz realized the other officers in the dugout were staring at him in silence. Finally one of them said: "Good news or bad?"

"Good!" said Fitz. "Wonderful, in fact. I have become a father."

They all shook his hand and slapped his back. Murray got out the whisky bottle, despite the early hour, and they drank the baby's health. "What'll he be called?" Murray asked.

"Viscount Aberowen, while I'm alive," Fitz said; then he realized that Murray was not asking about the baby's title, but his name. "George, for my father, and William for my grandfather. Bea's father was Petr Nikolaevich, so perhaps we'll add those as well."

Murray seemed amused. "George William Peter Nicholas Fitzherbert, Viscount Aberowen," he said. "Quite enough names to be going on with!"

Fitz nodded good-humoredly. "Especially as he probably weighs about seven pounds."

He was bursting with pride and good cheer, and he felt an urge to share his news. "I might go along to the front line," he said when they had finished their whisky. "Pass out a few cigars to the men."

He left the dugout and walked along the communication trench. He felt euphoric. There was no gunfire, and the air tasted crisp and clean, except when he passed the latrine. He found himself thinking not about Bea but about Ethel. Had she had her baby yet? Was she happy in her house, having extorted the money from Fitz to buy it? Although he was taken aback by the tough way she had bargained with him, he could not help remembering that it was his child she was carrying. He hoped she would deliver her baby safely, as Bea had.

All such thoughts flew from his mind when he reached the front. As he turned the corner into the frontline trench, he got a shock.

There was no one there.

He walked along the trench, zigzagging around one traverse, then another, and saw no one. It was like a ghost story, or one of those ships found floating undamaged with not a soul aboard.

There had to be an explanation. Had there been an attack that somehow Fitz had not been told about?

It occurred to him to look over the parapet.

This was not to be done casually. Many men were killed on their first day at the front because they took a quick look over the top.

Fitz picked up one of the short-handled spades called entrenching tools. He pushed the blade gradually up over the edge of the parapet. Then he climbed onto the fire step and slowly raised his head until he was looking out through the narrow gap between the parapet and the blade.

What he saw astonished him.

The men were all in the cratered desert of no-man's-land. But they were not fighting. They were standing around in groups, talking.

There was something odd about their appearance, and after a moment Fitz realized that some of the uniforms were khaki and others field gray.

The men were talking to the enemy.

Fitz dropped the entrenching tool, raised his head fully over the parapet, and stared. There were hundreds of soldiers in no-man's-land, stretching as far as he could see to left and right, British and Germans intermingled.

What the hell was going on?

He found a trench ladder and scrambled up over the parapet. He marched across the churned earth. The men were showing photographs of their families and sweethearts, offering cigarettes, and trying to communicate, saying things like: "Me Robert. Who you?"

He spotted two sergeants, one British and one German, deep in conversation. He tapped the Brit on the shoulder. "You!" he said. "What the devil are you doing?"

The man answered him in the flat guttural accent of the Cardiff docks. "I don't know how it happened, sir, exactly. Some of the Jerries got up on their parapet, unarmed, and shouted, 'Happy Christmas'; then one of our boys done the same, then they started walking toward one another and before you could say chips everyone was doing it."

"But there's no one in the trenches!" Fitz said angrily. "Don't you see this could be a trick?"

The sergeant looked up and down the line. "No, sir, if I'm honest, I can't say that I do see that," he said coolly.

The man was right. How could the enemy possibly take advantage of the fact that the frontline forces of both sides had become friends?

The sergeant pointed to the German. "This is Hans Braun, sir," he said. "Used to be a waiter at the Savoy Hotel in London. Speaks English!"

The German sergeant saluted Fitz. "Glad to make your acquaintance, Major," he said. "Happy Christmas." He had less of an accent than the sergeant from Cardiff. He proffered a flask. "Would you care for a drop of schnapps?"

"Good God," said Fitz, and walked away.

There was nothing he could do. This would have been difficult to stop even with the support of the noncommissioned officers such as that Welsh sergeant. Without their help it was impossible. He decided he had better report the situation to a superior and make it someone else's problem.

But before he could leave the scene he heard his name called. "Fitz! Fitz! Is that really you?"

The voice was familiar. He turned to see a German approaching. As the man came close, he recognized him. "Von Ulrich?" he said in amazement.

"The very same!" Walter smiled broadly and held out his hand. Automatically Fitz took it. Walter shook hands vigorously. He looked thinner, Fitz thought, and his fair skin was weathered. I suppose I've changed, too, Fitz thought.

Walter said: "This is amazing—what a coincidence!"

"I'm glad to see you fit and well," Fitz said. "Though I probably shouldn't be."

"Likewise!"

"What are we going to do about this?" Fitz waved a hand at the fraternizing soldiers. "I find it worrying."

"I agree. When tomorrow comes they may not wish to shoot at their new friends."

"And then what would we do?"

"We must have a battle soon to get them back to normal. If both sides start shelling in the morning, they'll soon start to hate each other again."

"I hope you're right."

"And how are you, my old friend?"

Fitz remembered his good news, and brightened. "I've become a father," he said. "Bea has given birth to a boy. Have a cigar."

They lit up. Walter had been on the eastern front, he revealed. "The Russians are corrupt," he said with disgust. "The officers sell supplies on the black market and let the infantry go hungry and cold. Half the population of East Prussia are wearing Russian army boots they bought cheap, while the Russian soldiers are barefoot."

Fitz said he had been in Paris. "Your favorite restaurant, Voisin's, is still open," he said.

The men started a football match, Britain versus Germany, piling up their uniform caps for goalposts. "I've got to report this," said Fitz.

"I, too," said Walter. "But first tell me, how is Lady Maud?"

"Fine, I think."

"I would most particularly like to be remembered to her."

Fitz was struck by the emphasis with which Walter uttered this otherwise routine remark. "Of course," he said. "Any special reason?"

Walter looked away. "Just before I left London . . . I danced with her at Lady Westhampton's ball. It was the last civilized thing I did before this *verdammten* war."

Walter seemed to be in the grip of emotion. There was a tremor in his voice, and it was highly unusual for him to mix German with English. Perhaps the Christmas atmosphere had got to him, too.

Walter went on: "I should very much like her to know that I was thinking of her on Christmas Day." He looked at Fitz with moist eyes. "Would you be sure to tell her, old friend?"

"I will," said Fitz. "I'm sure she'll be very pleased."

CHAPTER FOURTEEN

February 1915

"I went to the doctor," said the woman next to Ethel. "I said to him, 'I've got an itchy twat.'"

A ripple of laughter ran around the room. It was on the top floor of a small house in East London, near Aldgate. Twenty women sat at sewing machines in close-packed rows either side of a long workbench. There was no fire, and the one window was closed tight against the February cold. The floorboards were bare. The whitewashed plaster on the walls was crumbling with age, and the laths beneath showed through in places. With twenty women breathing the same air the room became stuffy, but it never seemed to warm up, and the women all wore hats and coats.

They had just stopped for a break, and the treadles under their feet were briefly silent. Ethel's neighbor was Mildred Perkins, a Cockney of her own age. Mildred was also Ethel's lodger. She would have been beautiful but for protruding front teeth. Dirty jokes were her specialty. She went on: "The doctor says to me, he goes, 'You shouldn't say that. It's a rude word.'"

Ethel grinned. Mildred managed to create moments of cheer in the grim twelve-hour working day. Ethel had never known such talk before. At Tŷ Gwyn the staff had been genteel. These London women would say anything. They were all ages and several nationalities, and some barely spoke English, including two refugees from German-occupied Belgium. The only thing they all had in common was that they were desperate enough to want the job.

"I says to him, 'What should I say, then, Doctor?' He says to me, 'Say you've got an itchy finger.'"

They were sewing British army uniforms, thousands of them, tunics and trousers. Day after day the pieces of thick khaki cloth came in from a cutting factory in the next street, big cardboard boxes full of sleeves and backs and legs, and the women here sewed them together and sent them to another small factory to have the buttons and buttonholes added. They were paid according to how many they finished.

"He says to me, 'Do your finger itch you all the time, Mrs. Perkins, or just now and again?'"

Mildred paused, and the women were silent, waiting for the punch line.

"I says, 'No, Doctor, only when I piss through it.'"

The women hooted with laughter and cheered.

A thin girl of twelve came through the door with a pole on her shoulder. Hanging from it were large mugs and tankards, twenty of them. She put the pole down gingerly on the workbench. The mugs contained tea, hot chocolate, clear soup, or watery coffee. Each woman had her own mug. Twice a day, midmorning and midafternoon, they gave their pennies and halfpennies to the girl, Allie, and she got their mugs filled at the café next door.

The women sipped their drinks, stretched their arms and legs, and rubbed their eyes. The work was not hard like coal mining, Ethel thought, but it was tiring, bent over your machine hour after hour, peering at the stitching. And it had to be done right. The boss, Mannie Litov, checked each piece, and if it was wrong you did not get paid, even though Ethel suspected he sent the faulty uniforms off anyway.

After five minutes Mannie came into the workroom, clapping his hands and saying: "Come on now, back to work." They drained their cups and turned back to the bench.

Mannie was a slave driver, but not the worst, the women said. At least he did not paw the girls or demand sexual favors. He was about thirty, with dark eyes and a black beard. His father was a tailor who had come over from Russia and opened a shop in the Mile End Road, making cheap suits for bank clerks and stockbrokers' runners. Mannie had learned the trade from his father, then started a more ambitious enterprise.

The war was good for business. A million men had volunteered for the army between August and Christmas, and
each one needed a uniform. Mannie was hiring every seamstress he could find. Fortunately Ethel had learned to use a
sewing machine at Tŷ Gwyn.

Ethel needed a job. Although her house was paid for,
and she was collecting rent from Mildred, she had to save
money for when the baby came along. But the experience
of looking for work had made her frustrated and irate.

All kinds of new jobs were opening up for women, but
Ethel had quickly learned that men and women were still
unequal. Jobs at which men earned three or four pounds
were being offered to women at a pound a week. And even
then the women had to put up with hostility and persecu-
tion. Male bus passengers would refuse to show their tickets to a woman conductor, male engineers would pour oil
into a woman's tool box, and women workers were barred
from the pub at the factory gate. What made Ethel even
more furious was that the same men would call a woman
lazy and shiftless if her children were dressed in rags.

In the end, reluctantly and angrily, she had opted for
an industry in which women were traditionally employed,
vowing she would change this unjust system before she
died.

She rubbed her back. Her baby was due in a week or
two, and she was going to have to stop work any day now.
Sewing was awkward with a great distended belly, but what
she found most difficult was the tiredness that threatened
to overcome her.

Two more women came through the door, one with a
bandage on her hand. The seamstresses frequently cut
themselves with sewing needles or with the sharp scissors
they used to trim their work.

Ethel said: "Look you, Mannie, you ought to keep a little medical kit here, with bandages and a bottle of iodine
and a few other bits and pieces in a tin."

He said: "What am I, made of money?" It was his stock
response to any demand by his workforce.

"But you must lose money every time one of us hurts
herself," Ethel said in a tone of sweet reason. "Here's two
women been away from their machines nearly an hour, because they had to go to the chemist's and get a cut seen to."

The woman with the bandage grinned and said: "Plus I had to stop at the Dog and Duck to steady my nerves."

Mannie said sarcastically to Ethel: "I suppose you want me to keep a bottle of gin in the medical kit as well."

Ethel ignored that. "I'll make you a list and find out what everything would cost. Then you can make up your mind, is it?"

"I'm not making any promises," said Mannie, which was as close as he ever came to making a promise.

"Right, then." Ethel turned back to her machine.

It was always she who asked Mannie for small improvements in the workplace, or protested when he made adverse changes such as asking them to pay to have their scissors sharpened. Without intending to, she seemed to have fallen into the kind of role her father played.

Outside the grimy window, the short afternoon was darkening. Ethel found the last three hours of the working day the hardest of all. Her back hurt, and the glare of the overhead lights made her head ache.

But, when seven o'clock came, she did not want to go home. The thought of spending the evening alone was too depressing.

When Ethel first came to London several young men had paid attention to her. She had not really fancied any of them, but she had accepted invitations to the cinema, the music hall, recitals, and evenings at pubs, and she had kissed one of them, though without much passion. However, as soon as her pregnancy began to show they had all lost interest. A pretty girl was one thing, and a woman with a baby quite another.

Fortunately, tonight there was a Labour Party meeting. Ethel had joined the Aldgate branch of the Independent Labour Party soon after buying her house. She often wondered what her father would have thought, had he known. Would he have wanted to exclude her from his party as he had from his house? Or would he have been secretly pleased? She would probably never know.

The scheduled speaker tonight was Sylvia Pankhurst, one of the leaders of the suffragettes, campaigners for votes for women. The war had split the famous Pankhurst family. Emmeline, the mother, had forsworn the campaign for the duration of the war. One daughter, Christabel, supported the mother, but the other, Sylvia, had broken with them and continued the campaign. Ethel was on Sylvia's side: women were oppressed in war as well as peace, and they would never get justice until they could vote.

On the pavement outside, she said good night to the other women. The gaslit street was busy with workers going home, shoppers putting together their evening meal, and revelers on the way to a night on the tiles. A breath of warm, yeasty air came from the open door of the Dog and Duck. Ethel understood the women who spent all evening in such places. Pubs were nicer than most people's homes, and there was friendly company and the cheap anesthetic of gin.

Next to the pub was a grocer's shop called Lippmann's, but it was closed: it had been vandalized by a patriotic gang because of its German name, and now it was boarded up. Ironically, the owner was a Jew from Glasgow with a son in the Highland Light Infantry.

Ethel caught a bus. It was two stops, but she was too tired to walk.

The meeting was at the Calvary Gospel Hall, the place where Lady Maud had her clinic. Ethel had come to Aldgate because it was the only district of London she had ever heard of, Maud having mentioned the name many times.

The hall was lit by cheerful gas mantels along the walls, and a coal stove in the middle of the room took the chill off the air. Cheap folding chairs had been put out in rows facing a table and a lectern. Ethel was greeted by the branch secretary, Bernie Leckwith, a studious, pedantic man with a good heart. Now he looked worried. "Our speaker has canceled," he said.

Ethel was disappointed. "What are we going to do?" she asked. She looked around the room. "You've already got more than fifty people here."

"They're sending a substitute, but she's not here yet, and I don't know if she'll be any good. She's not even a party member."

"Who is it?"

"Her name is Lady Maud Fitzherbert." Bernie added disapprovingly: "I gather she's from a coal-owning family."

Ethel laughed. "Fancy that!" she said. "I used to work for her."

"Is she a good speaker?"

"I've no idea."

Ethel was intrigued. She had not seen Maud since the fateful Tuesday when Maud had married Walter von Ulrich and Britain had declared war on Germany. Ethel still had the dress Walter had bought her, carefully wrapped in tissue paper and hanging in her wardrobe. It was pink silk with a gauzy overdress, and it was the most beautiful thing she had ever owned. Of course she could not fit into it now. Besides, it was too good for wearing to a Labour Party meeting. She still had the hat, too, in the original box from the shop in Bond Street.

She took her seat, grateful to get the weight off her feet, and settled to wait for the meeting to begin. She would never forget going to the Ritz, after the wedding, with Walter's handsome cousin Robert von Ulrich. Walking into the restaurant she had been the focus of hard looks from one or two of the women, and she guessed that, even though her dress was expensive, there was something about her that marked her as working class. But she hardly cared. Robert had made her laugh with catty comments about the other women's clothing and jewelry, and she had told him a bit about life in a Welsh mining town, which seemed stranger to him than the existence of the Eskimos.

Where were they now? Both Walter and Robert had gone to war, of course, Walter with the German army and Robert with the Austrian, and Ethel had no way of knowing whether they were dead or alive. She knew no more about Fitz. She presumed he had gone to France with the Welsh Rifles, but was not even sure of that. All the same, she scanned the casualty lists in the newspapers, fearfully looking for the name Fitzherbert. She hated him for the way he had treated her, but all the same she was deeply thankful when his name did not appear.

She could have remained in contact with Maud, simply by going to the Wednesday clinic, but how would she have explained her visit? Apart from a minor scare in July—a little spotting of blood in her underwear that Dr. Greenward had assured her was nothing to worry about—she had had nothing wrong with her.

However, Maud had not changed in six months. She walked into the hall as spectacularly well dressed as ever, in a huge wide-brimmed hat with a tall feather that stuck up out of the hatband like the mast of a yacht. Suddenly Ethel felt shabby in her old brown coat.

Maud caught her eye and came over. "Hello, Williams! Forgive me—I mean, Ethel. What a lovely surprise!"

Ethel shook her hand. "You'll excuse me if I don't get up," she said, patting her distended belly. "Just now I don't think I could manage to stand up for the king."

"Don't even think about it. Can we find a few minutes to chat after the meeting?"

"That would be lovely."

Maud went to the table, and Bernie opened the meeting. Bernie was a Russian Jew, like so many inhabitants of London's East End. In fact few East Enders were plain English. There were lots of Welsh, Scottish, and Irish. Before the war there had been many Germans; now there were thousands of Belgian refugees. The East End was where they got off the ship, so naturally they settled there.

Although they had a special guest, Bernie insisted on first going through apologies for absence, the minutes of the previous meeting, and other tedious routines. He worked for the local council in the libraries department, and he was a stickler for detail.

At last he introduced Maud. She spoke confidently and knowledgeably about the oppression of women. "A woman doing the same job as a man should be paid the same," she said. "But we are often told that the man has to support a family."

Several men in the audience nodded emphatically: that was what they always said.

"But what about the *woman* who has to support a family?"

This brought murmurs of agreement from the women.

"Last week in Acton I met a girl who is trying to feed and clothe her five children on two pounds a week, while her husband, who has run off and left her, is earning four pounds ten shillings making ships' propellers in Tottenham, and spending his money in the pub!"

"That's right!" said a woman behind Ethel.

"Recently I spoke to a woman in Bermondsey whose husband was killed at Ypres—she has to support his four children, yet she is paid a woman's wage."

"Shame!" said several women.

"If it's worth the employer's while to pay a man a shilling apiece to make gudgeon pins, it's worth his while to pay a woman at the same rate."

The men shifted uncomfortably in their seats.

Maud raked the audience with a steely gaze. "When I hear socialist men argue against equal pay, I say to them: Are you permitting greedy employers to treat women as cheap labor?"

Ethel thought it took a lot of courage and independence for a woman of Maud's background to have such views. She also envied Maud. She was jealous of her beautiful clothes and her fluent speaking style. On top of all that, Maud was married to the man she loved.

After the talk, Maud was questioned aggressively by the Labour Party men. The branch treasurer, a red-faced Scot called Jock Reid, said: "How can you keep on moaning about votes for women when our boys are dying in France?" There were loud sounds of agreement.

"I'm glad you asked me that, because it's a question that bothers many men and women, too," Maud said. Ethel admired the conciliatory tone of the answer, which contrasted nicely with the hostility of the questioner. "Should normal political activity go on during the war? Should you be attending a Labour Party meeting? Should trade unions continue to fight against exploitation of workers? Has the Conservative Party closed down for the duration? Have injustice and oppression been temporarily suspended? I say no, comrade. We must not permit the enemies of progress to take advantage of the war. It must not become an excuse for traditionalists to hold us back. As Mr. Lloyd George says, it's business as usual."

After the meeting, tea was made—by the women, of course—and Maud sat next to Ethel, taking off her gloves to hold a cup and saucer of thick blue earthenware pottery in her soft hands. Ethel felt it would be unkind to tell Maud the truth about her brother, so she gave her the latest version of her fictional saga, that "Teddy Williams" had been killed fighting in France. "I tell people we were married," she said, touching the cheap ring she wore. "Not that anyone cares these days. When boys are going off to war, girls want to please them, married or not." She lowered her voice. "I don't suppose you've heard from Walter."

Maud smiled. "The most amazing thing happened. You read in the newspapers about the Christmas truce?"

"Yes, of course—British and Germans exchanging presents and playing football in no-man's-land. It's a shame they didn't continue the truce, and refuse to fight on."

"Absolutely. But Fitz met Walter!"

"Well, now, that's marvelous."

"Of course, Fitz doesn't know we're married, so Walter had to be careful what he said. But he sent a message to say he was thinking of me on Christmas Day."

Ethel squeezed Maud's hand. "So he's all right!"

"He's been in the fighting in East Prussia, and now he's on the front line in France, but he hasn't been wounded."

"Thank heaven. But I don't suppose you'll hear from him again. Such luck doesn't repeat itself."

"No. My only hope is that for some reason he'll be sent to a neutral country, such as Sweden or the United States, where he can post a letter to me. Otherwise I'll have to wait until the war is over."

"And what about the earl?"

"Fitz is fine. He spent the first few weeks of the war living it up in Paris."

While I was looking for a job in a sweatshop, Ethel thought resentfully.

Maud went on: "Princess Bea had a baby boy."

"Fitz must be happy to have an heir."

"We're all pleased," Maud said, and Ethel remembered that she was an aristocrat as well as a rebel.

The meeting broke up. A cab was waiting for Maud, and they said good-bye. Bernie Leckwith got on the bus with Ethel. "She was better than I expected," he said. "Upper-class, of course, but quite sound. And friendly, especially to you. I suppose you get to know the family quite well when you're in service."

You don't know the half of it, Ethel thought.

Ethel lived on a quiet street of small terraced houses, old but well-built, mostly occupied by better-off workers, craftsmen and supervisors, and their families. Bernie walked her to her front door. He probably wanted to kiss her good night. She toyed with the idea of letting him, just because she was grateful there was one man in the world who still found her attractive. But common sense prevailed:

she did not want to give him false hope. "Good night, comrade!" she said cheerfully, and she went inside.

There was no sound or light upstairs: Mildred and her children were already asleep. Ethel undressed and got into bed. She was weary, but her mind was active, and she could not fall asleep. After a while she got up and made tea.

She decided to write to her brother. She opened her writing pad and began.

> My very dear young sister Libby,

In their childhood code, every third word counted, and familiar names were scrambled, so this meant simply *Dear Billy*.

She recalled that her method had been to write out the message she wanted to send, then fill in the spaces. She now wrote:

> Sitting alone feeling proper miserable.

Then she turned it into code.

> Where I'm sitting, if you're alone you're not feeling yourself either proper happy or miserable.

As a child she had loved this game, inventing an imaginary message to hide the real one. She and Billy had devised helpful tricks: crossed-out words counted, whereas underlined words did not.

She decided to write out the whole of her message, then go back and turn it into code.

> The streets of London are not paved with gold, at least not in Aldgate.

She thought about writing a cheerful letter, making light of her troubles. Then she thought: To hell with that. I can tell my brother the truth.

> I used to believe I was special, don't ask why. She thinks she's too good for Aberowen, they used to say, and they were right.

She had to blink back tears when she thought of those days: the crisp uniform, the hearty meals in the spotless servants' hall, and most of all the slim, beautiful body that had once been hers.

> Now look at me. I work twelve hours a day in Mannie Litov's sweatshop. I have a headache every evening and a permanent pain in my back. I'm having a baby no one wants. No one wants me, either, except a boring librarian with glasses.

She sucked the end of her pencil for a long, thoughtful moment; then she wrote:

> I might as well be dead.

{ II }

On the second Sunday of each month an Orthodox priest came from Cardiff on the train up the valley to Aberowen, carrying a suitcase full of carefully wrapped icons and candlesticks, to celebrate Divine Liturgy for the Russians.

Lev Peshkov hated priests, but he always attended the service—you had to, to get the free dinner afterward. The service took place in the reading room of the public library. It was a Carnegie library, built with a donation from the American philanthropist, according to a plaque in the lobby. Lev could read, but he did not really understand people who thought of it as a pleasure. The newspapers here were fixed to hefty wooden holders, so that they could not be stolen, and there were signs that read "Silence." How much fun could you have in such a place?

Lev disliked most things about Aberowen.

Horses were the same everywhere, but he hated working underground: it was always half dark, and the thick coal dust made him cough. Aboveground it rained all the time. He had never seen so much rain. It did not come in thunderstorms, or sudden cloudbursts, to be followed by the relief of clear skies and dry weather. Rather, it was a soft drizzle that drifted down all day, sometimes all week, creeping up the legs of his trousers and down the back of his shirt.

The strike had petered out in August, after the outbreak of war, and the miners had drifted back to work. Most had been rehired and given back their old houses. The exceptions were those the management branded troublemakers, most of whom had gone off to join the Welsh Rifles. The evicted widows had found places to live. The strikebreakers were no longer ostracized: the locals had come around to the view that the foreigners, too, had been manipulated by the capitalist system.

But it was not for this that Lev had escaped from St. Petersburg. Britain was better than Russia, of course: trade unions were allowed, the police were not completely out of control, and even Jews were free. All the same, he was not going to settle for a life of backbreaking work in a mining town on the edge of nowhere. This was not what he and Grigori had dreamed of. This was not America.

Even if he had been tempted to stay there, he owed it to Grigori to go on. He knew he had treated his brother badly, but he had sworn to send him the money for his own ticket. Lev had broken a lot of promises in his short life, but he intended to keep this one.

He had most of the price of a ticket from Cardiff to New York. The money was hidden under a flagstone in the kitchen of his house in Wellington Row, along with his gun and his brother's passport. He had not saved this out of his weekly wage, of course: that was barely enough to keep him in beer and tobacco. His savings came from the weekly card game.

Spirya was no longer his collaborator. The young man had left Aberowen after a few days and returned to Cardiff to seek easier work. But it was never difficult to find a greedy man, and Lev had befriended a colliery deputy called Rhys Price. Lev made sure Rhys won steadily, and afterward they shared the proceeds. It was important not to overdo things: other people had to win sometimes. If the miners worked out what was going on, not only would it be the end of the card school, but they would probably kill Lev. So the money accumulated slowly, and Lev could not afford to turn down a free meal.

The priest was always met at the station by the earl's

car. He was driven to Tŷ Gwyn, where he was given sherry and cake. If Princess Bea was in residence, she accompanied him to the library and entered the room a few seconds before him, which saved her having to wait too long with the common people.

Today it was a few minutes after eleven by the large clock on the reading room wall when she entered, wearing a white fur coat and hat against the February cold. Lev repressed a shudder: he could not look at her without feeling again the sheer terror of a six-year-old seeing his father hanged.

The priest followed in a cream-colored robe with a gold sash. Today, for the first time, he was accompanied by another man in the garb of a novice priest—and Lev was shocked and horrified to recognize his former partner in crime Spirya.

Lev's mind was in turmoil as the two clergymen prepared the five loaves and watered the red wine for the service. Had Spirya found God and changed his ways? Or was the clerical outfit just another cover for stealing and cheating?

The older priest sang the blessing. A few of the more devout men had formed a choir—a development their Welsh neighbors approved of heartily—and now they sang the first *amen.* Lev crossed himself when the others did, but his mind was anxiously on Spirya. It would be just like a priest to blurt out the truth and ruin everything: no more card games, no ticket to America, no money for Grigori.

Lev recalled the last day on the *Angel Gabriel,* when he had brutally threatened to throw Spirya overboard for merely talking about double-crossing him. Spirya might well remember that now. Lev wished he had not humiliated the man.

Lev studied Spirya throughout the service, trying to read his face. When he went up to the front to receive communion, he tried to catch his old friend's eye, but he saw no sign even of recognition: Spirya was totally caught up in the rite, or pretending to be.

Afterward the two clergy left in the car with the princess, and the thirty or so Russian Christians followed on foot. Lev wondered if Spirya would speak to him at Tŷ Gwyn, and fretted about what he might say. Would he pretend their scam had never happened? Would he spill the beans and bring the wrath of the miners down on Lev's head? Would he demand a price for his silence?

Lev was tempted to leave town immediately. There were trains to Cardiff every hour or two. If he had had more money he might have cut and run. But he did not have enough for the ticket, so he trudged up the hill out of town to the earl's palace for the midday dinner.

They were fed in the staff quarters below stairs. The food was hearty: mutton stew with as much bread as you could eat, and ale to wash it down. The princess's middle-aged Russian maid, Nina, joined them and acted as interpreter. She had a soft spot for Lev, and made sure he got extra ale.

The priest ate with the princess but Spirya came to the servants' hall and sat next to Lev. Lev turned on his most welcoming smile. "Well, old friend, this is a surprise!" he said in Russian. "Congratulations!"

Spirya refused to be charmed. "Are you still playing cards, my son?" he replied.

Lev kept the smile but lowered his voice. "I'll shut up about that if you will. Is that fair?"

"We'll talk after dinner."

Lev was frustrated. Which way was Spirya going to jump—righteousness or blackmail?

When the meal was over, Spirya went out through the back door, and Lev followed. Without speaking, Spirya led him to a white rotunda like a miniature Greek temple. From its raised platform they could see anyone approaching. It was raining, and the water dripped down the marble pillars. Lev shook the rain off his cap and put it back on his head.

Spirya said: "Do you recall my asking you, on the ship, what you would do if I refused to give you your half of the money?"

Lev had pushed Spirya half over the rail and threatened to break his neck and throw his body in the sea. "No, I don't remember," he lied.

"It doesn't matter," Spirya said. "I simply wished to forgive you."

Righteousness, then, Lev thought with relief.

"What we did was sinful," Spirya said. "I have confessed and received absolution."

"I won't ask your priest to play cards with me, then."

"Don't joke."

Lev wanted to grab Spirya by the throat, as he had on the ship, but Spirya no longer looked as if he could be bullied. The robe had given him balls, ironically.

Spirya went on: "I ought to reveal your crime to those you robbed."

"They won't thank you. They may take revenge on you as well as me."

"My priestly garments will protect me."

Lev shook his head. "Most of the people you and I robbed were poor Jews. They probably remember priests looking on with a smile while the Cossacks beat them up. They might kick you to death all the more eagerly in your robe."

The shadow of anger passed over Spirya's young face, but he forced a benign smile. "I'm more concerned about you, my son. I would not like to provoke violence against you."

Lev knew when he was being threatened. "What are you going to do?"

"The question is what you're going to do."

"Will you keep your mouth shut if I stop?"

"If you confess, make a sincere contrition, and cease your sin, God will forgive you—and then it will not be for me to punish you."

And you'll get away with it, too, Lev thought. "All right, I'll do it," he said. As soon as he had spoken, he realized he had given in too quickly.

Spirya's next words confirmed that he was not so easily fooled. "I will check," he said. "And if I find you have broken your promise to me and to God, I will reveal your crime to your victims."

"And they will kill me. Good work, Father."

"As far as I can see, it's the best way out of a moral dilemma. And my priest agrees. So take it or leave it."

"I have no choice."

"God bless you, my son," said Spirya.

Lev walked away.

He left the grounds of Tŷ Gwyn and headed through the rain back into Aberowen, fuming. How like a priest, he thought resentfully, to take away a man's chance of bettering himself. Spirya was comfortable now, food and clothing and accommodation all provided, forever, by the church and the hungry worshippers who gave money they could not afford. For the rest of his life, Spirya would have nothing to do but sing the services and fiddle with the altar boys.

What was Lev to do? If he gave up the card games, it would take him forever to save enough for his passage. He would be doomed to spend years tending pit ponies half a mile underground. And he would never redeem himself by sending Grigori the price of a ticket to America.

He had never chosen the safe path.

He made his way to the Two Crowns pub. In Sabbath-observing Wales, pubs were not allowed to open on Sundays, but the rules were lightly regarded in Aberowen. There was only one policeman in the town and, like most people, he took Sundays off. The Two Crowns closed its front door, for the sake of appearances, but regulars went in through the kitchen, and business was done as usual.

At the bar were the Ponti brothers, Joey and Johnny. They were drinking whisky, unusually. The miners drank beer. Whisky was a rich man's potion, and a bottle probably lasted the Two Crowns from one Christmas to the next.

Lev ordered a pot of beer and addressed the elder brother. "Aye, aye, Joey."

"Aye, aye, Grigori." Lev was still using his brother's name, which was on the passport.

"Feeling flush today, Joey, is it?"

"Aye. Me and the kid went to Cardiff yesterday for the boxing."

The brothers looked like boxers themselves, Lev thought: two broad-shouldered, bull-necked men with big hands. "Good, was it?" he said.

"Darkie Jenkins versus Roman Tony. We bet on Tony, being Italian like us. Odds of thirteen to one, and he knocked Jenkins out in three rounds."

Lev sometimes struggled with formal English, but he knew the meaning of "thirteen to one." He said: "You should come and play cards. You are . . ." He hesitated, then remembered the phrase. "You are making a lucky streak."

"Oh, I don't want to lose it as quick as I won it," Joey said.

However, when the card school assembled in the barn

half an hour later, Joey and Johnny were there. The rest of the players were a mixture of Russian and Welsh.

They played a local version of poker called three-card brag. Lev liked it. After the initial three, no further cards were dealt or exchanged, so the game went fast. If a player raised the bet, the next man in the circle had to match the raise immediately—he could not stay in the game by betting the original stake—so the pot grew quickly. Betting continued until there were only two players left, at which point one of them could end the round by doubling the previous bet, which forced his opponent to show his cards. The best hand was three of a kind, known as a prial, and the highest of all was a prial of treys, three threes.

Lev had a natural instinct for odds and would usually have won at cards without cheating, but that was too slow.

The deal moved to the left every hand, so Lev could fix the cards only once in a while. However, there were a thousand ways to cheat, and Lev had devised a simple code that enabled Rhys to indicate when he had a good hand. Lev would then stay in the betting, regardless of what he was holding, to force the stakes up and enlarge the pot. Most of the time everyone else would drop out, and Lev would then lose to Rhys.

As the first hand was dealt, Lev decided this would be his last game. If he cleaned out the Ponti brothers he would probably be able to buy his ticket. Next Sunday Spirya would make inquiries to find out whether Lev was still running a card school. By then Lev wanted to be at sea.

Over the next two hours Lev watched Rhys's winnings grow and told himself America was coming nearer with each penny. He did not usually like to clean anyone out, because he wanted them to come back next week. But today was the day to go for the jackpot.

As the afternoon began to darken outside he got the deal. He gave Joey Ponti three aces and Rhys three threes. In this game, threes beat aces. He gave himself a pair of kings, which justified him in betting high. He stayed in the betting until Joey was almost broke—he did not want to collect any IOUs. Joey used the last of his money to see Rhys's hand. The expression on Joey's face when Rhys showed a prial of treys was both comical and pitiful.

Rhys raked the money in. Lev stood up and said: "I'm

cleaned out." The game broke up and they all returned to the bar, where Rhys bought a round of drinks to soothe the feelings of the losers. The Ponti brothers reverted to drinking beer, and Joey said: "Ah, well, easy come, easy go, isn't it?"

A few minutes later, Lev went back outside and Rhys followed. There was no toilet at the Two Crowns, so the men used the lane at the back of the barn. The only illumination came from a distant streetlight. Rhys quickly handed Lev his half of the winnings, partly in coins and partly in the new colored banknotes, green for a pound and brown for ten shillings.

Lev knew exactly what he was owed. Arithmetic came naturally to him, like figuring the odds at cards. He would count the money later, but he was sure Rhys would not cheat him. The man had tried, once. Lev had found his share to be five shillings short—an amount that a careless man might have overlooked. Lev had gone to Rhys's house, stuck the barrel of his revolver into the man's mouth, and cocked the hammer. Rhys had soiled himself in fear. After that the money had always been correct to a halfpenny.

Lev stuffed the money into his coat pocket and they returned to the bar.

As they walked in, Lev saw Spirya.

He had taken off his robes and put on the overcoat he had worn on the ship. He stood at the bar, not drinking, but talking earnestly to a small group of Russians, including some of the card school.

Momentarily, he met Lev's eye.

Lev turned on his heel and went out, but he knew he was too late.

He walked quickly away, heading up the hill to Wellington Row. Spirya would betray him, he felt sure. Even now he might be explaining how Lev managed to cheat at cards and yet seem the loser. The men would be furious, and the Ponti brothers would want their money back.

As he approached his house, he saw a man coming the other way with a suitcase, and in the lamplight he recognized a young neighbor known as Billy-with-Jesus. "Aye, aye, Billy," he said.

"Aye, aye, Grigori."

The boy looked as if he was leaving town, and Lev was curious. "Off somewhere?"

"London."

Lev's interest quickened. "What train?"

"Six o'clock to Cardiff." Passengers for London had to change trains at Cardiff.

"What is it now?"

"Twenty to."

"So long, then." Lev went into his house. He would catch the same train as Billy, he decided.

He turned on the electric light in the kitchen and lifted the flagstone. He took out his savings, the passport with his brother's name and photograph, a box of brass bullets, and his gun, a Nagant M1895 he had won from an army captain in a card game. He checked the cylinder to make sure there was a live round in each chamber: used rounds were not automatically ejected, but had to be removed manually when reloading. He put the money, the passport, and the gun in the pockets of his coat.

Upstairs he found Grigori's cardboard suitcase with the bullet hole. Into it he packed the ammunition plus his other shirt, his spare underwear, and two packs of cards.

He had no watch, but he calculated that five minutes had passed since he saw Billy. That gave him fifteen minutes to walk to the station, which was enough.

From the street outside he heard the voices of several men.

He did not want a confrontation. He was tough, but the miners were, too. Even if he won the fight he would miss his train. He could use the gun, of course, but in this country the police were serious about catching murderers even when the victims were nobodies. At a minimum they would check passengers at the docks in Cardiff and make it difficult for him to buy a ticket. In every way it would be best if he could leave town without violence.

He went out of the back door and hurried along the lane, walking as quietly as he could in his heavy boots. The ground underfoot was muddy, as it almost always was in Wales, so fortunately his footsteps made little noise.

At the end of the lane he turned down an alley and emerged into the lights of the street. The toilets in the middle of the road shielded him from the view of anyone outside his house. He hurried away.

Two streets farther on he realized that his route took him

past the Two Crowns. He stopped and thought for a moment. He knew the layout of the town, and the only alternative route would require him to double back. But the men whose voices he had heard might still be near his house.

He had to risk the Two Crowns. He turned down another alley and took the back lane that passed behind the pub.

As he approached the barn where they had played cards, he heard voices and glimpsed two or more men, dimly outlined by the streetlamp at the far end of the lane. He was running out of time, but all the same he stopped and waited for them to go back inside. He stood close to a high wooden fence to make himself less visible.

They seemed to take forever. "Come on," he whispered. "Don't you want to get back into the warm?" The rain dripped off his cap and down the back of his neck.

At last they went inside, and Lev emerged from the shadows and hurried forward. He passed the barn without incident, but as he drew away from it he heard more voices. He cursed. The customers had been drinking beer since midday, and by this time of the afternoon they needed frequent visits to the lane. He heard someone call after him: "Aye, aye, butty." Their word for friend was "butty" or "butt." Its use meant he had not been recognized.

He pretended not to hear, and walked on.

He could hear a murmured conversation. Most of the words were unintelligible, but he thought one man said: "Looks like a Russky." Russian clothes were different from British, and Lev guessed they might be able to make out the cut of his coat and the shape of his cap by the light of the streetlamp, which he was quickly approaching. However, the call of nature was usually urgent for men coming out of a pub, and he thought they would not follow him before they had relieved themselves.

He turned down the next alley and disappeared from their view. Unfortunately, he doubted whether he had gone from their minds. Spirya must by now have told his story, and someone would soon realize the significance of a man in Russian clothes walking toward the town center with a suitcase in his hand.

He had to be on that train.

He broke into a run.

The railway line lay in the cleft of the valley, so the way to the station was all downhill. Lev ran easily, taking long strides. He could see, over the rooftops, the lights of the station and, as he came closer, the smoke from the funnel of a train standing at the platform.

He ran across the square and into the booking hall. The hands of the big clock stood at one minute to six. He hurried to the ticket window and fished money from his pocket. "Ticket, please," he said.

"Where would you like to go this evening?" the clerk said pleasantly.

Lev pointed urgently to the platform. "That train by there!"

"This train calls at Aberdare, Pontypridd—"

"Cardiff!" Lev glanced up and saw the minute hand click through its last segment and stop, trembling slightly, at the o'clock position.

"Single, or return?" said the clerk unhurriedly.

"Single, quickly!"

Lev heard the whistle. Desperately, he looked through the coins in his hand. He knew the fare—he had been to Cardiff twice in the last six months—and he put money on the counter.

The train began to move.

The clerk gave him his ticket.

Lev grabbed it and turned away.

"Don't forget your change!" said the clerk.

Lev strode the few paces to the barrier. "Ticket, please," said the collector, even though he had just watched Lev buy it.

Looking past the barrier, Lev saw the train gathering speed.

The collector punched his ticket and said: "Don't you want your change?"

The door of the booking hall burst open and the Ponti brothers rushed in. "There you are!" Joey cried, and he rushed at Lev.

Lev surprised him by stepping toward him and punching him directly in the face. Joey was stopped in his tracks. Johnny crashed into his older brother's back, and both fell to their knees.

Lev snatched his ticket from the collector and ran onto the

platform. The train was moving quite fast. He ran alongside it for a moment. Suddenly a door opened, and Lev saw the friendly face of Billy-with-Jesus.

Billy shouted: "Jump!"

Lev leaped for the train and got one foot on the step. Billy grabbed his arm. They teetered for a moment as Lev tried desperately to haul himself aboard. Then Billy gave a heave and pulled Lev inside.

He sank gratefully into a seat.

Billy pulled the door shut and sat opposite him.

"Thank you," Lev said.

"You cut it fine," Billy said.

"I made it, though," said Lev with a grin. "That's all that counts."

{ III }

At Paddington Station the next morning, Billy asked for directions to Aldgate. A friendly Londoner gave him a rapid stream of detailed instructions, every word of which he found completely incomprehensible. He thanked the man and walked out of the station.

He had never been to London but he knew that Paddington was in the west and poor people lived in the east, so he walked toward the midmorning sun. The city was even bigger than he had imagined, a great deal busier and more confusing than Cardiff, but he relished it: the noise, the rushing traffic, the crowds, and most of all the shops. He had not known there were so many shops in the world. How much was spent in London's shops every day? he wondered. It must be thousands of pounds—maybe millions.

He felt a sense of freedom that was quite heady. No one here knew him. In Aberowen, or even on his occasional trips to Cardiff, he was always liable to be observed by friends or relations. In London he might walk along a street holding hands with a pretty girl and his parents would never find out. He had no intention of doing so, but the thought that he could—and the fact that there were so many pretty well-dressed girls walking around—was intoxicating.

After a while he saw a bus with "Aldgate" written on its

front, and he jumped aboard. Ethel's letter had mentioned Aldgate.

When he decoded her letter he had been very worried. Of course he could not discuss it with his parents. He had waited until they left for the evening service at the Bethesda Chapel—which he no longer attended—then he had written a note.

> Dear Mam,
>   I am worried about our Eth and have gone to find her. Sorry to sneak off but I don't want a row.
>   Your loving son,
>   Billy

As it was Sunday, he was already bathed and shaved and dressed in his best clothes. His suit was a shabby hand-me-down from his father, but he had a clean white shirt and a black knitted tie. He had dozed in the waiting room at Cardiff station and caught the milk train in the early hours of Monday morning.

The bus conductor alerted him when they reached Aldgate, and he got off. It was a poor neighborhood, with crumbling slum houses, street stalls selling secondhand clothes, and barefoot children playing in noisome stairwells. He did not know where Ethel lived—her letter had not given an address. His only clue was *I work twelve hours a day in Mannie Litov's sweatshop.*

He looked forward to giving Eth all the news from Aberowen. She would know from the newspapers that the widows' strike had failed. Billy seethed when he thought of it. The bosses were able to behave outrageously because they held all the cards. They owned the mines and the houses, and they acted as if they owned the people. Because of various complex franchise rules, most miners did not have the vote, so Aberowen's member of Parliament was a Conservative who invariably sided with the company. Tommy Griffiths's father said nothing would ever change without a revolution like the one they had had in France. Billy's da said they needed a Labour government. Billy did not know who was right.

He went up to a friendly-looking young man and said: "Do you know the way to Mannie Litov's place?"

The man replied in a language that sounded like Russian.

He tried again, and this time got an English speaker who had never heard of Mannie Litov. Aldgate was not like Aberowen, where everyone on the street would know the way to every place of business in town. Had he come this far—and spent all that money on his train ticket—for nothing?

He was not yet ready to give up. He scanned the busy street for British-looking people who seemed to be about some kind of business, carrying tools or pushing carts. He questioned five more people without success, then came across a window cleaner with a ladder.

"Mannie Litov's?" the man repeated. He managed to say "Litov" without pronouncing the letter *t*, instead making a noise in his throat like a small cough. "Clouvin fectry?"

"Pardon me," Billy said politely. "What was that again?"

"Clouvin fectry. Plice where vey mikes clouvin—jickits an trahsies an at."

"Um . . . probably, yes," Billy said, feeling desperate.

The window cleaner nodded. "Strite on, quote of a ma, do a rye, Ark Rav Rahd."

"Straight on?" Billy replied. "Quarter of a mile?"

"Ass it. Ven do a rye."

"Turn right?"

"Ark Rav Rahd."

"Ark Rav Road?"

"Carn miss it."

The street name turned out to be Oak Grove Road. It had no grove of anything, let alone oaks. It was a narrow, winding lane of dilapidated brick buildings busy with people, horses, and handcarts. Two more inquiries brought Billy to a house squashed between the Dog and Duck pub and a boarded-up shop called Lippmann's. The front door stood open. Billy climbed the stairs to the top floor, where he found himself in a room with about twenty women sewing British army uniforms.

They continued working, operating their treadles, taking no apparent notice of him, until eventually one said: "Come in, love. We won't eat you—although, come to think of it, I might try a little taste." They all cackled with laughter.

"I'm looking for Ethel Williams," he said.

"She's not here," the woman said.

"Why not?" he said anxiously. "Is she ill?"

"What business is it of yours?" The woman got up from her machine. "I'm Mildred—who are you?"

Billy stared at her. She was pretty even though she had buckteeth. She wore bright red lipstick, and fair curls poked out from under her hat. She was wrapped in a thick, shapeless gray coat but, despite that, he could see the sway of her hips as she walked toward him. He was too taken with her to speak.

She said: "You're not the bastard who put her up the duff then scarpered, are you?"

Billy found his voice. "I'm her brother."

"Oh!" she said. "Fucking hell, are you Billy?"

Billy's jaw dropped. He had never heard a woman use that word.

She scrutinized him with a fearless gaze. "You are her brother, I can see it, though you look older than sixteen." Her tone softened in a way that made him feel warm inside. "You've got the same dark eyes and curly hair."

"Where can I find her?" he said.

She gave him a challenging look. "I happen to know that she doesn't want her family to find out where she's living."

"She's scared of my father," Billy said. "But she wrote me a letter. I was worried about her, so I came up on the train."

"All the way from that dump in Wales where she's from?"

"It's not a dump," Billy said indignantly. Then he shrugged and said: "Well, it is, really, I suppose."

"I love your accent," Mildred said. "To me it's like hearing someone sing."

"Do you know where she lives?"

"How did you find this place?"

"She said she worked at Mannie Litov's in Aldgate."

"Well, you're Sherlock bloody Holmes, aren't you?" she said, not without a note of reluctant admiration.

"If you don't tell me where she is, someone else will," he said with more confidence than he felt. "I'm not going home till I've seen her."

"She'll kill me, but all right," Mildred said. "Twenty-three Nutley Street."

Billy asked her for directions. He made her speak slowly.

"Don't thank me," she said as he took his leave. "Just protect me if Ethel tries to kill me."

"All right, then," said Billy, thinking how thrilling it would be to protect Mildred from something.

The other women shouted good-bye and blew kisses as he left, embarrassing him.

Nutley Street was an oasis of quiet. The terraced houses were built to a pattern that had become familiar to Billy after only one day in London. They were much larger than miners' cottages, with small front yards instead of a door opening onto the street. The effect of order and regularity was created by identical sash windows, each with twelve panes of glass, in rows all along the terrace.

He knocked at number 23 but no one answered.

He was worried. Why had she not gone to work? Was she ill? If not, why was she not at home?

He peered through the letterbox and saw a hallway with polished floorboards and a hat stand bearing an old brown coat that he recognized. It was a cold day: Ethel would not go out without her coat.

He stepped close to the window and tried to look inside, but he could not see through the net curtain.

He returned to the door and looked through the flap again. The scene inside was unchanged, but this time he heard a noise. It was a long, agonized groan. He put his mouth to the letterbox and shouted: "Eth! Is that you? It's Billy out here."

There was a long silence; then the groan was repeated.

"Bloody hell," he said.

The door had a Yale-type lock. That meant the catch was probably attached to the doorpost with two screws. He struck the door with the heel of his hand. It did not seem particularly stout, and he guessed the wood was cheap pine, many years old. He leaned back, lifted his right leg, and kicked the door with the heel of his heavy miner's boot. There was a sound of splintering. He kicked several more times, but the door did not open.

He wished he had a hammer.

He looked up and down the road, hoping to see a workman with tools, but the street was deserted except for two dirty-faced boys who were watching him with interest.

He walked down the short garden path to the gate,

turned, and ran at the door, hitting it with his right shoulder. It burst open and he fell inside.

He picked himself up, rubbing his hurt shoulder, and pushed the ruined door to. The house seemed silent. "Eth?" he called. "Where are you?"

The groaning came again, and he followed the sound into the front room on the ground floor. It was a woman's bedroom, with china ornaments on the mantelpiece and flowered curtains at the window. Ethel was on the bed, wearing a gray dress that covered her like a tent. She was not lying down, but on her hands and knees, groaning.

"What's wrong with you, Eth?" said Billy, and his voice came out as a terrified squeak.

She caught her breath. "The baby's coming."

"Oh, hell. I'd better fetch a doctor."

"Too late, Billy. Dear Jesus, it hurts."

"You sound like you're dying!"

"No, Billy, this is what childbirth is like. Come by here and hold my hand."

Billy knelt by the bed, and Ethel took his hand. She tightened her grip and began to groan again. The groan was longer and more agonized than before, and she gripped his hand so hard he thought she might break a bone. Her groan ended with a shriek; then she panted as if she had run a mile.

After a minute she said: "I'm sorry, Billy, but you're going to have to look up my skirt."

"Oh!" he said. "Oh, right." He did not really understand, but he thought he had better do as he was told. He lifted the hem of Ethel's dress. "Oh, Christ!" he said. The bedsheet beneath her was soaked in blood. There in the middle of it was a tiny pink thing covered in slime. He made out a big round head with closed eyes, two tiny arms, and two legs. "It's a baby!" he said.

"Pick it up, Billy," said Ethel.

"What, me?" he said. "Oh, right, then." He leaned over the bed. He got one hand under the baby's head and one under its little bum. It was a boy, he saw. The baby was slippery and slimy, but Billy managed to pick him up. There was a cord still attaching him to Ethel.

"Have you got it?" she said.

"Aye," he said. "I've got him. It's a boy."

"Is he breathing?"

"I dunno. How can you tell?" Billy fought down panic. "No, he's not breathing, I don't think."

"Smack his bum, not too hard."

Billy turned the baby over, held him easily in one hand, and sharply smacked his bottom. Immediately the child opened his mouth, breathed in, and yelled in protest. Billy was delighted. "Hark at that!" he said.

"Hold him a minute while I turn over." Ethel got herself into a sitting position and straightened her dress. "Give him to me."

Billy carefully handed him over. Ethel held the baby in the crook of her arm and wiped his face with her sleeve. "He's beautiful," she said.

Billy was not sure about that.

The cord attached to the baby's navel had been blue and taut, but now it shriveled and turned pale. Ethel said: "Open that drawer over by there and pass me the scissors and a reel of cotton."

Ethel tied two knots in the cord, then snipped it between the knots. "There," she said. She unbuttoned the front of her dress. "I don't suppose you'll be embarrassed, after what you've seen," she said, and she took out a breast and put the nipple to the baby's mouth. He began to suck.

She was right: Billy was not embarrassed. An hour ago he would have been mortified by the sight of his sister's bare breast, but such a feeling seemed trivial now. All he felt was enormous relief that the baby was all right. He stared, watching him suckle, marveling at the tiny fingers. He felt as if he had witnessed a miracle. His face was wet with tears, and he wondered when he had cried: he had no memory of doing so.

Quite soon the baby fell asleep. Ethel buttoned her dress. "We'll wash him in a minute," she said. Then she closed her eyes. "My God," she said. "I didn't know it was going to hurt that much."

Billy said: "Who's his father, Eth?"

"Earl Fitzherbert," she said. Then she opened her eyes. "Oh, bugger, I never meant to tell you that."

"The bloody swine," said Billy. "I'll kill him."

CHAPTER FIFTEEN

June to September 1915

As the ship entered New York harbor, it occurred to Lev Peshkov that America might not be as wonderful as his brother, Grigori, said. He steeled himself for a terrible disappointment. But that was unnecessary. America was all the things he had hoped for: rich, busy, exciting, and free.

Three months later, on a hot afternoon in June, he was working at a hotel in Buffalo, in the stables, grooming a guest's horse. The place was owned by Josef Vyalov, who had put an onion dome on top of the old Central Tavern and renamed it the St. Petersburg Hotel, perhaps out of nostalgia for the city he had left when he was a child.

Lev worked for Vyalov, as did many of Buffalo's Russian immigrants, but he had never met the man. If he ever did, he was not sure what he would say. The Vyalov family in Russia had cheated Lev by dumping him in Cardiff, and that rankled. On the other hand, the papers supplied by the St. Petersburg Vyalovs had got Lev through U.S. immigration without a hitch. And mentioning the name of Vyalov in a bar on Canal Street had got him a job immediately.

He had been speaking English every day for a year now, ever since he landed in Cardiff, and he was becoming fluent. Americans said he had a British accent, and they were not familiar with some of the expressions he had learned in Aberowen, such as *by here* and *by there,* or *is it?* and *isn't it?* at the ends of sentences. But he could say just about anything he needed to, and girls were charmed when he called them *my lovely*.

At a few minutes to six o'clock, shortly before he finished work for the day, his friend Nick came into the stable yard, a cigarette between his lips. "Fatima brand," he said. He drew in smoke with exaggerated satisfaction. "Turkish tobacco. Beautiful."

Nick's full name was Nicolai Davidovich Fomek, but here he was called Nick Forman. He occasionally played the role previously taken by Spirya and Rhys Price in Lev's card games, though mostly he was a thief.

"How much?" said Lev.

"In the stores, fifty cents for a tin of a hundred cigarettes. To you, ten cents. Sell them for a quarter."

Lev knew that Fatima was a popular brand. It would be easy to sell them at half price. He looked around the yard. The boss was nowhere to be seen. "All right."

"How many do you want? I've got a trunkful."

Lev had one dollar in his pocket. "Twenty tins," he said. "I'll give you a dollar now and a dollar later."

"I don't give credit."

Lev grinned and put his hand on Nick's shoulder. "Come on, buddy, you can trust me. Are we pals, or not?"

"Twenty it is. I'll be right back."

Lev found an old feed sack in a corner. Nick returned with twenty long green tins, each with a picture of a veiled woman on the lid. Lev put the tins in the sack and gave Nick a dollar. "Always nice to give a helping hand to a fellow Russian," Nick said, and he sauntered away.

Lev cleaned his curry comb and hoofpick. At five past six he said good-bye to the chief ostler and headed for the First Ward. He felt a little conspicuous, carrying a feed sack through the streets, and he wondered what he would say if a cop stopped him and demanded to see what was in the sack. But he was not very worried: he could talk his way out of most situations.

He went to a large, popular bar called the Irish Rover. He pushed through the crowd, bought a tankard of beer, and downed half of it thirstily. Then he sat next to a group of workingmen speaking a mixture of Polish and English. After a few moments he said: "Anyone here smoke Fatimas?"

A bald man in a leather apron said: "Yeah, I'll smoke a Fatima now and again."

"Want to buy a tin at half price? Twenty-five cents for a hundred smokes."

"What's wrong with them?"

"They got lost. Someone found them."

"Sounds a little risky."

"I tell you what. Put your money on the table. I won't pick it up until you tell me to."

The men were interested now. The bald man fished in his pocket and came up with a quarter. Lev took a tin from his sack and handed it over. The man opened the tin. He took out a small rectangle of folded paper and opened it to disclose a photograph. "Hey, it's even got a baseball card!" he said. He put one of the cigarettes in his mouth and lit it. "All right," he said to Lev. "Pick up your quarter."

Another man was watching over Lev's shoulder. "How much?" he said. Lev told him, and he bought two tins.

In the next half hour Lev sold all the cigarettes. He was pleased: he had turned two dollars into five in less than an hour. At work it took him a day and a half to earn three dollars. Maybe he would buy some more stolen tins from Nick tomorrow.

He bought another beer, drank it, and went out, leaving the empty sack on the floor. Outside, he turned toward the Lovejoy district, a poor neighborhood of Buffalo where most of the Russians lived, along with many Italians and Poles. He could buy a steak on the way home and fry it with potatoes. Or he could pick up Marga and take her dancing. Or he could buy a new suit.

He ought to save it toward Grigori's fare to America, he thought, guiltily knowing he would do no such thing. Three dollars was a drop in the bucket. What he needed was a really big score. Then he could send Grigori the money all in one go, before he was tempted to spend it.

He was startled out of his reverie by a tap on his shoulder.

His heart gave a guilty leap. He turned, half expecting to see a police uniform. But the person who had stopped him was no cop. He was a heavily built man in overalls, with a broken nose and an aggressive scowl. Lev tensed: such a man had only one function.

The man said: "Who told you to sell smokes in the Irish Rover?"

"I'm just trying to make a few bucks," Lev said with a smile. "I hope I didn't offend anyone."

"Was it Nicky Forman? I heard Nick knocked over a truckload of cigarettes."

Lev was not going to give that information to a stranger. "I never met anyone by that name," he said, still using a pleasant tone of voice.

"Don't you know the Irish Rover belongs to Mister V?"

Lev felt a surge of anger. Mister V had to be Josef Vyalov. He dropped the conciliatory tone. "So put up a sign."

"You don't sell stuff in Mister V's bars 'less he tells you."

Lev shrugged. "I didn't know that."

"Here's something to help you remember," the man said, and he swung his fist.

Lev was expecting the blow, and he stepped back sharply. The thug's arm swept through empty space and he staggered, off balance. Lev stepped forward and kicked him in the shin. A fist was a poor weapon, generally, nowhere near as hard as a booted foot. Lev kicked as powerfully as he could, but it was not enough to break a bone. The man roared with anger, swung again, and missed again.

There was no point hitting such a man in the face—he had probably lost all feeling there. Lev kicked him in the groin. Both his hands went to his crotch and he gasped for breath, bending forward. Lev kicked him in the stomach. The man opened and closed his mouth like a goldfish, unable to breathe. Lev stepped to one side and kicked the man's legs from under him. He went down on his back. Lev aimed carefully and kicked his knee, so that when he got up he would not be able to move fast.

Panting with exertion, he said: "Tell Mister V he should be more polite."

He walked away, breathing hard. Behind him he heard someone say: "Hey, Ilya, what the fuck happened?"

Two streets away his breathing eased and his heartbeat slowed. To hell with Josef Vyalov, he thought. The bastard cheated me and I won't be bullied.

Vyalov would not know who had beaten up Ilya. No one in the Irish Rover knew Lev. Vyalov might get mad but there was nothing he could do about it.

Lev started to feel elated. I put Ilya on the ground, he thought, and there's not a mark on me!

He still had a pocket full of money. He stopped to buy two steaks and a bottle of gin.

He lived on a street of dilapidated brick houses subdivided into small apartments. Outside the house next door Marga was sitting on the stoop filing her nails. She was a pretty black-haired Russian girl of about nineteen with a sexy grin. She worked as a waitress but hoped for a career as a singer. He had bought her drinks a couple of times and kissed her once. She had kissed him back enthusiastically.

"Hi, kid!" he shouted.

"Who are you calling a kid?"

"What are you doing tonight?"

"I've got a date," she said.

Lev did not necessarily believe her. She would never admit that she had nothing to do. "Throw him over," he said. "He has bad breath."

She grinned. "You don't even know who it is!"

"Come and see me." He hefted his paper bag. "I'm cooking steak."

"I'll think about it."

"Bring ice." He went into his building.

His apartment was a low-rent place, by American standards, but it seemed spacious and luxurious to Lev. It had a bed-sitting-room and a kitchen, with running water and electric light—and he had it all to himself! In St. Petersburg such an apartment would have housed ten or more people.

He took off his jacket, rolled up his sleeves, and washed his hands and face at the kitchen sink. He hoped Marga would come. She was his kind of girl, always ready to laugh or dance or have a party, never worrying too much about the future. He peeled and sliced some potatoes, then put a frying pan on the hot plate and dropped in a lump of lard. While the potatoes were frying, Marga came in with a tankard of chipped ice. She made drinks with gin and sugar.

Lev sipped his drink, then kissed her lightly on the lips. "Tastes good!" he said.

"You're fresh," she said, but it was not a serious protest. He began to wonder if he might get her into bed later.

He started to fry the steaks. "I'm impressed," she said. "Not many guys can cook."

"My father died when I was six, and my mother when I was eleven," Lev said. "I was raised by my brother, Grigori. We learned to do everything for ourselves. Not that we ever had steak, in Russia."

She asked him about Grigori, and he told her his life story over dinner. Most girls were touched by the tale of two motherless boys struggling to get by, working in a huge locomotive factory and renting space in a bed. He guiltily omitted the part of the story where he abandoned his pregnant girlfriend.

They had their second drink in the bed-sitting-room. By the time they started on the third it was getting dark outside and she was sitting on his lap. Between sips, Lev kissed her. When she opened her mouth to his tongue, he put his hand on her breast.

At that moment the door burst open.

Marga screamed.

Three men walked in. Marga jumped off Lev's lap, still screaming. One of the men hit her backhanded across the mouth and said: "Shut the fuck up, bitch." She ran for the door, both hands to her bleeding lips. They let her go.

Lev sprang to his feet and lashed out at the man who had hit Marga. He got in one good punch, striking the man over the eye. Then the other two grabbed his arms. They were strong men, and he could not break free. While they held him the first man, who seemed to be their leader, punched him in the mouth, then in the stomach, several times. He spat blood and vomited his steak.

When he was weakened and in agony, they frog-marched him down the stairs and out of the building. A blue Hudson stood at the curb with its engine running. They threw him onto the floor in the back. Two of them sat with their feet on him and the other got in the front and drove.

He was in too much pain to think about where they were going. He assumed these men worked for Vyalov, but how had they found him? And what were they going to do with him? He tried not to give in to fear.

After a few minutes the car stopped and he was hauled out. They were outside a warehouse. The street was deserted and dark. He could smell the lake, so he knew they were near the waterfront. It was a good place to murder someone, he thought with grim fatalism. There would be no witnesses, and the body could go into Lake Erie, tied inside a sack, with a few bricks to make sure it sank to the bottom.

They dragged him into the building. He tried to pull himself together. This was the worst scrape he had ever been in. He was not sure he could talk his way out of it. Why do I do these things? he asked himself.

The warehouse was full of new tires piled fifteen or twenty high. They took him through the stacks to the back and stopped outside a door that was guarded by yet another heavyset man who held up an arm to stop them.

No words were spoken.

After a minute, Lev said: "Seems we have a few minutes to wait. Anybody got a pack of cards?"

No one even smiled.

Eventually the door opened and Nick Forman came out. His upper lip was swollen and one eye was closed. When he saw Lev he said: "I had to do it. They would have killed me."

So, Lev thought, they found me through Nick.

A thin man in spectacles came to the door of the office. Surely this could not be Vyalov, Lev thought; he was too weedy. "Bring him in, Theo," he said.

"Sure thing, Mr. Niall," said the leader of the thugs.

The office reminded Lev of the peasant hut in which he had been born. It was too warm and the air was full of smoke. In a corner was a little table with icons of saints.

Behind a steel desk sat a middle-aged man with unusually broad shoulders. He wore an expensive-looking lounge suit with a collar and tie, and there were two rings on the hand that held his cigarette. He said: "What is that fucking smell?"

"I'm sorry, Mister V—it's puke," said Theo. "He acted up, and we had to calm him down a little. Then he lunged up his lunch."

"Let him go."

They released Lev's arms, but stayed near.

Mister V looked at him. "I got your message," he said. "Telling me I should be more polite."

Lev summoned his courage. He was not going to die sniveling. He said: "Are you Josef Vyalov?"

"By Christ, you've got some nerve," the man said. "Asking me who I am."

"I been looking for you."

"*You* have been looking for *me*?"

"The Vyalov family sold me a ticket from St. Petersburg to New York, then dumped me in Cardiff," Lev said.

"So?"

"I want my money back."

Vyalov stared at him for a long moment; then he laughed. "I can't help it," he said. "I like you."

Lev held his breath. Did this mean Vyalov was not going to kill him?

"Do you have a job?" Vyalov said.

"I work for you."

"Where?"

"At the Hotel St. Petersburg, in the stables."

Vyalov nodded. "I think we can offer you something better than that," he said.

{ II }

In June 1915 America came one step closer to war.

Gus Dewar was appalled. He did not think the United States should join in the European war. The American people felt the same, and so did President Woodrow Wilson. But somehow the danger loomed closer.

The crisis came about in May when a German submarine torpedoed the *Lusitania,* a British ship carrying 173 tons of rifles, ammunition, and shrapnel shells. It also carried two thousand passengers, including 159 U.S. citizens.

Americans were as shocked as if there had been an assassination. The newspapers went into convulsions of indignation. "People are asking you to do the impossible!" Gus said indignantly to the president, standing in the Oval Office. "They want you to get tough with the Germans, but not to risk going to war."

Wilson nodded agreement. Looking up from his typewriter, he said: "There's no rule that says public opinion has to be consistent."

Gus found his boss's calm admirable, but a bit frustrating. "How the heck do you deal with that?"

Wilson smiled, showing his bad teeth. "Gus, did someone tell you politics was easy?"

In the end Wilson sent a stern note to the German government, demanding that they stop attacking shipping. He and his advisers, including Gus, hoped the Germans would agree to some compromise. But if they decided to be defiant, Gus did not see how Wilson could avoid escalation. It was a dangerous game to play, and Gus found he was not able to remain as coolly detached about the risk as Wilson appeared to be.

While the diplomatic telegrams crossed the Atlantic, Wilson went to his summer place in New Hampshire and Gus went to Buffalo, where he stayed at his parents' mansion on Delaware Avenue. His father had a house in Washington, but Gus lived in his own apartment there, and when he came home to Buffalo he relished the comforts of a house run by his mother: the silver bowl of cut roses on his nightstand; the hot rolls at breakfast; the crisp white linen tablecloth fresh at every meal; the way a suit would appear sponged and pressed in his wardrobe without his having noticed that it had been taken away.

The house was furnished in a consciously plain manner, his mother's reaction against the ornate fashions of her parents' generation. Much of the furniture was Biedermeier, a utilitarian German style that was enjoying a revival. The dining room had one good painting on each of the four walls, and a single three-branched candlestick on the table. At lunch on the first day, his mother said: "I suppose you're planning to go to the slums and watch prizefights?"

"There's nothing wrong with boxing," Gus said. It was his great enthusiasm. He had even tried it himself, as a foolhardy eighteen-year-old: his long arms had given him a couple of victories, but he lacked the killer instinct.

"So canaille," she said disdainfully. This was a snobby expression she had picked up in Europe that meant low-class.

"I'd like to take my mind off international politics, if I can."

"There's a lecture on Titian, with magic-lantern slides, at the Albright this afternoon," she said. The Albright Art Gallery, a white classical building set in Delaware Park, was one of Buffalo's most important cultural institutions.

Gus had grown up surrounded by Renaissance paintings, and he particularly liked Titian's portraits, but he was not very interested in going to a lecture. However, it was just the kind of event to be patronized by the city's wealthy young men and women, so there was a good chance he would be able to renew old friendships.

The Albright was a short drive up Delaware Avenue. He entered the pillared atrium and took a seat. As he had expected, there were several people he knew in the audience. He found himself sitting next to a strikingly pretty girl who seemed familiar.

He smiled vaguely at her, and she said brightly: "You've forgotten who I am, haven't you, Mr. Dewar?"

He felt foolish. "Ah . . . I've been out of town for a while."

"I'm Olga Vyalov." She held out a white-gloved hand.

"Of course," he said. Her father was a Russian immigrant whose first job had been throwing drunks out of a bar on Canal Street. Now he owned Canal Street. He was a city councilor and a pillar of the Russian Orthodox Church. Gus had met Olga several times, though he did not remember her looking quite so enchanting: perhaps she had suddenly grown up, or something. She was about twenty, he guessed, with pale skin and blue eyes, and she wore a pink jacket with a turned-up collar and a cloche hat with pink silk flowers.

"I hear you're working for the president," she said. "What do you think of Mr. Wilson?"

"I admire him enormously," Gus replied. "He's a practical politician who hasn't abandoned his ideals."

"How exciting to be at the center of power."

"It is exciting, but strangely enough it doesn't feel like the center of power. In a democracy the president is subject to the voters."

"But surely he doesn't just do what the public wants."

"Not exactly, no. President Wilson says a leader must treat public opinion the way a sailor deals with the wind, using it to blow the ship in one direction or another, but never trying to go directly against it."

She sighed. "I would have loved to study these things, but my father wouldn't let me go to college."

Gus grinned. "I suppose he thinks you would learn to smoke cigarettes and drink gin."

"And worse, I've no doubt," she said. It was a risqué remark for an unmarried woman, and the surprise must have shown on his face, for she said: "I'm sorry. I've shocked you."

"Not at all." In fact he was feeling captivated. To keep her talking he said: "What would you study if you could go to college?"

"History, I think."

"I love history. Any particular period?"

"I'd like to understand my own past. Why did my father have to leave Russia? Why is America so much better? There must be reasons for these things."

"Exactly!" Gus was thrilled that such a pretty girl should also share his intellectual curiosity. He saw a sudden vision of them as a married couple, in her dressing room after a party, talking about world affairs while they got ready for bed, himself in pajamas, sitting and watching while she unhurriedly took off her jewelry and slipped out of her clothes . . . Then he caught her eye, and got the feeling that she had guessed what he was thinking, and he felt embarrassed. He searched for something to say, but found himself tongue-tied.

Then the lecturer arrived, and the audience fell silent.

He enjoyed the talk more than he had expected. The speaker had made Autochrome color transparencies of some of Titian's canvases, and his magic lantern projected them onto a big white screen.

When it was over he wanted to talk some more to Olga, but he was prevented. Chuck Dixon, a man he knew from school, came up to them. Chuck had an easy charm that Gus envied. They were the same age, twenty-five, but Chuck made Gus feel like an awkward schoolboy. "Olga, you have to meet my cousin," he said jovially. "He's been staring at you across the room." He smiled amiably at Gus. "Sorry to deprive you of such bewitching company, Dewar, but you can't have her all afternoon, you know." He put a possessive arm around Olga's waist and led her away.

Gus felt bereft. He had been getting on so well with her, he felt. For him those first conversations with a girl were usually the hardest, but with Olga small talk had seemed easy. And now Chuck Dixon, who had always been bottom of the class at school, had just walked away with her as easily as he would have taken a drink from a waiter's tray.

While Gus was looking around for someone else he knew, he was approached by a girl with one eye.

The first time he met Rosa Hellman—at a fund-raising

dinner for the Buffalo Symphony Orchestra, in which her brother played—he thought she was winking at him. In fact one eye was permanently closed. Her face was otherwise pretty, which made her disfigurement more striking. Furthermore, she always dressed stylishly, as if in defiance. Today she wore a straw boater set at a jaunty angle, and managed to look cute.

Last time he saw her she had been the editor of a small-circulation radical newspaper called the *Buffalo Anarchist*, and Gus said: "Are anarchists interested in art?"

"I work for the *Buffalo Advertiser* now," she said.

Gus was surprised. "Does the editor know about your political views?"

"My views aren't quite as extreme as they used to be, but he knows my history."

"I guess he figured that if you can make a success of an anarchist newspaper, you must be good."

"He says he gave me the job because I have more balls than any two of his male reporters."

Gus knew she liked to shock, but even so his mouth dropped open.

Rosa laughed. "But he still sends me to cover art exhibitions and fashion shows." She changed the subject. "What's it like working in the White House?"

Gus was conscious that anything he said might appear in her paper. "Tremendously exciting," he said. "I think Wilson is a great president, maybe the greatest ever."

"How can you say that? He's dangerously close to getting us involved in a European war."

Rosa's attitude was common among ethnic Germans, who naturally saw the German side of the story, and among left-wingers, who wanted to see the tsar defeated. However, plenty of people who were neither German nor left-wing took the same view. Gus replied carefully: "When German submarines are killing American citizens, the president can't—" He was about to say *turn a blind eye*. He hesitated, flushed, and said: "Can't ignore it."

She did not seem to notice his embarrassment. "But the British are blockading German ports—in violation of international law—and German women and children are starving as a result. Meanwhile, the war in France is at a stalemate: neither side has changed its position by more than a few yards for the last six months. The Germans *have* to sink British ships. Otherwise they lose the war."

She had an impressive grasp of the complexities: that was why Gus always enjoyed talking to her. "I studied international law," he said. "Strictly speaking, the British aren't acting illegally. Naval blockades were banned by the Declaration of London of 1909, but that was never ratified."

She was not so easily sidetracked. "Never mind the legalities. The Germans warned Americans not to travel on British liners. They put an advertisement in the papers, for goodness' sake! What else can they do? Imagine that we were at war with Mexico, and the *Lusitania* had been a Mexican ship carrying armaments intended to kill American soldiers. Would we have let it pass?"

It was a good question, and Gus had no reasonable answer. He said: "Well, Secretary of State Bryan agreed with you." William Jennings Bryan had resigned over Wilson's note to the Germans. "He thought all we needed to do was warn Americans not to travel on the ships of combatant nations."

She was not willing to let him off the hook. "Bryan sees that Wilson has taken a grave risk," she said. "If the Germans don't back down now, we can hardly avoid war with them."

Gus was not going to admit to a journalist that he shared these misgivings. Wilson had demanded that the German government disavow the attacks on merchant shipping, make reparations, and prevent any recurrence—in other words, allow the British the freedom of the seas while accepting that Germany's own ships were trapped in dock by the blockade. It was hard to see any government agreeing to such demands. "But public opinion approves what the president has done."

"Public opinion can be wrong."

"But the president can't ignore it. Look, Wilson is walking a tightrope. He wants to keep us out of the war, but he doesn't want America to appear weak in international diplomacy. I think he's struck the right balance for the present."

"But in the future?"

That was the worrying question. "No one can predict the future," Gus said. "Not even Woodrow Wilson."

She laughed. "A politician's answer. You'll go far in Washington." Someone spoke to her, and she turned away.

Gus moved off, feeling a bit as if he had been in a boxing match that had ended in a draw.

Some of the audience were invited to take tea with the lecturer. Gus was among the privileged because his mother was a patron of the museum. He left Rosa and headed for a private room. When he entered, he was delighted to see Olga there. No doubt her father also gave money.

He got a cup of tea and then approached her. "If you're ever in Washington, I'd love to show you around the White House," he said.

"Oh! Could you introduce me to the president?"

He wanted to say, *Yes, anything!* But he hesitated to promise what he might not be able to deliver. "Probably," he said. "It would depend on how busy he happened to be. When he gets behind that typewriter and starts to write speeches or press releases, no one is allowed to disturb him."

"I was so sad when his wife passed away," Olga said. Ellen Wilson had died almost a year ago, shortly after the outbreak of war in Europe.

Gus nodded. "He was devastated."

"But I hear he's romancing a wealthy widow already."

Gus was discomfited. It was an open secret in Washington that Wilson had fallen passionately, boyishly in love, only eight months after the death of his wife, with the voluptuous Mrs. Edith Galt. The president was fifty-eight, his paramour forty-one. Right now they were together in New Hampshire. Gus was among a very small group who also knew that Wilson had proposed marriage a month ago, but Mrs. Galt had not yet given him an answer. He said to Olga: "Who told you that?"

"Is it true?"

He was desperate to impress her with his inside knowledge, but he managed to resist the temptation. "I can't talk about that sort of thing," he said reluctantly.

"Oh, how disappointing. I was hoping you'd give me the inside gossip."

"I'm sorry to be such a letdown."

"Don't be silly." She touched his arm, giving him a thrill like an electric shock. "I'm having a tennis party tomorrow afternoon," she said. "Do you play?"

Gus had long arms and legs, and was a fairly good player. "I do," he said. "I love the game."

"Will you come?"

"I'd be delighted," he said.

{ III }

Lev learned to drive in a day. The other main skill of a chauffeur, changing punctured tires, took him a couple of hours to master. By the end of a week he could also fill the tank, change the oil, and adjust the brakes. If the car would not go he knew how to check for a flat battery or a blocked fuel line.

Horses were the transport of the past, Josef Vyalov told him. Stablehands were low-paid: there were plenty of them. Chauffeurs were scarce, and earned high wages.

In addition, Vyalov liked to have a driver who was tough enough to double as a bodyguard.

Vyalov's car was a brand-new Packard Twin Six, a seven-passenger limousine. Other chauffeurs were impressed. The model had been launched only a few weeks ago, and its twelve-cylinder engine was the envy even of drivers of the Cadillac V8.

Lev was not so taken with Vyalov's ultramodern mansion. To him it looked like the world's largest cowshed. It was long and low, with broad overhanging eaves. The head gardener told him it was a "prairie house" in the latest fashion.

"If I had a house this big, I'd want it to *look* like a palace," Lev said.

He thought of writing to Grigori and telling him all about Buffalo and the job and the car; but he hesitated. He would want to say that he had put aside some money for Grigori's ticket, but in fact he had nothing saved. When he had a little stash he would write, he vowed. Meanwhile Grigori could not write because he did not know Lev's address.

There were three people in the Vyalov family: Josef himself; his wife, Lena, who rarely spoke; and Olga, a pretty daughter of about Lev's age with a bold look in her eye. Josef was attentive and courteous with his wife, even though he spent most evenings out with his cronies. To his daughter he was affectionate but strict. He often drove home at midday to have lunch with Lena and Olga. After lunch he and Lena would take a nap.

While Lev was waiting to drive Josef back downtown, he sometimes talked to Olga.

She liked to smoke cigarettes, something that was forbidden by her father, who was fiercely determined that she should be a respectable young lady and marry into the Buffalo social elite. There were a few places on the property where Josef never went, and the garage was one of them, so Olga came there to smoke. She would sit in the backseat of the Packard, her silk dress on the new leather, and Lev would lean on the door, with his foot up on the runningboard, and chat with her.

He was aware that he looked handsome in the chauffeur's uniform, and he wore the cap tilted jauntily back. He soon discovered that the way to please Olga was to compliment her on being high-class. She loved to be told that she walked like a princess, talked like a president's wife, and dressed like a Parisian socialite. She was a snob, and so was her father. Most of the time Josef was a bully and a thug, but Lev noticed how he became well-mannered, almost deferential, when talking to high-status men such as bank presidents and congressmen.

Lev had a quick intuition, and soon had Olga figured out. She was an overprotected rich girl who had no outlet for her natural romantic and sexual impulses. Unlike the girls Lev had known in the slums of St. Petersburg, Olga could not slip out to meet a boy at twilight and let him feel her up in the darkness of a shop doorway. She was twenty years old and a virgin. It was even possible she had never been kissed.

Lev watched the tennis party from a distance, drinking in the sight of Olga's strong, slim body, and the way her breasts moved under the light cotton of her dress as she flew across the court. She was playing against a very tall man in white flannel trousers. Lev felt a jolt of recognition. Staring at the man, he eventually recalled where he had seen him before. It was at the Putilov works. Lev had tricked him out of a dollar and Grigori had asked him if Josef Vyalov really was a big man in Buffalo. What was his name? It was the same as a brand of whisky. Dewar, that was it. Gus Dewar.

A group of half a dozen young people were watching the game, the girls in bright summer dresses, the men wearing straw boaters. Mrs. Vyalov looked out from under her parasol with a pleased smile. A uniformed maid was serving lemonade.

Gus Dewar defeated Olga and they left the court. Their places were immediately taken by another couple. Olga daringly accepted a cigarette from her opponent. Lev watched him light it for her. Lev ached to be one of them, playing tennis in beautiful clothes and drinking lemonade.

A wild stroke sent the ball his way. He picked it up and, instead of throwing it back, carried it to the court and handed it to one of the players. He looked at Olga. She was deep in conversation with Dewar, charming him in a flirtatious way, just as she did with Lev in the garage. He felt a stab of jealousy and wanted to punch the tall guy in the mouth. He caught Olga's eye and gave her his most charming smile, but she looked away without acknowledging him. The other young people totally ignored him.

It was perfectly normal, he told himself: a girl could be friendly with the chauffeur while smoking in the garage, then treat him like a piece of furniture when she was with her friends. All the same, his pride was wounded.

He turned away—and saw her father walking down the gravel path toward the tennis court. Vyalov was dressed for business in a lounge suit with a waistcoat. He had come to greet his daughter's guests before returning downtown, Lev guessed.

Any second now he would see Olga smoking, and then there would be hell to pay.

Lev was inspired. In two strides he crossed to where Olga was sitting. With a swift motion he snatched the lighted cigarette from between her fingers.

"Hey!" she protested.

Gus Dewar frowned and said: "What the devil are you up to?"

Lev turned away, putting the cigarette between his lips. A moment later Vyalov spotted him. "What are you doing here?" he said crossly. "Get my car out."

"Yes, sir," said Lev.

"And put out that damned cigarette when you're talking to me."

Lev pinched out the coal and put the butt in his pocket. "Sorry, Mr. Vyalov, sir. I forgot myself."

"Don't let it happen again."

"Yes, sir."

"Now clear off."

Lev hurried away, then looked back over his shoulder. The young men had jumped to their feet, and Vyalov was jovially shaking hands all round. Olga, looking guilty, was introducing her friends. She had almost been caught. She met Lev's eye and shot him a grateful look.

Lev winked at her and walked on.

{ IV }

Ursula Dewar's drawing room contained a few ornaments, all precious in different ways: a marble head by Elie Nadelman, a first edition of the Geneva Bible, a single rose in a cut-glass vase, and a framed photograph of her grandfather, who had opened one of the first department stores in America. When Gus came into the room at six o'clock she was sitting in a silk evening dress, reading a new novel called *The Good Soldier*.

"How's the book?" he asked her.

"It is extraordinarily good, although I hear, paradoxically, that the author is a frightful cad."

He mixed an old-fashioned for her, the way she liked it, with bitters but no sugar. He felt nervous. At my age I shouldn't be afraid of my mother, he thought. But she could be scathing. He handed her the drink.

"Thank you," she said. "Are you enjoying your summer break?"

"Very much."

"I was afraid that by now you'd be itching to get back to the excitement of Washington and the White House."

Gus had expected that, too; but the holiday had brought unexpected pleasures. "I'll return as soon as the president does, but meanwhile I'm having a great time."

"Is Woodrow going to declare war on Germany, do you think?"

"I hope not. The Germans are willing to back down, but they want Americans to stop selling arms to the Allies."

"And will we stop?" Ursula was of German ancestry, as were some half the population of Buffalo, but when she said "we," she meant America.

"Absolutely not. Our factories are making too much money from British orders."

"Is it a deadlock, then?"

"Not yet. We're still dancing around one another. Meanwhile, as if to remind us of the pressures on neutral countries, Italy has joined the Allies."

"Will that make any difference?"

"Not enough." Gus took a deep breath. "I played tennis at the Vyalovs' place this afternoon," he said. His voice did not sound as casual as he had hoped.

"Did you win, dear?"

"Yes. They have a prairie house. It's very striking."

"So nouveau riche."

"I suppose we were nouveau riche once, weren't we? Perhaps when your grandfather opened his store?"

"I find it tiresome when you talk like a socialist, Angus, even though I know you don't mean it." She sipped her drink. "Mm, this is perfect."

He took a deep breath. "Mother, would you do something for me?"

"Of course, dear, if I can."

"You won't like it."

"What is it?"

"I want you to invite Mrs. Vyalov to tea."

His mother put her drink down slowly and carefully. "I see," she said.

"Aren't you going to ask why?"

"I know why," she said. "There is only one possible reason. I have met the ravishingly pretty daughter."

"You're not to be cross. Vyalov is a leading man in this city, and very wealthy. And Olga is an angel."

"Or, if not an angel, at least a Christian."

"The Vyalovs are Russian Orthodox," Gus said. Might as well get all the bad news on the table, he thought. "They go to the Church of Saints Peter and Paul on Ideal Street." The Dewars were Episcopalians.

"But not Jewish, thank God." Mother had once feared that Gus might marry Rachel Abramov, whom he had liked enormously but never loved. "And I suppose we can be grateful that Olga is not a fortune hunter."

"Indeed not. I should think Vyalov must be richer than Father."

"I'm sure I have no idea." Women such as Ursula were not supposed to know about money. Gus suspected they knew the net worth of their own and each others' husbands to the nearest dime, but they had to pretend ignorance.

She was not as cross as he had feared. "So you'll do it?" he said with trepidation.

"Of course. I'll send Mrs. Vyalov a note."

Gus felt elated, but a new fear struck him. "Mind you, you're not to invite your snobbish friends to make Mrs. Vyalov feel inferior."

"I have no snobbish friends."

That remark was too ludicrous even to be acknowledged. "Ask Mrs. Fischer—she's amiable. And Aunt Gertrude."

"Very well."

"Thank you, Mother." Gus felt great relief, as if he had survived an ordeal. "I know Olga is not the bride you may have dreamed of for me, but I feel sure you're going to become very fond of her in no time at all."

"My dear son, you're almost twenty-six years old. Five years ago I might have tried to talk you out of marriage to the daughter of a shady businessman. But lately I have been wondering if I'm ever to have grandchildren. If at this point you announced that you wanted to marry a divorced Polish waitress, I fear my first concern might be whether she were young enough to bear children."

"Don't jump the gun—Olga hasn't agreed to marry me. I haven't even asked her."

"How could she resist you?" She stood up and kissed him. "Now make me another drink."

{ V }

"You saved my life!" Olga said to Lev. "Father would have killed me."

Lev grinned. "I saw him coming. I had to act fast."

"I'm so grateful," Olga said, and she kissed his lips.

He was startled. She pulled away before he could take advantage, but he felt himself to be on a completely different footing with her immediately. He looked nervously around the garage, but they were alone.

She took out a pack of cigarettes and put one in her mouth. He lit it, copying what Gus Dewar had done yesterday. It was an intimate gesture, obliging the woman to dip her head and allowing the man to stare at her lips. It felt romantic.

She leaned back in the seat of the Packard and blew out smoke. Lev got into the car and sat beside her. She made no objection. He lit a cigarette for himself. They sat for a while in the half dark, their smoke mingling with the smells of oil and leather and a flowery perfume Olga was wearing.

To break the silence, Lev said: "I hope you enjoyed your tennis party."

She sighed. "All the boys in this town are frightened of my father," she said. "They think he'll shoot them if they kiss me."

"Will he shoot them?"

She laughed. "Probably."

"I'm not afraid of him." This was near to the truth. Lev was not really unafraid; he just ignored his fears, always hoping he could talk his way out of trouble.

But she looked skeptical. "Really?"

"That's why he hired me." This, too, was only one step removed from reality. "Ask him."

"I might do that."

"Gus Dewar really likes you."

"My father would love it if I married him."

"Why?"

"He's rich, his family are old Buffalo aristocracy, and his father is a senator."

"Do you always do what your pa wants?"

She drew thoughtfully on her cigarette. "Yes," she said, and blew out smoke.

Lev said: "I love to watch your lips when you smoke."

She made no reply, but gave him a speculative look.

That was invitation enough for Lev, and he kissed her.

She gave a little moan at the back of her throat, and

pushed feebly at his chest with her hand, but neither protest was serious. He tossed his cigarette out of the car and put his hand on her breast. She grasped his wrist, as if to shove his hand away, then instead pressed it harder against her soft flesh.

Lev touched her closed lips with his tongue. She pulled away and gave him a startled look. He realized she did not know about kissing this way. She really was inexperienced. "It's okay," he said. "Trust me."

She threw away her cigarette, pulled him nearer, closed her eyes, and kissed him with her mouth open.

After that it happened very fast. There was a desperate urgency about her desire. Lev had been with several women, and he believed it was wise to let them set the pace. A hesitant woman could not be hurried, and an impatient one should not be held back. When he found his way through Olga's underwear and stroked the soft mound of her sex, she became so aroused that she sobbed with passion. If it were true that she had reached the age of twenty without being kissed by any of the timid boys of Buffalo, she must have a lot of stored-up frustration, he guessed. She lifted her hips eagerly for him to pull down her drawers. When he kissed her between her legs, she cried out with shock and excitement. She had to be a virgin, but he was too heated for such a thought to give him pause.

She lay back with one foot on the seat and the other on the floor, her skirt around her waist, her thighs spread ready for him. Her mouth was open and she was breathing hard. She watched him with wide eyes as he unbuttoned. He entered her cautiously, knowing how easy it was to hurt a girl there, but she grasped his hips and pulled him inside her impatiently, as if she feared she might be cheated at the last minute of what she wanted. He felt the membrane of her virginity resist him briefly, then break easily, with only a little gasp from her, as of a tinge of pain that went as quickly as it had come. She moved against him in a rhythm of her own, and again he let her take the lead, sensing that she was answering a call that would not be denied.

This was more thrilling, for him, than the act of love had ever been before. Some girls were knowing; some were innocent, but keen to please; some were careful to satisfy the man before seeking their own fulfillment. But Lev had never come across such raw need as Olga's, and it inflamed him beyond measure.

He held himself back. Olga cried out loud, and he put a hand over her mouth to muffle the sound. She bucked like a pony, then buried her face in his shoulder. With a stifled scream she reached her climax, and a moment later he did the same.

He rolled off her and sat on the floor. She lay still, panting. Neither of them spoke for a minute. Eventually she sat upright. "Oh, God," she said. "I didn't know it would be like that."

"Usually it's not," he replied.

There was a long, reflective pause; then she said in a quieter voice: "What have I done?"

He made no answer.

She picked up her drawers from the floor of the car and pulled them on. She sat still a moment longer, catching her breath; then she got out of the car.

Lev stared at her, waiting for her to say something, but she did not. She walked to the rear door of the garage, opened it, and went out.

But she came back the next day.

{ VI }

Edith Galt accepted President Wilson's proposal of marriage on June 29. In July the president returned to the White House temporarily. "I have to go back to Washington for a few days," Gus said to Olga as they strolled through the Buffalo Zoo.

"How many days?"

"As long as the president needs me."

"How thrilling!"

Gus nodded. "It's the best job in the world. But it does mean that I'm not my own master. If the crisis with Germany escalates, it could be a long time before I come back to Buffalo."

"We'll miss you."

"And I'll miss you. We've been such pals since I came back." They had gone boating on the lake in Delaware Park and bathing at Crystal Beach; they had taken steamers up the river to Niagara and across the lake to the Canadian side; and they had played tennis every other day—always with a group of young friends, and chaperoned by at least one watchful mother. Today Mrs. Vyalov was with them, walking a few paces behind and talking to Chuck Dixon. Gus went on: "I wonder if you have any idea how much I'll miss you."

Olga smiled, but made no reply.

Gus said: "This has been the happiest summer of my life."

"And mine!" she said, twirling her red-and-white polka-dot parasol.

That delighted Gus, although he was not sure it was his company that had made her happy. He still could not make her out. She always seemed pleased to see him, and was glad to talk to him hour after hour. But he had seen no emotion, no sign that her feelings for him might be passionate rather than merely friendly. Of course, no respectable girl ought to show such signs, at least until she was engaged; but all the same Gus felt at sea. Perhaps that was part of her appeal.

He recalled vividly that Caroline Wigmore had communicated her needs to him with unmistakable clarity. He found himself thinking a lot about Caroline, who was the only other woman he had ever loved. If she could say what she wanted, why not Olga? But Caroline had been a married woman, whereas Olga was a virgin who had had a sheltered upbringing.

Gus stopped in front of the bear pit, and they looked through the steel bars at a small brown bear sitting on its haunches staring back at them. "I wonder if all our days could be this happy," Gus said.

"Why not?" she said.

Was that encouragement? He looked at her. She did not return his gaze, but watched the bear. He studied her blue eyes, the soft curve of her pink cheek, the delicate skin of her neck. "I wish I were Titian," he said. "I'd paint you."

Her mother and Chuck went by and strolled on, leaving Gus and Olga behind. They were as alone as they would ever be.

She turned her gaze on him at last, and he thought he

saw something like fondness in her eyes. That gave him courage. He thought: If a president who has been a widower less than a year can do it, surely I can?

He said: "I love you, Olga."

She said nothing, but continued to look at him.

He swallowed. Once again he could not make her out. He said: "Is there any chance . . . May I hope that one day you might love me, too?" He stared at her, holding his breath. At this moment she held his life in her hands.

There was a long pause. Was she thinking? Weighing him in the balance? Or just hesitating before a life-changing decision?

At last she smiled and said: "Oh, yes."

He could hardly believe it. "Really?"

She laughed happily. "Really."

He took her hand. "Do you love me?"

She nodded.

"You have to say it."

"Yes, Gus, I love you."

He kissed her hand. "I'll speak to your father before I go to Washington."

She smiled. "I think I know what he will say."

"After that we can tell everyone."

"Yes."

"Thank you," he said fervently. "You have made me very happy."

{ VII }

Gus called at Josef Vyalov's office in the morning and formally asked permission to propose to his daughter. Vyalov pronounced himself delighted. Although that was the answer Gus expected, he found himself weak with relief afterward.

Gus was on his way to the station to catch a train to Washington, so they agreed to celebrate as soon as he could get back. Meanwhile, Gus was happy to leave it to Olga's mother and his to plan the wedding.

Entering Central Station on Exchange Street with a spring in his step, he ran into Rosa Hellman coming out, wearing a red hat, carrying a small overnight bag. "Hello," he said. "May I help you with your luggage?"

"No, thanks. It's light," she said. "I was only away one night. I went for an interview with one of the wire services."

He raised his eyebrows. "For a job as a reporter?"

"Yes—and I got it."

"Congratulations! Forgive me if I sound surprised—I didn't think they employed women writers."

"It's unusual, but not unknown. *The New York Times* hired its first female reporter in 1869. Her name was Maria Morgan."

"What will you be doing?"

"I'll be the assistant to their Washington correspondent. The truth is, the president's love life has made them think they need a woman there. Men are liable to miss romantic stories."

Gus wondered if she had mentioned that she was friendly with one of Wilson's closest aides. He guessed she had: reporters were never coy. No doubt it had helped her get the job. "I'm on my way back," he said. "I guess we'll see each other there."

"I hope so."

"I have some good news, too," he said happily. "I proposed to Olga Vyalov—and she accepted me. We're getting married."

She gave him a long look; then she said: "You fool."

He could not have been more shocked if she had slapped him. He stared at her openmouthed.

"You goddamn fool," she said, and she walked away.

{ VIII }

Two more Americans died on August 19 when the Germans torpedoed another large British liner, the *Arabic*.

Gus was sorry for the victims but even more aghast at America's being pulled inexorably into the European conflict. He felt that the president was on the brink. Gus wanted to get married in a world of peace and happiness; he dreaded a future blighted by the mayhem and cruelty and destruction of war.

On Wilson's instructions, Gus told a few reporters, off the record, that the president was on the point of breaking off diplomatic relations with Germany. Meanwhile the new secretary of state, Robert Lansing, tried to make some kind of deal with the German ambassador, Count Johann von Bernstorff.

It could go horribly wrong, Gus thought. The Germans could call Wilson's bluff and defy him. Then what would he do? If he did nothing he would look stupid. He told Gus that breaking off diplomatic relations would not *necessarily* lead to war. Gus was left with the frightening feeling that the crisis was out of control.

But the kaiser did not want war with America and, to Gus's immense relief, Wilson's gamble paid off. At the end of August the Germans promised not to attack passenger ships without warning. It was not a fully satisfactory reassurance, but it ended the standoff.

The American newspapers, missing all the nuances, were ecstatic. On September 2 Gus triumphantly read aloud to Wilson a paragraph from a laudatory article in that day's New York *Evening Post:* "'Without mobilizing a regiment or assembling a fleet, by sheer, dogged, unwavering persistence in advocating the right, he has compelled the surrender of the proudest, the most arrogant, the best armed of nations.'"

"They haven't surrendered yet," said the president.

{ IX }

One evening in late September they took Lev to the warehouse, stripped him naked, and tied his hands behind his back. Then Vyalov came out of his office. "You dog," he said. "You mad dog."

"What have I done?" Lev pleaded.

"You know what you've done, you filthy cur," said Vyalov.

Lev was terrified. He could not talk his way out of this if Vyalov would not listen.

Vyalov took off his jacket and rolled up his shirtsleeves. "Bring it to me," he said.

Norman Niall, his weedy accountant, went into the office and returned with a knout.

Lev stared at it. It was the standard Russian pattern, traditionally used to punish criminals. It had a long wooden handle and three hardened leather thongs each terminating in a lead ball. Lev had never been flogged, but he had seen it done. In the countryside it was a common punishment for petty theft or adultery. In St. Petersburg the knout was often used on political offenders. Twenty lashes could cripple a man; a hundred would kill him.

Vyalov, still wearing his waistcoat with the gold watch chain, hefted the knout. Niall giggled. Ilya and Theo looked on with interest.

Lev cowered away, turning his back, pressing himself up against a stack of tires. The whip came down with a cruel swish, biting into his neck and shoulders, and he screamed in pain.

Vyalov brought the whip down again. This time it hurt more.

Lev could not believe what a fool he had been. He had fucked the virgin daughter of a powerful and violent man. What had he been thinking of? Why could he never resist temptation?

Vyalov lashed again. This time Lev flung himself away from the knout, trying to dodge the blow. Only the very ends of the thongs connected, but they still dug agonizingly into his flesh, and he cried out in pain again. He tried to get away, but Vyalov's men pushed him back, laughing.

Vyalov raised the whip again, started to bring it down, stopped in midswipe as Lev dodged, then struck. Lev's legs were slashed, and he saw blood pouring from the cuts. When Vyalov lashed again, Lev desperately flung himself away, then stumbled and fell to the concrete floor. As he lay on his back, losing strength rapidly, Vyalov whipped his front, striking his belly and thighs. Lev rolled over, too agonized and terror-struck to get to his feet, but the knout kept coming down. He summoned the energy to crawl a short way on his knees, like a baby, but he slipped in his own blood, and the whip came down again. He stopped screaming: he had no breath. Vyalov was going to flog him to death, he decided. He longed for oblivion to come.

But Vyalov denied him that relief. He dropped the

knout, panting with exertion. "I ought to kill you," he said when he had caught his breath. "But I can't."

Lev was baffled. He lay in a pool of blood, staring at his torturer.

"She's pregnant," Vyalov said.

In a haze of fear and pain, Lev tried to think. They had used condoms. You could buy them in any big American city. He had always put one on—except for that first time, of course, when he had not been expecting anything . . . and the time she had been showing him around the empty house and they had done it on the big bed in the guest room . . . and once in the garden after dark . . .

There had been several times, he realized.

"She was going to marry Senator Dewar's boy," Vyalov said, and Lev could hear bitterness as well as rage in his harsh voice. "My grandson might have been a president."

It was hard for Lev to think straight, but he realized that the wedding would have to be called off. Gus Dewar would not marry a girl who was pregnant with someone else's baby, no matter how much he loved her. Unless . . .

Lev managed to croak a few words. "She doesn't have to have the baby. . . . There are doctors right here in town. . . ."

Vyalov snatched up the knout, and Lev cowered away. Vyalov screamed: "Never even think about that! It's against the will of God!"

Lev was amazed. Every Sunday he drove the Vyalov family to church, but he had assumed religion was a sham for Josef. The man lived by dishonesty and violence. Yet he could not bear to hear mention of abortion! Lev wanted to ask whether his church did not prohibit bribery and beating people up.

Vyalov said: "Can you imagine the humiliation you're causing me? Every newspaper in town reported the engagement." His face reddened and his voice rose to a roar. "What am I going to say to Senator Dewar? I've booked the church! I've hired caterers! The invitations are at the printers! I can just see Mrs. Dewar, that proud old cunt, laughing at me behind her wrinkled hand. And all because of a fucking chauffeur!"

He raised the knout again, then threw it away with a violent gesture. "I can't kill you." He turned to Theo. "Take this piece of shit to the doctor," he said. "Get him patched up. He's going to marry my daughter."

CHAPTER SIXTEEN

June 1916

Billy's father said: "Can we have a chat, boyo?"

Billy was astonished. For almost two years, ever since Billy had stopped attending the Bethesda Chapel, they had hardly spoken. There was always tension in the air at the little house in Wellington Row. Billy had almost forgotten what it was like to hear soft voices talking amiably in the kitchen—or even loud voices raised in the passionate arguments they used to have. The bad atmosphere was half the reason Billy had joined the army.

Da's tone now was almost humble. Billy looked carefully at his face. His expression told the same story: no aggression, no challenge, just a plea.

All the same, Billy was not prepared to dance to his tune. "What for?" he said.

Da opened his mouth to snap a retort, then visibly controlled himself. "I've acted proud," he said. "It's a sin. You may have been proud, too, but that's between you and the Lord, and it's no excuse for me."

"It's taken you two years to work that out."

"It would have took me longer if you hadn't gone in the army."

Billy and Tommy had volunteered last year, lying about their age. They had joined the Eighth Battalion of the Welsh Rifles, known as the Aberowen Pals. The Pals' battalions were a new idea. Men from the same town were kept together, to train and fight alongside people with whom they had grown up. It was thought to be good for morale.

Billy's group had done a year's training, mostly at a new camp outside Cardiff. He had enjoyed himself. It was easier than coal mining and a lot less dangerous. As well as a certain amount of grinding boredom—*training* often meant the same as *waiting*—there had been sports and games and the camaraderie of a group of young men learning new ways. During a long period with nothing to do he had picked up a book at random and found himself reading the play *Macbeth*. To his surprise he had found the story thrilling and the poetry strangely fascinating. Shakespeare's language was not difficult for someone who had spent so many hours studying the seventeenth-century English of the Protestant Bible. He had since gone through the complete works, rereading the best plays several times.

Now training was over, and the Pals had two days' leave before going to France. Da thought this might be the last time he saw Billy alive. That would be why he was humbling himself to talk.

Billy looked at the clock. He had come here only to say good-bye to his mother. He was planning to spend his leave in London, with his sister, Ethel, and her sexy lodger. Mildred's pretty face, with her red lips and bunny teeth, had remained vividly in his mind ever since she had shocked him by saying, *Fucking hell, are you Billy?* His kit bag stood on the floor by the door, packed and ready. His complete Shakespeare was in it. Tommy was waiting for him at the station. "I've got a train to catch," he said.

"There are plenty of trains," Da said. "Sit down, Billy . . . please."

Billy was not comfortable with his father in this mood. Da might be righteous, arrogant, and harsh, but at least he was strong. Billy did not want to see him weaken.

Gramper was in his usual chair, listening. "Be a good boy, now, Billy," he said persuasively. "Give your da a chance, is it?"

"All right, then." Billy sat at the kitchen table.

His mother came in from the scullery.

There was a moment of silence. Billy knew he might never enter this house again. Coming back from an army camp, he had seen for the first time that his home was small, the rooms dark, the air heavy with coal dust and cooking smells. Most of all, after the free-and-easy banter of the barracks, he understood that in this house he had been raised to a Bible-black respectability in which much that was human and natural found no expression. And yet the thought of going made him sad. It was not just the place; it was the life he was leaving. Everything had been simple here. He had believed in God, obeyed his father, and trusted his workmates down the pit. The coal owners were wicked, the union protected the men, and socialism offered a brighter future. But life was not that simple. He might return to Wellington Row, but he would never again be the boy who had lived here.

Da folded his hands, closed his eyes, and said: "Oh, Lord, help thy servant to be humble and meek as Jesus was." Then he opened his eyes and said: "Why did you do it, Billy? Why did you join up?"

"Because we're at war," Billy said. "Like it or not, we have to fight."

"But can't you see—" Da stopped and held up his hands in a pacific gesture. "Let me start again. You don't believe what you read in the newspapers about the Germans being evil men who rape nuns, do you?"

"No," said Billy. "Everything the papers ever said about coal miners was lies, so I don't suppose they're telling the truth about the Germans."

"The way I see it, this is a capitalist war that has got nothing to do with the workingman," Da said. "But you may disagree."

Billy was amazed by the effort his father was making to be conciliatory. Never before had he heard Da say, *You may disagree.* He replied: "I don't know much about capitalism, but I expect you're right. All the same, the Germans have got to be stopped. They think they're entitled to rule the world!"

Da said: "We're British. Our empire holds sway over more than four hundred million people. Hardly any of them are entitled to vote. They have no control over their own countries. Ask the average British man why, and he'll say it's our destiny to govern inferior peoples." Da spread both hands in a gesture that meant *Isn't it obvious?* "Billy boy, it's not the Germans who think they should rule the world—it's us!"

Billy sighed. He agreed with all this. "But we're under attack. The reasons for the war may be wrong, but we have to fight, regardless."

"How many have died in the last two years?" Da said. "Millions!" His voice went up a notch, but he was not angry so much as sad. "It will go on as long as young men are willing to kill one another *regardless,* as you say."

"It will go on until someone wins, I suppose."

His mother said: "I expect you're afraid people will think you're scared."

"No," he said, but she was right. His rational explanations for joining up were not the whole story. As usual, Mam saw into his heart. For almost two years he had been hearing and reading that able-bodied young men such as himself were cowards if they did not fight. It was in the newspapers; people said it in shops and pubs; in Cardiff city center pretty girls handed out white feathers to any boy not in uniform, and recruiting sergeants jeered at young civilians on the streets. Billy knew it was propaganda, but it affected him just the same. He found it hard to bear the thought that people believed him to be a coward.

He fantasized explaining, to those girls with white feathers, that coal mining was more dangerous than being in the army. Apart from frontline troops, most soldiers were less likely to be killed or injured than miners. And Britain needed the coal. It fueled half the navy. The government had actually said it did not want miners to join up. None of this made any difference. Since he had put on the itchy khaki tunic and trousers, the new boots and the peaked cap, he had felt better.

Da said: "People think there's a big push coming at the end of the month."

Billy nodded. "The officers won't say a word, but everyone else is talking about it. I expect that's why there's a sudden rush to get more men over there."

"The newspapers say this could be the battle that turns the tide—the beginning of the end."

"Let's hope so, anyhow."

"You should have enough ammunition now, thanks to Lloyd George."

"Aye." Last year there had been a shortage of shells. Newspaper agitation about the Shell Scandal had almost brought down Prime Minister Asquith. He had formed a coalition government, created the new post of minister of munitions, and given the job to the most popular man in the cabinet, David Lloyd George. Since then, production had soared.

"Try to take care of yourself," Da said.

Mam said: "Don't be a hero. Leave that to them that started the war—the upper classes, the Conservatives, the officers. Do as you're told and no more."

Gramper said: "War is war. There's no safe way to do it."

They were saying their good-byes. Billy felt an urge to cry, and repressed it harshly. "Right, then," he said, standing up.

Gramper shook his hand. Mam kissed him. Da shook hands, then yielded to an impulse and hugged him. Billy could not remember the last time his father had done that.

"God bless you and keep you, Billy," Da said. There were tears in his eyes.

Billy's self-control almost broke. "So long, then," he said. He picked up his kit bag. He heard his mother sob. Without looking back, he went out, closing the door behind him.

He took a deep breath and composed himself. Then he set off down the steep street toward the station.

{ II }

The river Somme meandered from east to west across France on its way to the sea. The front line, running north to south, crossed the river not far from Amiens. South of there, the Allied line was held by French troops all the way to Switzerland. To its north most of the forces were British and Commonwealth.

From this point a range of hills ran northwest for twenty miles. The German trenches in this sector had been dug into the slopes of the hills. From one such trench, Walter von Ulrich looked through powerful Zeiss *Doppelfernrohr* binoculars down to the British positions.

It was a sunny day in early summer, and he could hear birdsong. In a nearby orchard that had so far escaped shelling, apple trees were blossoming bravely. Men were the only animals that slaughtered their own kind by the million, and turned the landscape into a waste of shell craters and barbed wire. Perhaps the human race would wipe itself out completely, and leave the world to the birds and trees, Walter thought apocalyptically. Perhaps that would be for the best.

The high position had many advantages, he thought, coming back to practical matters. The British would have to attack uphill. Even more useful was the ability of the Germans to see everything the British were doing. And Walter felt sure that right now they were preparing a major assault.

Such activity could hardly be concealed. For months, ominously, the British had been improving the roads and railways in this previously sleepy area of the French countryside. Now they were using those supply lines to bring forward hundreds of heavy guns, thousands of horses, and tens of thousands of men. Behind the front lines, trucks and trains in constant streams were unloading crates of ammunition, barrels of fresh water, and bales of hay. Walter focused his lenses on a communications detail, digging a narrow trench and unspooling a huge reel of what was undoubtedly telephone wire.

They must have high hopes, he thought with cold apprehension. The expenditure of men, money, and effort was colossal. It could only be justified if the British thought this was the decisive attack of the war. Walter hoped it was— one way or the other.

Whenever he looked into enemy territory he thought of Maud. The picture he carried in his wallet, cut out of the *Tatler* magazine, showed her in a dramatically simple ball gown at the Savoy Hotel, over the caption *Lady Maud Fitzherbert is always dressed in the latest fashion.* He guessed she was not doing much dancing now. Had she found some role in the war effort, as Walter's sister, Greta, had in Berlin, bringing small luxuries to wounded men in army hospitals? Or had she retired to the country, like Walter's mother, and planted her flower beds with potatoes because of the food shortage?

He did not know whether the British were short of food. Germany's navy was trapped in port by the British blockade, so there had been no imports by sea for almost two years. But the British continued to get supplies from America. German submarines attacked transatlantic ships intermittently, but the high command held back from an all-out effort—what was called USW, for "unrestricted submarine warfare"—for fear of bringing the Americans into the war. So, Walter guessed, Maud was not as hungry as he was. And he was better off than German civilians. There had been strikes and demonstrations against the food shortage in some cities.

He had not written to her, nor she to him. There was no postal service between Germany and Britain. The only chance would come if one of them traveled to a neutral country, the United States or Sweden perhaps, and posted a letter from there; but that opportunity had not yet arisen for him nor, presumably, for her.

It was torment not to know anything about her. He was tortured by the fear that she might be ill in a hospital without his knowledge. He longed for the end of the war so that he could be with her. He desperately wanted Germany to win, of course, but there were times when he felt he would not care about losing as long as Maud was all right. His nightmare was that the end came, and he went to London to find her, only to be told that she was dead.

He pushed the frightening thought to the back of his mind. He lowered his sights, focused his lenses nearer, and examined the barbed-wire defenses on the German side of no-man's-land. There were two belts of it, each fifteen feet wide. The wire was firmly fixed to the ground with iron stakes so that it could not easily be moved. It made a reassuringly formidable barrier.

He climbed down from the trench parapet and turned down a long flight of wooden steps to a deep dugout. The disadvantage of the hillside position was that the trenches were more visible to enemy artillery; so, to compensate, the dugouts in this sector had been cut far into the chalky soil, deep enough to provide protection from anything but a direct hit from the largest type of shell. There was room to shelter every man in the trench garrison during a bombardment. Some dugouts were interconnected, providing an alternative way out if shelling blocked the entrance.

Walter sat on a wooden bench and took out his notebook. For a few minutes he wrote abbreviated reminders of everything he had seen. His report would confirm other intelligence sources. Secret agents had been warning of what the British called a "big push."

He made his way through the maze of trenches to the rear. The Germans had constructed three lines of trenches two or three kilometers apart, so that if they were driven out of the front line, they could fall back on another trench and, failing that, a third. Whatever happened, he thought with considerable satisfaction, there would be no quick victory for the British.

Walter found his horse and rode back to Second Army headquarters, arriving at lunchtime. In the officers' mess he was surprised to encounter his father. The old man was a senior officer on the general staff, and now dashed from one battlefield to another just as, in peacetime, he had gone from one European capital to the next.

Otto looked older. He had lost weight—all Germans had lost weight. His monkish fringe was cut so short that he looked bald. But he seemed spry and cheerful. War suited him. He liked the excitement, the hurry, the quick decisions, and the sense of constant emergency.

He never mentioned Maud.

"What have you seen?" he asked.

"There will be a major assault in this area within the next few weeks," Walter said.

His father shook his head skeptically. "The Somme sector is the best-defended part of our line. We hold the upper ground and we have three lines of trenches. In war you attack at your enemy's weakest point, not his strongest—even the British know that."

Walter related what he had just seen: the trucks, the trains, and the communications detail laying telephone lines.

"I believe it's a ruse," said Otto. "If this were the real site of the attack, they would be doing more to conceal their efforts. There will be a feint here, followed by the real assault farther north, in Flanders."

Walter said: "What does von Falkenhayn believe?" Erich von Falkenhayn had been chief of staff for almost two years.

His father smiled. "He believes what I tell him."

{ III }

As coffee was served at the end of lunch, Lady Maud asked Lady Hermia: "In an emergency, Aunt, would you know how to get in touch with Fitz's lawyer?"

Aunt Herm looked mildly shocked. "My dear, what should I have to do with lawyers?"

"You never know." Maud turned to the butler as he put the coffeepot down on a silver trivet. "Grout, be so kind as to bring me a sheet of paper and a pencil." Grout went out and returned with writing materials. Maud wrote down the name and address of the family lawyer.

"Why do I need this?" Aunt Herm said.

"I may get arrested this afternoon," Maud said cheerfully. "If so, do please ask him to come and get me out of jail."

"Oh!" said Aunt Herm. "You can't mean it!"

"No, I'm sure it won't happen," Maud said. "But, you know, just in case . . ." She kissed her aunt and left the room.

Aunt Herm's attitude infuriated Maud, but most women were the same. It was unladylike even to know the name of your lawyer, let alone to understand your rights under the law. No wonder women were mercilessly exploited.

Maud put on her hat and gloves and a light summer coat, then went out and caught a bus to Aldgate.

She was alone. Chaperoning rules had relaxed since the outbreak of war. It was no longer scandalous for a single woman to go out unescorted in the daytime. Aunt Herm disapproved of the change, but she could not lock Maud up, and she could not appeal to Fitz, who was in France, so she had to accept the situation, albeit with a sour face.

Maud was editor of *The Soldier's Wife,* a small-circulation newspaper that campaigned for better treatment for the dependents of servicemen. A Conservative member of Parliament had described the journal as "a pestilential nuisance to the government," a quotation that was emblazoned on the masthead of every edition thereafter. Maud's campaigning rage was fueled by her indignation at the subjection of women combined with her horror at the pointless slaughter of war. Maud subsidized the newspaper out of her small inheritance. She hardly needed the money anyway: Fitz always paid for everything she needed.

Ethel Williams was the paper's manager. She had eagerly left the sweatshop for a better wage and a campaigning role. Ethel shared Maud's rage, but had a different set of skills. Maud understood politics at the top—she met cabinet ministers socially and talked to them about the issues of the day. Ethel knew a different political world: the National Union of Garment Workers, the Independent Labour Party, strikes and lockouts and street marches.

As appointed, Maud met Ethel across the road from the Aldgate office of the Soldiers' and Sailors' Families Association.

Before the war this well-meaning charity had enabled well-off ladies to graciously give help and advice to the hard-up wives of servicemen. Now it had a new role. The government paid one pound and one shilling to a soldier's wife with two children separated from her husband by the war. This was not much—about half what a coal miner earned—but it was enough to raise millions of women and children out of grinding poverty. The Soldiers' and Sailors' Families Association administered this separation allowance.

But the allowance was payable only to women of "good behavior" and the charity ladies sometimes withheld the government money from wives who rejected their advice about child rearing, household management, and the perils of visiting music halls and drinking gin.

Maud thought such women would be better off without the gin, but that did not give anyone the right to push them into penury. She was driven into a fury of outrage by comfortable middle-class people passing judgment on soldiers' wives and depriving them of the means to feed their children. Parliament would not permit such abuse, she thought, if women had the vote.

With Ethel were a dozen working-class women plus one man, Bernie Leckwith, secretary of the Aldgate Independent Labour Party. The party approved of Maud's paper and supported its campaigns.

When Maud joined the group on the pavement, Ethel was talking to a young man with a notebook. "The separation allowance is not a charitable gift," she said. "Soldiers' wives receive it as of right. Do you have to pass a good-conduct test before you get your wages as a reporter? Is Mr. Asquith questioned about how much Madeira he drinks before he can draw his salary as a member of Parliament? These women are entitled to the money just as if it was a wage."

Ethel had found her voice, Maud reflected. She expressed herself simply and vividly.

The reporter looked admiringly at Ethel: he seemed half in love with her. Rather apologetically he said: "Your opponents say that a woman should not receive support if she is unfaithful to her soldier husband."

"Are you checking on the husbands?" Ethel said indignantly. "I believe there are houses of ill fame in France and Mesopotamia and other places where our men are serving. Does the army take the names of married men entering such houses, and withdraw their wages? Adultery is a sin, but it is not a reason to impoverish the sinner and let her children starve."

Ethel was carrying her child, Lloyd, on her hip. He was now sixteen months old and able to walk, or at least stagger. He had fine dark hair and green eyes, and was as pretty as his mother. Maud put out her hands to take him, and he came to her eagerly. She felt a pang of longing: she almost wished she had become pregnant during her one night with Walter, despite all the trouble it would have caused.

She had heard nothing of Walter since the Christmas before last. She did not know whether he was alive or dead. She might already be a widow. She tried not to brood, but dreadful thoughts crept up on her unawares, sometimes, and then she had to keep from crying.

Ethel finished charming the reporter, then introduced Maud to a young woman with two children clinging to her skirts. "This is Jayne McCulley, who I told you about." Jayne had a pretty face and a determined look.

Maud shook hands. "I hope we can get justice for you today, Mrs. McCulley," she said.

"Very kind of you, I'm sure, ma'am." The habit of deference died hard even in egalitarian political movements.

"If we're all ready?" said Ethel.

Maud handed Lloyd back to Ethel, and together the group crossed the road and went in at the front door of the charity office. There was a reception area where a middle-aged woman sat behind a desk. She looked frightened by the crowd.

Maud said to her: "There's nothing to worry about. Mrs. Williams and I are here to see Mrs. Hargreaves, your manager."

The receptionist stood up. "I'll see if she's in," she said nervously.

Ethel said: "I know she's in—I saw her walk through the door half an hour ago."

The receptionist scurried out.

The woman who returned with her was less easily intimidated. Mrs. Hargreaves was a stout woman in her forties, wearing a French coat and skirt and a fashionable hat decorated with a large pleated bow. The ensemble lost all its continental chic on her stocky figure, Maud thought cattily, but the woman had the confidence that came with money. She also had a large nose. "Yes?" she said rudely.

In the struggle for female equality, Maud reflected, sometimes you had to fight women as well as men. "I have come to see you because I'm concerned about your treatment of Mrs. McCulley."

Mrs. Hargreaves looked startled, no doubt by Maud's upper-class accent. She gave Maud an up-and-down scrutiny. She was probably noting that Maud's clothes were as expensive as her own. When she spoke again, her tone was less arrogant. "I'm afraid I can't discuss individual cases."

"But Mrs. McCulley has asked me to speak to you—and she's here to prove it."

Jayne McCulley said: "Don't you remember me, Mrs. Hargreaves?"

"As a matter of fact, I do. You were very discourteous to me."

Jayne turned to Maud. "I told her to go and poke her nose into someone else's business."

The women giggled at the reference to the nose, and Mrs. Hargreaves blushed.

Maud said: "But you cannot refuse an application for a separation allowance on the grounds that the applicant was rude to you." Maud controlled her anger and tried to speak with icy disapproval. "Surely you know that?"

Mrs. Hargreaves tilted her chin defensively. "Mrs. McCulley was seen in the Dog and Duck public house, and at the Stepney Music Hall, on both occasions with a young man. The separation allowance is for wives of good conduct. The government does not wish to finance unchaste behavior."

Maud wanted to strangle her. "You seem to misunderstand your role," she said. "It is not for you to refuse payment on suspicion."

Mrs. Hargreaves looked a little less sure of herself.

Ethel put in: "I suppose Mr. Hargreaves is safe at home, is it?"

"No, he's not," the woman replied quickly. "He's with the army in Egypt."

"Oh!" said Ethel. "So you receive a separation allowance, too."

"That's neither here nor there."

"Does someone come to your house, Mrs. Hargreaves, to check on your conduct? Do they look at the level of the sherry in the decanter on your sideboard? Are you questioned about your friendship with your grocer's deliveryman?"

"How dare you!"

Maud said: "Your indignation is understandable—but perhaps now you will appreciate why Mrs. McCulley reacted as she did to your questioning."

Mrs. Hargreaves raised her voice. "That's ridiculous—there's no comparison!"

"No comparison?" Maud said angrily. "Her husband, like yours, is risking his life for his country. Both you and she claim the separation allowance. But you have the right to judge her behavior and refuse her the money—while no one judges you. Why not? Officers' wives sometimes drink too much."

Ethel said: "They commit adultery, too."

"That's it!" shouted Mrs. Hargreaves. "I refuse to be insulted."

"So does Jayne McCulley," said Ethel.

Maud said: "The man you saw with Mrs. McCulley was her brother. He was home on leave from France. He had only two days, and she wanted him to enjoy himself before going back to the trenches. That was why she took him to the pub and the music hall."

Mrs. Hargreaves looked abashed, but she put on a defiant air. "She should have explained that when I questioned her. And now I must ask you please to leave the premises."

"Now that you know the truth, I trust you will approve Mrs. McCulley's application."

"We'll see."

"I insist that you do it here and now."

"Impossible."

"We're not leaving until you do."

"Then I shall call the police."

"Very well."

Mrs. Hargreaves retreated.

Ethel turned to the admiring reporter. "Where is your photographer?"

"Waiting outside."

A few minutes later, a burly middle-aged police constable came in. "Now, now, ladies," he said. "No trouble, please. Just leave quietly."

Maud stepped forward. "I am refusing to leave," she said. "Never mind about the others."

"And who would you be, madam?"

"I am Lady Maud Fitzherbert, and if you want me to go you'll have to carry me out."

"If you insist," said the policeman, and he picked her up.

As they left the building, the photographer took a picture.

{ IV }

"Aren't you scared?" Mildred said.

"Aye," Billy admitted. "I am, a bit."

He could talk to Mildred. She seemed to know all about him anyway. She had been living with his sister for a couple of years, and women always told each other everything. However, there was something else about Mildred that made him feel comfortable. Aberowen girls were always trying to impress boys, saying things for effect and checking their appearance in mirrors, but Mildred was just herself. She said outrageous things sometimes, and made Billy laugh. He felt he could tell her anything.

He was almost overwhelmed by how attractive she was. It was not her fair curly hair or her blue eyes, but her devil-may-care attitude that mesmerized him. Then there was the age difference. She was twenty-three, and he was still not quite eighteen. She seemed very worldly-wise, yet she was frankly interested in him, and that was highly flattering. He looked longingly at her across the room, hoping he would get a chance to talk to her alone, wondering if he would dare to touch her hand, put his arm around her, and kiss her.

They were sitting around the square table in Ethel's kitchen: Billy, Tommy, Ethel, and Mildred. It was a warm evening, and the door was open to the backyard. On the flagstone floor Mildred's two little girls were playing with Lloyd. Enid and Lillian were three and four years old, but Billy had not yet worked out which was which. Because of the children, the women had not wanted to go out, so Billy and Tommy had fetched some bottles of beer from the pub.

"You'll be all right," Mildred said to Billy. "You've been trained."

"Aye." The training had not done much for Billy's confidence. There had been a lot of marching up and down, saluting, and doing bayonet drills. He did not feel he had been taught how to survive.

Tommy said: "If the Germans all turn out to be stuffed dummies tied to posts, we'll know how to stick our bayonets in them."

Mildred said: "You can shoot your guns, can't you?"

For a while they had trained with rusted and broken rifles stamped "D.P." for "drill purposes," which meant they were not on any account to be fired. But eventually each of them had been given a bolt-action Lee Enfield rifle with a detachable magazine holding ten rounds of .303 ammunition. It turned out that Billy could shoot well, being able to empty the magazine in under a minute and still hit a man-size target at three hundred yards. The Lee Enfield was renowned for its rapid rate of fire, the trainees had been told: the world record was thirty-eight rounds a minute.

"The equipment is all right," Billy said to Mildred. "It's the officers that worry me. So far I haven't met one I'd trust in an emergency down the pit."

"The good ones are all out in France, I expect," Mildred said optimistically. "They let the wankers stay home and do the training."

Billy laughed at her choice of words. She had no inhibitions. "I hope you're right."

What he was really afraid of was that when the Germans

started shooting at him he might turn and run away. That scared him most of all. The humiliation would be worse than a wound, he thought. Sometimes he felt so wrought up about it that he longed for the terrible moment to come, so that he would know, one way or the other.

"Anyway, I'm glad you're going to shoot those wicked Germans," Mildred said. "They're all rapists."

Tommy said: "If I were you, I wouldn't believe everything you read in the *Daily Mail.* They'd have you think all trade unionists are disloyal. I know that's not true—most of the members of my union branch have volunteered. So the Germans may not be as bad as the *Mail* paints them."

"Yeah, you're probably right." Mildred turned back to Billy. "Have you seen *The Tramp*?"

"Aye, I love Charlie Chaplin."

Ethel picked up her son. "Say good night to Uncle Billy." The toddler wriggled in her arms, not wanting to go to bed.

Billy remembered him newborn, and the way he had opened his mouth and wailed. How big and strong he seemed now. "Good night, Lloyd," he said.

Ethel had named him after Lloyd George. Billy was the only person who knew that he also had a middle name: Fitzherbert. It was on his birth certificate, but Ethel had not told anyone else.

Billy would have liked to get Earl Fitzherbert in the sights of his Lee Enfield.

Ethel said: "He looks like Gramper, doesn't he?"

Billy could not see the resemblance. "I'll let you know when he grows a mustache."

Mildred put her two to bed at the same time. Then the women announced that they wanted supper. Ethel and Tommy went to buy oysters, leaving Billy and Mildred alone.

As soon as they had gone, Billy said: "I really like you, Mildred."

"I like you, too," she said; so he moved his chair next to hers and kissed her.

She kissed him back with enthusiasm.

He had done this before. He had kissed several girls in the back row of the Majestic cinema in Cwm Street. They always opened their mouths straightaway, and he did the same now.

Mildred pushed him away gently. "Not so fast," she said.

"Do this." And she kissed him with her mouth closed, her lips brushing his cheek and his eyelids and his neck, and then his lips. It was strange but he liked it. She said: "Do the same to me." He followed her instructions. "Now do this," she said, and he felt the tip of her tongue on his lips, touching them as lightly as possible. Once again he copied her. Then she showed him yet another way to kiss, nibbling his neck and his earlobes. He felt he could do this forever.

When they paused for breath she stroked his cheek and said: "You're a quick learner."

"You're lovely," he said.

He kissed her again and squeezed her breast. She let him do it for a while, but when he started to breathe heavily, she took his hand away. "Don't get too worked up," she said. "They'll be back any minute."

A moment later he heard the front door. "Oh, dammo," he said.

"Be patient," she whispered.

"Patient?" he said. "I'm going to France tomorrow."

"Well, it ain't tomorrow yet, is it?"

Billy was still wondering what she meant when Ethel and Tommy came into the room.

They ate their supper and finished the beer. Ethel told them the story of Jayne McCulley, and how Lady Maud had been carried out of the charity office by a policeman. She made it sound like a comedy, but Billy was bursting with pride for his sister and the way she stood up for the rights of poor women. And she was the manager of a newspaper and the friend of Lady Maud! He was determined that one day he, too, would be a champion for ordinary people. It was what he admired about his father. Da was narrow-minded and stubborn, but all his life he had fought for the workingman.

Darkness fell and Ethel announced it was bedtime. She used cushions to improvise beds on the kitchen floor for Billy and Tommy. They all retired.

Billy lay awake, wondering what Mildred had meant by *It ain't tomorrow yet.* Perhaps she was just promising to kiss him again in the morning, when he left to catch the train to Southampton. But she had seemed to imply more. Could it really be that she wanted to see him again tonight?

The thought of going to her room inflamed him so much that he could not sleep. She would be wearing a nightdress, and under the sheets her body would be warm to the touch, he thought. He imagined her face on the pillow, and envied the pillowcase because it was touching her cheek.

When Tommy's breathing seemed regular, Billy slipped out of his sheets.

"Where are you going?" said Tommy, not as fast asleep as Billy had thought.

"Toilet," Billy whispered. "All that beer."

Tommy grunted and turned over.

In his underwear, Billy crept up the stairs. There were three doors off the landing. He hesitated. What if he had misinterpreted Mildred? She might scream at the sight of him. How embarrassing that would be.

No, he thought; she's not the screaming type.

He opened the first door he came to. There was a faint light from the street, and he could see a narrow bed with the blond heads of two little girls on the pillow. He closed the door softly. He felt like a burglar.

He tried the next door. In this room, a candle was burning, and it took him a moment to adjust to its unsteady light. He saw a bigger bed, with one head on the pillow. Mildred's face was toward him, but he could not see whether her eyes were open. He waited for her protest, but no sound came.

He stepped inside and closed the door behind him.

He whispered hesitantly: "Mildred?"

In a clear voice she said: "About bloody time, Billy. Get into bed, quick."

He slipped between the sheets and put his arms around her. She was not wearing the nightdress he had expected. In fact, he realized with a thrilling shock, she was naked.

Suddenly he felt nervous. He said: "I've never . . ."

"I know," she said. "You'll be my first virgin."

{ V }

In June of 1916, Major the Earl Fitzherbert was assigned to the Eighth Battalion of the Welsh Rifles and put in charge of B Company, one hundred twenty-eight men and four lieutenants. He had never commanded men in battle, and he was secretly racked with anxiety.

He was in France, but the battalion was still in Britain. They were recruits who had just finished their training. They would be stiffened with a sprinkling of veterans, the brigadier explained to Fitz. The professional army that had been sent to France in 1914 no longer existed—more than half of them were dead—and this was Kitchener's New Army. Fitz's lot were called the Aberowen Pals. "You'll probably know most of them," said the brigadier, who seemed not to realize how wide was the gulf that separated earls from coal miners.

Fitz got his orders at the same time as half a dozen other officers, and he bought a round of drinks in the mess to celebrate. The captain who had been given A Company raised his whisky glass and said: "Fitzherbert? You must be the coal owner. I'm Gwyn Evans, the shopkeeper. You probably buy all your sheets and towels from me."

There were a lot of these cocky businessmen in the army now. It was typical of that type to speak as if he and Fitz were equals who just happened to be in different lines of business. But Fitz also knew that the organizational skills of commercial men were valued by the army. In calling himself a shopkeeper, the captain was indulging in a little false modesty. Gwyn Evans was the name over department stores in the larger towns of South Wales. There were many more people on his payroll than in A Company. Fitz himself had never organized anything more complicated than a cricket team, and the daunting complexity of the war machine made him vividly aware of his inexperience.

"This is the attack that was agreed upon in Chantilly, I presume," Evans said.

Fitz knew what he meant. Back in December Sir John French had at last been fired and Sir Douglas Haig had taken over as commander in chief of the British army in France, and a few days later Fitz—still doing liaison work—had attended an Allied conference at Chantilly. The French had proposed a massive offensive on the western front during 1916, and the Russians had agreed to a similar push in the east.

Evans went on: "What I heard then was that the French would attack with forty divisions and us with twenty-five. That's not going to happen now."

Fitz did not like this negative talk—he was already apprehensive enough—but unfortunately Evans was right. "It's because of Verdun," Fitz said. Since the December agreement, the French had lost a quarter of a million men defending the fortress city of Verdun, and they had few to spare for the Somme.

Evans said: "Whatever the reason, we're virtually on our own."

"I'm not sure it makes any difference," Fitz said with an air of detachment that he did not in the least feel. "We will attack along our stretch of the front, regardless of what they do."

"I disagree," said Evans, with a confidence that was not quite insolent. "The French withdrawal frees up a lot of German reserves. They can all be pulled into our sector as reinforcements."

"I think we'll move too fast for that."

"Do you, really, sir?" said Evans coolly, again remaining just the right side of disrespect. "If we get through the first line of German barbed wire, we've still got to fight our way through a second and third."

Evans was beginning to annoy Fitz. This kind of talk was bad for morale. "The barbed wire will be destroyed by our artillery," Fitz said.

"In my experience, artillery is not very effective against barbed wire. A shrapnel shell fires steel balls downward and forward—"

"I know what shrapnel is, thank you."

Evans ignored that. "—so it has to explode just a few yards above and before the target. Otherwise it has no effect. Our guns just aren't that accurate. And a high-explosive shell goes off when it hits the ground, so even a direct hit sometimes just throws the wire up in the air and down again without actually damaging it."

"You're underestimating the sheer scale of our barrage." Fitz's irritation with Evans was sharpened by a nagging suspicion that he might have a point. Worse, that suspicion fed Fitz's nervousness. "There will be nothing left afterward. The German trenches will be completely destroyed."

"I hope you're right. If they hide in their dugouts during the barrage, then come out again afterward with their machine guns, our men will be mown down."

"You don't seem to understand," Fitz said angrily.

"There has never been a bombardment this intense in the history of warfare. We have one gun for every twenty yards of front line. We plan to fire more than a million shells! Nothing will be left alive."

"Well, we're in agreement about one thing, anyway," said Captain Evans. "This has never been done before, as you say; so none of us can be sure how it will work out."

{ VI }

Lady Maud appeared at Aldgate Magistrates Court in a large red hat with ribbons and ostrich feathers, and was fined one guinea for disturbing the peace. "I hope Prime Minister Asquith will take notice," she said to Ethel as they left the courtroom.

Ethel was not optimistic. "We have no way of compelling him to act," she said with exasperation. "This kind of thing will go on until women have the power to vote a government out of office." The suffragettes had planned to make women's votes the big issue of the general election of 1915, but the wartime Parliament had postponed elections. "We may have to wait until the war is over."

"Not necessarily," said Maud. They stopped to pose for a photograph on the courthouse steps, then headed for the office of *The Soldier's Wife*. "Asquith is struggling to hold the Liberal-Conservative coalition together. If it falls apart, there will have to be an election. And that's what gives us a chance."

Ethel was surprised. She had thought the issue of women's votes was moribund. "Why?"

"The government has a problem. Under the present system, serving soldiers can't vote because they aren't householders. That didn't matter much before the war, when there were only a hundred thousand men in the army. But today there are more than a million. The government wouldn't dare to hold an election and leave them out—these men are dying for their country. There would be a mutiny."

"And if they reform the system, how can they leave women out?"

"Right now the spineless Asquith is looking for a way to do just that."

"But he can't! Women are just as much part of the war effort as men: they make munitions, they take care of wounded soldiers in France, and they do so many jobs that used to be done only by men."

"Asquith is hoping to weasel his way out of having that argument."

"Then we must make sure he is disappointed."

Maud smiled. "Exactly," she said. "I think that's our next campaign."

{ VII }

"I joined up to get out of Borstal," said George Barrow, leaning on the rail of the troopship as it steamed out of Southampton. A Borstal was a jail for underage offenders. "I was done for housebreaking when I was sixteen, and got three years. After a year I got tired of sucking the warden's cock, so I said I wanted to volunteer. He marched me to the recruiting station and that was it."

Billy looked at him. He had a bent nose, a mutilated ear, and a scar on his forehead. He looked like a retired boxer. "How old are you now?" said Billy.

"Seventeen."

Boys were not allowed to join the army under eighteen, and had to be nineteen before they were sent overseas, officially. Both laws were constantly broken by the army. Recruiting sergeants and medical officers were each paid half a crown for every man passed, and they rarely questioned boys who claimed to be older than they seemed. There was a boy in the battalion called Owen Bevin who looked about fifteen.

"Was that an island we just passed?" said George.

"Aye," said Billy. "That's the Isle of Wight."

"Oh," said George. "I thought it was France."

"No, that's a lot farther."

The voyage took them until early the following morning, when they disembarked at Le Havre. Billy stepped off the gangplank and set foot on foreign soil for the first time in his life. In fact it was not soil but cobblestones, which proved difficult to march over in hobnailed boots. They passed through the town, watched listlessly by the French population. Billy had heard stories of pretty French girls gratefully embracing the arriving Brits, but he saw only apathetic middle-aged women in head scarves.

They marched to a camp, where they spent the night. Next morning they boarded a train. Being abroad was less exciting than Billy had hoped. Everything was different, but only slightly. Like Britain, France was mostly fields and villages, roads and railways. The fields had fences rather than hedges, and the cottages seemed larger and better built, but that was all. It was an anticlimax. At the end of the day they reached their billets in a huge new encampment of hastily built barracks.

Billy had been made a corporal, so he was in charge of his section, eight men including Tommy, young Owen Bevin, and George Barrow the Borstal boy. They were joined by the mysterious Robin Mortimer, who was a private despite looking thirty years old. As they sat down to tea with bread and jam in a long hall containing about a thousand men, Billy said: "So, Robin, we're all new here, but you seem more experienced. What's your story?"

Mortimer replied in the faintly accented speech of an educated Welshman, but he used the language of the pit. "None of your fucking business, Taffy," he said, and he went off to sit somewhere else.

Billy shrugged. "Taffy" was not much of an insult, especially coming from another Welshman.

Four sections made a platoon, and their platoon sergeant was Elijah Jones, age twenty, the son of John Jones the Shop. He was considered a hardened veteran because he had been at the front for a year. Jones belonged to the Bethesda Chapel and Billy had known him since they were both at school, where he had been dubbed Prophet Jones because of his Old Testament name.

Prophet overheard the exchange with Mortimer. "I'll have a word with him, Billy," he said. "He's a stuck-up old beggar, but he can't speak to a corporal like that."

"What's he so grumpy about?"

"He used to be a major. I dunno what he done, but he was court-martialed and cashiered, which means he lost his rank as an officer. Then, being eligible for war service, he was immediately conscripted as a private soldier. It's what they do to officers who misbehave."

After tea they met their platoon leader, Second Lieutenant James Carlton-Smith, a boy the same age as Billy. He was stiff and embarrassed, and seemed too young to be in charge of anyone. "Men," he said in a strangled upper-class accent, "I am honored to be your leader, and I know you will be brave as lions in the coming battle."

"Bloody wart," muttered Mortimer.

Billy knew that second lieutenants were called warts, but only by other officers.

Carlton-Smith then introduced the commander of B Company, Major the Earl Fitzherbert.

"Bloody hell," said Billy. He stared openmouthed as the man he hated most in the world stood on a chair to address the company. Fitz wore a well-tailored khaki uniform and carried the ash wood walking stick some officers affected. He spoke with the same accent as Carlton-Smith, and uttered the same kind of platitude. Billy could hardly believe his rotten luck. What was Fitz doing here—impregnating French maidservants? That this hopeless wastrel should be his commanding officer was hard to bear.

When the officers had gone, Prophet spoke quietly to Billy and Mortimer. "Lieutenant Carlton-Smith was at Eton until a year ago," he said. Eton was a posh school: Fitz had gone there too.

Billy said: "So why is he an officer?"

"He was a popper at Eton. It means a prefect."

"Oh, good," said Billy sarcastically. "We'll be all right, then."

"He doesn't know much about warfare, but he's got the sense not to throw his weight around, so he'll be fine so long as we keep an eye on him. If you see him about to do something really stupid, speak to me." He fixed his eye on Mortimer. "You know what it's like, don't you?"

Mortimer gave a surly nod.

"I'm counting on you, now."

A few minutes later it was lights-out. There were no cots, just straw palliasses in rows on the floor. Lying awake, Billy thought admiringly of what Prophet had done with Mortimer. He was dealing with a difficult subordinate by making an ally of him. That was the way Da would handle a troublemaker.

Prophet had given Billy and Mortimer the same message. Had Prophet also identified Billy as a rebel? He recalled that Prophet had been in the congregation the Sunday that Billy had read out the story of the woman taken in adultery. Fair enough, he thought; I am a troublemaker.

Billy did not feel drowsy, and it was still light outside, but he fell asleep immediately. He was awakened by a terrific noise like a thunderstorm overhead. He sat upright. A dull dawn light came in through the rain-streaked windows, but there was no storm.

The other men were equally startled. Tommy said: "Jesus H. Christ, what was that?"

Mortimer was lighting a cigarette. "Artillery fire," he said. "Our own guns. Welcome to France, Taffy."

Billy was not listening. He was looking at Owen Bevin, in the bed opposite. Owen was sitting up with a corner of the sheet in his mouth, crying.

{ VIII }

Maud dreamed that Lloyd George put his hand up her skirt, whereupon she told him she was married to a German, and he informed the police, who had come to arrest her and were banging on her bedroom window.

She sat up in bed, confused. After a moment she realized how unlikely it was that the police would bang on a second-floor bedroom window even if they did want to arrest her. The dream faded away, but the noise continued. There was also a deep bass rumble as of a distant railway train.

She turned on the bedside lamp. The art nouveau silver clock on her mantelpiece said it was four in the morning. Had there been an earthquake? An explosion in a munitions factory? A train crash? She threw back the embroidered coverlet and stood up.

She drew back heavy green-and-navy striped curtains and looked out of the window down to the Mayfair street. In the dawn light she saw a young woman in a red dress, probably a prostitute on her way home, speaking anxiously to the driver of a horse-drawn milk cart. There was no one else in sight. Maud's window continued to rattle for no apparent reason. It was not even windy.

She pulled a watered silk robe over her nightgown and glanced into her cheval glass. Her hair was untidy but otherwise she looked respectable enough. She stepped into the corridor.

Aunt Herm stood there in a nightcap, beside Sanderson, Maud's maid, whose round face was pale with fear. Then Grout appeared on the stairs. "Good morning, Lady Maud; good morning, Lady Hermia," he said with imperturbable formality. "No need for alarm. It's the guns."

"What guns?" said Maud.

"In France, my lady," said the butler.

{ IX }

The British artillery barrage went on for a week.

It was supposed to last five days, but only one of those days enjoyed fine weather, to Fitz's consternation. Even though it was summer, for the rest of the time there was low cloud and rain. This made it difficult for the gunners to fire accurately. It also meant the spotter planes could not survey the results and help the gunners adjust their aim. This made matters especially difficult for those dedicated to counter-battery—destroying the German artillery— because the Germans wisely kept moving their guns, so that the British shells would fall harmlessly on vacated positions.

Fitz sat in the damp dugout that was battalion headquarters, gloomily smoking cigars and trying not to listen to the unending boom. In the absence of aerial photographs, he and other company commanders organized trench raids. These at least allowed eyeball observation of the enemy. However, it was a hazardous business, and raiding parties that stayed too long never returned. So the men had to hastily observe a short section of the line and scurry home.

To Fitz's great annoyance, they brought back conflicting reports. Some German trenches were destroyed; others remained intact. Some barbed wire had been cut, but by no means all of it. Most worrying was that some patrols were driven back by enemy fire. If the Germans were still able to shoot, clearly the artillery had not succeeded in its task of wiping out their positions.

Fitz knew that exactly twelve German prisoners had been taken by the Fourth Army during the barrage. All had been interrogated but, infuriatingly, they gave conflicting evidence. Some said their dugouts had been destroyed, others that the Germans were sitting safe and sound beneath the earth while the British wasted their ammunition overhead.

So unsure were the British of the effects of their shells that Haig postponed the attack, which had been scheduled for June 29. But the weather continued poor.

"It will have to be canceled," said Captain Evans at breakfast on the morning of June 30.

"Unlikely," Fitz commented.

"We don't attack until we have confirmation that the enemy defenses have been destroyed," Evans said. "That's an axiom of siege warfare."

Fitz knew that this principle had been agreed upon early in the planning, but later dropped. "Be realistic," he said to Evans. "We've been preparing this offensive for six months. This is our major action for 1916. All our effort has been put into it. How could it be canceled? Haig would have to resign. It might even bring down Asquith's government."

Evans seemed angered by that remark. His cheeks flushed and his voice went up in pitch. "Better for the government to fall than for us to send our men up against entrenched machine guns."

Fitz shook his head. "Look at the millions of tons of supplies that have been shipped, the roads and railways we've built to bring them here, the hundreds of thousands of men trained and armed and brought here from all over Britain. What will we do—send them all home?"

There was a long silence; then Evans said: "You're right, of course, Major." His words were conciliatory but his tone was one of barely suppressed rage. "We won't send them home," he said through clenched teeth. "We will bury them here."

At midday the rain stopped and the sun came out. A little later, confirmation came down the line: we attack tomorrow.

CHAPTER SEVENTEEN

July 1, 1916

Walter von Ulrich was in hell.

The British bombardment had been going on for seven days and nights. Every man in the German trenches looked ten years older than he had a week ago. They huddled in their dugouts—man-made caves deep in the ground behind the trenches—but the noise was still deafening, and the earth beneath their feet shook continually. Worst of all, they knew that a direct hit from the largest-caliber shell might destroy even the strongest of dugouts.

Whenever it stopped they climbed out into the trenches, ready to repel the big attack that everyone expected. As soon as they were satisfied that the British were not yet advancing, they would look at the damage. They would find a trench caved in, a dugout entrance buried under a pile of earth, and—on one sorry afternoon—a smashed canteen full of broken crockery, dripping jam tins, and liquid soap. Wearily they would shovel away the soil, patch the revetment with new planks, and order more stores.

The ordered stores did not come. Very little came to the front line. The bombardment made all approaches dangerous. The men were hungry and thirsty. Walter had gratefully drunk rainwater from a shell hole more than once.

The men could not stay in the dugouts between bombardments. They had to be in the trenches, ready for the British. Sentries kept constant watch. The rest sat in or near the dugout entrances, ready either to run down the steps and shelter underground when the big guns opened up, or to rush to the parapet to defend their position if the attack came. Machine guns had to be carried underground every time, then brought back up and returned to their emplacements.

In between barrages the British attacked with trench mortars. Although these small bombs made little noise when fired, they were powerful enough to splinter the timber of the revetment. However, they came across no-man's-land in a slow arc, and it was possible to see them coming and take cover. Walter had dodged one, getting far enough away to escape injury, although it had sprayed earth all over his dinner, forcing him to throw away a good bowlful of hearty pork stew. That had been the last hot meal he got, and if he had it now he would eat it, he thought, dirt, too.

Shells were not all. This sector had suffered a gas attack. The men had gas masks, but the bottom of the trench was littered with the bodies of rats, mice, and other small creatures killed by the chlorine. Rifle barrels had turned greenish-black.

Soon after midnight on the seventh night of the bombardment, the shelling eased up, and Walter decided to go out on a patrol.

He put on a wool cap and rubbed earth on his face to darken it. He drew his pistol, the standard nine-millimeter Luger issued to German officers. He ejected the magazine from the butt and checked the ammunition. It was fully loaded.

He climbed a ladder and went over the parapet, a death-defying act by daylight but relatively safe in the dark. He ran, bent double, down the gentle slope as far as the German barbed-wire entanglement. There was a gap in the wire, placed—by design—directly in front of a German machine-gun emplacement. He crawled through the gap on his knees.

It reminded him of the adventure stories he used to read as a schoolboy. Usually they featured square-jawed young Germans menaced by Red Indians, pygmies with blowpipes, or sly English spies. He recalled a lot of crawling through undergrowth, jungle, and prairie grass.

There was not much undergrowth here. Eighteen months of war had left only a few patches of grass and bushes and the occasional small tree dotted around a wasteland of mud and shell holes.

Which made it worse, because there was no cover. Tonight was moonless, but the landscape was occasionally lit by the flash of an explosion or the fierce bright light of a flare. All Walter could do then was fall flat and freeze. If he happened to be in a crater he might be hard to see. Otherwise he just had to hope no one was looking his way.

There were a lot of unexploded British shells on the ground. Walter calculated that something like a third of their ammunition were duds. He knew that Lloyd George had been put in charge of munitions, and guessed that the crowd-pleasing demagogue had prioritized volume over quality. Germans would never make such a mistake, he thought.

He reached the British wire, crawled laterally until he found a gap, and passed through.

As the British line began to appear, like the smear of a black paintbrush against a wash of dark gray sky, he dropped to his belly and tried to move silently. He had to get close: that was the point. He wanted to hear what the men in the trenches were saying.

Both sides sent out patrols every night. Walter usually dispatched a couple of bright-looking soldiers who were bored enough to relish an adventure, albeit a dangerous one. But sometimes he went himself, partly to show that he was willing to risk his own life, partly because his own observations were generally more detailed.

He listened, straining to hear a cough, a few muttered words, perhaps a fart followed by a sigh of satisfaction. He seemed to be in front of a quiet section. He turned left, crawled fifty yards, and stopped. Now he could hear an unfamiliar sound a bit like the hum of distant machinery.

He crawled on, trying hard to keep his bearings. It was easy to lose all sense of direction in the dark. One night, after a long crawl, he had come up against the barbed wire he had passed half an hour earlier, and realized he had gone around in a circle.

He heard a voice say quietly: "Over by here." He froze. A masked flashlight bobbed into his field of view, like a firefly. In its faint reflected light he made out three soldiers in British-style steel helmets thirty yards away. He was tempted to roll away from them, but decided the movement was more likely to give him away. He drew his pistol: if he was going to die, he would take some of the enemy with him. The safety catch was on the left side just above the grip. He thumbed it up and forward. It made a click that sounded to him like a thunderclap, but the British soldiers did not appear to hear it.

Two of them were carrying a roll of barbed wire. Walter guessed they were going to renew a section that had been flattened by German artillery during the day. Maybe I should shoot them quickly, he thought, one-two-three. They will try to kill me tomorrow. But he had more important work to do, and he refrained from pulling the trigger as he watched them go by and recede into darkness.

He thumbed back the safety catch, holstered his gun, and crawled closer to the British trench.

Now the noise was louder. He lay still for a moment, concentrating. It was the sound of a crowd. They were trying to be quiet, but men in the mass could always be heard. It was a sound formed of shuffling feet, rustling clothes, sniffing and yawning and belching. Over that there was the occasional quiet word spoken in a voice of authority.

But what intrigued and startled Walter was that it seemed such a big crowd. He could not estimate how many. Lately the British had dug new, broader trenches, as if to hold vast quantities of stores, or very large artillery pieces. But perhaps they were for crowds.

Walter had to see.

He crawled forward. The sound grew. He had to look inside the trench, but how could he do so without being seen himself?

He heard a voice behind him, and his heart stopped.

He turned and saw the glowworm flashlight. The barbed-wire detail was returning. He pushed himself into the mud, then slowly drew his pistol.

They were hurrying, not troubling to be quiet, glad their task was done and keen to get back to safety. They came close, but did not look at him.

When they had passed, he was inspired, and leaped to his feet.

Now, if anyone should shine a light and see him, he would appear to be part of the group.

He followed them. He did not think they would hear his steps clearly enough to distinguish them from their own. None of them looked back.

He peered toward the source of the noise. He could see into the trench, now, but at first he could make out only a few points of light, presumably flashlights. But his eyes gradually adjusted, and at last he worked out what he was seeing, and then he was astonished.

He was looking at thousands of men.

He stopped. The broad trench, whose purpose had not been clear, was now revealed to be an assembly trench. The British were massing their troops for the big push. They stood waiting, fidgeting, the light from the officers' flashlights glinting off bayonets and steel helmets, line after line of them. Walter tried to count: ten lines of ten men was a hundred, the same again made two hundred, four hundred, eight . . . There were sixteen hundred men within his field of vision; then the darkness closed in over the others.

The assault was about to begin.

He had to get back as fast as possible with this information. If the German artillery opened up now, they could kill thousands of the enemy right here, behind British lines, before the attack got started. It was an opportunity sent by heaven, or perhaps by the devils who threw the cruel dice of war. As soon as he reached his own lines he would telephone headquarters.

A flare went up. In its light he saw a British sentry looking over the parapet, rifle at the ready, staring at him.

Walter dropped to the ground and buried his face in the mud.

A shot rang out. Then one of the barbed-wire detail shouted: "Don't shoot, you mad bastard. It's us!" The accent put Walter in mind of the staff at Fitz's house in Wales, and he guessed this was a Welsh regiment.

The flare died. Walter leaped to his feet and ran, heading for the German side. The sentry would be unable to see for a few seconds, his vision spoiled by the flare. Walter ran faster than he ever had, expecting the rifle to fire again at any moment. In half a minute he came to the British wire and dropped gratefully to his knees. He crawled rapidly forward through a gap. Another flare went up. He was still within rifle range, but no longer easily visible. He dropped to the ground. The flare was directly above him, and a dangerous lump of burning magnesium dropped a yard from his hand, but there were no more gunshots.

When the flare had burned out he got to his feet and ran all the way to the German line.

{ II }

Two miles behind the British front line, Fitz watched anxiously as the Eighth Battalion formed up shortly after two a.m. He was afraid these freshly trained men would disgrace him, but they did not. They were in a subdued mood and obeyed orders with alacrity.

The brigadier, sitting on his horse, addressed the men briefly. He was lit up from below by a sergeant's flashlight, and looked like the villain in an American moving picture. "Our artillery has wiped out the German defenses," he said. "When you reach the other side, you will find nothing but dead Germans."

A Welsh voice from somewhere nearby murmured: "Marvelous, isn't it, how these Germans can shoot back at us even when they're fucking dead."

Fitz raked the lines to identify the speaker but he could not in the dark.

The brigadier went on: "Take and secure their trenches, and the field kitchens will follow and give you a hot dinner."

B Company marched off toward the battlefield, led by the platoon sergeants. They went across the fields, leaving the roads clear for wheeled transport. As they left they started to sing "Guide Me O Thou Great Jehovah." Their voices lingered in the night air for some minutes after they disappeared into the darkness.

Fitz returned to battalion headquarters. An open truck was waiting to take the officers to the front line. Fitz sat next to Lieutenant Roland Morgan, son of the Aberowen colliery manager.

Fitz did all he could to discourage defeatist talk, but he could not help wondering if the brigadier had gone too far the other way. No army had ever mounted an offensive like this one, and nobody could be sure how it would turn out. Seven days of artillery bombardment had *not* obliterated the enemy's defenses: the Germans were still shooting back, as that anonymous soldier had sarcastically pointed out. Fitz had actually said the same thing in a report, whereupon Colonel Hervey had asked him if he was scared.

Fitz was worried. When the general staff closed their eyes to bad news, men died.

As if to prove his point, a shell exploded in the road behind. Fitz looked back and saw parts of a lorry just like this one flying through the air. A car following it swerved into a ditch, and in its turn was hit by another truck. It was a scene of carnage, but the driver of Fitz's truck quite correctly did not stop to help. The wounded had to be left to the medics.

More shells fell in the fields to the left and right. The Germans were targeting approaches to the front line, rather than the line itself. They must have worked out that the big assault was about to begin—such a huge movement of men could hardly be hidden from their intelligence branch—and with deadly efficiency they were killing men who had not yet even reached the trenches. Fitz fought down a feeling of panic, but his fear remained. B Company might not even make it to the battlefield.

He reached the marshaling area without further incident. Several thousand men were there already, leaning on their rifles and talking in low voices. Fitz heard that some groups had already been decimated by shelling. He waited, wondering grimly whether his company still existed. But eventually the Aberowen Pals arrived intact, to his relief, and formed up. Fitz led them the last few hundred yards to the frontline assembly trench.

Then they had nothing to do but wait for zero hour. There was water in the trench, and Fitz's puttees were soon soaked. No singing was permitted now: it might be heard at the enemy lines. Smoking was forbidden, too. Some of the men were praying. A tall soldier took out his pay book and began to fill out the "Last Will and Testament" page in the narrow beam of Sergeant Elijah Jones's flashlight. He wrote with his left hand, and Fitz recognized him as Morrison, a former footman at Tŷ Gwyn and left-handed bowler in the cricket team.

Dawn came early—midsummer was only a few days past. With the light, some men took out photographs and stared at them or kissed them. It seemed sentimental, and

Fitz hesitated to copy the men, but after a while he did. His picture showed his son, George, whom they called Boy. He was now eighteen months old, but the photo had been taken on his first birthday. Bea must have taken him to a photographer's studio, for behind him there was a backdrop, in poor taste, of a flowery glade. He did not look much of a boy, dressed as he was in a white frock of some kind and a bonnet; but he was whole and healthy, and he was there to inherit the earldom if Fitz died today.

Bea and Boy would be in London now, Fitz assumed. It was July, and the social season went on, albeit in a lower key: girls had to make their debuts, for how else would they meet suitable husbands?

The light strengthened; then the sun appeared. The steel helmets of the Aberowen Pals shone, and their bayonets flashed reflections of the new day. Most of them had never been in battle. What a baptism they would have, win or lose.

A mammoth British artillery barrage began with the light. The gunners were giving their all. Perhaps this last effort would finally destroy the German positions. That must be what General Haig was praying for.

The Aberowen Pals were not in the first wave, but Fitz went forward to look at the battlefield, leaving the lieutenants in charge of B Company. He pushed through the crowds of waiting men to the frontline trench, where he stood on the fire step and looked through a peephole in the sandbagged parapet.

A morning mist was dispersing, chased by the rays of the rising sun. The blue sky was blotched by the dark smoke of exploding shells. It was going to be fine, Fitz saw, a beautiful French summer day. "Good weather for killing Germans," he said to no one in particular.

He remained at the front as zero hour approached. He wanted to see what happened to the first wave. There might be lessons to be learned. Although he had been an officer in France for almost two years, this would be the first time he commanded men in battle, and he was more nervous about that than about getting killed.

A ration of rum was given out to each man. Fitz drank some. Despite the warmth of the spirit in his stomach, he felt himself becoming more tense. Zero hour was seven thirty. When seven o'clock passed, the men grew still.

At seven twenty the British guns fell silent.

"No!" Fitz said aloud. "Not yet—this is too soon!" No one was listening, of course. But he was aghast. This would tell the Germans that an attack was imminent. They would now be piling out of their dugouts, hauling up their machine guns, and taking their positions. Our gunners had given the enemy a clear ten minutes to prepare! They should have kept up the fire until the last possible moment, seven twenty-nine and fifty-nine seconds.

But nothing could be done about it now.

Fitz wondered grimly how many men would die just because of that blunder.

Sergeants barked commands, and the men around Fitz climbed the scaling ladders and scrambled over the parapet. They formed up on the near side of the British wire. They were about a quarter of a mile from the German line, but no one fired at them yet. To Fitz's surprise the sergeants barked: "Dressing by numbers, right dress—one!" The men began to dress off as if on the parade ground, carefully adjusting the distances between them until they were ranged as perfectly as skittles in a bowling alley. To Fitz's mind this was madness—it just gave the Germans more time to get ready.

At seven thirty a whistle blew, all the signalers dropped their flags, and the first line moved forward.

They did not sprint, being weighed down by their equipment: extra ammunition, a waterproof sheet, food and water, and two Mills bombs per man, hand grenades weighing almost two pounds each. They moved at a jog, splashing through the shell holes, and passed through the gaps in the British wire. As instructed, they re-formed into lines and went on, shoulder-to-shoulder, across no-man's-land.

When they were halfway, the German machine guns opened up.

Fitz saw men begin to fall a second before his ears picked up the familiar rattling sound. One went down, then a dozen, then twenty, then more. "Oh, my God," Fitz said as they fell, fifty of them, a hundred more. He stared aghast at the slaughter. Some men threw up their hands when hit; others screamed, or convulsed; others just went limp and fell to the ground like dropped kit bags.

This was worse than the pessimistic Gwyn Evans had predicted, worse than Fitz's most terrible fears.

Before they reached the German wire, most of them had fallen.

Another whistle blew, and the second line advanced.

{ III }

Private Robin Mortimer was angry. "This is fucking stupid," he said when they heard the crackle of machine guns. "We should have gone over in the dark. You can't cross no-man's-land in broad fucking daylight. They're not even laying down a smoke screen. It's fucking suicide."

The men in the assembly trench were unnerved. Billy was worried by the fall in morale among the Aberowen Pals. On the march from their billet to the front line, they had experienced their first artillery attack. They had not suffered a direct hit, but groups ahead and behind had been massacred. Almost as bad, they had marched past a series of newly dug pits, all exactly six feet deep, and had worked out that these were mass graves, ready to receive the day's dead.

"The wind is wrong for a smoke screen," said Prophet Jones mildly. "That's why they're not using gas, either."

"Fucking insane," Mortimer muttered.

George Barrow said cheerfully: "The higher-ups know best. They been bred to rule. Leave it to them, I say."

Tommy Griffiths could not let that pass. "How can you believe that, when they sent you to Borstal?"

"They got to put people like me in jail," George said stoutly. "Otherwise everyone would be thieving. I might get robbed myself!"

Everyone laughed, except the morose Mortimer.

Major Fitzherbert reappeared, looking grim, carrying a jug of rum. The lieutenant gave them all a ration, pouring it into the mess tins they held out. Billy drank his without enjoyment. The fiery spirit cheered the men up, but not for long.

The only time Billy had felt like this was on his first day down the mine, when Rhys Price had left him alone and his lamp had gone out. A vision had helped him then. Unfortunately, Jesus appeared to boys with fevered imaginations, not sober, literal-minded men. Billy was on his own today.

The supreme test was almost on him, perhaps minutes

away. Would he keep his nerve? If he failed—if he curled up in a ball on the ground and closed his eyes, or broke down in tears, or ran away—he would feel ashamed for the rest of his life. I'd rather die, he thought, but will I feel that way when the shooting starts?

They all moved a few steps forward.

He took out his wallet. Mildred had given him a photo of herself. She was dressed in a coat and hat: he would have preferred to remember her the way she had been the evening he went to her bedroom.

He wondered what she was doing now. Today was Saturday, so presumably she would be at Mannie Litov's, sewing uniforms. It was midmorning, and the women would be stopping for a break about now. Mildred might tell them all a funny story.

He thought about her all the time. Their night together had been an extension of the kissing lesson. She had stopped him going at things like a bull at a gate, and had taught him slower, more playful ways, caresses that had been exquisitely pleasurable, more so than he could have imagined. She had kissed his peter, and then asked him to do the equivalent to her. Even better, she had shown him how to do it so that it made her cry out in ecstasy. At the end, she had produced a condom from her bedside drawer. He had never seen one, though the boys talked about them, calling them rubber johnnies. She had put it on him, and even that had been thrilling.

It seemed like a daydream, and he had to keep reminding himself that it had really happened. Nothing in his upbringing had prepared him for Mildred's carefree, eager attitude to sex, and it had come to him like a revelation. His parents and most people in Aberowen would call her "unsuitable," with two children and no sign of a husband; but Billy would not have minded if she had six children. She had opened the gates of paradise to him, and all he wanted to do was go there again. More than anything else, he wanted to survive today so that he could see Mildred again and spend another night with her.

As the Pals shuffled forward, slowly getting nearer to the frontline trench, Billy found he was sweating.

Owen Bevin began to cry. Billy said gruffly: "Pull yourself together, now, Private Bevin. No good crying, is it?"

The boy said: "I want to go home."

"So do I, boyo. So do I."

"Please, Corporal, I didn't think it would be like this."

"How old are you anyway?"

"Sixteen."

"Bloody hell," said Billy. "How did you get recruited?"

"I told the doctor how old I was, and he said: 'Go away, and come back in the morning. You're tall for your age—you might be eighteen by tomorrow.' And he gave me a wink, see, so I knew I had to lie."

"Bastard," said Billy. He looked at Owen. The boy was not going to be any use on the battlefield. He was shaking and sobbing.

Billy spoke to Lieutenant Carlton-Smith. "Sir, Bevin is only sixteen, sir."

"Good God," said the lieutenant.

"He should be sent back. He'll be a liability."

"I don't know about that." Carlton-Smith looked baffled and helpless.

Billy recalled how Prophet Jones had tried to make an ally of Mortimer. Prophet was a good leader, thinking ahead and acting to prevent problems. Carlton-Smith, by contrast, seemed to be of no account, yet he was the superior officer. That's why it's called the class system, Da would have said.

After a minute, Carlton-Smith went to Fitzherbert and said something in a low voice. The major shook his head in negation, and Carlton-Smith shrugged helplessly.

Billy had not been brought up to look on cruelty without a protest. "The boy is only sixteen, sir!"

"Too late to say that now," said Fitzherbert. "And don't speak until you're spoken to, Corporal."

Billy knew that Fitzherbert did not recognize him. Billy was just one of hundreds of men who worked in the earl's pits. Fitzherbert did not know he was Ethel's brother. All the same, the casual dismissal angered Billy. "It's against the law," he said stubbornly. In other circumstances Fitzherbert would have been the first person to pontificate about respect for the law.

"I'll be the judge of that," said Fitz irritably. "That's why I'm the officer."

Billy's blood began to boil. Fitzherbert and Carlton-

Smith stood there in their tailored uniforms, glaring at Billy in his itchy khaki, thinking that they could do anything. "The law is the law," Billy said.

Prophet spoke quietly. "I see you've forgotten your stick this morning, Major Fitzherbert. Shall I send Bevin back to headquarters to get it for you?"

It was a face-saving compromise, Billy thought. Well done, Prophet.

But Fitzherbert was not buying it. "Don't be ridiculous," he said.

Suddenly Bevin darted away. He slipped into the crowd of men behind and disappeared from sight in a moment. It was so surprising that some of the men laughed.

"He won't get far," said Fitzherbert. "And when they catch him, it won't be very funny."

"He's a child!"

Fitzherbert fixed him with a look. "What's your name?" he said.

"Williams, sir."

Fitzherbert looked startled, but recovered fast. "There are hundreds of Williamses," he said. "What's your first name?"

"William, sir. They call me Billy Twice."

Fitzherbert gave him a hard stare.

He knows, Billy thought. He knows Ethel has a brother called Billy Williams. He stared straight back.

Fitzherbert said: "One more word out of you, Private William Williams, and you'll be on a charge."

There was a whistling sound above. Billy ducked. From behind him came a deafening bang. A hurricane blew all around him: clods of earth and fragments of planking flew past. He heard screams. Abruptly he found himself flat on the ground, not sure whether he had been knocked over or had thrown himself down. Something heavy hit his head, and he cursed. Then a boot thumped to the ground beside his face. There was a leg attached to the boot, but nothing else. "Oh, Christ," he said.

He got to his feet. He was uninjured. He looked around at the members of his section: Tommy, George Barrow, Mortimer . . . they were all standing up. Everyone pushed forward, suddenly seeing the front line as an escape route.

Major Fitzherbert shouted: "Hold your positions, men!"

Prophet Jones said: "As you were, as you were."

The surge forward was halted. Billy tried to brush mud off his uniform. Then another shell landed behind them. If anything, this one was farther back, but that made little difference. There was a bang, a hurricane, and a rain of debris and body parts. The men started scrambling out of the assembly trench at the front and to either side. Billy and his section joined in. Fitzherbert, Carlton-Smith, and Roland Morgan were screaming at the men to stay where they were, but no one was listening.

They ran forward, trying to get a safe distance from where the shells were landing. As they approached the British barbed wire, they slowed down, and stopped at the near edge of no-man's-land, realizing that ahead was a danger as great as the one from which they were fleeing.

Making the best of it, the officers joined them. "Form a line!" shouted Fitzherbert.

Billy looked at Prophet. The sergeant hesitated, then went along with it. "Line up, line up!" he called.

"Look at that," Tommy said to Billy.

"What?"

"Beyond the wire."

Billy looked.

"The bodies," Tommy said.

Billy saw what he meant. The ground was littered with corpses in khaki, some of them horribly mangled, some lying peacefully as if asleep, some intertwined like lovers.

There were thousands of them.

"Jesus help us," Billy whispered.

He felt sickened. What kind of world was this? What could be God's purpose in letting this happen?

A Company lined up, and Billy and the rest of B Company shuffled into place behind them.

Billy's horror turned to anger. Earl Fitzherbert and his like had planned this. They were in charge, and they were to blame for this slaughter. They should be shot, he thought furiously, every bloody one of them.

Lieutenant Morgan blew a whistle, and A Company ran on like rugby forwards. Carlton-Smith blew his whistle, and Billy set off at a jog.

Then the German machine guns opened up.

The men of A Company started to fall, and Morgan was

the first. They had not fired their weapons. This was not battle; it was massacre. Billy looked at the men around him. He felt defiant. The officers had failed. The men had to make their own decisions. To hell with orders. "Sod this," he shouted. "Take cover!" And he threw himself into a shell hole.

The sides were muddy and there was stinking water at the bottom, but he pressed himself gratefully to the clammy earth as the bullets flew over his head. A moment later Tommy landed by his side, then the rest of the section. Men from other sections copied Billy's.

Fitzherbert ran past their hole. "Keep moving, you men!" he shouted.

Billy said: "If he insists, I'm going to shoot the bastard."

Then Fitzherbert was hit by machine-gun fire. Blood spurted from his cheek, and one leg crumpled beneath him. He fell to the ground.

Officers were in as much danger as men. Billy was no longer angry. Instead he felt ashamed of the British army. How could it be so completely useless? After all the effort that had been put in, the money they had spent, the months of planning—the big assault was a fiasco. It was humiliating.

Billy looked around. Fitz lay still, unconscious. Neither Lieutenant Carlton-Smith nor Sergeant Jones was in sight. The other men in the section were looking at Billy. He was only a corporal, but they expected him to tell them what to do.

He turned to Mortimer, who had once been an officer. "What do you think—"

"Don't look at me, Taffy," said Mortimer sourly. "You're the fucking corporal."

Billy had to come up with a plan.

He was not going to lead them back. He hardly considered that option. It would be a waste of the lives of the men who had already died. We must gain something from all this, he thought; we must give some kind of account of ourselves.

On the other hand, he was not going to run into machine-gun fire.

The first thing he needed to do was survey the scene.

He took off his steel helmet, held it at arm's length, and raised it over the lip of the crater as a decoy, just in case a German had his sights on this hole. But nothing happened.

He raised his head over the edge, expecting at any moment to be shot through the skull. He survived that, too.

He looked across the divide and up the hill, over the German barbed wire to their front line, dug into the hillside. He could see rifle barrels poking through gaps in the parapet. "Where's that fucking machine gun?" he said to Tommy.

"Not sure."

C Company ran past. Some took cover, but others held the line. The machine gun opened up again, raking the line, and the men fell like skittles. Billy was no longer shocked. He was searching for the source of the bullets.

"Got it," said Tommy.

"Where?"

"Take a straight line from here to that clump of bushes at the top of the hill."

"Right."

"See where that line crosses the German trench?"

"Aye."

"Then go a bit to your right."

"How far . . . Never mind. I see the bastards." Ahead and a little to Billy's right, something that might have been a protective iron shield stuck up above the parapet, and the distinctive barrel of a machine gun protruded over it. Billy thought he could make out three German helmets around it, but it was hard to be sure.

They must be concentrating on the gap in the British wire, Billy thought. They repeatedly fired on men as they surged forward from that point. The way to attack them might be from a different angle. If his section could work its way diagonally across no-man's-land, they could come at the gun from the Germans' left, while the Germans were looking right.

He plotted a route using three large craters, the third just beyond a flattened section of German wire.

He had no idea whether this was correct military strategy. But correct strategy had got thousands of men killed this morning, so to hell with that.

He ducked down again and looked at the men around him. George Barrow was a steady shot with the rifle despite his youth. "Next time that machine gun opens up, get ready to fire. As soon as it stops, you start. With a bit of luck, they'll take cover. I'll be running to that shell hole over by there. Shoot steady and empty your magazine. You've got ten shots—make them last half a minute. By the time the Germans raise their heads, I should be in the next hole." He looked at the others. "Wait for another pause. Then all of you run while Tommy covers you. Third time, I'll cover and Tommy can run."

D Company ran into no-man's-land. The machine gun opened up. Rifles and trench mortars fired at the same time. But the carnage was less because more men were taking cover in shell holes instead of running into the hail of bullets.

Any minute now, Billy thought. He had told the men what he was going to do, and it would be too shameful to back out. He gritted his teeth. Better to die than be a coward, he told himself again.

The machine-gun fire ceased.

In an instant Billy leaped to his feet. Now he was a clear target. He bent over and ran.

Behind him he heard Barrow shooting. His life was in the hands of a seventeen-year-old Borstal boy. George fired steadily: bang, two, three, bang, two, three, just as ordered.

Billy charged across the field as fast as he could, loaded down as he was with kit. His boots stuck in the mud, his breath came in ragged gasps, his chest hurt, but his mind was empty of all thought except the desire to go faster. He was as close to death as he had ever been.

When he was a couple of yards from the shell hole, he threw his gun into it and dived as if tackling a rugby opponent. He landed on the rim of the crater and tumbled forward into the mud. He could hardly believe he was still alive.

He heard a ragged cheer. His section was applauding his run. He was amazed they could be so upbeat amid such carnage. How strange men were.

When he had caught his breath, he cautiously looked over the rim. He had run about a hundred yards. It was going to take some time to cross no-man's-land this way. But the alternative was suicide.

The machine gun opened up again. When it stopped, Tommy started shooting. He followed George's example and paused between shots. How fast we learn when our lives are in danger, Billy thought. As the tenth and last bullet in Tommy's magazine was fired, the rest of the section fell into the pit beside Billy.

"Come this side," he shouted, beckoning them forward. The German position was uphill from here, and Billy feared the enemy might be able to see into the back half of the crater.

He rested his rifle on the rim and sighted at the machine gun. After a while the Germans opened up again. When they stopped, Billy fired. He willed Tommy to run fast. He cared more about Tommy than the rest of the section put together. He held his rifle steady and fired at intervals of about five seconds. It did not matter whether he hit anyone, as long as he forced the Germans to keep their heads down while Tommy ran.

His rifle clicked on empty, and Tommy landed beside him.

"Bloody hell," said Tommy. "How many times have we got to do that?"

"Two more, I reckon," Billy said, reloading. "Then we'll either be close enough to throw a Mills bomb . . . or we'll all be fucking dead."

"Don't swear, now, Billy, please," said Tommy straight-faced. "You know I finds it distasteful."

Billy chuckled. Then he wondered how he could. I'm in a shell hole with the German army shooting at me and I'm laughing, he thought. God help me.

They moved in the same way to the next shell hole, but it was farther off, and this time they lost a man. Joey Ponti was hit in the head while running. George Barrow picked him up and carried him, but he was dead, a bloody hole in his skull. Billy wondered where his kid brother, Johnny, was: he had not seen him since leaving the assembly trench. I'll have to be the one to tell him the news, Billy thought. Johnny worshipped his big brother.

There were other dead men in this hole. Three khaki-clad bodies floated in the scummy water. They must have been among the first to go over the top. Billy wondered how they had got this far. Perhaps it was just the odds. The guns were bound to miss a few in the first sweep, and mop them up on the return.

Other groups were coming closer to the German line

now by following similar tactics. Either they were copying Billy's group or, more likely, they had gone through the same thought process, abandoning the foolish line charge ordered by the officers and devising their own more sensible tactics. The upshot was that the Germans no longer had things all their own way. Under fire themselves, they were not able to keep up the same relentless storm of gunfire. Perhaps for that reason, Billy's group made it to the last shell hole without further losses.

In fact they gained a man. A total stranger lay down next to Billy. "Where the fuck did you come from?" Billy said.

"I lost my group," the man said. "You seem to know what you're doing, so I followed you. I sure hope you don't mind."

He spoke with an accent Billy guessed might be Canadian. "Are you a good thrower?" Billy asked.

"Played for my high school baseball team."

"Right. When I give the word, see if you can hit that machine-gun emplacement with a Mills bomb."

Billy told Spotty Llewellyn and Alun Pritchard to throw their grenades while the rest of the section gave covering fire. Once again, they waited until the machine gun stopped. "Now!" Billy yelled, and he stood up.

There was a small flurry of rifle fire from the German trench. Spotty and Alun, spooked by the bullets, threw wildly. Neither bomb reached the trench, which was fifty yards away; they fell short and exploded harmlessly. Billy cursed: they had simply left the machine gun undamaged and, sure enough, it opened up again and, a moment later, Spotty convulsed horribly as a hail of bullets tore into his body.

Billy felt strangely calm. He took a second to focus on his target and draw his arm all the way back. He calculated the distance as if he were throwing a rugby ball. He was dimly aware that the Canadian, standing next to him, was equally cool. The machine gun rattled and spat and swung toward them.

They threw at the same time.

Both bombs went into the trench close to the emplacement. There was a double whump. Billy saw the barrel of the machine gun fly through the air, and he yelled in triumph. He pulled the pin from his second grenade and dashed up the slope, screaming: "Charge!"

Exhilaration ran in his veins like a drug. He hardly knew he was in danger. He had no idea how many Germans might be in that trench pointing their rifles at him. The others followed him. He threw his second grenade, and they copied him. Some flew wild, others landed in the trench and exploded.

Billy reached the trench. At that point he realized that his rifle was slung over his shoulder. By the time he could move it to the firing position, a German could shoot him dead.

But there were no Germans left alive.

The grenades had done terrible damage. The floor of the trench was littered with dead bodies and—worse to look at—parts of bodies. If any Germans had survived the onslaught, they had retreated. Billy jumped down into the trench and at last got his rifle in both hands in the ready stance. But he did not need it. There was no one left to shoot at.

Tommy leaped down beside him. "We done it!" he shouted ecstatically. "We took a German trench!"

Billy felt a savage glee. They had tried to kill him, but instead he had killed them. It was a feeling of profound satisfaction, like nothing he had known before. "You're right," he said to Tommy. "We done it."

Billy was struck by the quality of the German fortifications. He had a miner's eye for a secure structure. The walls were braced with planks, the traverses were square, and the dugouts were surprisingly deep, twenty and sometimes thirty feet down, with neatly framed doorways and wooden steps. That explained how so many Germans had survived seven days of relentless shelling.

The Germans presumably dug their trenches in networks, with communications trenches linking the front to storage and service areas in the rear. Billy needed to make sure there were no enemy troops waiting in ambush. He led the others on an exploratory patrol, rifles at the ready, but they found no one.

The network ended at the top of the hill. From there Billy looked around. Left of their position, beyond an area of heavy shell damage, other British troops had taken the next sector; to their right, the trench ended and the ground fell away into a little valley with a stream.

He looked east into enemy territory. He knew that a mile or two away was another trench system, the Germans' second line of defense. He was ready to lead his little group forward, but he hesitated. He could not see any other British troops advancing, and he guessed that his men had used up most of their ammunition. At any moment, he presumed, supply trucks would come bumping across the shell holes with more ammunition and orders for the next phase.

He looked up at the sky. It was midday. The men had not eaten since last night. "Let's see if the Germans left any food behind," he said. He stationed Suet Hewitt at the top of the hill as a lookout in case the Germans counterattacked.

There was not much to forage. It seemed the Germans were not very well-fed. They found stale black bread and hard salami-style sausage. There was not even any beer. The Germans were supposed to be famous for their beer.

The brigadier had promised that field kitchens would follow the advancing troops, but when Billy looked impatiently back over no-man's-land, he saw no sign of supplies.

They settled down to eat their rations of hard biscuits and bully beef.

He should send someone back to report. But before he could do so, the German artillery changed its aim. They had begun by shelling the British rear. Now they focused on no-man's-land. Volcanoes of earth were erupting between the British and German lines. The bombardment was so intense that no one could have got back alive.

Luckily, the gunners were avoiding their own front line. Presumably they did not know which sectors had been taken by the British and which remained in German hands.

Billy's group was stuck. They could not advance without ammunition, and they could not retreat because of the bombardment. But Billy seemed to be the only one worried by their position. The others started looking for souvenirs. They picked up pointed helmets, cap badges, and pocketknives. George Barrow examined all the dead Germans and took their watches and rings. Tommy took an officer's nine-millimeter Luger and a box of ammunition.

They began to feel lethargic. It was not surprising: they had been up all night. Billy posted two lookouts and let the rest of them doze. He felt disappointed. On his first day of battle he had won a little victory, and he wanted to tell someone about it.

In the evening the barrage let up. Billy considered whether to retreat. There seemed no point in doing anything else, but he was afraid of being accused of desertion in the face of the enemy. There was no telling what superior officers might be capable of.

However, the decision was made for him by the Germans. Suet Hewitt, the lookout on the ridge, saw them advancing from the east. Billy saw a large force—fifty or a hundred men—running across the valley toward him. His men could not defend the ground they had taken without fresh ammunition.

On the other hand, if they retreated they might be blamed.

He summoned his handful of men. "Right, boys," he said. "Fire at will. Then retreat when you run out of ammo." He emptied his rifle at the advancing troops, who were still half a mile out of range, then turned and ran. The others did the same.

They scrambled across the German trenches and back over no-man's-land toward the setting sun, jumping over the dead and dodging the stretcher parties who were picking up the wounded. But no one shot at them.

When Billy reached the British side he jumped into a trench that was crowded with dead bodies, wounded men, and exhausted survivors like himself. He saw Major Fitzherbert lying on a stretcher, his face bloody but his eyes open, alive and breathing. There's one I wouldn't have minded losing, he thought. Many men were just sitting or lying in the mud, staring into space, dazed by shock and paralyzed by weariness. The officers were trying to organize the return of men and bodies to the rear sections. There was no sense of triumph. No one was moving forward; the officers were not even looking at the battlefield. The great attack had been a failure.

The remaining men of Billy's section followed him into the trench.

"What a cock-up," Billy said. "What a God-almighty cock-up."

{ IV }

A week later Owen Bevin was court-martialed for cowardice and desertion.

He was given the option of being defended, at the trial, by an officer appointed to act as the "prisoner's friend," but he declined. Because the offense carried the death penalty, a plea of Not Guilty was automatically entered. However, Bevin said nothing in his defense. The trial took less than an hour. Bevin was convicted.

He was sentenced to death.

The papers were passed to general headquarters for review. The commander in chief approved the death sentence. Two weeks later, in a muddy French cow pasture at dawn, Bevin stood blindfolded before a firing squad.

Some of the men must have aimed to miss, because after they fired Bevin was still alive, though bleeding. The officer in charge of the firing squad then approached, drew his pistol, and fired two shots point-blank into the boy's forehead.

Then, at last, Owen Bevin died.

CHAPTER EIGHTEEN

Late July 1916

Ethel thought a lot about life and death after Billy went off to France. She knew she might never see him again. She was glad he had lost his virginity with Mildred. "I let your little brother have his wicked way with me," Mildred had said lightheartedly after he left. "Sweet boy. Have you got any more like that down there in Wales?" But Ethel suspected Mildred's feelings were not as superficial as she pretended, for in their nightly prayers Enid and Lillian now asked God to watch over Uncle Billy in France and bring him safely home again.

Lloyd developed a bad chest infection a few days later, and in an agony of desperation Ethel rocked him in her arms while he struggled to breathe. Fearing he might die, she bitterly regretted that her parents had never seen him. When he got better, she decided to take him to Aberowen.

She returned exactly two years after she had left. It was raining.

The place had not changed much, but it struck her as dismal. For the first twenty-one years of her life she had not seen it that way but now, after living in London, she noticed that Aberowen was all the same color. Everything was gray: the houses, the streets, the slag heaps, and the low rain clouds drifting disconsolately along the ridge of the mountain.

She felt tired as she emerged from the railway station in the middle of the afternoon. Taking a child of eighteen months on an all-day journey was hard work. Lloyd had been well-behaved, charming fellow passengers with his toothy grin. All the same he had to be fed in a rocking carriage, changed in a smelly toilet, and lulled to sleep when he became grizzly, and it was a strain with strangers looking on.

With Lloyd on her hip and a small suitcase in her hand, she set off across the station square and up the slope of Clive Street. Soon she was panting for breath. That was something else she had forgotten. London was mostly flat, but in Aberowen you could hardly go anywhere without walking up or down a steep hill.

She did not know what had happened here since she had left. Billy was her only source of news, and men were no good for gossip. No doubt she herself had been the main topic of conversation for some time. However, new scandals must have come along since.

Her return would be big news. Several women gave her frank stares as she walked up the street with her baby. She knew what they were thinking. Ethel Williams, believed she was better than us, coming back in an old brown dress with a toddler in her arms and no husband. Pride comes before a fall, they would say, their malice thinly disguised as pity.

She went to Wellington Row, but not to her parents' house. Her father had told her never to come back. She had written to Tommy Griffiths's mother, who was called Mrs. Griffiths Socialist on account of her husband's fiery politics. (In the same street there was a Mrs. Griffiths Church.) The Griffithses were not chapelgoers, and they disapproved of Ethel's father's hard line. Ethel had put Tommy up for the night in London, and Mrs. Griffiths was happy to reciprocate. Tommy was an only child, so while he was in the army there was a spare bed.

Da and Mam did not know Ethel was coming.

Mrs. Griffiths welcomed Ethel warmly and cooed over Lloyd. She had had a daughter of Ethel's age who had died of whooping cough—Ethel could just about remember her, a blond girl called Gwenny.

Ethel fed and changed Lloyd, then sat down in the kitchen for a cup of tea. Mrs. Griffiths noticed her wedding ring. "Married, is it?" she said.

"Widow," Ethel said. "He died at Ypres."

"Ah, pity."

"He was a Mr. Williams, so I didn't have to change my name."

This story would go all around the town. Some would question whether there really had been a Mr. Williams and if he had actually married Ethel. It did not matter whether they believed her. A woman who pretended to be married was acceptable; a mother who admitted to being single was a brazen hussy. The people of Aberowen had their principles.

Mrs. Griffiths said: "When are you going to see your mam?"

Ethel did not know how her parents would react to her. They might throw her out again, they might forgive everything, or they might find some way of condemning her sin without banishing her from their sight. "I dunno," she said. "I'm nervous."

Mrs. Griffiths looked sympathetic. "Aye, well, your da can be a Tartar. He loves you, though."

"People always think that. Your father loves you really, they say. But if he can throw me out of the house, I don't know why it's called love."

"People do things in haste, when their pride is hurt," Mrs. Griffiths said soothingly. " 'Specially men."

Ethel stood up. "Well, no point in putting it off, I suppose." She scooped Lloyd up from the floor. "Come here, my lovely. Time you found out you've got grandparents."

"Good luck," said Mrs. Griffiths.

The Williams house was only a few doors away. Ethel was hoping her father would be out. That way she could at least have some time with her mother, who was less harsh.

She thought of knocking at the door, then decided that would be ridiculous, so she walked straight in.

She entered the kitchen where she had spent so many of her days. Neither of her parents was there, but Gramper was dozing in his chair. He opened his eyes, looked puzzled, then said warmly: "It's our Eth!"

"Hello, Gramper."

He stood up and came to her. He had become more frail: he leaned on the table just to cross the little room. He kissed her cheek and turned his attention to the baby. "Well, now, who is this?" he said with delight. "Could it be my first great-grandchild?"

"This is Lloyd," said Ethel.

"What a fine name!"

Lloyd hid his face in Ethel's shoulder. "He's shy," she said.

"Ah, he's scared of the strange old man with the white mustache. He'll get used to me. Sit down, my lovely, and tell me all about everything."

"Where's our mam?"

"Gone down the Co-op for a tin of jam." The local grocery was a cooperative store, sharing profits among its customers. Such shops were popular in South Wales, although no one knew how to pronounce *co-op*, variations ranging from *cop* to *quorp*. "She'll be back now in a minute."

Ethel put Lloyd on the floor. He began to explore the room, going unsteadily from one handhold to the next, a bit like Gramper. Ethel talked about her job as manager of *The Soldier's Wife*: working with the printer, distributing the bundles of newspapers, collecting unsold copies, getting people to place advertisements. Gramper wondered how she knew what to do, and she admitted that she and Maud just made it up as they went along. She found the printer difficult—he did not like taking instructions from women—but she was good at selling advertising space. While they talked, Gramper took off his watch chain and dangled it from his hand, not looking at Lloyd. The child stared at the bright chain, then reached for it. Gramper let him grab it. Soon Lloyd was leaning on Gramper's knees for support while he investigated the watch.

Ethel felt strange in the old house. She had imagined it would be comfortably familiar, like a pair of boots that have taken the shape of the feet that have worn them for years. But in fact she was vaguely uneasy. It seemed more like the home of familiar old neighbors. She kept looking at the faded samplers with their tired biblical verses and wondering why her mother had not changed them in decades. She did not feel that this was her place.

"Have you heard anything from our Billy?" she asked Gramper.

"No, have you?"

"Not since he left for France."

"I should think he's in this big battle by the river Somme."

"I hope not. They say it's bad."

"Aye, terrible, if you believe the rumors."

Rumors were all people had, for newspaper accounts were cheerfully vague. But many of the wounded were back in British hospitals, and their bloodcurdling accounts of incompetence and slaughter were passed from mouth to mouth.

Mam came in. "They stand talking in that shop as if they got nothing else to do— Oh!" She stopped short. "Oh, my heavens, is that our Eth?" She burst into tears.

Ethel hugged her.

Gramper said: "Look, Cara, here's your grandson, Lloyd."

Mam wiped her eyes and picked him up. "Isn't he beautiful?" she said. "Such curly hair! He looks just like Billy at that age." Lloyd stared fearfully at Mam for a long moment, then cried.

Ethel took him. "He's turned into a real mummy's boy lately," she said apologetically.

"They all do at that age," Mam said. "Make the most of it—he'll soon change."

"Where's Da?" Ethel said, trying not to sound too anxious.

Mam looked tense. "Gone to Caerphilly for a union meeting." She checked the clock. "He'll be home for his tea now in a minute, unless he's missed his train."

Ethel guessed Mam was hoping he would be late. She felt the same. She wanted more time with her mother before the crisis came.

Mam made tea and put a plate of sugary Welsh cakes on the table. Ethel took one. "I haven't had these for two years," she said. "They're lovely."

Gramper said happily: "Now, I call this nice. I got my daughter, my granddaughter, and my great-grandson, all in the same room. What more could a man ask of life?" He took a Welsh cake.

Ethel reflected that some people would think it was not much of a life Gramper led, sitting in a smoky kitchen all day in his only suit. But he was grateful for his lot, and she had made him happy today, at least.

Then her father came in.

Mam was halfway through a sentence. "I had a chance to

go to London once, when I was your age, but your gramper said—" The door opened and she stopped dead. They all looked as Da came in from the street, wearing his meeting suit and a flat miner's cap, perspiring from the walk up the hill. He took a step into the room, then stopped, staring.

"Look who's here," Mam said with forced brightness. "Ethel, and your grandson." Her face was white with strain.

He said nothing. He did not take off his cap.

Ethel said: "Hello, Da. This is Lloyd."

He did not look at her.

Gramper said: "The little one resembles you, Dai boy— around the mouth, see what I mean?"

Lloyd sensed the hostility in the room and began to cry.

Still Da said nothing. Ethel knew then that she had made a mistake springing this on him. She had not wanted to give him the chance to forbid her to come. But now she saw that the surprise had put him on the defensive. He had a cornered look. It was always a mistake to back Da up against the wall, she remembered.

His face became stubborn. He looked at his wife and said: "I have no grandson."

"Oh, now," said Mam appealingly.

His expression remained rigid. He stood still, staring at Mam, not speaking. He was waiting for something, and he would not move until Ethel left. She began to cry.

Gramper said: "Oh, dammo."

Ethel picked up Lloyd. "I'm sorry, Mam," she sobbed. "I thought perhaps . . ." She choked up and could not finish the sentence. With Lloyd in her arms she pushed past her father. He did not meet her eye.

Ethel went out and slammed the door.

{ II }

In the morning, after the men had gone to work down the pit and the children had been sent to school, the women usually did jobs outside. They washed the pavement, polished the doorstep, or cleaned the windows. Some went to the shop or ran other errands. They needed to see the world beyond their small houses, Ethel thought, something to remind them that life was not bound within four jerry-built walls.

She stood in the sunshine outside the front door of Mrs. Griffiths Socialist, leaning against the wall. All up and down the street, women had found reasons to be out in the sun. Lloyd was playing with a ball. He had seen other children throw balls and he was trying to do the same, but failing. What a complicated action a throw was, Ethel reflected, using shoulder and arm, wrist and hand together. The fingers had to relax their grip just before the arm reached its longest stretch. Lloyd had not mastered this, and he released the ball too soon, sometimes dropping it behind his shoulder, or too late, so that it had no momentum. But he kept trying. He would get it right, eventually, Ethel supposed, and then he would never forget it. Until you had a child, you did not understand how much they had to learn.

She could not comprehend how her father could reject this little boy. Lloyd had done nothing wrong. Ethel herself was a sinner, but so were most people. God forgave their sins, so who was Da to sit in judgment? It made her angry and sad at the same time.

The boy from the post office came up the street on his pony and tied it up near the toilets. His name was Geraint Jones. His job was to bring parcels and telegrams, but today he did not appear to be carrying any packages. Ethel felt a sudden chill, as if a cloud had hidden the sun. In Wellington Row telegrams were rare, and they usually brought bad news.

Geraint walked down the hill, away from Ethel. She felt relieved: the news was not for her family.

Her mind drifted to a letter she had received from Lady Maud. Ethel and Maud and other women had mounted a campaign to ensure that votes for women would be part of any discussion of franchise reform for soldiers. They had got enough publicity to ensure that Prime Minister Asquith could not duck the issue.

Maud's news was that he had sidestepped their thrust by handing the whole problem over to a committee called the Speaker's Conference. But this was good, Maud said. There would be a calm private debate instead of histrionic speeches in the chamber of the House of Commons. Perhaps common sense would prevail. All the same she was trying hard to find out whom Asquith was putting on the committee.

A few doors up, Gramper emerged from the Williams house, sat on the low windowsill, and lit his first pipe of the day. He spotted Ethel, smiled, and waved.

On the other side Minnie Ponti, the mother of Joey and Johnny, started beating a rug with a stick, knocking the dust out of it and making herself cough.

Mrs. Griffiths came out with a shovelful of ashes from the kitchen range and dropped them in a pothole in the dirt road.

Ethel said to her: "Can I do anything? I could go to the Co-op for you if you like." She had already made the beds and washed the breakfast dishes.

"All right," said Mrs. Griffiths. "I'll make you a list now in a minute." She leaned on the wall, panting. She was a heavy woman, and any exertion made her breathless.

Ethel became aware of a commotion at the bottom end of the street. Several voices were raised. Then she heard a scream.

She and Mrs. Griffiths looked at each other. Then Ethel picked up Lloyd and they hurried to find out what was happening on the far side of the toilets.

The first thing Ethel saw was a small group of women clustered around Mrs. Pritchard, who was wailing at the top of her voice. The other women were trying to calm her. But she was not the only one. Stumpy Pugh, an ex-miner who had lost a leg in a roof collapse, sat in the middle of the road as if knocked down, with two neighbors either side of him. Across the street Mrs. John Jones the Shop stood in her doorway sobbing, holding a sheet of paper.

Ethel saw Geraint the post office boy, white in the face and near to tears himself, cross the road and knock at another house.

Mrs. Griffiths said: "Telegrams from the War Office— Oh, God help us."

"The battle of the Somme," said Ethel. "The Aberowen Pals must be in it."

"Alun Pritchard must be dead, and Clive Pugh, and Prophet Jones. He was a sergeant. His parents were so proud . . ."

"Poor Mrs. Jones Shop—her other son died in the explosion down the pit."

"Let my Tommy be all right, please, God," Mrs. Griffiths

prayed, even though her husband was a notorious atheist. "Oh, spare Tommy."

"And Billy," said Ethel; and then, whispering in Lloyd's tiny ear, she added: "And your daddy."

Geraint had a canvas sack slung across his shoulder. Ethel wondered fearfully how many more telegrams were in it. The boy crisscrossed the street, the angel of death in a post office cap.

By the time he passed the toilets and came to the upper half of the street, everyone was on the pavement. The women had stopped whatever work they were doing and stood waiting. Ethel's parents had come out—Da had not yet gone to work. They stood with Gramper, silent and afraid.

Geraint approached Mrs. Llewellyn. Her son Arthur must be dead. He was known as Spotty, Ethel recalled. The poor boy did not need to worry about his complexion now.

Mrs. Llewellyn held up her hands as if to ward Geraint off. "No!" she cried. "No, please!"

He held out her telegram. "I can't help it, Mrs. Llewellyn," he said. He was only about seventeen. "It's got your address on the front, see?"

Still she would not take the envelope. "No!" she said, turning her back and burying her face in her hands.

The boy's lip trembled. "Please take it," he said. "I got all these others to do. And there's more in the office, hundreds! It's ten o'clock now and I don't know how I'm going to get them all done before tonight. Please."

Her next-door neighbor, Mrs. Parry Price, said: "I'll take it for her. I haven't got any sons."

"Thank you very much, Mrs. Price," said Geraint, and he moved on.

He took another telegram from his sack, looked at the address, and walked past the Griffithses' house. "Oh, thank God," said Mrs. Griffiths. "My Tommy's all right, thank God." She began to cry with relief. Ethel switched Lloyd to her other hip and put an arm around her.

The boy approached Minnie Ponti. She did not scream, but tears ran down her face. "Which one?" she said in a cracked voice. "Joey or Johnny?"

"I dunno, Mrs. Ponti," said Geraint. "You'll have to read what it says by here."

She ripped open the envelope. "I can't see!" she cried.

She rubbed her eyes, trying to clear her vision of tears, and looked again. "Giuseppe!" she said. "My Joey's dead. Oh, my poor little boy!"

Mrs. Ponti lived almost at the end of the street. Ethel waited, heart pounding, to see whether Geraint would go to the Williams house. Was Billy alive or dead?

The boy turned away from the weeping Mrs. Ponti. He looked across the street and saw Da, Mam, and Gramper staring at him in dreadful anticipation. He looked in his sack, then glanced up.

"No more for Wellington Row," he said.

Ethel almost collapsed. Billy was alive.

She looked at her parents. Mam was crying. Gramper was trying to light his pipe, but his hands were shaking.

Da was staring at her. She could not read the look on his face. He was in the grip of some emotion, but she could not tell what.

He took a step toward her.

It was not much, but it was enough. With Lloyd in her arms, she ran to Da.

He put his arms around both of them. "Billy's alive," he said. "And so are you."

"Oh, Da," she said. "I'm so sorry I let you down."

"Never mind that," he said. "Never mind, now." He patted her back as he had when she was a little girl and she fell down and scraped her knees. "There, there," he said. "Better now."

{ III }

An interdenominational service was a rare event among Aberowen's Christians, Ethel knew. To the Welsh, doctrinal differences were never minor. One group refused to celebrate Christmas, on the grounds that there was no biblical evidence of the date of Christ's birth. Another banned voting in elections, because the Apostle Paul wrote: "Our citizenship is in heaven." None of them liked to worship side by side with people who disagreed with them.

However, after Telegram Wednesday such differences came, briefly, to seem trivial.

The rector of Aberowen, the Reverend Thomas Ellis-

Thomas, suggested a joint service of remembrance. When all the telegrams had been delivered there were two hundred and eleven dead and, as the battle was still going on, one or two more sad notifications arrived each day. Every street in town had lost someone, and in the close-packed rows of miners' hovels there was a bereavement every few yards.

The Methodists, the Baptists, and the Catholics agreed to the suggestion of the Anglican rector. The smaller groups might have preferred to remain aloof: the Full Gospel Baptists, the Jehovah's Witnesses, the Second Coming Evangelicals, and the Bethesda Chapel. Ethel saw her father wrestle with his conscience. But no one wanted to be left out of what promised to be the largest religious service in the town's history, and in the end they all joined in. There was no synagogue in Aberowen, but young Jonathan Goldman was among the dead, and the town's handful of practising Jews decided to attend, even though no concessions would be made to their religion.

The service was held on Sunday afternoon at half past two in a municipal park known as the Reck, short for Recreation Ground. A temporary platform was built by the town council for the clergy to stand on. It was a fine, sunny day, and three thousand people turned up.

Ethel scanned the crowd. Perceval Jones was there in a top hat. As well as being mayor of the town he was now its member of Parliament. He was also honorary commanding officer of the Aberowen Pals, and had led the recruiting drive. Several other directors of Celtic Minerals were with him—as if they had anything to do with the heroism of the dead, Ethel thought sourly. Maldwyn "Gone to Merthyr" Morgan showed up, with his wife, but they had a right, she thought, for their son Roland had died.

Then she saw Fitz.

At first she did not recognize him. She saw Princess Bea, in a black dress and hat, followed by a nurse carrying the young Viscount Aberowen, a boy the same age as Lloyd. With Bea was a man on crutches with his left leg in plaster and a bandage over one side of his head, covering his left eye. After a long moment Ethel realized it was Fitz, and she cried out in shock.

"What is it?" said her mam.

"Look at the earl!"

"Is that him? Oh, my word, the poor man."

Ethel stared at him. She was not in love with him anymore—he had been too cruel. But she could not be indifferent. She had kissed the face under that bandage, and caressed the long, strong body that was so woefully maimed. He was a vain man—it was the most pardonable of his weaknesses—and she knew that his mortification at looking in the mirror would hurt him more than his wounds.

"I wonder he didn't stay at home," Mam said. "People would have understood."

Ethel shook her head. "Too proud," she said. "He led the men to their deaths. He had to come."

"You know him well," Mam said, with a look that made Ethel wonder whether she suspected the truth. "But I expect he also wants people to see that the upper classes suffered, too."

Ethel nodded. Mam was right. Fitz was arrogant and high-handed, but paradoxically he also craved the respect of ordinary people.

Dai Chops, the butcher's son, came up. "It's very nice to see you back in Aberowen," he said.

He was a small man in a neat suit. "How are you, Dai?" she said.

"Very well, thank you. There's a new Charlie Chaplin film starting tomorrow. Do you like Chaplin?"

"I haven't got time to go to the pictures."

"Why don't you leave the little boy with your mam tomorrow night and come with me?"

Dai had put his hand up Ethel's skirt in the Palace Cinema in Cardiff. It was five years ago, but she could tell from the look in his eye that he had not forgotten. "No, thank you, Dai," she said firmly.

He was not ready to give up yet. "I'm working down the pit now, but I'll take over the shop when my da retires."

"You'll do very well, I know."

"There's some men wouldn't look at a girl with a baby," he said. "Not me, though."

That was a bit condescending, but Ethel decided not to take offense. "Good-bye, Dai. It was very nice of you to ask me."

He smiled ruefully. "You're still the prettiest girl I've ever met." He touched his cap and walked away.

Mam said indignantly: "What's wrong with him? You need a husband, and he's a catch!"

What *was* wrong with him? He was a bit short, but he made up for that with charm. He had good prospects and he was willing to take on another man's child. Ethel wondered why she was so unhesitatingly sure that she did not want to go to the pictures with him. Did she still think, in her heart, that she was too good for Aberowen?

There was a row of chairs at the front for the elite. Fitz and Bea took their seats alongside Perceval Jones and Maldwyn Morgan, and the service began.

Ethel believed vaguely in the Christian religion. She supposed there must be a God, but she suspected He was more reasonable than her father imagined. Da's ardent disagreements with the established churches had come down to Ethel merely as a mild dislike of statues, incense, and Latin. In London she occasionally went to the Calvary Gospel Hall on Sunday mornings, mainly because the pastor there was a passionate socialist who allowed his church to be used for Maud's clinic and Labour Party meetings.

There was no organ at the Reck, of course, so the puritans did not have to suppress their objection to musical instruments. Ethel knew, from Da, that there had been trouble about who was to lead the singing—a role that, in this town, was more important than preaching the sermon. In the end the Aberowen Male Voice Choir was placed at the front and its conductor, who belonged to no particular church, was put in charge of the music.

They began with Handel's "He Shall Feed His Flock Like a Shepherd," a popular anthem with elaborate part singing that the congregation performed faultlessly. As hundreds of tenor voices soared across the park with the line "And gather the lambs with his arm," Ethel realized that she missed this thrilling music when she was in London.

The Catholic priest recited Psalm 129, "De Profundis," in Latin. He shouted as loud as he could, but those at the edge of the crowd could hardly hear. The Anglican rector read the Collect Order for the Burial of the Dead from the *Book of Common Prayer*. Dilys Jones, a young Methodist, sang "Love Divine, All Loves Excelling," a hymn written by Charles Wesley. The Baptist pastor read I Corinthians 15 from verse 20 to the end.

One preacher had to represent the independent groups, and the choice had fallen on Da.

He began by reading a single verse from Romans 8: "'If the spirit of Him that raised up Jesus from the dead dwell in you, He that raised up Christ from the dead shall also quicken your mortal bodies by His Spirit that dwelleth in you.'" Da had a big voice that carried strongly all across the park.

Ethel was proud of him. This honor acknowledged his status as one of the principal men of the town, a spiritual and political leader. He looked smart, too: Mam had bought him a new black tie, silk, from the Gwyn Evans department store in Merthyr.

He spoke about resurrection and the afterlife, and Ethel's attention drifted: she had heard it all before. She assumed there was life after death, but she was not sure, and anyway she would find out soon enough.

A stirring in the crowd alerted her that Da might have diverted from the usual themes. She heard him say: "When this country decided to go to war, I hope that every member of Parliament searched his conscience, sincerely and prayerfully, and sought the Lord's guidance. But who put those men in Parliament?"

He's going to get political, Ethel thought. Good for you, Da. That will take the smug look off the rector's face.

"Every man in this country is liable, in principle, for military service. But not every man is allowed a part in the decision to go to war."

There were shouts of agreement from the crowd.

"The rules of the franchise exclude more than half the men in this country!"

Ethel said loudly: "And all the women!"

Mam said: "Hush, now! It's your da that's preaching, not you."

"More than two hundred Aberowen men were killed on the first day of July, there on the banks of the Somme River. I have been told that the total of British casualties is over fifty thousand!"

There was a gasp of horror from the crowd. Not many people knew that figure. Da had got it from Ethel. Maud had been told by her friends in the War Office.

"Fifty thousand casualties, of which twenty thousand are

dead," Da went on. "And the battle goes on. Day after day, more young men are being massacred." There were sounds of dissent from the crowd, but they were mostly drowned out by the shouts of agreement. Da held up his hand for quiet. "I do not say who is to blame. I say only this. Such slaughter cannot be right when men have been denied a part in the decision to go to war."

The rector stepped forward, trying to interrupt Da, and Perceval Jones tried unsuccessfully to climb up onto the platform.

But Da was almost done. "If ever we are asked again to go to war, it shall not be done without the consent of *all* the people."

"Women as well as men!" Ethel cried, but her voice was lost in the cheers of support from the miners.

Several men were now standing in front of Da, remonstrating with him, but his voice rang out over the commotion. "Never again will we wage war on the say-so of a minority!" he roared. "Never! Never! Never!"

He sat down, and the cheering was like thunder.

CHAPTER NINETEEN

July to October 1916

Kovel was a railway junction in the part of Russia that had once been in Poland, near the old border with Austria-Hungary. The Russian army assembled twenty miles east of the city, on the banks of the river Stokhod. The entire area was a swamp, hundreds of square miles of bog interlaced with footpaths. Grigori found a patch of drier ground and ordered his platoon to make camp. They had no tents: Major Azov had sold them all three months ago to a dressmaking factory in Pinsk. He said the men did not need tents in the summer, and by winter they would all be dead.

By some miracle, Grigori was still alive. He was a sergeant and his friend Isaak a corporal. Those few left of the 1914 intake were now mostly NCOs, noncommissioned officers. Grigori's battalion had been decimated, transferred, reinforced, and decimated again. They had been sent everywhere but home.

Grigori had killed many men in the last two years, with rifle, bayonet, or hand grenade, most of them close enough for him to see them die. Some of his comrades had nightmares about it, particularly the better-educated ones, but not Grigori. He had been born into the brutality of a peasant village and had survived as an orphan on the streets of St. Petersburg: violence did not give him bad dreams.

What had shocked him was the stupidity, callousness, and corruption of the officers. Living and fighting alongside the ruling class had made him a revolutionary.

He had to stay alive. There was no one else to take care of Katerina.

He wrote to her regularly, and received occasional letters, penned in a neat schoolgirl hand with many mistakes and crossings-out. He had kept every one, tied in a neat bundle in his kit bag, and when a long period went by with no letter, he reread the old ones.

In the first she had told him she had given birth to a boy, Vladimir, now eighteen months old—Lev's son. Grigori longed to see him. He vividly remembered his brother as a baby. Did Vladimir have Lev's irresistible gummy smile? he wondered. But he must have teeth by now, and be walking, and speaking his first words. Grigori wanted the child to learn to say "Uncle Grishka."

He often thought about the night Katerina had come to his bed. In his daydreams he sometimes changed the course of events so that, instead of throwing her out, he took her in his arms, kissed her generous mouth, and made love to her. But in real life he knew that her heart belonged to his brother.

Grigori had heard nothing from Lev, who had been gone more than two years. He feared that some catastrophe had befallen him in America. Lev's weaknesses often got him into scrapes, although somehow he seemed always to slip out of trouble. The problem stemmed from the way he had been brought up, living from hand to mouth with no proper discipline and only Grigori as a poor substitute for a parent. Grigori wished he had done better, but he had been only a boy himself.

The upshot was that Katerina had no one to look after her and her baby except Grigori. He was fiercely determined to keep himself alive, despite the chaotic inefficiency of the Russian army, so that he could one day return home to Katerina and Vladimir.

The commander in the zone was General Brusilov, a professional soldier—unlike so many of the generals who were courtiers. Under Brusilov's orders the Russians had made gains in June, driving the Austrians back in confusion. Grigori and his men fought hard when the orders made some kind of sense. Otherwise they devoted their energies to staying out of the line of fire. Grigori had become good at that, and in consequence had won the loyalty of his platoon.

In July the Russian advance had slowed, dragged back as always by lack of supplies. But now the Guard Army had arrived as reinforcements. The Guards were an elite group, the tallest and fittest of Russian soldiers. Unlike the rest of the army they had fine uniforms—dark green with gold braid—and new boots. But they had a poor commander, General Bezobrazov, another courtier. Grigori felt that Bezobrazov would not take Kovel, no matter how tall the Guards were.

It was Major Azov who brought the orders at dawn. He was a tall, heavy man in a tight uniform, and as usual his eyes were red this early in the morning. With him was Lieutenant Kirillov. The lieutenant summoned the sergeants and Azov told them to ford the river and follow the footpaths through the swamp toward the west. The Austrians were emplaced in the swamp, though not entrenched: the ground was too soggy for trenches.

Grigori could see a disaster in the making. The Austrians would be lying in wait, behind cover, in positions they had been able to choose with care. The Russians would be concentrated on the pathways and would not be able to move quickly on the boggy ground. They would be massacred.

In addition, they were low on bullets.

Grigori said: "Your Highness, we need an issue of ammunition."

Azov moved fast for a fat man. Without warning he punched Grigori in the mouth. Burning pain flared in Grigori's lips and he fell back. "That will keep you quiet for a while," Azov said. "You'll get ammunition when your officers say you need it." He turned to the others. "Form up in lines and advance when you hear the signal."

Grigori got to his feet, tasting blood. Touching his face gingerly, he found he had lost a front tooth. He cursed his carelessness. In an absentminded moment he had stood too close to an officer. He should have known better: they lashed out at the slightest provocation. He was lucky Azov had not been holding a rifle, or it would have been the butt that struck Grigori in the face.

He called his platoon together and got them in a ragged line. He planned to hold back and let others get ahead, but to his disappointment, Azov sent his company off early, and Grigori's platoon was among the leaders.

He would have to think of something else.

He waded into the river and the thirty-five men of his platoon followed. The water was cold but the weather was sunny and warm, so the men did not much mind getting wet. Grigori moved slowly, and his men did the same, staying behind him, waiting to see what he would do.

The Stokhod was broad and shallow, and they reached the far side without getting wet above their thighs. They had already been overtaken by keener men, Grigori saw with satisfaction.

Once on the narrow path through the swamp Grigori's platoon had to go at the same pace as everyone else, and he could not carry out his plan of falling behind. He began to worry. He did not want his men to be part of this crowd when the Austrians opened fire.

After they had gone a mile or so the path narrowed again and the pace slowed as the men ahead squeezed into single file. Grigori saw an opportunity. As if impatient with the delay, he moved off the path into the watery mud. The rest of his men quickly followed suit. The platoon behind moved up and closed the gap.

The water was up to Grigori's chest, and the mud was glutinous. Walking through the bog was very slow, and—as Grigori had anticipated—his platoon fell behind.

Lieutenant Kirillov saw what was happening and shouted angrily: "You men there! Get back on the path!"

Grigori called back: "Yes, Excellency." But he led his men farther away, as if searching for firmer ground.

The lieutenant cursed and gave up.

Grigori was scanning the terrain ahead as carefully as any of the officers, though for a different purpose. They were looking for the Austrian army; he was looking for a place to hide.

He kept moving forward while letting hundreds of troops overtake him. The Guards are so proud of themselves, he thought; let them do the fighting.

Around midmorning he heard the first shots from up ahead. The vanguard had engaged the enemy. It was time to take refuge.

Grigori came to a slight rise where the ground was drier. The rest of Major Azov's company was now out of sight far ahead. At the top of the rise Grigori shouted: "Take cover! Enemy emplacement ahead to the left!"

There was no enemy emplacement, and his men knew that, but they got down on the ground, behind bushes and trees, and aimed their rifles across the downside of the slope. Grigori shot one exploratory round into a clump of vegetation five hundred yards away, just in case he had unluckily picked a spot where there really were some Austrians; but no fire was returned.

They were safe, Grigori thought with satisfaction, as long as they stayed here. As the day wore on, one of two things would happen. Most likely, in a few hours' time Russian soldiers would come stumbling back through the swamp carrying their wounded, chased by the enemy—in which case Grigori's platoon would join the retreat. Alternatively, toward nightfall Grigori would conclude that the Russians had won the battle, and take his group forward to join the victory celebrations.

Meanwhile the only problem was forcing the men to maintain the pretense of engagement with an Austrian emplacement. It was boring to lie on the ground hour after hour staring ahead as if raking the landscape for enemy troops. The men tended to start eating and drinking, smoking, playing cards, or taking naps, which spoiled the illusion.

But before they had time to get comfortable, Lieutenant Kirillov appeared a couple of hundred yards to Grigori's right on the far side of a pond. Grigori groaned: this could ruin everything. "What are you men doing?" Kirillov shouted.

"Keep down, Excellency!" Grigori shouted back.

Isaak fired his rifle into the air, and Grigori ducked. Kirillov ducked, too, then retreated back the way he had come.

Isaak chuckled. "Works every time."

Grigori was not so sure. Kirillov had looked annoyed, not pleased, as if he knew he was being fooled but could not decide what to do about it.

Grigori listened to the boom and clatter and roar of battle up ahead. He thought it was about a mile away, and not moving in any direction.

The sun rose higher and dried his wet clothing. He began to feel hungry, and gnawed on a piece of hardtack from his ration tin, avoiding the sore place where Azov had knocked out his tooth.

After the mist had burned off, he saw German planes flying low about a mile ahead. Judging by the sound, Grigori could tell they were machine-gunning the troops on the ground. The Guards, crowded onto narrow paths or wading through mud, must have made dreadfully easy targets. Grigori was doubly glad he had made sure he and his men were not there.

Around the middle of the afternoon the sound of battle seemed to come nearer. The Russians were being pushed back. He got ready to order his men to join the fleeing forces—but not yet. He did not want to be conspicuous. Retreating slowly was almost as important as advancing slowly.

He saw a few scattered men away to his left and right, splashing through the swamp back toward the river, some evidently wounded. The retreat had begun, but the army was not yet in full flight.

From somewhere nearby he heard a neigh. A horse meant an officer. Grigori immediately fired at imaginary Austrians. His men followed suit, and there was a rattle of scattered fire. Then he looked around and saw Major Azov on a big gray hunter splashing through the mud. Azov was shouting at a group of retreating soldiers, telling them to return to the fray. They argued with him until he drew his pistol, a Nagant revolver—just like Lev's, Grigori thought irrelevantly—and pointed it at them, whereupon they turned around and reluctantly headed back the way they had come.

Azov holstered the gun and trotted up to Grigori's position. "What are you fools doing here?" he said.

Grigori remained lying on the ground but rolled over and reloaded his rifle, pushing his last five-round clip into place, making a show of haste. "Enemy emplacement in that clump of trees ahead, Your Highness," he said. "You'd better dismount, sir—they can see you."

Azov remained on his horse. "So what are you doing—hiding from them?"

"His Excellency Lieutenant Kirillov told us to take them out. I've sent a patrol to come at them from the side while we give covering fire."

Azov was not completely stupid. "They don't seem to be shooting back."

"We've got them pinned down."

He shook his head. "They've retreated—if they were ever there in the first place."

"I don't think so, Your Highness. They were blazing away at us a moment ago."

"There's no one there." Azov raised his voice. "Cease fire! You men, cease fire."

Grigori's platoon stopped shooting and looked at the major.

"On my signal, charge!" he said. He drew his pistol.

Grigori was not sure what to do. The battle had clearly been the disaster he had forecast. Having avoided it all day he did not want to risk lives when it was clearly over. But direct conflict with officers was dangerous.

At that moment, a group of soldiers broke through the vegetation in the place Grigori had been pretending was an enemy emplacement. Grigori stared in surprise. However, they were not Austrians, he saw as soon as he could make out their uniforms; they were retreating Russians.

But Azov did not change his mind. "Those men are cowardly deserters!" he screeched. "Charge them!" And he fired his pistol at the approaching Russians.

The men of the platoon were bewildered. Officers often threatened to shoot troops who seemed reluctant to go into battle, but Grigori's men had never before been ordered to attack their own side. They looked to him for guidance.

Azov aimed his pistol at Grigori. "Charge!" he screamed. "Shoot those traitors!"

Grigori made a decision. "Right, men!" he called. He scrambled to his feet. Turning his back to the approaching Russians, he looked to left and right and hefted his rifle. "You heard what the major said!" He swung his rifle, as if turning, then pointed it at Azov.

If he was going to shoot at his own side, he would kill an officer rather than a soldier.

Azov stared at him for a frozen moment, and in that second Grigori pulled the trigger.

His first shot hit Azov's horse, and it stumbled. That saved Grigori's life, for Azov fired at him, but the horse's sudden movement caused the shot to go wide. Automatically, Grigori worked the bolt of his rifle and fired again.

His second shot missed. Grigori swore. He was in real danger now. But so was the major.

Azov was struggling with his horse and unable to aim his weapon. Grigori followed his jerky movements with the sight of his rifle, fired a third time, and shot Azov in the chest. He stared as the major slowly fell off his horse. He felt a jolt of grim satisfaction as the heavy body plunged into a muddy puddle.

The horse walked away unsteadily, then suddenly sat down on its hindquarters like a dog.

Grigori went up to Azov. The major lay on his back in the mud, looking up, unmoving but still alive, bleeding from the right side of his chest. Grigori looked around. The retreating soldiers were still too far away to see clearly what was going on. His own men were completely trustworthy: he had saved their lives many times. He put the barrel of his rifle against Azov's forehead. "This is for all the good Russians you've killed, you murdering dog," he said. He grimaced, baring his teeth. "And for my front tooth," he added, and he pulled the trigger.

The major went limp and stopped breathing.

Grigori looked at his men. "The major has unfortunately been killed by enemy fire," he said. "Retreat!"

They cheered and began to run.

Grigori went up to the horse. It tried to rise, but Grigori could see it had a broken leg. He put his rifle to its ear and fired his last round. The horse fell sideways and lay still.

Grigori felt more pity for the horse than for Major Azov.

He ran after his retreating men.

{ II }

After the Brusilov Offensive slowed to a halt, Grigori was redeployed to the capital, now renamed Petrograd because "St. Petersburg" sounded too German. Battle-hardened troops were required to protect the tsar's family and his ministers from the angry citizens, it seemed. The remains of the battalion were merged with the elite First Machine Gun Regiment, and Grigori moved into their barracks in Samsonievsky Prospekt in the Vyborg district, a working-class neighborhood of factories and slums. The First Machine Guns were well fed and housed, in an attempt to keep them contented enough to defend the hated regime.

He was happy to be back, and yet the prospect of seeing Katerina filled him with apprehension. He longed to look at her, hear her voice, and hold her baby, his nephew. But his lust for her made him anxious. She was his wife, but that was a technicality. The reality was that she had chosen Lev, and her baby was Lev's child. Grigori had no right to love her.

He even toyed with the idea of not telling her he was back. In a city of more than two million people there was a good chance they would never meet by accident. But he would have found that too hard to bear.

On his first day back he was not allowed out of the barracks. He felt frustrated at not being able to go to Katerina. Instead, that evening he and Isaak made contact with other Bolsheviks at the barracks. Grigori agreed to start a discussion group.

Next morning his platoon became part of a squad assigned to guard the home of Prince Andrei, his former overlord, during a banquet. The prince lived in a pink-and-yellow palace on the English Embankment overlooking the Neva River. At midday the soldiers lined up on the steps. Low rain clouds darkened the city, but light shone from every window of the house. Behind the glass, framed by velvet curtains like a play at the theater, footmen and maids in clean uniforms hurried by, carrying bottles of wine, platters of delicacies, and silver trays piled with fruit. There was a small orchestra in the hall, and the strains of a symphony could be heard outside. The big shiny cars drew up at the foot of the steps, footmen hurried to open the car doors, and the guests emerged, the men in their black coats and tall hats, the women swathed in furs. A small crowd gathered on the other side of the street to watch.

It was a familiar scene, but there was a difference. Every time someone got out of a car the crowd booed and jeered. In the old days, the police would have broken up the mob with their nightsticks in a minute. Now there were no police, and the guests walked as quickly as they could up the steps between the two lines of soldiers and darted in through the grand doorway, clearly nervous of staying long in the open.

Grigori thought the bystanders were quite right to jeer at the nobility who had made such a mess of the war. If trouble broke out, he would be inclined to take the side of the crowd. He certainly did not intend to shoot at them, and he guessed many of the soldiers felt the same.

How could noblemen throw lavish parties at a time like this? Half Russia was starving and even the soldiers at the front were on short rations. Men like Andrei deserved to be murdered in their beds. If I see him, Grigori thought, I'm going to have to restrain myself from shooting him the way I shot Major Azov.

The procession of cars came to an end without incident, and the crowd got bored and drifted off. Grigori spent the afternoon looking hard at the faces of women passing by, eagerly hoping against the odds to see Katerina. By the time the guests began to leave it was getting dark and cold, and no one wanted to stand around on the street, so there was no more booing.

After the party the soldiers were invited to the back door to eat such of the leftovers as had not been consumed by the household staff: scraps of meat and fish, cold vegetables, half-eaten bread rolls, apples and pears. The food was thrown on a trestle table and unpleasantly mixed up, slices of ham smeared with fish pâté, fruit in gravy, bread dusted with cigar ash. But they had eaten worse in the trenches, and it was a long time since their breakfast of porridge and salt cod, so they tucked in hungrily.

At no time did Grigori see the hated face of Prince Andrei. Perhaps it was just as well.

When they had marched back to the barracks and handed in their weapons, they were given the evening off. Grigori was elated: it was his chance to visit Katerina. He went to the back door of the barracks kitchen and begged some bread and meat to take to her: a sergeant had his privileges. Then he shined his boots and went out.

Vyborg, where the barracks stood, was in the northeast of the city, and Katerina lived diagonally opposite in the southwestern district of Narva, assuming she still had his old room near the Putilov works.

He walked south along Samsonievsky Prospekt and over the Liteiny Bridge into the city center. Some of the swanky shops were still open, their windows bright with electric light, but many were closed. In the more mundane stores there was little for sale. A baker's window contained a single cake and a handwritten sign reading: "No bread until tomorrow."

The broad boulevard of Nevsky Prospekt reminded him of walking along here with his mother, on that fateful day in 1905 when he had seen her shot down by the tsar's soldiers. Now he was one of the tsar's soldiers. But he would not be shooting at women and children. If the tsar tried that now there would be trouble of a different kind.

He saw ten or twelve thuggish young men in black coats and black caps carrying a portrait of Tsar Nicholas as a young man, his dark hair not yet receding, his gingery beard luxuriant. One of them shouted: "Long live the tsar!" and they all stopped, raised their caps, and cheered. Several passersby raised their hats.

Grigori had encountered such bands before. They were called the Black Hundreds, part of the Union of the Russian People, a right-wing group that wanted to return to the golden age when the tsar was the unchallenged father of his people and Russia had no liberals, no socialists, and no Jews. Their newspapers were financed by the government and their pamphlets were printed in the basement of police headquarters, according to information the Bolsheviks got from their contacts in the police.

Grigori walked past with a glance of contempt, but one of them accosted him. "Hey, you! Why is your hat on?"

Grigori walked on without replying, but another member of the gang grabbed his arm. "What are you, a Jew?" the second man said. "Doff your cap!"

Grigori said quietly: "Touch me again and I'll tear your fucking head off, you loudmouthed schoolboy."

The man backed off, then offered Grigori a pamphlet. "Read this, friend," he said. "It explains how the Jews are betraying you soldiers."

"Get out of my way, or I'll shove that stupid pamphlet all the way up your arse," said Grigori.

The man looked to his comrades for support, but they had started beating up a middle-aged man in a fur hat. Grigori walked away.

As he passed the doorway of a boarded-up shop, a woman spoke to him. "Hey, big boy," she said. "You can fuck me for a ruble." Her words were standard prostitute's talk, but her voice surprised him: she sounded educated. He glanced her way. She was wearing a long coat, and when he looked at her, she opened it to show that she had nothing on underneath, despite the cold. She was in her thirties, with big breasts and a round belly.

Grigori felt a surge of desire. He had not been with a woman for years. The trench prostitutes were vile, dirty, and diseased. But this woman looked like someone he could embrace.

She closed her coat. "Yes or no?"

"I haven't got any money," Grigori said.

"What's in that bag?" She nodded at the sack he was carrying.

"A few scraps of food."

"I'll do you for a loaf of bread," the woman said. "My children are starving."

Grigori thought of those plump breasts. "Where?"

"In the back room of the shop."

At least, Grigori thought, I won't be mad with sexual frustration when I meet Katerina. "All right."

She opened the door, led him in, and closed and bolted it. They walked through the empty shop and into another room. Grigori saw, in the dim illumination from the streetlight, that there was a mattress on the floor covered with a blanket.

The woman turned to face him, letting her coat fall open again. He stared at the thatch of dark hair at her groin. She put out her hand. "The bread first, please, Sergeant."

He took a big loaf of black bread from his sack and gave it to her.

"I'll be back in a moment," she said.

She ran up a flight of stairs and opened a door. Grigori heard a child's voice. Then a man coughed, a hacking rasp from deep in his chest. There were muffled sounds of movement and low voices for a few moments. Then he heard the door again, and she came down the stairs.

She took off her coat, lay back on the mattress, and parted her legs. Grigori lay beside her and put his arms around her. She had an attractive, intelligent face lined with strain. She said: "Mm, you're so strong!"

He stroked her soft skin, but all desire had left him. The

entire scene was too pathetic: the empty shop, the sick husband, the hungry children, and the woman's false coquetry.

She unbuttoned his trousers and grasped his limp penis. "Do you want me to suck it?"

"No." He sat upright and handed her the coat. "Put this back on."

In a frightened voice she said: "You can't have the bread back—it's already half-eaten."

He shook his head. "What happened to you?"

She put her coat on and fastened the buttons. "Have you got any cigarettes?"

He gave her a cigarette and took one himself.

She blew out smoke. "We had a shoe shop—high quality at reasonable prices for the middle class. My husband is a good businessman and we lived well." Her tone was bitter. "But no one in this town, apart from the nobility, has bought new shoes for two years."

"Couldn't you do something else?"

"Yes." Her eyes flashed anger. "We didn't just sit back and helplessly accept our fate. My husband found he could provide good boots for soldiers at half the price the army was paying. All the small factories that used to supply the shop were desperate for orders. He went to the War Industries Committee."

"What's that?"

"You've been away for a while, haven't you, Sergeant? Nowadays, everything that works here is run by independent committees: the government is too incompetent to do anything. The War Industries Committee supplies the army—or it did, while Polivanov was war minister."

"What went wrong?"

"We got the order, my husband put all his savings into paying the bootmakers, and then the tsar fired Polivanov."

"Why?"

"Polivanov allowed workers' elected representatives on the committee, so the tsaritsa thought he must be a revolutionist. Anyway, the order was canceled—and we went bankrupt."

Grigori shook his head in disgust. "And I thought it was just the commanders at the front who were mad."

"We tried other things. My husband was willing to do any job, waiter or streetcar driver or road mender, but no one was hiring, and then with the worry and lack of food he fell ill."

"So now you do this."

"I'm not very good at it. But some men are kind, like you. Others . . ." She shuddered and looked away.

Grigori finished his cigarette and got to his feet. "Good-bye. I won't ask your name."

She got up. "Because of you, my family is still alive." There was a catch in her voice. "And I don't need to go on the street again until tomorrow." She stood on tiptoe and kissed his lips lightly. "Thank you, Sergeant."

Grigori went out.

It was getting colder. He hurried through the streets to the Narva district. As he got farther away from the shop-keeper's wife, his libido returned, and he thought with regret of her soft body.

It occurred to him that like him, Katerina had physical needs. Two years was a long time to go without romance, for a young woman—she was still only twenty-three. She had little reason to be faithful to either Lev or Grigori. A woman with a baby was enough to scare off many men, but on the other hand she was very alluring, or she had been two years ago. She might not be alone this evening. How dreadful that would be.

He made his way to his old home by the railway line. Was it his imagination, or did the street appear shabbier than it had two years ago? In the interim nothing seemed to have been painted, repaired, or even cleaned. He noticed a queue outside the bakery on the corner, even though the shop was closed.

He still had his key. He entered the house.

He felt fearful as he went up the stairs. He did not want to find her with a man. Now he wished he had sent word in advance, so that she could have arranged to be alone.

He knocked on the door.

"Who is it?"

The sound of her voice nearly brought tears to his eyes. "A visitor," he said gruffly, and he opened the door.

She was standing by the fireplace holding a pan. She dropped the pan, spilling milk, and her hands went to her mouth. She let out a small scream.

"It's only me," said Grigori.

On the floor beside her sat a little boy with a tin spoon in his hand. He appeared to have just stopped banging on an empty can. He stared at Grigori for a startled moment, then began to cry.

Katerina picked him up. "Don't cry, Volodya," she said, rocking him. "No need to be afraid." He quieted. Katerina said: "This is your daddy."

Grigori was not sure he wanted Vladimir to think he was his father, but this was not the moment to argue. He stepped into the room and closed the door behind him. He put his arms around them, kissed the child, then kissed Katerina's forehead.

He stood back and looked at them. She was no longer the fresh-faced kid he had rescued from the unwelcome attentions of Police Captain Pinsky. She was thinner and had a tired, strained look.

Strangely, the child did not look much like Lev. There was no sign of Lev's good looks, nor his winning smile. If anything, Vladimir had the intense blue-eyed gaze that Grigori saw when he looked in a mirror.

Grigori smiled. "He's beautiful."

Katerina said: "What happened to your ear?"

Grigori touched what remained of his right ear. "I lost most of it at the Battle of Tannenberg."

"And your tooth?"

"I displeased an officer. But he's dead now, so I got the better of him in the end."

"You're not so handsome."

She had never said he was handsome before. "They're minor wounds. I'm lucky to be alive."

He looked around his old room. It was subtly different. On the mantelpiece over the fireplace, where Grigori and Lev had kept pipes, tobacco in a jar, matches, and spills, Katerina had put a pottery vase, a doll, and a color postcard of Mary Pickford. There was a curtain at the window. It was made of scraps, like a quilt, but Grigori had never had any curtain. He also noticed the smell, or lack of it, and realized the place used to have a thick atmosphere of tobacco smoke, boiling cabbage, and unwashed men. Now it smelled fresh.

Katerina mopped up the spilled milk. "I've thrown away Volodya's supper," she said. "I don't know what I'll feed him. There's no milk in my breasts."

"Don't worry." From his sack Grigori took a length of sausage, a cabbage, and a tin of jam. Katerina stared in disbelief. "From the barracks kitchen," he explained.

She opened the jam and fed some to Vladimir on a spoon. He ate it and said: "More?"

Katerina ate a spoonful herself, then gave the child more. "This is like a fairy tale," she said. "All this food! I won't have to sleep outside the bakery."

Grigori frowned. "What do you mean?"

She swallowed more jam. "There's never enough bread. As soon as the bakery opens in the morning, it's all sold. The only way to get bread is to queue up. And if you don't join the queue before midnight, they'll be sold out before you get to the head of the line."

"My God." He hated the thought of her sleeping on the pavement. "What about Volodya?"

"One of the other girls listens for him while I'm out. He sleeps all night now anyway."

No wonder the shopkeeper's wife had been willing to have sex with Grigori for a loaf. He had probably overpaid her. "How do you manage?"

"I get twelve rubles a week at the factory."

He was puzzled. "But that's double what you were earning when I left!"

"But the rent for this room used to be four rubles a week—now it's eight. That leaves me four rubles for everything else. And a sack of potatoes used to be one ruble, but now it's seven."

"Seven rubles for a sack of potatoes!" Grigori was appalled. "How do people live?"

"Everyone is hungry. Children fall ill and die. Old people just fade away. It gets worse every day, and no one does anything."

Grigori felt heartsick. While he was suffering in the army, he had consoled himself with the thought that Katerina and the baby were better off, with a warm place to sleep and enough money for food. He had been fooling himself. It filled him with rage to think of her leaving Vladimir here while she slept outside the bakery.

They sat at the table and Grigori sliced the sausage with his knife. "Some tea would be nice," he said.

Katerina smiled. "I haven't had tea for a year."

"I'll bring some from the barracks."

Katerina ate the sausage. Grigori could see that she had to restrain herself from gobbling it. He picked up Vladimir and fed him more jam. The boy was still a bit young for sausage.

An easy contentment crept over Grigori. While at the front he had daydreamed this scene: the little room, the table with food, the baby, Katerina. Now it had come true. "This should not be so hard to find," he said ruminatively.

"What do you mean?"

"You and I are fit and strong and we work hard. All I want is this: a room, something to eat, rest at the end of the day. It should be ours every day."

"We've been betrayed by German-supporters at the royal court," she said.

"Really? How so?"

"Well, you know the tsaritsa is a German."

"Yes." The tsar's wife had been born Princess Alix of Hesse and Rhine in the German Empire.

"And Stürmer is obviously a German."

Grigori shrugged. Prime Minister Stürmer had been born in Russia, as far as Grigori knew. Many Russians had German names, and vice versa: inhabitants of the two countries had been crisscrossing the border for centuries.

"And Rasputin is pro-German."

"Is he?" Grigori suspected the mad monk was mainly interested in mesmerizing women at court and gaining influence and power.

"They're all in it together. Stürmer has been paid by the Germans to starve the peasantry. The tsar telephones his cousin Kaiser Wilhelm and tells him where our troops are going to be next. Rasputin wants us to surrender. And the tsaritsa and her lady-in-waiting Anna Vyrubova both sleep with Rasputin at the same time."

Grigori had heard most of these rumors. He did not believe the court was pro-German. They were just stupid and incompetent. But a lot of soldiers believed such stories, and to judge by Katerina some civilians did, too. It was the task of the Bolsheviks to explain the true reasons why Russians were losing the war and starving to death.

But not tonight. Vladimir yawned, so Grigori stood up and began to rock him, walking up and down, while Katerina talked. She told him about life at the factory, the other tenants in the house, and people he knew. Captain Pinsky was now a lieutenant with the secret police, ferreting out dangerous liberals and democrats. There were thousands of orphaned children on the streets, living by theft and prostitution or dying of starvation and cold. Konstantin, Grigori's closest friend at the Putilov works, was now a member of the Petrograd Bolshevik Committee. The Vyalov family were the only people getting richer: no matter how bad the shortages were, they could always sell you vodka, caviar, cigarettes, and chocolate. Grigori studied her wide mouth and full lips. It was a joy to watch her talk. She had a determined chin and bold blue eyes, yet to him she always looked vulnerable.

Vladimir fell asleep, lulled by Grigori's rocking and Katerina's voice. Grigori carefully put him down in a bed Katerina had improvised in a corner. It was just a sack filled with rags and covered by a blanket, but he curled up on it comfortably and put his thumb in his mouth.

A church clock struck nine, and Katerina said: "What time do you have to be back?"

"At ten," Grigori said. "I'd better go."

"Not just yet." She put her arms around his neck and kissed him.

It was a sweet moment. Her lips on his were soft and mobile. He closed his eyes for a second and inhaled the scent of her skin. Then he pulled away. "This is wrong," he said.

"Don't be stupid."

"You love Lev."

She looked him in the eye. "I was a peasant girl twenty years old and new to the city. I liked Lev's smart suits, his cigarettes and vodka, his openhandedness. He was charming and handsome and fun. But now I'm twenty-three and I have a child—and where is Lev?"

Grigori shrugged. "We don't know."

"But you're here." She stroked his cheek. He knew he should push her away, but he could not. "You pay the rent, and you bring food for my baby," she said. "Don't you think I see what a fool I was to love Lev instead of you? Don't you realize I know better now? Can't you understand that I've learned to love you?"

Grigori stared at her, unable to believe what he had heard.

Those blue eyes stared back at him candidly. "That's right," she said. "I love you."

He groaned, closed his eyes, took her in his arms, and surrendered.

CHAPTER TWENTY

November to December 1916

Ethel Williams anxiously scanned the casualty list in the newspaper. There were several Williamses, but no Corporal William Williams of the Welsh Rifles. With a silent prayer of thanks she folded the paper, handed it to Bernie Leckwith, and put the kettle on for cocoa.

She could not be sure Billy was alive. He might have been killed in the last few days or hours. She was haunted by the memory of Telegram Wednesday in Aberowen, and the women's faces twisted with fear and grief, faces that would carry forever the cruel marks of the news heard that day. She was ashamed of herself for feeling glad Billy was not among the dead.

The telegrams had kept coming to Aberowen. The Battle of the Somme did not end on that first day. Throughout July, August, September, and October the British army threw its young soldiers across no-man's-land to be mown down by machine guns. Again and again the newspapers hailed a victory, but the telegrams told another story.

Bernie was in Ethel's kitchen, as he was most evenings. Little Lloyd was fond of "Uncle" Bernie. Usually he sat on Bernie's lap, and Bernie read aloud to him from the newspaper. The child had little idea what the words meant but he seemed to like it anyway. Tonight, however, Bernie was on edge, for some reason, and paid no attention to Lloyd.

Mildred from upstairs came in carrying a teapot. "Lend us a spoonful of tea, Eth," she said.

"Help yourself. You know where it is. Do you want a cup of cocoa instead?"

"No, thanks. Cocoa makes me fart. Hello, Bernie. How's the revolution?"

Bernie looked up from the paper, smiling. He liked Mildred. Everyone did. "The revolution is slightly delayed," he said.

Mildred put tea leaves into her pot. "Any word from Billy?"

"Not lately," Ethel said. "You?"

"Not for a couple of weeks."

Ethel picked up the post from the hall floor in the morning, so she knew that Mildred received frequent letters from Billy. Ethel presumed they were love letters: why else would a boy write to his sister's lodger? Mildred apparently returned Billy's feelings: she asked regularly for news of him, assuming a casual air that failed to mask her anxiety.

Ethel liked Mildred, but she wondered whether Billy at eighteen was ready to take on a twenty-three-year-old woman and two stepchildren. True, Billy had always been extraordinarily mature and responsible for his age. And he might be a few years older before the war ended. Anyway, all Ethel wanted was for him to come home alive. After that, nothing mattered much.

Ethel said: "His name's not on the list of casualties in today's paper, thank God."

"I wonder when he'll get leave."

"He's only been gone five months."

Mildred put down the teapot. "Ethel, can I ask you something?"

"Of course."

"I'm thinking of going out on my own—as a seamstress, I mean."

Ethel was surprised. Mildred was the supervisor now at Mannie Litov's, so she was earning a better wage.

Mildred went on: "I've got a friend who can get me work trimming hats—putting on the veils, ribbons, feathers, and beads. It's skilled work and it pays a lot better than sewing uniforms."

"Sounds great."

"Only thing is, I'd have to work at home, at least at first.

Long-term, I'd like to employ other girls and get a small place."

"You're really looking ahead!"

"Got to, haven't you? When the war's over they won't want no more uniforms."

"True."

"So you wouldn't mind me using upstairs as my workshop, for a while?"

"Of course not. Good luck to you!"

"Thanks." Impulsively she kissed Ethel's cheek; then she picked up the teapot and went out.

Lloyd yawned and rubbed his eyes. Ethel lifted him up and put him to bed in the front room. She watched him fondly for a minute or two as he drifted into sleep. As always, his helplessness tugged at her heart. It will be a better world when you grow up, Lloyd, she promised silently. We'll make sure of that.

When she returned to the kitchen, she tried to draw Bernie out of his mood. "There should be more books for children," she said.

He nodded. "I'd like every library to have a little section of children's books." He spoke without looking up from the paper.

"Perhaps if you librarians do that, it will encourage the publishers to bring out more."

"That's what I'm hoping."

Ethel put more coal on the fire and poured cocoa for them both. It was unusual for Bernie to be withdrawn. Normally she enjoyed these cozy evenings. They were two outsiders, a Welsh girl and a Jew, not that there was any scarcity of Welsh people or Jews in London. Whatever the reason, in the two years she had been living in London, he had become a close friend, along with Mildred and Maud.

She had an idea what was on his mind. Last night a bright young speaker from the Fabian Society had addressed the local Labour Party on the subject of "postwar socialism." Ethel had argued with him and he had obviously been rather taken with her. After the meeting he had flirted with her, even though everyone knew he was married, and she had enjoyed the attention, not taking it at all seriously. But perhaps Bernie was jealous.

She decided to leave him to be quiet if that was what

he wanted. She sat at the kitchen table and opened a large envelope full of letters written by men on the front line. Readers of *The Soldier's Wife* sent their husbands' letters to the paper, which paid a shilling for each one published. They gave a truer picture of life at the front than anything in the mainstream press. Most of *The Soldier's Wife* was written by Maud, but the letters had been Ethel's idea and she edited that page, which had become the paper's most popular feature.

She had been offered a better-paid job, as a full-time organizer for the National Union of Garment Workers, but she had turned it down, wanting to stay with Maud and continue campaigning.

She read half a dozen letters, then sighed and looked at Bernie. "You would think people would turn against the war," she said.

"But they haven't," he replied. "Look at the results of that election."

Last month in Ayrshire there had been a by-election—a ballot in a single constituency, caused by the death of the sitting member of Parliament. The Conservative, Lieutenant-General Hunter-Weston, who had fought at the Somme, had been opposed by a Peace candidate, Reverend Chalmers. The army officer had won overwhelmingly, 7,149 votes to 1,300.

"It's the newspapers," Ethel said with frustration. "What can our little publication do to promote peace, against the propaganda put out by the bloody Northcliffe press?" Lord Northcliffe, a gung-ho militarist, owned *The Times* and the *Daily Mail*.

"It's not just the newspapers," Bernie said. "It's the money."

Bernie paid a lot of attention to government finance, which was odd in a man who had never had more than a few shillings. Ethel saw an opportunity to bring him out of his mood, and said: "What do you mean?"

"Before the war, our government used to spend about half a million pounds a day on everything—the army, courts and prisons, education, pensions, running the colonies, everything."

"So much!" She smiled at him affectionately. "That's the kind of statistic my father always knew."

He drank his cocoa, then said: "Guess how much we spend now."

"Double that? A million a day? It sounds impossible."

"You're nowhere near. The war costs five million pounds a day. That's ten times the normal cost of running the country."

Ethel was shocked. "Where does the money come from?"

"That's the problem. We borrow it."

"But the war has been going on for more than two years. We must have borrowed . . . nearly four thousand million pounds!"

"Something like that. Twenty-five years' normal expenditure."

"How will we ever pay it back?"

"We can never pay it back. A government that tried to bring in taxes sufficient to repay the loan would cause a revolution."

"So what will happen?"

"If we lose the war, our creditors—mainly Americans—will go bankrupt. And if we win, we'll make the Germans pay. 'Reparations' is the word they use."

"How will *they* manage it?"

"They will starve. But nobody cares what happens to the losers. Anyway, the Germans did the same to the French in 1871." He stood up and put his cup in the kitchen sink. "So you see why we can't make peace with Germany. Who then would pay the bill?"

Ethel was aghast. "And so we have to keep sending boys to die in the trenches. Because we can't pay the bill. Poor Billy. What a wicked world we live in."

"But we're going to change it."

I hope so, Ethel thought. Bernie believed it would take a revolution. She had read about the French Revolution and knew that such things did not always turn out the way people intended. All the same, she was determined that Lloyd would have a better life.

They sat in silence for a while; then Bernie stood up. He went to the door, as if to leave, then changed his mind. "That speaker last night was interesting."

"Aye," she said.

"Clever, too."

"Yes, he was clever."

Bernie sat down again. "Ethel . . . two years ago you told me you wanted friendship, not romance."

"I was very sorry to hurt your feelings."

"Don't be sorry. Our friendship is the best thing that ever happened to me."

"I like it, too."

"You said I'd soon forget all that lovey-dovey stuff, and we would just be pals. But you were wrong." He leaned forward in his chair. "As I've got to know you better, I've just come to love you more than ever."

Ethel could see the yearning in his eyes, and she felt desperately sorry that she could not return his feelings. "I'm very fond of you, too," she said. "But not in that way."

"What's the point of being alone? We like each other. We're such a good team! We have the same ideals, the same aims in life, similar opinions—we belong together."

"There's more to marriage than that."

"I know. And I long to take you in my arms." He moved his arm, as if about to reach out and touch her, but she crossed her legs and turned aside in her chair. He withdrew his hand, and a bitter smile twisted his usually amiable expression. "I'm not the handsomest man you've ever met. But I believe no one has ever loved you as I do."

He was right about that, she reflected sadly. Many men had fancied her, and one had seduced her, but none had shown the patient devotion of Bernie. If she married him she could be sure it would be forever. And somewhere in her soul she longed for that.

Sensing her hesitation, Bernie said: "Marry me, Ethel. I love you. I'll spend my life making you happy. It's all I want."

Did she need a man at all? She was not unhappy. Lloyd was a constant joy, with his stumbling walk, his attempts at speech, and his boundless curiosity. He was enough for her.

Bernie said: "Little Lloyd needs a father."

That gave her a pang of guilt. Bernie was already playing that role part-time. Should she marry Bernie for Lloyd's sake? It was not too late for him to start calling Bernie "Daddy."

It would mean giving up what little hope she had left of finding again the overwhelming passion she had felt with Fitz. She still suffered a spasm of longing when she thought about it. But, she asked herself, trying to think objectively despite her feelings, what did I get out of that love affair? I was disappointed by Fitz, rejected by my family, and exiled to another country. Why would I want that again?

Hard as she struggled, she could not bring herself to accept Bernie's proposal. "Let me think," she said.

He beamed. Clearly that was a more positive answer than he had dared to hope for. "Think as long as you want," he said. "I'll wait."

She opened the front door. "Good night, Bernie."

"Good night, Ethel." He leaned forward and she gave him her cheek to kiss. His lips lingered a moment on her skin. She drew back immediately. He caught her wrist. "Ethel . . ."

"Sleep well, Bernie," she said.

He hesitated, then nodded. "You, too," he said, and he went out.

{ II }

On election night in November 1916, Gus Dewar thought his career in politics had come to an end.

He was in the White House, fielding phone calls and passing messages to President Wilson, who was at Shadow Lawn, the new summer White House in New Jersey, with his second wife, Edith. Papers were sent from Washington to Shadow Lawn every day by the U.S. Postal Service, but sometimes the president needed to get the news faster.

By nine o'clock that evening it was clear that the Republican, a Supreme Court justice called Charles Evans Hughes, had won four swing states: New York, Indiana, Connecticut, and New Jersey.

But the reality did not hit Gus until a messenger brought him the early editions of the New York newspapers and he saw the headline:

PRESIDENT-ELECT HUGHES

He was shocked. He thought Woodrow Wilson was winning. Voters had not forgotten Wilson's deft handling of the *Lusitania* crisis: he had managed to get tough with the Germans while at the same time staying neutral. Wilson's campaign slogan was "He kept us out of war."

Hughes had accused Wilson of failing to prepare America for war, but this had backfired. Americans were more determined than ever to remain nonaligned after Britain's brutal suppression of the Easter Rising in Dublin. Britain's treatment of the Irish was no better than Germany's treatment of the Belgians, so why should America take sides?

When he had read the papers, Gus loosened his tie and napped on the couch in the study next to the Oval Office. He was unnerved by the prospect of leaving the White House. Working for Wilson had become his bedrock. His love life was a train wreck, but at least he knew he was valuable to the president of the United States.

His concern was not just selfish. Wilson was determined to create an international order in which wars could be avoided. Just as next-door neighbors no longer settled boundary disputes with six-guns, so the time must come when countries, too, submitted their quarrels to independent judgment. The British foreign secretary, Sir Edward Grey, had used the words "a league of nations" in a letter to Wilson, and the president had liked the phrase. If Gus could help bring that about his life would mean something.

But now it looked as if that dream was not going to come true, he thought, and he drifted into a disappointed sleep.

He was woken early in the morning by a cable saying that Wilson had won Ohio—a blue-collar state that had liked the president's stand on the eight-hour day—and Kansas, too. Wilson was back in the running. A little later he won Minnesota by fewer than a thousand votes.

It was not over after all, and Gus's spirits lifted.

By Wednesday evening Wilson was ahead with 264 electoral votes against 254, a lead of 10. But one state, California, had not yet declared a result, and it carried 13 electoral votes. Whoever won California would be president.

Gus's phone went quiet. There was nothing much for him to do. The counting in Los Angeles was slow. Every unopened box was guarded by armed Democrats, who believed that tampering had robbed them of a presidential victory in 1876.

The result was still hanging in the balance when the

lobby called to tell Gus he had a visitor. To his surprise it was Rosa Hellman, the former editor of the *Buffalo Anarchist*. Gus was pleased: Rosa was always interesting to talk to. He recalled that an anarchist had assassinated President McKinley in Buffalo in 1901. However, President Wilson was far away in New Jersey, so he brought Rosa up to the study and offered her a cup of coffee.

She was wearing a red coat. When he helped her off with it, he towered over her. He caught the aroma of a light flowery perfume.

"Last time we met you told me I was a goddamn fool to get engaged to Olga Vyalov," he said as he hung her coat on the hat stand.

She looked embarrassed. "I apologize."

"Ah, but you were right." He changed the subject. "So now you're working for a wire service?"

"That's right."

"As their Washington correspondent."

"No, I'm his one-eyed girl assistant."

She had never before mentioned her deformity. Gus hesitated, then said: "I used to wonder why you didn't wear a patch. But now I'm glad you don't. You're just a beautiful woman with one closed eye."

"Thank you. You're a kind man. What sort of thing do you do for the president?"

"Apart from pick up the phone when it rings . . . I read the State Department's mealymouthed reports, then tell Wilson the truth."

"For example . . . ?"

"Our ambassadors in Europe say that the Somme Offensive is achieving some but not all its objectives, with heavy casualties on both sides. It's almost impossible to prove that statement wrong—and it tells the president nothing. So I tell him the Somme is a disaster for the British." He shrugged. "Or I used to. My job may be over." He was concealing his real feelings. The prospect that Wilson could lose was dreadful to him.

She nodded. "They're counting again in California. Almost a million people voted, and the difference is about five thousand."

"So much hangs on the decisions of a small number of poorly educated people."

"That's democracy."

Gus smiled. "A terrible way to run a country, but every other system is worse."

"If Wilson wins, what will be his top priority?"

"Off the record?"

"Of course."

"Peace in Europe," Gus said without hesitation.

"Really?"

"He was never really comfortable with the slogan 'He kept us out of war.' The matter isn't entirely in his hands. We may be dragged in whether we like it or not."

"But what can he do?"

"He'll put pressure on both sides to find a compromise."

"Can he succeed?"

"I don't know."

"Surely they can't go on slaughtering one another as they have been at the Somme."

"God knows." He changed the subject again. "Tell me the news from Buffalo."

She gave him a candid look. "Do you want to know about Olga, or is it too embarrassing?"

Gus looked away. What could be more embarrassing? First he had received a note from Olga, calling the engagement off. She had been abjectly apologetic but had given no explanation. Gus had been unwilling to accept this and had written back demanding to see her in person. He could not understand it and speculated that someone was putting pressure on her. But later that same day his mother had discovered, through her network of gossiping friends, that Olga was going to marry her father's driver. "But why?" Gus had said in anguish, and Mother had replied: "My darling boy, there is only one reason a girl marries the chauffeur." He had stared uncomprehendingly, and Mother had at last said: "She must be pregnant." It was the most humiliating moment of Gus's life, and even a year later he winced with pain every time he recalled it.

Rosa read his face. "I shouldn't have mentioned her. I'm sorry."

Gus felt he might as well know what everyone else knew. He touched Rosa's hand lightly. "Thank you for being direct. I prefer it. And yes, I'm curious about Olga."

"Well, they got married at that Russian Orthodox

church on Ideal Street, and the reception took place at the
Statler Hotel. Six hundred people were invited, and Josef
Vyalov hired the ballroom *and* the dining room, and served
caviar to everyone. It was the most lavish wedding in the
history of Buffalo."

"And what is her husband like?"

"Lev Peshkov is handsome, charming, and completely
untrustworthy. You know as soon as you look at him that
he's a rogue. And now he's the son-in-law of one of the
richest men in Buffalo."

"And the child?"

"A girl, Darya, but they call her Daisy. She was born
in March. And Lev is no longer the chauffeur, of course. I
think he runs one of Vyalov's nightclubs."

They talked for an hour; then Gus walked her downstairs and hailed a cab to take her home.

Early the next morning Gus got the California result
by cable. Wilson had won by 3,777 votes. He had been re-
elected president.

Gus was elated. Four more years to try to achieve all
they aimed for. They could change the world in four years.

While he was still staring at the telegram, his phone rang.

He picked it up and heard the switchboard operator say:
"A call from Shadow Lawn. The president wants to speak
to you, Mr. Dewar."

"Thank you."

A moment later he heard Wilson's familiar voice.
"Good morning, Gus."

"Congratulations, Mr. President."

"Thank you. Pack a bag. I want you to go to Berlin."

{ III }

When Walter von Ulrich came home on leave, his mother
gave a party.

There were not many parties in Berlin. It was difficult
to buy food, even for a wealthy woman with an influential
husband. Susanne von Ulrich was not well: she was thin,
and had a permanent cough. However, she badly wanted to
do something for Walter.

Otto had a cellar full of good wine he had bought before the war. Susanne decided to have an afternoon reception, so that she would not have to provide a full dinner. She served little snacks of smoked fish and cheese on triangles of toast, and made up for the poor food with unlimited magnums of champagne.

Walter was grateful for the thought, but he did not really want a party. He had two weeks away from the battlefield, and he just wanted a soft bed, dry clothes, and the chance to lounge all day in the elegant salon of his parents' town house, looking out of the window and thinking about Maud, or sitting at the Steinway grand piano and playing Schubert's "Frühlingsglaube": "Now everything, everything must change."

How glibly he and Maud had said, back in August 1914, that they would be reunited by Christmas! It was now more than two years since he had looked at her lovely face. And it was probably going to take Germany another two years to win the war. Walter's best hope was that Russia would collapse, allowing the Germans to concentrate their forces on a massive final westward sweep.

Meanwhile Walter sometimes had trouble visualizing Maud, and had to look at the worn and fading magazine photograph he carried: *Lady Maud Fitzherbert is always dressed in the latest fashion.* He did not relish a party without her. As he got ready, he wished his mother had not troubled.

The house looked drab. There were not enough servants to keep the place spick-and-span. The men were in the army, the women had become streetcar conductors and mail deliverers, and the elderly staff who remained were struggling to maintain Mother's standards of cleanliness and polish. And the house was cold as well as grubby. The coal allowance was not enough to run the central heating, so Mother had put freestanding stoves in the hall, the dining room, and the drawing room, but they were inadequate against the chill of November in Berlin.

However, Walter cheered up when the cold rooms filled with young people and a small band began to play in the hall. His younger sister, Greta, had invited all her friends. He realized how much he missed social life. He liked seeing girls in beautiful gowns and men in immaculate suits. He enjoyed the joking and flirting and gossip. He had loved being a diplomat—the life suited him. It was easy for him to be charming and make small talk.

The von Ulrich house had no ballroom, but people began to dance on the tiled floor of the hall. Walter danced several times with Greta's best friend, Monika von der Helbard, a tall, willowy redhead with long hair who reminded him of pictures by the English artists who called themselves pre-Raphaelites.

He got her a glass of champagne and sat down with her. She asked him what it was like in the trenches, as they all did. He usually said it was a hard life but the men were in good spirits and they would win in the end. For some reason he told Monika the truth. "The worst thing about it is that it's pointless," he said. "We've been in the same positions, give or take a few yards, for two years, and I can't see how that will be changed by anything the high command is doing—or even by anything they might do. We're cold, hungry, sick with coughs and trench foot and stomachache, and bored to tears—all for nothing."

"That's not what we read in the newspapers," she said. "How very sad." She squeezed his arm sympathetically. The touch affected him like a mild electric shock. No woman outside his family had touched him for two years. He suddenly thought how wonderful it would be to take Monika in his arms, press her warm body to his, and kiss her lips. Her amber eyes looked back at him with a candid gaze, and after a moment he realized she had read his mind. Women often did know what men were thinking, he had found. He felt embarrassed, but clearly she did not care, and that thought made him more aroused.

Someone approached them, and Walter looked up irritably, guessing the man wanted to ask Monika to dance. Then he recognized a familiar face. "My God!" he said. The name came back to him: he had an excellent memory for people, like all good diplomats. He said in English: "Is it Gus Dewar?"

Gus replied in German. "It is, but we can speak German. How are you?"

Walter stood up and shook hands. "May I present Fräulein Monika von der Helbard? This is Gus Dewar, an adviser to President Woodrow Wilson."

"How delightful to meet you, Mr. Dewar," she said. "I shall leave you gentlemen to talk."

Walter watched her go with regret mingled with guilt. For a moment he had forgotten that he was a married man.

He looked at Gus. He had immediately liked the American when they met at Tŷ Gwyn. Gus was odd-looking, with a big head on a long thin body, but he was as sharp as a tack. Just out of Harvard then, Gus had had a charming shyness, but two years working in the White House had given him a degree of self-assurance. The shapeless style of lounge suit that Americans wore actually looked smart on him. Walter said: "I'm glad to see you. Not many people come here on holiday nowadays."

"It's not really a holiday," Gus said.

Walter waited for Gus to say more and, when he did not, prompted him. "What, then?"

"More like putting my toe in the water to see whether it's warm enough for the president to swim."

So this was official business. "I understand."

"To come to the point." Gus hesitated again, and Walter waited patiently. At last Gus spoke in a lowered voice. "President Wilson wants the Germans and the Allies to hold peace talks."

Walter's heart beat fast, but he raised a skeptical eyebrow. "He sent *you* to say this to *me*?"

"You know how it is. The president can't risk a public rebuff—it makes him look weak. Of course, he could tell our ambassador here in Berlin to speak to your foreign minister. But then the whole thing would become official, and sooner or later it would get out. So he asked his most junior adviser—me—to come to Berlin and use some of the contacts I made back in 1914."

Walter nodded. A lot was done in this fashion in the diplomatic world. "If we turn you down, no one needs to know."

"And even if the news gets out, it's just some low-ranking young men acting on their own initiative."

This made sense, and Walter began to feel excited. "What exactly does Mr. Wilson want?"

Gus took a deep breath. "If the kaiser were to write to the Allies suggesting a peace conference, then President Wilson would publicly support the proposal."

Walter suppressed a feeling of elation. This unexpected private conversation could have world-shaking consequences. Was it really possible that the nightmare of the trenches could be brought to an end? And that he might see Maud again in months rather than years? He told himself not to get carried away. Unofficial diplomatic feelers like this usually came to nothing. But he could not help being enthusiastic. "This is big, Gus," he said. "Are you sure Wilson means it?"

"Absolutely. It was the first thing he said to me after he won the election."

"What's his motivation?"

"He doesn't want to take America to war. But there's a danger we'll be dragged in anyway. He wants peace. And then he wants a new international system to make sure that a war like this never happens again."

"I'll vote for that," said Walter. "What do you want me to do?"

"Speak to your father."

"He may not like this proposal."

"Use your powers of persuasion."

"I'll do my best. Can I reach you at the American embassy?"

"No. This is a private visit. I'm staying at the Hotel Adlon."

"Of course you are, Gus," said Walter with a grin. The Adlon was the best hotel in the city and had once been called the most luxurious in the world. He felt nostalgic for those last years of peace. "Will we ever again be two young men with nothing on our minds except catching the waiter's eye to order another bottle of champagne?"

Gus took the question seriously. "No, I don't believe those days will ever come back, at least not in our lifetime."

Walter's sister, Greta, appeared. She had curly blond hair that shook fetchingly when she tossed her head. "What are you men looking so miserable about?" she said gaily. "Mr. Dewar, come and dance with me!"

Gus brightened. "Gladly!" he said.

She whisked him off.

Walter returned to the party, but as he chatted to friends and relations, half his mind was on Gus's proposal and how best to promote it. When he spoke to his father, he would try not to seem too keen. Father could be contrary. Walter would play the role of neutral messenger.

When the guests had gone, his mother cornered him in the salon. The room was decorated in the rococo style that was still the choice of old-fashioned Germans: ornate mirrors, tables with spindly curved legs, a big chandelier. "What a nice girl that Monika von der Helbard is," she said.

"Very charming," Walter agreed.

His mother wore no jewelry. She was chair of the gold-collection committee, and had given her baubles to be sold. All she had left was her wedding ring. "I must invite her again, with her parents next time. Her father is the Markgraf von der Helbard."

"Yes, I know."

"It's a very good family. They belong to the *Uradel,* the ancient nobility."

Walter moved to the door. "At what time do you expect Father to return home?"

"Soon. Walter, sit down and talk to me for a moment."

Walter had made it obvious he wanted to get away. The reason was that he needed to spend a quiet hour thinking about Gus Dewar's message. But he had been discourteous to his mother, whom he loved, and now he set about making amends. "With pleasure, Mother." He drew up a chair for her. "I imagined you might want to rest but, if not, I'd love to talk." He sat opposite her. "That was a super party. Thank you very much for organizing it."

She nodded acknowledgment, but changed the subject. "Your cousin Robert is missing," she said. "He was lost during the Brusilov Offensive."

"I know. He may have been taken prisoner by the Russians."

"And he may be dead. And your father is sixty years old. You could soon be the Graf von Ulrich."

Walter was not seduced by this possibility. Aristocratic titles mattered less and less nowadays. Perhaps he might be proud to be a count, but it might turn out to be a disadvantage in the postwar world.

Anyway, he did not have the title yet. "There has been no confirmation of Robert's death."

"Of course. But you must prepare yourself."

"In what way?"

"You should get married."

"Oh!" Walter was surprised. I should have seen that coming, he thought.

"You must have an heir, to assume the title when you die. And you may die soon, though I pray—" Her voice caught in her throat, and she stopped. She closed her eyes for a moment to regain her composure. "Though I pray to heaven every day to protect you. It would be best if you were to father a son as soon as possible."

She was afraid of losing him, but he was just as fearful of losing her. He looked fondly at her. She was blond and pretty like Greta, and perhaps she had once been equally vivacious. Indeed, right now her eyes were bright and her cheeks were flushed from the excitement of the party and the champagne. However, just climbing the stairs made her breathless these days. She needed a holiday, and plenty of good food, and freedom from worry. Because of the war, she could have none of those things. It was not only soldiers who died, Walter thought worriedly.

"Please consider Monika," his mother said.

He longed to tell her about Maud. "Monika is a delightful girl, Mother, but I don't love her. I hardly know her."

"There isn't time for that! In war the proprieties may be overlooked. See her again. You've got ten more days of leave. See her every day. You could propose on your last day."

"What about her feelings? She may not want to marry me."

"She likes you." Mother looked away. "And she will do as her parents tell her."

Walter did not know whether to be annoyed or amused. "You two mothers have fixed this up, haven't you?"

"These are desperate times. You could get married three months from now. Your father will make sure you get special leave for the wedding and the honeymoon."

"He said that?" Normally, Father was angrily hostile to special privileges for well-connected soldiers.

"He understands the need for an heir to the title."

Father had been talked around. How long had that taken? He did not give in easily.

Walter tried not to squirm in his seat. He was in an impossible position. Married to Maud, he could not even pretend to be interested in marrying Monika—but he was not able to explain why. "Mother, I'm sorry to disappoint you, but I am not going to propose to Monika von der Helbard."

"But why not?" she cried.

He felt bad. "All I can say is that I wish I could make you happy."

She gave him a hard look. "Your cousin Robert never married. None of us were surprised, in his case. I hope there isn't a problem of that nature . . ."

Walter felt embarrassed by this reference to Robert's homosexuality. "Oh, Mother, please! I know exactly what you mean about Robert, and I'm not like him in that respect, so set your mind at rest."

She looked away. "I'm sorry to have mentioned it. But what is it? You're thirty years old!"

"It's hard to find the right girl."

"Not that hard."

"I'm looking for someone just like you."

"Now you're teasing me," she said crossly.

Walter heard a male voice outside the room. A moment later his father entered, in uniform, rubbing cold hands together. "It will snow," he said. He kissed his wife and nodded to Walter. "I trust the party was a success? I could not possibly attend—a whole afternoon of meetings."

"It was splendid," Walter said. "Mother conjured up tasty snacks out of nothing at all, and the Perrier-Jouët was superb."

"What vintage did you have?"

"The eighteen ninety-nine."

"You should have had the ninety-two."

"There's not much of it left."

"Ah."

"I had an intriguing conversation with Gus Dewar."

"I remember him—the American whose father is close to President Wilson."

"The son is even closer, now. Gus is working at the White House."

"What did he have to say?"

Mother stood up. "I'll leave you men to talk," she said. They stood up.

"Please think about what I said, Walter, darling," she said as she went out.

A moment later the butler came in with a tray bearing a goblet with a stiff measure of golden-brown brandy. Otto took the glass. "One for you?" he said to Walter.

"No, thank you. I'm full of champagne."

Otto drank the brandy and stretched his legs toward the fire. "So, young Dewar appeared—with some kind of message?"

"In strictest confidence."

"Of course."

Walter could not feel much affection for his father. Their disagreements were too passionate, and Father was too flintily intransigent. He was narrow-minded, outdated, and deaf to reason, and he persisted in these faults with a kind of gleeful obstinacy that Walter found repellent. The consequence of his foolishness, and the foolishness of his generation in all European countries, was the slaughter of the Somme. Walter could not forgive that.

All the same, he spoke to his father with a soft voice and a friendly manner. He wanted this conversation to be as amiable and reasonable as possible. "The American president doesn't want to be drawn into the war," he began.

"Good."

"In fact, he would like us to make peace."

"Ha!" It was a shout of derision. "The cheap way to defeat us! What a nerve the man has."

Walter was dismayed by such immediate scorn, but he persisted, choosing his words with care. "Our enemies claim that German militarism and aggression caused this war, but of course that is not so."

"Indeed not," said Otto. "We were threatened by Russian mobilization on our eastern border and French mobilization to the west. The Schlieffen Plan was the only possible solution." As usual, Otto was speaking as if Walter were still twelve years old.

Walter answered patiently. "Exactly. I recall you saying that for us this was a defensive war, a response to an intolerable threat. We had to protect ourselves."

If Otto was surprised to hear Walter repeating the clichés of war justification, he did not show it. "Correct," he said.

"And we have done so," Walter said, playing his ace. "We have now achieved our aims."

His father was startled. "What do you mean?"

"The threat has been dealt with. The Russian army is destroyed, and the tsar's regime teeters on the brink of collapse. We have conquered Belgium, invaded France, and fought the French and their British allies to a standstill. We have done what we set out to do. We have protected Germany."

"A triumph."

"What more do we want, then?"

"Total victory!"

Walter leaned forward in his chair, looking intently at his father. "Why?"

"Our enemies must pay for their aggression! There must be reparations, perhaps border adjustments, colonial concessions."

"These were not our original war aims . . . were they?"

But Otto wanted to have it both ways. "No, but now that we have expended so much effort and money, and the lives of so many fine young Germans, we must have something in return."

It was a weak argument, but Walter knew better than to try to change his father's mind. Anyway, he had made the point that Germany's war aims had been achieved. Now he changed tack. "Are you quite sure that total victory is attainable?"

"Yes!"

"Back in February we launched an all-out assault on the French fortress of Verdun. We failed to take it. The Russians attacked us in the east, and the British threw everything into their offensive at the river Somme. These huge efforts by both sides have failed to end the stalemate." He waited for a response.

Grudgingly, Otto said: "So far, yes."

"Indeed, our own high command has acknowledged this. Since August, when von Falkenhayn was fired and Ludendorff became chief of staff, we have changed our tactics from attack to defense in depth. How do you imagine defense in depth will lead to total victory?"

"Unrestricted submarine warfare!" Otto said. "The Allies are being sustained by supplies from America, while our ports are blockaded by the British navy. We have to cut off their lifeline—then they'll give in."

Walter had not wanted to get into this, but now that he had

begun, he had to go on. Gritting his teeth, he said as mildly as he could: "That would certainly draw America into the war."

"Do you know how many men there are in the United States Army?"

"It's only about a hundred thousand, but—"

"Correct. They can't even pacify Mexico! They're no threat to us."

Otto had never been to America. Few men of his generation had. They just did not know what they were talking about. "The United States is a big country with great wealth," Walter said, seething with frustration but keeping his tone conversational, trying to maintain the pretense of an amiable discussion. "They can build up their army."

"But not quickly. It will take them at least a year. By that time, the British and French will have surrendered."

Walter nodded. "We've had this discussion before, Father," he said in a conciliatory tone. "So has everyone connected with war strategy. There are arguments on both sides."

Otto could hardly deny that, so he just grunted disapprovingly.

Walter said: "Anyway, I'm sure it's not for me to decide Germany's response to this informal approach from Washington."

Otto took the hint. "Nor for me, of course."

"Wilson says that if Germany will write formally to the Allies proposing peace talks, he will publicly support the proposal. I suppose it's our duty to pass this message on to our sovereign."

"Indeed," said Otto. "The kaiser must decide."

{ IV }

Walter wrote a letter to Maud on a plain sheet of white paper with no letterhead.

> My dearest darling,
>   It is winter in Germany and in my heart.

He wrote in English. He did not put his address at the top, nor did he use her name.

> I cannot tell you how much I love you and how
> badly I miss you.

It was hard to know what to say. The letter might be read by inquisitive policemen, and he had to make sure neither Maud nor he could be identified.

> I am one of a million men separated from the
> women we love, and the north wind blows through
> all our souls.

His idea was that this might be a letter from any soldier living away from his family because of the war.

> It is a cold, bleak world for me, as it must be for
> you, but the hardest part to bear is our separation.

He wished he could tell her about his work in battlefield intelligence, about his mother trying to make him marry Monika, about the scarcity of food in Berlin, even about the book he was reading, a family saga called *Buddenbrooks*. But he was afraid that any specifics would put him or her in danger.

> I cannot say much, but I want you to know that I
> am faithful to you—

He broke off, thinking guiltily of the urge he had felt to kiss Monika. But he had not yielded.

> —and to the sacred promises we made to each
> other the last time we were together.

It was as near as he could get to mentioning their marriage. He did not want to risk someone at her end reading it and learning the truth.

> I think every day of the moment when we will
> meet again, and look into each other's eyes and say:
> "Hello, my beloved."
> Until then, remember me.

He did not sign his name.

He put the letter in an envelope and slipped it into the inside breast pocket of his jacket.

There was no postal service between Germany and England.

He left his room, went downstairs, put on a hat and a heavy overcoat with a fur collar, and went out into the shivering streets of Berlin.

He met Gus Dewar in the bar of the Adlon. The hotel maintained a shadow of its prewar dignity, with waiters in evening dress and a string quartet, but there were no imported drinks—no Scotch, no brandy, no English gin—so they ordered schnapps.

"Well?" said Gus eagerly. "How was my message received?"

Walter was full of hope; but he knew that the grounds for optimism were slight, and he wanted to play down his excitement. The news he had for Gus was positive, but only just. "The kaiser is writing to the president," he said.

"Good! What is he going to say?"

"I have seen a draft. I'm afraid the tone is not very conciliatory."

"What do you mean?"

Walter closed his eyes, remembering, then quoted: "'The most formidable war in history has been raging for two and a half years. In that conflict, Germany and her allies have given proof of our indestructible strength. Our unshakable lines resist ceaseless attacks. Recent events show that continuation of the war cannot break our resisting power ...' There's a lot more like that."

"I see why you say it's not very conciliatory."

"Eventually it gets to the point." Walter brought the next part to mind. "'Conscious of our military and economic strength and ready to carry on to the end, if we must, the struggle that is forced upon us, but animated at the same time by the desire to stem the flow of blood and bring the horrors of war to an end'—here comes the important part—'we propose even now to enter into peace negotiations.'"

Gus was elated. "That's great! He says yes!"

"Quietly, please!" Walter looked around nervously, but it seemed no one had noticed. The sound of the string quartet muffled their conversation.

"Sorry," Gus said.

"You're right, though." Walter smiled, allowing his feeling of sanguinity to show a little. "The tone is arrogant, combative, and scornful—but he proposes peace talks."

"I can't tell you how grateful I am."

Walter held up a warning hand. "Let me tell you something very frankly. Powerful men close to the kaiser who are against peace have supported this proposal cynically, merely to look good in the eyes of your president, feeling sure the Allies will reject it anyway."

"Let's hope they're wrong!"

"Amen to that."

"When will they send the letter?"

"They're still arguing about the wording. When that is agreed, the letter will be handed to the American ambassador here in Berlin, with a request that he pass it to the Allied governments." This diplomatic game of pass-the-parcel was necessary because enemy governments had no official means of communication.

"I'd better go to London," Gus said. "Perhaps I can do something to prepare for its reception."

"I thought you might say that. I have a request."

"After what you've done to help me? Anything!"

"It's strictly personal."

"No problem."

"It requires me to let you into a secret."

Gus smiled. "Intriguing!"

"I would like you to take a letter from me to Lady Maud Fitzherbert."

"Ah." Gus looked thoughtful. He knew there could be only one reason for Walter to be writing secretly to Maud. "I see the need for discretion. But that's okay."

"If your belongings are searched when you are leaving Germany or entering England, you will have to say that it is a love letter from an American man in Germany to his fiancée in London. The letter gives no names or addresses."

"All right."

"Thank you," Walter said fervently. "I can't tell you how much it means to me."

{ V }

There was a shooting party at Tŷ Gwyn on Saturday, December 2. Earl Fitzherbert and Princess Bea were delayed in London, so Fitz's friend Bing Westhampton acted as host, and Lady Maud as hostess.

Before the war, Maud had loved such parties. Women did not shoot, of course, but she liked the house full of guests, the picnic lunch at which the ladies joined the men, and the blazing fires and hearty food they all came home to at night. But she found herself unable to enjoy such pleasure when soldiers were suffering in the trenches. She told herself that one couldn't spend one's whole life being miserable, even in wartime; but it did not work. She pasted on her brightest smile, and encouraged everyone to eat and drink heartily, but when she heard the shotguns she could only think of the battlefields. Lavish food was left untouched on her plate, and glasses of Fitz's priceless old wines were taken away untasted.

She hated to be at leisure, these days, because all she did was think about Walter. Was he alive or dead? The Battle of the Somme was over, at last. Fitz said the Germans had lost half a million men. Was Walter one of them? Or was he lying in a hospital somewhere, maimed?

Perhaps he was celebrating victory. The newspapers could not quite conceal the fact that the British army's major effort for 1916 had gained a paltry seven miles of territory. The Germans might feel entitled to congratulate themselves. Even Fitz was saying, quietly and in private, that Britain's best hope now was that the Americans might join in. Was Walter lounging in a brothel in Berlin, with a bottle of schnapps in one hand and a pretty blond fräulein in the other? I'd rather he was wounded, she thought; then she felt ashamed of herself.

Gus Dewar was among the guests at Tŷ Gwyn, and at teatime he sought Maud out. All the men wore plus fours, tweed trousers buttoned just below the knee, and the tall American looked particularly foolish in them. He held a cup of tea precariously in one hand as he crossed the crowded morning room to where she sat.

She suppressed a sigh. When a single man approached

her he usually had romance on his mind, and she had to fight him off without admitting she was married, which was sometimes difficult. Nowadays, so many eligible upper-class bachelors had been killed in the war that the most unprepossessing men fancied their chances with her: younger sons of bankrupt barons, weedy clergymen with bad breath, even homosexuals looking for a woman to give them respectability.

Not that Gus Dewar was such a poor prospect. He was not handsome, nor did he have the easy grace of such men as Walter and Fitz, but he had a sharp mind and high ideals, and he shared Maud's passionate interest in world affairs. And the combination of his slight awkwardness, physical and social, with a certain blunt honesty somehow amounted to a kind of charm. If she had been single he might even have had a chance.

He folded his long legs beside her on a yellow silk sofa. "Such a pleasure to be at Tŷ Gwyn again," he said.

"You were here shortly before the war," Maud recalled. She would never forget that weekend in January 1914, when the king had come to stay and there had been a terrible disaster at the Aberowen pit. What she remembered most vividly—she was ashamed to realize—was kissing Walter. She wished she could kiss him now. What fools they had been to do no more than kiss! She wished now that they had made love, and she had got pregnant, so that they were obliged to marry in undignified haste, and had been sent away to live in perpetual social disgrace somewhere frightful like Rhodesia or Bengal. All the considerations that had inhibited them—parents, society, career—seemed trivial by comparison with the awful possibility that Walter might be killed and she would never see him again. "How can men be so stupid as to go to war?" she said to Gus. "And to continue fighting when the dreadful cost in men's lives has long ago dwarfed any conceivable gain?"

He said: "President Wilson believes the two sides should consider peace without victory."

She was relieved that he did not want to tell her what fine eyes she had, or some such rubbish. "I agree with the president," she said. "The British army has already lost a million men. The Somme alone cost us four hundred thousand casualties."

"But what do the British people think?"

Maud considered. "Most of the newspapers are still pretending the Somme was a great victory. Any attempt at a realistic assessment is labeled unpatriotic. I'm sure Lord Northcliffe would really rather live under a military dictatorship. But most of our people know we're not making much progress."

"The Germans may be about to propose peace talks."

"Oh, I hope you're right."

"I believe a formal approach may be made soon."

Maud stared at him. "Pardon me," she said. "I assumed you were making polite conversation. But you're not." She felt excited. Peace talks? Could it happen?

"No, I'm not making conversation," Gus said. "I know you have friends in the Liberal government."

"It's not really a Liberal government anymore," she said. "It's a coalition, with several Conservative ministers in the cabinet."

"Excuse me. I misspoke. I did know about the coalition. All the same, Asquith is still prime minister, and he is a Liberal, and I know you are close to many leading Liberals."

"Yes."

"So I've come here to ask your opinion as to how the German proposal might be received."

She considered carefully. She knew who Gus represented. The president of the United States was asking her this question. She had better be exact. As it happened, she had a key item of information. "Ten days ago the cabinet discussed a paper by Lord Lansdowne, a former Conservative foreign secretary, arguing that we cannot win the war."

Gus lit up. "Really? I had no idea."

"Of course you didn't. It was secret. However, there have been rumors, and Northcliffe has been fulminating against what he calls defeatist talk of negotiated peace."

Gus said eagerly: "And how was Lansdowne's paper received?"

"I'd say there are four men inclined to sympathize with him: the foreign secretary, Sir Edward Grey; the chancellor, McKenna; the president of the Board of Trade, Runciman; and the prime minister himself."

Gus's face brightened with hope. "That's a powerful faction!"

"Especially now that the aggressive Winston Churchill has gone. He never recovered from the catastrophe of the Dardanelles expedition, which was his pet project."

"Who in the cabinet was against Lansdowne?"

"David Lloyd George, secretary for war, the most popular politician in the country. And Lord Robert Cecil, minister for blockade; Arthur Henderson, the paymaster general, who is also leader of the Labour Party; and Arthur Balfour, first lord of the Admiralty."

"I saw the interview Lloyd George gave to the papers. He said he wanted to see a fight to the knockout."

"Most people agree with him, unfortunately. Of course, they get little chance to hear any other point of view. People who argue against the war—such as the philosopher Bertrand Russell—are constantly harassed by the government."

"But what was the conclusion of the cabinet?"

"There was none. Asquith's meetings often end that way. People complain that he's indecisive."

"How frustrating. However, it seems a peace proposal won't fall on deaf ears."

It was so refreshing, Maud thought, to talk to a man who took her completely seriously. Even those who spoke intelligently to her tended to condescend a little. Walter was really the only other man who conversed with her as an equal.

At that moment Fitz came into the room. He was wearing black-and-gray London clothes, and had obviously just got off the train. He had an eye patch and walked with a stick. "I'm so sorry to have let you all down," he said, addressing everyone. "I had to stay last night in town. London is in a ferment over the latest political developments."

Gus spoke up. "What developments? We haven't seen today's newspapers yet."

"Yesterday Lloyd George wrote to Asquith demanding a change in the way we manage the war. He wants an all-powerful war council of three ministers to make all the decisions."

Gus said: "And will Asquith agree?"

"Of course not. He replied saying that if there were such a body, the prime minister would have to be its chairman."

Fitz's impish friend Bing Westhampton was sitting on a

window seat with his feet up. "That defeats the object," he said. "Any council of which Asquith is the chair will be just as feeble and indecisive as the cabinet." He looked around apologetically. "Begging the pardon of government ministers here present."

"You're right, though," said Fitz. "The letter is really a challenge to Asquith's leadership, especially as Lloyd George's friend Max Aitken has given the story to all the newspapers. There's no possibility of compromise now. It's a fight to the knockout, as Lloyd George would say. If he doesn't get his way, he'll have to resign from the cabinet. And if he does get his way, Asquith will go—and then we'll have to choose a new prime minister."

Maud caught Gus's eye. They shared the same unspoken thought, she knew. With Asquith in Downing Street, the peace initiative had a chance. If the belligerent Lloyd George won this contest, everything would be different.

The gong rang in the hall, telling guests it was time to change into evening dress. The tea party broke up. Maud went to her room.

Her clothes had been laid out ready. The dress was one she had got in Paris for the London season of 1914. She had bought few clothes since. She took off her tea gown and slipped on a silk wrap. She would not ring for her maid yet: she had a few minutes to herself. She sat at the dressing table and looked at her face in the mirror. She was twenty-six, and it showed. She had never been pretty, but people had called her handsome. With wartime austerity she had lost what little she had of girlish softness, and the angles of her face had become more pronounced. What would Walter think when he saw her—if they ever met again? She touched her breasts. They were still firm, at least. He would be pleased about that. Thinking about him made her nipples stiffen. She wondered if she had time to—

There was a tap at the door, and she guiltily dropped her hands. "Who is it?" she called.

The door opened, and Gus Dewar stepped in.

Maud stood up, pulling the wrap tightly around her, and said in her most forbidding voice: "Mr. Dewar, please leave at once!"

"Don't be alarmed," he said. "I have to see you in private."

"I can't imagine what possible reason—"

"I saw Walter in Berlin."

Maud fell silent, shocked. She stared at Gus. How could he know about her and Walter?

Gus said: "He gave me a letter for you." He reached inside his tweed jacket and drew out an envelope.

Maud took it with a trembling hand.

Gus said: "He told me he had not used your name or his, for fear the letter might be read at the border, but in fact no one searched my baggage."

Maud held the letter uneasily. She had longed to hear from him, but now she feared bad news. Walter might have taken a lover, and the letter might beg her understanding. Perhaps he had married a German girl, and wrote to ask her to keep the earlier marriage secret forever. Worst of all, perhaps he had started divorce proceedings.

She tore open the envelope.

She read:

> My dearest darling,
>   It is winter in Germany and in my heart. I cannot tell you how much I love you and how badly I miss you.

Her eyes filled with tears. "Oh!" she said. "Oh, Mr. Dewar, thank you for bringing this!"

He took a tentative step closer to her. "There, there," he said. He patted her arm.

She tried to read the rest of the letter but she could not see the words on the paper. "I'm so happy," she wept.

She dropped her head to Gus's shoulder, and he put his arms around her. "It's all right," he said.

Maud gave in to her feelings and began to sob.

CHAPTER TWENTY-ONE

December 1916

Fitz was working at the Admiralty in Whitehall. It was not the job he wanted. He longed to return to the Welsh Rifles in France. Much as he hated the dirt and discomfort of the trenches, he could not feel good about being safe in London while others were risking their lives. He had a horror of being thought a coward. However, the doctors insisted that his leg was not yet strong enough, and the army would not let him return.

Because Fitz spoke German, Smith-Cumming of the Secret Service Bureau—the man who called himself "C"—had recommended him to naval intelligence, and he had been temporarily posted to a department known as Room 40. The last thing he wanted was a desk job, but to his surprise, he found that the work was highly important to the war effort.

On the first day of the war a post office ship called the CS *Alert* had gone out into the North Sea, dredged up the Germans' heavy-duty seabed telecommunications cables, and severed them all. With that sly stroke the British had forced the enemy to use wireless for most messages. Wireless signals could be intercepted. The Germans were not stupid, and they sent all their messages in code. Room 40 was where the British tried to break the codes.

Fitz worked with an assortment of people—some of them quite odd, most not very military—who struggled to decipher the gibberish picked up by listening stations on the coast. Fitz was no good at the crossword-puzzle challenge of decoding—he could never even work out the murderer in a Sherlock Holmes mystery—but he was able to translate the decrypts into English and, more important, his battlefield experience enabled him to judge which were significant.

Not that it made much difference. At the end of 1916 the western front had hardly moved from its position at the beginning of the year, despite huge efforts by both sides— the relentless German assault at Verdun and the even more costly British attack at the Somme. The Allies desperately needed a boost. If the United States joined in they could tip the balance—but so far there was no sign of that.

Commanders in all armies issued their orders late at night or first thing in the morning, so Fitz started early and worked intensely until midday. On the Wednesday after the shooting party he left the Admiralty at half past twelve and took a taxi home. The uphill walk from Whitehall to Mayfair, though short, was too much for him.

The three women he lived with—Bea, Maud, and Aunt Herm—were just sitting down to lunch. He handed his walking stick and uniform cap to Grout and joined the ladies. After the utilitarian environment of his office, he took a warm pleasure in his home: the rich furnishings, the soft-footed servants, the French china on the snowy tablecloth.

He asked Maud what the political news was. A battle was raging between Asquith and Lloyd George. Yesterday Asquith had dramatically resigned as prime minister. Fitz was worried: he was no admirer of the Liberal Asquith, but what if the new man was seduced by facile talk of peace?

"The king has seen Bonar Law," Maud said. Andrew Bonar Law was the leader of the Conservatives. The last remnant of royal power in British politics was the monarch's right to appoint a prime minister—although his chosen candidate still had to win the support of Parliament.

Fitz said: "What happened?"

"Bonar Law declined to be prime minister."

Fitz bridled. "How could he refuse the king?" A man should obey his monarch, Fitz believed, especially a Conservative.

"He thinks it has to be Lloyd George. But the king doesn't want Lloyd George."

Bea put in: "I should hope not. The man is not much better than a socialist."

"Indeed," said Fitz. "But he's got more aggression than the rest of them put together. At least he would inject some energy into the war effort."

Maud said: "I fear he won't make the most of any chance of peace."

"Peace?" said Fitz. "I don't think you need to worry too much about that." He tried not to sound heated, but defeatist talk of peace made him think of all the lives that had been lost: poor young Lieutenant Carlton-Smith, so many Aberowen Pals, even the wretched Owen Bevin, shot by a firing squad. Was their sacrifice to have been for nothing? The thought seemed blasphemous to him. Forcing himself to speak in a conversational tone, he said: "There won't be peace until one side or the other has won."

Anger flashed in Maud's eyes but she, too, controlled herself. "We might get the best of both worlds: energetic leadership of the war by Lloyd George as chairman of the War Council, and a statesmanlike prime minister such as Arthur Balfour to negotiate peace if we decide that's what we want."

"Hmm." Fitz did not like that idea at all, but Maud had a way of putting things that made it hard to disagree. Fitz changed the subject. "What are you planning to do this afternoon?"

"Aunt Herm and I are going to the East End. We host a soldiers' wives club. We give them tea and cake—paid for by you, Fitz, for which we thank you—and try to help them with their problems."

"Such as?"

Aunt Herm answered. "Getting a clean place to live and finding a reliable child minder are the usual ones."

Fitz was amused. "You surprise me, Aunt. You used to disapprove of Maud's adventures in the East End."

"It's wartime," Lady Hermia said defiantly. "We must all do what we can."

On impulse Fitz said: "Perhaps I'll come with you. It's good for them to see that earls get shot just as easily as stevedores."

Maud looked taken aback, but she said: "Well, of course, yes, if you'd like to."

He could tell she was not keen. No doubt there was a certain amount of left-wing rubbish talked at her club—

votes for women and suchlike tosh. However, she could not refuse him, as he paid for the whole thing.

Lunch ended and they went off to get ready. Fitz went to his wife's dressing room. Bea's gray-haired maid, Nina, was helping her off with the dress she had worn at lunch. Bea murmured something in Russian, and Nina replied in the same language, which irritated Fitz as it seemed intended to exclude him. He spoke in Russian, hoping they would think he understood everything, and said to the maid: "Leave us alone, please." She curtsied and went out.

Fitz said: "I haven't seen Boy today." He had left the house early this morning. "I must go to the nursery before he's taken out for his walk."

"He's not going out at the moment," Bea said anxiously. "He's got a little cough."

Fitz frowned. "He needs fresh air."

To his surprise, she suddenly looked tearful. "I'm afraid for him," she said. "With you and Andrei both risking your lives in the war, Boy may be all I have left."

Her brother, Andrei, was married but had no children. If Andrei and Fitz died, Boy would be all the family Bea had. It explained why she was overprotective of the child. "All the same, it won't do him good to be mollycoddled."

"I don't know this word," she said sulkily.

"I think you know what I mean."

Bea stepped out of her petticoats. Her figure was more voluptuous than it used to be. Fitz watched her untie the ribbons that held up her stockings. He imagined biting the soft flesh of her inner thigh.

She caught his eye. "I'm tired," she said. "I must sleep for an hour."

"I could join you."

"I thought you were going slumming with your sister."

"I don't have to."

"I really need to rest."

He stood up to go, then changed his mind. He felt angry and rejected. "It's been a long time since you welcomed me into your bed."

"I haven't been counting the days."

"I have, and it's weeks, not days."

"I'm sorry. I feel so worried about everything." She was close to tears again.

Fitz knew she was fearful for her brother, and he sympathized with her helpless anxiety, but millions of women were going through the same agonies, and the nobility had a duty to be stoical. "I hear you started attending services at the Russian embassy while I was away in France." There was no Russian Orthodox church in London, but there was a chapel in the embassy.

"Who told you that?"

"Never mind who told me." It had been Aunt Herm. "Before we married, I asked you to convert to the Church of England, and you did."

She would not meet his eye. "I didn't think it would do any harm for me to go to one or two services," she said quietly. "I'm so sorry to have displeased you."

Fitz was suspicious of foreign clergymen. "Does the priest there tell you it's a sin to take pleasure in lying with your husband?"

"Of course not! But when you're away, and I feel so alone, so far away from everything I grew up with . . . it's a comfort to me to hear familiar Russian hymns and prayers."

Fitz felt sorry for her. It must be difficult. He certainly could not contemplate going to live permanently in a foreign country. And he knew, from conversations with other married men, that it was not unusual for a wife to resist her husband's advances after she had borne a child.

But he hardened his heart. Everyone had to make sacrifices. Bea should be grateful she did not have to run into machine-gun fire. "I think I have done my duty by you," he said. "When we married, I paid off your family's debts. I called in experts, Russian and English, to plan the reorganization of the estates." They had told Andrei to drain swamps to produce more farmland, and prospect for coal and other minerals, but he had never done anything. "It's not my fault that Andrei wasted every opportunity."

"Yes, Fitz," she said. "You did everything you promised."

"And I ask that you do your duty. You and I must produce heirs. If Andrei dies without fathering children, our son will inherit two huge estates. He will be one of the greatest landowners in the world. We must have more sons in case—God forbid—something should happen to Boy."

She kept her eyes cast down. "I know my duty."

Fitz felt dishonest. He talked about an heir—and everything he had said was true—but he was not telling her that he hungered to see her soft body spread-eagled for him on the bedsheets, white on white, and her fair hair spilling over the pillow. He repressed the vision. "If you know your duty, please do it. Next time I come into your room I shall expect to be welcomed like the loving husband that I am."

"Yes, Fitz."

He left. He was glad he had put his foot down, but he also felt an uneasy sense that he had done something wrong. It was ridiculous: he had pointed out to Bea the error of her ways, and she had accepted his reproof. That was how things ought to be between man and wife. But he could not feel as satisfied as he should.

He pushed Bea out of his mind when he met up with Maud and Aunt Herm in the hall. He put on his uniform cap and glanced in the mirror, then quickly looked away. He tried these days not to think much about his appearance. The bullet had damaged the muscles on the left side of his face, and his eyelid had a permanent droop. It was a minor disfigurement, but his vanity would never recover. He told himself to be grateful that his eyesight was unaffected.

The blue Cadillac was still in France, but he had managed to get hold of another. His chauffeur knew the way: he had obviously driven Maud to the East End before. Half an hour later they pulled up outside the Calvary Gospel Hall, a mean little chapel with a tin roof. It might have been transplanted from Aberowen. Fitz wondered if the pastor was Welsh.

The tea party was already under way and the place was packed with young women and their children. It smelled worse than a barracks, and Fitz had to resist the temptation to hold a handkerchief over his nose.

Maud and Herm went to work immediately, Maud seeing women one by one in the back office and Herm marshaling them. Fitz limped from one table to the next, asking the women where their husbands were serving and what their experiences had been, while their children rolled on the floor. Young women often became giggly and tongue-tied when Fitz spoke to them, but this group was not so easily flustered. They asked him what regiment he served in and how he had got his wounds.

It was not until he was halfway round the room that he saw Ethel.

He had noticed that there were two offices at the back of the hall, one Maud's, and he had vaguely wondered who was in the second. He happened to look up when the door opened and Ethel stepped out.

He had not seen her for two years, but she had not changed much. Her dark curls bounced as she walked, and her smile was a sunbeam. Her dress was drab and worn, like the clothes of all the women except Maud and Herm, but she had the same trim figure, and he could not help thinking about the petite body he had known so well. Without even looking at him she cast her spell. It was as if no time had passed since they had rolled around, giggling and kissing, on the bed in the Gardenia Suite.

She spoke to the only other man in the room, a stooped figure in a dark gray lounge suit of some heavy cloth, sitting at a table making notes in a ledger. He wore thick glasses, but even so Fitz could see the adoration in the man's eyes when he looked up at Ethel. She spoke to him with easy amiability, and Fitz wondered if they were married.

Ethel turned around and caught Fitz's eye. Her eyebrows went up and her mouth made an O of surprise. She took a step back, as if nervous, and bumped into a chair. The woman sitting in the chair looked up with an expression of irritation. Ethel mouthed: "Sorry!" without looking at her.

Fitz rose from his seat, not an easy matter with his busted leg, all the time gazing steadily at Ethel. She dithered visibly, not sure whether to approach him or flee to the safety of her office. He said: "Hello, Ethel." His words did not carry across the noisy room, but she could probably see his lips move and guess what he said.

She made a decision and walked toward him.

"Good afternoon, Lord Fitzherbert," she said, and her lilting Welsh accent made the routine phrase sound like a melody. She held out her hand and they shook. Her skin was rough.

He followed her in reverting to formality. "How are you, Mrs. Williams?"

She pulled up a chair and sat down. As he lowered himself into his seat he realized she had deftly put them on a footing of equality without intimacy.

"I seen you at the service in the Aberowen Reck," she

said. "I was very sorry—" Her voice caught in her throat. She looked down and started again. "I was very sorry to see you wounded. I hope you're getting better."

"Slowly." He could tell that her concern was genuine. She did not hate him, it seemed, despite everything that had happened. His heart was touched.

"How did you get your injuries?"

He had told the story so often that it bored him. "It was the first day of the Somme. I hardly saw any fighting. We went over the top, got past our own barbed wire, and started across no-man's-land, and the next thing I remember is being carried on a stretcher, and hurting like hell."

"My brother saw you fall."

Fitz remembered the insubordinate Corporal William Williams. "Did he? What happened to him?"

"His section captured a German trench, then had to abandon it when they ran out of ammunition."

Fitz had missed all the debriefing, being in hospital. "Did he get a medal?"

"No. The colonel told him he should have defended his position to the death. Billy said: 'What, like you did?' and he was put on a charge."

Fitz was not surprised. Williams was trouble. "So what are you doing here?"

"I work with your sister."

"She didn't tell me."

Ethel gave him a level look. "She wouldn't think you'd be interested in news of your former servants."

It was a jibe, but he ignored it. "What do you do?"

"I'm managing editor of *The Soldier's Wife*. I arrange printing and distribution, and edit the letters page. And I take care of the money."

He was impressed. It was a big step up from housekeeper. But she had always been an extraordinarily capable organizer. "My money, I suppose?"

"I don't think so. Maud is careful. She knows you don't mind paying for tea and cake, and doctoring for soldiers' children, but she wouldn't use your money for antiwar propaganda."

He kept the conversation going just for the pleasure of watching her face as she talked. "Is that what is in the newspaper?" he asked. "Antiwar propaganda?"

"We discuss publicly what you speak of only in secret: the possibility of peace."

She was right. Fitz knew that senior politicians in both major parties had been talking about peace, and it angered him. But he did not want to have a row with Ethel. "Your hero, Lloyd George, is in favor of fighting harder."

"Will he become prime minister, do you think?"

"The king doesn't want him. But he may be the only candidate who can unite Parliament."

"I fear he may prolong the war."

Maud came out of her office. The tea party was breaking up, the women clearing up the cups and saucers and marshaling their children. Fitz marveled to see Aunt Herm carrying a stack of dirty plates. How the war had changed people!

He looked again at Ethel. She was still the most attractive woman he had ever met. He yielded to an impulse. Speaking in a lowered voice he said: "Will you meet me tomorrow?"

She looked shocked. "What for?" she said quietly.

"Yes or no?"

"Where?"

"Victoria Station. One o'clock. At the entrance to platform three."

Before she could reply the man in thick glasses came over, and Ethel introduced him. "Earl Fitzherbert, may I present Mr. Bernie Leckwith, chairman of the Aldgate branch of the Independent Labour Party."

Fitz shook hands. Leckwith was in his twenties. Fitz guessed that poor eyesight had kept him out of the armed forces.

"I'm sorry to see you wounded, Lord Fitzherbert," Leckwith said in a Cockney accent.

"I was one of thousands, and lucky to be alive."

"With hindsight, is there anything we could have done differently at the Somme, that would have greatly altered the outcome?"

Fitz thought for a moment. It was a damned good question.

While he considered, Leckwith said: "Did we need more men and ammunition, as the generals claim? Or more flexible tactics and better communications, as the politicians say?"

Fitz said thoughtfully: "All those things would have helped but, frankly, I don't think they would have brought us victory. The assault was doomed from the start. But we could not possibly have known that in advance. We had to try."

Leckwith nodded, as if his own view had been confirmed. "I appreciate your candor," he said, almost as if Fitz had made a confession.

They left the chapel. Fitz handed Aunt Herm and Maud into the waiting car, then got in himself, and the chauffeur drove away.

Fitz found himself breathing hard. He had suffered a small shock. Three years ago Ethel had been counting pillowcases at Tŷ Gwyn. Today she was the managing editor of a newspaper that, although small, was considered by senior ministers to be a thorn in the flesh of the government.

What was her relationship with the surprisingly intelligent Bernie Leckwith? "Who was that chap Leckwith?" he asked Maud.

"An important local politician."

"Is he Williams's husband?"

Maud laughed. "No, though everyone thinks he should be. He's a clever man who shares her ideals, and he's devoted to her son. I don't know why Ethel didn't marry him long ago."

"Perhaps he doesn't make her heart beat faster."

Maud raised her eyebrows, and Fitz realized he had been dangerously candid.

He added hastily: "Girls of that type want romance, don't they? She'll marry a war hero, not a librarian."

"She's not a *girl of that type* or any other type," Maud said rather frostily. "She's nothing if not exceptional. You don't meet two like her in a lifetime."

Fitz looked away. He knew that was true.

He wondered what the child was like. It must have been one of the dirty-faced toddlers playing on the floor of the chapel. He had probably seen his own son this afternoon. He was strangely moved by the thought. For some reason it made him want to cry.

The car was passing through Trafalgar Square. He told the driver to stop. "I'd better drop in at the office," he explained to Maud.

He limped into the Old Admiralty Building and up the stairs. His desk was in the diplomatic section, which inhabited Room 45. Sublieutenant Carver, a student of Latin and Greek who had come down from Cambridge to help decode German signals, told him that not many intercepts had come in during the afternoon, as usual, and there was nothing he needed to deal with. However, there was some political news. "Have you heard?" said Carver. "The king has summoned Lloyd George."

{ II }

All the next morning, Ethel told herself she was not going to meet Fitz. How dared he suggest such a thing? For more than two years she had heard nothing from him. Then when they met he had not even asked about Lloyd—his own child! He was the same selfish, thoughtless deceiver as always.

All the same, she had been thrown into a whirl. Fitz had looked at her with his intense green eyes, and asked her questions about her life that made her feel she was important to him—contrary to all the evidence. He was no longer the perfect godlike man he had once been: his beautiful face was marred by one half-closed eye, and he stooped over his walking stick. But his weakness only made her want to take care of him. She told herself she was a fool. He had all the care money could buy. She would not go to meet him.

At twelve noon she left the premises of *The Soldier's Wife*—two small rooms over a print shop, shared with the Independent Labour Party—and caught a bus. Maud was not at the office that morning, which saved Ethel the trouble of inventing an excuse.

It was a long journey by bus and underground train from Aldgate to Victoria, and Ethel arrived at the rendezvous a few minutes after one o'clock. She wondered if Fitz might have grown impatient and left, and the thought made her feel slightly ill; but he was there, wearing a tweed suit as if he were going into the country, and she immediately felt better.

He smiled. "I was afraid you weren't coming," he said.

"I don't know why I did," she replied. "Why did you ask me?"

"I want to show you something." He took her arm.

They walked out of the station. Ethel felt foolishly pleased to be arm in arm with Fitz. She wondered at his boldness. He was an easily recognizable figure. What if they ran into one of his friends? She supposed they would pretend not to see each other. In Fitz's social class, a man who had been married a few years was not expected to be faithful.

They rode a bus a few stops and got off in the raffish suburb of Chelsea, a low-rent neighborhood of artists and writers. Ethel wondered what he wanted her to see. They walked along a street of small villas. Fitz said: "Have you ever watched a debate in Parliament?"

"No," she said. "But I'd love to."

"You have to be invited by an M.P. or a peer. Shall I arrange it?"

"Yes, please!"

He looked happy that she had accepted. "I'll check when there's going to be something interesting. You might like to see Lloyd George in action."

"Yes!"

"He is putting his government together today. I should think he will kiss the king's hand as prime minister tonight."

Ethel gazed about her thoughtfully. In parts, Chelsea still looked like the country village it had been a hundred years ago. The older buildings were cottages and farmhouses, low-built with large gardens and orchards. There was not much greenery in December, but even so the neighborhood had a pleasant semirural feel. "Politics is a funny business," she said. "I've wanted Lloyd George for prime minister ever since I was old enough to read the newspaper, but now that it's happened, I'm dismayed."

"Why?"

"He's the most belligerent senior figure in the government. His appointment might kill off any chance of peace. On the other hand . . ."

Fitz looked intrigued. "What?"

"He's the only man who could agree to peace talks without being crucified by Northcliffe's bloodthirsty newspapers."

"That's a point," Fitz said, looking worried. "If anyone else did it, the headlines would scream: 'Fire Asquith—or Balfour, or Bonar Law—and bring in Lloyd George!' But if they attack Lloyd George there's no one left."

"So maybe there is a hope of peace."

He allowed his tone of voice to become testy. "Why aren't you hoping for victory, rather than peace?"

"Because that's how we got into this mess," she said equably. "What are you going to show me?"

"This." He unlatched a gate and held it open. They entered the grounds of a detached two-story house. The garden was overgrown and the place needed painting, but it was a charming medium-size home, the kind of place that might be owned by a successful musician, Ethel imagined, or perhaps a well-known actor. Fitz took a key from his pocket and opened the door. They stepped inside, and he closed the door and kissed her.

She gave herself up to it. She had not been kissed for a long time, and she felt like a thirsty traveler in a desert. She stroked his long neck and pressed her breasts against his chest. She sensed that he was as desperate as she. Before she lost control she pushed him away. "Stop," she said breathlessly. "Stop."

"Why?"

"Last time we did this I ended up talking to your bloody lawyer." She moved away from him. "I'm not as innocent as I used to be."

"It will be different this time," he said, panting. "I was a fool to let you go. I see that now. I was young, too."

To help her calm down she looked into the rooms. They were full of dowdy old furniture. "Whose house is this?" she said.

"Yours," he replied. "If you want it."

She stared at him. What did he mean?

"You could live here with the baby," he explained. "It was occupied for years by an old lady who used to be my father's housekeeper. She died a few months ago. You could redecorate it and buy new furniture."

"Live here?" she said. "As what?"

He could not quite bring himself to say it.

"As your mistress?" she said.

"You can have a nurse, and a couple of housemaids, and

a gardener. Even a motorcar with a chauffeur, if that appeals to you."

The part of it that appealed to her was him.

He misinterpreted her thoughtful look. "Is the house too small? Would you prefer Kensington? Do you want a butler and a housekeeper? I'll give you anything you want, don't you understand? My life is empty without you."

He meant it, she saw. At least, he meant it now, when he was aroused and unsatisfied. She knew from bitter experience how fast he could change.

The trouble was, she wanted him just as badly.

He must have seen that in her face, for he took her in his arms again. She turned up her face to be kissed. I want more of this, she thought.

Once again she broke the embrace before she lost control.

"Well?" he said.

She could not make a sensible decision while he was kissing her. "I've got to be alone," she said. She forced herself to walk away from him before it was too late. "I'm going home," she said. She opened the door. "I need time to think." She hesitated on the doorstep.

"Think as long as you want," he said. "I'll wait."

She closed the door and ran away.

{ III }

Gus Dewar was in the National Gallery in Trafalgar Square, standing in front of Rembrandt's *Self-Portrait at the Age of Sixty-three,* when a woman standing next to him said: "Extraordinarily ugly man."

Gus turned and was surprised to recognize Maud Fitzherbert. He said: "Me, or Rembrandt?" and she laughed.

They strolled through the gallery together. "What a delightful coincidence," he said. "Meeting you here."

"As a matter of fact, I saw you and followed you in," she said. She lowered her voice. "I wanted to ask you why the Germans haven't yet made the peace offer you told me was coming."

He did not know the answer. "They may have changed

their minds," he said gloomily. "There as here, there is a peace faction and a war faction. Perhaps the war faction has gained the upper hand, and succeeded in changing the kaiser's mind."

"Surely they must see that battles no longer make a difference!" she said with exasperation. "Did you read in this morning's papers that the Germans have taken Bucharest?"

Gus nodded. Rumania had declared war in August, and for a while the British had hoped their new partner might strike a mighty blow, but Germany had invaded back in September and now the Rumanian capital had fallen. "In fact the upshot is good for Germany, which now has Rumania's oil."

"Exactly," said Maud. "It's the same old one step forward, one step back. When will we learn?"

"The appointment of Lloyd George as prime minister isn't encouraging," Gus said.

"Ah. There you might be wrong."

"Really? He has built his political reputation on being more aggressive than everyone else. It would be hard for him to make peace after that."

"Don't be so sure. Lloyd George is unpredictable. He could do a volte-face. It would surprise only those naïve enough to have thought him sincere."

"Well, that's hopeful."

"All the same, I wish we had a woman prime minister."

Gus did not think that was ever likely to happen, but he did not say so.

"There's something else I want to ask you," she said, and she halted.

Gus turned to face her. Perhaps because the paintings had sensitized him, he found himself admiring her face. He noticed the sharp lines of her nose and chin, the high cheekbones, the long neck. The angularity of her features was softened by her full lips and large green eyes. "Anything you like," he said.

"What did Walter tell you?"

Gus's mind went back to that surprising conversation in the bar of the Adlon Hotel in Berlin. "He said he was obliged to let me into a secret. But then he didn't tell me what the secret was."

"He thought you would be able to guess."

"I guessed he must be in love with you. And from your reaction when I gave you the letter at Tŷ Gwyn, I could see that his love is returned." Gus smiled. "If I may say so, he's a lucky man."

She nodded, and Gus read something like relief on her face. There must be more to the secret, he realized; that was why she needed to find out how much he knew. He wondered what else they were hiding. Perhaps they were engaged.

They walked on. I understand why he loves you, Gus thought. I could fall for you in a heartbeat.

She surprised him again by suddenly saying: "Have you ever been in love, Mr. Dewar?"

It was an intrusive question, but he answered anyway. "Yes, I have—twice."

"But no longer."

He felt an urge to confide in her. "The year the war broke out, I was wicked enough to fall in love with a woman who was already married."

"Did she love you?"

"Yes."

"What happened?"

"I asked her to leave her husband for me. That was very wrong of me, and you will be shocked, I know. But she was a better person than I, and she rejected my immoral offer."

"I'm not so easily shocked. When was the second time?"

"Last year I became engaged to someone in my hometown, Buffalo; but she married someone else."

"Oh! I'm so sorry. Perhaps I should not have asked. I have revived a painful memory."

"Extremely painful."

"Forgive me if I say that makes me feel better. It's just that you know what sorrow love can bring."

"Yes, I do."

"But perhaps there will be peace after all, and my sorrow will soon be over."

"I very much hope so, Lady Maud," said Gus.

{ IV }

Ethel agonized for days over Fitz's proposition. As she stood freezing in her backyard, turning the mangle to wring out the washing, she imagined herself in that pretty house in Chelsea, with Lloyd running around the garden watched over by an attentive nurse. "I'll give you anything you want," Fitz had said, and she knew it was true. He would put the house in her name. He would take her to Switzerland and the south of France. If she set her mind to it, she could make him give her an annuity so that she would have an income until she died, even if he got bored with her— although she also knew she could make sure he never got bored.

It was shameful and disgusting, she told herself sternly. She would be a woman paid for sex, and what else did the word *prostitute* mean? She could never invite her parents to her Chelsea hideaway: they would know immediately what it meant.

Did she care about that? Perhaps not, but there were other things. She wanted more from life than comfort. As a millionaire's mistress she could hardly continue to campaign on behalf of working-class women. Her political life would be over. She would lose touch with Bernie and Mildred, and it would be awkward even to see Maud.

But who was she, to ask for so much from life? She was Ethel Williams, born in a coal miner's cottage! How could she turn up her nose at a lifetime of ease? You should be so lucky, she told herself, using one of Bernie's sayings.

And then there was Lloyd. He would have a governess, and later Fitz would pay for him to go to a posh school. He would grow up among the elite and lead a life of privilege. Did Ethel have the right to deny him that?

She was no nearer an answer when she opened the newspapers in the office she shared with Maud and learned of another dramatic offer. On December 12 the German chancellor, Theobald von Bethmann-Hollweg, proposed peace talks with the Allies.

Ethel was elated. Peace! Was it really possible? Might Billy come home?

The French premier immediately described the note as

a crafty move, and the Russian foreign minister denounced the Germans' "lying proposals," but Ethel believed it was the British reaction that would count.

Lloyd George was not making public speeches of any kind, claiming he had a sore throat. In London in December half the population had coughs and colds, but all the same Ethel suspected Lloyd George just wanted time to think. She took that as a good sign. An immediate response would have been a rejection; anything else was hopeful. He was at least considering peace, she thought optimistically.

Meanwhile President Wilson threw America's weight into the balance on the side of peace. He suggested that as a preliminary to talks all the warring powers state their aims—what they were trying to achieve by fighting.

"That's embarrassed them," said Bernie Leckwith that evening. "They've forgotten why they started it. They're fighting now just because they want to win."

Ethel remembered what Mrs. Dai Ponies had said about the strike: *These men—once they get into a fight, all they care about is winning. They won't give in, whatever the cost.* She wondered how a woman prime minister might have reacted to a peace proposal.

But Bernie was right, she realized over the next few days. President Wilson's suggestion met with a strange silence. No country answered immediately. That made Ethel more angry. How could they carry on if they did not even know what they were fighting for?

At the end of the week Bernie organized a public meeting to debate the German note. On the day of the meeting, Ethel woke up to see her brother standing beside her bed in his khaki uniform. "Billy!" she cried. "You're alive!"

"And on a week's leave," he said. "Get out of bed, you lazy cow."

She jumped up, put on a dressing gown over her nightdress, and hugged him. "Oh, Billy, I'm so happy to see you." She noticed the stripes on his sleeve. "Sergeant, now, is it?"

"Aye."

"How did you get into the house?"

"Mildred opened the door. Actually, I been here since last night."

"Where did you sleep?"

He looked bashful. "Upstairs."

Ethel grinned. "Lucky lad."

"I really like her, Eth."

"So do I," Ethel said. "Mildred is solid gold. Are you going to marry her?"

"Aye, if I survive the war."

"You don't mind about the age difference?"

"She's twenty-three. It's not like she's really old, thirty or something."

"And the children?"

Billy shrugged. "They're nice kids, but even if they weren't I'd put up with them for her sake."

"You really do love her."

"It's not difficult."

"She's started a little business. You must have seen all the hats up there in her room."

"Aye. Going well, too, it is, she says."

"Very well. She's a hard worker. Is Tommy with you?"

"He come over on the boat with me, but now he've gone to Aberowen on the train."

Lloyd woke up, saw a strange man in the room, and began to cry. Ethel picked him up and quieted him. "Come in the kitchen," she said to Billy. "I'll make us some breakfast."

Billy sat and read the paper while she made porridge. After a moment he said: "Bloody hell."

"What?"

"Bloody Fitzherbert's been opening his big mouth, I see." He glanced at Lloyd, almost as if the baby might be offended at this scornful reference to his father.

Ethel looked over his shoulder. She read:

PEACE: A SOLDIER'S PLEA

"Don't Give Up on Us Now!"
Wounded Earl Speaks Out

A moving speech was made yesterday in the House of Lords against the current proposal of the German Chancellor for peace talks. The speaker was Earl Fitzherbert, a Major in the Welsh Rifles, who is in London recovering from wounds received at the Battle of the Somme.

Lord Fitzherbert said that to talk peace with the Germans would be a betrayal of all the men who have given their lives in the war. "We believe we are winning and can achieve complete victory provided you don't give up on us now," he said.

Wearing his uniform, with an eye patch, and leaning on a crutch, the earl made a striking figure in the debating chamber. He was listened to in absolute silence, and cheered when he sat down.

There was a lot more of the same. Ethel was aghast. It was sentimental claptrap, but it would be effective. Fitz did not normally wear the eye patch—he must have put it on for effect. The speech would prejudice a lot of people against the peace plan.

She ate breakfast with Billy, then dressed Lloyd and herself and went out. Billy was going to spend the day with Mildred, but he promised to come to the meeting that evening.

When Ethel arrived at the office of *The Soldier's Wife,* she saw that all the newspapers had reported Fitz's speech. Several made it the subject of a leading article. They took different views, but agreed he had struck a powerful blow.

"How can anyone be against the mere *discussion* of peace?" she said to Maud.

"You can ask him yourself," Maud said. "I invited him to tonight's meeting, and he accepted."

Ethel was startled. "He'll get a warm reception!"

"I certainly hope so."

The two women spent the day working on a special edition of the newspaper with the front-page headline SMALL DANGER OF PEACE. Maud liked the irony but Ethel thought it was too subtle. Late in the afternoon Ethel collected Lloyd from the child minder, took him home, fed him, and put him to bed. She left him in the care of Mildred, who did not go to political meetings.

The Calvary Gospel Hall was filling up when Ethel arrived, and soon there was standing room only. The audience included many soldiers and sailors in uniform. Bernie chaired the meeting. He opened with a speech of his own that managed to be dull even though short—he was no orator. Then he called on the first speaker, a philosopher from Oxford University.

Ethel knew the arguments for peace better than the philosopher did, and as he spoke she studied the two men on the platform who were wooing her. Fitz was the product of hundreds of years of wealth and culture. As always, he was beautifully dressed, his hair well-cut, his hands white, and his fingernails clean. Bernie came from a tribe of persecuted nomads who survived by being cleverer than those who tormented them. He was wearing his only suit, the heavy dark gray serge. Ethel had never seen him in anything else: when the weather was warm he simply took off the jacket.

The audience listened quietly. The Labour movement was divided over peace. Ramsay MacDonald, who had spoken against the war in Parliament on August 3, 1914, had resigned as Labour Party leader when war was declared two days later, and since then the party's M.P.s had supported the war, as did most of their voters. But Labour supporters tended to be the most skeptical of working-class people, and there was a strong minority in favor of peace.

Fitz began by speaking of Britain's proud traditions. For hundreds of years, he said, Britain had maintained the balance of power in Europe, generally by siding with weaker nations to make sure no one country dominated. "The German chancellor has not said anything about the terms of a peace settlement, but any discussion would have to start from the status quo," he said. "Peace now means that France is humiliated and robbed of territory and Belgium becomes a satellite. Germany would dominate the continent by sheer military force. We cannot allow that to happen. We must fight for victory."

When the discussion opened, Bernie said: "Earl Fitzherbert is here in a purely personal capacity, not as an army officer, and he has given me his word of honor that serving soldiers in the audience will not be disciplined for anything they say. Indeed, we would not have invited the earl to attend the meeting on any other basis."

Bernie himself asked the first question. As usual, it was a good one. "If France is humiliated and loses territory, then that will destabilize Europe, according to your analysis, Lord Fitzherbert."

Fitz nodded.

"Whereas if Germany is humiliated and loses the territories of Alsace and Lorraine—as she undoubtedly would—then that will stabilize Europe."

Fitz was momentarily stumped, Ethel could see. He had not expected to have to deal with such sharp opposition here in the East End. Intellectually he was no match for Bernie. She felt a bit sorry for him.

"Why the difference?" Bernie finished, and there was a murmur of approval from the peace faction in the audience.

Fitz recovered rapidly. "The difference," he said, "is that Germany is the aggressor, brutal, militaristic, and cruel, and if we make peace now we will be rewarding that behavior—and encouraging it in the future!"

That brought a cheer from the other section of the audience, and Fitz's face was saved, but it was a poor argument, Ethel thought, and Maud stood up to say so. "The outbreak of war was not the fault of any single nation!" she said. "It has become the conventional wisdom to blame Germany, and our militaristic newspapers encourage this fairy tale. We remember Germany's invasion of Belgium and talk as if it was completely unprovoked. We have forgotten the mobilization of six million Russian soldiers on Germany's border. We have forgotten the French refusal to declare neutrality." A few men booed her. You never get cheered for telling people the situation is not as simple as they think, Ethel reflected wryly. "I don't say Germany is innocent!" Maud protested. "I say no country is innocent. I say we are not fighting for the stability of Europe, or for justice for the Belgians, or to punish German militarism. We are fighting because we are too proud to admit we made a mistake!"

A soldier in uniform stood up to speak, and Ethel saw with pride that it was Billy. "I fought at the Somme," he began, and the audience went quiet. "I want to tell you why we lost so many men there." Ethel heard their father's strong voice and quiet conviction, and she realized Billy would have made a great preacher. "We were told by our officers"—here he stretched out his arm and pointed an accusing finger at Fitz—"that the assault would be a walk in the park."

Ethel saw Fitz shift uncomfortably in his chair on the platform.

Billy went on: "We were told that our artillery had destroyed the enemy positions, wrecked their trenches and demolished their dugouts, and when we got to the other side we would see nothing but dead Germans."

He was not addressing the people on the platform, Ethel observed, but looking all around him, sweeping the audience with an intense gaze, making sure all eyes were on him.

"Why did they tell us those things?" Billy said, and now he looked straight at Fitz and spoke with deliberate emphasis. "Things that were not true." There was a mutter of agreement from the audience.

Ethel saw Fitz's face darken. She knew that for men of Fitz's class an accusation of lying was the worst of all insults. Billy knew it, too.

Billy said: "The German positions had not been destroyed, as we discovered when we ran into machine-gun fire."

The audience reaction became less muted. Someone called out: "Shame!"

Fitz stood up to speak, but Bernie said: "One moment, please, Lord Fitzherbert. Let the present speaker finish." Fitz sat down, shaking his head vigorously from side to side.

Billy raised his voice. "Did our officers check, by aerial reconnaissance and by sending out patrols, how much damage the artillery had in fact done to the German lines? If not, why not?"

Fitz stood up again, furious. Some of the audience cheered; others booed. He began to speak. "You don't understand!" he said.

But Billy's voice prevailed. "If they knew the truth," he cried, "why did they tell us otherwise?"

Fitz began to shout, and half the audience were calling out, but Billy's voice could be heard over everything else. "I ask one simple question!" he roared. "Are our officers fools—or liars?"

{ V }

Ethel received a letter in Fitz's large, confident handwriting on his expensive crested notepaper. He did not mention the meeting in Aldgate, but invited her to the Palace of Westminster on the following day, Tuesday, December 19, to sit in the gallery of the House of Commons and hear

Lloyd George's first speech as prime minister. She was excited. She had never thought she would see the inside of Westminster Palace, let alone hear her hero speak.

"Why do you suppose he's invited you?" said Bernie that evening, asking the key question as usual.

Ethel did not have a plausible answer. Sheer unadulterated kindness had never been part of Fitz's character. He could be generous when it suited him. Bernie was shrewdly wondering if he wanted something in return.

Bernie was cerebral rather than intuitive, but he had sensed some connection between Fitz and Ethel, and he had responded by becoming a bit amorous. It was nothing dramatic, for Bernie was not a dramatic man, but he held her hand an instant longer than he should have, stood an inch closer to her than was comfortable, patted her shoulder when speaking to her, and held her elbow as she went down a step. Suddenly insecure, Bernie was instinctively making gestures that said she belonged to him. Unfortunately, she found it hard not to flinch when he did so. Fitz had reminded her cruelly of what she did *not* feel about Bernie.

Maud came into the office at half past ten on Tuesday, and they worked side by side all morning. Maud could not write the front page of the next edition until Lloyd George had spoken, but there was a lot else in the paper: jobs, advertisements for child minders, advice on women's and children's health written by Dr. Greenward, recipes, and letters.

"Fitz is beside himself with rage after that meeting," Maud said.

"I told you they would give him a hard time."

"He doesn't mind that," she said. "But Billy called him a liar."

"You're sure it's not just that Billy got the better of the argument?"

Maud smiled ruefully. "Perhaps."

"I just hope he doesn't make Billy suffer for it."

"He won't do that," Maud said firmly. "It would be breaking his word."

"Good."

They had lunch in a café in the Mile End Road—"A Good Pull-In for Car Men," according to its signboard, and it was indeed full of lorry drivers. Maud was greeted cheer-fully by the counter staff. They had beef and oyster pie, the cheap oysters added to eke out the scarce beef.

Afterward they took a bus across London to the West End. Ethel looked up at the giant dial of Big Ben and saw that it was half past three. Lloyd George was due to speak at four. He had it in his power to end the war and save mil-lions of lives. Would he do it?

Lloyd George had always fought for the workingman. Before the war he had done battle with the House of Lords and the king to bring in old-age pensions. Ethel knew how much that meant to penniless old people. On the first day the pension was paid out she had seen retired miners—once-strong men now bent and trembling—come out of the Aberowen post office openly weeping for joy that they were no longer destitute. That was when Lloyd George had become a working-class hero. The Lords had wanted to spend the money on the Royal Navy.

I could write his speech today, she thought. I would say: "There are moments in the life of a man, and of a nation, when it is right to say: I have done my utmost, and I can do no more. Therefore I will cease my striving, and seek an-other road. Within the last hour I have ordered a cease-fire along the entire length of the British line in France. Gentle-men, the guns have fallen silent."

It could be done. The French would be furious, but they would have to join in the cease-fire, or take the risk that Britain might make a separate peace and leave them to certain defeat. The peace settlement would be hard on France and Belgium, but not as hard as the loss of millions more lives.

It would be an act of great statesmanship. It would also be the end of Lloyd George's political career: voters would not elect the man who lost the war. But what a way to go out!

Fitz was waiting in the Central Lobby. Gus Dewar was with him. No doubt he was as eager as everyone else to find out how Lloyd George would respond to the peace initiative.

They climbed the long staircase to the gallery and took their seats overlooking the debating chamber. Ethel had Fitz on her right and Gus on her left. Below them, the rows of green leather benches on both sides were already full of M.P.s, except for the few places in the front row tradition-ally reserved for the cabinet.

"Every M.P. a man," Maud said loudly.

An usher, wearing full formal court dress complete with velvet knee breeches and white stockings, officiously hissed: "Quiet, please!"

A backbencher was on his feet, but hardly anyone was listening to him. They were all waiting for the new prime minister. Fitz spoke quietly to Ethel. "Your brother in-sulted me."

"You poor thing," Ethel said sarcastically. "Are your feelings hurt?"

"Men used to fight duels for less."

"Now there's a sensible idea for the twentieth century."

He was unmoved by her scorn. "Does he know who is the father of Lloyd?"

Ethel hesitated, not wanting to tell him but reluctant to lie.

Her hesitation told him what he wanted to know. "I see," he said. "That would explain his vituperation."

"I don't think you need to look for an ulterior motive," she said. "What happened at the Somme is enough to make soldiers angry, don't you think?"

"He should be court-martialed for insolence."

"But you promised not to—"

"Yes," he said crossly. "Unfortunately, I did."

Lloyd George entered the chamber.

He was a small, slight figure in formal morning dress, the overlong hair a bit unkempt, the bushy mustache now entirely white. He was fifty-three, but there was a spring in his step, and as he sat down and said something to a backbencher, Ethel saw the grin familiar from newspaper photographs.

He began speaking at ten past four. His voice was a little hoarse, and he said he had a sore throat. He paused, then said: "I appear before the House of Commons today with the most terrible responsibility that can fall on the shoul-ders of any living man."

That was a good start, Ethel thought. At least he was not going to dismiss the German note as an unimportant trick or diversion, in the way the French and Russians had.

"Any man or set of men who wantonly, or without sufficient cause, prolonged a terrible conflict like this would have on his soul a crime that oceans could not cleanse."

That was a biblical touch, Ethel thought, a Baptist-chapel reference to sins being washed away.

But then, like a preacher, he made the contrary statement. "Any man or set of men who, out of a sense of weariness or despair, abandoned the struggle without the high purpose for which we had entered into it being nearly fulfilled, would have been guilty of the costliest act of poltroonery ever perpetrated by any statesman."

Ethel fidgeted anxiously. Which way was he going to jump? She thought of Telegram Wednesday in Aberowen, and saw again the faces of the bereaved. Surely Lloyd George—of all politicians—would not let heartbreak of that nature continue if he could help it? If he did, what was the point of his being in politics at all?

He quoted Abraham Lincoln. "'We accepted this war for an object, and a worthy object, and the war will end when that object is attained.'"

That was ominous. Ethel wanted to ask him what the object was. Woodrow Wilson had asked that question and as yet had got no reply. No answer was given now. Lloyd George said: "Are we likely to achieve that object by accepting the invitation of the German chancellor? That is the only question we have to put to ourselves."

Ethel felt frustrated. How could this question be discussed if no one knew what the object of the war was?

Lloyd George raised his voice, like a preacher about to speak of hell. "To enter at the invitation of Germany, proclaiming herself victorious, without any knowledge of the proposals she proposes to make, into a conference"—here he paused and looked around the chamber, first to the Liberals behind him and to his right, then across the floor to the Conservatives on the opposition side—"is to put our heads into a noose with the rope end in the hands of Germany!"

There was a roar of approval from the M.P.s.

He was rejecting the peace offer.

Beside Ethel, Gus Dewar buried his face in his hands.

Ethel said loudly: "What about Alun Pritchard, killed at the Somme?"

The usher said: "Quiet, there!"

Ethel stood up. "Sergeant Prophet Jones, dead!" she cried.

Fitz said: "Be quiet and sit down, for God's sake!"

Down in the chamber, Lloyd George continued speaking, though one or two M.P.s were looking up at the gallery.

"Clive Pugh!" she shouted at the top of her voice.

Two ushers came toward her, one from each side.

"Spotty Llewellyn!"

The ushers grabbed her arms and hustled her away.

"Joey Ponti!" she screamed, and then they dragged her out through the door.

CHAPTER TWENTY-TWO

January and February 1917

Walter von Ulrich dreamed he was in a horse-drawn carriage on his way to meet Maud. The carriage was going downhill, and began to travel dangerously fast, bouncing on the uneven road surface. He shouted, "Slow down! Slow down!" but the driver could not hear him over the drumming of hooves, which sounded oddly like the running of a motorcar engine. Despite this anomaly, Walter was terrified that the runaway carriage would crash and he would never reach Maud. He tried again to order the driver to slow down, and the effort of shouting woke him.

In reality he was in an automobile, a chauffeur-driven Mercedes 37/95 Double Phaeton, traveling at moderate speed along a bumpy road in Silesia. His father sat beside him, smoking a cigar. They had left Berlin in the early hours of the morning, both wrapped in fur coats—it was an open car—and they were on their way to the eastern headquarters of the high command.

The dream was easy to interpret. The Allies had scornfully rejected the peace offer that Walter had worked so hard to promote. The rejection had strengthened the hand of the German military, who wanted to resume unrestricted submarine warfare, sinking every ship in the war zone, military or civilian, passenger or freight, combatant or neutral, in order to starve Britain and France into submission. The politicians, notably the chancellor, feared that was the way to defeat, for it was likely to bring the United States into the war, but the submariners were winning the argument. The kaiser had shown which way he leaned by promoting the aggressive Arthur Zimmermann to foreign minister. And Walter dreamed of charging downhill to disaster.

Walter believed that the greatest danger to Germany was the United States. The aim of German policy should be to keep America out of the war. True, Germany was being starved by the Allied naval blockade. But the Russians could not last much longer, and when they capitulated, Germany would overrun the rich western and southern regions of the Russian Empire, with their vast cornfields and bottomless oil wells. And the entire German army would then be able to concentrate on the western front. That was the only hope.

But would the kaiser see that?

The final decision would be made today.

A bleak winter daylight was breaking over countryside patchworked with snow. Walter felt like a shirker, being so far from the fighting. "I should have returned to the front line weeks ago," he said.

"Clearly the army wants you in Germany," said Otto. "You are valued as an intelligence analyst."

"Germany is full of older men who could do the job at least as well as I. Have you pulled strings?"

Otto shrugged. "I think if you were to marry and have a son, you could then be transferred anywhere you like."

Walter said incredulously: "You're keeping me in Berlin to make me marry Monika von der Helbard?"

"I don't have the power to do that. But it may be that there are men in the high command who understand the need to maintain noble bloodlines."

That was disingenuous, and a protest came to Walter's lips, but then the car turned off the road, passed through an ornamental gateway, and started up a long drive flanked by leafless trees and snow-covered lawn. At the end of the drive was a huge house, the largest Walter had ever seen in Germany. "Castle Pless?" he said.

"Correct."

"It's vast."

"Three hundred rooms."

They got out of the car and entered a hall like a railway station. The walls were decorated with boars' heads framed with red silk, and a massive marble staircase led up to the state rooms on the first floor. Walter had spent half his life in splendid buildings, but this was exceptional.

A general approached them, and Walter recognized von Henscher, a crony of his father's. "You've got time to wash and brush up, if you're quick," he said with amiable urgency. "You're expected in the state dining room in forty minutes." He looked at Walter. "This must be your son."

Otto said: "He's in the intelligence department."

Walter gave a brisk salute.

"I know. I put his name on the list." The general addressed Walter. "I believe you know America."

"I spent three years in our embassy in Washington, sir."

"Good. I have never been to the United States. Nor has your father. Nor, indeed, have most of the men here—with the notable exception of our new foreign minister."

Twenty years ago, Arthur Zimmermann had returned to Germany from China via the States, crossing from San Francisco to New York by train, and on the basis of this experience was considered an expert on America. Walter said nothing.

Von Henscher said: "Herr Zimmermann has asked me to consult you both on something." Walter was flattered but puzzled. Why would the new foreign minister want his opinion? "But we will have more time for that later." Von Henscher beckoned to a footman in old-fashioned livery, who showed them to a bedroom.

Half an hour later they were in the dining room, now converted to a conference room. Looking around, Walter was awestruck to see that just about every man who counted for anything in Germany was present, including the chancellor, Theobald von Bethmann-Hollweg, his close-cropped hair now almost white at age sixty.

Most of Germany's senior military commanders were sitting around a long table. For lesser men, including Walter, there were rows of hard chairs against the wall. An aide passed around a few copies of a two-hundred-page memorandum. Walter looked over his father's shoulder at the file. He saw charts of tonnage moving in and out of British ports, tables of freight rates and cargo space, the calorific value of British meals, even a calculation of how much wool there was in a lady's skirt.

They waited two hours; then Kaiser Wilhelm came in, wearing a general's uniform. Everyone sprang to their feet. His Majesty looked pale and ill-tempered. He was a few days from his fifty-eighth birthday. As ever, he held his withered left arm motionless at his side, attempting to make it inconspicuous. Walter found it difficult to summon up that emotion of joyous loyalty that had come so easily to him as a boy. He could no longer pretend the kaiser was the wise father of his people. Wilhelm II was too obviously an unexceptional man completely overwhelmed by events. Incompetent, bewildered, and miserably unhappy, he was a standing argument against hereditary monarchy.

The kaiser looked around, nodding to one or two special favorites, including Otto; then he sat down and made a gesture at Henning von Holtzendorff, white-bearded chief of the admiralty staff.

The admiral began to speak, quoting from his memorandum: the number of submarines the navy could maintain at sea at any one time, the tonnage of shipping required to keep the Allies alive, and the speed at which they could replace sunk vessels. "I calculate we can sink six hundred thousand tons of shipping per month," he said. It was an impressive performance, every statement backed up by a number. Walter was skeptical only because the admiral was too precise, too certain: surely war was never that predictable?

Von Holtzendorff pointed to a ribbon-tied document on the table, presumably the imperial order to begin unrestricted submarine warfare. "If Your Majesty approves my plan today, I guarantee the Allies will capitulate in precisely five months." He sat down.

The kaiser looked at the chancellor. Now, Walter thought, we will hear a more realistic assessment. Bethmann had been chancellor for seven years, and unlike the monarch he had a sense of the complexity of international relations.

Bethmann spoke gloomily of American entry into the war and the USA's uncounted resources of manpower, supplies, and money. In his support he quoted the opinions of every senior German who was familiar with the United States. But to Walter's disappointment he looked like a man going through the motions. He must believe the kaiser had already made up his mind. Was this meeting merely to ratify a decision already taken? Was Germany doomed?

The kaiser had a short attention span for people who disagreed with him, and while his chancellor was speaking he fidgeted, grunting impatiently and making disapproving faces. Bethmann began to dither. "If the military authorities consider the U-boat war essential, I am not in a position to contradict them. On the other hand—"

He never got to say what was on the other hand. Von Holtzendorff jumped to his feet and interrupted. "I guarantee on my word as a naval officer that no American will set foot upon the Continent!" he said.

That was absurd, Walter thought. What did his word as a naval officer have to do with anything? But it went down better than all his statistics. The kaiser brightened, and several other men nodded approval.

Bethmann seemed to give up. His body slumped in the chair, the tension went out of his face, and he spoke in a defeated voice. "If success beckons, we must follow," he said.

The kaiser made a gesture, and von Holtzendorff pushed the beribboned document across the table.

No, Walter thought, we can't possibly make this fateful decision on such inadequate grounds!

The kaiser picked up a pen and signed: "Wilhelm I.R."

He put down the pen and stood up.

Everyone in the room jumped to their feet.

This can't be the end, Walter thought.

The kaiser left the room. The tension was broken, and a buzz of talk broke out. Bethmann remained in his seat, staring down at the table. He looked like a man who has met his doom. He was muttering something, and Walter stepped closer to hear. It was a Latin phrase: *Finis Germaniae*—the end of the Germans.

General von Henscher appeared and said to Otto: "If you would care to come with me, we will have lunch privately. You, too, young man." He led them into a side room where a cold buffet was laid out.

Castle Pless served as a residence for the kaiser, so the food was good. Walter was angry and depressed, but like everyone else in Germany he was hungry, and he piled his plate high with cold chicken, potato salad, and white bread.

"Today's decision was anticipated by Foreign Minister

Zimmermann," said von Henscher. "He wants to know what we can do to discourage the Americans."

Small chance of that, Walter thought. If we sink American ships and drown American citizens, there's not much we can do to soften the blow.

The general went on: "Can we, for example, foment a protest movement among the one point three million Americans who were born here in Germany?"

Walter groaned inwardly. "Absolutely not," he said. "It's a stupid fairy tale."

His father snapped: "Careful how you speak to your superiors."

Von Henscher made a calming gesture. "Let the boy speak his mind, Otto. I might as well have his frank opinion. Why do you say that, Major?"

Walter said: "They don't love the fatherland. Why do you think they left? They may eat wurst and drink beer, but they're Americans and they'll fight for America."

"What about the Irish-born?"

"Same thing. They hate the British, of course, but when our submarines kill Americans they'll hate us more."

Otto said irritably: "How can President Wilson declare war on us? He has just won reelection as the man who kept America out of war!"

Walter shrugged. "In some ways that makes it easier. People will believe he had no option."

Von Henscher said: "What might hold him back?"

"Protection for ships of neutral countries—"

"Out of the question," his father interrupted. "Unrestricted means unrestricted. That's what the navy wanted, and that's what His Majesty has given them."

Von Henscher said: "If domestic issues aren't likely to trouble Wilson, is there any chance he may be distracted by foreign affairs in his own hemisphere?" He turned to Otto. "Mexico, for example?"

Otto smiled, looking pleased. "You're remembering the *Ypiranga*. I must admit, that was a small triumph of aggressive diplomacy."

Walter had never shared his father's glee over the incident of the shipload of arms sent by Germany to Mexico. Otto and his cronies had made President Wilson look foolish, and they could yet come to regret it.

"And now?" said von Henscher.

"Most of the U.S. Army is either in Mexico or stationed on the border," said Walter. "Ostensibly they're chasing a bandit called Pancho Villa, who raids across the border. President Carranza is bursting with indignation at the violation of his sovereign territory, but there isn't much he can do."

"If he had help from us, would that change anything?"

Walter considered. This kind of diplomatic mischief-making struck him as risky, but it was his duty to answer the questions as accurately as he could. "The Mexicans feel they were robbed of Texas, New Mexico, and Arizona. They have a dream of winning those territories back, much like the French pipe dream of winning back Alsace and Lorraine. President Carranza may be stupid enough to believe it could be done."

Otto said eagerly: "In any event, the attempt would certainly take American attention away from Europe!"

"For a while," Walter agreed reluctantly. "In the long-term our interference might strengthen those Americans who would like to join in the war on the Allied side."

"The short term is what interests us. You heard von Holtzendorff—our submarines are going to bring the Allies to their knees in five months. All we want is to keep the Americans busy that long."

Von Henscher said: "What about Japan? Is there any chance the Japs might be persuaded to attack the Panama Canal, or even California?"

"Realistically, no," Walter said firmly. The discussion was venturing further into the land of fantasy.

But von Henscher persisted. "Nevertheless, the mere threat might tie up more American troops on the West Coast."

"I suppose it could, yes."

Otto patted his lips with his napkin. "This is all most interesting, but I must see whether His Majesty needs me."

They all stood up. Walter said: "If I may say so, General . . ."

His father sighed, but von Henscher said: "Please."

"I believe all this is very dangerous, sir. If word got out that German leaders were even talking about fomenting strife in Mexico, and encouraging Japanese aggression in

California, American public opinion would be so outraged that the declaration of war could come much sooner, if not immediately. Forgive me if I am stating the obvious, but this conversation should remain highly secret."

"Quite all right," said von Henscher. He smiled at Otto. "Your father and I are the older generation, of course, but we still know a thing or two. You may rely on our discretion."

{ II }

Fitz was pleased that the German peace proposal had been spurned, and proud of his part in the process, but when it was over he had doubts.

He thought it over, walking—or, rather, limping—along Piccadilly on the morning of Wednesday, January 17, on his way to his office in the Admiralty. Peace talks would have been a sneaky way for the Germans to consolidate their gains, legitimizing their hold over Belgium, northeastern France, and parts of Russia. For Britain to take part in such talks would have amounted to an admission of defeat. But Britain still had not won.

Lloyd George's talk of a knockout went down well in the newspapers, but all sensible people knew it was a day-dream. The war would go on, perhaps for a year, perhaps longer. And, if the Americans continued to remain neutral, it might end in peace talks after all. What if no one *could* win this war? Another million men would be killed for no purpose. The thought that haunted Fitz was that Ethel might have been right after all.

And what if Britain lost? There would be a financial crisis, unemployment, and destitution. Working-class men would take up Ethel's father's cry and say that they had never been allowed to vote for the war. The people's rage against their rulers would be boundless. Protests and marches would turn into riots. It was only a little more than a century ago that Parisians had executed their king and much of the nobility. Would Londoners do the same? Fitz imagined himself, bound hand and foot, carried on a cart to the place of execution, spat upon and jeered at by the crowd. Worse, he saw the same happening to Maud, and

Aunt Herm, and Bea, and Boy. He pushed the nightmare out of his mind.

What a little spitfire Ethel was, he thought with mingled admiration and regret. He had been mortified with embarrassment when his guest was ejected from the gallery during Lloyd George's speech, but at the same time he found himself even more attracted to her.

Unfortunately, she had turned against him. He had followed her out and caught up with her in the Central Lobby, and she had berated him, blaming him and his kind for prolonging the war. From the way she talked you would think every soldier who died in France had been killed by Fitz personally.

That was the end of his Chelsea scheme. He had sent her a couple of notes but she had not replied. The disappointment hit him hard. When he thought of the delightful afternoons they might have spent in that love nest, he felt the loss like an ache in his chest.

However, he had some consolation. Bea had taken his reprimand to heart. She now welcomed him to her bedroom, dressed in pretty nightwear, offering him her scented body as she had when they were first married. In the end she was a well-brought-up aristocratic woman and she knew what a wife was for.

Musing on the compliant princess and the irresistible activist, he entered the Old Admiralty Building to find a partly decoded German telegram on his desk.

It was headed:

Berlin zu Washington. W.158. 16 January 1917.

Fitz looked automatically at the foot of the decrypt to see who it was from. The name at the end was:

Zimmermann.

His interest was piqued. This was a message from the German foreign minister to his ambassador in the United States. With a pencil Fitz wrote a translation, putting squiggles and question marks where code groups had not been decrypted.

Most secret for Your Excellency's personal information and to be handed on to the imperial minister in (?Mexico?) with xxxx by a safe route.

The question marks indicated a code group whose meaning was not certain. The decoders were guessing. If they were right, this message was for the German ambassador in Mexico. It was simply being sent via the Washington embassy.

Mexico, Fitz thought. How odd.

The next sentence was completely decoded.

> We propose to begin on 1 February unrestricted submarine warfare.

"My God!" Fitz said aloud. It was fearfully expected, but this was firm confirmation—and with a date! The news would be a coup for Room 40.

> In doing so however we shall endeavor to keep America neutral xxxx. If we should not we propose to (?Mexico?) an alliance upon the following basis: conduct of war, conclusion of peace.

"An alliance with Mexico?" Fitz said to himself. "This is strong stuff. The Americans are going to be hopping mad!"

> Your Excellency should for the present inform the president secretly war with the USA xxxx and at the same time to negotiate between us and Japan xxxx our submarines will compel England to peace within a few months. Acknowledge receipt.

Fitz looked up and caught the eye of young Carver, who—he now saw—was bursting with excitement. "You must be reading the Zimmermann intercept," the sublieutenant said.

"Such as it is," Fitz said calmly. He was just as euphoric as Carver, but better at concealing it. "Why is the decrypt so scrappy?"

"It's in a new code that we haven't completely cracked. All the same, the message is hot stuff, isn't it?"

Fitz looked again at his translation. Carver was not exaggerating. This appeared very much like an attempt to get Mexico to ally with Germany against the United States. It was sensational.

It might even make the American president angry enough to declare war on Germany.

Fitz's pulse quickened. "I agree," he said. "And I'm going to take this straight to Blinker Hall." Captain William Reginald Hall, the director of naval intelligence, had a chronic facial tic, hence the nickname; but there was nothing wrong with his brain. "He will ask questions, and I need to have some answers ready. What are the prospects for getting a complete decrypt?"

"It's going to take us several weeks to master the new code."

Fitz gave a grunt of exasperation. The reconstruction of new codes from first principles was a painstaking business that could not be hurried.

Carver went on: "But I notice that the message is to be forwarded from Washington to Mexico. On that route, they're still using an old diplomatic code we broke more than a year ago. Perhaps we could get a copy of the forwarded cable?"

"Perhaps we could!" Fitz said eagerly. "We have an agent in the telegraph office in Mexico City." He thought ahead. "When we reveal this to the world . . ."

Carver said anxiously: "We can't do that."

"Why not?"

"The Germans would know we're reading their traffic."

Fitz saw that he was right. It was the perennial problem of secret intelligence: how to use it without compromising the source. He said: "But this is so important we might want to take the risk."

"I doubt it. This department has provided too much reliable information. They won't put that in jeopardy."

"Damn! Surely we can't come across something like this and then be powerless to use it?"

Carver shrugged. "It happens in this line of work."

Fitz was not prepared to accept that. The entry of America could win the war. That was surely worth any sacrifice. But he knew enough about the army to realize that some men would show more courage and resourcefulness defending a department than a redoubt. Carver's objection had to be taken seriously. "We need a cover story," he said.

"Let's say the Americans intercepted the cable," Carver said.

Fitz nodded. "It is to be forwarded from Washington to Mexico, so we could say the U.S. government got it from Western Union."

"Western Union may not like it . . ."

"To hell with them. Now: how, exactly, do we use this information to the maximum effect? Does our government make the announcement? Do we give it to the Americans? Do we get some third party to challenge the Germans?"

Carver put up both hands in a gesture of surrender. "I'm out of my depth."

"I'm not," said Fitz, suddenly inspired. "And I know just the person to help."

{ III }

Fitz met Gus Dewar at a south London pub called the Ring.

To Fitz's surprise, Dewar was a lover of boxing. As a teenager he had attended a waterfront arena in Buffalo, and in his travels across Europe, back in 1914, he had watched prizefights in every capital city. He kept his enthusiasm quiet, Fitz thought wryly: boxing was not a popular topic of conversation at teatime in Mayfair.

However, all classes were represented at the Ring. Gentlemen in evening dress mingled with dockers in torn coats. Illegal bookmakers took bets in every corner while waiters brought loaded trays of beer in pint glasses. The air was thick with the smoke of cigars, pipes, and cigarettes. There were no seats and no women.

Fitz found Gus deep in conversation with a broken-nosed Londoner, arguing about the American fighter Jack Johnson, the first black world heavyweight champion, whose marriage to a white woman had caused Christian ministers to call for him to be lynched. The Londoner had riled Gus by agreeing with the clergymen.

Fitz nourished a secret hope that Gus might fall for Maud. It would be a good match. They were both intellectuals, both liberals, both frightfully serious about everything, always reading books. The Dewars came from what Americans called Old Money, the nearest thing they had to an aristocracy.

In addition, both Gus and Maud were in favor of peace. Maud had always been strangely passionate about ending the war; Fitz had no idea why. And Gus revered his boss, Woodrow Wilson, who had made a speech a month ago calling for "peace without victory," a phrase that had infuriated Fitz and most of the British and French leadership.

But the compatibility Fitz had seen between Gus and Maud had not led anywhere. Fitz loved his sister, but he wondered what was wrong with her. Did she want to be an old maid?

When Fitz had detached Gus from the man with the broken nose, he raised the subject of Mexico.

"It's a mess," Gus said. "Wilson has withdrawn General Pershing and his troops, in an attempt to please President Carranza, but it hasn't worked—Carranza won't even discuss policing the border. Why do you ask?"

"I'll tell you later," Fitz said. "The next bout is starting."

As they watched a fighter called Benny the Yid pounding the brains out of Bald Albert Collins, Fitz resolved to avoid the topic of the German peace offer. He knew that Gus was heartbroken at the failure of Wilson's initiative. Gus asked himself constantly whether he could have handled matters better, or done something further to support the president's plan. Fitz thought the plan had been doomed from the start because neither side really wanted peace.

In the third round Bald Albert went down and stayed down.

"You caught me just in time," Gus said. "I'm about to head for home."

"Looking forward to it?"

"If I get there. I might be sunk by a U-boat on the way."

The Germans had resumed unrestricted submarine warfare on February 1, exactly as foretold in the Zimmermann intercept. This had angered the Americans, but not as much as Fitz had hoped. "President Wilson's reaction to the submarine announcement was surprisingly mild," he said.

"He broke off diplomatic relations with Germany. That's not mild."

"But he did not declare war." Fitz had been devastated by this. He had fought hard against peace talks, but Maud and Ethel and their pacifist friends were right to say there was no hope of victory in the foreseeable future—without extra help from somewhere. Fitz had felt sure that unrestricted submarine warfare would bring the Americans in. So far it had not.

Gus said: "Frankly, I think President Wilson was infuriated by the submarine decision, and is now ready to declare war. He's tried everything else, for goodness' sake. But he won reelection as the man who kept us out. The only way he can switch is if he is swept into war on a tide of public enthusiasm."

"In that case," said Fitz, "I believe I have something that might help him."

Gus raised an eyebrow.

"Since I was wounded, I've been working in a unit that decodes intercepted German wireless messages." Fitz took from his pocket a sheet of paper covered with his own handwriting. "Your government will be given this officially in the next few days. I'm showing it to you now because we need advice on how to handle it." He gave it to Gus.

The British spy in Mexico City had got hold of the relayed message in the old code, and the paper Fitz handed to Gus was a complete decrypt of the Zimmermann intercept. In full, it read:

Washington to Mexico, 19 January 1917

We intend to begin on 1 February unrestricted submarine warfare. We shall endeavour in spite of this to keep the USA neutral. In the event of this not succeeding we make Mexico a proposal of alliance on the following terms:

Make war together.

Make peace together.

Generous financial support and an undertaking on our part that Mexico is to reconquer the lost territory in Texas, New Mexico, and Arizona. The settlement in detail is left to you.

You will inform the president of the above most secretly as soon as the outbreak of war with the USA is certain, and add the suggestion that he should on his own initiative invite Japan to immediate adherence and at the same time mediate between Japan and ourselves.

Please call the president's attention to the fact that the ruthless employment of our submarines now offers the prospect of compelling England in a few months to make peace.

Gus read a few lines, holding the sheet close to his eyes in the low light of the boxing arena, and said: "Alliance? My God!"

Fitz glanced around. A new bout had begun, and the noise of the crowd was too loud for people nearby to overhear Gus.

Gus read on. "Reconquer Texas?" he said with incredulity. And then, angrily: "Invite Japan?" He looked up from the paper. "This is outrageous!"

This was the reaction Fitz had been hoping for, and he had to quell his elation. "Outrageous is the word," he said with forced solemnity.

"The Germans are offering to pay Mexico to invade the United States!"

"Yes."

"And they're asking Mexico to try to get Japan to join in!"

"Yes."

"Wait till this gets out!"

"That's what I want to talk to you about. We want to make sure it's publicized in a manner favorable to your president."

"Why doesn't the British government simply reveal it to the world?"

Gus was not thinking this through. "Two reasons," Fitz said. "One, we don't want the Germans to know we're reading their cables. Two, we may be accused of forging this intercept."

Gus nodded. "Pardon me. I was too angry to think. Let's look at this coolly."

"If possible, we would like you to say that the United States government obtained a copy of the cable from Western Union."

"Wilson won't tell a lie."

"Then get a copy from Western Union, and it won't be a lie."

Gus nodded. "That should be possible. As for the second problem, who could release the telegram without being suspected of forgery?"

"The president himself, I presume."

"That's one possibility."

"But you have a better idea?"

"Yes," Gus said thoughtfully. "I believe I do."

{ IV }

Ethel and Bernie got married in the Calvary Gospel Hall. Neither of them had strong views about religion, and they both liked the pastor.

Ethel had not communicated with Fitz since the day of Lloyd George's speech. Fitz's public opposition to peace had reminded her harshly of his true nature. He stood for everything she hated: tradition, conservatism, exploitation of the working class, unearned wealth. She could not be the lover of such a man, and she felt ashamed of herself for even being tempted by the house in Chelsea. Her true soul mate was Bernie.

Ethel wore the pink silk dress and flowered hat that Walter von Ulrich had bought her for Maud Fitzherbert's wedding. There were no bridesmaids, but Mildred and Maud served as matrons of honor. Ethel's parents came up from Aberowen on the train. Sadly, Billy was in France and could not get leave. Little Lloyd wore a pageboy outfit specially made for him by Mildred, sky blue with brass buttons and a cap.

Bernie surprised Ethel by producing a family no one knew about. His elderly mother spoke nothing but Yiddish and muttered under her breath all through the service. She lived with Bernie's prosperous older brother, Theo, who— Mildred discovered, flirting with him—owned a bicycle factory in Birmingham.

Afterward tea and cake were served in the hall. There were no alcoholic drinks, which suited Da and Mam, and smokers had to go outside. Mam kissed Ethel and said: "I'm glad to see you settled at last, anyway." That word *anyway* carried a lot of baggage, Ethel thought. It meant: "Congratulations, even though you're a fallen woman, and you've got an illegitimate child whose father no one knows, and you're marrying a Jew, and living in London, which is the same as Sodom and Gomorrah." But Ethel accepted Mam's qualified blessing and vowed never to say such things to her own child.

Mam and Da had bought cheap day-return tickets, and they left to catch their train. When the majority of guests had gone, the remainder went to the Dog and Duck for a few drinks.

Ethel and Bernie went home when it was Lloyd's bedtime. That morning, Bernie had put his few clothes and many books into a handcart and wheeled it from his rented lodgings to Ethel's house.

To give themselves one night alone, they put Lloyd to bed upstairs with Mildred's children, which Lloyd regarded as a special treat. Then Ethel and Bernie had cocoa in the kitchen and went to bed.

Ethel had a new nightdress. Bernie put on clean pajamas. When he got into bed beside her, he broke into a nervous sweat. Ethel stroked his cheek. "Although I'm a scarlet woman, I haven't got much experience," she said. "Just my first husband, and that was only for a few weeks before he went away." She had not told Bernie about Fitz and never would. Only Billy and the lawyer Albert Solman knew the truth.

"You're better off than me," Bernie said, but already she could feel him beginning to relax. "Just a few fumbles."

"What were their names?"

"Oh, you don't want to know."

She grinned. "Yes, I do. How many women? Six? Ten? Twenty?"

"Good God, no. Three. The first was Rachel Wright, in school. Afterward she said we would have to get married, and I believed her. I was so worried."

Ethel giggled. "What happened?"

"The next week she did it with Micky Armstrong, and I was off the hook."

"Was it nice with her?"

"I suppose it was. I was only sixteen. Mainly I just wanted to be able to say I had done it."

She kissed him gently, then said: "Who was next?"

"Carol McAllister. She was a neighbor. I paid her a shilling. It was a bit brief—I think she knew what to do and say to get it over quickly. The part she liked was taking the money."

Ethel frowned disapprovingly, then recalled the house in Chelsea, and realized she had contemplated doing the same as Carol McAllister. Feeling uncomfortable, she said: "Who was the other one?"

"An older woman. She was my landlady. She came to my bed at night when her husband was away."

"Was it nice with her?"

"Lovely. It was a happy time for me."

"What went wrong?"

"Her husband got suspicious and I had to leave."

"And then?"

"Then I met you, and I lost all interest in other women."

They began to kiss. Soon he pushed up the skirt of her nightdress and got on top of her. He was gentle, worried about hurting her, but he entered her easily. She felt a surge of affection for him, for his kindness and intelligence and devotion to her and her child. She put her arms around him and hugged his body to hers. Quite soon, his climax came. Then they both lay back, content, and went to sleep.

{V}

Women's skirts had changed, Gus Dewar realized. They now showed the ankles. Ten years ago, a glimpse of ankle had been arousing; now it was mundane. Perhaps women covered their nakedness to make themselves more alluring, not less.

Rosa Hellman was wearing a dark-red coat that fell in pleats from the yoke at the back, rather fashionable. It was trimmed with black fur, which he guessed was welcome in Washington in February. Her gray hat was small and round with a red hatband and a feather, not very practical, but when was the last time American women's hats had been designed for practical purposes? "I'm honored by this invitation," she said. He could not be sure whether she was mocking him. "You're only just back from Europe, aren't you?"

They were having lunch in the dining room of the Willard Hotel, two blocks east of the White House. Gus had invited her for a specific purpose. "I've got a story for you," he said as soon as they had ordered.

"Oh, good! Let me guess. The president is going to divorce Edith and marry Mary Peck?"

Gus frowned. Wilson had had a dalliance with Mary Peck while he was married to his first wife. Gus doubted whether they had actually committed adultery, but Wilson had been foolish enough to write letters that showed more affection than was seemly. Washington gossips knew all about it, but nothing had been printed. "I'm talking about something serious," Gus said sternly.

"Oh, sorry," said Rosa. She composed her face in a solemn expression that made Gus want to laugh.

"The only condition is going to be that you can't say you got the information from the White House."

"Agreed."

"I'm going to show you a telegram from the German foreign minister, Arthur Zimmermann, to the German ambassador in Mexico."

She looked astonished. "Where did you get that?"

"From Western Union," he lied.

"Isn't it in code?"

"Codes can be broken." He handed her a typewritten copy of the full English translation.

"Is this off the record?" she said.

"No. The only thing I want you to keep to yourself is where you got it."

"Okay." She began to read. After a moment, her mouth dropped open. She looked up. "Gus," she said. "Is this real?"

"When did you know me to play a practical joke?"

"The last time was never." She read on. "The Germans are going to pay Mexico to invade Texas?"

"That's what Herr Zimmermann says."

"This isn't a story, Gus—this is the scoop of the century!"

He allowed himself a small smile, trying not to appear as triumphant as he felt. "That's what I thought you'd say."

"Are you acting independently, or on behalf of the president?"

"Rosa, do you imagine I would do a thing like this without approval from the very top?"

"I guess not. Wow. So this comes to me from President Wilson."

"Not officially."

"But how do I know it's true? I don't think I can write the story based only on a scrap of paper and your word."

Gus had anticipated this snag. "Secretary of State Lansing will personally confirm the authenticity of the telegram to your boss, provided the conversation is confidential."

"Good enough." She looked down at the sheet of paper again. "This changes everything. Can you imagine what the American people will say when they read it?"

"I think it will make them more inclined to join in the war and fight against Germany."

"Inclined?" she said. "They're going to be foaming at the mouth! Wilson will have to declare war."

Gus said nothing.

After a moment, Rosa interpreted his silence. "Oh, I see. That's why you're releasing the telegram. The president *wants* to declare war."

She was dead right. He smiled, enjoying this dance of wits with a bright woman. "I'm not saying that."

"But this telegram will anger the American people so much that they will demand war. And Wilson will be able to say he did not renege on his election promises—he was forced by public opinion to change his policy."

She was in fact a bit too bright for his purposes. He said anxiously: "That's not the story you'll write, is it?"

She smiled. "Oh, no. That's just me refusing to take anything at face value. I was an anarchist once, you know."

"And now?"

"Now I'm a reporter. And there's only one way to write this story."

He felt relieved.

The waiter brought their food: poached salmon for her, steak and mashed potatoes for him. Rosa stood up. "I have to get back to the office."

Gus was startled. "What about your lunch?"

"Are you serious?" she said. "I can't eat. Don't you understand what you've done?"

He thought he did, but he said: "Tell me."

"You've just sent America to war."

Gus nodded. "I know," he said. "Go write the story."

"Hey," she said. "Thanks for picking me."

A moment later she was gone.

CHAPTER TWENTY-THREE

March 1917

That winter in Petrograd was cold and hungry. The thermometer outside the barracks of the First Machine Gun Regiment stayed at minus fifteen degrees centigrade for a full month. Bakers stopped making pies, cakes, pastries, and anything else other than bread, but still there was not enough flour. Armed guards were posted at the barracks kitchen door because so many soldiers tried to beg or steal extra food.

One bitterly cold day early in March, Grigori got an afternoon pass and decided to go and see Vladimir, who would be with the landlady while Katerina was at work. He put on his army greatcoat and set off through icy streets. On Nevsky Prospekt he caught the eye of a child beggar, a girl of about nine, standing on a corner in an arctic wind. Something about her bothered him, and he frowned as he walked past. A minute later he realized what had struck him. She had given him a look of sexual invitation. He was so shocked that he stopped in his tracks. How could she be a whore at that age? He turned around, intending to question her, but she was gone.

He walked on with a troubled mind. He knew, of course, that there were men who wanted sex with children: he had learned that when he and little Lev sought help from a priest, all those years ago. But somehow the picture of that nine-year-old pathetically imitating a come-hither smile wrenched at his heart. It made him want to weep for his country. We are turning our children into prostitutes, he thought: can it possibly get any worse?

He was in a grim mood when he reached his old lodgings. As soon as he entered the house he heard Vladimir bawling. He went up to Katerina's room and found the child alone, his face red and contorted with crying. He picked him up and rocked him.

The room was clean and tidy, and smelled of Katerina. Grigori came here most Sundays. They had a routine: they went out in the morning, then came home and made lunch, with food Grigori brought from the barracks when he could get any. Afterward, while Vladimir had his nap, they made love. On Sundays when there was enough to eat, Grigori was blissfully happy in this room.

Vladimir's yelling became a droning discontented grizzle. With the child in his arms, Grigori went to look for the landlady, who was supposed to be watching Vladimir. He found her in the laundry, a low-built extension at the back of the house, running wet bedsheets through a mangle. She was a woman of about fifty with gray hair tied up in a scarf. She had been plump back in 1914 when Grigori left to go in the army, but now her throat was scraggy and her jowls hung loose. Even landladies were hungry these days.

She looked startled and guilty when she saw him. Grigori said: "Didn't you hear the child crying?"

"I can't rock him all day," she said defensively, and went on turning the handle of the wringer.

"Perhaps he's hungry."

"He's had his milk," she said quickly. Her response was suspiciously rapid, and Grigori guessed she had drunk the milk herself. He wanted to strangle her.

In the cold air of the unheated laundry he felt Vladimir's soft baby skin radiating heat. "I think he's got a fever," he said. "Didn't you notice his temperature?"

"Am I a doctor, now, too?"

Vladimir stopped crying and fell into a state of lassitude that Grigori found more worrying. He was normally an alert, busy child, curious and mildly destructive, but now he lay still in Grigori's arms, his face flushed, his eyes staring.

Grigori put him back on his bed in the corner of Katerina's room. He took a jug from Katerina's shelf, left the house, and hurried to the next street, where there was a general store. He bought some milk, a little sugar in a twist of paper, and an apple.

When he got back Vladimir was the same.

He warmed the milk, dissolved the sugar in it, and broke a crust of stale bread into the mixture, then fed morsels of soaked bread to Vladimir. He recalled his mother giving this to baby Lev when he was sick. Vladimir ate as if he was hungry and thirsty.

When all the bread and milk were gone, Grigori took out the apple. With his pocketknife he cut it into segments and peeled a slice. He ate the peel himself and offered the rest to Vladimir, saying: "Some for me, some for you." In the past the boy had been amused by this procedure, but now he was indifferent, and let the apple fall from his mouth.

There was no doctor nearby, and anyway Grigori could not afford the fee, but there was a midwife a few streets away. She was Magda, the pretty wife of Grigori's old friend Konstantin, the secretary of the Putilov Bolshevik Committee. Grigori and Konstantin played chess whenever they got the chance—Grigori usually won.

Grigori put a clean diaper on Vladimir, then wrapped him in the blanket from Katerina's bed, leaving only his eyes and nose visible. They went out into the cold.

Konstantin and Magda lived in a two-room apartment with Magda's aunt, who watched their three small children. Grigori was afraid Magda would be out delivering a baby, but he was in luck and she was at home.

Magda was knowledgeable and kindhearted, though a bit brisk. She felt Vladimir's forehead and said: "He has an infection."

"How bad?"

"Does he cough?"

"No."

"What are his stools like?"

"Runny."

She took off Vladimir's clothes and said: "I suppose Katerina's breasts have no milk."

"How did you know that?" Grigori said in surprise.

"It's common. A woman cannot feed a baby unless she herself is fed. Nothing comes from nothing. That's why the child is so thin."

Grigori did not know Vladimir was thin.

Magda poked Vladimir's belly and made him cry. "Inflammation of the bowels," she said.

"Will he be all right?"

"Probably. Children get infections all the time. They usually survive."

"What can we do?"

"Bathe his forehead with tepid water to bring down his temperature. Give him plenty to drink, all he wants. Don't worry about whether he eats. Feed Katerina, so that she can nurse him. Mother's milk is what he needs."

Grigori took Vladimir home. He bought more milk on the way, and warmed it up on the fire. He gave it to Vladimir on a teaspoon, and the boy drank it all. Then he warmed a pan of water and bathed Vladimir's face with a rag. It seemed to work: the child lost the flushed, staring look and began to breathe normally.

Grigori was feeling less anxious when Katerina came home at half past seven. She looked tired and cold. She had bought a cabbage and a few grams of pork fat, and Grigori put them in a saucepan to make stew while she rested. He told her about Vladimir's fever, the negligent landlady, and Magda's prescription. "What can I do?" Katerina said with weary despair. "I have to go to the factory. There is no one else to watch Volodya."

Grigori fed the child with the broth from the stew, then put him down to sleep. When Grigori and Katerina had eaten they lay on the bed together. "Don't let me sleep too long," Katerina said. "I have to join the bread queue."

"I'll go for you," Grigori said. "You rest." He would be late back to the barracks, but he could probably get away with that: the officers were too fearful of mutiny, these days, to make a fuss about minor transgressions.

Katerina took him at his word, and fell into a deep sleep.

When he heard the church clock strike two, he put on his boots and greatcoat. Vladimir seemed to be sleeping normally. Grigori left the house and walked to the bakery. To his surprise there was already a long queue, and he realized he had left it a bit late. There were about a hundred people in line, muffled up, stamping their feet in the snow. Some had brought chairs or stools. An enterprising young man with a brazier was selling porridge, washing the bowls in the snow when they were done with. A dozen more people joined the queue behind Grigori.

They gossiped and grumbled while they waited. Two

women ahead of Grigori argued about who was to blame for the bread shortage: one said Germans at court, the other Jews hoarding flour. "Who rules?" Grigori said to them. "If a streetcar overturns, you blame the driver, because he was in charge. The Jews don't rule us. The Germans don't rule us. It's the tsar and the nobility." This was the Bolshevik message.

"Who would rule, if there was no tsar?" said the younger woman skeptically. She was wearing a yellow felt hat.

"I think we should rule ourselves," said Grigori. "As they do in France and America."

"I don't know," said the older woman. "It can't go on like this."

The shop opened at five. A minute later the news came down the line that customers were rationed to one loaf per person. "All night, just for one loaf!" said the woman in the yellow hat.

It took another hour to shuffle to the head of the queue. The baker's wife was admitting customers one at a time. The older of the two women ahead of Grigori went in; then the baker's wife said: "That's all. No more bread."

The woman in the yellow hat said: "No, please! Just one more!"

The baker's wife wore a stony expression. Perhaps this had happened before. "If he had more flour, he'd bake more bread," she said. "It's all gone, do you hear me? I can't sell you bread if I haven't got any."

The last customer came out of the shop with her loaf under her coat and hurried away.

The woman in the yellow hat began to cry.

The baker's wife slammed the door.

Grigori turned and walked away.

{ II }

Spring came to Petrograd on Thursday, March 8, but the Russian Empire clung obstinately to the calendar of Julius Caesar, so they called it February 23. The rest of Europe had been using the modern calendar for three hundred years.

The rise in temperature coincided with International

Women's Day, and the female workers from the textile mills came out on strike and marched from the industrial suburbs into the city center to protest against the bread queues, the war, and the tsar. Bread rationing had been announced, but it seemed to have made the shortage worse.

The First Machine Gun Regiment, like all army units in the city, was detailed to help the police and the mounted Cossacks keep order. What would happen, Grigori wondered, if the soldiers were ordered to fire on the marchers? Would they obey? Or would they turn their rifles on their officers? In 1905 they had obeyed orders and shot workers. But since then the Russian people had suffered a decade of tyranny, repression, war, and hunger.

However, there was no trouble, and Grigori and his section returned to barracks that evening without having fired a shot.

On Friday more workers came out on strike.

The tsar was at army headquarters, four hundred miles away at Mogilev. In charge of the city was the commander of the Petrograd Military District, General Khabalov. He decided to keep marchers out of the center by stationing soldiers at the bridges. Grigori's section was posted close to the barracks, guarding the Liteiny Bridge that led across the Neva River to Liteiny Prospekt. But the water was still frozen solid, and the marchers foiled the army by simply walking across the ice—to the delight of the watching soldiers, most of whom, like Grigori, sympathized with the marchers.

None of the political parties had organized the strike. The Bolsheviks, like the other leftist revolutionary parties, found themselves following rather than leading the working class.

Once again Grigori's section saw no action, but it was not the same everywhere. When he got back to barracks on Saturday night, he learned that police had attacked demonstrators outside the railway station at the far end of Nevsky Prospekt. Surprisingly, the Cossacks had defended the marchers against the police. Men were talking about the Comrade Cossacks. Grigori was skeptical. The Cossacks had never really been loyal to anyone but themselves, he thought; they just loved a fight.

On Sunday morning Grigori was awakened at five, long before first light. At breakfast there was a rumor that the tsar had instructed General Khabalov to put a stop to strikes and marches using whatever force was necessary. That was an ominous phrase, Grigori thought: *whatever force was necessary.*

After breakfast the sergeants were given their orders. Each platoon was to guard a different point in the city: not just bridges but intersections, railway stations, and post offices. The pickets would be connected by field telephones. The nation's capital was to be secured like a captured enemy city. Worst of all, the regiment was to set up machine guns at likely trouble spots.

When Grigori relayed the instructions to his men, they were horrified. Isaak said: "Is the tsar really going to order the army to machine-gun his own people?"

Grigori said: "If he does, will soldiers obey him?"

Grigori's mounting excitement was paralleled by fear. He was heartened by the strikes, for he knew the Russian people had to defy their rulers. Otherwise the war would drag on, the people would starve, and there was no prospect that Vladimir might live a better life than Grigori and Katerina. It was this conviction that had caused Grigori to join the party. On the other hand, he cherished a secret hope that if soldiers simply refused to obey orders, the revolution might go off without too much bloodshed. But when his own regiment was ordered to set up machine-gun emplacements on Petrograd street corners, he began to feel that his hope had been foolish.

Was it even possible that the Russian people could ever escape from the tyranny of the tsars? Sometimes it seemed like a pipe dream. Yet other nations had had revolutions, and overthrown their oppressors. Even the English had killed their king once.

Petrograd was like a pan of water on the fire, Grigori thought: there were wisps of steam and a few bubbles of violence, and the surface shimmered with intense heat, but the water seemed to hesitate, and the proverbial watched pot did not boil.

His platoon was sent to the Tauride Palace, the vast summer town house of Catherine II, now home to Russia's toothless parliament, the Duma. The morning was quiet: even starving people liked to sleep late on Sunday. But the weather continued sunny, and at midday they started to come in from the suburbs, on foot and in streetcars. Some gathered in the large garden of the Tauride Palace. They were not all factory workers, Grigori noticed. There were middle-class men and women, students, and a few prosperous-looking businessmen. Some had brought their children. Were they on a political demonstration, or just going for a walk in the park? Grigori guessed they themselves were not sure.

At the entrance to the palace he saw a well-dressed young man whose handsome face was familiar from photographs in the newspapers, and he recognized the Trudovik deputy Alexander Fedorovich Kerensky. The Trudoviks were a moderate breakaway faction from the Socialist Revolutionaries. Grigori asked him what was going on inside. "The tsar formally dissolved the Duma today," Kerensky told him.

Grigori shook his head in disgust. "A characteristic reaction," he said. "Repress those who complain, rather than address their discontents."

Kerensky looked at him sharply. Perhaps he had not been expecting such an analysis from a soldier. "Quite," he said. "Anyway, we deputies are ignoring the tsar's edict."

"What will happen?"

"Most people think the demonstrations will peter out as soon as the authorities manage to restore the supply of bread," Kerensky said, and he went inside.

Grigori wondered what made the moderates think that was going to happen. If the authorities were able to restore the supply of bread, would they not have done so, instead of rationing it? But moderates always seemed to deal in hopes rather than facts.

Early in the afternoon Grigori was surprised to see the smiling faces of Katerina and Vladimir. He normally spent Sunday with them, but had assumed he would not see them today. Vladimir looked well and happy, much to Grigori's relief. Evidently the boy had got over the infection. It was warm enough for Katerina to wear her coat open, showing her voluptuous figure. He wished he could caress her. She smiled at him, making him think of how she would kiss his face as they lay on the bed, and Grigori felt a stab of yearning that was almost unbearable. He hated to miss that Sunday afternoon embrace.

"How did you know I would be here?" he asked her.

"It was a lucky guess."

"I'm glad to see you, but it's dangerous for you to be in the city center."

Katerina looked at the crowds strolling through the park. "It seems safe enough to me."

Grigori could not dispute that. There was no sign of trouble.

Mother and child went off to walk around the frozen lake. Grigori's breath caught in his throat as he watched Vladimir toddle away and almost immediately fall over. Katerina picked him up, soothed him, and walked on. They looked so vulnerable. What was going to happen to them?

When they returned, Katerina said she was taking Vladimir home for his nap.

"Go by the backstreets," Grigori said. "Keep away from crowds. I don't know what might happen."

"All right," she said.

"Promise."

"I promise."

Grigori saw no bloodshed that day, but at the barracks in the evening he heard a different story from other groups. In Znamenskaya Square soldiers had been ordered to shoot demonstrators, and forty people had died. Grigori felt a cold hand on his heart. Katerina might have been killed just walking along the street!

Others were equally outraged, and in the mess hall feelings were running high. Sensing the mood of the men, Grigori stood on a table and took charge, calling for order and inviting soldiers to speak in turn. Supper turned rapidly into a mass meeting. He called first on Isaak, who was well known as the star of the regimental soccer team.

"I joined the army to kill Germans, not Russians," Isaak said, and there was a roar of approval. "The marchers are our brothers and sisters, our mothers and fathers—and their only crime is to ask for bread!"

Grigori knew all the Bolsheviks in the regiment, and he called on several of them to speak, but he was careful to point to others, too, not to seem overly biased. Normally the men were cautious about expressing their opinions, for fear their remarks would be reported and they would be punished; but today they did not seem to care.

The speaker who made the greatest impression was Yakov, a tall man with shoulders like a bear. He stood on the table beside Grigori with tears in his eyes. "When they told us to fire, I didn't know what to do," he said. He seemed unable to raise his voice, and the room went quiet as the other men strained to hear him. "I said: 'God, please guide me now,' and I listened in my heart, but God sent me no answer." The men were silent. "I raised my rifle," Yakov said. "The captain was screaming: 'Shoot! Shoot!' But who should I shoot at? In Galicia we knew who our enemies were because they were firing at us. But today in the square no one was attacking us. The people were mostly women, some with children. Even the men had no weapons."

He fell silent. The men were as still as stones, as if they feared that any movement might break the spell. After a moment Isaak prompted him. "What happened next, Yakov Davidovich?"

"I pulled the trigger," Yakov said, and the tears ran from his eyes into his bushy black beard. "I didn't even aim the gun. The captain was screaming at me and I fired just to shut him up. But I hit a woman. A girl, really—about nineteen, I suppose. She had a green coat. I shot her in the chest, and the blood went all over the coat, red on green. Then she fell down." He was weeping openly now, speaking in gasps. "I dropped my gun and tried to go to her, to help her, but the crowd went for me, punching and kicking, though I hardly felt it." He wiped his face with his sleeve. "I'm in trouble, now, for losing my rifle." There was another long pause. "Nineteen," he said. "I think she must have been about nineteen."

Grigori had not noticed the door opening, but suddenly Lieutenant Kirillov was there. "Get off that damn table, Yakov," he shouted. He looked at Grigori. "You, too, Peshkov, you troublemaker." He turned and spoke to the men, sitting on benches at their trestle tables. "Return to your barracks, all of you," he said. "Anyone still in this room one minute from now gets a flogging."

No one moved. The men stared surlily at the lieutenant. Grigori wondered if this was how a mutiny started.

But Yakov was too lost in his misery to realize what a moment of drama he had created; he got down clumsily from the table, and the tension was released. Some of the men close to Kirillov stood up, looking sullen but scared.

Grigori remained defiantly standing on the table a few moments longer, but he sensed that the men were not quite angry enough to turn on an officer, so in the end he got down. The men started to leave the room. Kirillov remained where he was, glaring at everyone.

Grigori returned to barracks and soon the bell rang for lights-out. As a sergeant, he had the privilege of a curtained niche at the end of his platoon's dormitory. He could hear the men speaking in low voices.

"I won't shoot women," said one.

"Me neither."

A third voice said: "If you don't, some of these bastard officers will shoot you for disobedience!"

"I'm going to aim to miss," said another voice.

"They might see."

"You only have to aim a bit above the heads of the crowd. No one can be sure what you're doing."

"That's what I'm going to do," said another voice.

"Me, too."

"Me, too."

We'll see, Grigori thought as he drifted off to sleep. Brave words came easily in the dark. Daylight might tell a different story.

{ III }

On Monday Grigori's platoon was marched the short distance along Samsonievsky Prospekt to the Liteiny Bridge and ordered to prevent demonstrators crossing the river to the city center. The bridge was four hundred yards long, and rested on massive stone piers set into the frozen river like stranded icebreakers.

This was the same job they had had on Friday, but the orders were different. Lieutenant Kirillov briefed Grigori. He spoke these days as if he was in a constant bad temper, and perhaps he was: officers probably disliked being lined up against their own countrymen just as much as the men did. "No marchers are to cross the river, either by the bridge or on the ice, do you understand? You will shoot people who flout your instructions."

Grigori hid his contempt. "Yes, Excellency!" he said smartly.

Kirillov repeated the orders, then disappeared. Grigori thought the lieutenant was scared. Doubtless he feared being held responsible for what happened, whether his orders were obeyed or defied.

Grigori had no intention of obeying. He would allow the leaders of the march to engage him in discussion while their followers crossed the ice, exactly as it had played out on Friday.

However, early in the morning his platoon was joined by a detachment of police. To his horror, he saw that they were led by his old enemy Mikhail Pinsky. The man did not appear to be suffering from the shortage of bread: his round face was fatter than ever, and his police uniform was tight around the middle. He was carrying a megaphone. His weasel-faced sidekick, Kozlov, was nowhere in sight.

"I know you," Pinsky said to Grigori. "You used to work at the Putilov factory."

"Until you had me conscripted," Grigori said.

"Your brother is a murderer, but he escaped to America."

"So you say."

"No one is going to cross the river here today."

"We shall see."

"I expect full cooperation from your men. Is that understood?"

Grigori said: "Aren't you afraid?"

"Of the rabble? Don't be stupid."

"No, I mean of the future. Suppose the revolutionaries get their way. What do you think they will do to you? You've spent your life bullying the weak, beating people up, harassing women, and taking bribes. Don't you fear a day of retribution?"

Pinsky pointed a gloved finger at Grigori. "I'm reporting you as a damned subversive," he said, and he walked away.

Grigori shrugged. It was not as easy as it used to be for the police to arrest anyone they liked. Isaak and others might mutiny if Grigori was jailed, and the officers knew it.

The day started quietly, but Grigori noted that few workers were on the streets. Many factories were closed because they could not get fuel for their steam engines and furnaces. Other places were on strike, the employees de-

manding more money to pay inflated prices, or heating for
ice-cold workshops, or safety rails around dangerous machinery. It looked as if almost no one was actually going to
work today. But the sun rose cheerfully, and people were
not going to stay indoors. Sure enough, at midmorning
Grigori saw, coming along Samsonievsky Prospekt, a large
crowd of men and women in the blue tunics and ragged
coats of industrial workers.

Grigori had thirty men and two corporals. He had stationed them in four lines of eight across the road, blocking
the end of the bridge. Pinsky had about the same number
of men, half on foot and half on horseback, and he placed
them at the sides of the road.

Grigori peered anxiously at the oncoming march. He
could not predict what would happen. On his own he could
have prevented bloodshed, by offering only token resistance, then letting the demonstrators pass. But he did not
know what Pinsky was going to do.

The marchers came nearer. There were hundreds of
people—no, thousands. Most wore red armbands or red
ribbons. Their banners read *Down with the Tsar* and *Bread,
Peace, and Land*. This was no longer merely a protest, Grigori concluded: it had become a political movement.

As the leaders came nearer, he sensed the tightening
anxiety among his waiting men.

He walked forward to meet the marchers. At their head,
to his surprise, was Varya, the mother of Konstantin. Her
gray hair was tied up in a red scarf, and she carried a red
flag on a hefty stick. "Hello, Grigori Sergeivich," she said
amiably. "Are you going to shoot me?"

"No, I'm not," he replied. "But I can't speak for the
police."

Although Varya stopped, the others came on, pressed
from behind by thousands more. Grigori heard Pinsky urge
his mounted men forward. These horseback policemen,
called Pharaohs, were the most hated section of the force.
They were armed with whips and clubs.

Varya said: "All we want is to make a living and feed our
families. Isn't that what you want, too, Grigori?"

The marchers were not confronting Grigori's soldiers, or
attempting to get past them onto the bridge. Instead they
were spreading out along the embankment on both sides.

Pinsky's Pharaohs nervously walked their horses along the towpath, as if to bar the way to the ice, but there were not enough of them to form a continuous barrier. However, no marcher wanted to be the first to make a dash for it, and there was a moment of stalemate.

Lieutenant Pinsky put his megaphone to his mouth. "Go back!" he shouted. The instrument was no more than a piece of tin shaped like a cone, and made his voice only a little louder. "You may not enter the city center. Return to your workplaces in orderly fashion. This is a police command. Go back."

Nobody went back—most people could not even hear—but the marchers started to jeer and boo. Someone deep in the crowd threw a stone. It struck the rump of a horse, and the beast started. Its rider, taken by surprise, almost fell off. Furious, he pulled himself upright, sawed on the reins, and lashed the horse with his whip. The crowd laughed, which made him angrier, but he brought his horse under control.

A brave marcher took advantage of the diversion, dodged past a Pharaoh on the embankment, and ran onto the ice. Several more people on both sides of the bridge did the same. The Pharaohs deployed their whips and clubs, wheeling and rearing their horses as they lashed out. Some of the marchers fell to the ground, but more got through, and others were emboldened to try. In seconds, thirty or more people were running across the frozen river.

For Grigori, that was a happy outcome. He could say that he had attempted to enforce the ban, and he had in fact kept people off the bridge, but the number of demonstrators was too great and it had proved impossible to stop people crossing the ice.

Pinsky did not see it that way.

He turned his megaphone to the armed police and said: "Take aim!"

"No!" Grigori shouted, but it was too late. The police took up the firing position, on one knee, and raised their rifles. Marchers at the front of the crowd tried to go back, but they were pushed forward by the thousands behind them. Some ran for the river, braving the Pharaohs.

Pinsky shouted: "Fire!"

There was a crackle of shots like fireworks, followed by

shouts of fear and screams of pain as marchers fell dead and wounded.

Grigori was taken back twelve years. He saw the square in front of the Winter Palace, the hundreds of men and women kneeling in prayer, the soldiers with their rifles, and his mother lying on the ground with her blood spreading on the snow. In his mind he heard eleven-year-old Lev scream: "She's dead! Ma's dead, my mother is dead!"

"No," Grigori said aloud. "I will not let them do this again." He turned the safety knob on his Mosin-Nagant rifle, unlocking the bolt; then he raised the gun to his shoulder.

The crowd was screaming and running in all directions, trampling the fallen. The Pharaohs were out of control, lashing out at random. The police fired indiscriminately into the crowd.

Grigori aimed carefully at Pinsky, targeting the middle of the body. He was not a very good shot, and Pinsky was sixty yards away, but he had a chance of hitting him. He pulled the trigger.

Pinsky continued to yell through his megaphone.

Grigori had missed. He lowered his sights—the rifle kicked up a little when fired—and squeezed the trigger again.

He missed again.

The carnage went on, police shooting wildly into the crowd of fleeing men and women.

There were five rounds in the magazine of Grigori's rifle. He could usually hit something with one of the five. He fired a third time.

Pinsky gave a shout of pain that was amplified by his megaphone. His right knee seemed to fold under him. He dropped the megaphone and fell to the ground.

Grigori's men followed his example. They attacked the police, some firing and some using their rifles as clubs. Others pulled the Pharaohs off their horses. The marchers drew courage and joined in. Some of those on the ice turned around and came back.

The fury of the mob was ugly. For as long as anyone could remember, the Petrograd police had been sneering brutes, undisciplined and uncontrolled, and now the people took their revenge. Policemen on the ground were kicked and trampled, those on their feet were knocked down, and the Pharaohs had their horses shot from under them. The police resisted for only a few moments; then those who could fled.

Grigori saw Pinsky struggle to his feet. Grigori took aim again, eager now to finish the bastard off, but a Pharaoh got in the way, heaved Pinsky up onto his horse's neck, and galloped off.

Grigori stood back, watching the police run away.

He was in the worst trouble of his life.

His platoon had mutinied. In direct contravention of their orders, they had attacked the police, not the marchers. And he had led them, by shooting Lieutenant Pinsky, who had survived to tell the tale. There was no way to cover this up, no excuse he could offer that would make any difference, and no escape from punishment. He was guilty of treason. He could be court-martialed and executed.

Despite that, he felt happy.

Varya pushed through the crowd. There was blood on her face, but she was smiling. "What now, Sergeant?"

Grigori was not going to resign himself to his punishment. The tsar was murdering his people. Well, his people would shoot back. "To the barracks," Grigori said. "Let's arm the working class!" He snatched her red flag. "Follow me!"

He strode back along Samsonievsky Prospekt. His men came after him, marshaled by Isaak, and the crowd fell in behind them. Grigori was not sure exactly what he was going to do, but he did not feel the need of a plan: as he marched at the head of the crowd he had the sense that he could do anything.

The sentry opened the barracks gates for the soldiers, then was unable to close them on the marchers. Feeling invincible, Grigori led the procession across the parade ground to the arsenal. Lieutenant Kirillov came out of the headquarters building, saw the crowd, and turned toward them, breaking into a run. "You men!" he shouted. "Halt! Stop right there!"

Grigori ignored him.

Kirillov came to a standstill and drew his revolver. "Halt!" he said. "Halt, or I shoot!"

Two or three of Grigori's platoon raised their rifles and

fired at Kirillov. Several bullets struck him and he fell to the ground, bleeding.

Grigori went on.

The arsenal was guarded by two sentries. Neither of them tried to stop Grigori. He used the last two rounds in his magazine to shoot out the lock on the heavy wooden doors. The crowd burst into the arsenal, pushing and shoving to get at the weapons. Some of Grigori's men took charge, opening wooden cases of rifles and revolvers and passing them out along with boxes of ammunition.

This is it, Grigori thought. This is a revolution. He was exhilarated and terrified at the same time.

He armed himself with two of the Nagant revolvers that were issued to officers, reloaded his rifle, and filled his pockets with ammunition. He was not sure what he intended to do, but now that he was a criminal he needed weapons.

The rest of the soldiers in the barracks joined in the looting of the arsenal, and soon everyone was armed to the teeth.

Carrying Varya's red flag, Grigori led the crowd out of the barracks. Demonstrations always went toward the city center. With Isaak, Yakov, and Varya he marched across the bridge to Liteiny Prospekt, heading for the affluent heart of Petrograd. He felt as if he were flying, or dreaming, as if he had drunk a large mouthful of vodka. For years he had talked about defying the authority of the regime, but today he was doing it, and that made him feel like a new man, a different creature, a bird of the air. He remembered the words of the old man who had spoken to him after his mother was shot dead. "May you live long," the man had said, as Grigori walked away from Palace Square with his mother's body in his arms. "Long enough to take revenge on the bloodstained tsar for the evil he has done this day." Your wish may come true, old man, he thought exultantly.

The First Machine Guns were not the only regiment to have mutinied this morning. When he reached the far side of the bridge he was even more elated to see that the streets were full of soldiers wearing their caps backward or their coats unbuttoned in merry defiance of regulations. Most sported red armbands or red lapel ribbons to show they were revolutionaries. Commandeered cars roared around, erratically driven, rifle barrels and bayonets sticking out of the windows, laughing girls sitting on the soldiers' knees inside. The pickets and checkpoints of yesterday had vanished. The streets had been taken over by the people.

Grigori saw a wine shop with its windows broken and its door battered down. A soldier and a girl came out, bottles in both hands, trampling over broken glass. Next door a café proprietor had put plates of smoked fish and sliced sausage on a table outside, and stood beside it with a red ribbon in his lapel, smiling nervously and inviting soldiers to help themselves. Grigori guessed he was trying to make sure his place was not broken into and looted like the wine shop.

The carnival atmosphere grew as they neared the center. Some people were already quite drunk, although it was only midday. Girls seemed happy to kiss anyone with a red armband, and Grigori saw a soldier openly fondling the large breasts of a smiling middle-aged woman. Some girls had dressed in soldiers' uniforms, and swaggered along the streets in caps and oversize boots, evidently feeling liberated.

A shiny Rolls-Royce car came along the street and the crowd tried to stop it. The chauffeur put his foot on the gas but someone opened the door and pulled him out. People shoved one another trying to get into the car. Grigori saw Count Maklakov, one of the directors of the Putilov works, scramble out of the backseat. Grigori recalled how Maklakov had been so entranced with Princess Bea the day she visited the factory. The crowd jeered but did not molest the count as he hurried away, pulling his fur collar up around his ears. Nine or ten people crammed into his car and someone drove it off, honking blithely.

At the next corner a handful of people were tormenting a tall man in the trilby hat and well-worn greatcoat of a middle-class professional. A soldier poked him with his rifle barrel, an old woman spat at him, and a young man in worker's overalls threw a handful of rubbish. "Let me pass!" the man said, trying to sound commanding, but they just laughed. Grigori recognized the thin figure of Kanin, supervisor of the casting section at the Putilov works. His hat fell off, and Grigori saw that he had gone bald.

Grigori pushed through the little crowd. "There's nothing wrong with this man!" he shouted. "He's an engineer. I used to work with him."

Kanin recognized him. "Thank you, Grigori Sergeivich," he said. "I'm just trying to make my way to my mother's house, to see if she's all right."

Grigori turned to the crowd. "Let him pass," he said. "I vouch for him." He saw a woman carrying a reel of red ribbon—looted, presumably, from a haberdashery—and asked her for a length. She cut some off with a pair of scissors, and Grigori tied it around Kanin's left sleeve. The crowd cheered.

"Now you'll be safe," Grigori said.

Kanin shook his hand and walked away, and they let him pass.

Grigori's group came out onto Nevsky Prospekt, the broad shopping street that ran from the Winter Palace to Nikolaevsky Station. It was full of people drinking from bottles, eating, kissing, and firing guns into the air. Those restaurants that were open had signs reading, "Free food for revolutionaries!" and "Eat what you like, pay what you can!" Many shops had been broken into, and there was smashed glass all over the cobblestones. One of the hated streetcars—priced too high for workers to use—had been overturned in the middle of the road, and a Renault automobile had crashed into it.

Grigori heard a rifle shot, but it was one of many, and he thought nothing of it for a second; but then Varya, by his side, staggered and fell down. Grigori and Yakov knelt either side of her. She seemed unconscious. They turned the heavy body over, not without difficulty, and saw immediately that she was beyond help: a bullet had entered her forehead, and her eyes stared up sightlessly.

Grigori did not allow himself to feel sorrow, either on his own account or for Varya's son, his best friend, Konstantin. He had learned on the battlefield to fight back first and grieve later. But was this a battlefield? Who could possibly want to kill Varya? Yet the wound was so exactly placed that he could hardly believe she was the victim of a stray bullet fired at random.

His question was answered a moment later. Yakov keeled over, bleeding from his chest. His heavy body hit the cobbles with a thump.

Grigori stepped away from the two bodies, saying: "What the hell?" He dropped into a crouch, making himself a smaller target, and rapidly looked around for somewhere he could take cover.

He heard another shot, and a passing soldier with a red scarf around his cap fell to the ground holding his stomach.

There was a sniper, and he was targeting revolutionaries.

Grigori ran three paces and dived behind the overturned streetcar.

A woman screamed, then another. People saw the bleeding bodies and began to run away.

Grigori lifted his head and scanned the surrounding buildings. The shooter had to be a police rifleman, but where was he? It seemed to Grigori that the crack of the rifle had come from the other side of the street and less than a block away. The buildings were bright in the afternoon sunlight. There was a hotel, a jewelry store with steel shutters closed, a bank, and on the corner, a church. He could see no open windows, so the sniper had to be on a roof. None of the roofs offered cover—except that of the church, which was a stone building in the baroque style with towers, parapets, and an onion dome.

Another shot rang out, and a woman in the clothes of a factory worker screamed and fell clutching her shoulder. Grigori felt sure the sound had come from the church, but he saw no smoke. That must mean the police had issued their snipers with smokeless ammunition. This really was war.

A whole block of Nevsky Prospekt was now deserted.

Grigori aimed his rifle at the parapet that ran along the top of the side wall of the church. That was the firing position he would have chosen, commanding the whole street. He watched carefully. Out of the corner of his eye he saw two more rifles pointing in the same direction as his, held by soldiers who had taken cover nearby.

A soldier and a girl came staggering along the street, both drunk. The girl was dancing a jig, raising the skirt of her dress to show her knees, while her boyfriend waltzed around her, holding his rifle to his neck and pretending to play it like a violin. Both wore red armbands. Several people shouted warnings, but the revelers did not hear. As they passed the church, happily oblivious to the danger, two shots rang out, and the soldier and his girl fell down.

Once again Grigori saw no wisp of smoke, but all the

same he fired angrily at the parapet above the church door, emptying his magazine. His bullets chipped the stonework and sent up puffs of dust. The other two rifles cracked, and Grigori saw that they were shooting in the same direction, but there was no sign that either of them had hit anything.

It was impossible, Grigori thought as he reloaded. They were firing at an invisible target. The sniper must be lying flat, well back from the edge, so that no part of his gun needed to poke through the bars.

But he had to be stopped. He had already killed Varya, Yakov, two soldiers, and an innocent girl.

There was only one way to reach him, and that was to get up on the roof.

Grigori fired at the parapet again. As he expected, that caused the other two soldiers to do the same. Assuming the sniper must have put his head down for a few seconds, Grigori stood up, abandoning the shelter of the overturned streetcar, and ran to the far side of the street, where he flattened himself up against the window of a bookshop—one of the few stores that had not been looted.

Keeping within the afternoon shadow cast by the buildings, he made his way along the street to the church. It was separated by an alley from the bank next door. He waited patiently for several minutes, until the shooting started again, then darted across the alley and stood with his back to the east end of the church.

Had the sniper seen him run, and guessed what he was planning? There was no way to tell.

Staying close to the wall, he edged around the church until he came to a small door. It was unlocked. He slipped inside.

It was a rich church, gorgeously decorated with red, green, and yellow marble. There was no service taking place at that moment, but twenty or thirty worshippers stood or sat with bowed heads, holding their own private devotions. Grigori scanned the interior, looking for a door that might lead to a staircase. He hurried down the aisle, fearful that more people were being murdered every minute he delayed.

A young priest, dramatically handsome with black hair and white skin, saw his rifle and opened his mouth to voice a protest, but Grigori ignored him and hurried past.

In the vestibule he spotted a small wooden door set into a wall. He opened it and saw a spiral staircase leading up. Behind him, a voice said: "Stop there, my son. What are you doing?"

He turned to see the young priest. "Does this lead to the roof?"

"I am Father Mikhail. You can't bring that weapon into the house of God."

"There's a sniper on your roof."

"He is a police officer!"

"You know about him?" Grigori stared at the priest with incredulity. "He's killing people!"

The priest made no reply.

Grigori ran up the stairs.

A cold wind was coming from somewhere above. Clearly Father Mikhail was on the side of the police. Was there any way the priest could warn the sniper? Not short of running out into the street and waving—which would probably get him shot.

After a long climb in near-darkness, Grigori saw another door.

When his eyes were on a level with the bottom of the door, so that he presented a very small target, he opened it an inch, using his left hand, keeping his rifle in his right. Bright sunlight shone through the gap. He pushed it wide.

He could not see anyone.

He screwed up his eyes against the sun to scan the area visible through the small rectangle of doorway. He was in the bell tower. The door opened south. Nevsky Prospekt was on the north side of the church. The sniper was on the other side—unless he had moved to ambush Grigori.

Cautiously, Grigori ascended one step, then another, and put his head out.

Nothing happened.

He stepped through the door.

Under his feet the roof sloped gently to a gutter that ran alongside a decorative parapet. Wooden duckboards permitted workmen to move around without treading on the roof tiles. At his back the tower rose to a belfry.

Gun in hand, he edged around the tower.

At the first corner he found himself looking west the length of Nevsky Prospekt. In the clear light he could see the Alexander Garden and the Admiralty at the far end. In the middle distance the street was crowded, but nearby it was empty. The sniper must still be at work.

Grigori listened, but heard no shots.

He sidled farther around the tower until he could look around the next corner. Now he could see all along the north wall of the church. He had felt sure he would find the sniper there, flat on his belly, shooting between the uprights of the parapet—but there was no one in sight. Beyond the parapet he could see the wide street below, with people crouching in doorways and skulking around corners, waiting to see what would happen.

A moment later, the sniper's rifle rang out. A scream from the street told Grigori the man had hit his target.

The shot had come from above Grigori's head.

He looked up. The bell tower was pierced by glassless windows and flanked by open turrets placed diagonally at the corners. The shooter was up there somewhere, firing out of one of the many available openings. Fortunately, Grigori had remained hard up against the wall, where he could not have been seen by the sniper.

Grigori went back inside. Within the confined space of the stairwell his rifle felt big and clumsy. He put it down and took out one of his pistols. He knew by its weight that it was empty. He cursed: loading the Nagant M1895 was slow. He took a box of cartridges from the pocket of his uniform coat and inserted seven of them, one by one, through the revolver's awkward loading gate into the cylinder. Then he cocked the hammer.

Leaving the rifle behind, he went up the spiral stairs, treading softly. He moved at a steady pace, not wanting to exert himself so much that his breathing would become audible. He kept his revolver in his right hand pointing up the stairs.

After a few moments he smelled smoke.

The sniper was having a cigarette. But the pungent smell of burning tobacco could travel a long way, and Grigori could not be sure how close the man was.

Ahead and above he saw reflected sunlight. He crept upward, ready to fire. The light was coming through a glassless window. The sniper was not there.

Grigori climbed farther and saw light again. The smell

of smoke grew stronger. Was it his imagination, or could he sense the presence of the sniper just a little farther around the curve of the stairwell? And, if so, could the man sense him?

He heard a sharp intake of breath. It shocked him so much that he almost pulled the trigger. Then he realized it was the noise a man made when inhaling smoke. A moment later he heard the softer, satisfied sound of the smoker blowing out.

He hesitated. He did not know which way the sniper was looking or where his gun might be pointing. He wanted to hear the rifle fire again, for that would tell him that the sniper's attention was directed outward.

Waiting might mean another death, another Yakov or Varya bleeding on the cold cobblestones. On the other hand, if Grigori failed now how many more people would be brought down by the sniper this afternoon?

Grigori forced himself to be patient. It was like being on the battlefield. You did not rush to save a wounded comrade and thereby sacrifice your life. You took chances only when the reasons were overwhelming.

He heard another intake of breath, followed by a long exhalation, and a moment later a crushed cigarette stub came down the staircase, bouncing off the wall and landing at his feet. There was the sound of a man shifting position in a confined space. Then Grigori heard a low muttering, the words sounding mostly like imprecations: "Swine ... revolutionaries ... stinking Jews ... diseased whores ... retards ..." The sniper was winding himself up to kill again.

If Grigori could stop him now it would save at least one life.

He went up a step.

The muttering continued: "Cattle ... Slavs ... thieves and criminals ..." The voice was vaguely familiar, and Grigori wondered if this was a man he had met before.

He took another step, and saw the man's feet, shod in shiny new police-pattern black leather boots. They were small feet: the sniper was a diminutive man. He was down on one knee, the most stable position for shooting. Grigori could now see that he had positioned himself inside one of the corner turrets, so that he could fire in three different directions.

One more step, Grigori thought, and I will be able to shoot him dead.

He took another step, but tension caused him to miss his footing. He stumbled, fell, and dropped his gun. It hit the stone step with a clang.

The sniper uttered a loud, frightened curse and looked around.

With astonishment, Grigori recognized him as Pinsky's sidekick, Ilya Kozlov.

Grigori grabbed for his dropped gun and missed. The revolver fell down the stone staircase with agonizing slowness, one step at a time, until it came to rest well out of reach.

Kozlov began to turn, but he could not do so quickly from his kneeling position.

Grigori regained his balance and went up another step.

Kozlov tried to swing his rifle around. It was the standard Mosin-Nagant, but with a telescope attached. It was well more than a yard long even without the bayonet, and Kozlov could not bring it to bear fast enough. Moving quickly, Grigori got close, so that the barrel of the rifle struck his left shoulder. Kozlov pulled the trigger uselessly, and a bullet ricocheted around the curved inside wall of the stairwell.

Kozlov sprang to his feet with surprising agility. Some part of Grigori's mind guessed that the ugly little man had become a sniper to get revenge on all the bigger boys—and girls—who had ever pushed him around.

Grigori got his hands on the rifle and the two men struggled for possession, face-to-face in the cramped little turret, next to the glassless window. Grigori heard excited shouting, and guessed they must be visible to people on the street.

Grigori was bigger and stronger, and knew that he would win possession of the gun. Kozlov realized it, too, and suddenly let go. Grigori staggered back. In a flash the policeman drew his short wooden club and struck out, hitting Grigori on the head. For a moment Grigori saw stars. In a blur, he saw Kozlov raise the club again. He lifted the rifle and the club landed on the barrel. Before the policeman could strike again, Grigori dropped the gun, grabbed the front of Kozlov's coat with both hands, and lifted him.

The man was slight and his weight was little. Grigori held him off the floor for a moment. Then, with all his might, he threw him out of the window.

Kozlov seemed to fall through the air very slowly. The sunlight picked out the green facings of his uniform as he sailed over the parapet of the church roof. A long scream of pure terror rang out in the silence. Then he hit the ground with a thump that could be heard in the bell tower, and the scream was abruptly cut off.

After a moment of quiet, a huge cheer went up.

Grigori realized the people were cheering him. They could see the police uniform on the ground and the army uniform in the turret, and they had worked out what had happened. As he watched, they came out of doorways and around corners and stood in the street, looking up at him, shouting and applauding. He was a hero.

He did not feel comfortable about that. He had killed several people in the war, and was no longer squeamish about it, but all the same he found it hard to celebrate another death, much as Kozlov had deserved to die. He stood there a few moments longer, letting them applaud but feeling uneasy. Then he ducked back inside and went down the spiral staircase.

He picked up his revolver and his rifle on the way down. When he emerged into the church, Father Mikhail was waiting, looking scared. Grigori pointed the revolver at him. "I ought to shoot you," he said. "That sniper you allowed onto your roof killed two of my friends and at least three other people, and you're a murdering devil for letting him do it." The priest was so shocked to be called a devil that he was lost for words. But Grigori could not bring himself to shoot an unarmed civilian, so he grunted in disgust and went outside.

The men of his platoon were waiting for him, and roared their approval as he stepped into the sunshine. He could not stop them lifting him onto their shoulders and carrying him in procession.

From his elevated viewpoint he saw that the atmosphere in the street had changed. People were more drunk, and on every block there were one or two passed out in doorways. He was startled to see men and women doing a lot more than just kissing in the alleyways. Everyone had a gun: clearly the mob had raided other arsenals and perhaps arms factories, too. At every intersection there were crashed cars, some with ambulances and doctors attending to the injured. Children as well as adults were on the streets, the small boys having a particularly good time, stealing food and smoking cigarettes and playing in abandoned automobiles.

Grigori saw a fur shop being looted with an efficiency that appeared professional, and he spotted Trofim, a former associate of Lev's, carrying armfuls of coats out of the store and loading them onto a handcart, watched by another crony of Lev's, the dishonest policeman Fyodor, now wearing a peasant-style overcoat to hide his uniform. The city's criminals saw the revolution as an opportunity.

After a while Grigori's men put him down. The afternoon light was growing dim, and several bonfires had been lit in the street. People gathered around them, drinking and singing songs.

Grigori was appalled to see a boy of about ten take a pistol from a soldier who had passed out. It was a long-barreled Luger P08 machine pistol, a gun issued to German artillery crew: the soldier must have taken it from a prisoner at the front. The boy held it in both hands, grinning, and pointed it at the man on the ground. As Grigori moved to take the gun away, the boy pulled the trigger, and a bullet thudded into the drunk soldier's chest. The boy screamed, but in his fright he kept the trigger pulled back, so that the machine pistol continued firing. The recoil jerked the boy's arms upward, and he sprayed bullets, hitting an old woman and another soldier, until the eight-round magazine was empty. Then he dropped the gun.

Before Grigori could react to this horror he heard a shout, and turned. In the doorway of a closed hat shop, a couple were having full sexual intercourse. The woman had her back to the wall and her skirt up around her waist, her legs spread apart and her booted feet firmly planted on the ground. The man, who wore the uniform of a corporal, stood between her legs, knees bent, trousers unbuttoned, thrusting. Grigori's platoon stood around them cheering.

The man appeared to reach his climax. He withdrew hastily, turned away, and buttoned his fly, while the woman pushed her skirts down. A soldier called Igor said: "Wait a minute—my turn!" He pulled up the woman's skirts, showing her white legs.

The others cheered.

"No!" the woman said, and tried to push him away. She was drunk, but not helpless.

Igor was a short, wiry man of unexpected strength. He pushed her up against the wall and grabbed her wrists. "Come on," he said. "One soldier's as good as another."

The woman struggled, but two other soldiers grabbed her and held her still.

Her original partner said: "Hey, leave her alone!"

"You've had your turn—now it's mine," said Igor, unbuttoning.

Grigori was revolted by this scene. "Stop it!" he shouted.

Igor gave him a challenging look. "Are you giving me an order as an officer, Grigori Sergeivich?"

"Not as an officer—as a human being!" Grigori said. "Come on, Igor, you can see she doesn't want you. There are plenty more women."

"I want this one." Igor looked around. "We all want this one—don't we, boys?"

Grigori stepped forward and stood with his hands on his hips. "Are you men, or dogs?" he cried. "The woman said no!" He put his arm around the angry Igor. "Tell me something, comrade," he said. "Is there anywhere around here where a man can get a drink?"

Igor grinned, the soldiers cheered, and the woman slipped away.

Grigori said: "I see a small hotel across the street. Shall we ask the proprietor whether, by any chance, he has any vodka?"

The men cheered again, and they all went into the hotel.

In the lobby a frightened proprietor was serving free beer. Grigori thought he was wise. It took men longer to drink beer than vodka, and they were less likely to become violent.

He accepted a glass and drank a mouthful. His elation had vanished. He felt as if he had been drunk and sobered up. The incident with the woman in the doorway had appalled him, and the small boy firing the machine pistol had been horrendous. Revolution was not a simple matter of throwing off your chains. There were dangers in arming the people. Allowing soldiers to commandeer the cars of the bourgeoisie was almost as lethal. Even the apparently harmless freedom to kiss anyone who took your fancy had led, in a few hours, to Grigori's platoon attempting a gang rape.

It could not go on.

There had to be order. Grigori did not want to go back to the old days, of course. The tsar had given them bread queues, brutal police, and soldiers without boots. But there had to be freedom without chaos.

Grigori mumbled an excuse about needing to piss and slipped away from his men. He walked back the way he had come along Nevsky Prospekt. The people had won today's battle. The tsar's police and army officers had been defeated. But if that led only to an orgy of violence, it would not be long before people clamored for a return of the old regime.

Who was in charge? The Duma had defied the tsar and refused to close, according to what Kerensky had told Grigori yesterday. The parliament was more or less impotent, but at least it symbolized democracy. Grigori decided to go to the Tauride Palace and see if anything was happening there.

He walked north to the river, then east to the Tauride Gardens. Night had fallen by the time he got there. The classical façade of the palace had dozens of windows, and they were all lit up. Several thousand people had had the same idea as Grigori, and the broad front courtyard was crammed with soldiers and workers milling around.

A man with a megaphone was making an announcement, repeating it over and over again. Grigori worked his way to the front so that he could hear.

"The Workers' Group of the War Industry Committee has been released from the Kresty Prison," the man shouted.

Grigori was not sure who they were, but their name sounded good.

"Together with other comrades, they have formed the provisional executive committee of the Soviet of Workers' Deputies."

Grigori liked that idea. A soviet was a council of representatives. There had been a St. Petersburg soviet in 1905.

Grigori had been only sixteen at the time, but he knew the soviet had been elected by factory workers and had organized strikes. It had had a charismatic leader, Leon Trotsky, since exiled.

"All of this will be officially announced in a special edition of the newspaper *Izvestiia*. The executive committee has formed a food supply commission to ensure that workers and soldiers are fed. It has also created a military commission to defend the revolution."

There was no mention of the Duma. The crowd was cheering, but Grigori wondered whether soldiers would take orders from a self-elected military commission. Where was the democracy in all this?

His question was answered by the final sentence of the announcement. "The committee appeals to workers and soldiers to elect representatives to the soviet as quickly as possible, and to send their representatives here to the palace to take part in the new revolutionary government!"

That was what Grigori had wanted to hear. The new revolutionary government—a soviet of workers and soldiers. Now there would be change without disorder. Full of enthusiasm, he left the courtyard and headed back toward the barracks. Sooner or later, the men would come back to their beds. He could hardly wait to tell them the news.

Then, for the first time, they would have an election.

{ IV }

On the morning of the next day, the First Machine Gun Regiment gathered on the parade ground to elect a representative to the Petrograd soviet. Isaak proposed Sergeant Grigori Peshkov.

He was elected unopposed.

Grigori was pleased. He knew what life was like for soldiers and workers, and he would bring the machine-oil smell of real life to the corridors of power. He would never forget his roots and put on a top hat. He would make sure that unrest led to improvements, not to random violence. Now he had a real chance to make a better life for Katerina and Vladimir.

He walked quickly across the Liteiny Bridge, alone this time, and headed for the Tauride Palace. His urgent priority had to be bread. Katerina, Vladimir, and the other two and a half million inhabitants of Petrograd had to eat. And now, as he assumed responsibility—at least in his imagination—he began to feel daunted. The farmers and the millers in the countryside had to send more flour to the Petrograd bakers immediately—but they would not do so unless they were paid. How was the soviet going to make sure there was enough money? He began to wonder whether over-throwing the government might have been the easy part.

The palace had a long central façade and two wings. Grigori discovered that both the Duma and the soviet were in session. Appropriately, the Duma—the old middle-class parliament—was in the right wing and the soviet in the left. But who was in charge? No one knew. That would have to be resolved first, Grigori thought impatiently, before they could start on the real problems.

On the steps of the palace Grigori spotted the broom-stick figure and bushy black hair of Konstantin. He realized with a shock that he had not made any attempt to tell Konstantin of the death of Varya, his mother. But he saw immediately that Konstantin knew. As well as his red armband, Konstantin was wearing a black scarf tied around his hat.

Grigori embraced him. "I saw it happen," he said.

"Was it you who killed the police sniper?"

"Yes."

"Thank you. But her real revenge will be the revolution."

Konstantin had been elected as one of two deputies from the Putilov works. During the afternoon more and more deputies arrived until, by early evening, there were three thousand of them crammed into the huge Catherine Hall. Nearly all were soldiers. Troops were already orga-nized into regiments and platoons, and Grigori guessed it had been easier for them to arrange elections than for the factory workers, many of whom were locked out of their workplaces. Some deputies had been elected by a few dozen people, others by thousands. Democracy was not as simple as it seemed.

Someone proposed that they should rename themselves the Petrograd Soviet of Workers' and Soldiers' Deputies, and the idea was approved by thunderous applause. There seemed to be no procedure. There was no agenda, no proposing or seconding of resolutions, no voting mechanism. People just stood up and spoke, often more than one at a time. On the platform, several suspiciously middle-class-looking men were scribbling notes, and Grigori guessed these were the members of the executive committee formed yesterday. At least someone was taking minutes.

Despite the worrying chaos, there was tremendous excitement. They all felt they had fought a battle and won. For better or worse, they were making a new world.

But no one was talking about bread. Frustrated by the inaction of the soviet, Grigori and Konstantin left the Catherine Hall during a particularly chaotic moment and walked across the palace to find out what the Duma was up to. On the way they saw troops with red armbands stockpiling food and ammunition in the hallway as if for a siege. Of course, Grigori thought, the tsar is not simply going to accept what has happened. At some point he will try to regain control by force. And that would mean attacking this building.

In the right wing they came across Count Maklakov, a director of the Putilov works. He was a delegate for a right-of-center party, but he spoke to them politely enough. He told them that yet another committee had been formed, the Temporary Committee of Duma Members for the Restoration of Order in the Capital and the Establishment of Relations with Individuals and Institutions. Despite its ludicrous title, Grigori felt it was an ominous attempt by the Duma to take control. He became more worried when Maklakov told him the committee had appointed a Colonel Engelhardt as commandant of Petrograd.

"Yes," said Maklakov with satisfaction. "And they have instructed all soldiers to return to barracks and obey orders."

"What?" Grigori was shocked. "But that would destroy the revolution. The tsar's officers would regain control!"

"The members of the Duma do not believe there is a revolution."

"The members of the Duma are idiots," Grigori said angrily.

Maklakov put his nose in the air and walked away.

Konstantin shared Grigori's anger. "This is a counter-revolution!" he said.

"And it must be stopped," said Grigori.

They hurried back to the left wing. In the big hall, a chairman was attempting to control a debate. Grigori leaped onto the platform. "I have an emergency announcement!" he shouted.

"Everyone has," said the chairman wearily. "But what the hell, go ahead."

"The Duma is ordering soldiers to return to barracks—and to accept the authority of their officers!"

A shout of protest went up from the delegates.

"Comrades!" Grigori shouted, trying to quiet them. "We are not going back to the old ways!"

They roared their agreement.

"The people of the city must have bread. Our women must feel safe on the streets. The factories must reopen and the mills must roll—but not in the same old way."

They were listening to him now, unsure where he was going.

"We soldiers must stop beating up the bourgeoisie, stop harassing women on the street, and stop looting wine shops. We must return to our barracks, sober up, and resume our duties, but"—he paused dramatically—"under our own conditions!"

There was a rumble of assent.

"What should those conditions be?"

Someone shouted: "Elected committees to issue orders, instead of officers!"

Another said: "No more 'Your Excellency' and 'Most High Radiance'—they should be called Colonel and General."

"No saluting!" cried another.

Grigori did not know what to do. Everyone had his own suggestion. He could not hear them all, let alone remember them.

The chairman came to his rescue. "I propose that all those with suggestions should form a group with Comrade Sokolov." Grigori knew that Nikolai Sokolov was a left-wing lawyer. That's good, he thought—we need someone to draft our proposal in correct legal terms. The chairman went on: "When you have agreed what you want, bring your proposal to the soviet for approval."

"Right." Grigori jumped off the platform. Sokolov was

sitting at a small table to one side of the hall. Grigori and Konstantin approached him, along with a dozen or more deputies.

"Very well," said Sokolov. "Who is this addressed to?"

Grigori was baffled again. He was about so say *To the world.* But a soldier said: "To the Petrograd Garrison."

Another said: "And all the soldiers of the guard, army, and artillery."

"And the fleet," said someone else.

"Very good," said Sokolov, writing. "For immediate and precise execution, I presume?"

"Yes."

"And to the workers of Petrograd for information?"

Grigori became impatient. "Yes, yes," he said. "Now, who proposed elected committees?"

"That was me," said a soldier with a gray mustache. He sat on the edge of the table directly in front of Sokolov. As if giving dictation, he said: "All troops should set up committees of their elected representatives."

Sokolov, still writing, said: "In all companies, battalions, regiments . . ."

Someone added: "Depots, batteries, squadrons, warships . . ."

The gray mustache said: "Those who have not yet elected deputies must do so."

"Right," said Grigori impatiently. "Now. Weapons of all kinds, including armored cars, are under the control of the battalion and company committees, not the officers."

Several of the soldiers voiced their agreement.

"Very good," said Sokolov.

Grigori went on: "A military unit is subordinate to the Soviet of Workers' and Soldiers' Deputies and its committees."

For the first time, Sokolov looked up. "That would mean the soviet controls the army."

"Yes," said Grigori. "The orders of the military commission of the Duma are to be followed only when they do not contradict the decisions of the soviet."

Sokolov continued to look at Grigori. "This makes the Duma as powerless as it always was. Before, it was subject to the whim of the tsar. Now, every decision will require the approval of the soviet."

"Exactly," said Grigori.

"So the soviet is supreme."

"Write it down," said Grigori.

Sokolov wrote it down.

Someone said: "Officers are forbidden to be rude to other ranks."

"All right," said Sokolov.

"And must not address them as *tyi* as if we were animals or children."

Grigori thought these clauses were trivial. "The document needs a title," he said.

Sokolov said: "What do you suggest?"

"How have you headed previous orders by the soviet?"

"There are no previous orders," said Sokolov. "This is the first."

"That's it, then," said Grigori. "Call it 'Order Number One.'"

{ V }

It gave Grigori profound satisfaction to have passed his first piece of legislation as an elected representative. Over the next two days there were several more, and he became deeply absorbed in the minute-by-minute work of a revolutionary government. But he thought all the time about Katerina and Vladimir, and on Thursday evening he at last got a chance to slip away and check on them.

His heart was full of foreboding as he walked to the southwest suburbs. Katerina had promised to stay away from trouble, but the women of Petrograd believed this was their revolution as much as the men's. After all, it had started on International Women's Day. This was nothing new. Grigori's mother had died in the failed revolution of 1905. If Katerina had decided to go into the city center with Vladimir on her hip to see what was going on, she would not have been the only mother to do so. And many innocent people had died—shot by the police, trampled in crowds, run over by drunk soldiers in commandeered cars, or hit by stray bullets. As he entered the old house, he dreaded being met by one of the tenants, with a solemn face and tears in her eyes, saying, *Something terrible has happened.*

He went up the stairs, tapped on her door, and walked in. Katerina leaped from her chair and threw herself into his arms. "You're alive!" she said. She kissed him eagerly. "I've been so worried! I don't know what we would do without you."

"I'm sorry I couldn't come sooner," Grigori said. "But I'm a delegate to the soviet."

"A delegate!" Katerina beamed with pride. "My husband!" She hugged him.

Grigori had actually impressed her. He had never done that before. "A delegate is only a representative of the people who elected him," he said modestly.

"But they always choose the cleverest and most reliable."

"Well, they try to."

The room was dimly lit by an oil lamp. Grigori put a parcel on the table. With his new status he had no trouble getting food from the barracks kitchen. "There are some matches and a blanket in there, too," he said.

"Thank you!"

"I hope you've been staying indoors as much as you can. It's still dangerous on the streets. Some of us are making a revolution, but others are just going wild."

"I've hardly been out. I've been waiting to hear from you."

"How's our little boy?" Vladimir was asleep in the corner.

"He misses his daddy."

She meant Grigori. It was not Grigori's wish that Vladimir should call him Daddy, but he had accepted Katerina's fancy. It was not likely that any of them would ever see Lev again—there had been no word from him for almost three years—so the child would never know the truth, and perhaps that was better.

Katerina said: "I'm sorry he's asleep. He loves to see you."

"I'll talk to him in the morning."

"You can stay the night? How wonderful!"

Grigori sat down, and Katerina knelt in front of him and pulled off his boots. "You look tired," she said.

"I am."

"Let's go to bed. It's late."

She began to unbutton his tunic, and he sat back and let her. "General Khabalov is hiding out in the Admiralty," he said. "We were afraid he might recapture the railway stations, but he didn't even try."

"Why not?"

Grigori shrugged. "Cowardice. The tsar ordered Ivanov to march on Petrograd and set up a military dictatorship, but Ivanov's men became mutinous and the expedition was canceled."

Katerina frowned. "Has the old ruling class just given up?"

"It seems that way. Strange, isn't it? But clearly there isn't going to be a counterrevolution."

They got into bed, Grigori in his underwear, Katerina with her dress still on. She had never stripped naked in front of him. Perhaps she felt she had to hold something back. It was a peculiarity of hers that he accepted, not without regret. He took her in his arms and kissed her. When he entered her, she said: "I love you," and he felt he was the luckiest man in the world.

Afterward she said sleepily: "What will happen next?"

"There's going to be a constituent assembly, elected by what they called the four-tail suffrage: universal, direct, secret, and equal. Meanwhile the Duma is forming a provisional government."

"Who will be its leader?"

"Lvov."

Katerina sat upright. "A prince! Why?"

"They want the confidence of all classes."

"To hell with all classes!" Indignation made her even more beautiful, bringing color to her face and a sparkle to her eyes. "The workers and soldiers have made the revolution—why do we need the confidence of anyone else?"

This question had bothered Grigori, too, but the answer had convinced him. "We need businessmen to reopen factories, wholesalers to recommence supplying the city, shopkeepers to open their doors again."

"And what about the tsar?"

"The Duma is demanding his abdication. They have sent two delegates to Pskov to tell him so."

Katerina was wide-eyed. "Abdication? The tsar? But that would be the end."

"Yes."

"Is it possible?"

"I don't know," said Grigori. "We'll find out tomorrow."

{ VI }

In the Catherine Hall of the Tauride Palace on Friday, the debate was desultory. Two or three thousand men and a few women packed the room, and the air was full of tobacco smoke and the smell of unwashed soldiers. They were waiting to hear what the tsar would do.

The debate was frequently interrupted for announcements. Often they were less than urgent—a soldier would stand up to say that his battalion had formed a committee and arrested the colonel. Sometimes they were not even announcements, but speeches calling for the defense of the revolution.

But Grigori knew something was different when a gray-haired sergeant jumped onto the platform, pink-faced and breathless, with a sheet of paper in his hand, and called for silence.

Slowly and loudly he said: "The tsar has signed a document . . ."

The cheering began after those few words.

The sergeant raised his voice: ". . . abdicating the crown . . ."

The cheer rose to a roar. Grigori was electrified. Had it really happened? Had the dream come true?

The sergeant held up his hand for quiet. He had not yet finished.

". . . and because of the poor health of his twelve-year-old son, Alexei, he has named as his successor the grand duke Mikhail, the tsar's younger brother."

The cheers turned to howls of protest. "No!" Grigori shouted, and his voice was lost among thousands.

When after several minutes they began to quieten, a greater roar was heard from outside. The crowd in the courtyard must have heard the same news, and were receiving it with the same indignation.

Grigori said to Konstantin: "The provisional government must not accept this."

"Agreed," said Konstantin. "Let's go and tell them so."

They left the soviet and crossed the palace. The ministers of the newly formed government were meeting in the room where the old temporary committee had met—indeed, they were to a worrying degree the same men. They were already discussing the tsar's statement.

Pavel Miliukov was on his feet. The monocled moderate was arguing that the monarchy had to be preserved as a symbol of legitimacy. "Horseshit," Grigori muttered. The monarchy symbolized incompetence, cruelty, and defeat, but not legitimacy. Fortunately, others felt the same way. Kerensky, who was now minister of justice, proposed that Grand Duke Mikhail should be told to refuse the crown, and to Grigori's relief the majority agreed.

Kerensky and Prince Lvov were mandated to go to see Mikhail immediately. Miliukov glared through his monocle and said: "And I should go with them, to represent the minority view!"

Grigori assumed this foolish suggestion would be trodden upon, but the other ministers weakly assented. At that point Grigori stood up. Without forethought he said: "And I shall accompany the ministers as an observer from the Petrograd soviet."

"Very well, very well," said Kerensky wearily.

They left the palace by a side door and got into two waiting Renault limousines. The former president of the Duma, the hugely fat Mikhail Rodzianko, also came. Grigori could not quite believe this was happening to him. He was part of a delegation going to order a crown prince to refuse to become tsar. Less than a week ago he had got down from a table because Lieutenant Kirillov had ordered him to. The world was changing so fast it was hard to keep up.

Grigori had never been inside the home of a wealthy aristocrat, and it was like entering a dream world. The large house was stuffed with possessions. Everywhere he looked there were gorgeous vases, elaborate clocks, silver candelabra, and jeweled ornaments. If he had grabbed a golden bowl and run out of the front door, he could have sold it for enough money to buy himself a house—except that right now no one was buying golden bowls. They just wanted bread.

Prince Georgy Lvov, a silver-haired man with a huge bushy beard, clearly was not impressed by the decor, nor intimidated by the solemnity of his errand, but everyone else seemed nervous. They waited in the drawing room, frowned upon by ancestral portraits, shuffling their feet on the thick rugs.

At last Grand Duke Mikhail appeared. He was a prematurely balding man of thirty-eight with a little mustache. To Grigori's surprise he appeared to be more nervous than the delegation. He seemed shy and bewildered, despite a haughty tilt to his head. He eventually summoned enough courage to say: "What do you have to tell me?"

Lvov replied: "We have come to ask you not to accept the crown."

"Oh, dear," said Mikhail, and seemed not to know what to do next.

Kerensky retained his presence of mind. He spoke clearly and firmly. "The people of Petrograd have reacted with outrage to the decision of His Majesty the tsar," he said. "Already a huge contingent of soldiers is marching on the Tauride Palace. There will be a violent uprising followed by a civil war unless we announce immediately that you have refused to take over as tsar."

"Oh, my goodness," said Mikhail mildly.

The grand duke was not very bright, Grigori realized. Why am I surprised? he thought. If these people were intelligent they would not be on the point of losing the throne of Russia.

The monocled Miliukov said: "Your Royal Highness, I represent the minority view in the provisional government. In our opinion, the monarchy is the only symbol of authority accepted by the people."

Mikhail looked even more bewildered. The last thing he needed was a choice, Grigori thought; that only made matters worse. The grand duke said: "Would you mind if I had a word alone with Rodzianko? No, don't all leave—we will just retire to a side room."

When the dithering tsar-designate and the fat president had left, the others talked in low voices. No one spoke to Grigori. He was the only working-class man in the room, and he sensed they were a bit frightened of him, suspecting—rightly—that the pockets of his sergeant's uniform were stuffed with guns and ammunition.

Rodzianko reappeared. "He asked me whether we could guarantee his personal safety if he became tsar," he said. Grigori was disgusted but not surprised that the grand duke was concerned about himself rather than his country. "I told him we could not," Rodzianko finished.

Kerensky said: "And . . . ?"

"He will rejoin us in a moment."

There was a pause that seemed endless; then Mikhail came back. They all fell silent. For a long moment, no one said anything.

At last Mikhail said: "I have decided to decline the crown."

Grigori's heart seemed to stop. Eight days, he thought. Eight days ago the women of Vyborg marched across the Liteiny Bridge. Today the rule of the Romanovs has ended.

He recalled the words of his mother on the day she died: "I will not rest until Russia is a republic." Rest now, Mother, he thought.

Kerensky was shaking the grand duke's hand and saying something pompous, but Grigori was not listening.

We have done it, he thought. We made a revolution.

We have deposed the tsar.

{ VII }

In Berlin, Otto von Ulrich opened a magnum of the 1892 Perrier-Jouët champagne.

The von Ulrichs had invited the von der Helbards to lunch. Monika's father, Konrad, was a *Graf*, or count, and her mother was therefore a *Gräfin*, or countess. Gräfin Eva von der Helbard was a formidable woman with gray hair piled in an elaborate coiffure. Before lunch she cornered Walter and told him that Monika was an accomplished violin player and had been top of her school class in all subjects. Out of the corner of his eye he saw his father talking to Monika, and guessed she was getting a school report about him.

He was irritated with his parents for persisting in foisting Monika on him. The fact that he found himself strongly attracted to her made matters worse. She was intelligent as well as beautiful. Her hair was always carefully dressed, but he could not help imagining her unpinning it at night and shaking her head to liberate her curls. Sometimes, these days, he found it hard to picture Maud.

Now Otto raised his glass. "Good-bye to the tsar!" he said.

"I'm surprised at you, Father," said Walter irritably. "Are you really celebrating the overthrow of a legitimate monarch by a mob of factory workers and mutinous soldiers?"

Otto went red in the face. Walter's sister, Greta, patted her father's arm soothingly. "Take no notice, Daddy," she said. "Walter just says these things to annoy you."

Konrad said: "I got to know Tsar Nicholas when I was at our embassy in Petrograd."

Walter said: "And what did you think of him, sir?"

Monika answered for her father. Giving Walter a conspiratorial grin, she said: "Daddy used to say that if the tsar had been born to a different station in life, he might, with an effort, have become a competent postman."

"This is the tragedy of inherited monarchy." Walter turned to his father. "But you must surely disapprove of democracy in Russia."

"Democracy?" said Otto derisively. "We shall see. All we know is that the new prime minister is a liberal aristocrat."

Monika said to Walter: "Do you think Prince Lvov will try to make peace with us?"

It was the question of the hour. "I hope so," said Walter, trying not to look at Monika's breasts. "If all our troops on the eastern front could be switched to France, we could overrun the Allies."

She raised her glass and looked over its rim into Walter's eyes. "Then let's drink to that," she said.

❋

In a cold, wet trench in northeastern France, Billy's platoon was drinking gin.

The bottle had been produced by Robin Mortimer, the cashiered officer. "I've been saving this," he said.

"Well, knock me down with a feather," said Billy, using one of Mildred's expressions. Mortimer was a surly beggar and had never been known to buy anyone a drink.

Mortimer splashed liquor into their mess tins. "Here's to bloody revolution," he said, and they all drank, then held out their tins for refills.

Billy had been in high spirits even before drinking the gin. The Russians had proved it was still possible to overthrow tyrants.

They were singing "The Red Flag" when Earl Fitzherbert came limping around the traverse, splashing through the mud. He was a colonel now, and more arrogant than ever. "Be quiet, you men!" he shouted.

The singing died down gradually.

Billy said: "We're celebrating the overthrow of the tsar of Russia!"

Fitz said angrily: "He was a legitimate monarch, and those who deposed him are criminals. No more singing."

Billy's contempt for Fitz went up a notch. "He was a tyrant who murdered thousands of his subjects, and all civilized men are rejoicing today."

Fitz looked more closely at him. The earl no longer wore an eye patch, but his left eyelid had a permanent droop. However, it did not seem to affect his eyesight. "Sergeant Williams—I might have guessed. I know you—and your family."

And how, Billy thought.

"Your sister's a peace agitator."

"So's yours, sir," said Billy, and Robin Mortimer laughed raucously, then shut up suddenly.

Fitz said to Billy: "One more insolent word out of you and you'll be on a charge."

"Sorry, sir," said Billy.

"Now calm down, all of you. And no more singing." Fitz walked away.

Billy said quietly: "Long live the revolution."

Fitz pretended not to hear.

❊

In London, Princess Bea screamed: "No!"

"Try to stay calm," said Maud, who had just told her the news.

"They cannot!" Bea screamed. "They cannot make our beloved tsar abdicate! He is the father of his people!"

"It may be for the best—"

"I don't believe you! It's a wicked lie!"

The door opened and Grout put his head in, looking worried.

Bea picked up a Japanese bottle-vase containing an arrangement of dried grasses and hurled it across the room. It hit the wall and smashed.

Maud patted Bea's shoulder. "There, there," she said. She was not sure what else to do. She herself was delighted that the tsar had been overthrown, but all the same she sympathized with Bea, for whom an entire way of life had been destroyed.

Grout crooked a finger and a maid came in, looking frightened. He pointed at the broken vase, and the maid began to pick up the pieces.

The tea things were on a table: cups, saucers, teapots, jugs of milk and cream, bowls of sugar. Bea swept them all violently to the floor. "Those revolutionaries are going to kill everyone!"

The butler knelt down and began to clear up the mess.

"Don't excite yourself," Maud said.

Bea began to cry. "The poor tsaritsa! And her children! What will become of them?"

"Perhaps you should lie down for a while," Maud said. "Come on, I'll walk you to your room." She took Bea's elbow, and Bea allowed herself to be led away.

"It's the end of everything," Bea sobbed.

"Never mind," said Maud. "Perhaps it's a new beginning."

✳

Ethel and Bernie were in Aberowen. It was a sort of honeymoon. Ethel was enjoying showing Bernie the places of her childhood: the pithead, the chapel, the school. She even showed him around Tŷ Gwyn—Fitz and Bea were not in residence—though she did not take him to the Gardenia Suite.

They were staying with the Griffiths family, who had again offered Ethel Tommy's room, which saved disturbing Gramper. They were in Mrs. Griffiths's kitchen when her husband, Len, atheist and revolutionary socialist, burst in waving a newspaper. "The tsar have abdicated!" he said.

They all cheered and clapped. For a week they had been hearing of riots in Petrograd, and Ethel had been wondering how it would end.

Bernie asked: "Who's took over?"

"Provisional government under Prince Lvov," said Len.

"Not quite a triumph for socialism, then," said Bernie.

"No."

Ethel said: "Cheer up, you men—one thing at a time! Let's go to the Two Crowns and celebrate. I'll leave Lloyd with Mrs. Ponti for a while."

The women put on their hats and they all went to the pub. Within an hour the place was crammed. Ethel was astonished to see her mother and father come in. Mrs. Griffiths saw them, too, and said: "What the 'ell are they doing here?"

A few minutes later, Ethel's da stood on a chair and called for quiet. "I know some of you are surprised to see me here, but special occasions call for special actions." He showed them a pint glass. "I haven't changed my habits of a lifetime, but the landlord has been kind enough to give me a glass of tap water." They all laughed. "I'm here to share with my neighbors the triumph that have took place in Russia." He held up his glass. "A toast—to the revolution!"

They all cheered and drank.

"Well!" said Ethel. "Da in the Two Crowns! I never thought I'd see the day."

In Josef Vyalov's ultramodern prairie house in Buffalo, Lev Peshkov helped himself to a drink from the cocktail cabinet. He no longer drank vodka. Living with his wealthy father-in-law, he had developed a taste for Scotch whisky. He liked it the way Americans drank it, with lumps of ice.

Lev did not like living with his in-laws. He would have preferred for Olga and him to have a place of their own. But Olga liked it this way, and her father paid for everything. Until Lev could build up a stash of his own, he was stuck.

Josef was reading the paper and Lena was sewing. Lev

raised his glass to them. "Long live the revolution!" he said exuberantly.

"Watch your words," said Josef. "It's going to be bad for business."

Olga came in. "Pour me a little glass of sherry, please, darling," she said.

Lev suppressed a sigh. She loved to ask him to perfom little services, and in front of her parents he could not refuse. He poured sweet sherry into a small glass and handed it to her, bowing like a waiter. She smiled prettily, missing the irony.

He drank a mouthful of Scotch and savored the taste and the burn of it.

Mrs. Vyalov said: "I feel sorry for the poor tsaritsa and her children. What will they do?"

Josef said: "They'll all be killed by the mob, I shouldn't wonder."

"Poor things. What did the tsar ever do to those revolutionaries, to deserve this?"

"I can answer that question," Lev said. He knew he should shut up, but he could not, especially with whisky warming his guts. "When I was eleven years old, the factory where my mother worked went on strike."

Mrs. Vyalov tutted. She did not believe in strikes.

"The police rounded up all the children of the strikers. I'll never forget it. I was terrified."

"Why would they do a thing like that?" said Mrs. Vyalov.

"The police flogged us all," Lev said. "On our bottoms, with canes. To teach our parents a lesson."

Mrs. Vyalov had gone white. She could not bear cruelty to children or animals.

"That's what the tsar and his regime did to me, Mother," said Lev. He clinked ice in his glass. "That's why I toast the revolution."

✻

"What do you think, Gus?" said President Wilson. "You're the only person around here who's actually been to Petrograd. What's going to happen?"

"I hate to sound like a State Department official, but it could go either way," said Gus.

The president laughed. They were in the Oval Office, Wilson behind the desk, Gus standing in front of it. "Come on," Wilson said. "Take a guess. Will the Russians pull out of the war or not? It's the most important question of the year."

"Okay. All the ministers in the new government belong to scary-sounding political parties with *socialist* and *revolutionary* in their names, but in fact they're middle-class businessmen and professionals. What they really want is a bourgeois revolution that gives them freedom to promote industry and commerce. But the people want bread, peace, and land: bread for the factory workers, peace for the soldiers, and land for the peasants. None of that really appeals to men like Lvov and Kerensky. So, to answer your question, I think Lvov's government will try for gradual change. In particular, they will carry on fighting the war. But the workers will not be satisfied."

"And who will win in the end?"

Gus recalled his trip to St. Petersburg, and the man who had demonstrated the casting of a locomotive wheel in a dirty, tumbledown foundry at the Putilov factory. Later, Gus had seen the same man in a fight with a cop over some girl. He could not remember the man's name, but he could picture him now, his big shoulders and strong arms, one finger a stump, but most of all his fierce blue-eyed look of unstoppable determination. "The Russian people," Gus said. "They will win in the end."

CHAPTER TWENTY-FOUR

April 1917

On a mild day in early spring Walter walked with Monika von der Helbard in the garden of her parents' town house in Berlin. It was a grand house and the garden was large, with a tennis pavilion, a bowling green, a riding school for exercising horses, and a children's playground with swings and a slide. Walter remembered coming here as a child and thinking it was paradise. However, it was no longer an idyllic playground. All but the oldest horses had gone to the army. Chickens scratched on the flagstones of the broad terrace. Monika's mother was fattening a pig in the tennis pavilion. Goats grazed the bowling green, and it was rumored that the *Gräfin* milked them herself.

However, the old trees were coming into leaf, the sun was shining, and Walter was in his waistcoat and shirtsleeves with his coat slung over his shoulder—a state of undress that would have displeased his mother, but she was in the house, gossiping with the *Gräfin*. His sister, Greta, had been walking with Walter and Monika, but she had made an excuse and left them alone—another thing Mother would have deplored, at least in theory.

Monika had a dog called Pierre. It was a standard poodle, long-legged and graceful, with a lot of curly rust-colored hair and light brown eyes, and Walter could not help thinking that it looked a little like Monika, beautiful though she was.

He liked the way she acted with her dog. She did not pet

it or feed it scraps or talk to it in a baby voice, as some girls did. She just let it walk at her heel, and occasionally threw an old tennis ball for it to fetch.

"It's so disappointing about the Russians," she said.

Walter nodded. Prince Lvov's government had announced they would continue to fight. Germany's eastern front was not to be relieved, and there would be no reinforcements for France. The war would drag on. "Our only hope now is that Lvov's government will fall and the peace faction will take over," Walter said.

"Is that likely?"

"It's hard to say. The left revolutionaries are still demanding bread, peace, and land. The government has promised a democratic election for a constituent assembly—but who will win?" He picked up a twig and threw it for Pierre. The dog bounded after it, and proudly brought it back. Walter bent down to pat its head, and when he straightened up Monika was very close to him.

"I like you, Walter," she said, looking very directly at him with her amber eyes. "I feel as if we would never run out of things to talk about."

He had the same feeling, and he knew that if he tried to kiss her now, she would let him.

He stepped away. "I like you, too," he said. "And I like your dog." He laughed, to show that he was speaking lightheartedly.

All the same he could see that she was hurt. She bit her lip and turned away. She had been about as bold as was possible for a well-brought-up girl, and he had rejected her.

They walked on. After a long silence Monika said: "What is your secret, I wonder?"

My God, he thought, she's sharp. "I have no secrets," he lied. "Do you?"

"None worth telling." She reached up and brushed something off his shoulder. "A bee," she said.

"It's too soon in the year for bees."

"Perhaps we shall have an early summer."

"It's not that warm."

She pretended to shiver. "You're right. It's chilly. Would you fetch me a wrap? If you go to the kitchen and ask a maid, she will find one."

"Of course." It was not chilly, but a gentleman never refused such a request, no matter how whimsical. She obviously wanted a minute alone. He strolled back to the house. He had to spurn her advances, but he was sorry to hurt her. They *were* well suited—their mothers were quite right—and clearly Monika could not understand why he kept pushing her away.

He entered the house and went down the back stairs to the basement, where he found an elderly housemaid in a black dress and a lace cap. She went off to look for a shawl.

Walter waited in the hall. The house was decorated in the up-to-date *Jugendstil*, which did away with the rococo flourishes loved by Walter's parents and favored well-lit rooms with gentle colors. The pillared hall was all cool gray marble and mushroom-colored carpet.

It seemed to him as if Maud was a million miles away on another planet. And in a way she was, for the prewar world would never come back. He had not seen his wife nor heard from her for almost three years, and he might never meet her again. Although she had not faded from his mind—he would never forget the passion they had shared—he did find, to his distress, that he could no longer recall the fine details of their times together: what she was wearing, where they were when they kissed or held hands, or what they ate and drank and talked about when they met at those endlessly similar London parties. Sometimes it crossed his mind that the war had in a way divorced them. But he pushed the thought aside: it was shamefully disloyal.

The maid brought him a yellow cashmere shawl. He returned to Monika, who was sitting on a tree stump with Pierre at her feet. Walter gave her the shawl and she put it around her shoulders. The color suited her, making her eyes gleam and her skin glow.

She had a strange look on her face, and she handed him his wallet. "This must have fallen out of your coat," she said.

"Oh, thank you." He returned it to the inside pocket of the coat that he still had slung over his shoulder.

She said: "Let's go back to the house."

"As you wish."

Her mood had changed. Perhaps she had simply decided to give up on him. Or had something else happened?

He was struck by a frightening thought. Had his wallet really fallen out of his coat? Or had she taken it, like a pickpocket, when she brushed that unlikely bee off his shoulder? "Monika," he said, and he stopped and turned to face her. "Did you look inside my wallet?"

"You said you had no secrets," she said, and she blushed bright red.

She must have seen the newspaper clipping he carried: *Lady Maud Fitzherbert is always dressed in the latest fashion.* "That was most ill-mannered of you," he said angrily. He was mainly angry with himself. He should not have kept the incriminating photo. If Monika could figure out its significance, so could others. Then he would be disgraced and drummed out of the army. He might be accused of treason and jailed or even shot.

He had been foolish. But he knew he would never throw the picture away. It was all he had of Maud.

Monika put a hand on his arm. "I have never done anything like that in my whole life, and I'm ashamed. But you must see that I was desperate. Oh, Walter, I could fall in love with you so easily, and I can tell that you could love me, too—I can see it, in your eyes and the way you smile when you see me. But you said nothing!" There were tears in her eyes. "It was driving me out of my mind."

"I'm sorry for that." He could no longer feel indignant. She had now gone beyond the bounds of propriety, and opened her heart to him. He felt terribly sad for her, sad for both of them.

"I just had to understand why you kept turning away from me. Now I do, of course. She's beautiful. She even looks a bit like me." She wiped her tears. "She found you before I did, that's all." She stared at him with those penetrating amber eyes. "I suppose you're engaged."

He could not lie to someone who was being so honest with him. He did not know what to say.

She guessed the reason for his hesitation. "Oh, my goodness!" she said. "You're married, aren't you?"

This was disastrous. "If people found out, I would be in serious trouble."

"I know."

"I hope I may trust you to keep my secret?"

"How can you ask?" she said. "You're the best man I've ever met. I wouldn't do anything to harm you. I will never breathe a word."

"Thank you. I know you'll keep your promise."

She looked away, fighting back the tears. "Let's go inside."

In the hall she said: "You go ahead. I must wash my face."

"All right."

"I hope—" Her voice broke into a sob. "I hope she knows how lucky she is," she whispered. Then she turned away and slipped into a side room.

Walter put on his coat and composed himself, then went up the marble staircase. The drawing room was done in the same understated style, with blond wood and pale blue-green curtains. Monika's parents had better taste than his, he decided.

His mother looked at him and knew instantly something was wrong. "Where is Monika?" she said sharply.

He raised an eyebrow at her. It was not like her to ask a question to which the answer might be *Gone to the toilet*. She was obviously tense. He said quietly: "She will join us in a few minutes."

"Look at this," said his father, waving a sheet of paper. "Zimmermann's office just sent it to me for my comments. Those Russian revolutionaries want to cross Germany. The nerve!" He had had a couple of glasses of schnapps, and was in an exuberant mood.

Walter said politely: "Which revolutionaries would those be, Father?" He did not really care, but was grateful for a topic of conversation.

"The ones in Zurich! Martov and Lenin and that crowd. There's supposed to be freedom of speech in Russia, now that the tsar has been deposed, so they want to go home. But they can't get there!"

Monika's father, Konrad von der Helbard, said thoughtfully: "I suppose they can't. There's no way to get from Switzerland to Russia without passing through Germany—any other overland route would involve crossing battle lines. But there are still steamers going from England across the North Sea to Sweden, aren't there?"

Walter said: "Yes, but they won't risk going via Britain. The British detained Trotsky and Bukharin. And France or Italy would be worse."

"So they're stuck!" said Otto triumphantly.

Walter said: "What will you advise Foreign Minister Zimmermann to do, Father?"

"Refuse, of course. We don't want that filth contaminating our folk. Who knows what kind of trouble those devils would stir up in Germany?"

"Lenin and Martov," Walter said musingly. "Martov is a Menshevik, but Lenin is a Bolshevik." German intelligence took a lively interest in Russian revolutionaries.

Otto said: "Bolsheviks, Mensheviks, socialists, revolutionaries, they're all the same."

"No, they're not," said Walter. "The Bolsheviks are the toughest."

Monika's mother said with spirit: "All the more reason to keep them out of our country!"

Walter ignored that. "More important, the Bolsheviks abroad tend to be more radical than those at home. The Petrograd Bolsheviks support the provisional government of Prince Lvov, but their comrades in Zurich do not."

His sister, Greta, said: "How do you know a thing like that?"

Walter knew because he had read intelligence reports from German spies in Switzerland who were intercepting the revolutionaries' mail. But he said: "Lenin made a speech in Zurich a few days ago in which he repudiated the provisional government."

Otto made a dismissive noise, but Konrad von der Helbard leaned forward in his chair. "What are you thinking, young man?"

Walter said: "By refusing the revolutionaries permission to pass through Germany, we are protecting Russia from their subversive ideas."

Mother looked bewildered. "Explain, please."

"I'm suggesting we should help these dangerous men get home. Once there, either they will try to undermine the Russian government and cripple its ability to make war, or alternatively they will take power and make peace. Either way, Germany gains."

There was a moment of silence while they all thought about that. Then Otto laughed loudly and clapped his hands. "My own son!" he said. "There is a bit of the old man in him after all!"

{ II }

My dearest darling,
    Zurich is a cold city by a lake,

Walter wrote,

> but the sun shines on the water, on the leafy hill-
> sides all around, and on the Alps in the distance. The
> streets are laid out in a grid with no bends: the Swiss
> are even more orderly than the Germans! I wish you
> were here, my beloved friend, as I wish you were
> with me wherever I am!!!

The exclamation marks were intended to give the postal
censor the impression that the writer was an excitable girl.
Although Walter was in neutral Switzerland, he was still
being careful that the text of the letter did not identify either the sender or the recipient.

> I wonder whether you suffer the embarrassment of
> unwanted attention from eligible bachelors. You are so
> beautiful and charming that you must. I have the same
> problem. I don't have beauty or charm, of course, but
> despite that I receive advances. My mother has cho-
> sen someone for me to marry, a chum of my sister's, a
> person I have always known and liked. It was very dif-
> ficult for a while, and I'm afraid that in the end the per-
> son discovered that I have a friendship that excludes
> marriage. However, I believe our secret is safe.

If a censor bothered to read this far, he would now conclude that the letter was from a lesbian to her lover. The
same conclusion would be reached by anyone in England
who read the letter. This hardly mattered: undoubtedly
Maud, being a feminist and apparently single at twenty-six,
was already suspected of Sapphic tendencies.

> In a few days' time I will be in Stockholm, an-
> other cold city beside the water, and you could send
> me a letter at the Grand Hotel there.

Sweden, like Switzerland, was a neutral country with a postal service to England.

> I would love to hear from you!!!
>> Until then, my wonderful darling,
>> remember your beloved—
>> Waltraud

{ III }

The United States declared war on Germany on Friday, April 6, 1917.

Walter had been expecting it, but all the same he felt the blow. America was rich, vigorous, and democratic: he could not imagine a worse enemy. The only hope now was that Russia would collapse, giving Germany a chance to win on the western front before the Americans had time to build up their forces.

Three days later, thirty-two exiled Russian revolutionaries met at the Zähringerhof Hotel in Zurich: men, women, and one child, a four-year-old boy called Robert. They walked from there to the baroque arch of the railway station to board a train for home.

Walter had been afraid they would not go. Martov, the Menshevik leader, had refused to leave without permission from the provisional government in Petrograd—an oddly deferential attitude for a revolutionary. Permission had not been given, but Lenin and the Bolsheviks decided to go anyway. Walter was keen that there should be no snags on the trip, and he accompanied the group to the riverside station and boarded the train with them.

This is Germany's secret weapon, Walter thought: thirty-two malcontents and misfits who want to bring down the Russian government. God help us.

Vladimir Ilyich Ulyanov, known as Lenin, was forty-six years old. He was a short, stocky figure, dressed neatly but without elegance, too busy to waste time on style. He had once been a redhead, but he had lost his hair early, and now he had a shiny dome with a vestigial fringe, and a carefully trimmed Vandyke beard, ginger streaked with gray. On first acquaintance Walter had found him unimpressive, without charm or good looks.

Walter was posing as a lowly official in the Foreign Office who had been given the job of making all the practical arrangements for the Bolsheviks' journey through Germany. Lenin had given him a hard, appraising look, clearly guessing that he was in reality some kind of intelligence operative.

They traveled to Schaffhausen, on the border, where they transferred to a German train. They all spoke some German, having been living in the German-speaking region of Switzerland. Lenin himself spoke it well. He was a remarkable linguist, Walter learned. He was fluent in French, spoke passable English, and read Aristotle in ancient Greek. Lenin's idea of relaxation was to sit down with a foreign-language dictionary for an hour or two.

At Gottmadingen they changed again, to a train with a sealed carriage specially prepared for them as if they were carriers of an infectious disease. Three of its four doors were locked shut. The fourth door was next to Walter's sleeping compartment. This was to reassure overanxious German authorities, but it was not necessary: the Russians had no desire to escape; they wanted to go home.

Lenin and his wife, Nadya, had a room to themselves, but the others were crowded four to a compartment. So much for egalitarianism, Walter thought cynically.

As the train crossed Germany from south to north, Walter began to sense the force of character beneath Lenin's dull exterior. Lenin had no interest in food, drink, comfort, or possessions. Politics consumed his entire day. He was always arguing about politics, writing about politics, or thinking about politics and making notes. In arguments, Walter noted, Lenin always appeared to know more than his comrades and to have thought longer and harder than they—unless the subject under discussion was nothing to do with Russia or politics, in which case he was rather ill-informed.

He was a real killjoy. The first evening, the bespectacled young Karl Radek was telling jokes in the next compartment. "A man was arrested for saying, 'Nicholas is a moron.' He told the policeman: 'I meant another Nicholas, not our beloved tsar.' The policeman said: 'Liar! If you say *moron* you obviously mean the tsar!'" Radek's companions hooted with laughter. Lenin came out of his compartment with a face like thunder and ordered them to keep quiet.

Lenin did not like smoking. He himself had given it up, on his mother's insistence, thirty years ago. In deference to him, people smoked in the toilet at the end of the carriage. As there was only one toilet for thirty-two people, this led to queues and squabbles. Lenin turned his considerable intellect to solving this problem. He cut up some paper and issued everyone tickets of two kinds, some for normal use of the toilet and a smaller number for smoking. This reduced the queue and ended the arguments. Walter was amused. It worked, and everyone was happy, but there was no discussion, no attempt at collective decision-making. In this group, Lenin was a benign dictator. If he ever gained real power, would he manage the Russian Empire the same way?

But would he win power? If not, Walter was wasting his time.

There was only one way he could think of to improve Lenin's prospects, and he made up his mind to do something about it.

He left the train at Berlin, saying he would be back to rejoin the Russians for the last leg. "Don't be long," one of them said. "We leave again in an hour."

"I'll be quick," said Walter. The train would depart when Walter said, but the Russians did not know that.

The carriage was in a siding at the Potsdamer station, and it took him only a few minutes to walk from there to the Foreign Office at 76 Wilhelmstrasse in the heart of old Berlin. His father's spacious room had a heavy mahogany desk, a painting of the kaiser, and a glass-fronted cabinet containing his collection of ceramics, including the eighteenth-century creamware fruit bowl he had bought on his last trip to London. As Walter had hoped, Otto was at his desk.

"There's no doubt of Lenin's beliefs," he told his father over coffee. "He says they have got rid of the symbol of oppression—the tsar—without changing Russian society. The workers have failed to take control: the middle class still runs everything. On top of that, Lenin personally hates Kerensky for some reason."

"But can he overthrow the provisional government?"

Walter spread his hands in a helpless gesture. "He is highly intelligent, determined, and a natural leader, and he never does anything except work. But the Bolsheviks are just another little political party among a dozen or more vying for power, and there's no way to tell who will come out on top."

"So all this effort may have been for nothing."

"Unless we do something to help the Bolsheviks win."

"Such as?"

Walter took a deep breath. "Give them money."

"What?" Otto was outraged. "The government of Germany, to give money to socialist revolutionaries?"

"I suggest a hundred thousand rubles, initially," Walter said coolly. "Preferably in gold ten-ruble pieces, if you can get them."

"The kaiser would never agree."

"Does he have to be told? Zimmermann could approve this on his own authority."

"He would never do such a thing."

"Are you sure?"

Otto stared at Walter in silence for a long time, thinking. Then he said: "I'll ask him."

{ IV }

After three days on the train, the Russians left Germany. At Sassnitz, on the coast, they bought tickets for the ferry *Queen Victoria* to take them across the Baltic Sea to the southern tip of Sweden. Walter went with them. The crossing was rough and everyone was seasick except Lenin, Radek, and Zinoviev, who were on deck having an angry political argument and did not seem to notice the heavy seas.

They took an overnight train to Stockholm, where the socialist Borgmastare gave them a welcome breakfast. Walter checked into the Grand Hotel, hoping to find a letter from Maud waiting for him. There was nothing.

He was so disappointed that he wanted to throw himself into the cold water of the bay. This had been his only chance to communicate with his wife in almost three years, and something had gone wrong. Had she even received his letter?

Unhappy fantasies tormented him. Did she still care for him? Had she forgotten him? Was there perhaps a new man in her life? He was completely in the dark.

Radek and the well-dressed Swedish socialists took Lenin, somewhat against his will, to the menswear section of the PUB department store. The hobnailed mountain boots the Russian had been wearing vanished. He got a coat with a velvet collar and a new hat. Now, Radek said, he was at least dressed like someone who could lead his people.

That evening, as night fell, the Russians went to the station to board yet another train for Finland. Walter was leaving the group here, but he went with them to the station. Before the train left, he had a meeting alone with Lenin.

They sat in a compartment under a dim electric light that gleamed off Lenin's bald head. Walter was tense. He had to do this just right. It would be no good to beg or plead with Lenin, he felt sure. And the man certainly could not be bullied. Only cold logic would persuade him.

Walter had a prepared speech. "The German government is helping you to return home," he said. "You know we are not doing this out of goodwill—"

Lenin interrupted in fluent German. "You think it will be to the detriment of Russia!" he barked.

Walter did not contradict him. "And yet you have accepted our help."

"For the sake of the revolution! This is the only standard of right and wrong."

"I thought you would say that." Walter was carrying a heavy suitcase, and now he put it down on the floor of the railway carriage with a thump. "In the false bottom of this case you will find one hundred thousand rubles in notes and coins."

"What?" Lenin was normally imperturbable, but now he looked startled. "What is it for?"

"For you."

Lenin was offended. "A bribe?" he said indignantly.

"Certainly not," said Walter. "We have no need to bribe you. Your aims are the same as ours. You have called for the overthrow of the provisional government and an end to the war."

"What, then?"

"For propaganda. To help you spread your message. It is the message that we, too, would like to broadcast. Peace between Germany and Russia."

"So that you can win your capitalist-imperialist war against France!"

"As I said before, we are not helping you out of goodwill—nor would you expect us to. It's practical politics, that's all. For the moment, your interests coincide with ours."

Lenin looked as he had when Radek insisted on buying him new clothes: he hated the idea, but could not deny that it made sense.

Walter said: "We'll give you a similar amount of money once a month—as long, of course, as you continue to campaign effectively for peace."

There was a long silence.

Walter said: "You say that the success of the revolution is the only standard of right and wrong. If that is so, you should take the money."

Outside on the platform, a whistle blew.

Walter stood up. "I must leave you now. Good-bye, and good luck."

Lenin stared at the suitcase on the floor and did not reply.

Walter left the compartment and got off the train.

He turned and looked back at the window of Lenin's compartment. He half-expected the window to open and the suitcase to come flying out.

There was another whistle and a hoot. The carriages jerked and moved, and slowly the train steamed out of the station, with Lenin, the other Russian exiles, and the money on board.

Walter took the handkerchief from the breast pocket of his coat and wiped his forehead. Despite the cold, he was sweating.

{ V }

Walter walked from the railway station along the water-front to the Grand Hotel. It was dark, and a cold east wind blew off the Baltic. He should have been rejoicing: he had bribed Lenin! But he felt a sense of anticlimax. And he was more depressed than he should have been over the silence from Maud. There were a dozen possible reasons why she had not sent him a letter. He should not assume the worst. But he had come dangerously close to falling for Monika, so why should Maud not do something similar? He could not help feeling she must have forgotten him.

He decided he would get drunk tonight.

At the front desk he was given a typewritten note: "Please call at suite 201, where someone has a message for you." He guessed it was an official from the Foreign Office. Perhaps they had changed their minds about supporting Lenin. If so, they were too late.

He walked up the stairs and tapped on the door of 201. From inside a muffled voice said in German: "Yes?"

"Walter von Ulrich."

"Come in. It's open."

He stepped inside and closed the door. The suite was lit by candles. "Someone has a message for me?" he said, peering into the gloom. A figure rose from a chair. It was a woman, and she had her back to him, but something about her made his heart skip. She turned to face him.

It was Maud.

His mouth fell open and he stood paralyzed.

She said: "Hello, Walter."

Then her self-control broke and she threw herself into his arms.

The familiar smell of her filled his nostrils. He kissed her hair and stroked her back. He could not speak for fear he might cry. He crushed her body to his own, hardly able to believe that this was really her, that he was really holding her and touching her, something he had longed for so painfully for almost three years. She looked up at him, her eyes full of tears, and he stared at her face, drinking it in. She was the same but different: thinner, with the faintest of lines under her eyes where there had been none before, yet with that familiar piercingly intelligent gaze.

She said in English: "'He falls to such perusal of my face, as he would draw it.'"

He smiled. "We're not Hamlet and Ophelia, so please don't go to a nunnery."

"Dear God, I've missed you."

"And I you. I was hoping for a letter—but this! How did you manage it?"

"I told the passport office I planned to interview Scandinavian politicians about votes for women. Then I met the home secretary at a party and had a word in his ear."

"How did you get here?"

"There are still passenger steamers."

"But it's so dangerous—our submarines are sinking everything."

"I know. I took the risk. I was desperate." She began to cry again.

"Come and sit down." With his arm still around her waist, he walked her across the room to the couch.

"No," she said when they were about to sit. "We waited too long, before the war." She took his hand and led him through an inner door to a bedroom. Logs crackled in the fireplace. "Let's not waste any more time. Come to bed."

{ VI }

Grigori and Konstantin were part of the delegation from the Petrograd soviet that went to the Finland Station late in the evening of Monday, April 16, to welcome Lenin home.

Most of them had never seen Lenin, who had been in exile for all but a few months of the last seventeen years. Grigori had been eleven years old when Lenin left. Nevertheless he knew him by reputation, and so, it seemed, did thousands more people, who gathered at the station to greet him. Why so many? Grigori wondered. Perhaps they, like him, were dissatisfied with the provisional government, suspicious of its middle-class ministers, and angry that the war had not ended.

The Finland Station was in the Vyborg district, close to

the textile mills and the barracks of the First Machine Gun Regiment. There was a crowd in the square. Grigori did not expect treachery, but he had told Isaak to bring a couple of platoons and several armored cars to stand guard just in case. There was a searchlight on the station roof, and someone was playing it over the mass of people waiting in the dark.

Inside, the station was full of workers and soldiers, all carrying red flags and banners. A military band played. Twenty minutes before midnight, two sailors' units formed up on the platform as a guard of honor. The delegation from the soviet loitered in the grand waiting room formerly reserved for the tsar and the royal family, but Grigori went out onto the platform with the crowd.

It was about midnight when Konstantin pointed up the line and Grigori, following his finger, saw the distant lights of a train. A rumble of anticipation rose from those waiting. The train steamed into the station, puffing smoke, and hissed to a halt. It had the number 293 painted on its front.

After a pause a short, stocky man got off the train wearing a double-breasted wool coat and a Homburg hat. Grigori thought this could not be Lenin—surely he would not be wearing the clothes of the boss class? A young woman stepped forward and handed him a bouquet, which he accepted with an ungracious frown. This was Lenin.

Behind him was Lev Kamenev, who had been sent by the Bolshevik Central Committee to meet Lenin at the border in case of problems—though in fact Lenin had been admitted without trouble. Now Kamenev indicated with a gesture that they should go to the royal waiting room.

Lenin rather rudely turned his back on Kamenev and addressed the sailors. "Comrades!" he shouted. "You have been deceived! You have made a revolution—and its fruits have been stolen from you by the traitors of the provisional government!"

Kamenev went white. It was the policy of almost everyone on the left to support the provisional government, at least temporarily.

Grigori was delighted, however. He did not believe in bourgeois democracy. The parliament allowed by the tsar in 1905 had been a trick, disempowered when the unrest came to an end and everyone went back to work. This provisional government was headed the same way.

And now at last someone had the guts to say so.

Grigori and Konstantin followed Lenin and Kamenev into the reception room. The crowd squeezed in after them until the room was crammed. The chairman of the Petrograd soviet, the balding, rat-faced Nikolai Chkeidze, stepped forward. He shook Lenin's hand and said: "In the name of the Petrograd soviet and the revolution, we hail your arrival in Russia. But . . ."

Grigori raised his eyebrows at Konstantin. This "but" seemed inappropriately early in a speech of welcome. Konstantin shrugged his bony shoulders.

"But we believe that the main task of revolutionary democracy consists now of defending our revolution against all attacks . . ." Chkeidze paused, then said with emphasis: " . . . whether internal or external."

Konstantin murmured: "This is not a welcome—it's a warning."

"We believe that to accomplish this, not disunity but unity is necessary on the part of all revolutionists. We hope that, in agreement with us, you will pursue these aims."

There was polite applause from some of the delegation.

Lenin paused before replying. He looked at the faces around him and at the lavishly decorated ceiling. Then, in a gesture that seemed a deliberate insult, he turned his back on Chkeidze and spoke to the crowd.

"Comrades, soldiers, sailors, and workers!" he said, pointedly excluding middle-class parliamentarians. "I salute you as the vanguard of the world proletarian army. Today, or perhaps tomorrow, all of European imperialism may collapse. The revolution you have made has opened up a new epoch. Long live the world socialist revolution!"

They cheered. Grigori was startled. They had only just achieved a revolution in Petrograd—and the results of that were still in doubt. How could they think about a *world* revolution? But the idea thrilled him all the same. Lenin was right: all people should turn on the masters who had sent so many men to die in this pointless world war.

Lenin marched away from the delegation and out into the square.

A roar went up from the waiting crowd. Isaak's troops lifted Lenin onto the reinforced roof of an armored car. The searchlight was trained on him. He took off his hat.

His voice was a monotonous bark, but his words were electric. "The provisional government has betrayed the revolution!" he shouted.

They cheered. Grigori was surprised: he had not known how many people thought the way he did.

"The war is a predatory imperialist war. We want no part in this shameful imperialist slaughter of men. With the overthrow of the capital we can conclude a democratic peace!"

That got a bigger roar.

"We do not want the lies or frauds of a bourgeois parliament! The only possible form of government is a soviet of workers' deputies. All banks must be taken over and brought under the control of the soviet. All private land must be confiscated. And all army officers must be elected!"

That was exactly what Grigori thought, and he cheered and waved along with almost everyone else in the crowd.

"Long live the revolution!"

The crowd went wild.

Lenin clambered off the roof and got into the armored car. It drove off at a walking pace. The crowd surrounded and followed it, waving red flags. The military band joined in the procession, playing a march.

Grigori said: "This is the man for me!"

Konstantin said: "Me, too."

They followed the procession.

CHAPTER TWENTY-FIVE

May and June 1917

The Monte Carlo nightclub in Buffalo looked dreadful by daylight, but Lev Peshkov loved it just the same. The woodwork was scratched, the paint was chipped, the upholstery was stained, and there were cigarette butts all over the carpet; yet Lev thought it was paradise. As he walked in he kissed the hat-check girl, gave the doorman a cigar, and told the barman to be careful lifting a crate.

The job of nightclub manager was ideal for him. His main responsibility was to make sure no one was stealing. As a thief himself, he knew how to do that. Otherwise he just had to see that there was enough drink behind the bar and a decent band onstage. As well as his salary, he had free cigarettes and all the booze he could take without falling down. He always wore formal evening dress, which made him feel like a prince. Josef Vyalov left him alone to run the place. As long as the profits were coming in, his father-in-law had no other interest in the club, except to turn up occasionally with his cronies and watch the show.

Lev had only one problem: his wife.

Olga had changed. For a few weeks, back in the summer of 1915, she had been a sexpot, always hungry for his body. But that had been uncharacteristic, he now knew. Since they got married, everything he did displeased her. She wanted him to bathe every day and use a toothbrush and stop farting. She did not like dancing or drinking and she asked him not to smoke. She never came to the club.

They slept in separate beds. She called him low-class. "I am low-class," he had said to her one day. "That's why I was the chauffeur." She continued dissatisfied.

So he had hired Marga.

His old flame was onstage now, rehearsing a new number with the band, while two black women in head scarves wiped the tables and swept the floor. Marga wore a tight dress and red lipstick. Lev had given her a job as a dancer, having no idea whether she was good. She had turned out to be not just good but a star. Now she was belting out a suggestive number about waiting all night for her man to come.

> *Though I suffer from frustrations*
> *The anticipation's*
> *A boost to our relations*
> *When he comes*

Lev knew exactly what she meant.

He watched her until she was done. She came offstage and kissed his cheek. He got two bottles of beer and followed her to her dressing room. "That's a great number," he said as he went in.

"Thanks." She put the bottle in her mouth and tilted it. Lev watched her red lips on the neck. She took a long drink. She caught him watching her, swallowed, and grinned. "That remind you of something?"

"You bet it does." He embraced her and ran his hands over her body. After a couple of minutes she knelt down, unbuttoned his pants, and took him into her mouth. She was good at this, the best he had ever known. Either she really liked it, or she was the greatest actor in America. He closed his eyes and sighed with pleasure.

The door opened and Josef Vyalov came in.

"So it's true!" he said furiously.

Two of his thugs, Ilya and Theo, followed him in.

Lev was scared half to death. He hastily tried to button his pants and apologize at the same time.

Marga stood up quickly and wiped her mouth. "You're in my dressing room!" she protested.

Vyalov said: "And you're in my nightclub. But not for much longer. You're fired." He turned to Lev. "When you're married to my daughter, you don't screw the help!"

Marga said defiantly: "He wasn't screwing me, Vyalov. Didn't you notice that?"

Vyalov punched her in the mouth. She cried out and fell back, her lip bleeding. "You've been fired," he said to her. "Fuck off."

She picked up her bag and left.

Vyalov looked at Lev. "You asshole," he said. "Haven't I done enough for you?"

Lev said: "I'm sorry, Pa." He was terrified of his father-in-law. Vyalov would do anything: people who displeased him might be flogged, tortured, maimed, or murdered. He had no mercy and no fear of the law. In his way he was as powerful as the tsar.

"Don't tell me it's the first time, either," said Vyalov. "I been hearing these rumors ever since I put you in charge here."

Lev said nothing. The rumors were true. There had been others, although not since Marga was hired.

"I'm moving you," Vyalov said.

"What do you mean?"

"I'm taking you out of the club. Too many goddamn girls here."

Lev's heart sank. He loved the Monte Carlo. "But what would I do?"

"I own a foundry down by the harbor. There are no women employees. The manager got sick—he's in the hospital. You can keep an eye on it for me."

"A foundry?" Lev was incredulous. "Me?"

"You worked at the Putilov factory."

"In the stables!"

"And in a coal mine."

"Same thing."

"So, you know the environment."

"And I hate it!"

"Did I ask you what you like? Jesus Christ, I just caught you with your pants down. You're lucky not to get worse."

Lev shut up.

"Go outside and get in the goddamn car," said Vyalov.

Lev left the dressing room and walked through the club, with Vyalov following. He could hardly believe he was leaving for good. The barman and the hat-check girl stared, sensing something wrong. Vyalov said to the barman: "You're in charge tonight, Ivan."

"Yes, boss."

Vyalov's Packard Twin Six was waiting at the curb. A new chauffeur stood proudly beside it, a kid from Kiev. The commissionaire hurried to open the rear door for Lev. At least I'm still riding in the back, Lev thought.

He was living like a Russian nobleman, if not better, he reminded himself for consolation. He and Olga had the nursery wing of the spacious prairie house. Rich Americans did not keep as many servants as the Russians, but their houses were cleaner and brighter than Petrograd palaces. They had modern bathrooms, iceboxes and vacuum cleaners, and central heating. The food was good. Vyalov did not share the Russian aristocracy's love of champagne, but there was always whisky on the sideboard. And Lev had six suits.

Whenever he felt oppressed by his bullying father-in-law, he cast his mind back to the old days in Petrograd: the single room he shared with Grigori, the cheap vodka, the coarse black bread, and the turnip stew. He remembered thinking what a luxury it would be to ride the streetcars instead of walking everywhere. Stretching out his legs in the back of Vyalov's limousine, he looked at his silk socks and shiny black shoes, and told himself to be grateful.

Vyalov got in after him and they drove to the waterfront. Vyalov's foundry was a small version of the Putilov works: same dilapidated buildings with broken windows, same tall chimneys and black smoke, same drab workers with dirty faces. Lev's heart sank.

"It's called the Buffalo Metal Works, but it makes only one thing," Vyalov said. "Fans." The car drove through the narrow gateway. "Before the war it was losing money. I bought it and cut the men's pay to keep it going. Lately business has picked up. We've got a long list of orders for airplane and ship propellers and fans for armored car engines. They want a pay raise now, but I need to get back some of what I've spent before I start giving money away."

Lev was dreading working here, but his fear of Vyalov was stronger, and he did not want to fail. He resolved that he would not be the one to give the men a raise.

Vyalov showed him around the factory. Lev wished he were not wearing his tuxedo. But the place was not like the Putilov works inside. It was a lot cleaner. There were no children running around. Apart from the furnaces, everything worked by electric power. Where the Russians would get twelve men hauling on a rope to lift a locomotive boiler, here a mighty ship's propeller was raised by an electric hoist.

Vyalov pointed to a bald man wearing a collar and tie under his overalls. "That's your enemy," he said. "Brian Hall, secretary of the local union branch."

Lev studied Hall. The man was adjusting a heavy stamping machine, turning a nut with a long-handled wrench. He had a pugnacious air and, when he glanced up and saw Lev and Vyalov, he gave them a challenging look, as if he might be about to ask whether they wanted to make trouble.

Vyalov shouted over the noise of a nearby grinder. "Come here, Hall."

The man took his time, replacing the wrench in a toolbox and wiping his hands on a rag before approaching.

Vyalov said: "This is your new boss, Lev Peshkov."

"How do," Hall said to Lev; then he turned back to Vyalov. "Peter Fisher got a nasty cut on his face from a flying shard of steel this morning. Had to be taken to the hospital."

"I'm sorry to hear that," Vyalov said. "Metalworking is a hazardous industry, but no one is forced to work here."

"It just missed his eye," Hall said indignantly. "We ought to have goggles."

"No one has lost an eye in my time here."

Hall became angry quickly. "Do we have to wait until someone is blinded before we get goggles?"

"How else will I know you need them?"

"A man who has never been robbed still puts a lock on the door of his house."

"But he's paying for it himself."

Hall nodded as if he had been expecting nothing better and, with an air of weary wisdom, returned to his machine.

"They're always asking for something," Vyalov said to Lev.

Lev gathered that Vyalov wanted him to be tough. Well, he knew how to do that. It was the way all factories were run in Petrograd.

They left the plant and drove up Delaware Avenue. Lev guessed they were going home to dinner. It would never occur to Vyalov to ask whether that was okay with Lev. Vyalov made decisions for everyone.

In the house Lev took off his shoes, which were dirty from the foundry, and put on a pair of embroidered slippers Olga had given him for Christmas; then he went to the baby's room. Olga's mother, Lena, was there with Daisy.

Lena said: "Look, Daisy, here's your father!"

Lev's daughter was now fourteen months old and just beginning to walk. She came staggering across the room toward him, smiling, then fell over and cried. He picked her up and kissed her. He had never before taken the least interest in babies or children, but Daisy had captured his heart. When she was fractious and did not want to go to bed, and no one else could soothe her, he would rock her, murmuring endearments and singing fragments of Russian folk songs, until her eyes closed, her tiny body went limp, and she fell asleep in his arms.

Lena said: "She looks just like her handsome daddy!"

Lev thought she looked like a baby, but he did not contradict his mother-in-law. Lena adored him. She flirted with him, touched him a lot, and kissed him at every opportunity. She was in love with him, though she undoubtedly thought she was showing nothing more than normal family affection.

On the other side of the room was a young Russian girl called Polina. She was the nurse, but she was not overworked: Olga and Lena spent most of their time taking care of Daisy. Now Lev handed the baby to Polina. As he did so, Polina gave him a direct look. She was a classic Russian beauty, with blond hair and high cheekbones. Lev wondered briefly whether he could have an affair with her and get away with it. She had her own tiny bedroom. Could he sneak in without anyone noticing? It might be worth the risk: that look had shown eagerness.

Olga came in, making him feel guilty. "What a surprise!" she said when she saw him. "I didn't expect you back until three in the morning."

"Your father has moved me," Lev said sourly. "I'm running the foundry now."

"But why? I thought you were doing well at the club."

"I don't know why," Lev lied.

"Maybe because of the draft," Olga said. President Wilson had declared war on Germany and was about to introduce conscription. "The foundry will be classified as an essential war industry. Daddy wants to keep you out of the army."

Lev knew from the newspapers that conscription would be run by local draft boards. Vyalov was sure to have at least one crony on the board who would fix anything he asked for. That was how this town worked. But Lev did not disabuse Olga. He needed a cover story that did not involve Marga, and Olga had invented one. "Sure," he said. "I guess that must be it."

Daisy said: "Dadda."

"Clever girl!" Polina said.

Lena said: "I'm sure you'll make a good job of managing the foundry."

Lev gave her his best aw-shucks American grin. "Guess I'll do my best," he said.

{ II }

Gus Dewar felt his European mission for the president had been a failure. "Failure?" said Woodrow Wilson. "Heck, no! You got the Germans to make a peace offer. It's not your fault the British and French told them to drop dead. You can lead a horse to water, but you can't make it drink." All the same, the truth was that Gus had not succeeded in bringing the two sides together even for preliminary discussions.

So he was all the more eager to succeed in the next major task Wilson gave him. "The Buffalo Metal Works has been closed by a strike," the president said. "We have ships and planes and military vehicles stuck on production lines waiting for the propellers and fans they make. You come from Buffalo—go up there and get them back to work."

On his first night back in his hometown, Gus went to dinner at the home of Chuck Dixon, once his rival for the affections of Olga Vyalov. Chuck and his new wife, Doris, had a Victorian mansion on Elmwood Avenue, which ran parallel to Delaware, and Chuck took the Belt Line railway every morning to work in his father's bank.

Doris was a pretty girl who looked a bit like Olga, and as Gus watched the newlyweds he wondered how much he would like this life of domesticity. He had once dreamed of waking up every morning next to Olga, but that was two years ago, and now that her enchantment had worn off he thought he might prefer his bachelor apartment on Sixteenth Street in Washington.

When they sat down to their steaks and mashed potatoes, Doris said: "What happened to President Wilson's promise to keep us out of the war?"

"You have to give him credit," Gus said mildly. "For three years he's been campaigning for peace. They just wouldn't listen."

"That doesn't mean we have to join in the fighting."

Chuck said impatiently: "Honey, the Germans are sinking American ships!"

"Then tell American ships to stay out of the war zone!" Doris looked cross, and Gus guessed they had had this argument before. No doubt her anger was fueled by the fear that Chuck would be conscripted.

To Gus, these issues were too nuanced for passionate declarations of right and wrong. He said gently: "Okay, that's an alternative, and the president considered it. But it means accepting Germany's power to tell us where American ships can and can't go."

Chuck said indignantly: "We can't be pushed around that way by Germany or anyone else!"

Doris was adamant. "If it saves lives, why not?"

Gus said: "Most Americans seem to feel the way Chuck does."

"That doesn't make it right."

"Wilson believes a president must treat public opinion the way a sailing ship treats the wind, using it but never going directly against it."

"Then why must we have conscription? That makes slaves of American men."

Chuck chipped in again. "Don't you think it's fair that we should all be equally responsible for fighting for our country?"

"We have a professional army. At least those men joined voluntarily."

Gus said: "We have an army of a hundred and thirty

thousand men. That's nothing in this war. We're going to need at least a million."

"A lot more men to die," Doris said.

Chuck said: "We're damn glad at the bank, I can tell you. We have a lot of money out on loan to American companies supplying the Allies. If the Germans win, and the Brits and the Froggies can't pay their debts, we're in trouble."

Doris looked thoughtful. "I didn't know that."

Chuck patted her hand. "Don't worry about it, honey. It's not going to happen. The Allies are going to win, especially with the U.S. of A. helping out."

Gus said: "There's another reason for us to fight. When the war is over, the U.S. will be able to take part as an equal in the postwar settlement. That may not sound very important, but Wilson's dream is to set up a league of nations to resolve future conflicts without us killing one another." He looked at Doris. "You must be in favor of that, I guess."

"Certainly."

Chuck changed the subject. "What brings you home, Gus? Apart from the desire to explain the president's decisions to us common folk."

He told them about the strike. He spoke lightly, as this was dinner-party talk, but in truth he was worried. The Buffalo Metal Works was vital to the war effort, and he was not sure how to get the men back to work. Wilson had settled a national rail strike shortly before his reelection and seemed to think that intervention in industrial disputes was a natural element of political life. Gus found it a heavy responsibility.

"You know who owns that place, don't you?" said Chuck.

Gus had checked. "Vyalov."

"And who runs it for him?"

"No."

"His new son-in-law, Lev Peshkov."

"Oh," said Gus. "I didn't know that."

{ III }

Lev was furious about the strike. The union was trying to take advantage of his inexperience. He felt sure Brian Hall and the men had decided he was weak. He was determined to prove them wrong.

He had tried being reasonable. "Mr. V needs to make back some of the money he lost in the bad years," he had said to Hall.

"And the men need to make back some of what *they* lost in reduced wages!" Hall had replied.

"It's not the same."

"No, it's not," Hall had agreed. "You're rich and they're poor. It's harder for them." The man was infuriatingly quick-witted.

Lev was desperate to get back into his father-in-law's good books. It was dangerous to let a man such as Josef Vyalov remain displeased with you for long. The trouble was that charm was Lev's only asset, and it did not work on Vyalov.

However, Vyalov was being supportive about the foundry. "Sometimes you have to let them strike," he had said. "It doesn't do to give in. Just stick it out. They become more reasonable when they start to get hungry." But Lev knew how fast Vyalov could change his mind.

However, Lev had a plan of his own to hasten the collapse of the strike. He was going to use the power of the press.

Lev was a member of the Buffalo Yacht Club, thanks to his father-in-law, who had got him elected. Most of the town's leading businessmen belonged, including Peter Hoyle, editor of the *Buffalo Advertiser*. One afternoon Lev approached Hoyle in the clubhouse at the foot of Porter Avenue.

The *Advertiser* was a conservative newspaper that always called for stability and blamed all problems on foreigners, Negroes, and socialist troublemakers. Hoyle, an imposing figure with a black mustache, was a crony of Vyalov's. "Hello, young Peshkov," he said. His voice was loud and harsh, as if he was used to shouting over the noise of a printing press. "I hear the president has sent Cam Dewar's son up here to settle your strike."

"I believe so, but I haven't heard from him yet."

"I know him. He's naïve. You don't have much to worry about."

Lev agreed. He had taken a dollar from Gus Dewar in Petrograd in 1914, and more recently he had taken Gus's fiancée just as easily. "I wanted to talk to you about the strike," he said, sitting in the leather armchair opposite Hoyle.

"The *Advertiser* has already condemned the strikers as un-American socialists and revolutionaries," Hoyle said. "What more can we do?"

"Call them enemy agents," Lev said. "They're holding up the production of vehicles that our boys are going to need when they get to Europe—but the workers themselves are exempt from the draft!"

"That's an angle." Hoyle frowned. "But we don't yet know how the draft is going to work."

"It's sure to exclude war industries."

"That's true."

"And yet they're demanding more money. A lot of people would take less for a job that keeps them out of the army."

Hoyle took a notebook from his jacket pocket and began to write. "Take less money for a draft-exempt job," he muttered.

"Maybe you want to ask: whose side are they on?"

"Sounds like a headline."

Lev was surprised and pleased. It had been easy.

Hoyle looked up from his notebook. "I presume Mr. V knows we're having this conversation?"

Lev had not anticipated this question. He grinned to cover his confusion. If he said no, Hoyle would drop the whole thing immediately. "Yes, of course," he lied. "In fact it was his idea."

{ IV }

Vyalov asked Gus to meet him at the yacht club. Brian Hall proposed a conference at the Buffalo office of the union. Each wanted to meet on his own ground, where he would feel confident and in charge. So Gus took a meeting room at the Statler Hotel.

Lev Peshkov had attacked the strikers as draft dodgers, and the *Advertiser* had put his comments on the front page, under the headline WHOSE SIDE ARE THEY ON? When Gus saw the paper he had been dismayed: such aggressive talk could only escalate the dispute. But Lev's effort had backfired. This morning's papers reported a storm of protest from workers in other war industries, indignant at the suggestion that they should receive low wages on account of their privileged status, and furious at being labeled draft dodgers. Lev's clumsiness heartened Gus, but he knew that Vyalov was his real enemy, and that made him nervous.

Gus brought all the papers with him to the Statler and put them out on a side table in the meeting room. In a prominent position he placed a popular rag with the headline WILL *YOU* JOIN UP, LEV?

Gus had asked Brian Hall to get there a quarter of an hour before Vyalov. The union leader showed up on the dot. He wore a smart suit and a gray felt hat, Gus noted. That was good tactics. It was a mistake to look inferior, even if you represented the workers. Hall was as formidable, in his own way, as Vyalov.

Hall saw the newspapers and grinned. "Young Lev made a mistake," he said with satisfaction. "He's fetched himself a pile of trouble."

"Manipulating the press is a dangerous game," Gus said. He got right down to business. "You're asking for a dollar-a-day increase."

"It's only ten cents more than my men were getting before Vyalov bought the plant, and—"

"Never mind all that," Gus interrupted, showing more boldness than he felt. "If I can get you fifty cents, will you take it?"

Hall looked dubious. "I'd have to put it to the men—"

"No," Gus said. "You have to decide now." He prayed his nervousness was not showing.

Hall prevaricated. "Has Vyalov agreed to this?"

"I'll worry about Vyalov. Fifty cents, take it or leave it." Gus resisted an urge to wipe his forehead.

Hall gave Gus a long, appraising stare. Behind the pugnacious look there was a shrewd brain, Gus suspected. At last Hall said: "We'll take it—for now."

"Thank you." Gus managed not to let out his breath in a long sigh of relief. "Would you like coffee?"

"Sure."

Gus turned away, grateful to be able to hide his face, and pressed the bell for a waiter.

Josef Vyalov and Lev Peshkov walked in. Gus did not shake hands. "Sit down," he said curtly.

Vyalov's eyes went to the newspapers on the side table, and a look of anger crossed his face. Gus guessed that Lev was already in trouble over those headlines.

He tried not to stare at Lev. This was the chauffeur who had seduced Gus's fiancée—but that must not be allowed to cloud Gus's judgment. He would have liked to punch Lev in the face. However, if this meeting went according to plan, the result would be more humiliating to Lev than a punch—and much more satisfying to Gus.

A waiter appeared, and Gus said: "Bring coffee for my guests, please, and a plate of ham sandwiches." He deliberately did not ask them what they wanted. He had seen Woodrow Wilson act like this with people he wanted to intimidate.

He sat down and opened a folder. It contained a blank sheet of paper. He pretended to read it.

Lev sat down and said: "So, Gus, the president has sent you up here to negotiate with us."

Now Gus allowed himself to look at Lev. He stared at him for a long moment without speaking. Handsome, yes, he thought, but also untrustworthy and weak. When Lev began to look embarrassed, Gus spoke at last. "Are you out of your fucking mind?"

Lev was so shocked that he actually pushed his chair back from the table as if fearing a blow. "What the hell . . . ?"

Gus made his voice harsh. "America is at war," he said. "The president is not going to *negotiate* with you." He looked at Brian Hall. "Or you," he said, even though he had made a deal with Hall only ten minutes ago. Finally he looked at Vyalov. "Not even with you," he said.

Vyalov looked steadily back at him. Unlike his son-in-law, he was not intimidated. However, he had lost the look of amused contempt with which he began the meeting. After a long pause, he said: "So what are you here for?"

"I'm here to tell you what's going to happen," Gus said in the same voice. "And when I'm done, you'll accept it."

Lev said: "Huh!"

Vyalov said: "Shut up, Lev. Go on, Dewar."

"You're going to offer the men a raise of fifty cents a day," Gus said. He turned to Hall. "And you're going to accept his offer."

Hall kept his face blank and said: "Is that so?"

"And I want your men back at work by noon today."

Vyalov said: "And why the hell should we do what you tell us?"

"Because of the alternative."

"Which is?"

"The president will send an army battalion to the foundry to take it over, secure it, release all finished products to customers, and continue to run it with army engineers. After the war, he might give it back." He turned to Hall. "And your men can probably have their jobs back then, too." Gus wished he had run this past Woodrow Wilson first, but it was too late now.

Lev said with amazement: "Does he have the right to do that?"

"Under wartime legislation, yes," said Gus.

"So you say," said Vyalov skeptically.

"Challenge us in court," said Gus. "Do you think there's a judge in this country who will side with you—and our country's enemies?" He sat back and stared at them with an arrogance he did not feel. Would this work? Would they believe him? Or would they call his bluff, laugh at him, and walk out?

There was a long silence. Hall's face was expressionless. Vyalov was thoughtful. Lev looked sick.

At last Vyalov turned to Hall. "Are you willing to settle for fifty cents?"

Hall just said: "Yes."

Vyalov looked back at Gus. "Then we accept, too."

"Thank you, gentlemen." Gus closed his folder, trying to still the shaking of his hands. "I'll tell the president."

{ V }

Saturday was sunny and warm. Lev told Olga he was needed at the foundry; then he drove to Marga's place. She lived in a small room in Lovejoy. They embraced, but when Lev started to unbutton her blouse she said: "Let's go to Humboldt Park."

"I'd rather screw."

"Later. Take me to the park, and I'll show you something special when we come back. Something we haven't done before."

Lev's throat went dry. "Why do I have to wait?"

"It's such a beautiful day."

"What if we're seen?"

"There'll be a million people there."

"Even so . . ."

"I suppose you're afraid of your father-in-law?"

"Hell, no," Lev said. "Listen, I'm the father of his grandchild. What's he going to do, shoot me?"

"Let me change my dress."

"I'll wait in the car. If I watch you undress I might lose control."

He had a new Cadillac three-passenger coupe, not the swankiest car in town but a good place to start. He sat at the wheel and lit a cigarette. He *was* afraid of Vyalov, of course. But all his life he had taken risks. He was not Grigori, after all. And things had worked out pretty well for him so far, he thought, sitting in his car, wearing a summer-weight blue suit, about to take a pretty girl to the park. Life was good.

Before he had finished his smoke, Marga came out of the building and got into the car beside him. She was wearing a daring sleeveless dress and had her hair coiled over her ears in the latest fashion.

He drove to Humboldt Park, on the east side of town. They sat together on a slatted wooden park seat, enjoying the sunshine and watching the children playing in the pond. Lev could not stop touching Marga's bare arms. He loved the envious looks he got from other men. She's the prettiest girl in the park, he thought, and she's with me. How about that?

"I'm sorry about your lip," he said. Her lower lip was

still swollen where Vyalov had punched her. It looked quite sexy.

"Not your fault," Marga said. "Your father-in-law is a pig."

"That's the truth."

"The Hot Spot offered me a job right away. I'll start there as soon as I can sing again."

"How does it feel?"

She tried a few bars.

> *I run my fingers through my hair*
> *Play a little solitaire*
> *Waiting for my millionaire*
> *To come*

She touched her mouth gingerly. "Still hurts," she said.

He leaned toward her. "Let me kiss it better." She turned her face up to his and he kissed her gently, hardly touching.

She said: "You can be a little firmer than that."

He grinned. "Okay, how about this?" He kissed her again, and this time he let the tip of his tongue caress the inside of her lips.

After a minute she said: "That's okay, too," and she giggled.

"In that case . . ." This time he put his tongue all the way inside her mouth. She responded eagerly—she always did. Her tongue and his met; then she put her hand behind his head and stroked his neck. He heard someone say: "Disgusting." He wondered whether people walking by could see his erection.

Smiling at Marga, he said: "We're shocking the towns-people." He glanced up to see whether anyone was watching, and met the eyes of his wife, Olga.

She was staring at him in shock, her mouth forming a silent O.

Beside her stood her father, in a suit with a vest and a straw boater. He was carrying Daisy. Lev's daughter had a white bonnet to shade her face from the sun. The nurse, Polina, was behind them.

Olga said: "Lev! What . . . Who is she?"

Lev felt he might have talked himself out of even this situation if Vyalov had not been there.

He got up. "Olga . . . I don't know what to say."

Vyalov said harshly: "Don't say a damn thing."

Olga began to cry.

Vyalov handed Daisy to the nurse. "Take my grand-daughter to the car right away."

"Yes, Mr. Vyalov."

Vyalov grasped Olga's arm and moved her away. "Go with Polina, honey."

Olga put her hand over her eyes to hide her tears and followed the nurse.

"You piece of shit," Vyalov said to Lev.

Lev clenched his fists. If Vyalov struck him he would fight back. Vyalov was built like a bull, but he was twenty years older. Lev was taller, and had learned to fight in the slums of Petrograd. He was not going to take a beating.

Vyalov read his mind. "I'm not going to fight you," he said. "It's beyond that."

Lev wanted to say: *So what are you going to do?* He kept his mouth clamped shut.

Vyalov looked at Marga. "I should have hit you harder," he said.

Marga picked up her bag, opened it, put her hand inside, and left it there. "If you move one inch toward me, so help me God, I'll shoot you in the gut, you pig-faced Russian peasant," she said.

Lev could not help admiring her nerve. Few people had the balls to threaten Josef Vyalov.

Vyalov's face darkened in anger, but he turned away from Marga and spoke to Lev. "You know what you're going to do?"

What the hell was coming now?

Lev said nothing.

Vyalov said: "You're going in the goddamn army."

Lev went cold. "You don't mean it."

"When was the last time you heard me say something I didn't mean?"

"I'm not going in the army. How can you make me?"

"Either you'll volunteer, or you'll get conscripted."

Marga burst out: "You can't do that!"

"Yes, he can," Lev said in desolation. "He can fix anything in this town."

"And you know what?" said Vyalov. "You might be my son-in-law, but I hope to God you get killed."

{ VI }

Chuck and Doris Dixon gave an afternoon party in their garden at the end of June. Gus went with his parents. All the men wore suits, but the women dressed in summer outfits and extravagant hats, and the crowd looked colorful. There were sandwiches and beer, lemonade and cake. A clown gave out candy and a schoolteacher in shorts organized the children to run jokey races: a sack race, an egg-and-spoon race, a three-legged race.

Doris wanted to talk to Gus about the war, again. "There are rumors of mutiny in the French army," she said.

Gus knew that the truth was worse than the rumors: there had been mutinies in fifty-four French divisions, and twenty thousand men had deserted. "I assume that's why they've switched their tactics from offense to defense," he said neutrally.

"Apparently the French officers treat their men badly." Doris relished bad news about the war because it gave support to her opposition. "And the Nivelle Offensive has been a disaster."

"The arrival of American troops will buck them up." The first Americans had boarded ships to sail to France.

"But so far we have sent only a token force. I hope that means we're going to play only a small part in the fighting."

"No, it does not mean that. We have to recruit, train, and arm at least a million men. We can't do that instantly. But next year we will send them in the hundreds of thousands."

Doris looked over Gus's shoulder and said: "Goodness, here comes one of our new recruits."

Gus turned and saw the Vyalov family: Josef and Lena with Olga, Lev, and a little girl. Lev was wearing an army uniform. He looked dashing, but his handsome face was sulky.

Gus was embarrassed but his father, wearing his public persona as senator, shook hands cordially with Josef and said something that made him laugh. Mother spoke graciously to Lena and cooed over the baby. Gus realized his parents had anticipated this meeting and decided to act as if they had forgotten that he and Olga had once been engaged.

He caught Olga's eye and nodded politely. She blushed.

Lev was as brash as ever. "So, Gus, is the president pleased with you for settling the strike?"

The others heard this question and went quiet, listening to hear Gus's answer.

"He's pleased with you for being reasonable," Gus said tactfully. "I see you joined the army."

"I volunteered," Lev said. "I'm doing officer training."

"How are you finding it?"

Suddenly Gus was aware that he and Lev had an audience around them in a ring: the Vyalovs, the Dewars, and the Dixons. Since the engagement had been broken off, the two men had not been seen together in public. Everyone was curious.

"I'll get accustomed to the army," Lev said. "How about you?"

"What about me?"

"Are you going to volunteer? After all, you and your president got us into the war."

Gus said nothing, but he felt ashamed. Lev was right.

"You can always wait and see whether you get drafted," Lev said, turning the knife. "You never know—you could get lucky. Anyway, if you go back to Washington, I guess the president can get you exempted." He laughed.

Gus shook his head. "No," he said. "I've been thinking about this. You're right. I'm part of the government that brought in the draft. I could hardly evade it."

He saw his father nod, as if he had anticipated this; but his mother said: "But, Gus, you work for the president! What better way could there be for you to help the war effort?"

Lev said: "I guess it would seem kind of cowardly."

"Exactly," said Gus. "So I won't be going back to Washington. That part of my life is over for now."

He heard his mother say: "Gus, no!"

"I've already spoken to General Clarence of the Buffalo Division," he said. "I'm joining the National Army."

His mother began to cry.

CHAPTER TWENTY-SIX

Mid-June 1917

Ethel had never thought about women's rights until she stood in the library at Tŷ Gwyn, unmarried and pregnant, while the slimy lawyer Solman told her the facts of life. She was to spend her best years struggling to feed and care for Fitz's child, but there was no obligation upon the father to help in any way. The unfairness of it had made her want to murder Solman.

Her rage had been further inflamed by looking for work in London. A job would be open to her only if no man wanted it, and then she would be offered half a man's wages or less.

But her angry feminism had set as hard as concrete during years of living alongside the tough, hardworking, dirt-poor women of London's East End. Men often told a fairy tale in which there was a division of labor in families, the man going out to earn money, the woman looking after home and children. Reality was different. Most of the women Ethel knew worked twelve hours a day and looked after home and children as well. Underfed, overworked, living in hovels, and dressed in rags, they could still sing songs and laugh and love their children. In Ethel's view one of those women had more right to vote than any ten men.

She had been arguing this for so long that she felt quite strange when votes for women became a real possibility in the middle of 1917. As a little girl she had asked: "What will it be like in heaven?" and had never got a satisfactory answer.

Parliament agreed to a debate in mid-June. "It's the result of two compromises," Ethel said excitedly to Bernie when she read the report in *The Times*. "The Speaker's Conference, which Asquith called to sidestep the issue, was desperate to avoid a row."

Bernie was giving Lloyd his breakfast, feeding him toast dipped in sweet tea. "I assume the government is afraid that women will start chaining themselves to railings again."

Ethel nodded. "And if the politicians get caught up in that kind of fuss, people will say they're not concentrating on winning the war. So the committee recommended giving the vote only to women over thirty who are householders or the wives of householders. Which means I'm too young."

"That was the first compromise," said Bernie. "And the second?"

"According to Maud, the cabinet was split." The War Cabinet consisted of four men plus the prime minister, Lloyd George. "Curzon is against us, obviously." Earl Curzon, the leader of the House of Lords, was proudly misogynist. He was president of the League for Opposing Woman Suffrage. "So is Milner. But Henderson supports us." Arthur Henderson was the leader of the Labour Party, whose M.P.s supported the women, even though many Labour Party men did not. "Bonar Law is with us, though lukewarm."

"Two in favor, two against, and Lloyd George as usual wanting to keep everyone happy."

"The compromise is that there will be a free vote." That meant the government would not order its supporters to vote one way or the other.

"So that whatever happens it won't be the government's fault."

"No one ever said Lloyd George was ingenuous."

"But he's given you a chance."

"A chance is all it is. We've got some campaigning work to do."

"I think you'll find attitudes have changed," Bernie said optimistically. "The government is desperate to get women into industry to replace all the men sent to France, so they've put out a lot of propaganda about how great women are as bus drivers and munitions workers. That makes it more difficult for people to say that women are inferior."

"I hope you're right," Ethel said fervently.

They had been married four months, and Ethel had no regrets. Bernie was clever, interesting, and kind. They believed in the same things and worked together to achieve them. Bernie would probably be the Labour candidate for Aldgate in the next general election—whenever that might be: like so much else, it had to wait for the end of the war. Bernie would make a good member of Parliament, hardworking and intelligent. However, Ethel did not know whether Labour could win Aldgate. The current M.P. was a Liberal, but much had changed since the last election in 1910. Even if the clause about votes for women did not pass, the other proposals of the Speaker's Conference would give the vote to many more working-class men.

Bernie was a good man, but to her shame Ethel still occasionally thought longingly of Fitz, who was not clever, nor interesting, nor kind, and whose beliefs were opposite to hers. When she had these thoughts she felt she was no better than the type of man that hankered after girls who danced the can-can. Such men were inflamed by stockings and petticoats and frilly knickers; she was entranced by Fitz's soft hands and clipped accent and the clean, slightly scented smell of him.

But she was Eth Leckwith now. Everyone spoke of Eth and Bernie the way they said horse-and-cart or bread-and-dripping.

She put Lloyd's shoes on and took him to the child minder, then walked to the office of *The Soldier's Wife*. The weather was fine and she felt hopeful. We *can* change the world, she thought. It's not easy, but it can be done. Maud's newspaper would whip up support for the bill among working-class women, and make sure all eyes were on M.P.s when they voted.

Maud was at their pokey office already, having come in early, no doubt because of the news. She sat at an old stained table, wearing a lilac summer gown and a hat like a fore-and-aft cap with one dramatically long feather stuck through its peak. Most of her clothes were prewar, but she still dressed elegantly. She looked too thoroughbred for this place, like a racehorse in a farmyard.

"We must bring out a special edition," she said, scribbling on a pad. "I'm writing the front page."

Ethel felt a wave of excitement. This was what she liked: action. She sat on the other side of the table and said: "I'll make sure the other pages are ready. How about a column on how readers can help?"

"Yes. Come to our meeting, lobby your member of Parliament, write a letter to a newspaper, that sort of thing."

"I'll draft something." She picked up a pencil and took a pad from a drawer.

Maud said: "We have to mobilize women against this bill."

Ethel froze, pencil in hand. "What?" she said. "Did you say against?"

"Of course. The government is going to *pretend* to give women the vote—but still withhold it from most of us."

Ethel looked across the table and saw the headline Maud had written: VOTE AGAINST THIS TRICK! "Just a minute." She did not see it as a trick. "This may not be all that we want, but it's better than nothing."

Maud looked at her angrily. "It's worse than nothing. This bill only pretends to make women equal."

Maud was being too theoretical. Of course it was wrong in principle to discriminate against younger women. But right now that was not important. This was about practical politics. Ethel said: "Look, sometimes reform has to go step by step. The vote has been extended to men very gradually. Even now only about half of men can vote—"

Maud interrupted her imperiously. "Have you thought about who the left-out women are?"

It was a fault of Maud's that she could occasionally seem high-handed. Ethel tried not to be offended. Mildly, she said: "Well, I'm one of them."

Maud did not soften her tone. "The majority of female munitions workers—such an essential part of the war effort—would be too young to vote. So would most of the nurses who have risked their lives caring for wounded soldiers in France. War widows could not vote, despite the terrible sacrifice they have made, if they happen to live in furnished lodgings. Can't you see that the purpose of this bill is to turn women into a minority?"

"So you want to campaign *against* the bill?"

"Of course!"

"That's crazy." Ethel was surprised and upset to find

herself disagreeing violently with someone who had been a friend and colleague for so long. "I'm sorry. I just don't see how we can ask members of Parliament to vote against something we've been demanding for decades."

"That is *not* what we're doing!" Maud's anger mounted. "We've been campaigning for equality, and this is not it. If we fall for this ruse we'll be on the sidelines for another generation!"

"It's not a question of falling for a ruse," Ethel said tetchily. "I'm not being *fooled*. I understand the point you're making—it's not even particularly subtle. But your judgment is wrong."

"Is it, indeed?" Maud said stiffly, and Ethel suddenly saw her resemblance to Fitz: brother and sister held opposing opinions with a similar obstinacy.

Ethel said: "Just think of the propaganda the other side will put out! 'We always knew women couldn't make up their minds,' they'll say. 'That's why they can't vote.' They will make fun of us, yet again."

"Our propaganda must be better than theirs," Maud said airily. "We just have to explain the situation very clearly to everyone."

Ethel shook her head. "You're wrong. These things are too emotional. For years we've been campaigning against the rule that women can't vote. That's the barrier. Once it's broken down, people will see further concessions as mere technicalities. It will be relatively easy to get the voting age lowered and other restrictions eased. You must see that."

"No, I do not," Maud said icily. She did not like being told that she *must* see something. "This bill is a step backward. Anyone who supports it is a traitor."

Ethel stared at Maud. She felt wounded. She said: "You can't mean that."

"Please don't instruct me as to what I can and cannot mean."

"We've worked and campaigned together for two years," Ethel said, and tears came to her eyes. "Do you really believe that if I disagree with you I must be disloyal to the cause of women's suffrage?"

Maud was implacable. "I most certainly do."

"Very well," said Ethel; and, not knowing what else she could possibly do, she walked out.

{ II }

Fitz caused his tailor to make him six new suits. All the old ones hung loosely on his thin frame and made him look old. He put on his new evening clothes: black tailcoat, white waistcoat, and wing collar with white bow tie. He looked in the cheval glass in his dressing room and thought: That's better.

He went down to the drawing room. He could manage without a cane indoors. Maud poured him a glass of Madeira. Aunt Herm said: "How do you feel?"

"The doctors say the leg's getting better, but it's slow." Fitz had returned to the trenches earlier this year, but the cold and damp had proved too much for him, and he was back on the convalescent list, and working in intelligence.

Maud said: "I know you'd rather be over there, but we're not sorry you missed the spring fighting."

Fitz nodded. The Nivelle Offensive had been a failure, and the French general Nivelle had been fired. French soldiers were mutinous, defending their trenches but refusing to advance when ordered. So far this had been another bad year for the Allies.

But Maud was wrong to think Fitz would rather be on the front line. The work he was doing in Room 40 was probably even more important than the fighting in France. Many people had feared that German submarines would strangle Britain's supply lines. But Room 40 was able to find out where the U-boats were and forewarn ships. This information, combined with the tactic of sending ships in convoys escorted by destroyers, rendered the submarines much less effective. It was a triumph, albeit one that few people knew about.

The danger now was Russia. The tsar had been deposed, and anything could happen. So far, the moderates had remained in control, but could that last? It was not just Bea's family and Boy's inheritance that were in danger. If extremists took over the Russian government they might make peace, and free hundreds of thousands of German troops to fight in France.

Fitz said: "At least we haven't lost Russia."

"Yet," said Maud. "The Germans are hoping the Bolsheviks will triumph—everyone knows that."

As she spoke Princess Bea came in, wearing a low-cut dress in silver silk and a suite of diamond jewelry. Fitz and Bea were going to a dinner party, then a ball: it was the London season. Bea heard Maud's remark and said: "Don't underestimate the Russian royal family. There may yet be a counterrevolution. After all, what have the Russian people gained? The workers are still starving, the soldiers are still dying, and the Germans are still advancing."

Grout came in with a bottle of champagne. He opened it inaudibly and poured a glass for Bea. As always, she took one sip and set it down.

Maud said: "Prince Lvov has announced that women will be able to vote in the election for the Constituent Assembly."

"If it ever happens," Fitz said. "The provisional government is making a lot of announcements, but is anyone listening? As far as I can make out, every village has set up a soviet and is running its own affairs."

"Imagine it!" said Bea. "Those superstitious, illiterate peasants, pretending to govern!"

"It's very dangerous," Fitz said angrily. "People have no idea how easily they could slip into anarchy and barbarism." The subject made him irate.

Maud said: "How ironic it will be if Russia becomes more democratic than Great Britain."

"Parliament is about to debate votes for women," Fitz said.

"Only for women over thirty who are householders, or the wives of householders."

"Still, you must be pleased to have made progress. I read an article about it by your comrade Ethel in one of the journals." Fitz had been startled, sitting in the drawing room of his club looking at the *New Statesman,* to find he was reading the words of his former housekeeper. The uncomfortable thought had occurred to him that he might not be capable of writing such a clear and well-argued piece. "Her line is that women should accept this on the grounds that something is better than nothing."

"I'm afraid I disagree," Maud said frostily. "I will not wait until I am thirty to be considered a member of the human race."

"Have you two quarreled?"

"We have agreed to go our separate ways."

Fitz could see Maud was furious. To cool the atmosphere he turned to Lady Hermia. "If the British Parliament gives the vote to women, Aunt, for whom will you cast your ballot?"

"I'm not sure I shall vote at all," said Aunt Herm. "Isn't it a bit vulgar?"

Maud looked annoyed, but Fitz grinned. "If ladies of good family think that way, the only voters will be the working class, and they will put the socialists in," he said.

"Oh, dear," said Herm. "Perhaps I'd better vote, after all."

"Would you support Lloyd George?"

"A Welsh solicitor? Certainly not."

"Perhaps Bonar Law, the Conservative leader."

"I expect so."

"But he's Canadian."

"Oh, my goodness."

"This is the problem of having an empire. Riffraff from all over the world think they're part of it."

The nurse came in with Boy. He was two and a half years old now, a plump toddler with his mother's thick fair hair. He ran to Bea, and she sat him on her lap. He said: "I had porridge and Nursie dropped the sugar!" and laughed. That had been the big event of the day in the nursery.

Bea was at her best with the child, Fitz thought. Her face softened and she became affectionate, stroking and kissing him. After a minute he wriggled off her lap and waddled over to Fitz. "How's my little soldier?" said Fitz. "Going to grow up and shoot Germans?"

"Bang! Bang!" said Boy.

Fitz saw that his nose was running. "Has he got a cold, Jones?" he asked sharply.

The nurse looked frightened. She was a young girl from Aberowen, but she had been professionally trained. "No, my lord, I'm sure—it's June!"

"There's such a thing as a summer cold."

"He's been perfectly well all day. It's just a runny nose."

"It's certainly that." Fitz took a linen handkerchief from the inside breast pocket of his evening coat and wiped Boy's nose. "Has he been playing with common children?"

"No, sir, not at all."

"What about in the park?"

"There's none but children from good families in the parts we visit. I'm most particular."

"I hope you are. This child is heir to the Fitzherbert title, and may be a Russian prince, too." Fitz put Boy down and he ran back to the nurse.

Grout reappeared with an envelope on a silver tray. "A telegram, my lord," he said. "Addressed to the princess."

Fitz made a gesture indicating that Grout should give the cable to Bea. She frowned anxiously—telegrams made everyone nervous in wartime—and ripped it open. She scanned the sheet of paper and gave a cry of distress.

Fitz jumped up. "What is it?"

"My brother!"

"Is he alive?"

"Yes—wounded." She began to cry. "They have amputated his arm, but he is recovering. Oh, poor Andrei."

Fitz took the cable and read it. The only additional information was that Prince Andrei had been taken home to Bulovnir, his country estate in Tambov province southeast of Moscow. He hoped Andrei really was recovering. Many men died of infected wounds, and amputation did not always halt the spread of the gangrene.

"My dear, I'm most frightfully sorry," said Fitz. Maud and Herm stood on either side of Bea, trying to comfort her. "It says a letter will follow, but God knows how long it will take to get here."

"I must know how he is!" Bea sobbed.

Fitz said: "I will ask the British ambassador to make careful inquiries." An earl still had privileges, even in this democratic age.

Maud said: "Let us take you up to your room, Bea."

Bea nodded and stood up.

Fitz said: "I'd better go to Lord Silverman's dinner—Bonar Law is going to be there." Fitz wanted one day to be a minister in a Conservative government, and he was glad of any opportunity to chat with the party leader. "But I'll skip the ball and come straight home."

Bea nodded, and allowed herself to be taken upstairs.

Grout came in and said: "The car is ready, my lord."

During the short drive to Belgrave Square, Fitz brooded over the news. Prince Andrei had never been good at managing the family lands. He would probably use his disability as an excuse to take even less care of business. The estate would decline further. But there was nothing Fitz could do, fifteen hundred miles away in London. He felt frustrated and worried. Anarchy was always just around the corner, and slackness by noblemen such as Andrei was what gave revolutionists their chance.

When he reached the Silverman residence Bonar Law was already there—and so was Perceval Jones, the member of Parliament for Aberowen and chairman of Celtic Minerals. Jones was a turkey-cock at the best of times, and tonight he was bursting with pride at being in such distinguished company, talking to Lord Silverman with his hands in his pockets, a massive gold watch chain stretched across his wide waistcoat.

Fitz should not have been so surprised. This was a political dinner, and Jones was rising in the Conservative party: no doubt he, too, hoped to be a minister when and if Bonar Law should become prime minister. All the same, it was a bit like meeting your head groom at the Hunt Ball, and Fitz had an unnerving feeling that Bolshevism might be coming to London, not by revolution but by stealth.

At the table Jones shocked Fitz by saying he was in favor of votes for women. "For heaven's sake, why?" said Fitz.

"We have conducted a survey of constituency chairmen and agents," Jones replied, and Fitz saw Bonar Law nodding. "They are two to one in favor of the proposal."

"Conservatives are?" Fitz said incredulously.

"Yes, my lord."

"But why?"

"The bill will give the vote only to women over thirty who are householders or the wives of householders. Most women factory workers are excluded, because they tend to be younger. And all those dreadful female intellectuals are single women who live in other people's homes."

Fitz was taken aback. He had always regarded this as an issue of principle. But principle did not matter to jumped-up businessmen such as Jones. Fitz had never thought about electoral consequences. "I still don't see . . ."

"Most of the new voters will be mature middle-class mothers of families." Jones tapped the side of his nose in a vulgar gesture. "Lord Fitzherbert, they are the most conservative group of people in the country. This bill will give our party six million new votes."

"So you're going to support woman suffrage?"

"We must! We need those Conservative women. At the next election there will be three million new working-class male voters, a lot of them coming out of the army, most of them not on our side. But our new women will outnumber them."

"But the principle, man!" Fitz protested, though he sensed this was a losing battle.

"Principle?" said Jones. "This is practical politics." He gave a condescending smile that infuriated Fitz. "But then, if I may say so, you always were an idealist, my lord."

"We're all idealists," said Lord Silverman, smoothing over the conflict like a good host. "That's why we're in politics. People without ideals don't bother. But we have to confront the realities of elections and public opinion."

Fitz did not want to be labeled an impractical dreamer, so he quickly said: "Of course we do. Still, the question of a woman's place touches the heart of family life, something I should have thought dear to Conservatives."

Bonar Law said: "The issue is still open. Members of Parliament have a free vote. They will follow their consciences."

Fitz nodded submissively, and Silverman began speaking of the mutinous French army.

Fitz remained quiet for the rest of the dinner. He found it ominous that this bill had the support of both Ethel Leckwith and Perceval Jones. There was a dangerous possibility that it might pass. He thought Conservatives should defend traditional values, and not be swayed by short-term vote-winning considerations; but he had seen clearly that Bonar Law did not feel the same, and Fitz had not wanted to show himself out of step. The result was that he was ashamed of himself for not being completely honest, a feeling he hated.

He left Lord Silverman's house immediately after Bonar Law. He returned home and went upstairs. He took off his dress coat, put on a silk dressing gown, and went to Bea's room.

He found her sitting up in bed with a cup of tea. He could see that she had been crying, but she had put a little powder on her face and dressed in a flowered nightdress and a pink knitted bed jacket with puffed sleeves. He asked her how she was feeling.

"I am devastated," she said. "Andrei is all that is left of my family."

"I know." Both her parents were dead and she had no other close relatives. "It's worrying—but he will probably pull through."

She put down her cup and saucer. "I have been thinking very hard, Fitz."

That was an unusual thing for her to say.

"Please hold my hand," she said.

He took her left hand in both of his. She looked pretty, and despite the sad topic of conversation, he felt a stirring of desire. He could feel her rings, a diamond engagement ring and a gold wedding band. He had an urge to put her hand in his mouth and bite the fleshy part at the base of the thumb.

She said: "I want you to take me to Russia."

He was so startled that he dropped her hand. "What?"

"Don't refuse yet—think about it," she said. "You'll say it's dangerous—I know that. All the same there are hundreds of British people in Russia right now: diplomats at the embassy, businessmen, army officers and soldiers at our military missions there, journalists, and others."

"What about Boy?"

"I hate to leave him, but Nurse Jones is excellent, Hermia is devoted to him, and Maud can be relied upon to make sensible decisions in a crisis."

"We would need visas . . ."

"You could have a word in the right ear. My goodness, you've just dined with at least one member of the cabinet."

She was right. "The Foreign Office would probably ask me to write a report on the trip—especially as we'll be traveling through the countryside, where our diplomats rarely venture."

She took his hand again. "My only living relative is severely wounded and may die. I must see him. Please, Fitz. I'm begging you."

The truth was that Fitz was not as reluctant as she assumed. His perception of what was dangerous had been altered by the trenches. After all, most people survived an artillery barrage. A trip to Russia, though hazardous, was nothing by comparison. All the same he hesitated. "I understand your desire," he said. "Let me make some inquiries."

She took that for consent. "Oh, thank you!" she said.

"Don't thank me yet. Let me find out how practicable this is."

"All right," she said, but he could see that she was already assuming the outcome.

He stood up. "I must get ready for bed," he said, and went to the door.

"When you've put on your nightclothes . . . please come back. I want you to hold me."

Fitz smiled. "Of course," he said.

{ III }

On the day Parliament debated votes for women, Ethel organized a rally in a hall near the Palace of Westminster.

She was now employed by the National Union of Garment Workers, which had been eager to hire such a well-known activist. Her main job was recruiting women members in the sweatshops of the East End, but the union believed in fighting for its members in national politics as well as in the workplace.

She felt sad about the end of her relationship with Maud. Perhaps there had always been something artificial about a friendship between an earl's sister and his former housekeeper, but Ethel had hoped they could transcend the class divide. However, deep in her heart Maud had believed—without being conscious of it—that she was born to command and Ethel to obey.

Ethel hoped the vote in Parliament would take place before the end of the rally, so that she could announce the result, but the debate went on late, and the meeting had to break up at ten. Ethel and Bernie went to a pub in Whitehall used by Labour M.P.s and waited for news.

It was after eleven and the pub was closing when two M.P.s rushed in. One of them spotted Ethel. "We won!" he shouted. "I mean, you won. The women."

She could hardly believe it. "They passed the clause?"

"By a huge majority—three eighty-seven to fifty-seven!"

"We won!" Ethel kissed Bernie. "We won!"

"Well done," he said. "Enjoy your victory. You deserve it."

They could not have a drink to celebrate. New wartime rules forced pubs to stop serving at set hours. This was supposed to improve the productivity of the working class. Ethel and Bernie went out into Whitehall to catch a bus home.

Waiting at the bus stop, Ethel was euphoric. "I can't take it in. After all these years—votes for women!"

A passerby heard her, a tall man in evening dress walking with a cane.

She recognized Fitz.

"Don't be so sure," he said. "We'll vote you down in the House of Lords."

CHAPTER TWENTY-SEVEN

June to September 1917

Walter von Ulrich climbed out of the trench and, taking his life in his hands, began to walk across no-man's-land.

New grass and wildflowers were growing in the shell holes. It was a mild summer evening in a region that had once been Poland, then Russia, and was now partly occupied by German troops. Walter wore a nondescript coat over a corporal's uniform. He had dirtied his face and hands for authenticity. He wore a white cap, like a flag of truce, and carried on his shoulder a cardboard box.

He told himself there was no point being scared.

The Russian positions were dimly visible in the twilight. There had been no firing for weeks, and Walter thought his approach would be regarded with more curiosity than suspicion.

If he was wrong, he was dead.

The Russians were preparing an offensive. German reconnaissance aircraft and scouts reported fresh troops being deployed to the front lines and truckloads of ammunition being unloaded. This had been confirmed by starving Russian soldiers who had crossed the lines and surrendered in the hope of getting a meal from their German captors.

The evidence of the approaching offensive had come as a big disappointment to Walter. He had hoped that the new Russian government would be unable to fight on. In Petrograd, Lenin and the Bolsheviks were vociferously calling for peace, and pouring out a flood of newspapers and pamphlets—paid for with German money.

The Russian people did not want war. An announcement by Pavel Miliukov, the monocled foreign minister, that Russia was still aiming for "decisive victory" had brought enraged workers and soldiers out onto the streets again. The theatrical young war minister, Kerensky, who was responsible for the expected new offensive, had reinstated flogging in the army and restored the authority of officers. But would the Russian soldiers fight? That was what the Germans needed to know and Walter was risking his life to find out.

The signs were mixed. In some sections of the front, Russian soldiers had hoisted white flags and unilaterally declared an armistice. Other sections seemed quiet and disciplined. It was one such area that Walter had decided to visit.

He had at last got away from Berlin. Probably Monika von der Helbard had told her parents bluntly that there was not going to be a wedding. Anyway, Walter was on the front line again, gathering intelligence.

He shifted the box to the other shoulder. Now he could see half a dozen heads sticking up over the edge of a trench. They wore caps—Russian soldiers did not have helmets. They stared at him but did not point their weapons, yet.

He felt fatalistic about death. He thought he could die happy after his joyous night in Stockholm with Maud. Of course, he would prefer to live. He wanted to make a home with Maud and have children. And he hoped to do so in a prosperous, democratic Germany. But that meant winning the war, which in turn meant risking his life, so he had no choice.

All the same his stomach felt watery as he got within rifle range. It was so easy for a soldier to aim his gun and pull the trigger. That was what they were here for, after all.

He carried no rifle, and he hoped they had noticed that. He did have a nine-millimeter Luger stuffed into his belt at the back, but they could not see it. What they could see was the box he was carrying. He hoped it looked harmless.

He felt grateful for every step he survived, but conscious that each took him farther into danger. Any second now, he thought philosophically. He wondered whether a man heard the shot that killed him. What Walter feared most was being wounded and bleeding slowly to death, or succumbing to infection in a filthy field hospital.

He could now see the faces of the Russians, and he read amusement, astonishment, and lively wonderment in their expressions. He looked anxiously for signs of fear: that was the greatest danger. A scared soldier might shoot just to break the tension.

At last he had ten yards to go, then nine, eight . . . He came to the lip of the trench. "Hello, comrades," he said in Russian. He put down the box.

He held out his hand to the nearest soldier. Automatically, the man reached out and helped him jump into the trench. A small group gathered around him.

"I have come to ask you a question," he said.

Most educated Russians spoke some German, but the troops were peasants, and few understood any language other than their own. As a boy Walter had learned Russian as part of his preparation, rigidly enforced by his father, for a career in the army and the foreign ministry. He had never used his Russian much, but he thought he could remember enough for this mission.

"First a drink," he said. He brought the box into the trench, ripped open the top, and took out a bottle of schnapps. He pulled the cork, took a swig, wiped his mouth, and gave the bottle to the nearest soldier, a tall corporal of eighteen or nineteen. The man grinned, drank, and passed the bottle on.

Walter covertly studied his surroundings. The trench was poorly constructed. The walls slanted, and were not braced by timber. The floor was irregular and had no duckboards, so even now in summer it was muddy. The trench did not even follow a straight line—although that was probably a good thing, as there were no traverses to contain the blast of an artillery hit. There was a foul smell: obviously the men did not always bother to walk to the latrine. What was wrong with these Russians? Everything they did was slapdash, disorganized, and half-finished.

While the bottle was going around, a sergeant appeared. "What's going on, Feodor Igorovich?" he said, addressing the tall corporal. "Why are you talking to a cow-fucking German?"

Feodor was young, but his mustache was luxuriant and curled across his cheeks. For some reason he had a nautical cap, which he wore at a jaunty angle. His air of self-confidence bordered on arrogance. "Have a drink, Sergeant Gavrik."

The sergeant drank from the bottle like the rest, but he was not as nonchalant as his men. He gave Walter a mistrustful look. "What the fuck are you doing here?"

Walter had rehearsed what he would say. "On behalf of German workers, soldiers, and peasants, I come to ask why you are fighting us."

After a moment of surprised silence, Feodor said: "Why are *you* fighting *us*?"

Walter had his answer ready. "We have no choice. Our country is still ruled by the kaiser—we have not yet made our revolution. But you have. The tsar is gone, and Russia is now ruled by its people. So I have come to ask the people: Why are you fighting us?"

Feodor looked at Gavrik and said: "It's the question we keep asking ourselves!"

Gavrik shrugged. Walter guessed he was a traditionalist who was carefully keeping his opinions to himself.

Several more men came along the trench and joined the group. Walter opened another bottle. He looked around the circle of thin, ragged, dirty men who were rapidly getting drunk. "What do Russians want?"

Several men answered.

"Land."

"Peace."

"Freedom."

"More booze!"

Walter took another bottle from the box. What they really needed, he thought, was soap, good food, and new boots.

Feodor said: "I want to go home to my village. They're dividing up the prince's land, and I need to make sure my family gets its fair share."

Walter asked: "Do you support a political party?"

A soldier said: "The Bolsheviks!" The others cheered.

Walter was pleased. "Are you party members?"

They shook their heads.

Feodor said: "I used to support the Socialist Revolutionaries, but they have let us down." Others nodded agreement. "Kerensky has brought back flogging," Feodor added.

"And he has ordered a summer offensive," Walter said. He could see, in front of his eyes, a stack of ammunition boxes, but he did not refer to them, for fear of calling the Russians' attention to the obvious possibility that he was a spy. "We can see from our aircraft," he added.

Feodor said to Gavrik: "Why do we need to attack? We can make peace just as well from where we are now!" There was a mutter of agreement.

Walter said: "So what will you do if the order to advance is given?"

Feodor said: "There will have to be a meeting of the soldiers' committee to discuss it."

"Don't talk shit," said Gavrik. "Soldiers' committees are no longer allowed to debate orders."

There was a rumble of discontent, and someone at the edge of the circle muttered: "We'll see about that, comrade Sergeant."

The crowd continued to grow. Perhaps Russians could smell booze at a distance. Walter handed out two more bottles. By way of explanation to the new arrivals, he said: "German people want peace just as much as you. If you don't attack us, we won't attack you."

"I'll drink to that!" said one of the newcomers, and there was a ragged cheer.

Walter feared the noise would attract the attention of an officer, and wondered how he could get the Russians to keep their voices down despite the schnapps; but he was already too late. A loud, authoritative voice said: "What's going on here? What are you men up to?" The crowd parted to give passage to a big man in the uniform of a major. He looked at Walter and said: "Who the hell are you?"

Walter's heart sank. It was undoubtedly the officer's duty to take him prisoner. German intelligence knew how the Russians treated their POWs. Being captured by them was a sentence of lingering death by starvation and cold.

He forced a smile and offered the last unopened bottle. "Have a drink, Major."

The officer ignored him and turned to Gavrik. "What do you think you're doing?"

Gavrik was not intimidated. "The men have had no dinner today, Major, so I couldn't make them refuse a drink."

"You should have taken him prisoner!"

Feodor said: "We can't take him prisoner, now that we've
drunk his booze." He was slurring already. "It wouldn't be
fair!" he finished, and the others cheered.

The major said to Walter: "You're a spy, and I ought to
blow your damned head off." He touched the holstered gun
at his belt.

The soldiers shouted protests. The major continued to
look angry, but he said no more, clearly not wanting a clash
with the men.

Walter said to them: "I'd better leave you. Your major is
a bit unfriendly. Besides, we have a brothel just behind our
front line, and there's a blond girl with big tits who may be
feeling a bit lonely . . ."

They laughed and cheered. It was half true: there was a
brothel, but Walter had never visited it.

"Remember," he said. "We won't fight if you don't!"

He scrambled out of the trench. This was the moment
of greatest danger. He got to his feet, walked a few paces,
turned, waved, and walked on. They had satisfied their curiosity and all the schnapps was gone. Now they might just
take it into their heads to do their duty and shoot the enemy. He felt as if his coat had a target printed on the back.

Darkness was falling. Soon he would be out of sight. He
was only a few yards from safety. It took all his willpower
not to break into a sprint—but he felt that might provoke a
shot. Gritting his teeth, he walked with even strides through
the litter of unexploded shells.

He glanced back. He could not see the trench. That
meant they could not see him. He was safe.

He breathed easier and walked on. It had been worth
the risk. He had learned a lot. Although this section was
showing no white flags, the Russians were in poor shape for
battle. Clearly the men were discontented and rebellious,
and the officers had only a weak hold on discipline. The sergeant had been careful not to cross them and the major had
not dared to take Walter prisoner. In that frame of mind it
was impossible for soldiers to put up a brave fight.

He came within sight of the German line. He shouted
his name and a prearranged password. He dropped down

into the trench. A lieutenant saluted him. "Successful sortie, sir?"

"Yes, thanks," said Walter. "Very successful indeed."

{ II }

Katerina lay on the bed in Grigori's old room, wearing only a thin shift. The window was open, letting in the warm July air and the thunder of the trains that passed a few steps away. She was six months pregnant.

Grigori ran a finger along the outline of her body, from her shoulder, over one swollen breast, down again to her ribs, up over the gentle hill of her belly, and down her thigh. Before Katerina he had never known this easygoing joy. His youthful relations with women had been hasty and short-lived. To him it was a new and thrilling experience to lie beside a woman after sex, touching her body gently and lovingly but without urgency or lust. Perhaps this was what marriage meant, he thought. "You're even more beautiful pregnant," he said, speaking in a low murmur so as not to wake Vlad.

For two and a half years he had acted as father to his brother's son, but now he was going to have a child of his own. He would have liked to name the baby after Lenin, but they already had a Vladimir. The pregnancy had made Grigori a hardliner in politics. He had to think about the country in which the child would grow up, and he wanted his son to be free. (For some reason he thought of the baby as a boy.) He had to be sure Russia would be ruled by its people, not by a tsar or a middle-class parliament or a coalition of businessmen and generals who would bring back the old ways in new disguises.

He did not really like Lenin. The man lived in a permanent rage. He was always shouting at people. Anyone who disagreed with him was a swine, a bastard, a cunt. But he worked harder than anyone else, he thought about things for a long time, and his decisions were always right. In the past, every Russian "revolution" had led to nothing but dithering. Grigori knew Lenin would not let that happen.

The provisional government knew it, too, and there

were signs they wanted to target Lenin. The right-wing press had accused him of being a spy for Germany. The accusation was ridiculous. However, it was true that Lenin had a secret source of finance. Grigori, as one of those who had been Bolsheviks since before the war, was part of the inner circle, and he knew the money came from Germany. If the secret got out it would fuel suspicion.

He was dozing off when he heard footsteps in the hall followed by a loud, urgent knock at the door. Pulling on his trousers he shouted: "What is it?" Vlad woke up and cried.

A man's voice said: "Grigori Sergeivich?"

"Yes." Grigori opened the door and saw Isaak. "What's happened?"

"They've issued arrest warrants for Lenin, Zinoviev, and Kamenev."

Grigori went cold. "We have to warn them!"

"I've got an army car outside."

"I'll put my boots on."

Isaak went. Katerina picked up Vlad and comforted him. Grigori hastily pulled his clothes on, kissed them both, and ran down the stairs.

He jumped into the car beside Isaak and said: "Lenin is the most important." The government was right to target him. Zinoviev and Kamenev were sound revolutionaries, but Lenin was the engine that drove the movement. "We must warn him first. Drive to his sister's place. Fast as you can go."

Isaak headed off at top speed.

Grigori held tight while the car screeched around a corner. As it straightened up, he said: "How did you find out?"

"From a Bolshevik in the Ministry of Justice."

"When were the warrants signed?"

"This morning."

"I hope we're in time." Grigori was terrified that Lenin might already have been seized. No one else had his inflexible determination. He was a bully, but he had transformed the Bolsheviks into the leading party. Without him, the revolution could fall back into muddle and compromise.

Isaak drove to Shirokaya Street and pulled up outside a middle-class apartment building. Grigori jumped out, ran inside, and knocked at the Yelizarov flat. Anna Yelizarova, Lenin's elder sister, opened the door. She was in her fifties,

with graying hair parted in the center. Grigori had met her
before: she worked on *Pravda*. "Is he here?" Grigori said.

"Yes. Why? What's happened?"

Grigori felt a wave of relief. He was not too late. He
stepped inside. "They're going to arrest him."

Anna slammed the door. "Volodya!" she called, using
the familiar form of Lenin's first name. "Come quickly!"

Lenin appeared, dressed as always in a shabby dark suit
with a collar and tie. Grigori explained the situation rapidly.

"I'll leave immediately," Lenin said.

Anna said: "Don't you want to throw a few things in
your suitcase—"

"Too risky. Send everything later. I'll let you know where
I am." He looked at Grigori. "Thank you for the warning,
Grigori Sergeivich. Do you have a car?"

"Yes."

Without another word Lenin went out into the hall.

Grigori followed him to the street and hurried to open
the car door. "They have also issued warrants for Zinoviev
and Kamenev," Grigori said as Lenin got in.

"Go back to the apartment and telephone them," Lenin
said. "Mark has a phone and he knows where they are." He
slammed the door. He leaned forward and said something
to Isaak that Grigori did not hear. Isaak drove off.

This was how Lenin was all the time. He barked orders
at everyone, and they did what he said because he always
made sense.

Grigori felt the pleasure of a great weight being lifted
from his shoulders. He looked up and down the street. A
group of men came out of a building on the other side.
Some were dressed in suits, others wore army officers'
uniforms. Grigori was shocked to recognize Mikhail Pinsky. The secret police had been abolished, in theory, but it
seemed men such as Pinsky were continuing their work as
part of the army.

These men must have come for Lenin—and just missed
him by going into the wrong building.

Grigori ran back inside. The door to the Yelizarovs'
apartment was still open. Just inside were Anna; her husband, Mark; her foster son, Gora; and the family servant,
a country girl called Anyushka, all looking shocked. Grigori
closed the door behind him. "He's safely away," he said.

"But the police are outside. I have to telephone Zinoviev and Kamenev quickly."

Mark said: "The phone is there on the side table."

Grigori hesitated. "How does it work?" He had never used a telephone.

"Oh, sorry," said Mark. He picked up the instrument, holding one piece to his ear and the other to his mouth. "It's quite new to us, but we use it so much that we take it for granted already." Impatiently he jiggled the sprung bar on top of the stand. "Yes, please, operator," he said, and gave a number.

There was a banging at the door.

Grigori held his finger to his lips, telling the others to be quiet.

Anna took Anyushka and the child into the back of the apartment.

Mark spoke rapidly into the phone. Grigori stood at the apartment door. A voice said: "Open up or we'll break down the door! We have a warrant!"

Grigori shouted back: "Just a minute—I'm putting my pants on." The police came often to the kinds of buildings where he had lived most of his life, and he knew all the pretexts for keeping them waiting.

Mark jiggled the bar again and asked for another number.

Grigori shouted: "Who is it? Who's at the door?"

"Police! Open up this instant!"

"I'm just coming—I have to lock the dog in the kitchen."

"Hurry up!"

Grigori heard Mark say: "Tell him to go into hiding. The police are at my door now." He replaced the earpiece on its hook and nodded to Grigori.

Grigori opened the door and stood back.

Pinsky stepped in. "Where is Lenin?" he said.

Several army officers followed him in.

Grigori said: "There is no one here by that name."

Pinsky stared at him. "What are you doing here?" he said. "I always knew you were a troublemaker."

Mark stepped forward and said calmly: "Show me the warrant, please."

Reluctantly, Pinsky handed over a piece of paper.

Mark studied it for a few moments, then said: "High treason? That's ridiculous!"

"Lenin is a German agent," Pinsky said. He narrowed his eyes at Mark. "You're his brother-in-law, aren't you?"

Mark handed the paper back. "The man you are looking for is not here," he said.

Pinsky could sense he was telling the truth, and he looked angry. "Why the hell not?" he said. "He lives here!"

"Lenin is not here," Mark repeated.

Pinsky's face reddened. "Was he warned?" He grabbed Grigori by the front of his tunic. "What are you doing here?"

"I am a deputy to the Petrograd soviet, representing the First Machine Guns, and unless you want the regiment to pay a visit to your headquarters, you'd better take your fat hands off my uniform."

Pinsky let go. "We'll take a look around anyway," he said.

There was a bookcase beside the phone table. Pinsky took half a dozen books off the shelf and threw them to the floor. He waved the officers toward the interior of the flat. "Tear the place apart," he said.

{ III }

Walter went to a village within the territory won from the Russians and gave an astonished and delighted peasant a gold coin for all his clothes: a filthy sheepskin coat, a linen smock, loose coarse trousers, and shoes made of bast, the woven bark of a beech tree. Fortunately Walter did not have to buy his underwear, for the man wore none.

Walter cut his hair with a pair of kitchen scissors and stopped shaving.

In a small market town he bought a sack of onions. He put a leather bag containing ten thousand rubles in coins and notes in the bottom of the sack under the onions.

One night he smeared his hands and face with earth; then, dressed in the peasant's clothes and carrying the onion sack, he crossed no-man's-land, slipped through the Russian lines, and walked to the nearest railway station, where he bought a third-class ticket.

He adopted an aggressive attitude, and snarled at anyone who spoke to him, as if he feared they wanted to steal his onions, which they probably did. He had a large knife, rusty but sharp, clearly visible at his belt, and a Mosin-Nagant pistol, taken from a captured Russian officer, concealed under his smelly coat. On two occasions when a policeman spoke to him, he grinned stupidly and offered an onion, a bribe so contemptible that both times the policeman grunted with disgust and walked off. If a policeman had insisted on looking into the sack, Walter was ready to kill him, but it was never necessary. He bought tickets for short journeys, three or four stops at a time, for a peasant would not go hundreds of miles to sell his onions.

He was tense and wary. His disguise was thin. Anyone who spoke to him for more than a few seconds would know he was not really Russian. The penalty for what he was doing was death.

At first he was scared, but that eventually wore off, and by the second day he was bored. He had nothing to occupy his mind. He could not read, of course: indeed, he had to be careful not to look at timetables posted at stations, or do more than glance at advertisements, for most peasants were illiterate. As a series of slow trains rattled and shook through the endless Russian forests, he entered into an elaborate daydream about the apartment he and Maud would live in after the war. It would have modern decor, with pale wood and neutral colors, like that of the von der Helbard house, rather than the heavy, dark look of his parents' home. Everything would be easy to clean and maintain, especially in the kitchen and laundry, so that they could employ fewer servants. They would have a really good piano, a Steinway grand, for they both liked to play. They would buy one or two eye-catching modern paintings, perhaps by Austrian expressionists, to shock the older generation and establish themselves as a progressive couple. They would have a light, airy bedroom and lie naked on a soft bed, kissing and talking and making love.

In this way he journeyed to Petrograd.

The arrangement, made through a revolutionary socialist in the Swedish embassy, was that someone from the Bolsheviks would wait to collect the money from Walter at Petrograd's Warsaw Station every day at six p.m. for one hour. Walter arrived at midday, and took the opportunity to look around the city, with the aim of assessing the Russian people's ability to fight on.

He was shocked by what he saw.

As soon as he left the station, he was assailed by prostitutes, male and female, adult and child. He crossed a canal bridge and walked a couple of miles north into the city center. Most shops were closed, many boarded up, a few simply abandoned, with the smashed glass of their windows glittering on the street outside. He saw many drunks and two fistfights. Occasionally an automobile or a horse-drawn carriage dashed past, scattering pedestrians, its passengers hiding behind closed curtains. Most of the people were thin, ragged, and barefoot. It was much worse than Berlin.

He saw many soldiers, individually and in groups, most showing lapsed discipline: marching out of step or lounging at their posts, uniforms unbuttoned, chatting to civilians, apparently doing as they pleased. Walter was confirmed in the impression he had formed when he visited the Russian front line: these men were in no mood to fight.

This is all good news, he thought.

No one accosted him and the police ignored him. He was just another shabby figure shuffling about his own business in a city that was falling apart.

In high spirits, he returned to the station at six and quickly spotted his contact, a sergeant with a red scarf tied to the barrel of his rifle. Before making himself known, Walter studied the man. He was a formidable figure, not tall but broad-shouldered and thickset. He was missing his right ear, one front tooth, and the ring finger of his left hand. He waited with the patience of a veteran soldier, but he had a keen blue-eyed gaze that did not miss much. Although Walter intended to watch him covertly, the soldier met his eye, nodded, and turned and walked away. As was clearly intended, Walter followed him. They went into a large room full of tables and chairs and sat down.

Walter said: "Sergeant Grigori Peshkov?"

Grigori nodded: "I know who you are. Sit down."

Walter looked around the room. There was a samovar hissing in a corner, and an old woman in a shawl selling smoked and pickled fish. Fifteen or twenty people were sitting at tables. No one gave a second glance to a soldier and a peasant who was obviously hoping to sell his sack of onions. A young man in the blue tunic of a factory worker followed them in. Walter caught the man's eye briefly and watched him take a seat, light a cigarette, and open *Pravda*.

Walter said: "May I have something to eat? I'm starving, but a peasant probably can't afford the prices here."

Grigori got a plate of black bread and herrings and two glasses of tea with sugar. Walter tucked into the food. After watching him for a minute, Grigori laughed. "I'm amazed you've passed for a peasant," he said. "I'd know you for a bourgeois."

"How?"

"Your hands are dirty, but you eat in small bites and dab your lips with a rag as if it was a linen napkin. A real peasant shovels the food in and slurps tea before swallowing."

Walter was irritated by his condescension. After all, I've survived three days on a damn train, he thought. I'd like to see you try that in Germany. It was time to remind Peshkov that he had to earn his money. "Tell me how the Bolsheviks are doing," he said.

"Dangerously well," said Grigori. "Thousands of Russians have joined the party in the last few months. Leon Trotsky has at last announced his support for us. You should hear him. Most nights he packs out the Cirque Moderne." Walter could see that Grigori hero-worshipped Trotsky. Even the Germans knew that Trotsky's oratory was enchanting. He was a real catch for the Bolsheviks. "Last February we had ten thousand members—today we have two hundred thousand," Grigori finished proudly.

"This is good, but can you change things?" Walter said.

"We have a strong chance of winning the election for the Constituent Assembly."

"When will it be held?"

"It has been much delayed—"

"Why?"

Grigori sighed. "First the provisional government called together a council of representatives which, after two months, finally agreed on the composition of a sixty-member second council to draft the electoral law—"

"Why? Why such an elaborate process?"

Grigori looked irate. "They say they want the election to be absolutely unchallengeable—but the real reason is that the conservative parties are dragging their feet, knowing they stand to lose."

He was only a sergeant, Walter thought, but his analysis seemed quite sophisticated. "So when will the election be held?"

"September."

"And why do you think the Bolsheviks will win?"

"We are still the only group firmly committed to peace. And everyone knows that—thanks to all the newspapers and pamphlets we've produced."

"Why did you say you were doing 'dangerously' well?"

"It makes us the government's prime target. There's a warrant out for Lenin's arrest. He's had to go into hiding. But he's still running the party."

Walter believed that, too. If Lenin could keep control of his party from exile in Zurich, he could certainly do so from a hideaway in Russia.

Walter had made the delivery and gathered the information he needed. He had accomplished his mission. A sense of relief came over him. Now all he had to do was get home.

With his foot he pushed the sack containing the ten thousand rubles across the floor to Grigori.

He finished his tea and stood up. "Enjoy your onions," he said, and he walked to the door.

Out of the corner of his eye, he saw the man in the blue tunic fold his copy of *Pravda* and get to his feet.

Walter bought a ticket to Luga and boarded the train. He entered a third-class compartment. He pushed through a group of soldiers smoking and drinking vodka, a family of Jews with all their possessions in string-tied bundles, and some peasants with empty crates who had presumably sold their chickens. At the far end of the carriage he paused and looked back.

The blue tunic entered the carriage.

Walter watched for a second as the man pushed through the passengers, carelessly elbowing people out of his way. Only a policeman would do that.

Walter jumped off the train and hurriedly left the station. Recalling his tour of exploration that afternoon, he headed at a fast walk for the canal. It was the season of short summer nights, so the evening was light. He hoped he might have shaken his tail, but when he glanced over his shoulder he saw the blue tunic following him. He had presumably been following Peshkov, and had decided to investigate Grigori's onion-selling peasant friend.

The man broke into a jogging run.

If caught, Walter would be shot as a spy. He had no choice about what he had to do next.

He was in a low-rent neighborhood. All of Petrograd looked poor, but this district had the cheap hotels and dingy bars that clustered near railway stations all over the world. Walter started to run, and the blue tunic quickened his pace to keep up.

Walter came to a canalside brickyard. It had a high wall and a gate with iron bars, but next door was a derelict warehouse on an unfenced site. Walter turned off the street, raced across the warehouse site to the waterside, then scrambled over the wall into the brickyard.

There had to be a watchman somewhere, but Walter saw no one. He looked for a place of concealment. It was a pity the light was still so clear. The yard had its own quay with a small timber pier. All around him were stacks of bricks the height of a man, but he needed to see without being seen. He moved to a stack that was partly dismantled—some having been sold, presumably—and swiftly rearranged a few so that he could hide behind them and look through a gap. He eased the Mosin-Nagant revolver out of his belt and cocked the hammer.

A few moments later, he saw the blue tunic come over the wall.

The man was of medium height and thin, with a small mustache. He looked scared: he had realized he was no longer merely following a suspect. He was engaged in a manhunt, and he did not know whether he was the hunter or the quarry.

He drew a gun.

Walter pointed his own gun through the gap in the bricks and aimed at the blue tunic, but he was not close enough to be sure of hitting his target.

The man stood still for a moment, looking all around, clearly undecided about what to do next. Then he turned and walked hesitantly toward the water.

Walter followed him. He had turned the tables.

The man dodged from stack to stack, scanning the area.

Walter did the same, ducking behind bricks whenever the man stopped, getting nearer all the time. Walter did not want a prolonged gunfight, which might attract the attention of other policemen. He needed to down his enemy with one or two shots and get away fast.

By the time the man reached the canal end of the site, they were only ten yards apart. The man looked up and down the canal, as if Walter might have rowed away in a boat.

Walter stepped out of cover and drew a bead on the middle of the man's back.

The man turned away from the water and looked straight at Walter.

Then he screamed.

It was a high-pitched, girlish scream of shock and terror. Walter knew, in that instant, that he would remember the scream all his life.

He squeezed the trigger, the revolver banged, and the scream was cut off instantly.

Only one shot was needed. The secret policeman crumpled to the ground, lifeless.

Walter bent over the body. The eyes stared upward sightlessly. There was no heartbeat, no breath.

Walter dragged the body to the edge of the canal. He put bricks in the pockets of the man's trousers and tunic, to weight the corpse. Then he slid it over the low parapet and let it fall into the water.

It sank below the surface, and Walter turned away.

{ IV }

Grigori was in a session of the Petrograd soviet when the counterrevolution began.

He was worried, but not surprised. As the Bolsheviks gained popularity, the backlash had become more ruthless. The party was doing well in local elections, winning control of one provincial soviet after another, and had gained 33 percent of the votes for the Petrograd city council. In response the government—now led by Kerensky—arrested Trotsky and again deferred the long-delayed national elections for the Constituent Assembly. The Bolsheviks had said all along that the provisional government would never hold a national election, and this further postponement only added to Bolshevik credibility.

Then the army made its move.

General Kornilov was a shaven-headed Cossack who had the heart of a lion and the brains of a sheep, according to a famous remark by General Alexeev. On September 9 Kornilov ordered his troops to march on Petrograd.

The soviet responded quickly. The delegates immediately resolved to set up the Committee for Struggle Against the Counterrevolution.

A committee was nothing, Grigori thought impatiently. He got to his feet, holding down anger and fear. As the delegate for the First Machine Gun Regiment, he was listened to respectfully, especially on military matters. "There is no point in a committee if its members are just going to make speeches," he said passionately. "If the reports we have just heard are true, some of Kornilov's troops are not far from the city limits of Petrograd. They can be halted only by force." He always wore his sergeant's uniform, and carried his rifle and a pistol. "The committee will be pointless unless it mobilizes the workers and soldiers of Petrograd against the mutiny of the army."

Grigori knew that only the Bolshevik party could mobilize the people. And all the other deputies knew it, too, regardless of what party they belonged to. In the end it was agreed that the committee would have three Mensheviks, three Socialist Revolutionaries, and three Bolsheviks including Grigori; but everyone knew the Bolsheviks were the only ones who counted.

As soon as that was decided, the Committee for Struggle left the debating hall. Grigori had been a politician for six months, and he had learned how to work the system. Now he ignored the formal composition of the committee and invited a dozen useful people to join them, including Konstantin from the Putilov works and Isaak from the First Machine Guns.

The soviet had moved from the Tauride Palace to the Smolny Institute, a former girls' school, and the committee reconvened in a classroom, surrounded by framed embroidery and girlish watercolors.

The chairman said: "Do we have a motion for debate?"

This was rubbish, but Grigori had been a deputy long enough to know how to get around it. He moved immediately to take control of the meeting and get the committee focused on action instead of words.

"Yes, comrade Chairman, if I may," he said. "I propose there are five things we need to do." A numbered list was always a good idea: people felt they had to listen until you got to the end. "First: Mobilize the Petrograd soldiers against the mutiny of General Kornilov. How can we achieve this? I suggest that Corporal Isaak Ivanovich should draw up a list of the principal barracks with the names of reliable revolutionary leaders in each. Having identified our allies, we should send a letter instructing them to put themselves under the orders of this committee and get ready to repel the mutineers. If Isaak begins now he can bring list and letter back to this committee for approval in a few minutes' time."

Grigori paused briefly to allow people to nod; then, taking that for approval, he went on.

"Thank you. Carry on, Comrade Isaak. Second, we must send a message to Kronstadt." The naval base at Kronstadt, an island twenty miles offshore, was notorious for its brutal treatment of sailors, especially young trainees. Six months ago the sailors had turned on their tormentors, and had tortured and murdered many of their officers. The place was now a radical stronghold. "The sailors must arm themselves, deploy to Petrograd, and put themselves under our orders." Grigori pointed to a Bolshevik deputy whom he knew to be close to the sailors. "Comrade Gleb, will you undertake that task, with the committee's approval?"

Gleb nodded. "If I may, I will draft a letter for our chairman to sign, then take it to Kronstadt myself."

"Please do."

The committee members were now looking a bit bewildered. Things were moving faster than usual. Only the Bolsheviks were unsurprised.

"Third, we must organize factory workers into defensive units and arm them. We can get the guns from army arsenals and from armaments factories. Most workers will need some training in firearms and military discipline. I suggest this task be carried out jointly by the trade unions and the

Red Guards." The Red Guards were revolutionary soldiers and workers who carried firearms. Not all were Bolsheviks, but they usually obeyed orders from the Bolshevik committees. "I propose that Comrade Konstantin, the deputy from the Putilov works, take charge of this. He will know the leading union in each major factory."

Grigori knew that he was turning the population of Petrograd into a revolutionary army, and so did the other Bolsheviks on the committee, but would the rest of them figure that out? At the end of this process, assuming the counterrevolution was defeated, it was going to be very difficult for the moderates to disarm the force they had created and restore the authority of the provisional government. If they thought that far ahead they might try to moderate or reverse what Grigori was proposing. But at the moment they were focused on preventing a military takeover. As usual, only the Bolsheviks had a strategy.

Konstantin said: "Yes, indeed, I'll make a list." He would favor Bolshevik union leaders, of course, but they were nowadays the most effective anyway.

Grigori said: "Fourth, the Railwaymen's Union must do all it can to hamper the advance of Kornilov's army." The Bolsheviks had worked hard to gain control of this union, and now had at least one supporter in every locomotive shed. Bolshevik trade unionists always volunteered for duty as treasurer, secretary, or chairman. "Although some troops are on the way here by road, the bulk of the men and their supplies will have to come by rail. The union can make sure they get held up and sent on long diversions. Comrade Viktor, may the committee rely on you to do this?"

Viktor, a railwaymen's deputy, nodded agreement. "I will set up an ad hoc committee within the union to organize the disruption of the mutineers' advance."

"Finally, we should encourage other cities to set up committees like this one," Grigori said. "The revolution must be defended everywhere. Perhaps other members of this committee could suggest which towns we should communicate with?"

This was a deliberate distraction, but they fell for it. Glad to have something to do, the committee members called out the names of towns that should organize Committees for Struggle. That ensured they did not pick over Grigori's more important proposals, but let them go unchallenged; and they never thought about the long-term consequences of arming the citizens.

Isaak and Gleb drafted their letters and got them signed by the chairman without further discussion. Konstantin made his list of factory leaders and started sending messages to them. Viktor left to organize the railwaymen.

The committee began to argue about the wording of a letter to neighboring towns. Grigori slipped away. He had what he wanted. The defense of Petrograd, and of the revolution, was well under way. And the Bolsheviks were in charge of it.

What he needed now was reliable information about the whereabouts of the counterrevolutionary army. Were there really troops approaching the southern suburbs of Petrograd? If so they might have to be dealt with faster than the Committee for Struggle could act.

He walked from the Smolny Institute across the bridge the short distance to his barracks. There he found the troops already preparing to fight Kornilov's mutineers. He took an armored car, a driver, and three reliable revolutionary soldiers, and drove across the city to the south.

In the darkening autumn afternoon they zigzagged through the southern suburbs, looking for the invading army. After a couple of fruitless hours Grigori decided there was a good chance the reports of Kornilov's progress had been exaggerated. In any event he was likely to come across nothing more than an advance party. All the same, it was important to check them, and he persisted with his search.

They eventually found an infantry brigade making camp at a school.

He considered returning to barracks and bringing the First Machine Guns here to attack. But he thought there might be a better way. It was risky, but it would save a lot of bloodshed if it worked.

He was going to try to win by talking.

They drove past an apathetic sentry into the playground and Grigori got out of the car. As a precaution, he unfolded the spike bayonet at the end of his rifle and fixed it in the attack position. Then he slung the rifle over his shoulder. Feeling vulnerable, he forced himself to look relaxed.

Several soldiers approached him. A colonel said: "What are you doing here, Sergeant?"

Grigori ignored him and addressed a corporal. "I need to speak to the leader of your soldiers' committee, comrade," he said.

The colonel said: "There are no soldiers' committees in this brigade, *comrade*. Get back in your car and clear off."

But the corporal spoke up with nervous defiance. "I was the leader of my platoon committee, Sergeant—before the committees were banned, of course."

The colonel's face darkened with anger.

This was the revolution in miniature, Grigori realized. Who would prevail—the colonel or the corporal?

More soldiers drew near to listen.

"Then tell me," Grigori said to the corporal, "why are you attacking the revolution?"

"No, no," said the corporal. "We're here to defend it."

"Someone has been lying to you." Grigori turned and raised his voice to address the bystanders. "The prime minister, Comrade Kerensky, has sacked General Kornilov, but Kornilov won't go, and that's why he has sent you to attack Petrograd."

There was a murmur of disapproval.

The colonel looked awkward: he knew Grigori was right. "Enough of these lies!" he blustered. "Get out of here now, Sergeant, or I'll shoot you down."

Grigori said: "Don't touch your weapon, Colonel. Your men have a right to the truth." He looked at the growing crowd. "Don't they?"

"Yes!" said several of them.

"I don't like everything Kerensky has done," said Grigori. "He has brought back the death penalty and flogging. But he is our revolutionary leader. Whereas your General Kornilov wants to destroy the revolution."

"Lies!" the colonel said angrily. "Don't you men understand? This sergeant is a Bolshevik. Everyone knows they are in the pay of Germany!"

The corporal said: "How do we know who to believe? You say one thing, Sergeant, but the colonel says another."

"Then don't believe either of us," Grigori said. "Go and find out for yourselves." He raised his voice to make sure everyone could hear him. "You don't have to hide in this school. Go to the nearest factory and ask any worker. Speak to soldiers you see in the streets. You'll soon learn the truth."

The corporal nodded. "Good idea."

"You'll do no such thing," said the colonel furiously. "I'm ordering you all to stay within the grounds."

That was a big mistake, Grigori thought. He said: "Your colonel doesn't want you to inquire for yourselves. Doesn't that show you that he must be telling you lies?"

The colonel put his hand on his pistol and said: "That's mutinous talk, Sergeant."

The men stared at the colonel and at Grigori. This was the moment of crisis, and death was as near to Grigori as it had ever been.

Suddenly Grigori realized that he was at a disadvantage. He had been so caught up in the argument that he had failed to plan what to do when it ended. He had his rifle over his shoulder, but the safety lock was engaged. It would take several seconds to swing it off his shoulder, turn the awkward knob that unlocked the safety catch, and lift the rifle into firing position. The colonel could draw and shoot his pistol a lot faster. Grigori felt a wave of fear, and had to suppress an urge to turn and run.

"Mutiny?" he said, playing for time, trying not to let fear weaken the assertive tone of his voice. "When a sacked general marches on the capital, but his troops refuse to attack their legitimate government, who's the mutineer? I say it's the general—and those officers who attempt to carry out his treasonable orders."

The colonel drew his pistol. "Get out of here, Sergeant." He turned to the others. "You men, go into the school and assemble in the hall. Remember, disobedience is a crime in the army—and the death penalty has been restored. I'll shoot anyone who refuses."

He pointed his gun at the corporal.

Grigori saw that the men were about to obey the authoritative, confident, armed officer. There was now only one way out, he saw in desperation. He had to kill the colonel.

He would have to be very quick indeed, but he thought he could probably do it.

If he was wrong he would die.

He slipped his rifle off his left shoulder and, without pausing to switch it to his right hand, he thrust it forward as hard as he could into the colonel's side. The sharp point of the long bayonet ripped through the cloth of the uniform, and Grigori felt it sink into the soft stomach. The colonel gave a shout of pain, but he did not fall. Despite his wound he turned, swinging his gun hand around in an arc. He pulled the trigger.

The shot went wild.

Grigori pushed on the rifle, thrusting the bayonet in and up, aiming for the heart. The colonel's face twisted in agony and his mouth opened, but no sound came out, and he fell to the ground, still clutching his pistol.

Grigori withdrew the bayonet with a jerk.

The colonel's pistol fell from his fingers.

Everyone stared at the officer writhing in silent torment on the parched grass of the playground. Grigori unlocked the safety on his rifle, aimed at the colonel's heart, and fired at close range twice. The man became still.

"As you said, Colonel," Grigori said. "It's the death penalty."

{ V }

Fitz and Bea took a train from Moscow accompanied only by Bea's Russian maid, Nina, and Fitz's valet, Jenkins, a former boxing champion who had been rejected by the army because he could not see farther than ten yards.

They got off the train at Bulovnir, the tiny station that served Prince Andrei's estate. Fitz's experts had suggested that Andrei build a small township here, with a timber yard and grain stores and a mill; but nothing had been done, and the peasants still took their produce by horse and cart twenty miles to the old market town.

Andrei had sent an open carriage to meet them, with a surly driver who looked on while Jenkins lifted the trunks onto the back of the vehicle. As they drove along a dirt road through farmland, Fitz recalled his previous visit, when he had come as the new husband of the princess, and the villagers had stood at the roadside and cheered. There was a different atmosphere now. Laborers in the fields barely looked up as the carriage passed, and in villages and hamlets the inhabitants deliberately turned their backs.

This kind of thing irritated Fitz and made him bad-tempered, but his spirits were soothed by the sight of the timeworn stones of the old house, colored a buttery yellow by the low afternoon sun. A little flock of immaculately dressed servants emerged from the front door like ducks coming to be fed, and bustled about the carriage opening doors and manhandling luggage. Andrei's steward, Georgi, kissed Fitz's hand and said, in an English phrase he had obviously learned by rote: "Welcome back to your Russian home, Earl Fitzherbert."

Russian houses were often grandiose but shabby, and Bulovnir was no exception. The double-height hall needed painting, the priceless chandelier was dusty, and a dog had peed on the marble floor. Prince Andrei and Princess Valeriya were waiting beneath a large portrait of Bea's grandfather frowning sternly down on them.

Bea rushed to Andrei and embraced him.

Valeriya was a classical beauty with regular features and dark hair in a neat coiffure. She shook hands with Fitz and said in French: "Thank you for coming. We're so happy to see you."

When Bea detached herself from Andrei, wiping her tears, Fitz offered his hand to shake. Andrei gave him his left hand: the right sleeve of his jacket hung empty. He was pale and thin, as if suffering from a wasting illness, and there was a little gray in his black beard, although he was only thirty-three. "I can't tell you how relieved I am to see you," he said.

Fitz said: "Is something wrong?" They were speaking French, in which they were all fluent.

"Come into the library. Valeriya will take Bea upstairs."

They left the women and went into a dusty room full of leather-bound books that looked as if they were not often read. "I've ordered tea. I'm afraid we've no sherry."

"Tea will be fine." Fitz eased himself into a chair. His wounded leg ached after the long journey. "What's going on?"

"Are you armed?"

"Yes, as a matter of fact, I am. My service revolver is in

my luggage." Fitz had a Webley Mark V that had been issued to him in 1914.

"Please keep it close to hand. I wear mine constantly."
Andrei opened his jacket to reveal a belt and holster.

"You'd better tell me why."

"The peasants have set up a land committee. Some Socialist Revolutionaries have talked to them and given them
stupid ideas. They claim the right to take over any land I'm
not cultivating and divide it up among themselves."

"Haven't you been through this before?"

"In my grandfather's time. We hanged three peasants
and thought that was the end of the matter. But these
wicked ideas lie dormant, and sprout again years later."

"What did you do this time?"

"I gave them a lecture and showed them I'd lost my
arm defending them from the Germans, and they went
quiet—until a few days ago, when half a dozen local men
returned from service in the army. They claimed to have
been discharged, but I'm sure they've deserted. Impossible
to check, unfortunately."

Fitz nodded. The Kerensky Offensive had been a failure, and the Germans and Austrians had counterattacked.
The Russians had fallen to pieces, and the Germans were
now heading for Petrograd. Thousands of Russian soldiers
had walked away from the battlefield and returned to their
villages.

"They brought their rifles with them, and pistols they
must have stolen from officers, or taken from German prisoners. Anyway, they're heavily armed, and full of subversive ideas. There's a corporal, Feodor Igorovich, who seems
to be the ringleader. He told Georgi he did not understand
why I was still claiming any land at all, let alone the fallow."

"I don't understand what happens to men in the army,"
said Fitz with exasperation. "You'd think it would teach
them the value of authority and discipline—but it seems to
do the opposite."

"I'm afraid things came to a head this morning," Andrei
went on. "Corporal Feodor's younger brother, Ivan Igorovich, put his cattle to graze in my pasture. Georgi found out,
and he and I went to remonstrate with Ivan. We started to
turn his cattle out into the lane. He tried to close the gate to
prevent us. I was carrying a shotgun, and I gave him a clout

across the head with the butt end of it. Most of these damn peasants have heads like cannonballs, but this one was different, and the wretch fell down and died. The socialists are using that as an excuse to get everyone agitated."

Fitz politely concealed his distaste. He disapproved of the Russian practice of striking one's inferiors, and he was not surprised when it led to this kind of unrest. "Have you told anyone?"

"I sent a message to the town, reporting the death and asking for a detachment of police or troops to keep order, but my messenger hasn't returned yet."

"So for now, we're on our own."

"Yes. If things get any worse, I'm afraid we may have to send the ladies away."

Fitz was devastated. This was much worse than he had anticipated. They could all be killed. Coming here had been a dreadful mistake. He had to get Bea away as soon as possible.

He stood up. Conscious that Englishmen sometimes boasted to foreigners about their coolness in a crisis, he said: "I'd better go and change for dinner."

Andrei showed him up to his room. Jenkins had unpacked his evening clothes and pressed them. Fitz began to undress. He felt a fool. He had put Bea and himself into danger. He had gained a useful impression of the state of affairs in Russia, but the report he would write was hardly worth the risk he had taken. He had let himself be talked into it by his wife, and that was always a mistake. He resolved they would catch the first train in the morning.

His revolver was on the dresser with his cuff links. He checked the action, then broke it open and loaded it with .455 Webley cartridges. There was nowhere to put it in a dress suit. In the end he stuffed it into his trousers pocket, where it made an unsightly bulge.

He summoned Jenkins to put away his traveling clothes, then stepped into Bea's room. She stood at the mirror in her underwear, trying on a necklace. She looked more voluptuous than usual, her breasts and hips a little heavier, and Fitz suddenly wondered whether she might be pregnant. She had suffered an attack of nausea this morning in Moscow, he recalled, in the car going to the railway station. He was reminded of her first pregnancy, and that took him back to a time he now thought of as a golden moment, when he had Ethel and Bea, and there was no war.

He was about to tell her that they had to leave tomorrow when he glanced out of the window and stopped short.

The room was at the front of the house and had a view over the park and the fields beyond to the nearest village. What had caught Fitz's eye was a crowd of people. With deep foreboding he went to the window and peered across the grounds.

He saw a hundred or so peasants approaching the house across the park. Although it was still daylight, many carried blazing torches. Some, he saw, had rifles.

He said: "Oh, fuck."

Bea was shocked. "Fitz! Have you forgotten that I am here?"

"Look at this," he said.

Bea gasped. "Oh, no!"

Fitz shouted: "Jenkins! Jenkins, are you there?" He opened the communicating door and saw the valet, looking startled, putting the traveling suit on a hanger. "We're in mortal danger," Fitz said. "We have to leave in the next five minutes. Run to the stables, put the horses to a carriage, and bring it to the kitchen door as fast as you can."

Jenkins dropped the suit on the floor and dashed off.

Fitz turned to Bea. "Throw on a coat, any coat, and pick up a pair of sensible outdoor shoes, then go down the back stairs to the kitchen and wait for me there."

To her credit, there were no hysterics: she just did as she was told.

Fitz left the room and hurried, limping as fast as he could, to Andrei's bedroom. His brother-in-law was not there, nor was Valeriya.

Fitz went downstairs. Georgi and some of the male servants were in the hall, looking frightened. Fitz was scared, too, but he hoped he was not showing it.

Fitz found the prince and princess in the drawing room. There was an opened bottle of champagne on ice, and two glasses had been poured, but they were not drinking. Andrei stood in front of the fireplace and Valeriya was at the window, looking at the approaching crowd. Fitz stood beside her. The peasants were almost at the door. A few had firearms; most carried knives, hammers, and scythes.

Andrei said: "Georgi will attempt to reason with them, and if that fails I shall have to speak to them myself."

Fitz said: "For God's sake, Andrei, the time for talking is past. We have to leave now."

Before Andrei could reply, they heard raised voices in the hall.

Fitz went to the door and opened it a crack. He saw Georgi arguing with a tall young peasant who had a bushy mustache that stretched across his cheeks: Feodor Igorovich, he guessed. They were surrounded by men and a few women, some holding burning torches. More were pushing in through the front door. It was hard to understand their local accent, but one shouted phrase was repeated several times: "We *will* speak to the prince!"

Andrei heard it, too, and he stepped past Fitz and out into the hall. Fitz said: "No—" but it was too late.

The mob jeered and hissed when Andrei appeared in evening dress. Raising his voice, he said: "If you all leave quietly now, perhaps you won't be in such bad trouble."

Feodor shot back: "You're the one in trouble—you murdered my brother!"

Fitz heard Valeriya say quietly: "My place is beside my husband." Before he could stop her, she, too, had gone into the hall.

Andrei said: "I didn't intend Ivan to die, but he would be alive now if he had not broken the law and defied his prince!"

With a sudden quick movement, Feodor reversed his rifle and hit Andrei across the face with its butt.

Andrei staggered back, holding a hand to his cheek.

The peasants cheered.

Feodor shouted: "This is what you did to Ivan!"

Fitz reached for his revolver.

Feodor raised his rifle above his head. For a frozen moment the long Mosin-Nagant hovered in the air like an executioner's axe. Then he brought the rifle down, with a powerful blow, and hit the top of Andrei's head. There was a sickening crack, and Andrei fell.

Valeriya screamed.

Fitz, standing in the doorway with the door half closed, thumbed off the lock on the left side of his revolver's barrel and aimed at Feodor; but the peasants crowded around his target. They began to kick and beat Andrei, who lay on the floor unconscious. Valeriya tried to get to him to help him, but she could not push through the crowd.

A peasant with a scythe struck at the portrait of Bea's stern grandfather, slashing the canvas. One of the men fired a shotgun at the chandelier, which smashed into tinkling fragments. A set of drapes suddenly blazed up: someone must have put a torch to them.

Fitz had been on the battlefield and had learned that gallantry had to be tempered with cool calculation. He knew that on his own he could not save Andrei from the mob. But he might be able to rescue Valeriya.

He pocketed the gun.

He stepped into the hall. All attention was on the supine prince. Valeriya stood at the edge of the throng, beating ineffectually on the shoulders of the peasants in front of her. Fitz grabbed her by the waist, lifted her, and carried her away, stepping back into the drawing room. His bad leg hurt like fire under the burden, but he gritted his teeth.

"Let me go!" she screamed. "I must help Andrei!"

"We can't help Andrei!" Fitz said. He shifted his grip and slung his sister-in-law over his shoulder, easing the pressure on his leg. As he did so a bullet passed close enough for him to feel its wind. He glanced back and saw a grinning soldier in uniform aiming a pistol.

He heard a second shot, and sensed an impact. He thought for a moment that he had been hit, but there was no pain, and he dashed for the communicating door that led to the dining room.

He heard the soldier shout: "She's getting away!"

Fitz burst through the door as another bullet hit the woodwork. Ordinary soldiers were not trained with pistols and sometimes did not realize how much less accurate they were than rifles. Moving at a limping run, he went past the table elaborately laid with silver and crystal ready for four wealthy aristocrats to have dinner. Behind him he heard several pursuers. At the far end of the room a door led to the kitchen area. He passed into a narrow corridor and from there to the kitchen. A cook and several kitchen maids had stopped work and were standing around looking terrified.

Fitz's pursuers were too close behind him. As soon as

they got a clear shot he would be killed. He had to do something to slow them down.

He set Valeriya on her feet. She swayed, and he saw blood on her dress. She had been hit by a bullet, but she was alive and conscious. He sat her in a chair, then turned to the corridor. The grinning soldier was running toward him, firing wildly, followed by several more in single file in the narrow space. Behind them, in the dining room and drawing room, Fitz saw flames.

He drew his Webley. It was a double-action gun so it did not need to be cocked. Shifting all his weight to his good leg, he aimed carefully at the belly of the soldier running at him. He squeezed the trigger, the gun banged, and the man fell on the stone floor in front of him. In the kitchen, Fitz heard women screaming in terror.

Fitz immediately fired again at the next man, who also went down. He fired a third time at a third man, with the same result. The fourth man ducked back into the dining room.

Fitz slammed the kitchen door. The pursuers would now hesitate, wondering how they could check whether he was lying in wait for them, and that might just give him the time he needed.

He picked up Valeriya, who seemed to be losing consciousness. He had never been in the kitchens of this house, but he moved toward the back. Another corridor took him past storerooms and laundries. At last he opened a door that led to the outside.

Stepping out, panting, his bad leg hurting like the very devil, he saw the carriage waiting, with Jenkins in the driver's seat and Bea inside with Nina, who was sobbing uncontrollably. A frightened-looking stable boy was holding the horses.

He manhandled the unconscious Valeriya into the carriage, climbed in after her, and shouted at Jenkins: "Go! Go!"

Jenkins whipped the horses, the stable boy leaped out of the way, and the carriage moved off.

Fitz said to Bea: "Are you all right?"

"No, but I'm alive and unhurt. You . . . ?"

"No damage. But I fear for your brother's life." In reality he was quite sure Andrei was dead by now, but he did not want to say that to her.

Bea looked at the princess. "What happened?"

"She must have been hit by a bullet." Fitz looked more closely. Valeriya's face was white and still. "Oh, dear God," he said.

"She's dead, isn't she?" Bea said.

"You must be brave."

"I will be brave." Bea took her sister-in-law's lifeless hand. "Poor Valeriya."

The carriage raced down the drive and past the small dowager house where Bea's mother had lived after Bea's father died. Fitz looked back at the big house. There was a small crowd of frustrated pursuers outside the kitchen door. One of them was aiming a rifle, and Fitz pushed Bea's head down and ducked himself.

When next he looked they were out of range. Peasants and the staff were pouring out of the house by all its doors. The windows were strangely bright, and Fitz realized that the place was on fire. As he looked, smoke drifted from the front door, and an orange flame licked up from an open window and set fire to the creeper growing up the wall.

Then the carriage topped a rise and rattled downhill, and the old house disappeared from view.

CHAPTER TWENTY-EIGHT

October and November 1917

Walter said angrily: "Admiral von Holtzendorff promised us the British would starve in five months. That was nine months ago."

"He made a mistake," said his father.

Walter suppressed a scornful retort.

They were in Otto's room at the Foreign Office in Berlin. Otto sat in a carved chair behind a big desk. On the wall behind him hung a painting of Kaiser Wilhelm I, grandfather of the present monarch, being proclaimed German emperor in the Hall of Mirrors at Versailles.

Walter was infuriated by his father's half-baked excuses. "The admiral gave his word as an officer that no American would reach Europe," he said. "Our intelligence is that fourteen thousand of them landed in France in June. So much for the word of an officer!"

That stung Otto. "He did what he believed was best for his country," he said irately. "What more can a man do?"

Walter raised his voice. "You ask me what more a man can do? He can avoid making false promises. When he doesn't know for sure, he can refrain from saying he knows for sure. He can tell the truth, or keep his stupid mouth shut."

"Von Holtzendorff gave the best advice he could."

The feebleness of these arguments maddened Walter. "Such humility would have been appropriate *before* the event. But there was none. You were there, at Castle Pless—you know what happened. Von Holtzendorff gave his word. *He misled the kaiser.* He brought the Americans into the war against us. A man could hardly serve his monarch worse!"

"I suppose you want him to resign—but then who would take his place?"

"Resign?" Walter was bursting with fury. "I want him to put the barrel of his revolver in his mouth and pull the trigger."

Otto looked severe. "That's a wicked thing to say."

"His own death would be small retribution for all those who have died because of his smug foolishness."

"You youngsters have no common sense."

"You dare to talk to me about common sense? You and your generation took Germany into a war that has crippled us and killed millions—a war that, after three years, we still have not won."

Otto looked away. He could hardly deny that Germany had not yet won the war. The opposing sides were deadlocked in France. Unrestricted submarine warfare had failed to choke off supplies to the Allies. Meanwhile, the British naval blockade was slowly starving the German people. "We have to wait and see what happens in Petrograd," said Otto. "If Russia drops out of the war, the balance will change."

"Exactly," said Walter. "Everything now depends on the Bolsheviks."

{ II }

Early in October, Grigori and Katerina went to see the midwife.

Grigori now spent most nights in the one-room apartment near the Putilov works. They no longer made love—she found it too uncomfortable. Her belly was huge. The skin was as taut as a football, and her navel stuck out instead of in. Grigori had never been intimate with a pregnant woman, and he found it frightening as well as thrilling. He knew that everything was normal, but all the same he dreaded the thought of a baby's head cruelly stretching the narrow passage he loved so much.

They set out for the home of the midwife, Magda, the wife of Konstantin. Vladimir rode on Grigori's shoulders. The boy was almost three, but Grigori still carried him without effort. His personality was emerging: in his childish way he was intelligent and earnest, more like Grigori than his charming, wayward father, Lev. A baby was like a revolution, Grigori thought: you could start one, but you could not control how it would turn out.

General Kornilov's counterrevolution had been crushed before it got started. The Railwaymen's Union had made sure most of Kornilov's troops got stuck in sidings miles from Petrograd. Those who came anywhere near the city were met by Bolsheviks who undermined them simply by telling them the truth, as Grigori had in the schoolyard. Soldiers then turned on officers who were in on the conspiracy and executed them. Kornilov himself was arrested and imprisoned.

Grigori became known as the man who turned back Kornilov's army. He protested that this was an exaggeration, but his modesty only increased his stature. He was elected to the Central Committee of the Bolshevik Party.

Trotsky got out of jail. The Bolsheviks won 51 percent of the vote in the Moscow city elections. Party membership reached 350,000.

Grigori had an intoxicating feeling that anything could happen, including total disaster. Every day the revolution might be defeated. That was what he dreaded, for then his child would grow up in a Russia that was no better. Grigori thought of the milestones of his own childhood: the hanging of his father, the death of his mother outside the Winter Palace, the priest who took little Lev's trousers down, the grinding work at the Putilov factory. He wanted a different life for his child.

"Lenin is calling for an armed uprising," he told Katerina as they walked to Magda's place. Lenin had been in hiding outside the city, but he had been sending a constant stream of furious letters urging the party to action.

"I think he's right," said Katerina. "Everyone is fed up with governments who speak about democracy but do nothing about the price of bread."

As usual, Katerina said what most Petrograd workers were thinking.

Magda was expecting them and had made tea. "I'm sorry there's no sugar," she said. "I haven't been able to get sugar for weeks."

"I can't wait to get this over with," said Katerina. "I'm so tired of carrying all this weight."

Magda felt Katerina's belly and said she had about two weeks to go.

Katerina said: "It was awful when Vladimir was born. I had no friends, and the midwife was a hard-faced Siberian bitch called Kseniya."

"I know Kseniya," said Magda. "She's competent, but a bit stern."

"I'll say."

Konstantin was leaving for the Smolny Institute. Although the soviet was not in session every day, there were constant meetings of committees and ad hoc groups. Kerensky's provisional government was now so weak that the soviet gained authority by default. "I hear Lenin is back in town," Konstantin said to Grigori.

"Yes, he got back last night."

"Where is he staying?"

"It's a secret. The police are still keen to arrest him."

"What made him return?"

"We'll find out tomorrow. He's called a meeting of the Central Committee."

Konstantin left to catch a streetcar to the city center. Grigori walked Katerina home. When he was about to leave for the barracks, she said: "I feel better, knowing Magda will be with me."

"Good." Grigori still felt that childbirth seemed more dangerous than an armed uprising.

"And you'll be there, too," Katerina added.

"Not actually in the room," Grigori said nervously.

"No, of course not. But you'll be outside, pacing up and down, and that will make me feel safe."

"Good."

"You will be there, won't you?"

"Yes," he said. "Whatever happens, I'll be there."

When he got to the barracks an hour later, he found the place in turmoil. On the parade ground, officers were trying to get guns and ammunition loaded onto wagons, with little success: every battalion committee was either holding a meeting or preparing to hold one. "Kerensky has done it now!" said Isaak jubilantly. "He's trying to send us to the front."

Grigori's heart sank. "Send who?"

"The entire Petrograd garrison! The orders have come down. We're to change places with soldiers at the front."

"What's their reason?"

"They say it's because of the German advance." The Germans had taken the islands in the Gulf of Riga and were heading toward Petrograd.

"Rubbish," said Grigori angrily. "It's an attempt to undermine the soviet." And it was a clever attempt, he realized as he thought it through. If the troops in Petrograd were replaced by others coming back from the front, it would take days, perhaps weeks of organization to form new soldiers' committees and elect new deputies to the soviet. Worse, the new men would lack the experience of the last six months' political battles—which would have to be fought all over again. "What do the soldiers say?"

"They're furious. They want Kerensky to negotiate peace, not send them to die."

"Will they refuse to leave Petrograd?"

"I don't know. It will help if they get the backing of the soviet."

"I'll take care of that."

Grigori took an armored car and two bodyguards and drove over the Liteiny Bridge to the Smolny. This looked like a setback, he reflected, but it might turn into an opportunity. Until now, not all troops had supported the Bolsheviks, but Kerensky's attempt to send them to the front might swing the waverers over. The more he thought about it, the more he believed this could be Kerensky's big mistake.

The Smolny was a grand building that had been a school for daughters of the wealthy. Two machine guns from Grigori's regiment guarded the entrance. Red Guards attempted to verify everyone's identity—but, Grigori noted uneasily, the crowds going in and out were so numerous that the check was not rigorous.

The courtyard was a scene of frenetic activity. Armored cars, motorcycles, trucks, and cars came and went constantly, competing for space. A broad flight of steps led up to a row of arches and a classical colonnade. In an upstairs room Grigori found the executive committee of the soviet in session.

The Mensheviks were calling on the garrison soldiers to prepare to move to the front. As usual, Grigori thought with disgust, the Mensheviks were surrendering without a fight; and he suffered a sudden panicky fear that the revolution was slipping away from him.

He went into a huddle with the other Bolsheviks on the executive to compose a more militant resolution. "The only way to defend Petrograd against the Germans is to mobilize the workers," Trotsky said.

"As we did at the time of the Kornilov Putsch," Grigori said with enthusiasm. "We need another Committee for Struggle to take charge of the defense of the city."

Trotsky scribbled a draft, then stood up to propose the motion.

The Mensheviks were outraged. "You would be creating a second military command center alongside army headquarters!" said Mark Broido. "No man can serve two masters."

To Grigori's disgust, most committeemen agreed with that. The Menshevik motion was passed and Trotsky's was defeated. Grigori left the meeting in despair. Could the soldiers' loyalty to the soviet survive such a rebuff?

That afternoon the Bolsheviks met in Room 36 and decided they could not accept this decision. They agreed to propose their motion again that evening, at the meeting of the full soviet.

The second time, the Bolsheviks won the vote.

Grigori was relieved. The soviet had backed the soldiers and set up an alternative military command.

They were one large step closer to power.

{ III }

Next day, feeling optimistic, Grigori and the other leading Bolsheviks slipped quietly away from the Smolny in ones and twos, careful not to attract the attention of the secret police, and made their way to the large apartment of a comrade, Galina Flakserman, for the meeting of the Central Committee.

Grigori was nervous about the meeting and arrived early. He circled the block, looking for idlers who might be police spies, but he saw no one suspicious. Inside the building he reconnoitered the different exits—there were three—and determined the fastest way out.

The Bolsheviks sat around a big dining table, many wearing the leather coats that were becoming a kind of uniform for them. Lenin was not there, so they started without him. Grigori fretted about him—he might have been arrested—but he arrived at ten o'clock, disguised in a wig that kept slipping and almost made him look foolish.

However, there was nothing laughable about the resolution he proposed, calling for an armed uprising, led by the Bolsheviks, to overthrow the provisional government and take power.

Grigori was elated. Everyone wanted an armed uprising, of course, but most revolutionaries said the time was not yet ripe. At last the most powerful of them was saying *now*.

Lenin spoke for an hour. As always he was strident, banging the table, shouting, and abusing those who disagreed with him. His style worked against him—you wanted to vote down someone who was so rude. But despite that he was persuasive. His knowledge was wide, his political instinct was unerring, and few men could stand firm against the hammer blows of his logical arguments.

Grigori was on Lenin's side from the start. The important thing was to seize power and end the dithering, he thought. All other problems could be solved later. But would the others agree?

Zinoviev spoke against. Normally a handsome man, he, too, had changed his appearance to confuse the police. He had grown a beard and cropped his luxuriant thatch of curly black hair. He thought Lenin's strategy was too risky. He was afraid an uprising would give the right wing an excuse for a military coup. He wanted the Bolshevik party to concentrate on winning the elections for the Constituent Assembly.

This timid argument infuriated Lenin. "The provisional government is *never* going to hold a national election!" he said. "Anyone who thinks otherwise is a fool and a dupe."

Trotsky and Stalin backed the uprising, but Trotsky angered Lenin by saying they should wait for the All-Russia Congress of Soviets, scheduled to begin in ten days' time.

That struck Grigori as a good idea—Trotsky was always reasonable—but Lenin surprised him by roaring: "No!"

Trotsky said: "We're likely to have a majority among the delegates—"

"If the congress forms a government, it is bound to be a coalition!" Lenin said angrily. "The Bolsheviks admitted to the government will be centrists. Who could wish for that—other than a counterrevolutionary traitor?"

Trotsky flushed at the insult, but he said nothing.

Grigori realized Lenin was right. As usual, Lenin had thought further ahead than anyone else. In a coalition, the Mensheviks' first demand would be that the prime minister must be a moderate—and they would probably settle for anyone but Lenin.

It dawned on Grigori—and at the same time on the rest of the committee, he guessed—that the only way Lenin could become prime minister was by a coup.

The dispute raged until the small hours. In the end they voted by ten to two in favor of an armed uprising.

However, Lenin did not get all his own way. No date was set for the coup.

When the meeting was over, Galina produced a samovar and put out cheese, sausage, and bread for the hungry revolutionaries.

{ IV }

As a child on Prince Andrei's estate, Grigori had once witnessed the climax of a deer hunt. The dogs had brought down a stag just outside the village, and everyone had gone to look. When Grigori got there the deer was dying, the dogs already greedily eating the intestines spilling out of its ripped belly while the huntsmen on their horses swigged brandy in celebration. Yet even then the wretched beast had made one last attempt to fight back. It had swung its mighty antlers, impaling one dog and slashing another, and had, for a moment, almost looked as if it might struggle to its feet; then it had sunk back to the bloodstained earth and closed its eyes.

Grigori thought Prime Minister Kerensky, the leader of the provisional government, was like that stag. Everyone knew he was finished—except him.

As the bitter cold of a Russian winter closed around Petrograd like a fist, the crisis came to a head.

The Committee for Struggle, soon renamed the Military Revolutionary Committee, was dominated by the charismatic figure of Trotsky. He was not handsome, with his big nose, high forehead, and bulging eyes staring through rimless glasses, but he was charming and persuasive. Where Lenin shouted and bullied, Trotsky reasoned and beguiled. Grigori suspected that Trotsky was as tough as Lenin but better at hiding it.

On Monday, November 5, two days before the All-Russia Congress was due to start, Grigori went to a mass meeting, called by the Military Revolutionary Committee, of all the troops in the Peter and Paul Fortress. The meeting started at noon and went on all afternoon, hundreds of soldiers debating politics in the square in front of the fort while their officers fumed impotently. Then Trotsky arrived, to thunderous applause, and after listening to him they voted to obey the committee rather than the government, Trotsky, not Kerensky.

Walking away from the square, Grigori reflected that the government could not possibly tolerate a key army unit declaring its loyalty to someone else. The cannon of the fortress were directly across the river from the Winter Palace, where the provisional government was headquartered. Surely, he thought, Kerensky would now admit defeat and resign.

Next day Trotsky announced precautions against a counterrevolutionary coup by the army. He ordered Red Guards and troops loyal to the soviet to take over the bridges, railway stations, and police stations, plus the post office, the telegraph office, the telephone exchange, and the state bank.

Grigori was at Trotsky's side, turning the great man's stream of commands into detailed instructions for specific military units and dispatching the orders around the city by messengers on horseback, on bicycles, and in cars. He thought Trotsky's "precautions" seemed very similar to a takeover.

To his amazement and delight, there was little resistance.

A spy at the Marinsky Palace reported that Prime Minister Kerensky had asked the preparliament—the body that had so miserably failed in its task of setting up the Constituent Assembly—for a vote of confidence. The preparliament refused. No one took much notice. Kerensky was history, just another inadequate man who had tried and failed to rule Russia. He returned to the Winter Palace, where his impotent government continued to pretend to rule.

Lenin was hiding at the apartment of a comrade, Margarita Fofanova. The Central Committee had ordered him not to move about the city, fearing he would be arrested. Grigori was one of the few people who knew his location. At eight o'clock in the evening Margarita arrived at the Smolny with a note from Lenin ordering the Bolsheviks to launch an armed insurrection immediately. Trotsky said tetchily: "What does he imagine we're doing?"

But Grigori thought Lenin was right. In spite of everything, the Bolsheviks had not quite seized power. Once the Congress of Soviets assembled it would have all authority—and then, even if the Bolsheviks were in a majority, the result would be yet another coalition government based on compromise.

The congress was scheduled to begin tomorrow afternoon at two o'clock. Only Lenin seemed to understand the urgency of the situation, Grigori thought with a sense of desperation. He was needed here, at the heart of things.

Grigori decided to go get him.

It was a freezing night, with a north wind that seemed to blow straight through the leather coat Grigori wore over his sergeant's uniform. The center of the city was shockingly normal: well-dressed middle-class people were coming out of theaters and walking to brightly lit restaurants, while beggars pestered them for change and prostitutes smiled on street corners. Grigori nodded to a comrade who was selling a pamphlet by Lenin called *Will the Bolsheviks Be Able to Hold the Power?* Grigori did not buy one. He already knew the answer to that question.

Margarita's flat was on the northern edge of the Vyborg

district. Grigori could not drive there for fear of calling attention to Lenin's hideout. He walked to the Finland Station, then caught a streetcar. The journey was long, and he spent most of it wondering if Lenin would refuse to come.

However, to his great relief Lenin did not need much persuading. "Without you, I don't believe the other comrades will take the final decisive step," Grigori said, and that was all it took to convince Lenin to come.

He left a note on the kitchen table, so that Margarita would not imagine he had been arrested. It said: "I have gone where you wanted me not to go. Good-bye, Ilich." Party members called him Ilich, his middle name.

Grigori checked his pistol while Lenin put on his wig, a worker's cap, and a shabby overcoat. Then they set out.

Grigori kept a sharp lookout, fearful that they would run into a detachment of police or an army patrol and Lenin would be recognized. He made up his mind that, rather than let Lenin be arrested, he would shoot without hesitation.

They were the only passengers on the streetcar. Lenin questioned the conductress on what she thought of the latest political developments.

Walking from the Finland Station they heard hoofbeats and hid from what turned out to be a troop of loyalist cadets looking for trouble.

Grigori triumphantly delivered Lenin to the Smolny at midnight.

Lenin went at once to Room 36 and called a meeting of the Bolshevik Central Committee. Trotsky reported that Red Guards now controlled many of the city's key points. But that was not enough for Lenin. For symbolic reasons, he argued, the revolutionary troops had to seize the Winter Palace and arrest the ministers of the provisional government. That would be the act that convinced people that power had passed, finally and irrevocably, to the revolutionaries.

Grigori knew he was right.

So did everyone else.

Trotsky began to plan the taking of the Winter Palace.

Grigori did not get home to Katerina that night.

{ V }

There could be no mistakes.

The final act of the revolution had to be decisive, Grigori knew. He made sure the orders were clear and reached their destinations in good time.

The plan was not complicated, but Grigori worried that Trotsky's timetable was optimistic. The bulk of the attacking force would consist of revolutionary sailors. The majority were coming from Helsingfors, capital of the Finnish region, by train and ship. They left at three a.m. More were coming from Kronstadt, the island naval base twenty miles offshore.

The attack was scheduled to begin at twelve noon.

Like a battlefield operation, it would start with an artillery barrage: the guns of the Peter and Paul Fortress would fire across the river and batter down the walls of the palace. Then the sailors and soldiers would take over the building. Trotsky said it would be over by two o'clock, when the Congress of Soviets was due to start.

Lenin wanted to stand up at the opening and announce that the Bolsheviks had *already* taken power. It was the only way to prevent another indecisive, ineffective compromise government, the only way to ensure that Lenin ended up in charge.

Grigori worried that things might not go as fast as Trotsky hoped.

Security was poor at the Winter Palace, and at dawn Grigori was able to send Isaak inside to reconnoiter. He reported that there were about three thousand loyalist troops in the building. If they were properly organized and fought bravely, there would be a mighty battle.

Isaak also discovered that Kerensky had left town. Because the Red Guards controlled the railway stations he had been unable to leave by train, and he had eventually departed in a commandeered car. "What kind of prime minister can't catch a train in his own capital?" Isaak said.

"Anyway, he's gone," Grigori said with satisfaction. "And I don't suppose he'll ever come back."

However, Grigori's mood turned pessimistic when noon came around and none of the sailors had appeared.

He crossed the bridge to the Peter and Paul Fortress to

make sure the cannon were ready. To his horror he found that they were museum pieces, there only for show, and could not be fired. He ordered Isaak to find some working artillery.

He hurried back to the Smolny to tell Trotsky his plan was behind schedule. The guard at the door said: "There was someone here looking for you, comrade. Something about a midwife."

"I can't deal with that now," Grigori said.

Events were moving very fast. Grigori learned that the Red Guards had taken the Marinsky Palace and dispersed the preparliament without bloodshed. Those Bolsheviks in jail had been released. Trotsky had ordered all troops outside Petrograd to remain where they were, and they were obeying him, not their officers. Lenin was writing a manifesto that began: "To the citizens of Russia: The provisional government has been overthrown!"

"But the assault has not begun," Grigori told Trotsky miserably. "I don't see how it can be managed before three o'clock."

"Don't worry," said Trotsky. "We can delay the opening of the congress."

Grigori returned to the square in front of the Winter Palace. At two in the afternoon, at long last, he saw the minelayer *Amur* sail into the Neva with a thousand sailors from Kronstadt on its deck, and the workers of Petrograd lined the banks to cheer them.

If Kerensky had thought to put a few mines in the narrow channel, he could have kept the sailors out of the city and defeated the revolution. But there were no mines, and the sailors in their black pea jackets began to disembark, carrying their rifles. Grigori prepared to deploy them around the Winter Palace.

But the plan was still bedeviled by snags, to Grigori's immense exasperation. Isaak found a cannon and, with much effort, got it dragged into place, only to find that there were no shells for it. Meanwhile, loyalist troops at the palace were building barricades.

Maddened by frustration, Grigori drove back to the Smolny.

An emergency session of the Petrograd soviet was about to start. The spacious hall of the girls' school, painted a virginal white, was packed full with hundreds of delegates.

Grigori went up onto the stage and sat beside Trotsky, who was about to open the session. "The assault has been delayed by a series of problems," he said.

Trotsky took the bad news calmly. Lenin would have thrown a fit. Trotsky said: "When can you take the palace?"

"Realistically, six o'clock."

Trotsky nodded calmly and stood up to address the meeting. "On behalf of the Military Revolutionary Committee, I declare that the provisional government no longer exists!" he shouted.

There was a storm of cheering and shouting. Grigori thought: I hope I can make that lie true.

When the noise died down, Trotsky listed the achievements of the Red Guards: the overnight seizure of railway stations and other key buildings, and the dispersal of the preparliament. He also announced that several government ministers had been individually arrested. "The Winter Palace has not been taken, but its fate will be decided momentarily!" There were more cheers.

A dissenter shouted: "You are anticipating the will of the Congress of Soviets!"

This was the soft democratic argument, one that Grigori himself would have advanced in the old days, before he became a realist.

Trotsky's response was so quick that he must have expected this criticism. "The will of the congress has already been anticipated by the uprising of workers and soldiers," he replied.

Suddenly there was a murmur around the hall. People began to stand up. Grigori looked toward the door, wondering why. He saw Lenin walking in. The deputies began to cheer. The noise became thunderous as Lenin came up onto the stage. He and Trotsky stood side by side, smiling and bowing in acknowledgment of the standing ovation, as the crowd acclaimed the coup that had not yet taken place.

The tension between the victory being proclaimed in the hall and the reality of muddle and delay outside was too much for Grigori to bear, and he slipped away.

The sailors still had not arrived from Helsingfors, and the cannon at the fortress were not yet ready to fire. As night fell, a cold drizzling rain began. Standing at the edge of Palace Square, with the Winter Palace in front of him and general staff headquarters behind, Grigori saw a force of cadets emerge from the palace. Their uniform badges said they were from the Mikhailovsky Artillery School, and they were leaving, taking four heavy guns with them. Grigori let them go.

At seven o'clock he ordered a force of soldiers and sailors to enter general staff headquarters and seize control. They did so without opposition.

At eight o'clock the two hundred Cossacks on guard at the palace decided to return to their barracks, and Grigori let them through the cordon. He realized that the irksome delays might not be a total catastrophe: the forces he had to overcome were diminishing with time.

Just before ten, Isaak reported that the cannon were finally ready at the Peter and Paul Fortress. Grigori ordered one blank round to be fired, followed by a pause. As he had expected, more troops fled the palace.

Could it be this easy?

Out on the water, an alarm sounded aboard the *Amur*. Seeking the cause, Grigori looked downriver and saw the lights of approaching ships. His heart went cold. Had Kerensky succeeded in sending loyal forces to save his government at the last gasp? But then a cheer went up on the deck of the *Amur*, and Grigori realized the newcomers were the sailors from Helsingfors.

When they were safely anchored, he gave the order for the shelling to begin—at last.

There was a thunder of guns. Some shells exploded in midair, lighting up the ships on the river and the besieged palace. Grigori saw a hit on a third-floor corner window, and wondered if there had been anyone in the room. To his amazement, the brightly lit streetcars continued without interruption to trundle across the nearby Troitsky Bridge and Palace Bridge.

It was nothing like the battlefield, of course. At the front there were hundreds of guns firing, perhaps thousands; here, just four. There were long intervals between shots, and it was shocking to see how many were wasted, falling short and dropping harmlessly into the river.

Grigori called a halt and sent small groups of troops into the palace to reconnoiter. They came back to say that those few guards left were offering no resistance.

Shortly after midnight, Grigori led a larger contingent inside. In accordance with prearranged tactics they spread through the palace, running along the grand dark corridors, neutralizing opposition and searching for government ministers. The palace looked like a disorderly barracks, with soldiers' mattresses on the parquet floors of the gilded staterooms, and everywhere a filthy litter of cigarette ends, crusts of bread, and empty bottles with French labels that the guards had presumably taken from the costly cellars of the tsar.

Grigori heard a few scattered shots but there was not much fighting. He found no government ministers on the ground floor. The thought occurred to him they might have sneaked away, and he suffered a panicky moment. He did not want to have to report to Trotsky and Lenin that the members of Kerensky's government had slipped through his fingers.

With Isaak and two other men he ran up a broad staircase to check the next floor. Together they burst through a pair of double doors into a meeting room and there found what was left of the provisional government: a small group of frightened men in suits and ties, sitting at a table and on armchairs around the room, wide-eyed with apprehension.

One of them mustered a remnant of authority. "The provisional government is here—what do you want?" he said.

Grigori recognized Alexander Konovalov, the wealthy textile manufacturer who was Kerensky's deputy prime minister.

Grigori replied: "You are all under arrest." It was a good moment, and he savored it.

He turned to Isaak. "Write down their names." He recognized all of them. "Konovalov, Maliantovich, Nikitin, Tereschenko . . ." When the list was complete, he said: "Take them to the Peter and Paul Fortress and put them in the cells. I'll go to the Smolny and give Trotsky and Lenin the good news."

He left the building. Crossing Palace Square, he stopped for a minute, remembering his mother. She had died on this spot twelve years ago, shot by the tsar's guards. He turned around and looked at the vast palace, with its rows of white columns and the moonlight glinting off hundreds of windows. In a sudden fit of rage, he shook his fist at the building. "That's what you get, you devils," he said aloud. "That's what you get for killing her."

He waited until he felt calm again. I don't even know who I'm talking to, he thought. He jumped into his dust-colored armored car, waiting beside a dismantled barricade. "To the Smolny," he told the driver.

As he rode the short distance he began to feel elated. Now we really have won, he told himself. We are the victors. The people have overthrown their oppressors.

He ran up the steps of the Smolny and into the hall. The place was packed, and the Congress of Soviets had opened. Trotsky had not been able to keep on postponing it. That was bad news. It would be just like the Mensheviks, and the other milquetoast revolutionaries, to demand a place in the new government even though they had done nothing to overthrow the old.

A fog of tobacco smoke hung around the chandeliers. The members of the presidium were seated on the platform. Grigori knew most of them, and he studied the composition of the group. The Bolsheviks occupied fourteen of the twenty-five seats, he noted. That meant the party had the largest number of delegates. But he was horrified to see that the chairman was Kamenev—a moderate Bolshevik who had voted against an armed uprising! As Lenin had warned, the congress was shaping up for another feeble compromise.

Grigori scanned the delegates in the hall and spotted Lenin in the front row. He went over and said to the man in the next seat: "I have to talk to Ilich—let me have your chair." The man looked resentful, but after a moment he got up.

Grigori spoke into Lenin's ear. "The Winter Palace is in our hands," he said. He gave the names of the ministers who had been arrested.

"Too late," said Lenin bleakly.

That was what Grigori had feared. "What's happening here?"

Lenin looked black. "Martov proposed the motion." Julius Martov was Lenin's old enemy. Martov had always wanted the Russian Social Democratic Labour Party to be like the British Labour Party, and fight for working people by democratic means; and his quarrel with Lenin over this issue had split the SDLP, back in 1903, into its two factions, Lenin's Bolsheviks and Martov's Mensheviks. "He argued for an end to street fighting followed by negotiations for a democratic government."

"Negotiations?" Grigori said incredulously. "We've seized power!"

"We supported the motion," Lenin said tonelessly.

Grigori was surprised. "Why?"

"We would have lost if we opposed it. We have three hundred of the six hundred and seventy delegates. We're the largest party by a big margin, but we don't have an overall majority."

Grigori could have wept. The coup had come too late. There would be another coalition, its composition dictated by deals and compromises, and the government would dither on while Russians starved at home and died at the front.

"But they're attacking us anyway," Lenin added.

Grigori listened to the current speaker, someone he did not know. "This congress was called to discuss the new government, yet what do we find?" the man was saying angrily. "An irresponsible seizure of power has already occurred and the will of the congress has been preempted! We must save the revolution from this mad venture."

There was a storm of protest from the Bolshevik delegates. Grigori heard Lenin saying: "Swine! Bastard! Traitor!"

Kamenev called for order.

But the next speech was also bitterly hostile to the Bolsheviks and their coup, and it was followed by more in the same vein. Lev Khinchuk, a Menshevik, called for negotiations with the provisional government, and the eruption of indignation among the delegates was so violent that Khinchuk could not continue for some minutes. Finally, shouting over the noise, he said: "We leave the present congress!" Then he walked out of the hall.

Grigori saw that their tactic would be to say that the congress had no authority once they had withdrawn. "Deserters!" someone shouted, and the cry was taken up around the hall.

Grigori was appalled. They had waited so long for this congress. The delegates represented the will of the Russian people. But it was falling apart.

He looked at Lenin. To Grigori's astonishment, Lenin's eyes glittered with delight. "This is wonderful," he said. "We're saved! I never imagined they would make such a mistake."

Grigori had no idea what he was talking about. Had Lenin become irrational?

The next speaker was Mikhail Gendelman, a leading Socialist Revolutionary. He said: "Taking cognizance of the seizure of power by the Bolsheviks, holding them responsible for this insane and criminal action, and finding it impossible to collaborate with them, the Socialist Revolutionary faction is leaving the congress!" And he walked out, followed by all the Socialist Revolutionaries. They were jeered, booed, and whistled at by the remaining delegates.

Grigori was mortified. How could his triumph have degenerated, so quickly, into this kind of rowdyism?

But Lenin looked even more pleased.

A series of soldier-delegates spoke in favor of the Bolshevik coup, and Grigori began to brighten, but he still did not understand Lenin's jubilation. Ilich was now scribbling something on a notepad. As speech followed speech he corrected and rewrote. Finally he handed two sheets of paper to Grigori. "This must be presented to the congress for immediate adoption," he said.

It was a long statement, full of the usual rhetoric, but Grigori homed in on the key sentence: "The congress hereby resolves to take governmental power into its own hands."

That was what Grigori wanted.

"For Trotsky to read out?" said Grigori.

"No, not Trotsky." Lenin scanned the men—and one woman—on the platform. "Lunacharsky," he said.

Grigori guessed Lenin felt Trotsky had already gained enough glory.

Grigori took the proclamation to Lunacharsky, who made a signal to the chairman. A few minutes later Kamenev called on Lunacharsky, who stood up and read out Lenin's words.

Every sentence was greeted with a roar of approval.

The chairman called for a vote.

And now, at last, Grigori began to see why Lenin was happy. With the Mensheviks and the Socialist Revolutionaries out of the room, the Bolsheviks had an overwhelming majority. They could do anything they liked. There was no need for compromise.

A vote was taken. Only two delegates were against.

The Bolsheviks had the power, and now they had the legitimacy.

The chairman closed the session. It was five a.m. on Thursday, November 8. The Russian revolution was victorious. And the Bolsheviks were in charge.

Grigori left the room behind Josef Stalin, the Georgian revolutionary, and another man. Stalin's companion wore a leather coat and a cartridge belt, as did many of the Bolsheviks, but something about him rang an alarm bell in Grigori's memory. When the man turned to say something to Stalin, Grigori recognized him, and a tremor of shock and horror ran through him.

It was Mikhail Pinsky.

He had joined the revolution.

{ VI }

Grigori was exhausted. He had not slept for two nights. There had been so much to do that he had hardly noticed the passage of days. The armored car was the most uncomfortable vehicle he had ever traveled in, but all the same he fell asleep as it drove him home. When Isaak woke him, he saw that they were outside the house. He wondered how much Katerina knew of what had happened. He hoped she had not heard too much, for that would give him the pleasure of telling her about the triumph of the revolution.

He went into the house and stumbled up the stairs. There was a light under the door. "It's me," he said, and went into the room.

Katerina was sitting up in bed with a tiny baby in her arms.

Grigori was suffused with delight. "The baby came!" he said. "He's beautiful."

"It's a girl."

"A girl!"

"You promised you would be here," Katerina said accusingly.

"I didn't know!" He looked at the baby. "She has dark hair, like me. What shall we call her?"

"I sent you a message."

Grigori recalled the guard who had told him someone was looking for him. *Something about a midwife,* the man had said. "Oh, my God," Grigori said. "I was so busy . . ."

"Magda was attending to another birth," Katerina said. "I had to have Kseniya."

Grigori was concerned. "Did you suffer?"

"Of course I suffered," Katerina snapped.

"I'm so sorry. But listen! There's been a revolution! A real one, this time—we've taken power! The Bolsheviks are forming a government." He bent down to kiss her.

"That's what I thought," she said, and she turned her face away.

CHAPTER TWENTY-NINE

March 1918

Walter stood on the roof of a small medieval church in the village of Villefranche-sur-Oise, not far from St.-Quentin. For a while this had been a rest-and-recreation area in the German rear echelon and the French inhabitants, making the best of it, had sold omelettes and wine, when they could get any, to their conquerors. *"Malheur la guerre,"* they said. *"Pour nous, pour vous, pour tout le monde."* "Miserable war—for us, for you, for everyone." Small advances by the Allies had since driven the French residents away, flattened half the buildings, and brought the village closer to the front line: now it was an assembly zone.

Down below, on the narrow road through the center, German soldiers marched four abreast. They had been passing through hour after hour, thousands of them. They looked weary but happy, even though they must have known they were heading for the front line. They had been transferred here from the eastern front. France in March was an improvement on Poland in February, Walter guessed, whatever else might be in store.

The sight gladdened his heart. These men had been freed up by the armistice between Germany and Russia. In the last few days the negotiators at Brest-Litovsk had signed a peace treaty. Russia was out of the war permanently. Walter had played a part in making that happen, by giving support to Lenin and the Bolsheviks, and this was the triumphant result.

The German army in France now had 192 divisions, up from 129 this time last year, most of the increase being units switched from the eastern front. For the first time they had more men here than the Allies, who had 173 divisions, according to German intelligence. Many times in the last three and a half years, the German people had been told they were on the brink of victory. This time Walter thought it was true.

He did not share his father's belief that the Germans were a superior type of human, but on the other hand he could see that German mastery of Europe would be no bad thing. The French had many brilliant talents—cooking, painting, fashion, wine—but they were not good at government. French officials saw themselves as some kind of aristocracy, and thought it was perfectly all right to keep citizens waiting hours. A dose of German efficiency would do them a world of good. The same went for the disorderly Italians. Eastern Europe would benefit most of all. The old Russian Empire was still in the Middle Ages, with ragged peasants starving in hovels, and women flogged for adultery. Germany would bring order, justice, and modern agricultural methods. They had just started their first scheduled air service. Planes went from Vienna to Kiev and back like railway trains. There would be a network of flights all over Europe after Germany won the war. And Walter and Maud would raise their children in a peaceful and well-ordered world.

But this moment of battlefield opportunity would not last long. Americans had started to arrive in greater numbers. It had taken them almost a year to build their army, but now there were three hundred thousand American soldiers in France, and more were landing every day. Germany had to win now, conquer France and drive the Allies into the sea before the American reinforcements tipped the scales.

The imminent assault had been named the *Kaiserschlacht,* the Emperor's Battle. One way or another, it would be Germany's last offensive.

Walter had been reassigned to the battlefield. Germany needed every man to fight now, especially as so many officers had been killed. He had been given command of a *Sturmbataillon*—storm troopers—and had gone through a training course in the latest tactics with his men. Some were hardened veterans, others boys and old men recruited in desperation. Walter had grown to like them, in training, but he had to take care not to become too attached to men whom he might have to send to their deaths.

On the same training course had been Gottfried von Kessel, Walter's old rival from the German embassy in London. Despite his poor eyesight, Gottfried was a captain in Walter's battalion. War had done little to reduce his know-all pomposity.

Walter surveyed the surrounding countryside through his field glasses. It was a bright, cold day and he could see clearly. To the south the wide river Oise passed slowly through marshes. Northward, fertile land was dotted with hamlets, farmhouses, bridges, orchards, and small areas of woodland. A mile to the west was the network of German trenches, and beyond that the battleground. Here the same agricultural landscape had been devastated by war. Barren wheat fields were cratered like the moon; every village was a heap of stones; the orchards had been blasted and the bridges blown up. If he focused his binoculars carefully, he could see the rotting corpses of men and horses and the steel shells of burned-out tanks.

On the far side of this wasteland were the British.

A loud rumbling caused Walter to look eastward. The vehicle approaching was one he had never seen before, though he had heard talk. It was a self-propelled gun, with giant barrel and firing mechanism mounted on a chassis with its own one-hundred-horsepower engine. It was closely followed by a heavy-duty truck loaded, presumably, with proportionately huge ammunition. A second and a third gun came after. The artillery crews riding on the vehicles waved their caps as they passed by, as if they were on a victory parade.

Walter felt bucked. Such guns could be repositioned rapidly once the offensive got under way. They would give much better support to advancing infantry.

Walter had heard that an even bigger gun was shelling Paris from a distance of sixty miles. It hardly seemed possible.

The guns were followed by a Mercedes 37/95 Double Phaeton that looked distinctly familiar. It turned off the road and parked in the square in front of the church, and Walter's father got out.

What was he doing here?

Walter passed through the low doorway into the tower and hurried down the narrow spiral staircase to the ground. The nave of the disused church had become a dormitory. He picked his way through bedrolls and the upturned crates that served the men as tables and chairs.

Outside, the graveyard was packed with trench bridges, prefabricated wooden platforms that would enable artillery and supply trucks to cross captured British trenches in the wake of the storm troopers. They were stashed amid the tombstones so as not to be easily visible from the air.

The stream of men and vehicles passing through the village from east to west had now slowed to a trickle. Something was up.

Otto was in uniform, and saluted formally. Walter could see that his father was bursting with excitement. "A special visitor is coming!" Otto said immediately.

So that was it. "Who?"

"You'll see."

Walter guessed it was General Ludendorff, who was now in effect supreme commander. "What does he want to do?"

"Address the soldiers, of course. Please assemble the men in front of the church."

"How soon?"

"He's not far behind me."

"Right." Walter looked around the square. "Sergeant Schwab! Come here. You and Corporal Grunwald—and you men, come here." He dispatched messengers to the church, the canteen that had been set up in a large barn, and the tent village on the rise to the north. "I want every man in front of the church, properly dressed, in fifteen minutes. Quick!" They ran off.

Walter hurried around the village, informing the officers, ordering the men to the square, keeping an eye on the road from the east. He found his commanding officer, Generalmajor Schwarzkopf, in a cheese-smelling former dairy on the edge of the village, finishing a late breakfast of bread and tinned sardines.

Within a quarter of an hour two thousand men were

assembled, and ten minutes later they looked respectable, uniforms buttoned and caps on straight. Walter brought up a flatbed truck and backed it up in front of the men. He improvised steps up to the back of the truck using ammunition crates.

Otto produced a length of red carpet from the Mercedes and placed it on the ground leading to the steps.

Walter took Grunwald out of the line. The corporal was a tall man with big hands and feet. Walter sent him up onto the church roof with his field glasses and a whistle.

Then they waited.

Half an hour went by, then an hour. The men fidgeted, the lines became ragged, and conversation broke out.

After another hour, Grunwald blew his whistle.

"Get ready!" Otto barked. "Here he comes!"

A cacophony of shouted orders burst out. The men came quickly to attention. A motorcade swept into the square.

The door of an armored car opened, and a man in a general's uniform got out. However, it was not the balding, bullet-headed Ludendorff. The special visitor moved awkwardly, holding his left hand in the pocket of his tunic as if his arm were injured.

After a moment, Walter saw that it was the kaiser himself.

Generalmajor Schwarzkopf approached him and saluted.

As the men realized who their visitor was, there was a rumble of reaction that grew rapidly into an explosion of cheering. The generalmajor at first looked angry at the indiscipline, but the kaiser smiled benignly and Schwarzkopf quickly recomposed his face into an expression of approval.

The kaiser mounted the steps, stood on the bed of the truck, and acknowledged the cheers. When the noise at last died down, he began to speak. "Germans!" he said. "This is the hour of victory!"

They cheered all over again, and this time Walter cheered with them.

{ II }

At one o'clock in the morning on Thursday, March 21, the brigade was disposed in its forward positions, ready for the attack. Walter and his battalion officers sat in a dugout in the frontline trench. They were talking to relieve the strain of waiting to go into battle.

Gottfried von Kessel was expounding Ludendorff's strategy. "This westward thrust will drive a wedge between the British and the French," he said, with all the ignorant confidence he used to display when they worked together at the German embassy in London. "Then we will swing north, turning the British right flank, and drive them into the English Channel."

"No, no," said Lieutenant von Braun, an older man. "The smart thing to do, once we've broken through their front line, will be to go all the way to the Atlantic coast. Imagine that—a German line stretching all the way across the middle of France, separating the French army from their allies."

Von Kessel protested: "But then we would have enemies to our north and south!"

A third man, Captain Kellerman, joined in. "Ludendorff will swing south," he predicted. "We need to take Paris. That's all that counts."

"Paris is just symbolic!" von Kessel said scornfully.

They were speculating—no one knew. Walter felt too tense to listen to pointless conversation, so he went outside. The men were sitting on the ground in the trench, still and calm. The few hours before battle were a time of reflection and prayer. There had been beef in their barley stew yesterday evening, a rare treat. Morale was good—they all felt the end of the war was coming.

It was a bright starry night. Field kitchens were giving out breakfast: black bread and a thin coffee that tasted of yellow turnips. There had been some rain, but that had passed, and the wind had dropped to almost nothing. This meant poison gas shells could be fired. Both sides used gas, but Walter had heard that this time the Germans would be using a new mixture: deadly phosgene plus tear gas. The tear gas was not lethal, but it could penetrate the standard-issue British gas mask. The theory was that the irritation of tear gas would cause enemy soldiers to pull off their masks in order to rub their eyes, whereupon they would inhale the phosgene and die.

The big guns were ranged all along the near side of no-man's-land. Walter had never seen so much artillery. Their crews were stacking ammunition. Behind them a second line of guns stood ready to move, the horses already in their traces; they would be the next wave of the rolling barrage.

At half past four everything went still. The field kitchens disappeared; the gun crews sat on the ground, waiting; the officers stood in the trenches, looking across no-man's-land into the darkness where the enemy slept. Even the horses became quiet. This is our last chance of victory, Walter thought. He wondered if he should pray.

At four forty a white flare shot up into the sky, its glare making the twinkling stars go out. A moment later, the big gun near Walter went off with a flash of flame and a bang so loud that he staggered back as if pushed. But that was nothing. Within seconds all the artillery were firing. The noise was much louder than a thunderstorm. The flashes lit up the faces of the gun crews as they manhandled the heavy shells and cordite charges. Fumes and smoke filled the air, and Walter tried to breathe only through his nose. The ground under his feet trembled in shock.

Soon Walter saw explosions and flames on the British side, as German shells hit ammunition dumps and petrol tanks. He knew what it was like to be under artillery fire, and he felt sorry for the enemy. He hoped Fitz was not over there.

The guns became so hot they would burn the skin of anyone foolish enough to touch them. The heat distorted the barrels enough to spoil their aim, so the crews used wet sacks to cool them. Walter's troopers volunteered to carry buckets of water from nearby shell holes to keep the sacking drenched. Infantry were always eager to help gun crews before an attack: every enemy soldier killed by the guns was one less man to shoot at the ground troops when they advanced.

Daylight brought fog. Near the guns, the explosion of charges burned the vapor away, but in the distance nothing could be seen. Walter was troubled. The gunners would have to aim "by the map." Fortunately they had detailed, accurate plans of the British positions, most of which had been German positions only a year ago. But there was no substitute for correction by observation. It was a bad start.

The mist mingled with the gun smoke. Walter tied a handkerchief over his nose and mouth. There was no return fire from the British, at least in this section. Walter felt encouraged. Perhaps their artillery had already been destroyed. The only German killed near Walter was a mortar operator whose gun blew up, presumably because the shell exploded in the barrel. A stretcher party took the body away, and a medical team bandaged the wounds of bystanders hit by shards.

At nine o'clock in the morning he moved his men into their jump-off positions, the storm troopers lying on the ground behind the guns, the regular infantry standing in the trenches. Behind them were massed the next wave of artillery, the medical teams, the telephonists, the ammunition resuppliers, and the messengers.

The storm troopers wore the modern "coal scuttle" helmet. They had been the first to abandon the old spiked *pickelhaube*. They were armed with the Mauser K98 carbine. Its short barrel made it inaccurate over distances, but it was less cumbersome than longer rifles in close-quarters trench fighting. Each man had a bag slung across his chest containing a dozen stick grenades. The Tommies called these "tatermashers" after the potato-mashing tool used by their wives. Apparently there was one in every British kitchen. Walter had learned this by interrogating prisoners of war: he had never actually been inside a British kitchen.

Walter put on his gas mask, and gestured to his men to follow suit, so that they would not be afflicted by their own poison fumes when they reached the other side. Then, at nine thirty, he stood up. He slung his rifle across his back and held a stick grenade in each hand, which was correct for advancing storm troopers. He could not shout orders, for no one could hear anything, so he gestured with his arm and then ran.

His men followed him into no-man's-land.

The ground was firm and dry: there had been no heavy rain for weeks. That was good for the attackers, making it easier to move men and vehicles.

They ran bent over. The German guns were firing over their heads. Walter's men understood the danger of being hit by their own shells falling short, especially in fog when artillery observers were unable to correct the gunners' aim. But it was worth the risk. This way they could get so close to the enemy trench that, when the bombardment ended, the British would not have time to get into position and set up their machine-gun posts before the storm troopers fell on them.

As they ran farther across no-man's-land, Walter hoped the other side's barbed wire had been destroyed by artillery. If not, his men would be delayed cutting it.

There was an explosion to his right, and he heard a scream. A moment later, a gleam on the ground caught his eye, and he spotted a trip wire. He was in a previously undetected minefield. A wave of pure panic swept over him as he realized that he might blow himself up with the next step. Then he got himself under control again. "Watch out underfoot!" he yelled, but his words were lost in the thunder of the guns. They ran on: the wounded had to be left for the medical teams, as always.

A moment later, at nine forty, the guns stopped.

Ludendorff had abandoned the old tactic of several days of artillery fire before an attack: it gave the enemy too much time to bring up reserves. Five hours was calculated to be enough to confuse and demoralize the enemy without permitting him to reorganize.

In theory, Walter thought.

He straightened up and ran faster. He was breathing hard but steadily, hardly sweating, alert but calm. Contact with the enemy was now seconds away.

He reached the British wire. It had not been destroyed, but there were gaps, and he led his men through.

The company and platoon commanders ordered the men to spread out again, using gestures rather than words: they might be near enough to be heard.

Now the fog was their friend, hiding them from the enemy, Walter thought with a little frisson of glee. At this point they might have expected to face the hell of machine-gun fire. But the British could not see them.

He came to an area where the ground had been completely churned up by German shells. At first he could see nothing but craters and mounds of earth. Then he saw a section of trench, and realized he had reached the British line. But it had been wrecked: the artillery had done a good job.

Was there anyone in the trench? No shots had been fired. But it was best to make sure. Walter pulled a pin from a grenade and tossed it into the trench as a precaution. After it had exploded he looked over the parapet. There were several men lying on the ground, none moving. Any who had not been killed earlier by the artillery had been finished off by the grenade.

Lucky so far, Walter thought. Don't expect it to last.

He ran along the line to check on the rest of his battalion. He saw half a dozen British soldiers surrendering, their hands on their steel soup-bowl helmets, their weapons abandoned. They looked well-fed by comparison with their German captors.

Lieutenant von Braun was pointing his rifle at the captives, but Walter did not want his officers wasting time dealing with prisoners. He pulled off his gas mask: the British were not wearing them. "Keep moving!" he shouted in English. "That way, that way." He pointed to the German lines. The British walked forward, eager to get away from the fighting and save their lives. "Let them go," he shouted at von Braun. "Rear echelons will deal with them. You must keep advancing." That was the whole idea of storm troopers.

He ran on. For several hundred yards the story was the same: destroyed trenches, enemy casualties, no real resistance. Then he heard machine-gun fire. A moment later he came upon a platoon that had taken cover in shell craters. He lay down beside the sergeant, a Bavarian called Schwab. "We can't see the emplacement," said Schwab. "We're shooting at the noise."

Schwab had not understood the tactics. Storm troopers were supposed to bypass strong points, leaving them to be mopped up by the following infantry. "Keep moving!" Walter ordered him. "Go around the machine gun." When there was a pause in the firing, he stood up and gestured to the men. "Come on! Up, up!" They obeyed. He led them away from the machine gun and across an empty trench.

He ran into Gottfried again. The lieutenant had a tin

of biscuits and was stuffing them into his mouth as he ran along. "Incredible!" he shouted. "You should see the British food!"

Walter knocked the tin out of his hands. "You're here to fight, not eat, you damn fool," he yelled. "Get going."

He was startled by something running over his foot. He saw a rabbit disappearing into the fog. No doubt the artillery had destroyed their warrens.

He checked his compass to make sure he was still heading west. He did not know whether the trenches he was encountering might be communication or supply trenches, so their orientation did not tell him much.

He knew that the British had followed the Germans in creating multiple lines of trenches. Having passed the first he expected soon to come upon a well-defended trench they called the Red Line, then—if he could break through that—another trench a mile or so farther west called the Brown Line.

After that, there was nothing but open country all the way to the west coast.

Shells exploded in the mist ahead. Surely the British could not be responsible? They would be firing on their own defenses. It must be the next wave of the German rolling barrage. He and his men were in danger of outstripping their own artillery. He turned. Fortunately most of his people were behind him. He raised his arms. "Take cover!" he shouted. "Spread the word!"

They hardly needed telling, having come to the same conclusion as he. They ran back a few yards and jumped into some empty trenches.

Walter felt elated. This was going remarkably well.

There were three British soldiers lying on the trench floor. Two were motionless, one groaning. Where were the rest? Perhaps they had fled. Alternatively, this might be a suicide squad, left to defend an indefensible position in order to give their retreating comrades a better chance.

One of the dead Brits was an unusually tall man with big hands and feet. Grunwald immediately removed the corpse's boots. "My size!" he said to Walter by way of explanation. Walter did not have the heart to stop him: Grunwald's own boots had holes in them.

He sat down to catch his breath. Reviewing the first

phase in his mind, he could not think how it could have gone better.

After an hour, the German guns fell silent again. Walter rallied the men and moved on.

Halfway up a long slope, he heard voices. He held up a hand to halt the men near him. Ahead, someone said in English: "I can't see a fucking dicky bird."

There was something familiar about the accent. Was it Australian? It sounded more like Indian.

Another voice said in the same accent: "If they can't see you, they can't bloody shoot you!"

In a flash Walter was transported back to 1914, and Fitz's big country house in Wales. This was how the servants there spoke. The men in front of him, here in this devastated French field, were Welsh.

Up above, the sky seemed to brighten a little.

{ III }

Sergeant Billy Williams peered into the fog. The artillery had stopped, mercifully, but that only meant the Germans were coming. What was he supposed to do?

He had no orders. His platoon occupied a redoubt, a defensive post on a rise some distance behind the front line. In normal weather their position commanded a wide view of a long, gradual downward slope to a pile of rubble that must once have been farm buildings. A trench linked them to other redoubts, now invisible. Orders normally came from the rear, but none had arrived today. The phone was dead, the line presumably cut by the barrage.

The men stood or sat in the trench. They had come out of the dugout when the shelling stopped. Sometimes the field kitchen sent a wheeled cart with a great urn of hot tea along the trench at midmorning, but there was no sign of refreshments today. They had eaten their iron rations for breakfast.

The platoon had an American-designed Lewis light machine gun. It stood on the back wall of the trench over the dugout. It was operated by nineteen-year-old George Barrow, the Borstal boy, a good soldier whose education was so poor he thought the last invader of England was called Norman the Conqueror. George was sitting behind his gun, protected from stray bullets by the steel breech assembly, smoking a pipe.

They also had a Stokes mortar, a useful weapon that fired a three-inch-diameter bomb up to eight hundred yards. Corporal Johnny Ponti, brother of the Joey Ponti who died at the Somme, had become lethally proficient with this.

Billy climbed up to the machine gun and stood beside George, but he could not see any farther.

George said to him: "Billy, do other countries have empires like us?"

"Aye," said Billy. "The French have most of North Africa. Then there's the Dutch East Indies, German South-West Africa . . ."

"Oh," said George, somewhat deflated. "I heard that, but I didn't think it could be true."

"Why not?"

"Well, what right have they got to rule over other people?"

"What right have *we* got to rule over Nigeria and Jamaica and India?"

"Because we're British."

Billy nodded. George Barrow, who evidently had never seen an atlas, felt superior to Descartes, Rembrandt, and Beethoven. And he was not unusual. They had all endured years of propaganda in school, telling them about every British military victory and none of the defeats. They were taught about democracy in London, not about tyranny in Cairo. When they learned about British justice, there was no mention of flogging in Australia, starvation in Ireland, or massacre in India. They learned that Catholics burned Protestants at the stake, and it came as a shock if they ever found out that Protestants did the same to Catholics whenever they got the chance. Few of them had a father like Billy's da to tell them that the world depicted by their schoolteachers was a fantasy.

But Billy had no time today to set George straight. He had other worries.

The sky brightened a little, and it seemed to Billy that the fog might be clearing; then, suddenly, it lifted com-

pletely. George said: "Bloody hell!" A split second later
Billy saw what had shocked him. A quarter of a mile away,
coming up the slope toward him, were several hundred
German soldiers.

Billy jumped down into the trench. A number of men
had spotted the enemy at the same time, and their surprised
exclamations alerted the others. Billy looked through a slit
in a steel panel set into the parapet. The Germans were
slower to react, probably because the British in their trench
were less conspicuous. One or two of them halted, but most
came running on.

A minute later there was a crackle of rifle fire up and
down the trench. Some of the Germans fell. The rest hurled
themselves to the ground, seeking cover in shell holes and
behind a few stunted bushes. Above Billy's head, the Lewis
gun opened up with a noise like a football supporter's rattle. After a minute the Germans began to return fire. They
appeared to have no machine guns or trench mortars, Billy
noted gratefully. He heard one of his own men scream: a
sharp-eyed German had spotted someone indiscreetly
looking over the parapet, perhaps; or, more likely, a lucky
shooter had hit an unlucky British head.

Tommy Griffiths appeared beside Billy. "Dai Powell got
it," he said.

"Wounded?"

"Dead. Shot through the head."

"Oh, bugger," said Billy. Mrs. Powell was a prodigious
knitter who sent pullovers to her son in France. Who would
she knit for now?

"I've took his collection from his pocket," Tommy said.
Dai had a stack of pornographic postcards he had bought
from a Frenchman. They showed plump girls with masses
of pubic hair. Most of the men in the battalion had borrowed them at one time or another.

"Why?" said Billy distractedly as he surveyed the enemy.

"Don't want them sent home to Aberowen."

"Oh, aye."

"What shall I do with them?"

"Bloody hell, Tommy, ask me later, will you? I've got
a few hundred fucking Germans to worry about at the
moment."

"Sorry, Bill."

How many Germans were out there? Numbers were hard to estimate on the battlefield, but Billy thought he had seen at least two hundred, and presumably there were others out of sight. He guessed he was facing a battalion. His platoon of forty men was hopelessly outnumbered.

What was he supposed to do?

He had not seen an officer for more than twenty-four hours. He was the senior man here. He was in charge. He needed a plan.

He was long past getting angry about the incompetence of his superior officers. That was all part of the class system he had been brought up to despise. But on the rare occasions when the burden of command fell on him, he took little pleasure in it. Rather, he felt the weight of responsibility and the fear that he might make the wrong decisions and cause the deaths of his comrades.

If the Germans attacked frontally, his platoon would be overwhelmed. But the enemy did not know how weak he was. Could he make it look as if he had more men?

The thought of retreat crossed his mind. But soldiers were not supposed to run away the minute they were attacked. This was a defensive post, and he ought to try to hold it.

He would stand and fight, at least for now.

Once he had made that decision, others followed. "Give them another drum, George!" he shouted. As the Lewis gun opened up he ran along the trench. "Keep up a steady fire, boys," he said. "Make them think there's hundreds of us."

He saw Dai Powell's body lying on the ground, the blood already turning black around the hole in his head. Dai was wearing one of his mother's sweaters under his uniform tunic. It was a hideous brown thing, but it had probably kept him warm. "Rest in peace, boyo," Billy murmured.

Farther along the trench he found Johnny Ponti. "Deploy that Stokes mortar, Johnny bach," he said. "Make the buggers jump."

"Right," said Johnny. He set up his two-legged gun mount on the floor of the trench. "What's the range, five hundred yards?"

Johnny's partner was the pudding-faced boy called Suet Hewitt. He jumped up on the fire step and called back: "Aye, five to six hundred." Billy took a look for himself, but

Suet and Johnny had worked together before and he left the decision to them.

"Two rings, then, at forty-five degrees," said Johnny. The self-propelling bombs could be fitted with additional charges of propellant in rings to extend their range.

Johnny jumped up on the fire step for another look at the Germans, then adjusted his aim. The other soldiers in the vicinity stood well to the side. Johnny dropped a bomb in the barrel. When it hit the bottom of the barrel, a firing pin ignited the propellant and it was fired.

The bomb fell short and exploded some distance from the nearest enemy soldiers. "Fifty yards farther, and a touch to your right," Suet shouted.

Johnny made the adjustments and fired again. The second bomb landed in a shell hole where some Germans were sheltering. "That's it!" shouted Suet.

Billy could not see whether any of the enemy had been hit, but the firing was forcing them to keep their heads down. "Give them a dozen like that!" he said.

He came up behind Robin Mortimer, the cashiered officer, who was on the fire step shooting rhythmically. Mortimer stopped to reload, and caught Billy's eye. "Get some more ammo, Taffy," he said. As always, his tone was surly even when he was being helpful. "You don't want everyone to run out at the same time."

Billy nodded. "Good idea. Thanks." The ammunition store was a hundred yards to the rear along a communication trench. He picked out two recruits who could hardly shoot straight anyway. "Jenkins and Nosey, bring up more ammo, double quick." The two lads hurried away.

Billy took another look through the parapet peephole. As he did so, one of the Germans stood up. Billy guessed it might be their commanding officer about to launch an attack. His heart sank. They must have guessed they were up against no more than a few dozen men, and realized they could easily overwhelm them.

But he was wrong. The officer gestured to rearward, then began to run downhill. His men followed suit. Billy's platoon cheered and fired wildly at the running men, bringing down a few more before they got out of range.

The Germans reached the ruined farm buildings and took cover in the rubble.

Billy could not help grinning. He had driven off a force ten times the size of his own! I should be a bloody general, he thought. "Hold your fire!" he shouted. "They're out of range."

Jenkins and Nosey reappeared, carrying ammunition boxes. "Keep going, lads," Billy said. "They may be back."

But, when he looked out again, he saw that the Germans had a different plan. They had split into two groups and were heading left and right away from the ruins. As Billy watched, they began to circle around his position, staying out of range. "Oh, bugger," he said. They were going to slip between his position and neighboring redoubts, then come at him from both sides. Or, alternatively, they might bypass him, leaving him to be mopped up by their rearguard.

Either way, this position was going to fall to the enemy.

"Take down the machine gun, George," Billy said. "And you, Johnny, dismantle the mortar. Pick up your stuff, everyone. We're falling back."

They slung their rifles and backpacks, hurried to the nearest communication trench, and began to run.

Billy looked into the dugout to make sure there was no one inside. He pulled the pin out of a grenade and threw it in, to deny any remaining supplies to the enemy.

Then he followed his men into retreat.

{ IV }

At the end of the afternoon, Walter and his battalion were in possession of a rearward line of British trenches.

He was weary but triumphant. The battalion had had a few fierce skirmishes but no sustained battle. The storm troopers' tactics had worked even better than expected, thanks to the fog. They had wiped out weak opposition, bypassed strong points, and taken a great deal of ground.

Walter found a dugout and ducked into it. Several of his men followed. The place had a homely look, as if the Brits had been living there for some months: there were magazine pictures nailed to the walls, a typewriter on an upturned box, cutlery and crockery in old cake tins, and even a blanket spread like a tablecloth on a stack of crates. Walter guessed this had been a battalion headquarters.

His men immediately found the food. There were crackers, jam, cheese, and ham. He could not stop them eating, but he did forbid them to open any of the bottles of whisky. They broke open a locked cupboard and found a jar of coffee, and one of the men made a small fire outside and brewed a pot. He gave Walter a cup, adding sweetened milk from a can. It tasted heavenly.

Sergeant Schwab said: "I read in the newspaper that the British were short of food, just as we are." He held up the tin of jam he was eating with a spoon. "Some shortage!"

Walter had been wondering how long it would take them to work that out. He had long suspected the German authorities of exaggerating the effect of submarine war on Allied supplies. Now he knew the truth, and so did the men. Food was rationed in Britain, but the Brits did not look as if they were starving to death. The Germans did.

He found a map carelessly left behind by the retreating forces. Comparing it with his own, he saw that he was not far from the Crozat Canal. That meant that in one day the Germans had taken back all the territory so painfully won by the Allies during the five months of the Battle of the Somme the year before last.

Victory really was within the Germans' grasp.

Walter sat down at the British typewriter and began to compose his report.

CHAPTER THIRTY

Late March and April 1918

Fitz held a house party at Tŷ Gwyn over the Easter weekend. He had an ulterior motive. The men he invited were as violently opposed as he was to the new regime in Russia.

His star guest was Winston Churchill.

Winston was a member of the Liberal Party, and might have been expected to sympathize with the revolutionaries; but he was also the grandson of a duke, and he had an authoritarian streak. Fitz had long thought of him as a traitor to his class, but was now inclined to forgive him because his hatred of the Bolsheviks was passionate.

Winston arrived on Good Friday. Fitz sent the Rolls-Royce to Aberowen Station to meet him. He came bouncing into the morning room, a small, slight figure with red hair and a pink complexion. There was rain on his boots. He wore a well-cut suit of wheat-colored tweed and a bow tie the same blue as his eyes. He was forty-three, but there was still something boyish about him as he nodded to acquaintances and shook hands with guests he did not know.

Looking around at the linenfold paneling, the patterned wallpaper, the carved stone fireplace, and the dark oak furniture, he said: "Your house is decorated like the Palace of Westminster, Fitz!"

He had reason to be ebullient. He was back in the government. Lloyd George had made him minister of munitions. There was much talk about why the prime minister had brought back such a troublesome and unpredictable colleague, and the consensus was that he preferred to have Churchill inside the tent spitting out.

"Your coal miners support the Bolsheviks," Winston said, half-amused and half-disgusted, as he sat down and stretched his wet boots to the roaring coal fire. "There were red flags flying from half the houses I passed."

"They have no idea what they're cheering for," Fitz said with contempt. Beneath his scorn he was deeply anxious.

Winston accepted a cup of tea from Maud and took a buttered muffin from a plate offered by a footman. "You've suffered a personal loss, I gather."

"The peasants killed my brother-in-law, Prince Andrei, and his wife."

"I'm very sorry."

"Bea and I happened to be there at the time, and escaped by the skin of our teeth."

"So I heard!"

"The villagers have taken over his land—a very large estate that is rightfully the inheritance of my son—and the new regime has endorsed such theft."

"I'm afraid so. The first thing Lenin did was to pass his Decree on Land."

Maud said: "In fairness, Lenin has also announced an eight-hour day for workers and universal free education for their children."

Fitz was annoyed. Maud had no tact. This was not the moment to defend Lenin.

But Winston was a match for her. "And a Decree on the Press which bans newspapers from opposing the government," he shot back. "So much for socialist freedom."

"My son's birthright is not the only reason, or even the main reason, why I'm so concerned," Fitz said. "If the Bolsheviks get away with what they've done in Russia, where next? Welsh miners already believe the coal found deep underground doesn't really belong to the man who owns the land on the surface. You can hear 'The Red Flag' sung in half the pubs in Wales on any given Saturday night."

"The Bolshevik regime should be strangled at birth," Winston said. He looked thoughtful. "Strangled at birth," he repeated, pleased with the expression.

Fitz controlled his impatience. Sometimes Winston imagined he had devised a policy when all he had done was coin a phrase. "But we're doing nothing!" Fitz said in exasperation.

The gong sounded to tell everyone it was time to change for dinner. Fitz did not persist with the conversation: he had all weekend to make his point.

On his way to his dressing room it struck him that, contrary to custom, Boy had not been brought down to the morning room at teatime. Before changing, he walked down a long corridor to the nursery wing.

Boy was now three years and three months old, no longer a baby or even a toddler, but a walking, talking boy with Bea's blue eyes and blond curls. He was sitting near the fire, wrapped in a blanket, and pretty, young Nurse Jones was reading to him. The rightful lord of thousands of acres of Russian farmland was sucking his thumb. He did not jump up and run to Fitz as he normally would. "What's wrong with him?" Fitz said.

"He's got a bad tummy, my lord."

Nurse Jones reminded Fitz a bit of Ethel Williams, but she was not as bright. "Try to be more exact," Fitz said impatiently. "What is wrong with his stomach?"

"He have got the diarrhea."

"How the dickens did he get that?"

"I don't know. The toilet on the train was not very clean . . ."

That made it Fitz's fault, for dragging his family down to Wales for this house party. He suppressed a curse. "Have you summoned a doctor?"

"Dr. Mortimer is on his way."

Fitz told himself not to be so fretful. Children suffered minor infections all the time. How often had he himself had a bad tummy as a child? Yet children did, sometimes, die of gastroenteritis.

He knelt in front of the sofa, bringing himself down to his son's level. "How's my little soldier?"

Boy's tone was lethargic. "I got the trots."

He must have picked up that vulgar expression from the servants—indeed, there was the hint of a Welsh lilt in the way he said it. But Fitz decided not to make a fuss about that now. "The doctor will be here soon," he said. "He'll make you better."

"I don't want a bath."

"Perhaps you can skip your bath tonight." Fitz got up.

"Send for me when the doctor arrives," he said to Nurse. "I'd like to speak to the fellow myself."

"Very good, my lord."

He left the nursery and went to his dressing room. His valet had laid out his evening clothes, with the diamond studs in the shirtfront and the matching cuff links in the sleeves, a clean linen handkerchief in the coat pocket, and one silk sock placed inside each patent-leather shoe.

Before getting changed he went through to Bea's room.

She was eight months pregnant.

He had not seen her in this state when she was expecting Boy. He had left for France in August 1914, when she was only four or five months along, and he had not returned until after Boy had been born. He had not previously witnessed this spectacular swelling, nor marveled at the body's shocking ability to change and stretch.

She was sitting at her dressing table but not looking in the glass. She was leaning back, her legs apart, her hands resting on the bulge. Her eyes were closed and she looked pale. "I just can't get comfortable," she complained. "Standing, sitting, lying down, everything hurts."

"You ought to go along to the nursery and take a look at Boy."

"I will as soon as I can summon up the energy!" she snapped. "I should never have traveled to the country. It's ridiculous for me to host a house party in this state."

Fitz knew she was right. "But we need the support of these men if we're to do anything about the Bolsheviks."

"Is Boy's tummy still poorly?"

"Yes. The doctor is coming."

"You'd better send him to me while he's here—not that a country doctor is likely to know much."

"I'll tell the staff. I take it you won't be coming down to dinner."

"How can I, when I feel like this?"

"I was just asking. Maud can sit at the head of the table."

Fitz returned to his dressing room. Some men had abandoned tailcoats and white ties, and wore short tuxedo jackets and black ties at dinner, citing the war as their excuse. Fitz did not see the connection. Why should war oblige people to dress informally?

He put on his evening clothes and went downstairs.

{ II }

After dinner, as coffee was served in the drawing room, Winston said provocatively: "So, Lady Maud, you women have got the vote at last."

"Some of us have," she said.

Fitz knew she was disappointed that the bill had included only women over thirty who were householders or the wives of householders. Fitz himself was angry that it had passed at all.

Churchill went on mischievously: "You must thank, in part, Lord Curzon here, who surprisingly abstained when the bill went to the House of Lords."

Earl Curzon was a brilliant man whose stiffly superior air was made worse by a metal corset he wore for his back. There was a rhyme about him:

> *I am George Nathaniel Curzon*
> *I am a most superior person*

He had been viceroy of India and was now leader of the House of Lords and one of the five members of the War Cabinet. He was also president of the League for Opposing Woman Suffrage, so his abstention had astonished the political world and severely disappointed the opponents of votes for women, not least Fitz.

"The bill had been passed by the House of Commons," Curzon said. "I felt we could not defy elected members of Parliament."

Fitz was still annoyed about this. "But the Lords exist to scrutinize the decisions of the Commons, and to curb their excesses. Surely this was an exemplary case!"

"If we had voted down the bill, I believe the Commons would have taken umbrage and sent it back to us again."

Fitz shrugged. "We've had that kind of dispute before."

"But unfortunately the Bryce Committee is sitting."

"Oh!" Fitz had not thought of that. The Bryce Committee was considering the reform of the House of Lords. "So that was it?"

"They're due to report shortly. We can't afford a stand-up fight with the Commons before then."

"No." With great reluctance, Fitz had to concede the point. If the Lords made a serious attempt to defy the Commons, Bryce might recommend curbing the power of the upper chamber. "We might have lost all our influence—permanently."

"That is precisely the calculation that led me to abstain."

Sometimes Fitz found politics depressing.

Peel, the butler, brought Curzon a cup of coffee, and murmured to Fitz: "Dr. Mortimer is in the small study, my lord, awaiting your convenience."

Fitz had been worrying about Boy's stomachache, and welcomed the interruption. "I'd better see him," said Fitz. He excused himself and went out.

The small study was furnished with pieces that did not fit anywhere else in the house: an uncomfortable Gothic carved chair, a Scottish landscape no one liked, and the head of a tiger Fitz's father had shot in India.

Mortimer was a competent local physician who had a rather too confident air, as if he thought his profession made him in some way the equal of an earl. However, he was polite enough. "Good evening, my lord," he said. "Your son has a mild gastric infection, which will most likely do him no harm."

"Most likely?"

"I use the phrase deliberately." Mortimer spoke with a Welsh accent that had been moderated by education. "We scientists deal always in probabilities, never certainties. I tell your miners that they go down the pit every morning knowing there will *probably* be no explosion."

"Hmm." That was not much comfort to Fitz. "Did you see the princess?"

"I did. She, too, is not seriously ill. In fact she is not ill at all, but she is giving birth."

Fitz leaped up. "What?"

"She thought she was eight months pregnant, but she miscalculated. She is nine months pregnant, and happily will not continue pregnant many more hours."

"Who is with her?"

"Her servants are all around her. I have sent for a competent midwife, and I myself will attend the birth if you so wish."

"This is my fault," Fitz said bitterly. "I should not have persuaded her to leave London."

"Perfectly healthy babies are born outside London every day."

Fitz had a feeling he was being mocked, but he ignored it. "What if something should go wrong?"

"I know the reputation of your London doctor, Professor Rathbone. He is of course a physician of great distinction, but I think I can safely say that I have delivered more babies than he has."

"Miners' babies."

"Indeed, most of them; though at the moment of birth there is no apparent difference between them and the little aristocrats."

Fitz *was* being mocked. "I don't like your cheek," he said.

Mortimer was not intimidated. "I don't like yours," he said. "You've made it clear, without even a semblance of courtesy, that you consider me inadequate to treat your family. I will gladly take my leave." He picked up his bag.

Fitz sighed. This was a foolish quarrel. He was angry with the Bolsheviks, not with this touchy middle-class Welshman. "Don't be a fool, man."

"I try not to be." Mortimer went to the door.

"Aren't you supposed to put the interests of your patients first?"

Mortimer stopped at the door. "My God, you've got a bloody nerve, Fitzherbert."

Few people had ever talked to Fitz that way. But he suppressed the scathing retort that came to mind. It might take hours to find another doctor. Bea would never forgive him if he let Mortimer leave in a huff. "I'll forget you said that," Fitz said. "In fact I'll forget this whole conversation, if you will."

"I suppose that's the nearest thing to an apology that I'm likely to get."

It was, but Fitz said nothing.

"I'll go back upstairs," said the doctor.

{ III }

Princess Bea did not give birth quietly. Her screams could be heard throughout the principal wing of the house, where her room was. Maud played piano rags very loudly, to entertain the guests and drown out the noise, but one piano rag was much like the next, and she gave up after twenty minutes. Some of the guests went to bed, but as midnight struck, most of the men congregated in the billiard room. Peel offered cognac.

Fitz gave Winston an El Rey del Mundo cigar from Cuba. While Winston was getting it alight, Fitz said: "The government must do something about the Bolsheviks."

Winston glanced quickly around the room, as if to make sure that everyone present was completely trustworthy. Then he sat back in his chair and said: "Here is the situation. The British Northern Squadron is already in Russian waters off Murmansk. In theory their task is to make sure Russian ships there don't fall into German hands. We also have a small mission in Archangel. I'm pressing for troops to be landed at Murmansk. Longerterm, this could be the core of a counterrevolutionary force in northern Russia."

"It's not enough," Fitz said immediately.

"I agree. I'd like us to send troops to Baku, on the Caspian Sea, to make sure those vast oil fields are not taken over by the Germans, or indeed the Turks, and to the Black Sea, where there is already the nucleus of an anti-Bolshevik resistance in the Ukraine. Finally, in Siberia, we have thousands of tons of supplies at Vladivostok, worth perhaps a billion pounds, intended to support the Russians when they were our allies. We are entitled to send troops there to protect our property."

Fitz spoke half in doubt and half in hope. "Will Lloyd George do any of this?"

"Not publicly," said Winston. "The problem is those red flags flying from miners' houses. There is in our country a great well of support for the Russian people and their revolution. And I understand why, much as I loathe Lenin and his crew. With all due respect to the family of Princess Bea"—he glanced up at the ceiling as another scream began—"it cannot be denied that the Russian ruling class were slow to deal with their people's discontents."

Winston was an odd mix, Fitz thought: aristocrat and man of the people, a brilliant administrator who could never resist meddling in other people's departments, a charmer who was disliked by most of his political colleagues.

Fitz said: "The Russian revolutionaries are thieves and murderers."

"Indeed. But we have to live with the fact that not everyone sees them that way. So our prime minister cannot openly oppose the revolution."

"There's not much point in his opposing it in his mind," Fitz said impatiently.

"A certain amount may be done without his knowing about it, officially."

"I see." Fitz did not know whether that meant much.

Maud came into the room. The men stood up, a bit startled. In a country house women did not usually enter the billiard room. Maud ignored rules that did not suit her convenience. She came up to Fitz and kissed his cheek. "Congratulations, dear Fitz," she said. "You have another son."

The men cheered and clapped and gathered around Fitz, slapping him on the back and shaking his hand. "Is my wife all right?" he asked Maud.

"Exhausted but proud."

"Thank God."

"Dr. Mortimer has left, but the midwife says you may go and see the baby now."

Fitz went to the door.

Winston said: "I'll walk up with you."

As they left the room, Fitz heard Maud say: "Pour me some brandy, please, Peel."

In a lowered voice, Winston said: "You've been to Russia, of course, and you speak the language."

Fitz wondered where this was leading. "A bit," he said. "Nothing to boast about, but I can make myself understood."

"Have you come across a chap called Mansfield Smith-Cumming?"

"As it happens, I have. He runs ..." Fitz hesitated to mention the Secret Intelligence Service out loud. "He runs a special department. I've written a couple of reports for him."

"Ah, good. When you get back to town, you might have a word with him."

Now that *was* interesting. "I'll see him at any time, of course," said Fitz, trying not to show his eagerness.

"I'll ask him to get in touch. He may have another mission for you."

They were at the door to Bea's rooms. From inside, there came the distinctive cry of a newborn baby. Fitz was ashamed to feel tears come to his eyes. "I'd better go in," he said. "Good night."

"Congratulations, and a good night to you, too."

{ IV }

They named him Andrew Alexander Murray Fitzherbert. He was a tiny scrap of life with a shock of hair as black as Fitz's. They took him to London wrapped in blankets, traveling in the Rolls-Royce with two other cars following in case of breakdowns. They stopped for breakfast in Chepstow and lunch in Oxford, and reached their home in Mayfair in time for dinner.

A few days later, on a mild April afternoon, Fitz walked along the Embankment, looking at the muddy water of the river Thames, heading for a meeting with Mansfield Smith-Cumming.

The Secret Service had outgrown its flat in Victoria. The man called "C" had moved his expanding organization into a swanky Victorian building called Whitehall Court, on the river within sight of Big Ben. A private lift took Fitz to the top floor, where the spymaster occupied two apartments linked by a walkway on the roof.

"We've been watching Lenin for years," said C. "If we fail to depose him, he will be one of the worst tyrants the world has ever known."

"I believe you're right." Fitz was relieved that C felt the same as he did about the Bolsheviks. "But what can we do?"

"Let's talk about what you might do." C took from his desk a pair of steel dividers such as were used for measuring distances on maps. As if absentmindedly, he thrust the point into his left leg.

Fitz was able to check the cry of shock that came to his lips. This was a test, of course. He recalled that C had a wooden leg as a result of a car crash. He smiled. "A good trick," he said. "I almost fell for it."

C put down the dividers and looked hard at Fitz through his monocle. "There is a Cossack leader in Siberia who has overthrown the local Bolshevik regime," he said. "I need to know if it's worth our while to support him."

Fitz was startled. "Openly?"

"Of course not. But I have secret funds. If we can sustain a kernel of counterrevolutionary government in the east, it will merit the expenditure of, say, ten thousand pounds a month."

"Name?"

"Captain Semenov, twenty-eight years old. He's based in Manchuli, which lies astride the Chinese Eastern Railway near its junction with the Trans-Siberian Express."

"So this Captain Semenov controls one railway line and could control another."

"Exactly. And he hates the Bolsheviks."

"So we need to find out more about him."

"Which is where you come in."

Fitz was delighted at the chance of helping to overthrow Lenin. He thought of many questions: How was he to find Semenov? The man was a Cossack, and they were notorious for shooting first and asking questions later: would he talk to Fitz, or kill him? Of course Semenov would claim he could defeat the Bolsheviks, but would Fitz be able to assess the reality? Was there any way to ensure he would be spending British money to good effect?

The question he asked was: "Am I the right choice? Forgive me, but I'm a conspicuous figure, hardly anonymous even in Russia . . ."

"Frankly, we don't have a wide choice. We need someone fairly high-level in case you get to the stage of negotiating with Semenov. And there aren't many thoroughly trustworthy men who speak Russian. Believe me, you're the best available."

"I see."

"It will be dangerous, of course."

Fitz recalled the crowd of peasants battering Andrei to death. That could be him. He repressed a fearful shudder. "I understand the danger," he said in a level voice.

"So tell me: will you go to Vladivostok?"

"Of course," said Fitz.

CHAPTER THIRTY-ONE

May to September 1918

Gus Dewar did not take easily to soldiering. He was a gangling, awkward figure, and he had trouble marching and saluting and stamping his feet the army way. As for exercise, he had not done physical jerks since his school days. His friends, who knew of his liking for flowers on the dining table and linen sheets on his bed, had felt the army would come as a terrible shock. Chuck Dixon, who went through officer training with him, said: "Gus, at home you don't even run your own bath."

But Gus survived. At the age of eleven he had been sent to boarding school, so it was nothing new to him to be persecuted by bullies and ordered about by stupid superiors. He suffered a certain amount of mockery because of his wealthy background and careful good manners, but he bore it patiently.

In vigorous action, Chuck commented with surprise, Gus revealed a certain lanky grace, previously seen only on the tennis court. "You look like a goddamn giraffe," Chuck said, "but you run like one, too." Gus also did well at boxing, because of his long reach, although his sergeant instructor told him, regretfully, that he lacked the killer instinct.

Unfortunately, he turned out to be a terrible shot.

He wanted to do well in the army, partly because he knew people thought he could not hack it. He needed to prove to them, and perhaps to himself, that he was no wimp. But he had another reason. He believed in what he was fighting for.

President Wilson had made a speech, to Congress and the Senate, that had rung like a clarion around the world. He had called for nothing less than a new world order. "A general association of nations must be formed under specific covenants for the purpose of affording mutual guarantees of political independence and territorial integrity to great and small states alike."

A league of nations was a dream for Wilson, for Gus, and for many others—including, rather surprisingly, Sir Edward Grey, who had originated the idea while he was British foreign secretary.

Wilson had set out his program in fourteen points. He had spoken of reductions in armaments; the right of colonial people to a say in their own future; and freedom for the Balkan states, Poland, and the subject peoples of the Ottoman Empire. The speech had become known as Wilson's Fourteen Points. Gus envied the men who had helped the president write it. In the old days he would have had a hand in it himself.

"An evident principle runs through the whole program," Wilson had said. "It is the principle of justice to all peoples and nationalities, and their right to live on equal terms of liberty and safety with one another, whether they be strong or weak." Tears had come to Gus's eyes when he had read these words. "The people of the United States could act upon no other principle," Wilson had said.

Was it really possible that the nations could settle their arguments without war? Paradoxically, that was something worth fighting for.

Gus and Chuck and their machine-gun battalion traveled from Hoboken, New Jersey, on the *Corinna,* once a luxury liner, now converted to troop transport. The trip took two weeks. As second lieutenants, they shared a cabin on an upper deck. Although they had once been rivals for the affection of Olga Vyalov, they had become friends.

The ship was part of a convoy, with a navy escort, and the voyage was uneventful, except that several men died of Spanish flu, a new illness that was sweeping the world. The food was poor: the men said the Germans had given up submarine warfare and now aimed to win by poisoning them.

The *Corinna* waited a day and a half off Brest, on the northwest tip of France. They disembarked onto a dock crowded with men, vehicles, and stores, noisy with shouted orders and revving engines, busy with impatient officers and sweating stevedores. Gus made the mistake of asking a sergeant on the dock what the reason for the delay was. "Delay, sir?" he said, managing to make the word "sir" sound like an insult. "Yesterday we disembarked five thousand men, with their cars, guns, tents, and field kitchens, and transferred them to rail and road transport. Today we will disembark another five thousand, and the same tomorrow. There is no delay, sir. This is fucking fast."

Chuck grinned at Gus and murmured: "That's told you."

The stevedores were colored soldiers. Wherever black and white soldiers had to share facilities, there was trouble, usually caused by white recruits from the Deep South; so the army had given in. Rather than mix the races on the front line, the army assigned colored regiments to menial tasks in the rear. Gus knew that Negro soldiers complained bitterly about this: they wanted to fight for their country like everyone else.

Most of the regiment went on from Brest by train. They were not given passenger carriages, but crammed into a cattle truck. Gus amused the men by translating the sign on the side of a railcar: "Forty men or eight horses." However, the machine-gun battalion had its own vehicles, so Gus and Chuck went by road to their camp south of Paris.

In the States they had practiced trench warfare with wooden rifles, but now they had real weapons and ammunition. Gus and Chuck, as officers, had each been issued a Colt M1911 semiautomatic pistol with a seven-round magazine in the grip. Before leaving the States they had thrown away their Mountie-style hats and replaced them with more practical caps with a distinctive fore-and-aft ridge. They also had steel helmets the same soup-bowl shape as the British.

Now blue-coated French instructors trained them to fight in cooperation with heavy artillery, a skill the United States Army had not previously needed. Gus could speak French, so inevitably he was assigned to liaison duties. Relations between the two nationalities were good, though the French complained that the price of brandy went up as soon as the doughboys arrived.

The German offensive had continued successfully through April. Ludendorff had advanced so fast in Flanders that General Haig said the British had their backs to the wall—a phrase that sent shock waves through the Americans.

Gus was in no hurry to see action, but Chuck became impatient in the training camp. What were they doing, he wanted to know, rehearsing mock battles when they ought to be fighting real ones? The nearest section of German front was at the champagne city of Rheims, northeast of Paris; but Gus's commanding officer, Colonel Wagner, told him that Allied intelligence was confident there would be no German offensive in that sector.

In that prediction, however, Allied intelligence was dead wrong.

{ II }

Walter was jubilant. Casualties were high, but Ludendorff's strategy was working. The Germans were attacking where the enemy was weak, moving fast, leaving strong points behind to be mopped up later. Despite some clever defensive moves by General Foch, the new supreme commander of the Allied armies, the Germans were gaining territory faster than at any time since 1914.

The biggest problem was that the advance was held up every time German troops overran stocks of food. They just stopped and ate, and Walter found it impossible to get them to move until they were full. It was the strangest thing to see men sitting on the ground, sucking raw eggs, stuffing their faces with cake and ham at the same time, or guzzling bottles of wine, while shells landed around them and bullets whistled over their heads. He knew that other officers had the same experience. Some tried threatening the men with handguns, but even that would not persuade them to leave the food and run on.

That aside, the spring offensive was a triumph. Walter and his men were exhausted, after four years of war, but so were the French and British soldiers they encountered.

After the Somme and Flanders, Ludendorff's third attack of 1918 was planned for the sector between Rheims and Soissons. Here the Allies held a ridge called the Chemin des Dames, the Ladies' Way—so named because the road along it had been built for the daughters of Louis XV to visit a friend.

The final deployment took place on Sunday, May 26, a sunny day with a fresh northeasterly breeze. Once again, Walter felt proud as he watched the columns of men marching to the front line, the thousands of guns being maneuvered into position under harassing fire from French artillery, the telephone lines being laid from the command dugouts to the battery positions.

Ludendorff's tactics remained the same. That night at two a.m. thousands of guns opened up, firing gas, shrapnel, and explosives into the French lines on the summit of the ridge. Walter noticed with satisfaction that the French firing slackened off immediately, indicating that the German guns were hitting their targets. The barrage was short, in line with the new thinking, and at five forty a.m. it stopped.

The storm troopers advanced.

The Germans were attacking uphill, but despite that they met little resistance, and to Walter's surprise and delight he reached the road along the top of the ridge in less than an hour. It was now clear daylight, and he could see the French retreating all along the downhill slope.

The storm troopers followed at a steady speed, keeping pace with the rolling barrage of the artillery, but all the same they reached the river Aisne, in the cleft of the valley, before midday. Some farmers had destroyed their reaping machines and burned the early crops in their barns, but most had left in too much of a hurry, and there were rich rewards for the requisition parties in the rear of the German forces. To Walter's astonishment, the retreating French had not even blown up the bridges over the Aisne. That suggested they were panicking.

Walter's five hundred men advanced across the next ridge during the afternoon, and made camp on the far side of the river Vesle, having advanced twelve miles in a single day.

Next day they paused, waiting for reinforcements, but on the third day they advanced again, and on the fourth day, Thursday, May 30, having gained an amazing thirty miles since Monday, they reached the north bank of the river Marne.

Here, Walter recalled ominously, the German advance had been halted in 1914.

He vowed it would not happen again.

{ III }

Gus was with the American Expeditionary Force at the Chateauvillain training area south of Paris on May 30 when the Third Division was ordered to help with the defense of the river Marne. Most of the division began to entrain, even though the battered French railway system might take several days to move them. However, Gus and Chuck and the machine guns set off by road immediately.

Gus was excited and fearful. This was not like boxing, where there was a referee to enforce the rules and stop the fight if it got dangerous. How would he act when someone actually fired a weapon at him? Would he turn and run away? What would prevent him? He generally did the logical thing.

Cars were as unreliable as trains, and numerous vehicles broke down or ran out of gas. In addition they were delayed by civilians traveling in the opposite direction, fleeing the battle, some driving herds of cows, others with their possessions in handcarts and wheelbarrows.

Seventeen machine guns arrived at the leafy small town of Château-Thierry, fifty miles east of Paris, at six p.m. on Friday. It was a pretty little place in the evening sunshine. It straddled the Marne, with two bridges linking the southern suburb with the northern town center. The French held both banks, but the leading edge of the German advance had reached the northern city limits.

Gus's battalion was ordered to set up its armament along the south bank, commanding the bridges. Their crews were equipped with M1914 Hotchkiss heavy machine guns, each mounted on a sturdy tripod, fed by articulated metal cartridge belts holding 250 rounds. They also had rifle grenades, fired at a forty-five-degree angle from a bipod, and a few trench mortars of the British "Stokes" pattern.

As the sun set, Gus and Chuck were supervising the emplacement of their platoons between the two bridges. No training had prepared them to make these decisions: they just had to use their common sense. Gus picked a three-story building with a shuttered café on the ground floor. He broke in through the back door and climbed the stairs. There was a clear view from an attic window across the river and along a northward-leading street on the far side. He ordered a heavy machine-gun squad to set up there. He waited for the sergeant to tell him that was a stupid idea, but the man nodded approval and set about the task.

Gus placed three more machine guns in similar locations.

Looking for suitable cover for mortars, he found a brick boathouse on the riverbank, but was not sure whether it was in his sector or Chuck's, so he went looking for his friend to check. He spotted Chuck a hundred yards along the bank, near the east bridge, peering across the water through field glasses. He took two steps that way; then there was a terrific bang.

He turned in the direction of the noise, and in the next second there were several more deafening crashes. He realized the German artillery had opened up when a shell burst in the river, sending up a plume of water.

He looked again to where Chuck stood, just in time to see his friend disappear in an explosion of earth.

"Jesus Christ!" he said, and he ran toward the spot.

Shells and mortars burst all along the south bank. The men threw themselves flat. Gus reached the place where he had last seen Chuck and looked around in bewilderment. He saw nothing but piles of earth and stone. Then he spotted an arm poking out from the rubble. He moved a stone aside and found, to his horror, that the arm was not attached to a body.

Was it Chuck's arm? There had to be a way to tell, but Gus was too shocked to think how. He used the toe of his boot to push some loose earth aside ineffectually. Then he went down on his knees and began to dig with his hands. He saw a tan collar with a metal disc marked "US" and he groaned: "Oh, God." He quickly uncovered Chuck's face. There was no movement, no breath, no heartbeat.

He tried to remember what he was supposed to do next. Whom should he contact about a death? Something had to be done with the body, but what? Normally you would summon an undertaker.

He looked up to see a sergeant and two corporals staring at him. A mortar exploded on the street behind them, and they all ducked their heads reflexively, then looked at him again. They were waiting for his orders.

He stood up abruptly, and some of the training came back. It was not his job to deal with dead comrades, or even wounded ones. He was alive and well, and his duty was to fight. He felt a surge of irrational anger against the Germans who had killed Chuck. Hell, he thought, I'm going to fight back. He remembered what he had been doing: deploying the guns. He should get on with that. He would now have to take charge of Chuck's platoon as well.

He pointed at the sergeant in charge of the mortars. "Forget the boathouse—it's too exposed," he said. He pointed across the street to a narrow alleyway between a winery and livery stables. "Set up three mortars in that alley."

"Yes, sir." The sergeant hurried off.

Gus looked along the street. "See that flat roof, Corporal? Put a machine gun there."

"Sir, pardon me, that's an automobile repair shop—there may be a fuel tank below."

"Damn, you're right. Well spotted, Corporal. The tower of that church, then. Nothing but hymn books under that."

"Yes, sir, much better. Thank you, sir."

"The rest of you, follow me. We'll take cover while I figure out where to put everything else."

He led them across the road and down a side street. A narrow pathway or lane ran along the backs of the buildings. A shell landed in the yard of an establishment selling farm supplies, showering Gus with clouds of powdered fertilizer, as if to remind him that he was not out of range.

He hurried along the lane, trying when he could to shelter from the barrage behind walls, barking orders at his NCOs, deploying his machine guns in the tallest and most solid-looking structures and his mortars in the gardens between houses. Occasionally his subordinates made suggestions or disagreed with him. He listened, then made quick decisions.

In no time it was dark, making the job harder. The Germans sent a storm of ordnance across the town, much of it accurately aimed at the American position on the south bank. Several buildings were destroyed, making the waterfront street look like a mouthful of bad teeth. Gus lost three machine guns to shelling in the first few hours.

It was midnight before he was able to return to battalion headquarters, in a sewing-machine factory a few streets south. Colonel Wagner was with his French opposite number, poring over a large-scale map of the town. Gus reported that all his guns and Chuck's were in position. "Good work, Dewar," the colonel said. "Are you all right?"

"Of course, sir," Gus said, puzzled and a bit offended, thinking the colonel might believe he did not have the nerve for this work.

"It's just that there's blood all over you."

"Is there?" Gus looked down and saw that there was indeed a good deal of congealed blood on the front of his uniform. "I wonder where that came from."

"From your face, by the look of it. You've got a nasty cut."

Gus felt his cheek, and winced as his fingers touched raw flesh. "I don't know when that happened," he said.

"Go along to the dressing station and get it cleaned up."

"It's nothing much, sir. I'd rather—"

"Do as you're told, Lieutenant. It will be serious if it gets infected." The colonel gave a thin smile. "I don't want to lose you. You seem to have the makings of a useful officer."

{ IV }

At four o'clock the next morning the Germans launched a gas barrage. Walter and his storm troopers approached the northern edge of the town at sunrise, expecting the resistance from the French forces to be as weak as it had been for the past two months.

They would have preferred to bypass Château-Thierry, but it was not possible. The railway line to Paris went through the town, and there were two key bridges. It had to be taken.

Farmhouses and fields gave way to cottages and smallholdings, then to paved streets and gardens. As Walter came close to the first of the two-story houses, a burst of machine-gun fire came from an upper window, dotting the road at his feet like raindrops on a pond. He threw himself over a low fence into a vegetable patch and rolled until he found cover behind an apple tree. His men scattered likewise, all but two who fell in the road. One lay still; the other moaned in pain.

Walter looked back and spotted Sergeant Schwab. "Take six men, find the back entrance to that house, and destroy that machine-gun emplacement," he said. He located his lieutenants. "Von Kessel, go west one block and enter the town from there. Von Braun, come east with me."

He kept off the streets and moved through alleys and backyards, but there were riflemen and machine gunners in about every tenth house. Something had happened to give the French back their fighting spirit, Walter realized with trepidation.

All morning the storm troopers fought from house to house, taking heavy casualties. This was not how they were supposed to operate, bleeding for every yard. They were trained to follow the line of least resistance, penetrate deep behind enemy lines, and disrupt communications, so that the forces at the front would become demoralized and leaderless, and would quickly surrender to follow-up infantry. But that tactic had now failed, and they were slogging it out hand to hand with an enemy who seemed to have gained his second wind.

But they made progress, and at midday Walter stood on the ruins of the medieval castle that gave its name to the town. The castle was at the top of a hill, and the town hall stood at its foot. From there the main street ran in a straight line two hundred and fifty yards to a double-arched road bridge across the Marne. To the east, five hundred yards upriver, was the only other crossing, a railway bridge.

He could see all that with the naked eye. He took out his field glasses and focused on the enemy positions on the south bank. The men carelessly showed themselves, a sign that they were new to warfare: veterans stayed out of sight. They were young and energetic and well-fed and well-dressed, he noted. Their uniforms were not blue but tan, he saw with dismay.

They were Americans.

{ V }

During the afternoon, the French fell back to the north bank of the river, and Gus was able to bring his armament to bear, directing mortar and machine-gun fire over the heads of the French at the advancing Germans. The American guns sent a torrent of ammunition along the straight north-south avenues of Château-Thierry, turning them into killing lanes. All the same he could see the Germans advance fearlessly from bank to café, alley to shop doorway, overwhelming the French by sheer weight of numbers.

As afternoon turned to bloody evening, Gus watched from a high window and saw the tattered remnants of the blue-coated French falling back toward the west bridge. They made their last stand at the north end of the bridge and held it while the red sun went down behind the hills to the west. Then, in the dusk, they retreated across the bridge.

A small group of Germans saw what was happening and gave chase. Gus saw them run onto the bridge, barely visible in the twilight, gray moving on gray. Then the bridge exploded. The French had previously wired it for demolition, Gus realized. Bodies flew through the air and the northern arch of the bridge collapsed into a heap of rubble in the water.

Then it went quiet.

Gus lay down on a palliasse at headquarters and got some sleep, his first for almost forty-eight hours. He was awakened by the Germans' dawn barrage. Bleary-eyed, he hurried from the sewing-machine factory to the waterfront. In the pearly light of a June morning he saw that the Germans had occupied the entire north bank of the river and were shelling the American positions on the south bank at hellishly close range.

He arranged for the crews who had been up all night to be relieved by men who had got some rest. Then he went from position to position, always staying behind the waterfront buildings. He suggested ways of improving cover—moving a gun to a smaller window, using sheets of corrugated tin to protect crews from flying debris, or piling up rubble either side of the gun. But the best way for his men to protect themselves was to make life impossible for the enemy gunners. "Give the bastards hell," he said.

The men responded eagerly. The Hotchkiss fired four hundred and fifty rounds per minute, and its range was four thousand yards, so it was highly effective across the river. The Stokes mortar was less useful: its up-and-over trajectory was intended for trench warfare, where line-of-sight fire was ineffective. But the rifle grenades were highly destructive at short range.

The two sides pounded each other like bare-knuckle boxers fighting in a barrel. The noise of so much ammunition being fired was never less than deafening. Buildings collapsed, men screamed in the agony of wounds, bloodstained stretcher-bearers ran from the waterfront to the dressing station and back, and runners brought more ammunition and jugs of hot coffee to the weary soldiers manning the guns.

As the day wore on, Gus noticed, in a back-of-the-mind way, that he was not scared. He did not think about it often—there was too much to do. For a brief moment, in the middle of the day, as he stood in the canteen of the sewing-machine factory gulping down sweet milky coffee instead of lunch, he marveled at the strange person he had become. Could it really be Gus Dewar who ran from one building to the next through an artillery barrage, shouting at his men to give 'em hell? This man had been afraid he would lose his nerve and turn around and walk away from the battle. In the event, he hardly thought of his own safety, being too preoccupied with the danger to his men. How had that come about? Then a corporal came to tell him that his squad had lost the special wrench used to change overheated Hotchkiss barrels, and he swallowed the rest of his coffee and ran to deal with the problem.

He did suffer a moment of sadness that evening. It was dusk, and he happened to look out of a smashed kitchen window to the spot on the bank where Chuck Dixon had died. He no longer felt shocked by the way Chuck had disappeared in an explosion of earth: he had seen much more death and destruction in the last three days. What struck him now, with a different kind of shock, was the realization that one day he would have to speak about that awful moment to Chuck's parents, Albert and Emmeline, owners of a Buffalo bank, and to his young wife, Doris, who had been so against America's joining the war—probably because she feared exactly what had happened. What was Gus going to say to them? "Chuck fought bravely." Chuck had not fought at all: he had died in the first minute of his first battle, without firing a shot. It would hardly have mattered if he had been a coward—the result would have been the same. His life had just been wasted.

As Gus stared at the spot, lost in thought, his eye was caught by movement on the railway bridge.

His heart missed a beat. There were men coming onto the far end of the bridge. Their field-gray uniforms were only just visible in the half-light. They ran awkwardly along the rails, stumbling on the sleepers and the gravel. Their helmets were of the coal scuttle shape, and they carried their rifles slung. They were German.

Gus ran to the nearest machine-gun emplacement, behind a garden wall. The crew had not noticed the assault force. Gus tapped the gunner on the shoulder. "Fire at the bridge!" he shouted. "Look—Germans!" The gunner swung the barrel around to the new target.

Gus pointed to a soldier at random. "Run to headquarters and report an enemy incursion across the east bridge," he shouted. "Quick, quick!"

He found a sergeant. "Make sure everyone is firing at the bridge," he said. "Go!"

He headed west. Heavy machine guns could not be moved quickly—the Hotchkiss weighed eighty-eight pounds with its tripod—but he told all the rifle grenadiers and mortar crews to move to new positions from which they could defend the bridge.

The Germans began to be mown down, but they were determined, and kept coming. Through his glasses, Gus saw a tall man in the uniform of a major who looked familiar. He wondered if it was someone he had met before the war. As Gus looked, the major took a hit and fell to the ground.

The Germans were supported by a terrific barrage from their own artillery. It seemed as if every gun on the north bank had trained its sights on the south end of the railway bridge where the defending Americans were clustered. Gus saw his men fall one after another, but he replaced every killed or wounded gunner with a fresh man, and there was hardly a pause in the firing.

The Germans stopped running and began to take up positions, using the scant cover of dead comrades. The boldest of them advanced, but there was no place to hide, and they were swiftly brought down.

Darkness fell, but it made no difference: firing continued at maximum on both sides. The enemy became vague shapes lit by flashes of gunfire and exploding shells. Gus moved some of the heavy machine guns to new positions, feeling almost certain this incursion was not a feint to cover a river crossing somewhere else.

It was a stalemate, and at last the Germans began to retreat.

Seeing stretcher parties on the bridge, Gus ordered his men to stop firing.

In response, the German artillery went quiet.

"Christ Almighty," Gus said to no one in particular. "I think we've beaten them off."

{ VI }

An American bullet had broken Walter's shinbone. He lay on the railway line in agony, but he felt worse when he saw the men retreating and heard the guns fall silent. He knew then that he had failed.

He screamed when he was lifted onto the stretcher. It was bad for the men's morale to hear the wounded cry out, but he could not help it. They bumped him along the track and through the town to the dressing station, where someone gave him morphine and he passed out.

He woke up with his leg in a splint. He questioned everyone who passed his cot on the progress of the battle, but he got no details until Gottfried von Kessel came by to gloat over his wound. The German army had given up trying to cross the Marne at Château-Thierry, Gottfried told him. Perhaps they would try elsewhere.

Next day, just before he was put on a train home, he learned that the main body of the United States Third Division had arrived and taken up positions all along the south bank of the Marne.

A wounded comrade told him of a bloody battle in a

wood near the town called the Bois de Belleau. There had been terrible casualties on both sides, but the Americans had won.

Back in Berlin, the papers continued to tell of German victories, but the lines on the maps got no nearer to Paris, and Walter came to the bitter conclusion that the spring offensive had failed. The Americans had arrived too soon.

He was released from the hospital to convalesce in his old room at his parents' house.

On August 8 an Allied attack at Amiens used almost five hundred of the new "tanks." These ironclad vehicles were plagued with problems but could be unstoppable, and the British gained eight miles in a single day.

It was only eight miles, but Walter suspected the tide had turned, and he could tell by his father's face that the old man felt the same. No one in Berlin now spoke of winning the war.

One night at the end of September, Otto came home looking as if someone had died. There was nothing left of his natural ebullience. Walter even wondered if he was going to cry.

"The kaiser has returned to Berlin," he said.

Walter knew that Kaiser Wilhelm had been at army headquarters in the Belgian hill resort called Spa. "Why has he come back?"

Otto's voice dropped to a near-whisper, as if he could not bear to say what he had to say in a normal voice. "Ludendorff wants an armistice."

CHAPTER THIRTY-TWO

October 1918

Maud had lunch at the Ritz with her friend Lord Remarc, who was a junior minister in the War Office. Johnny was wearing a new lavender waistcoat. Over the pot-au-feu she asked him: "Is the war really coming to an end?"

"Everyone thinks so," Johnny said. "The Germans have suffered seven hundred thousand casualties this year. They can't go on."

Maud wondered miserably if Walter was one of the seven hundred thousand. He might be dead, she knew; and the thought was like a cold lump inside her where her heart should be. She had had no word from him since their idyllic second honeymoon in Stockholm. She guessed that his work no longer took him to neutral countries from which he could write. The awful truth was that he had probably returned to the battlefield for Germany's last, all-or-nothing offensive.

Such thoughts were morbid, but realistic. So many women had lost their loved ones: husbands, brothers, sons, fiancés. They had all lived through four years during which such tragedies happened daily. It was no longer possible to be too pessimistic. Grief was the norm.

She pushed her soup dish away. "Is there any other reason to hope for peace?"

"Yes. Germany has a new chancellor, and he has written to President Wilson, suggesting an armistice based on Wilson's famous Fourteen Points."

"That is hopeful! Has Wilson agreed?"

"No. He said Germany must first withdraw from all conquered territories."

"What does our government think?"

"Lloyd George is hopping mad. The Germans treat the Americans as the senior partners in the alliance—and President Wilson acts as if they could make peace without consulting us."

"Does it matter?"

"I'm afraid it does. Our government doesn't necessarily agree with Wilson's Fourteen Points."

Maud nodded. "I suppose we're against point five, about colonial peoples having a say in their own government."

"Exactly. What about Rhodesia, and Barbados, and India? We can't be expected to ask the natives' permission before we civilize them. Americans are far too liberal. And we're dead against point two, freedom of the seas in war and peace. British power is based on the navy. We would not have been able to starve Germany into submission if we had not been allowed to blockade their seagoing trade."

"How do the French feel about it?"

Johnny grinned. "Clemenceau said Wilson was trying to outdo the Almighty. 'God himself only came up with ten points,' he said."

"I get the impression that most ordinary British people actually like Wilson and his points."

Johnny nodded. "And European leaders can hardly tell the American president to stop making peace."

Maud was so eager to believe it that she frightened herself. She told herself not to be happy yet. There could be such heavy disappointment in store.

A waiter brought them sole Waleska and cast an admiring eye at Johnny's waistcoat.

Maud turned to her other worry. "What do you hear from Fitz?" Her brother's mission in Siberia was secret, but he had confided in her, and Johnny gave her bulletins.

"That Cossack leader turned out to be a disappointment. Fitz made a pact with him, and we paid him for a while, but he was nothing more than a warlord, really. However, Fitz is staying on, hoping to encourage the Russians to overthrow the Bolsheviks. Meanwhile, Lenin has moved his government from Petrograd to Moscow, where he feels safer from invasion."

"Even if the Bolsheviks were deposed, would a new regime resume the war against Germany?"

"Realistically? No." Johnny took a sip of Chablis. "But a lot of very powerful people in the British government just hate the Bolsheviks."

"Why?"

"Lenin's regime is brutal."

"So was the tsar's, but Winston Churchill never plotted to overthrow him."

"Underneath, they're frightened that if Bolshevism is a success over there, it will come here next."

"Well, if it's a success, why not?"

Johnny shrugged. "You can't expect people such as your brother to see it that way."

"No," said Maud. "I wonder how he's getting on?"

{ II }

"We're in Russia!" Billy Williams said when the ship docked and he heard the voices of the longshoremen. "What are we doing in fucking Russia?"

"How can we be in Russia?" said Tommy Griffiths. "Russia's in the east. We've been sailing west for weeks."

"We've gone halfway round the world and come at it from the other side."

Tommy was not convinced. He leaned over the rail, staring. "The people look a bit Chinesey," he said.

"They're speaking Russian, though. They sound like that pony driver, Peshkov, the one who cheated the Ponti brothers at cards, then scarpered."

Tommy listened. "Aye, you're right. Well, I never."

"This must be Siberia," Billy said. "No wonder it's fucking cold."

A few minutes later they learned they were in Vladivostok.

People took little notice of the Aberowen Pals marching through the town. There were already thousands of soldiers in uniform here. Most were Japanese but there were also Americans and Czechs and others. The town had a busy port, trams running along broad boulevards, modern hotels and theaters, and hundreds of shops. It was like Cardiff, Billy thought, but colder.

When they reached their barracks they met a battalion of elderly Londoners who had been shipped there from Hong Kong. It made sense, Billy thought, to send old codgers to this backwater. But the Pals, though depleted by casualties, had a core of hardened veterans. Who had pulled strings to have them withdrawn from France and sent to the other side of the globe?

He soon found out. After dinner the brigadier, a comfortable-looking man evidently close to retirement, told them they were to be addressed by Colonel the Earl Fitzherbert.

Captain Gwyn Evans, the owner of the department stores, brought a wooden crate that had once held cans of lard, and Fitz climbed up on it, not without difficulty on account of his bad leg. Billy watched without sympathy. He reserved his compassion for Stumpy Pugh and the many other crippled ex-miners who had been injured digging the earl's coal. Fitz was smug, arrogant, and a merciless exploiter of ordinary men and women. It was a shame the Germans had not shot him in the heart rather than the leg.

"Our mission is fourfold," Fitz began, raising his voice to address six hundred men. "First, we're here to protect our property. On your way out of the docks, passing the railway sidings, you may have noticed a large supply dump guarded by troops. That ten-acre site contains six hundred thousand tons of munitions and other military equipment sent here by Britain and the United States when the Russians were our allies. Now that the Bolsheviks have made peace with Germany, we do not want bullets paid for by our people to fall into their hands."

"That doesn't make sense," Billy said loud enough for Tommy and the others around him to hear. "Instead of bringing us here, why didn't they ship the stores home?"

Fitz glanced irritably in the direction of the noise, but continued. "Second, there are many Czech nationalists in this country, some prisoners of war and others who were working here prewar, who have formed themselves into the Czech Legion and are trying to take ship from Vladivostok to join our forces in France. They are being harassed by the

Bolsheviks and our job is to help them get away. Local Cossack community leaders will help us in this effort."

"Cossack community leaders?" Billy said. "Who is he trying to fool? They're bloody bandits."

Once again Fitz heard the dissident muttering. This time Captain Evans looked annoyed and walked down the mess hall to stand near Billy and his group.

"Here in Siberia there are eight hundred thousand Austrian and German prisoners of war who have been set free since the peace treaty. We must prevent them returning to the European battlefield. Finally, we suspect the Germans of eyeing up the oil fields of Baku, in the south of Russia. They must not be allowed to access that supply."

Billy said: "I've got a feeling Baku is quite a long way from here."

The brigadier said amiably: "Do any of you men have any questions?"

Fitz gave him a glare, but it was too late. Billy said: "I haven't read nothing about this in the papers."

Fitz replied: "Like many military missions, it is secret, and you will not be allowed to say where you are in your letters home."

"Are we at war with Russia, sir?"

"No, we are not." Fitz pointedly looked away from Billy. Perhaps he remembered how Billy had bested him at the peace talks meeting in the Calvary Gospel Hall. "Does anyone other than Sergeant Williams have a question?"

Billy persisted. "Are we trying to overthrow the Bolshevik government?"

There was an angry murmur from the troops, many of whom sympathized with the revolution.

"There is no Bolshevik government," Fitz said with mounting exasperation. "The regime in Moscow has not been recognized by His Majesty the king."

"Have our mission been authorized by Parliament?"

The brigadier looked troubled—he had not been expecting *this* type of question—and Captain Evans said: "That's enough from you, Sergeant—let the others have a chance."

But Fitz was not smart enough to shut up. Apparently it did not occur to him that Billy's debating skills, learned from a radical nonconformist father, might be superior to his own. "Military missions are authorized by the War Office, not by Parliament," Fitz argued.

"So this have been kept secret from our elected representatives!" Billy said indignantly.

Tommy murmured anxiously: "Careful, now, butty."

"Necessarily," said Fitz.

Billy ignored Tommy's advice—he was too angry now. He stood up and said in a clear, loud voice: "Sir, is what we're doing legal?"

Fitz colored, and Billy knew he had scored a hit.

Fitz began: "Of course it is—"

"If our mission have not been approved by the British people or the Russian people," Billy interrupted, "how can it be legal?"

Captain Evans said: "Sit down, Sergeant. This isn't one of your bloody Labour Party meetings. One more word and you'll be on a charge."

Billy sat down, satisfied. He had made his point.

Fitz said: "We have been invited here by the All-Russia Provisional Government, whose executive arm is a five-man directory based at Omsk, at the western edge of Siberia. And that," Fitz finished, "is where you're going next."

{ III }

It was dusk. Lev Peshkov waited, shivering, in a freight yard in Vladivostok, the ass end of the Trans-Siberian Railway. He wore an army greatcoat over his lieutenant's uniform, but Siberia was the coldest place he had ever been.

He was furious to be in Russia. He had been lucky to escape, four years ago, and even luckier to marry into a wealthy American family. And now he was back—all because of a girl. What's wrong with me? he asked himself. Why can't I be satisfied?

A gate opened, and a cart drawn by a mule came out of the supply dump. Lev jumped onto the seat beside the British soldier who was driving it. "Aye, aye, Sid," said Lev.

"Wotcher," said Sid. He was a thin man of about forty with a perpetual cigarette and a prematurely lined face. A Cockney, he spoke English with an accent quite different from that of South Wales or upstate New York. At first Lev had found him hard to understand.

"Have you got the whisky?"

"Nah, just tins of cocoa."

Lev turned around, leaned into the cart, and pulled back a corner of the tarpaulin. He was almost certain Sid was joking. He saw a cardboard box marked: "Fry's Chocolate and Cocoa." He said: "Not much demand for that among the Cossacks."

"Look underneath."

Lev moved the box aside and saw a different legend: "Teacher's Highland Cream—Perfection of Old Scotch Whisky." He said: "How many?"

"Twelve cases."

He covered the box. "Better than cocoa."

He directed Sid away from the city center. He checked behind frequently to see if anyone was following them, and looked with apprehension when he saw a senior U.S. Army officer, but no one questioned them. Vladivostok was crammed with refugees from the Bolsheviks, most of whom had brought a lot of money with them. They were spending it as if there were no tomorrow, which there probably was not for many of them. In consequence the shops were busy and the streets full of carts like this one delivering goods. As everything was scarce in Russia, much of what was on sale had been smuggled in from China or, like Sid's Scotch, stolen from the military.

Lev saw a woman with a little girl, and thought of Daisy. He missed her. She was walking and talking now, and investigating the world. She had a pout that melted everyone's heart, even Josef Vyalov's. Lev had not seen her for six months. She was two and a half now, and she must have changed in the time he had been away.

He also missed Marga. She was the one he dreamed about, her naked body wriggling against his in bed. It was because of her that he had got into trouble with his father-in-law and ended up in Siberia, but all the same he longed to see her again.

"Have you got a weakness, Sid?" said Lev. He felt he needed a closer friendship with the taciturn Sid: partners in crime required trust.

"Nah," said Sid. "Only money."

"Does your love of money lead you to take risks?"

"Nah, just thieving."

"And does thieving ever get you into trouble?"

"Not really. Prison, once, but that was only for six months."

"My weakness is women."

"Is it?"

Lev was used to this British habit of asking the question after the answer had been given. "Yes," he said. "I can't resist them. I have to walk into a nightclub with a pretty girl on my arm."

"Do you?"

"Yes. I can't help myself."

The cart entered a dockland neighborhood of dirt roads and sailors' hostels, places that had neither names nor addresses. Sid looked nervous.

Lev said: "You're armed, yeah?"

"Nah," said Sid. "I just got this." He pulled back his coat to reveal a huge pistol with a foot-long barrel stuck into his belt.

Lev had never seen a gun like it. "What the fuck is that?"

"Webley-Mars. Most powerful handgun in the world. Very rare."

"No need to pull the trigger—just wave it about. It'll scare people to death."

In this area no one was paid to clear the streets of snow, and the cart followed the tracks of previous vehicles, or slid on the ice of little-used lanes. Being in Russia made Lev think of his brother. He had not forgotten his promise to send Grigori the fare to America. He was making good money selling stolen military supplies to the Cossacks. With today's deal he would have enough for Grigori's passage.

He had done a lot of wicked things in his short life, but if he could make amends to his brother, he would feel better about himself.

They drove into an alley and turned behind a low building. Lev opened a cardboard box and took out one bottle of Scotch. "Stay here and guard the load," he said to Sid. "Otherwise it will be gone when we come out."

"Don't worry," said Sid, but he looked apprehensive.

Lev reached under his greatcoat to touch the holstered Colt .45 semiautomatic pistol on his belt; then he went in through the back door.

The place was what passed for a tavern in Siberia. There was a small room with a few chairs and a table. It had no bar, but an open door revealed a dirty kitchen with a shelf of bottles and a barrel. Three men sat near the log fire, dressed in ragged furs. Lev recognized the one in the middle, a man he knew as Sotnik. He wore baggy trousers tucked into riding boots. He had high cheekbones and slanted eyes, and he sported an elaborate mustache and side-whiskers. His skin was reddened and lined by the weather. He might have been any age between twenty-five and fifty-five.

Lev shook hands all round. He uncorked the bottle, and one of the men—presumably the bar owner—brought four nonmatching glasses. Lev poured generous measures, and they all drank.

"This is the best whisky in the world," Lev said in Russian. "It comes from a cold country, like Siberia, where the water in the mountain streams is pure melted snow. What a pity it is so expensive."

Sotnik's face was expressionless. "How much?"

Lev was not going to let him reopen the bargaining. "The price you agreed to yesterday," he said. "Payable in gold rubles, nothing else."

"How many bottles?"

"One hundred and forty-four."

"Where are they?"

"Nearby."

"You should be careful. There are thieves in the neighborhood."

This might have been a warning or a threat: Lev guessed the ambiguity was intentional. "I know about thieves," he said. "I'm one of them."

Sotnik looked at his two comrades; then, after a pause, he laughed. They laughed, too.

Lev poured another round. "Don't worry," he said. "Your whisky is safe—behind the barrel of a gun." That, too, was ambiguous. It might have been a reassurance or a warning.

"That's good," said Sotnik.

Lev drank his whisky, then looked at his watch. "A military police patrol is due in this neighborhood soon," he lied. "I have to go."

"One more drink," said Sotnik.

Lev stood up. "Do you want the whisky?" He let his irritation show. "I can easily sell it to someone else." This was true. You could always sell liquor.

"I'll take it."

"Money on the table."

Sotnik picked up a saddlebag from the floor and began counting out five-ruble pieces. The agreed price was sixty rubles a dozen. Sotnik slowly put the coins in piles of twelve until he had twelve stacks. Lev guessed he could not actually count up to 144.

When Sotnik had finished he looked at Lev. Lev nodded. Sotnik put the coins back in the saddlebag.

They went outside, Sotnik carrying the bag. Night had fallen, but there was a moon, and they could see clearly. Lev said to Sid in English: "Stay on the cart. Be alert." In an illegal transaction, this was always the dangerous moment—the buyer's chance to grab the goods and keep the money. Lev was not taking any chances with Grigori's ticket money.

Lev pulled the cover off the cart, then moved three boxes of cocoa aside to reveal the Scotch. He took a case from the cart and put it on the ground at Sotnik's feet.

The other Cossack went to the cart and reached for another case.

"No," said Lev. He looked at Sotnik. "The bag."

There was a long pause.

On the driving seat, Sid pulled back his coat to reveal his weapon.

Sotnik gave Lev the bag.

Lev looked inside, but decided not to count the money again. He would have seen if Sotnik had slyly extracted a few coins. He handed the bag to Sid, then helped the others unload the cart.

He shook hands all round and was about to get up on the cart when Sotnik stopped him. "Look," he said. He pointed at an opened box. "There's a bottle missing."

That bottle was on the table in the tavern, and Sotnik knew it. Why was he trying to pick a quarrel at this stage? This was dangerous.

He said to Sid in English: "Give me one gold piece."

Sid opened the bag and handed him a coin.

Lev balanced it on his closed fist, then threw it in the air, spinning it. The coin flashed in the moonlight. As Sotnik reached out reflexively to catch it, Lev jumped onto the seat of the cart.

Sid cracked the whip.

"Go with God," Lev called out as the cart jerked into motion. "And let me know when you need more whisky."

The mule trotted out of the yard and turned onto the road, and Lev breathed easier.

"How much did we get?" said Sid.

"What we asked for. Three hundred and sixty rubles each. Minus five. I'll stand the loss of that last coin. Got a bag?"

Sid produced a large leather purse. Lev counted seventy-two coins into it.

He said good-bye to Sid and jumped off the cart near the U.S. officers' accommodation. As he was making his way to his room, he was accosted by Captain Hammond. "Peshkov! Where have you been?"

Lev wished he were not carrying 355 rubles in a Cossack saddlebag. "A little sightseeing, sir."

"It's dark!"

"That's why I came back."

"We've been looking for you. The colonel wants you."

"Right away, sir." Lev headed for his room, to drop off the saddlebag, but Hammond said: "The colonel's office is the other way."

"Yes, sir." Lev turned around.

Colonel Markham did not like Lev. The colonel was a career soldier, not a wartime recruit. He felt Lev did not share his commitment to excellence in the United States Army, and he was right—110 percent, as the colonel himself might have put it.

Lev considered parking the saddlebag on the floor outside the colonel's office door, but it was too much money to leave lying around.

"Where the hell were you?" said Markham as soon as Lev walked in.

"Taking a look around town, sir."

"I'm reassigning you. Our British allies need interpreters and they've asked me to second you to them."

It sounded like a soft option. "Yes, sir."

"You'll be going with them to Omsk."

That was not so soft. Omsk was four thousand miles away in the barbaric heartland of Russia. "What for, sir?"

"They will brief you."

Lev did not want to go. It was too far from home. "Are you asking me to volunteer, sir?"

The colonel hesitated, and Lev realized the assignment *was* voluntary, insofar as anything was in the army. "Are you refusing the assignment?" said Markham threateningly.

"Only if it's voluntary, sir, of course."

"I'll tell you the situation, Lieutenant," said the colonel. "If you volunteer, I won't ask you to open that bag and show me what's inside."

Lev cursed under his breath. There was nothing he could do. The colonel was too damn sharp. And Grigori's fare to America was in the saddlebag.

Omsk, he thought. Hell.

"I'd be glad to go, sir," he said.

{ IV }

Ethel went upstairs to Mildred's apartment. The place was clean but not tidy, with toys on the floor, a cigarette burning in an ashtray, and knickers drying in front of the fire. "Can you keep an eye on Lloyd tonight?" Ethel asked. She and Bernie were going to a Labour Party meeting. Lloyd was nearly four now and quite capable of getting out of bed and going for a walk on his own if not watched.

"Of course," said Mildred. They frequently watched each other's children in the evenings. "I've got a letter from Billy," Mildred said.

"Is he all right?"

"Yes. But I don't think he's in France. He doesn't say anything about the trenches."

"He must be in the Middle East, then. I wonder if he's seen Jerusalem." The Holy City had been taken by British forces at the end of last year. "Our da will be pleased if he has."

"There's a message for you. He says he'll write later, but to tell you . . ." She reached into the pocket of her apron. "Let me get it right. 'Believe me, I feel I am badly informed here about events in politics in Russia.' Funny bloody message, really."

"It's in code," Ethel said. "Every third word counts. The message says, *I am here in Russia.* What's he doing there?"

"I didn't know our army was in Russia."

"Nor did I. Does he mention a song, or a book title?"

"Yeah—how did you know?"

"That's code, too."

"He says to remind you of a song you used to sing called 'I'm with Freddie in the Zoo.' I've never heard of it."

"Nor have I. It's the initials. 'Freddie in the Zoo' means . . . Fitz."

Bernie came in wearing a red tie. "He's fast asleep," he said, meaning Lloyd.

Ethel said: "Mildred's got a letter from Billy. He seems to be in Russia with Earl Fitzherbert."

"Aha!" said Bernie. "I wondered how long it would take them."

"What do you mean?"

"We've sent troops to fight the Bolsheviks. I knew it would happen."

"We're at war with the new Russian government?"

"Not officially, of course." Bernie looked at his watch. "We need to go." He hated to be late.

On the bus, Ethel said: "We can't be *unofficially* at war. Either we are or we aren't."

"Churchill and that crowd know the British people won't support a war against the Bolsheviks, so they're trying to do it secretly."

Ethel said thoughtfully: "I'm disappointed in Lenin—"

"He's just doing what he's got to do!" Bernie interrupted. He was a passionate supporter of the Bolsheviks.

Ethel went on: "Lenin could become just as much of a tyrant as the tsar—"

"That's ridiculous!"

"—but even so, he should be given a chance to show what he can do for Russia."

"Well, we're in agreement about that, at least."

"I'm not sure what we can do about it, though."

"We need more information."

"Billy will write to me soon. He'll give me the details."

Ethel felt indignant about the government's secret

war—if that was what it was—but she was in an agony of worry about Billy. He would not keep his mouth shut. If he thought the army was doing wrong, he would say so, and might get into trouble.

The Calvary Gospel Hall was full: the Labour Party had gained popularity during the war. This was partly because the Labour leader, Arthur Henderson, had been in Lloyd George's War Cabinet. Henderson had started work in a locomotive factory at the age of twelve, and his performance as a cabinet minister had killed off the Conservative argument that workers could not be trusted in government.

Ethel and Bernie sat next to Jock Reid, a red-faced Glaswegian who had been Bernie's best friend when he was single. The chairman of the meeting was Dr. Greenward. The main item on the agenda was the next general election. There were rumors that Lloyd George would call a national election as soon as the war ended. Aldgate needed a Labour candidate, and Bernie was the front runner.

He was proposed and seconded. Someone suggested Dr. Greenward as an alternative, but the doctor said he felt he should stick to medicine.

Then Jayne McCulley stood up. She had been a party member ever since Ethel and Maud had protested against the withdrawal of her separation allowance, and Maud had been carried off to jail in the arms of a policeman. Now Jayne said: "I read in the paper that women can stand in the next election, and I propose that Ethel Williams should be our candidate."

There was a moment of stunned silence; then everyone tried to speak at the same time.

Ethel was taken aback. She had not thought about this. Ever since she had known Bernie, he had wanted to be the local M.P. She had accepted that. Besides, it had never been possible for women to be elected. She was not sure it was possible now. Her first inclination was to refuse immediately.

Jayne had not finished. She was a pretty young woman, but the softness of her appearance was deceptive, and she could be formidable. "I respect Bernie, but he is an organizer and a meetings man," she said. "Aldgate has a Liberal M.P. who is quite well-liked and may be hard to defeat. We need a candidate who can win this seat for Labour, someone who can say to the people of the East End: 'Follow me to victory!' and they will. We need Ethel."

All the women cheered, and so did some of the men, though others muttered darkly. Ethel realized she would have a lot of support if she ran.

And Jayne was right: Bernie was probably the cleverest man in the room, but he was not an inspirational leader. He could explain how revolutions happened and why companies went bust, but Ethel could inspire people to join a crusade.

Jock Reid stood up. "Comrade Chairman, I believe the legislation does not permit women to stand."

Dr. Greenward said: "I can answer that question. The law that was passed earlier this year, giving the vote to certain women over thirty, did not provide for women to stand for election. But the government has admitted that this is an anomaly, and a further bill has been drafted."

Jock persisted. "But the law *as it stands today* forbids the election of women, so we can't nominate one." Ethel gave a wry smile: it was odd how men who called for world revolution could insist on following the letter of the law.

Dr. Greenward said: "The Parliament (Qualification of Women) Bill is clearly intended to become law before the next general election, so it seems perfectly in order for this branch to nominate a woman."

"But Ethel is under thirty."

"Apparently this new bill applies to women over twenty-one."

"Apparently?" said Jock. "How can we nominate a candidate if we don't know the rules?"

Dr. Greenward said: "Perhaps we should postpone nomination until the new legislation has been passed."

Bernie whispered something in Jock's ear, and Jock said: "Let's ask Ethel if she's willing to stand. If not, then there's no need to postpone the decision."

Bernie turned to Ethel with a confident smile.

"All right," said Dr. Greenward. "Ethel, if you were nominated, would you accept?"

Everyone looked at her.

Ethel hesitated.

This was Bernie's dream, and Bernie was her husband. But which of them would be the better choice for Labour?

As the seconds passed, a look of incredulity came over Bernie's face. He had expected her to decline the nomination instantly.

That hardened her resolve.

"I . . . I've never considered it," she said. "And, um, as the chairman said, it's not even a legal possibility yet. So it's a hard question to answer. I believe Bernie would be a good candidate . . . but all the same I'd like time to think about it. So perhaps we should accept the chairman's suggestion of a postponement."

She turned to Bernie.

He looked as if he could kill her.

CHAPTER THIRTY-THREE

November 11, 1918

At two o'clock in the morning, the phone rang at Fitz's house in Mayfair.

Maud was still up, sitting in the drawing room with a candle, the portraits of dead ancestors looking down on her, the drawn curtains like shrouds, the pieces of furniture around her dimly visible, like beasts in a field at night. For the last few days she had hardly slept. A superstitious foreboding told her Walter would be killed before the war ended.

She sat alone, with a cold cup of tea in her hands, staring into the coal fire, wondering where he was and what he was doing. Was he sleeping in a damp trench somewhere, or preparing for tomorrow's fighting? Or was he already dead? She could be a widow, having spent only two nights with her husband in four years of marriage. All she could be sure of was that he was not a prisoner of war. Johnny Remarc checked every list of captured officers for her. Johnny did not know her secret: he believed she was concerned only because Walter had been a dear friend of Fitz's before the war.

The telephone bell startled her. At first she thought it might be a call about Walter, but that would not make sense. News of a friend taken prisoner could wait until morning. It must be Fitz, she thought with agony: could he have been wounded in Siberia?

She hurried out to the hall but Grout got there first. She realized with a guilty start that she had forgotten to give the staff permission to go to bed.

"I will inquire whether Lady Maud is at home, my lord," Grout said into the apparatus. He covered the mouthpiece with his hand and said to Maud: "Lord Remarc at the War Office, my lady."

She took the phone from Grout and said: "It is Fitz? Is he hurt?"

"No, no," said Johnny. "Calm down. It's good news. The Germans have accepted the armistice terms."

"Oh, Johnny, thank God!"

"They're all in the forest of Compiègne, north of Paris, on two trains in a railway siding. The Germans have just gone into the dining car of the French train. They're ready to sign."

"But they haven't signed yet?"

"No, not yet. They're quibbling about the wording."

"Johnny, will you phone me again when they've signed? I shan't go to bed tonight."

"I will. Good-bye."

Maud gave the handset back to the butler. "The war may end tonight, Grout."

"I'm very happy to hear it, my lady."

"But you should go to bed."

"With your ladyship's permission, I'd like to stay up until Lord Remarc telephones again."

"Of course."

"Would you like some more tea, my lady?"

{ II }

The Aberowen Pals arrived in Omsk early in the morning.

Billy would always remember every detail of the four-thousand-mile journey along the Trans-Siberian Railway from Vladivostok. It had taken twenty-three days, even with an armed sergeant posted in the locomotive to make sure the driver and fireman kept maximum speed. Billy was cold all the way: the stove in the center of the railcar hardly took the chill off the Siberian mornings. They lived on black bread and bully beef. But Billy found every day a revelation.

He had not known there were places in the world as

beautiful as Lake Baikal. The lake was longer from one end to the other than Wales, Captain Evans told them. From the speeding train they watched the sun rise over the still blue water, lighting the tops of the mile-high mountains on the far side, the snow turning to gold on the peaks.

All his life he would cherish the memory of an endless caravan of camels alongside the railway line, the laden beasts plodding patiently through the snow, ignoring the twentieth century as it hurtled past them in a clash of iron and a shriek of steam. I'm a bloody long way from Aberowen, he thought at that moment.

But the most memorable incident was a visit to a high school in Chita. The train stopped there for two days while Colonel Fitzherbert parlayed with the local leader, a Cossack chieftain called Semenov. Billy attached himself to a party of American visitors on a tour. The principal of the school, who spoke English, explained that until a year ago he had taught only the children of the prosperous middle class, and that Jews had been banned even if they could afford the fees. Now, by order of the Bolsheviks, education was free to all. The effect was obvious. His classrooms were crammed to bursting with children in rags, learning to read and write and count, and even studying science and art. Whatever else Lenin might have done—and it was difficult to separate the truth from the conservative propaganda—at least, Billy thought, he was serious about educating Russian children.

On the train with him was Lev Peshkov. He had greeted Billy warmly, showing no sense of shame, as if he had forgotten being chased out of Aberowen as a cheat and a thief. Lev had made it to America and married a rich girl, and now he was a lieutenant, attached to the Pals as an interpreter.

The population of Omsk cheered the battalion as they marched from the railway station to their barracks. Billy saw numerous Russian officers on the streets, wearing fancy old-fashioned uniforms but apparently doing nothing military. There were also a lot of Canadian troops.

When the battalion was dismissed, Billy and Tommy strolled around town. There was not much to look at: a cathedral, a mosque, a brick fortress, and a river busy with freight and passenger traffic. They were surprised to see many locals wearing bits and pieces of British army uniform. A woman selling hot fried fish from a stall had on a khaki tunic; a deliveryman with a handcart wore thick army-issue serge trousers; a tall schoolboy with a satchel of books walked along the street in bright new British boots. "Where did they get them?" said Billy.

"We supply uniforms to the Russian army here, but Peshkov told me the officers sell them on the black market," Tommy said.

"Serves us bloody well right for supporting the wrong side," said Billy.

The Canadian YMCA had set up a canteen. Several of the Pals were already there: it seemed to be the only place to go. Billy and Tommy got hot tea and big wedges of apple tart, which North Americans called pie. "This town is the headquarters of the anti-Bolshevik reactionary government," Billy said. "I read it in *The New York Times*." The American papers, which had been available in Vladivostok, were more honest than the British.

Lev Peshkov came in. With him was a beautiful young Russian girl in a cheap coat. They all stared at him. How did he do it so fast?

Lev looked excited. "Hey, have you guys heard the rumor?"

Lev probably always heard rumors first, Billy thought.

Tommy said: "Yeah, we heard you're a homo."

They all laughed.

Billy said: "What rumor?"

"They've signed an armistice." Lev paused. "Don't you get it? The war is over!"

"Not for us," said Billy.

{ III }

Captain Dewar's platoon was attacking a small village called Aux Deux Eglises, east of the river Meuse. Gus had heard a rumor there would be a cease-fire at eleven a.m., but his commanding officer had ordered the assault, so he was carrying it out. He had moved his heavy machine guns forward to the edge of a spinney, and they were firing across a broad meadow at the outlying buildings, and giving the enemy plenty of time to retreat.

Unfortunately, the Germans were not taking the opportunity. They had set up mortars and light machine guns in the farmyards and orchards, and were shooting back energetically. One gun in particular, firing from the roof of a barn, was effectively keeping half of Gus's platoon pinned down.

Gus spoke to Corporal Kerry, the best shot in the unit. "Could you put a grenade into that barn roof?"

Kerry, a freckled youth of nineteen, said: "If I could get a bit closer."

"That's the problem."

Kerry surveyed the terrain. "There's a bit of a rise a third of the way across the meadow," he said. "From there I could do it."

"It's risky," Gus said. "Do you want to be a hero?" He looked at his watch. "The war could be over in five minutes, if the rumors are true."

Kerry grinned. "I'll give it a try, Captain."

Gus hesitated, reluctant to let Kerry risk his life. But this was the army, and they were still fighting, and orders were orders. "All right," Gus said. "In your own time."

He half hoped Kerry would delay, but the boy immediately shouldered his rifle and picked up a case of grenades.

Gus shouted: "All fire! Give Kerry as much cover as you can."

All the machine guns rattled, and Kerry began to run.

The enemy spotted him immediately, and their guns opened up. He zigzagged across the field like a hare chased by dogs. German mortars exploded around him but miraculously missed.

Kerry's "bit of a rise" was three hundred yards away.

He almost made it.

The enemy machine gunner got Kerry perfectly in his sights and let fly with a long burst. Kerry was struck by a dozen rounds within a heartbeat. He flung up his arms, dropped his mortars, and fell, momentum carrying him through the air until he landed a few paces from his rise. He lay quite still, and Gus thought he must have been dead before he hit the ground.

The enemy guns stopped. After a few moments, the

Americans stopped firing, too. Gus thought he could hear the sound of distant cheering. All the men near him fell silent, listening. The Germans were cheering, too.

German soldiers began to appear, emerging from their shelters in the distant village.

Gus heard the sound of an engine. An Indian-brand American motorcycle came through the woods driven by a sergeant with a major on the pillion. "Cease fire!" the major yelled. The motorcyclist was driving him along the line from one position to the next. "Cease fire!" he shouted again. "Cease fire!"

Gus's platoon began to whoop. The men took off their helmets and threw them in the air. Some danced jigs; others shook one another's hands. Gus heard singing.

Gus could not take his eyes off Corporal Kerry.

He walked slowly across the meadow and knelt beside the body. He had seen many corpses and he had no doubt Kerry was dead. He wondered what the boy's first name was. He rolled the body over. There were small bullet holes all over Kerry's chest. Gus closed the boy's eyes and stood up.

"God forgive me," he said.

{ IV }

As it happened, both Ethel and Bernie were home from work that day. Bernie was ill in bed with influenza, and so was Lloyd's child minder, so Ethel was looking after her husband and her son.

She felt very low. They had had a tremendous row about which of them was to be the parliamentary candidate. It was not merely the worst quarrel of their married life; it was the only one. And they had barely spoken to each other since.

Ethel knew she was justified, but she felt guilty all the same. She might well make a better M.P. than Bernie, and anyway the choice should be made by their comrades, not by themselves. Bernie had been planning this for years, but that did not mean the job was his by right. Although Ethel had not thought of it before, she was now eager to run. Women had won the vote, but there was more to be done. First, the age limit must be lowered so that it was the same as for men. Then women's pay and working conditions needed improvement. In most industries, women were paid less than men even when doing exactly the same work. Why should they not get the same?

But she was fond of Bernie, and when she saw the hurt on his face she wanted to give in immediately. "I expected to be undermined by my enemies," he had said to her one evening. "The Conservatives, the halfway-house Liberals, the capitalist imperialists, the bourgeoisie. I even expected opposition from one or two jealous individuals in the party. But there was one person I felt sure I could rely on. And she is the one who has sabotaged me." Ethel felt a pain in her chest when she thought about it.

She took him a cup of tea at eleven o'clock. Their bedroom was comfortable, if shabby, with cheap cotton curtains, a writing table, and a photograph of Keir Hardie on the wall. Bernie put down his novel, *The Ragged Trousered Philanthropists*, which all the socialists were reading. He said coldly: "What are you going to do tonight?" The Labour Party meeting was that evening. "Have you made a decision?"

She had. She could have told him two days ago, but she had not been able to bring herself to utter the words. Now that he had asked the question, she would answer it.

"It should be the best candidate," she said defiantly.

He looked wounded. "I don't know how you can do this to me and still say you love me."

She felt it was unfair of him to use such an argument. Why did it not apply in reverse? But that was not the point. "We shouldn't think of ourselves—we should think of the party."

"What about our marriage?"

"I'm not giving way to you just because I'm your wife."

"You've betrayed me."

"But I am giving way to you," she said.

"What?"

"I said, I am giving way to you."

Relief spread across his face.

She went on: "But it's not because I'm your wife. And it's not because you're the better candidate."

He looked mystified. "Why, then?"

Ethel sighed. "I'm pregnant."

"Oh, my word!"

"Yes. Just at the moment when a woman can become a member of Parliament, I've fallen for a baby."

Bernie smiled. "Well, then, everything's turned out for the best!"

"I knew you'd think that," Ethel said. At that moment she resented Bernie and the unborn baby and everything else about her life. Then she became aware that a church bell was ringing. She looked at the clock on the mantelpiece. It was five past eleven. Why were they ringing at this time on a Monday morning? Then she heard another. She frowned and went to the window. She could see nothing unusual in the street, but more bells began. To the west, in the sky over central London, she saw a red flare, the kind they called a maroon.

She turned back to Bernie. "It sounds as if every church in London is ringing its bells."

"Something's happened," he said. "I bet it's the end of the war. They must be ringing for peace!"

"Well," said Ethel sourly, "it's not for my bloody pregnancy."

{ V }

Fitz's hopes for the overthrow of Lenin and his bandits were centered on the All-Russia Provisional Government, based in Omsk. It was not just Fitz, but powerful men in most of the world's major governments, who looked to this town for the start of the counterrevolution.

The five-man directory was housed in a railway train on the outskirts of the city. A series of armored railcars guarded by elite troops contained, Fitz knew, the remains of the imperial treasury, many millions of rubles' worth of gold. The tsar was dead, killed by the Bolsheviks, but his money was here to give power and authority to the loyalist opposition.

Fitz felt he had a profound personal investment in the directory. The group of influential men he had assembled at Tŷ Gwyn back in April formed a discreet network within British politics, and they had managed to foster Britain's clandestine but weighty encouragement of the Russian resistance. That in turn had brought support from other nations, or at least discouraged them from helping Lenin's regime, he felt sure. But foreigners could not do everything: it was the Russians themselves who had to rise up.

How much could the directory achieve? Although it was anti-Bolshevik, its chairman was a Socialist Revolutionary, Nicholas D. Avkentsiev. Fitz deliberately ignored him. The Socialist Revoutionaries were almost as bad as Lenin's lot. Fitz's hopes lay with the right wing and the military. Only they could be relied upon to restore the monarchy and private property. He went to see General Boldyrev, commander in chief of the directory's Siberian army.

The rail carriages occupied by the government were furnished with fading tsarist splendor: worn velvet seats, chipped marquetry, stained lampshades, and elderly servants wearing dirty remnants of the elaborate braided and beaded livery of the old St. Petersburg court. In one carriage there was a lipsticked young woman in a silk dress smoking a cigarette.

Fitz was discouraged. He wanted to return to the old ways, but this setup seemed too backward-looking even for his taste. He thought with anger of Sergeant Williams's scornful mockery. "Is what we're doing legal?" Fitz knew the answer was doubtful. It was time he shut Williams up for good, he thought wrathfully: the man was practically a Bolshevik himself.

General Boldyrev was a big, clumsy-looking figure. "We have mobilized two hundred thousand men," he told Fitz proudly. "Can you equip them?"

"That's impressive," Fitz said, but he suppressed a sigh. This was the kind of thinking that had caused the Russian army of six million to be defeated by much smaller German and Austrian forces. Boldyrev even wore the absurd epaulets favored by the old regime, big round boards with fringes that made him look like a character in a comic opera by Gilbert and Sullivan. In his makeshift Russian Fitz went on: "But if I were you I'd send half the conscripts home."

Boldyrev was baffled. "Why?"

"At most we can equip a hundred thousand. And they

must be trained. Better to have a small, disciplined army than a great rabble who will retreat or surrender at the first opportunity."

"Ideally, yes."

"The supplies we give you must be issued to men in the front line first, not to those in the rear."

"Of course. Very sensible."

Fitz had a dismal feeling that Boldyrev was agreeing without really listening. But he had to plow on. "Too much of what we send is going astray, as I can see by the number of civilians on the streets wearing articles of British army uniform."

"Yes, quite."

"I strongly recommend that all officers not fit to serve be deprived of their uniforms and asked to return to their homes." The Russian army was plagued by amateurs and elderly dilettantes who interfered with decisions but stayed away from the fighting.

"Hmm."

"And I suggest you give wider powers to Admiral Kolchak as minister of war." The Foreign Office thought Kolchak was the most promising of the members of the directory.

"Very good, very good."

"Are you willing to do all these things?" Fitz said, desperate to get some kind of commitment.

"Definitely."

"When?"

"All in good time, Colonel Fitzherbert, all in good time."

Fitz's heart sank. It was a good thing that men such as Churchill and Curzon could not see how unimpressive were the forces ranged against Bolshevism, he thought dismally. But perhaps they would shape up, with British encouragement. Anyway, he had to do his best with the materials to hand.

There was a knock at the door and his aide-de-camp, Captain Murray, came in holding a telegram. "Sorry to interrupt, sir," he said breathlessly. "But I feel sure you'll want to hear this news as soon as possible."

{ VI }

Mildred came downstairs in the middle of the day and said to Ethel: "Let's go up west." She meant the West End of London. "Everyone's going," she said. "I've sent my girls home." She was now employing two young seamstresses in her hat-trimming business. "The whole East End is shutting up shop. It's the end of the war!"

Ethel was eager to go. Her giving in to Bernie had not improved the atmosphere in the house much. He had cheered up but she had become more bitter. It would do her good to get out of the house. "I'll have to bring Lloyd," she said.

"That's all right. I'll take Enid and Lil. They'll remember it all their lives—the day we won the war."

Ethel made Bernie a cheese sandwich for his lunch; then she dressed Lloyd warmly and they set off. They managed to get on a bus, but soon it was full, with men and boys hanging on the outside. Every house seemed to be flying a flag, not just Union Jacks but Welsh dragons, French tricolors, and the American Stars and Stripes. People were embracing strangers, dancing in the streets, kissing. It was raining, but no one cared.

Ethel thought of all the young men who were now safe from harm, and she began to forget her troubles and share the joyous spirit of the moment.

When they passed the theaters and entered the government district, the traffic slowed to a crawl. Trafalgar Square was a heaving mass of rejoicing humanity. The bus could go no farther, and they got off. They made their way along Whitehall to Downing Street. They could not get near number 10, because of the crush of people hoping for a sight of Prime Minister Lloyd George, the man who won the war. They went into St. James's Park, which was full of couples embracing in the bushes. On the far side of the park, thousands of people stood outside Buckingham Palace. They were singing "Keep the Home Fires Burning." When the song ended they began "Now Thank We All Our God." Ethel saw that a slim young woman in a tweed suit was conducting the singing, standing on top of a lorry, and she reflected that a girl would not have dared to do such a thing before the war.

They crossed the street to Green Park, hoping to get nearer the palace. A young man smiled at Mildred, and when she smiled back, he put his arms around her and kissed her. She returned the kiss enthusiastically.

"You seemed to enjoy that," Ethel said a bit enviously as the boy walked away.

"I did," said Mildred. "I'd have sucked him off if he'd asked me."

"I won't tell Billy that," Ethel said with a laugh.

"Billy's not daft—he knows what I'm like."

They circled the crowd and reached the street called Constitution Hill. The crush thinned out here, but they were at the side of Buckingham Palace, so they would not be able to see the king if he decided to come out onto the balcony. Ethel was wondering where to go next when a troop of mounted police came down the road, causing people to scurry out of the way.

Behind them came a horse-drawn open carriage and inside, smiling and waving, were the king and queen. Ethel recognized them immediately, remembering them vividly from their visit to Aberowen almost five years ago. She could hardly believe her luck as the carriage came slowly toward her. The king's beard was gray, she saw: it had been dark when he came to Tŷ Gwyn. He looked exhausted but happy. Beside him, the queen was holding an umbrella to keep the rain off her hat. Her famous bosom seemed even larger than before.

"Look, Lloyd!" Ethel said. "It's the king!"

The carriage came within inches of where Ethel and Mildred stood.

Lloyd called out loudly: "Hello, King!"

The king heard him and smiled. "Hello, young man," he said; and then he was gone.

{ VII }

Grigori sat in the dining car of the armored train and looked across the table. The man sitting opposite was chairman of the Revolutionary War Council and people's commissar for military and naval affairs. That meant he commanded the Red Army. His name was Lev Davidovich Bronstein, but like most of the leading revolutionaries he had adopted an alias, and he was known as Leon Trotsky. He was a few days past his thirty-ninth birthday, and he held the fate of Russia in his hands.

The revolution was a year old, and Grigori had never been so worried about it. The storming of the Winter Palace had seemed like a conclusion, but in fact it had been only the beginning of the struggle. The most powerful governments of the world were hostile to the Bolsheviks. Today's armistice meant they could now turn their full attention to destroying the revolution. And only the Red Army could stop them.

Many soldiers disliked Trotsky because they thought he was an aristocrat and a Jew. It was impossible to be both in Russia, but soldiers were not logical. Trotsky was no aristocrat, though his father had been a prosperous farmer, and Trotsky had had a good education. But his high-handed manners did him no favors, and he was foolish enough to travel with his own chef and clothe his staff in new boots and gold buttons. He looked older than his years. His great mop of curly hair was still black, but his face was now lined with strain.

He had worked miracles with the army.

The Red Guards who overthrew the provisional government had proved less effective on the battlefield. They were drunken and ill-disciplined. Deciding tactics by a show of hands at a soldiers' meeting had turned out to be a poor way to fight, even worse than taking orders from aristocratic dilettantes. The Reds had lost major battles against the counterrevolutionaries, who were beginning to call themselves the Whites.

Trotsky had reintroduced conscription, against howls of protest. He had drafted many former tsarist officers, called them "specialists," and put them back into their old posts. He had also brought back the death penalty for deserters. Grigori did not like these measures, but he saw the necessity. Anything was better than counterrevolution.

What kept the army together was a core of Bolshevik party members. They were carefully spread through all units to maximize their impact. Some were ordinary soldiers; some held command posts; some, such as Grigori, were political commissars, working alongside the military commanders and reporting back to the Bolshevik Central

Committee in Moscow. They maintained morale by reminding soldiers they were fighting for the greatest cause in the history of humankind. When the army was obliged to be ruthless and cruel, requisitioning grain and horses from desperately poor peasant families, the Bolsheviks would explain to the soldiers why it was necessary for the greater good. And they reported rumblings of discontent early, so that such talk could be crushed before it spread.

But would all this be enough?

Grigori and Trotsky were bent over a map. Trotsky pointed to the Transcaucasia region between Russia and Persia. "The Turks are still in control of the Caspian Sea, with some German help," he said.

"Threatening the oil fields," Grigori muttered.

"Denikin is strong in the Ukraine." Thousands of aristocrats, officers, and bourgeoisie fleeing the revolution had ended up in Novocherkassk, where they had formed a counterrevolutionary force under the renegade General Denikin.

"The so-called Volunteer Army," said Grigori.

"Exactly." Trotsky's finger moved to the north of Russia. "The British have a naval squadron at Murmansk. There are three battalions of American infantry at Archangel. They are supplemented by just about every other country: Canada, China, Poland, Italy, Serbia . . . It might be quicker to list the nations that *don't* have troops in the frozen north of our country."

"And then Siberia."

Trotsky nodded. "The Japanese and Americans have forces in Vladivostok. The Czechs control most of the Trans-Siberian Railway. The British and Canadians are in Omsk, supporting the so-called All-Russia Provisional Government."

Grigori had known much of this, but he had not previously looked at the picture as a whole. "Why, we're surrounded!" he said.

"Exactly. And now that the capitalist-imperialist powers have made peace, they will have millions of troops free."

Grigori sought for a ray of hope. "On the other hand, in the last six months we have increased the size of the Red Army from three hundred thousand to a million men."

"I know." Trotsky was not cheered by this reminder. "But it's not enough."

{ VIII }

Germany was in the throes of a revolution—and to Walter it looked horribly like the Russian revolution of a year ago.

It started with a mutiny. Naval officers ordered the fleet at Kiel to put to sea and attack the British in a suicide mission, but the sailors knew an armistice was being negotiated and they refused. Walter had pointed out to his father that the officers were going against the wishes of the kaiser, so they were the mutineers, and the sailors were the loyal ones. This argument had made Otto apoplectic with rage.

After the government tried to suppress the sailors, the city of Kiel was taken over by a workers' and soldiers' council modeled on the Russian soviets. Two days later Hamburg, Bremen, and Cuxhaven were controlled by soviets. The day before yesterday, the kaiser had abdicated.

Walter was fearful. He wanted democracy, not revolution. But on the day of the abdication, workers in Berlin had marched in their thousands, waving red flags, and the extreme leftist Karl Liebknecht had declared Germany a free socialist republic. Walter did not know how it would end.

The armistice was a dreadfully low moment. He had always believed the war to be a terrible mistake, but there was no satisfaction in being right. The fatherland had been defeated and humiliated, and his fellow countrymen were starving. He sat in the drawing room of his parents' house in Berlin, leafing through the newspapers, too depressed even to play the piano. The wallpaper was faded and the picture rail dusty. There were loose blocks in the aging parquet floor, but no craftsmen to repair it.

Walter could only hope that the world would learn a lesson. President Wilson's Fourteen Points provided a gleam of light that might just herald the rising sun. Was it possible that the giants among nations would find a way to resolve their differences peacefully?

He was infuriated by an article in a right-wing paper. "This fool of a journalist says the German army was never defeated," he said as his father came into the room. "He claims we were betrayed by Jews and socialists at home. We must stamp out that kind of nonsense."

Otto was angrily defiant. "Why should we?" he said.

"Because we know it's not true."

"I think we *were* betrayed by Jews and socialists."

"What?" Walter said incredulously. "It wasn't Jews and socialists who turned us back at the Marne, twice. We lost the war!"

"We were weakened by the lack of supplies."

"That was the British blockade. And whose fault was it that the Americans came in? It was not Jews and socialists who demanded unrestricted submarine warfare and sank ships with American passengers."

"It is the socialists who have given in to the Allies' outrageous armistice terms."

Walter was almost incoherent with rage. "You know perfectly well that it was Ludendorff who asked for an armistice. Chancellor Ebert was appointed only the day before yesterday—how can you blame him?"

"If the army was still in charge we would never have signed today's document."

"But you're not in charge, because you lost the war. You told the kaiser you could win it, and he believed you, and in consequence he lost his crown. How will we learn from our mistakes if you let the German people believe such lies as these?"

"They will be demoralized if they think we were defeated."

"They *should* be demoralized! The leaders of Europe did something wicked and foolish, and ten million men died as a result. At least let the people understand that, so that they will never let it happen again!"

"No," said his father.

PART THREE

THE
WORLD
MADE NEW

CHAPTER THIRTY-FOUR

November to December 1918

Ethel woke early on the morning after Armistice Day. Shivering in the stone-floored kitchen, waiting for the kettle to boil on the old-fashioned range, she made a resolution to be happy. There was a lot to be happy about. The war was over and she was going to have a baby. She had a faithful husband who adored her. Things had not turned out exactly how she wanted, but she would not let that make her miserable. She would paint her kitchen a cheerful yellow, she decided. Bright colors in kitchens were a new fashion.

But first she had to try to mend her marriage. Bernie had been mollified by her surrender, but she had continued to feel bitter, and the atmosphere in the house had remained poisoned. She was angry, but she did not want the rift to be permanent. She wondered if she could make friends.

She took two cups of tea into the bedroom and got back into bed. Lloyd was still asleep in his cot in the corner. "How do you feel?" she said as Bernie sat up and put his glasses on.

"Better, I think."

"Stay in bed another day. Make sure you've got rid of it completely."

"I might do that." His tone was neutral, neither warm nor hostile.

She sipped hot tea. "What would you like, a boy or a girl?"

He was silent, and at first she thought he was sulkily refusing to answer; but in fact he was just thinking for a few moments, as he often did before answering a question. At last he said: "Well, we've got a boy, so it would be nice to have one of each."

She felt a surge of affection for him. He always talked as if Lloyd was his own child. "We've got to make sure this is a good country for them to grow up in," she said. "Where they can get good schooling and a job and a decent house to bring up their own children in. And no more wars."

"Lloyd George will call a snap election."

"Do you think so?"

"He's the man who won the war. He'll want to get re-elected before that wears off."

"I think Labour will still do well."

"We've got a chance in places like Aldgate, anyway."

Ethel hesitated. "Would you like me to manage your campaign?"

Bernie looked doubtful. "I've asked Jock Reid to be my agent."

"Jock can deal with legal documents and finance," Ethel said. "I'll organize meetings and so on. I can do it much better." Suddenly she felt this was about their marriage, not just the campaign.

"Are you sure you want to?"

"Yes. Jock would just send you to make speeches. You'll have to do that, of course, but it's not your strong point. You're better sitting down with a few people, talking over a cup of tea. I'll get you into factories and warehouses where you can chat to the men informally."

"I'm sure you're right," Bernie said.

She finished her tea and put the cup and saucer on the floor beside the bed. "So you're feeling better?"

"Yes."

She took his cup and saucer, put them down, then pulled her nightdress over her head. Her breasts were not as perky as they had been before she got pregnant with Lloyd, but they were still firm and round. "How much better?" she said.

He stared. "A lot."

They had not made love since the evening Jayne Mc-Culley had proposed Ethel as candidate. Ethel was missing it badly. She held her breasts in her hands. The cold air in the room was making her nipples stand up. "Do you know what these are?"

"I believe they're your bosoms."

"Some people call them tits."

"I call them beautiful." His voice had become a little hoarse.

"Would you like to play with them?"

"All day long."

"I'm not sure about that," she said. "But make a start, and we'll see how we go."

"All right."

Ethel sighed happily. Men were so simple.

An hour later she went to work, leaving Lloyd with Bernie. There were not many people on the streets: London had a hangover this morning. She reached the office of the National Union of Garment Workers and sat at her desk. Peace would bring new industrial problems, she realized as she thought about the working day ahead of her. Millions of men leaving the army would be looking for employment, and they would want to elbow aside the women who had been doing their jobs for four years. But those women needed their wages. They did not all have a man coming home from France: a lot of their husbands were buried there. They needed their union, and they needed Ethel.

Whenever the election came, the union would naturally be campaigning for the Labour Party. Ethel spent most of the day in planning meetings.

The evening papers brought surprising news about the election. Lloyd George had decided to continue the coalition government into peacetime. He would not campaign as leader of the Liberals, but as head of the coalition. That morning he had addressed two hundred Liberal M.P.s at Downing Street and won their support. At the same time Bonar Law had persuaded Conservative M.P.s to back the idea.

Ethel was baffled. What were people supposed to vote for?

When she got home she found Bernie furious. "It's not an election—it's a bloody coronation," he said. "King David Lloyd George. What a traitor. He has a chance to bring in a radical left-wing government and what does he do? Sticks with his Conservative pals! He's a bloody turncoat."

"Let's not give up yet," said Ethel.

Two days later the Labour Party withdrew from the coalition and announced it would campaign against Lloyd George. Four Labour M.P.s who were government ministers refused to resign and were smartly expelled from the party. The date of the election was set for December 14. To give time for soldiers' ballots to be returned from France and counted, the results would not be announced until after Christmas.

Ethel started drawing up Bernie's campaigning schedule.

{ II }

On the day after Armistice Day, Maud wrote to Walter on her brother's crested writing paper and put the letter in the red pillar-box on the street corner.

She had no idea how long it would take for normal post to be resumed, but when it happened she wanted her envelope to be on top of the pile. Her message was carefully worded, just in case censorship continued: it did not refer to their marriage, but just said she hoped to resume their old relationship now that their countries were at peace. Perhaps the letter was risky all the same. But she was desperate to find out whether Walter was alive and, if he was, to see him.

She feared that the victorious Allies would want to punish the German people, but Lloyd George's speech to Liberal M.P.s that day was reassuring. According to the evening papers, he said the peace treaty with Germany must be fair and just. "We must not allow any sense of revenge, any spirit of greed, or any grasping desire to overrule the fundamental principles of righteousness." The government would set its face against what he called "a base, sordid, squalid idea of vengeance and avarice." That cheered her up. Life for the Germans now would be hard enough anyway.

However, she was horrified the following morning when she opened the *Daily Mail* at breakfast. The leading article was headed THE HUNS MUST PAY. The paper argued that food aid should be sent to Germany—only because "if Germany

were starved to death she could not pay what she owes."
The kaiser must be put on trial for war crimes, it added.
The paper fanned the flames of revenge by publishing at
the top of its letters column a diatribe from Viscountess
Templetown headed KEEP OUT THE HUNS. "How long are we
all supposed to go on hating one another?" Maud said to
Aunt Herm. "A year? Ten years? Forever?"

But Maud should not have been surprised. The *Mail*
had conducted a hate campaign against the thirty thousand
Germans who had been living in Britain at the outbreak
of war—most of them long-term residents who thought of
this country as their home. In consequence families had
been broken up and thousands of harmless people had
spent years in British concentration camps. It was stupid,
but people needed someone to hate, and the newspapers
were always ready to supply that need.

Maud knew the proprietor of the *Mail,* Lord Northcliffe. Like all great press men, he really believed the drivel
he published. His talent was to express his readers' most
stupid and ignorant prejudices as if they made sense, so
that the shameful seemed respectable. That was why they
bought the paper.

She also knew that Lloyd George had recently snubbed
Northcliffe personally. The self-important press lord had
proposed himself as a member of the British delegation
at the upcoming peace conference, and had been offended
when the prime minister turned him down.

Maud was worried. In politics, despicable people sometimes had to be pandered to, but Lloyd George seemed to
have forgotten that. She wondered anxiously how much effect the *Mail*'s malevolent propaganda would have on the
election.

A few days later she found out.

She went to an election meeting in a municipal hall in
the East End of London. Eth Leckwith was in the audience and her husband, Bernie, was on the platform. Maud
had not made up her quarrel with Ethel, even though they
had been friends and colleagues for years. In fact Maud
still trembled with anger when she recalled how Ethel and
others had encouraged Parliament to pass a law that kept
women at a disadvantage to men in elections. All the same
she missed Ethel's high spirits and ready smile.

The audience sat restlessly through the introductions. They were still mostly men, even though some women could now vote. Maud guessed that most women had not yet got used to the idea that they needed to take an interest in political discussions. But she also felt women would be put off by the tone of political meetings, in which men stood on a platform and ranted while the audience cheered or booed.

Bernie was the first speaker. He was no orator, Maud saw immediately. He spoke about the Labour Party's new constitution, in particular clause four, calling for public ownership of the means of production. Maud thought this was interesting, for it drew a clear line between Labour and the pro-business Liberals; but she soon realized she was in a minority. The man sitting next to her grew restless and eventually shouted: "Will you chuck the Germans out of this country?"

Bernie was thrown. He mumbled for a few moments, then said: "I would do whatever benefited the workingman." Maud wondered about the workingwoman, and guessed that Ethel must be thinking the same. Bernie went on: "But I don't see that action against Germans in Britain is a high priority."

That did not go down well; in fact it drew a few scattered boos.

Bernie said: "But to return to more important issues—"

From the other side of the hall, someone shouted: "What about the kaiser?"

Bernie made the mistake of replying to the heckler with a question. "What *about* the kaiser?" he rejoined. "He has abdicated."

"Should he be put on trial?"

Bernie said with exasperation: "Don't you understand that a trial means he will be entitled to defend himself? Do you really want to give the German emperor a platform to proclaim his innocence to the world?"

This was a compelling argument, Maud thought, but it was not what the audience wanted to hear. The booing grew louder, and there were shouts of "Hang the kaiser!"

British voters were ugly when riled, Maud thought; at least, the men were. Few women would ever want to come to meetings like this.

Bernie said: "If we hang our defeated enemies, we are barbarians."

The man next to Maud shouted again: "Will you make the Hun pay?"

That got the biggest reaction of all. Several people shouted out: "Make the Hun pay!"

"Within reason," Bernie began, but he got no further.

"Make the Hun pay!" The shout became common, and in a moment they were chanting in unison: "Make the Hun pay! Make the Hun pay!"

Maud got up from her seat and left.

{ III }

Woodrow Wilson was the first American president ever to leave the country during his term of office.

He sailed from New York on December 4. Nine days later Gus was waiting for him at the quayside in Brest, on the western tip of the Brittany panhandle. At midday the mist cleared and the sun came out, for the first time in days. In the bay, battleships from the French, British, and American navies formed an honor guard through which the president steamed in a U.S. Navy transport ship, the *George Washington*. Guns thundered a salute, and a band played "The Star-Spangled Banner."

It was a solemn moment for Gus. Wilson had come here to make sure there would never be another war like the one just ended. Wilson's Fourteen Points, and his League of Nations, were intended to change forever the way nations resolved their conflicts. It was a stratospheric ambition. In the history of human civilization, no politician had ever aimed so high. If he succeeded, the world would be made new.

At three in the afternoon the first lady, Edith Wilson, walked down the gangplank on the arm of General Pershing, followed by the president in a top hat.

The town of Brest received Wilson as a conquering hero. *Vive Wilson,* said the banners, *Defenseur du Droit des Peuples;* Long Live Wilson, Defender of People's Rights. Every building flew the Stars and Stripes. Crowds jammed the sidewalks, many of the women wearing the traditional Breton tall lace headdress. The sound of Breton bagpipes was everywhere. Gus could have done without the bagpipes.

The French foreign minister made a speech of welcome. Gus stood with the American journalists. He noticed a small woman wearing a big fur hat. She turned her head, and he saw that her pretty face was marred by one permanently closed eye. He smiled with delight: it was Rosa Hellman. He looked forward to hearing her view of the peace conference.

After the speeches, the entire presidential party boarded the night train for the four-hundred-mile journey to Paris. The president shook Gus's hand and said: "Glad to have you back on the team, Gus."

Wilson wanted familiar associates around him for the Paris Peace Conference. His main adviser would be Colonel House, the pale Texan who had been unofficially counseling him on foreign policy for years. Gus would be the junior member of the crew.

Wilson looked weary, and he and Edith retired to their suite. Gus was concerned. He had heard rumors that the president's health was poor. Back in 1906 a blood vessel had burst behind Wilson's left eye, causing temporary blindness, and the doctors had diagnosed high blood pressure and advised him to retire. Wilson had cheerfully ignored their advice and gone on to become president, of course— but lately he had been suffering from headaches that might be a new symptom of the same blood pressure problem. The peace conference would be taxing: Gus hoped Wilson could stand it.

Rosa was on the train. Gus sat opposite her on the brocaded upholstery in the dining car. "I wondered whether I might see you," she said. She seemed pleased they had met.

"I'm on detachment from the army," said Gus, who was still wearing the uniform of a captain.

"Back home, Wilson has been walloped for his choice of colleagues. Not you, of course—"

"I'm a small fish."

"But some people say he should not have brought his wife."

Gus shrugged. It seemed trivial. After the battlefield it

was going to be difficult to take seriously some of the stuff people worried about in peacetime.

Rosa said: "More important, he hasn't brought any Republicans."

"He wants allies on his team, not enemies," Gus said indignantly.

"He needs allies back home, too," Rosa said. "He's lost Congress."

She had a point, and Gus was reminded how smart she was. The midterm elections had been disastrous for Wilson. The Republicans had gained control of the Senate and the House of Representatives. "How did that happen?" he said. "I've been out of touch."

"Ordinary people are fed up with rationing and high prices, and the end of the war came just a bit too late to help. And liberals hate the Espionage Act. It allowed Wilson to jail people who disagreed with the war. He used it, too—Eugene Debs was sentenced to ten years." Debs had been a presidential candidate for the Socialists. Rosa sounded angry as she said: "You can't put your opponents in jail and still pretend to believe in freedom."

Gus remembered how much he enjoyed the cut and thrust of an argument with Rosa. "Freedom sometimes has to be compromised in war," he said.

"Obviously American voters don't think so. And there's another thing: Wilson segregated his Washington offices."

Gus did not know whether Negroes could ever be raised to the level of white people but, like most liberal Americans, he thought the way to find out was to give them better chances in life and see what happened. However, Wilson and his wife were Southerners, and felt differently. "Edith won't take her maid to London, for fear the girl will get spoiled," Gus said. "She says British people are too polite to Negroes."

"Woodrow Wilson is no longer the darling of the left in America," Rosa concluded. "Which means he's going to need Republican support for his League of Nations."

"I suppose Henry Cabot Lodge feels snubbed." Lodge was a right-wing Republican.

"You know politicians," Rosa said. "They're as sensitive as schoolgirls, and more vengeful. Lodge is chairman of the Senate Foreign Relations Committee. Wilson should have brought him to Paris."

Gus protested: "Lodge is against the whole idea of the League of Nations!"

"The ability to listen to smart people who disagree with you is a rare talent—but a president should have it. And bringing Lodge here would have neutralized him. As a member of the team, he couldn't go home and fight against whatever is agreed in Paris."

Gus guessed she was right. But Wilson was an idealist who believed that the force of righteousness would overcome all obstacles. He underestimated the need to flatter, cajole, and seduce.

The food was good, in honor of the president. They had fresh sole from the Atlantic in a buttery sauce. Gus had not eaten so well since before the war. He was amused to see Rosa tuck in heartily. She had a petite figure: where did she put it all?

At the end of the meal they were served strong coffee in small cups. Gus found he did not want to leave Rosa and retire to his sleeping compartment. He was much too interested in talking to her. "Wilson will be in a strong position in Paris, anyway," he said.

Rosa looked skeptical. "How so?"

"Well, first of all we won the war for them."

She nodded. "Wilson said: 'At Château-Thierry we saved the world.'"

"Chuck Dixon and I were in that battle."

"Was that where he died?"

"Direct hit from a shell. First casualty I saw. Not the last, sadly."

"I'm very sorry, especially for his wife. I've known Doris for years—we used to have the same piano teacher."

"I don't know if we saved the world, though," Gus went on. "There are many more French and British and Russians among the dead than Americans. But we tipped the balance. That ought to mean something."

She shook her head, tossing her dark curls. "I disagree. The war is over, and the Europeans no longer need us."

"Men such as Lloyd George seem to think that American military power cannot be ignored."

"Then he's wrong," said Rosa. Gus was surprised and intrigued to hear a woman speak so forcefully about such a subject. "Suppose the French and British simply refuse to go along with Wilson," she said. "Would he use the army to enforce his ideas? No. Even if he wanted to, a Republican Congress wouldn't let him."

"We have economic and financial power."

"It's certainly true that the Allies owe us huge debts, but I'm not sure how much leverage that gives us. There's a saying: 'If you owe a hundred dollars, the bank has you in its power; but if you owe a million dollars, you have the bank in your power.'"

Gus began to see that Wilson's task might be more difficult than he had imagined. "Well, what about public opinion? You saw the reception Wilson got in Brest. All over Europe, people are looking to him to create a peaceful world."

"That's his strongest card. People are sick of slaughter. 'Never again' is their cry. I just hope Wilson can deliver what they want."

They returned to their compartments and said good night. Gus lay awake a long time, thinking about Rosa and what she had said. She really was the smartest woman he had ever met. She was beautiful, too. Somehow you quickly forgot about her eye. At first it seemed a terrible deformity, but after a while Gus stopped noticing it.

She had been pessimistic about the conference, however. And everything she said was true. Wilson had a struggle ahead, Gus now realized. He was overjoyed to be part of the team, and determined to do what he could to turn the president's ideals into reality.

In the small hours of the morning he looked out of the window as the train steamed eastward across France. Passing through a town, he was startled to see crowds on the station platforms and on the road beside the railway line, watching. It was dark, but they were clearly visible by lamplight. There were thousands of them, men and women and children. There was no cheering: they were quite silent. The men and boys took off their hats, Gus saw, and that gesture of respect moved him almost to tears. They had waited half the night to see the passing of the train that held the hope of the world.

CHAPTER THIRTY-FIVE

December 1918 to February 1919

The votes were counted three days after Christmas. Eth and Bernie Leckwith stood in Aldgate town hall to hear the results, Bernie on the platform in his best suit, Eth in the audience.

Bernie lost.

He was stoical, but Ethel cried. For him it was the end of a dream. Perhaps it had been a foolish dream, but all the same he was hurt, and her heart ached for him.

The Liberal candidate had supported the Lloyd George coalition, so there had been no Conservative candidate. Consequently the Conservatives had voted Liberal, and the combination had been too much for Labour to beat.

Bernie congratulated his winning opponent and came down off the platform. The other Labour Party members had a bottle of Scotch and wanted to hold a wake, but Bernie and Ethel went home.

"I'm not cut out for this, Eth," Bernie said as she boiled water for cocoa.

"You did a good job," she said. "We were outwitted by that bloody Lloyd George."

Bernie shook his head. "I'm not a leader," he said. "I'm a thinker and a planner. Time and again I tried to talk to people the way you do, and fire them with enthusiasm for our cause, but I never could do it. When you talk to them, they love you. That's the difference."

She knew he was right.

Next morning the newspapers showed that the Aldgate result had been mirrored all over the country. The coalition had won 525 of the 707 seats, one of the largest majorities in the history of Parliament. The people had voted for the man who won the war.

Ethel was bitterly disappointed. The old men were still running the country. The politicians who had caused millions of deaths were now celebrating, as if they had done something wonderful. But what had they achieved? Pain and hunger and destruction. Ten million men and boys had been killed to no purpose.

The only glimmer of hope was that the Labour Party had improved its position. They had won sixty seats, up from forty-two.

It was the anti–Lloyd George Liberals who had suffered. They had won only thirty constituencies, and Asquith himself had lost his seat. "This could be the end of the Liberal Party," said Bernie as he spread dripping on his bread for lunch. "They've failed the people, and Labour is the opposition now. That may be our only consolation."

Just before they left for work, the post arrived. Ethel looked at the letters while Bernie tied the laces of Lloyd's shoes. There was one from Billy, written in their code. She sat at the kitchen table to decode it.

She underlined the key words with a pencil and wrote them on a pad. As she deciphered the message she became more and more fascinated.

"You know Billy's in Russia," she said to Bernie.

"Yes."

"Well, he says our army is there to fight against the Bolsheviks. The American army is there, too."

"I'm not surprised."

"Yes, but listen, Bern," she said. "We know the Whites can't beat the Bolsheviks—but what if foreign armies join in? Anything could happen!"

Bernie looked thoughtful. "They could bring back the monarchy."

"The people of this country won't stand for that."

"The people of this country don't know what's going on."

"Then we'd better tell them," said Ethel. "I'm going to write an article."

"Who will publish it?"

"We'll see. Maybe the *Daily Herald*." The *Herald* was left-wing. "Will you take Lloyd to the child minder?"

"Yes, of course."

Ethel thought for a minute; then, at the top of a sheet of paper, she wrote:

Hands Off Russia!

{ II }

Walking around Paris made Maud cry. Along the broad boulevards there were piles of rubble where German shells had fallen. Broken windows in the grand buildings were repaired with boards, reminding her painfully of her handsome brother with his disfigured eye. The avenues of trees were marred by gaps where an ancient chestnut or noble plane had been sacrificed for its timber. Half the women wore black for mourning, and on street corners crippled soldiers begged for change.

She was crying for Walter, too. She had received no reply to her letter. She had inquired about going to Germany, but that was impossible. It had been difficult enough to get permission to come to Paris. She had hoped Walter might come here with the German delegation, but there was no German delegation: the defeated countries were not invited to the peace conference. The victorious Allies intended to thrash out an agreement among themselves, then present the losers with a treaty for signing.

Meanwhile there was a shortage of coal, and all the hotels were freezing cold. She had a suite at the Majestic, where the British delegation was headquartered. To guard against French spies, the British had replaced all the staff with their own people. Consequently the food was dire: porridge for breakfast, overcooked vegetables, and bad coffee.

Wrapped in a prewar fur coat, Maud went to meet Johnny Remarc at Fouquet's on the Champs-Elysées. "Thank you for arranging for me to travel to Paris," she said.

"Anything for you, Maud. But why were you so keen to come here?"

She was not going to tell the truth, least of all to someone who loved to gossip. "Shopping," she said. "I haven't bought a new dress for four years."

"Oh, spare me," he said. "There's almost nothing to buy, and what there is costs a fortune. Fifteen hundred francs for a gown! Even Fitz might draw the line there. I think you must have a French paramour."

"I wish I did." She changed the subject. "I've found Fitz's car. Do you know where I might get petrol?"

"I'll see what I can do."

They ordered lunch. Maud said: "Do you think we're really going to make the Germans pay billions in reparations?"

"They're not in a good position to object," said Johnny. "After the Franco-Prussian War they made France pay five billion francs—which the French did in three years. And last March, in the Treaty of Brest-Litovsk, Germany made the Bolsheviks promise six billion marks, although of course it won't be paid now. All the same, the Germans' righteous indignation has the hollow ring of hypocrisy."

Maud hated it when people spoke harshly of the Germans. It was as if the fact that they had lost made them beasts. *What if we had been the losers,* Maud wanted to say—*would we have had to say the war was our fault, and pay for it all?* "But we're asking for so much more—twenty-four billion pounds, we say, and the French put it at almost double that."

"It's hard to argue with the French," Johnny said. "They owe us six hundred million pounds, and more to the Americans; but if we deny them German reparations, they'll say they can't pay us."

"Can the Germans pay what we're asking?"

"No. My friend Pozzo Keynes says they could pay about a tenth—two billion pounds—though it may cripple their country."

"Do you mean John Maynard Keynes, the Cambridge economist?"

"Yes. We call him Pozzo."

"I didn't know he was one of . . . your friends."

Johnny smiled. "Oh, yes, my dear, very much so."

Maud suffered a moment of envy for Johnny's cheerful depravity. She had fiercely suppressed her own need for physical love. It was almost two years since a man had touched her lovingly. She felt like an old nun, wrinkled and dried up.

"What a sad look!" Johnny did not miss much. "I hope you're not in love with Pozzo."

She laughed, then turned the conversation back to politics. "If we know the Germans can't pay, why is Lloyd George insisting?"

"I asked him that question myself. I've known him quite well since he was minister for munitions. He says all the belligerents will end up paying their own debts, and no one will get any reparations to speak of."

"So why this pretense?"

"Because in the end the taxpayers of every country will pay for the war—but the politician who tells them that will never win another election."

{ III }

Gus went to the daily meetings of the League of Nations Commission. This group had the job of drafting the covenant that would set up the league. Woodrow Wilson himself chaired the committee, and he was in a hurry.

Wilson had completely dominated the first month of the conference. He had swept aside a French agenda putting German reparations at the top and the league at the bottom, and insisted that the league must be part of any treaty signed by him.

The League Commission met at the luxurious Hotel Crillon on the Place de la Concorde. The hydraulic elevators were ancient and slow, and sometimes stopped between floors while the water pressure built up; Gus thought they were very like the European diplomats, who enjoyed nothing more than a leisurely argument, and never came to a decision until forced. He saw with secret amusement that both diplomats and lifts caused the American president to fidget and mutter in furious impatience.

The nineteen commissioners sat around a big table covered with a red cloth, their interpreters behind them whispering in their ears, their aides around the room with files and notebooks. Gus could tell that the Europeans were impressed by his boss's ability to drive the agenda forward. Some people had said the writing of the covenant would take months, if not years; and others said the nations would never reach agreement. However, to Gus's delight, after ten days they were close to completing a first draft.

Wilson had to return to the United States on February 14. He would be back soon, but he was determined to have a draft of the covenant to take home.

Unfortunately, the afternoon before he left, the French produced a major obstacle. They proposed that the League of Nations should have its own army.

Wilson's eyes rolled up in despair. "Impossible," he groaned.

Gus knew why. Congress would not allow American troops to be under someone else's control.

The French delegate, former prime minister Léon Bourgeois, argued that the league would be ignored if it had no means of enforcing its decisions.

Gus shared Wilson's frustration. There were other ways for the league to put pressure on rogue nations: diplomacy, economic sanctions, and in the last resort an ad hoc army, to be used for a specific mission, then disbanded when the job was done.

But Bourgeois said none of that would have protected France from Germany. The French could not focus on anything else. Perhaps it was understandable, Gus thought, but it was not the way to create a new world order.

Lord Robert Cecil, who had done a lot of the drafting, raised a bony finger to speak. Wilson nodded: he liked Cecil, who was a strong supporter of the league. Not everyone agreed: Clemenceau, the French prime minister, said that when Cecil smiled he looked like a Chinese dragon. "Forgive me for being blunt," Cecil said. "The French delegation seems to be saying that because the league may not be as strong as they hoped, they will reject it altogether. May I point out very frankly that in that case there will almost certainly be a bilateral alliance between Great Britain and the United States that would offer nothing to France."

Gus suppressed a smile. That's telling 'em, he thought.

Bourgeois looked shocked and withdrew his amendment.

Wilson shot a grateful look across the table at Cecil.

The Japanese delegate, Baron Makino, wanted to speak. Wilson nodded and looked at his watch.

Makino referred to the clause in the covenant, already agreed, that guaranteed religious freedom. He wished to add an amendment to the effect that all members would treat one another's citizens equally, without racial discrimination.

Wilson's face froze.

Makino's speech was eloquent, even in translation. Different races had fought side by side in the war, he pointed out. "A common bond of sympathy and gratitude has been established." The league would be a great family of nations. Surely they should treat one another as equals?

Gus was worried but not surprised. The Japanese had been talking about this for a week or two. It had already caused consternation among the Australians and the Californians, who wanted to keep the Japanese out of their territories. It had disconcerted Wilson, who did not for one moment think that American Negroes were his equals. Most of all it had upset the British, who ruled undemocratically over hundreds of millions of people of different races and did not want them to think they were as good as their white overlords.

Again it was Cecil who spoke. "Alas, this is a highly controversial matter," he said, and Gus could almost have believed in his sadness. "The mere suggestion that it might be discussed has already created discord."

There was a murmur of agreement around the table.

Cecil went on: "Rather than delay the agreement of a draft covenant, perhaps we should postpone discussion of, ah, racial discrimination to a later date."

The Greek prime minister said: "The whole question of religious liberty is a tricky subject, too. Perhaps we should drop that for the present."

The Portuguese delegate said: "My government has never yet signed a treaty that did not call on God!"

Cecil, a deeply religious man, said: "Perhaps this time we will all have to take a chance."

There was a ripple of laughter, and Wilson said with evident relief: "If that's agreed, let us move on."

{ IV }

Next day Wilson went to the French foreign ministry at the Quai d'Orsay and read the draft to a plenary session of the peace conference in the famous Clock Room under the enormous chandeliers that looked like stalactites in an Arctic cave. That evening he left for home. The following day was a Saturday, and in the evening Gus went dancing.

Paris after dark was a party town. Food was still scarce but there seemed to be plenty of booze. Young men left their hotel room doors open so that Red Cross nurses could wander in whenever they needed company. Conventional morality seemed to be put on hold. People did not try to hide their love affairs. Effeminate men cast off the pretense of masculinity. Larue's became the lesbian restaurant. It was said the coal shortage was a myth put about by the French so that everyone would keep warm at night by sleeping with their friends.

Everything was expensive, but Gus had money. He had other advantages, too: he knew Paris and could speak French. He went to the races at St. Cloud, saw *La Bohème* at the opera, and went to a risqué musical called *Phi Phi*. Because he was close to the president, he was invited to every party.

He found himself spending more and more time with Rosa Hellman. He had to be careful, when talking to her, to tell her only things that he would be happy to see printed, but the habit of discretion was automatic with him now. She was one of the smartest people he had ever met. He liked her, but that was as far as it went. She was always ready to go out with him, but what reporter would refuse an invitation from a presidential aide? He could never hold hands with her, or try to kiss her good night, in case she might think he was taking advantage of his position as someone she could not afford to offend.

He met her at the Ritz for cocktails. "What are cocktails?" she said.

"Hard liquor dressed up to be more respectable. I promise you, they're fashionable."

Rosa was fashionable, too. Her hair was bobbed. Her cloche hat came down over her ears like a German soldier's steel helmet. Curves and corsets had gone out of style, and her draped dress fell straight from the shoulders to a startlingly low waistline. By concealing her shape, paradoxically, the dress made Gus think about the body beneath. She wore lipstick and face powder, something European women still considered daring.

They had a martini each, then moved on. They drew a lot of stares as they walked together through the long lobby of the Ritz: the lanky man with the big head and his tiny one-eyed companion, him in white-tie-and-tails and her in silver-blue silk. They got a cab to the Majestic, where the British held Saturday night dances that everyone went to.

The ballroom was packed. Young aides from the delegations, journalists from all over the world, and soldiers freed from the trenches were "jazzing" with nurses and typists. Rosa taught Gus the fox-trot; then she left him and danced with a handsome dark-eyed man from the Greek delegation.

Feeling jealous, Gus drifted around the room chatting to acquaintances until he ran into Lady Maud Fitzherbert in a purple dress and pointed shoes. "Hello!" he said in surprise.

She seemed pleased to see him. "You look well."

"I was lucky. I'm all in one piece."

She touched the scar on his cheek. "Almost."

"A scratch. Shall we dance?"

He took her in his arms. She was thin: he could feel her bones through the dress. They did the hesitation waltz. "How is Fitz?" Gus asked.

"Fine, I think. He's in Russia. I'm probably not supposed to say that, but it's an open secret."

"I notice the British newspapers saying 'Hands Off Russia.'"

"That campaign is being led by a woman you met at Tŷ Gwyn, Ethel Williams, now Eth Leckwith."

"I don't remember her."

"She was the housekeeper."

"Good Lord!"

"She's becoming something of a force in British politics."

"How the world has changed."

Maud drew him closer and lowered her voice. "I don't suppose you have any news of Walter?"

Gus recalled the familiar-looking German officer he had seen fall at Château-Thierry, but he was far from certain that had been Walter, so he said: "Nothing, I'm sorry. It must be hard for you."

"No information is coming out of Germany and no one is allowed to go there!"

"I'm afraid you may have to wait until the peace treaty is signed."

"And when will that be?"

Gus did not know. "The league covenant is pretty much done, but they're a long way from agreement over how much Germany should pay in reparations."

"It's foolish," Maud said bitterly. "We need the Germans to be prosperous, so that British factories can sell them cars and stoves and carpet sweepers. If we cripple their economy, Germany will go Bolshevik."

"People want revenge."

"Do you remember 1914? Walter didn't want war. Nor did the majority of Germans. But the country wasn't a democracy. The kaiser was egged on by the generals. And once the Russians had mobilized, they had no choice."

"Of course I remember. But most people don't."

The dance ended. Rosa Hellman appeared, and Gus introduced the two women. They talked for a minute, but Rosa was uncharacteristically charmless, and Maud moved away.

"That dress cost a fortune," Rosa said grumpily. "It's by Jeanne Lanvin."

Gus was perplexed. "Didn't you like Maud?"

"You obviously do."

"What do you mean?"

"You were dancing very close."

Rosa did not know about Walter. All the same, Gus resented being falsely accused of flirting. "She wanted to talk about something rather confidential," he said with a touch of indignation.

"I bet she did."

"I don't know why you're taking this attitude," Gus said. "You went off with that oily Greek."

"He's very handsome, and not a bit oily. Why shouldn't I dance with other men? It's not as if you're in love with me."

Gus stared at her. "Oh," he said. "Oh, dear." He suddenly felt confused and uncertain.

"What's the matter now?"

"I've just realized something . . . I think."

"Are you going to tell me what it is?"

"I suppose I must," he said shakily. He paused.

She waited for him to speak. "Well?" she said impatiently.

"I am in love with you."

She looked back at him in silence. After a long pause she said: "Do you mean it?"

Although the thought had taken him by surprise, he had no doubt. "Yes. I love you, Rosa."

She smiled weakly. "Just fancy that."

"I think perhaps I've been in love with you for quite a long time without knowing it."

She nodded, as if having a suspicion confirmed. The band started a slow tune. She moved closer.

He took her in his arms automatically, but he was too wrought up to dance properly. "I'm not sure I can manage—"

"Don't worry." She knew what he was thinking. "Just pretend."

He shuffled a few steps. His mind was in turmoil. She had not said anything about her own feelings. On the other hand, she had not walked away. Was there any chance she might return his love? She obviously liked him, but that was not the same thing at all. Was she asking herself, at this very minute, how she felt? Or was she thinking up some gentle words of rejection?

She looked up at him, and he thought she was about to give him the answer; then she said: "Take me away from here, please, Gus."

"Of course."

She got her coat. The doorman summoned a red Renault taxi. "Maxim's," Gus said. It was a short drive, and they rode in silence. Gus longed to know what was in her mind, but he did not rush her. She would have to tell him soon.

The restaurant was packed, the few empty tables reserved for later customers. The headwaiter was *désolé*. Gus took out his wallet, extracted a hundred-franc note, and said: "A quiet table in a corner." A card saying *Réservée* was whipped away and they sat down.

They chose a light supper and Gus ordered a bottle of champagne. "You've changed so much," Rosa said.

He was surprised. "I don't think so."

"You were a diffident young man, back in Buffalo. I think you were even shy of me. Now you walk around Paris as if you own it."

"Oh, dear—that sounds arrogant."

"No, just confident. After all, you've worked for a president and fought a war—those things make a difference."

The food came but neither of them ate much. Gus was too tense. What was she thinking? Did she love him or not? Surely she must know? He put down his knife and fork, but instead of asking her the question on his mind he said: "You've always seemed self-confident."

She laughed. "Isn't that amazing?"

"Why?"

"I suppose I was confident until about the age of seven. And then ... well, you know what schoolgirls are like. Everyone wants to be friends with the prettiest. I had to play with the fat girls and the ugly ones and those dressed in hand-me-downs. That went on into my teenage years. Even working for the *Buffalo Anarchist* was kind of an outsider thing to do. But when I became editor I started to get my self-esteem back." She took a sip of champagne. "You helped."

"I did?" Gus was surprised.

"It was the way you talked to me, as if I was the smartest and most interesting person in Buffalo."

"You probably were."

"Except for Olga Vyalov."

"Ah." Gus blushed. Remembering his infatuation with Olga made him feel foolish, but he did not want to say so, for that would be running her down, which was ungentlemanly.

When they had finished their coffee and he called for the bill, he still did not know how Rosa felt about him.

In the taxi he took her hand and pressed it to his lips. She said: "Oh, Gus, you are very dear." He did not know what she meant by that. However, her face was turned up toward him in a way that almost seemed expectant. Did she want him to ... ? He screwed up his nerve and kissed her mouth.

There was a frozen moment when she did not respond, and he thought he had done the wrong thing. Then she sighed contentedly and parted her lips.

Oh, he thought happily; so that's all right, then.

He put his arms around her and they kissed all the way to her hotel. The journey was too short. Suddenly a commissionaire was opening the door of the cab. "Wipe your mouth," Rosa said as she got out. Gus pulled out a handkerchief and hastily rubbed at his face. The white linen came away red with her lipstick. He folded it carefully and put it back in his pocket.

He walked her to the door. "Can I see you tomorrow?" he said.

"When?"

"Early."

She laughed. "You never pretend, Gus, do you? I love that about you."

That was good. *I love that about you* was not the same as *I love you* but it was better than nothing. "Early it is," he said.

"What shall we do?"

"It's Sunday." He said the first thing that came into his head. "We could go to church."

"All right."

"Let me take you to Notre Dame."

"Are you Catholic?" she said in surprise.

"No, Episcopalian, if anything. You?"

"The same."

"It's all right—we can sit at the back. I'll find out what time mass is and phone your hotel."

She held out her hand and they shook like friends. "Thank you for a lovely evening," she said formally.

"It was such a pleasure. Good night."

"Good night," she said, and she turned away and disappeared into the hotel lobby.

CHAPTER THIRTY-SIX

March to April 1919

When the snow melted, and the iron-hard Russian earth turned to rich wet mud, the White armies made a mighty effort to rid their country of the curse of Bolshevism. Admiral Kolchak's force of one hundred thousand, patchily supplied with British uniforms and guns, came storming out of Siberia and attacked the Reds over a front that stretched seven hundred miles from north to south.

Fitz followed a few miles behind the Whites. He was leading the Aberowen Pals, plus some Canadians and a few interpreters. His job was to stiffen Kolchak by supervising communications, intelligence, and supply.

Fitz had high hopes. There might be difficulties, but it was unimaginable that Lenin and Trotsky would be allowed to steal Russia.

At the beginning of March he was in the city of Ufa on the European side of the Ural Mountains, reading a batch of week-old British newspapers. The news from London was mixed. Fitz was delighted that Lloyd George had appointed Winston Churchill as secretary for war. Of all the leading politicians, Winston was the most vigorous supporter of intervention in Russia. But some of the papers took the opposite side. Fitz was not surprised by the *Daily Herald* and the *New Statesman*, which in his view were more or less Bolshevik publications anyway. But even the Conservative *Daily Express* had a headline reading WITHDRAW FROM RUSSIA.

Unfortunately, they also had accurate details of what was going on. They even knew that the British had helped Kolchak with the coup that had abolished the directorate and made him supreme ruler. Where were they getting the information? He looked up from the paper. He was quartered in the city's commercial college, and his aide-de-camp sat at the opposite desk. "Murray," he said, "next time there's a batch of mail from the men to be sent home, bring it to me first."

This was irregular, and Murray looked dubious. "Sir?"

Fitz thought he had better explain. "I suspect information may be getting back from here. The censor must be asleep at the wheel."

"Perhaps they think they can slacken off now that the war in Europe has ended."

"No doubt. Anyway, I want to see whether the leak is in our section of the pipe."

The back page of the paper had a photograph of the woman leading the "Hands Off Russia" campaign, and Fitz was startled to see that it was Ethel. She had been a housemaid at Tŷ Gwyn but now, the *Express* said, she was general secretary of the National Garment Workers Union.

He had slept with many women since then—most recently, in Omsk, a stunning Russian blonde, the bored mistress of a fat tsarist general who was too drunk and lazy to fuck her himself. But Ethel shone out in his memory. He wondered what her child was like. Fitz probably had half a dozen bastards around the world, but Ethel's was the only one he knew of for sure.

And she was the one whipping up protest against intervention in Russia. Now Fitz knew where the information was coming from. Her damn brother was a sergeant in the Aberowen Pals. He had always been a troublemaker, and Fitz had no doubt he was briefing Ethel. Well, Fitz thought, I'll catch him out, and then there will be hell to pay.

Over the next few weeks the Whites raced ahead, driving before them the surprised Reds, who had thought the Siberian government a spent force. If Kolchak's armies could link up with their supporters in Archangel, in the north, and with Denikin's Volunteer Army in the south, they would form a semicircular force, a curved eastern scimitar a thousand miles long that would sweep irresistibly to Moscow.

Then, at the end of April, the Reds counterattacked.

By then Fitz was in Buguruslan, a grimly impoverished town in forest country a hundred miles or so east of the Volga River. The few dilapidated stone churches and municipal buildings poked up over the roofs of low-built wooden houses like weeds in a rubbish dump. Fitz sat in a large room in the town hall with the intelligence unit, sifting reports of prisoner interrogations. He did not know anything was wrong until he looked out of the window and saw the ragged soldiers of Kolchak's army streaming along the main road through the town in the wrong direction. He sent an American interpreter, Lev Peshkov, to question the retreating men.

Peshkov came back with a sorry story. The Reds had attacked in force from the south, striking the overstretched left flank of Kolchak's advancing army. To avoid his force being cut in two the local White commander, General Belov, had ordered them to retreat and regroup.

A few minutes later, a Red deserter was brought in for interrogation. He had been a colonel under the tsar. What he had to say dismayed Fitz. The Reds had been surprised by Kolchak's offensive, he said, but they had quickly regrouped and resupplied. Trotsky had declared that the Red Army must go on the offensive in the east. "Trotsky thinks that if the Reds falter, the Allies will recognize Kolchak as supreme ruler; and once they have done that, they will flood Siberia with men and supplies."

That was exactly what Fitz was hoping for. In his heavily accented Russian he asked: "So what did Trotsky do?"

The reply came fast, and Fitz could not understand what was said until he heard Peshkov's translation. "Trotsky drew on special levies of recruits from the Bolshevik party and the trade unions. The response was amazing. Twenty-two provinces sent detachments. The Novgorod Provincial Committee mobilized half its members!"

Fitz tried to imagine Kolchak summoning such a response from his supporters. It would never happen.

He returned to his quarters to pack his kit. He was almost too slow: the Pals got out only just ahead of the Reds, and a handful of men were left behind. By that evening Kolchak's Western Army was in full retreat and Fitz was on a train going back toward the Ural Mountains.

Two days later he was back in the commercial college at Ufa.

Over those two days, Fitz's mood turned black. He felt bitter with rage. He had been at war for five years, and he could recognize the turn of the tide—he knew the signs. The Russian civil war was as good as over.

The Whites were just too weak. The revolutionaries were going to win. Nothing short of an Allied invasion could turn the tables—and that was not going to happen: Churchill was in enough trouble for the little he was doing. Billy Williams and Ethel were making sure the needed reinforcements would never be sent.

Murray brought him a sack of mail. "You asked to see the men's letters home, sir," he said, with a hint of disapproval in his tone.

Fitz ignored Murray's scruples and opened the sack. He searched for a letter from Sergeant Williams. Someone, at least, could be punished for this catastrophe.

He found what he was looking for. Sergeant Williams's letter was addressed to E. Williams, her maiden name: no doubt he feared the use of her married name would call attention to his traitorous letter.

Fitz read it. Billy's handwriting was large and confident. At first sight the text seemed innocent, if a bit odd. But Fitz had worked in Room 40, and knew about codes. He settled down to crack this one.

Murray said: "On another matter, sir, have you seen the American interpreter, Peshkov, in the last day or two?"

"No," Fitz said. "What's happened to him?"

"We seem to have lost him, sir."

{ II }

Trotsky was immensely weary, but not discouraged. The lines of strain on his face did not diminish the light of hope in his eyes. Grigori thought admiringly that he was sustained by an unshakable belief in what he was doing. They all had that, Grigori suspected; Lenin and Stalin, too. Each felt sure he knew the right thing to do, whatever the problem might be, from land reform to military tactics.

Grigori was not like that. With Trotsky, he tried to work out the best response to the White armies, but he never felt sure they had made the right decision until the results were known. Perhaps that was why Trotsky was world-famous and Grigori was just another commissar.

As he had many times before, Grigori sat in Trotsky's personal train with a map of Russia on the table. "We hardly need worry about the counterrevolutionaries in the north," Trotsky said.

Grigori agreed. "According to our intelligence, there are mutinies among the British soldiers and sailors there."

"And they have lost all hope of linking up with Kolchak. His armies are running as fast as they can back to Siberia. We could chase them over the Urals—but I think we have more important business elsewhere."

"In the West?"

"That's bad enough. The Whites are bolstered by reactionary nationalists in Latvia, Lithuania, and Estonia. Kolchak has appointed Yudenich commander in chief there, and he's supported by a British navy flotilla that is keeping our fleet bottled up in Kronstadt. But I'm even more worried about the South."

"General Denikin."

"He has about a hundred and fifty thousand men, supported by French and Italian troops, and supplied by the British. We think he's planning a dash for Moscow."

"If I may say so, I think the key to defeating him is political, not military."

Trotsky looked intrigued. "Go on."

"Everywhere he goes, Denikin makes enemies. His Cossacks rob everyone. Whenever he takes a town, he rounds up all the Jews and just shoots them. If the coal mines fail to meet production targets, he kills one in ten miners. And, of course, he executes all deserters from his army."

"So do we," said Trotsky. "And we kill villagers who harbor deserters."

"And peasants who refuse to give up their grain." Grigori had had to harden his heart to accept this brutal necessity. "But I know peasants—my father was one. What they care about most is land. A lot of these people gained considerable tracts of land in the revolution, and they want to hold on to it—whatever else happens."

"So?"

"Kolchak has announced that land reform should be based on the principle of private property."

"Which means the peasants giving back the fields they have taken from the aristocracy."

"And everyone knows that. I'd like to print his proclamation and post it outside every church. No matter what our soldiers do, the peasants will prefer us to the Whites."

"Do it," said Trotsky.

"One more thing. Announce an amnesty for deserters. For seven days, any who return to the ranks will escape punishment."

"Another political move."

"I don't believe it will encourage desertion, because it's only for a week; but it might bring men back to us—especially when they find out the Whites want to take their land."

"Give it a try," said Trotsky.

An aide came in and saluted. "A strange report, Comrade Peshkov, that I thought you would want to hear."

"All right."

"It's about one of the prisoners we took at Buguruslan. He was with Kolchak's army, but wearing an American uniform."

"The Whites have soldiers from all over the world. The capitalist imperialists support the counterrevolution, naturally."

"It's not that, sir."

"What, then?"

"Sir, he says he's your brother."

{ III }

The platform was long, and there was a heavy morning mist, so that Grigori could not see the far end of the train. There was probably some mistake, he thought; a confusion of names or an error of translation. He tried to steel himself for a disappointment, but he was not successful: his heart beat faster and his nerves seemed to tingle. It was almost five years since he had seen his brother. He had often thought Lev must be dead. That could still be the awful truth.

He walked slowly, peering into the swirling haze. If this really was Lev, he would naturally be different. In the last five years Grigori had lost a front tooth and most of one ear, and had probably changed in other ways he was not aware of. How would Lev have altered?

After a few moments two figures emerged from the white mist: a Russian soldier, in ragged uniform and homemade shoes; and, beside him, a man who looked American. Was that Lev? He had a short American haircut and no mustache. He had the round-faced look of the well-fed American soldiers, with meaty shoulders under the smart new uniform. It was an officer's uniform, Grigori saw with growing incredulity. Could his brother be an American officer?

The prisoner was staring back at him, and as Grigori came close he saw that it was, indeed, his brother. He did look different, and it was not just the general air of sleek prosperity. It was the way he stood, the expression on his face, and most of all the look in his eyes. He had lost his boyish cockiness and acquired an air of caution. He had, in fact, grown up.

As they came within touching distance, Grigori thought of all the ways Lev had let him down, and a host of recriminations sprang to his lips; but he uttered none of them, and instead opened his arms and hugged Lev. They kissed cheeks, slapped each other on the back, and hugged again, and Grigori found that he was weeping.

After a while he led Lev onto the train and took him to the carriage he used as his office. Grigori told his aide to bring tea. They sat in two faded armchairs. "You're in the army?" Grigori said incredulously.

"They have conscription in America," Lev said.

That made sense. Lev would never have joined voluntarily. "And you're an officer!"

"So are you," said Lev.

Grigori shook his head. "We've abolished ranks in the Red Army. I'm a military commissar."

"But there are still some men who order tea and others who bring it," Lev said as the aide came in with cups. "Wouldn't Ma be proud?"

"Fit to bust. But why did you never write to me? I thought you were dead!"

"Aw, hell, I'm sorry," said Lev. "I felt so bad about taking your ticket that I wanted to write and say I can pay for your passage. I kept putting off the letter until I had more money."

It was a feeble excuse, but characteristic of Lev. He would not go to a party unless he had a fancy jacket to put on, and he refused to enter a bar if he did not have the money to buy a round of drinks.

Grigori recalled another betrayal. "You didn't tell me Katerina was pregnant when you left."

"Pregnant! I didn't know."

"Yes, you did. You told her not to tell me."

"Oh. I guess I forgot." Lev looked foolish, caught in a lie, but it did not take him long to recover and come up with his own counteraccusation. "That ship you sent me on didn't even go to New York! It put us all ashore at a dump called Cardiff. I had to work for months to save up for another ticket."

Grigori even felt guilty for a moment, then recalled how Lev had begged for the ticket. "Maybe I shouldn't have helped you escape from the police," he said crisply.

"I suppose you did your best for me," Lev said reluctantly. Then he gave the warm smile that always caused Grigori to forgive him. "As you always have," he added. "Ever since Ma died."

Grigori felt a lump in his throat. "All the same," he said, concentrating to make his voice steady, "we ought to punish the Vyalov family for cheating us."

"I got my revenge," Lev said. "There's a Josef Vyalov in Buffalo. I fucked his daughter and made her pregnant, and he had to let me marry her."

"My God! You're part of the Vyalov family now?"

"He regretted it, which is why he arranged for me to be conscripted. He's hoping I'll be killed in battle."

"Hell, do you still go wherever your dick leads you?"

Lev shrugged. "I guess."

Grigori had some revelations of his own, and he was nervous about making them. He began by saying carefully: "Katerina had a baby boy, your son. She called him Vladimir."

Lev looked pleased. "Is that so? I've got a son!"

Grigori did not have the courage to say that Vladimir

knew nothing of Lev, and called Grigori "Daddy." Instead he said: "I've taken good care of him."

"I knew you would."

Grigori felt a familiar stab of indignation at how Lev assumed that others would pick up the responsibilities he dropped. "Lev," he said, "I married Katerina." He waited for the outraged reaction.

But Lev remained calm. "I knew you'd do that, too."

Grigori was astonished. "What?"

Lev nodded. "You were crazy for her, and she needed a solid, dependable type to raise the child. It was in the cards."

"I went through agonies!" Grigori said. Had all that been for nothing? "I was tortured by the thought that I was being disloyal to you."

"Hell, no. I left her in the lurch. Good luck to you both."

Grigori was maddened by how casual Lev was about the whole thing. "Did you worry about us at all?" he asked pointedly.

"You know me, Grishka."

Of course Lev had not worried about them. "You hardly thought about us."

"Sure I thought about you. Don't be so holy. You wanted her. You held off for a while—maybe for years—but in the end you fucked her."

It was the crude truth. Lev had an annoying way of bringing everyone else down to his level. "You're right," Grigori said. "Anyway, we have another child now, a daughter, Anna. She's a year and a half old."

"Two adults and two children. It doesn't matter. I've got enough."

"What are you talking about?"

"I've been making money, selling whisky from British army stores to the Cossacks for gold. I've accumulated a small fortune." Lev reached inside his uniform shirt, unfastened a buckle, and pulled out a money belt. "There's enough here to pay for all four of you to come to America!" He gave the belt to Grigori.

Grigori was astonished and moved. Lev had not forgotten his family after all. He had saved up for a ticket. Naturally the handing over of the money had to be a flamboyant gesture—that was Lev's character. But he had kept his promise.

What a shame it was all for nothing.

"Thank you," Grigori said. "I'm proud of you for doing what you said you'd do. But, of course, it's not necessary now. I can get you released and help you return to normal Russian life." He handed the money belt back.

Lev took it and held it in his hands, staring at it. "What do you mean?"

Grigori saw that Lev looked hurt, and understood that he was wounded by the refusal of his gift. But there was a greater worry on Grigori's mind. What would happen when Lev and Katerina were reunited? Would she fall for the more attractive brother all over again? Grigori's heart was chilled by the thought that he could lose her, after all they had been through together. "We live in Moscow now," he said. "We have an apartment in the Kremlin, Katerina and Vladimir and Anna and me. I can get an apartment for you easily enough—"

"Wait a minute," said Lev, and there was a look of incredulity on his face. "You think I want to come back to Russia?"

"You already have," Grigori said.

"But not to stay!"

"You can't possibly want to return to America."

"Of course I do! And you should come with me."

"But there's no need! Russia's not like it used to be. The tsar is gone!"

"I like America," Lev said. "You'll like it, too, all of you, especially Katerina."

"But we're making history here! We've invented a new form of government, the soviet. This is the new Russia, the new world. You're missing everything!"

"You're the one who doesn't understand," Lev said. "In America I have my own car. There's more food than you can eat. All the booze I want, all the cigarettes I can smoke. I have five suits!"

"What's the point in having five suits?" Grigori said in frustration. "It's like having five beds. You can only use one at a time!"

"That's not how I see it."

What made the conversation so aggravating was that Lev clearly thought Grigori was the one who was missing the point. Grigori did not know what more he could say to change his brother's mind. "Is that really what you want? Cigarettes and too many clothes and a car?"

"It's what everyone wants. You Bolsheviks better remember that."

Grigori was not going to take lessons in politics from Lev. "Russians want bread, peace, and land."

"Anyway, I have a daughter in America. Her name is Daisy. She's three."

Grigori frowned doubtfully.

"I know what you're thinking," Lev said. "I didn't care about Katerina's child—what's his name?"

"Vladimir."

"I didn't care about him, you think, so why should I care about Daisy? But it's different. I never met Vladimir. He was just a speck when I left Petrograd. But I love Daisy, and what's more, she loves me."

Grigori could at least understand that. He was glad Lev had a good enough heart to feel attached to his daughter. And although he was bewildered by Lev's preference for America, in his heart he would be hugely relieved if Lev did not come home. For Lev would surely want to get to know Vladimir, and then how long would it be before Vladimir learned that Lev was his real father? And if Katerina decided to leave Grigori for Lev, and take Vladimir with her, what would happen to Anna? Would Grigori lose her, too? For himself, he thought guiltily, it was much better if Lev went back to America alone. "I believe you're making the wrong choice, but I'm not going to force you," he said.

Lev grinned. "You're afraid I'll take Katerina back, aren't you? I know you too well, brother."

Grigori winced. "Yes," he said. "Take her back, then discard her all over again, and leave me to pick up the pieces a second time. I know you, too."

"But you'll help me get back to America."

"No." Grigori could not help feeling a twitch of gratification at the look of fear that passed across Lev's face. But he did not prolong the agony. "I'll help you get back to the White Army. They can take you to America."

"What'll we do?"

"We'll drive to the front line, and a little beyond it. Then I'll release you into no-man's-land. After that you're on your own."

"I might get shot."

"We both might get shot. It's a war."

"I guess I'll have to take my chances."

"You'll be okay, Lev," said Grigori. "You always are."

{ IV }

Billy Williams was marched from the Ufa city jail, through the dusty streets of the city, to the commercial college being used as temporary accommodation by the British army.

The court-martial took place in a classroom. Fitz sat at the teacher's desk, with his aide-de-camp, Captain Murray, beside him. Captain Gwyn Evans was there with a notebook and pencil.

Billy was dirty and unshaven, and he had slept badly with the drunks and prostitutes of the town. Fitz wore a perfectly pressed uniform, as always. Billy knew he was in bad trouble. The verdict was a foregone conclusion: the evidence was clear. He had revealed military secrets in coded letters to his sister. But he was determined not to let his fear show. He was going to give a good account of himself.

Fitz said: "This is a field general court-martial, permitted when the accused is on active service or overseas and it is not possible to hold the more regular general court-martial. Only three officers are required to sit as judges, or two if no more are available. It may try a soldier of any rank on any offense, and has the power to impose the death penalty."

Billy's only chance was to influence the sentence. The possible punishments included penal servitude, hard labor, and death. No doubt Fitz would like to put Billy in front of a firing squad, or at least give him several years in prison. Billy's aim was to plant in the minds of Murray and Evans sufficient doubts about the fairness of the trial to make them plump for a short term in prison.

Now he said: "Where is my lawyer?"

"It is not possible to offer you legal representation," Fitz said.

"You're sure of that, are you, sir?"

"Speak when you're spoken to, Sergeant."

Billy said: "Let the record show that I was denied access

to a lawyer." He stared at Gwyn Evans, the only one with a notebook. When Evans did nothing, Billy said: "Or will the record of this trial be a lie?" He put heavy emphasis on the word *lie*, knowing it would offend Fitz. It was part of the code of the English gentleman always to tell the truth.

Fitz nodded to Evans, who made a note.

First point to me, Billy thought, and he cheered up a bit.

Fitz said: "William Williams, you stand accused under part one of the Army Act. The charge is that you knowingly, while on active service, committed an act calculated to imperil the success of His Majesty's forces. The penalty is death, or such lesser punishment as the court shall impose."

The repeated emphasis on the death penalty chilled Billy, but he kept his face stiff.

"How do you plead?"

Billy took a deep breath. He spoke in a clear voice, and put into his tone as much scorn and contempt as he could muster. "I plead how dare you," he said. "How dare you pretend to be an objective judge? How dare you act as if our presence in Russia is a legitimate operation? And how dare you make an accusation of treason against a man who has fought alongside you for three years? That's how I plead."

Gwyn Evans said: "Don't be insolent, Billy boy. You'll only make it worse for yourself."

Billy was not going to let Evans pretend to be benevolent. He said: "And my advice to you is to leave now and have nothing more to do with this kangaroo court. When the news gets out—and believe you me, this is going to be on the front page of the *Daily Mirror*—you will find that you're the one in disgrace, not me." He looked at Murray. "Every man who had anything to do with this farce is going to be disgraced."

Evans looked troubled. Clearly he had not thought there might be publicity.

"Enough!" said Fitz loudly and angrily.

Good, Billy thought; I've got his goat already.

Fitz went on: "Let's have the evidence, please, Captain Murray."

Murray opened a folder and took out a sheet of paper. Billy recognized his own handwriting. It was, as he expected, a letter to Ethel.

Murray showed it to him and said: "Did you write this letter?"

Billy said: "How did it come to your attention, Captain Murray?"

Fitz barked: "Answer the question!"

Billy said, "You went to Eton school, didn't you, Captain? A gentleman would never read someone else's mail, or so we're told. But as I understand it, only the official censor has the right to examine soldiers' letters. So I assume this was brought to your attention by the censor." He paused. As he expected, Murray was unwilling to answer. He went on: "Or was the letter obtained illegally?"

Murray repeated: "Did you write this letter?"

"If it was obtained illegally, then it can't be used in a trial. I think that's what a lawyer would say. But there are no lawyers here. That's what makes this a kangaroo court."

"Did you write this letter?"

"I will answer that question when you have explained how it came into your possession."

Fitz said: "You can be punished for contempt of court, you know."

I'm already facing the death penalty, Billy thought; how stupid of Fitz to think he can threaten me! But he said: "I am defending myself by pointing out the irregularity of the court and the illegality of the prosecution. Are you going to forbid that . . . sir?"

Murray gave up. "The envelope is marked with a return address and the name of Sergeant Billy Williams. If the accused wishes to claim he did not write it, he should say so now."

Billy said nothing.

"The letter is a coded message," Murray went on. "It may be decoded by reading every third word, and the initial capital letters of titles of songs and films." Murray handed the letter to Evans. "When so decoded, it reads as follows."

Billy's letter described the incompetence of the Kolchak regime, saying that despite all their gold they had failed to pay the staff of the Trans-Siberian Railway, and so were continuing to have supply and transport problems. It also detailed the help the British army was trying to give. The information had been kept secret from the British public, who were paying for the army and whose sons were risking their lives.

Murray said to Billy: "Do you deny sending this message?"

"I cannot comment on evidence that has been obtained illegally."

"The addressee, E. Williams, is in fact Mrs. Ethel Leckwith, leader of the 'Hands Off Russia' campaign, is she not?"

"I cannot comment on evidence that has been obtained illegally."

"Have you written previous coded letters to her?"

Billy said nothing.

"And she has used the information you gave her to generate hostile newspaper stories bringing discredit on the British army and imperiling the success of our actions here."

"Certainly not," said Billy. "The army has been discredited by the men who sent us on a secret and illegal mission without the knowledge or consent of Parliament. The 'Hands Off Russia' campaign is the necessary first step in returning us to our proper role as the defenders of Great Britain, rather than the private army of a little conspiracy of right-wing generals and politicians."

Fitz's chiseled face was red with anger, Billy saw to his great satisfaction. "I think we've heard enough," Fitz said. "The court will now consider its verdict." Murray murmured something, and Fitz said: "Oh, yes. Does the accused have anything to say?"

Billy stood up. "I call as my first witness Colonel the Earl Fitzherbert."

"Don't be ridiculous," said Fitz.

"Let the record show that the court refused to allow me to question a witness even though he was present at the trial."

"Get on with it."

"If I had not been denied my right to call a witness, I would have asked the colonel what his relationship with my family was. Did he not bear a personal grudge against me because of my father's role as a miners' leader? What was his relationship with my sister? Did he not employ her as his housekeeper, then mysteriously sack her?" Billy was tempted to say more about Ethel, but it would have been dragging her name through the mud, and besides, the hint was probably enough. "I would ask him about his personal interest in this illegal war against the Bolshevik government. Is his wife a Russian princess? Is his son heir to property here? Is the colonel in fact here to defend his personal financial interest? And are all these matters the real explanation of why he has convened this sham of a court? And does that not completely disqualify him from being a judge in this case?"

Fitz stared stony-faced, but both Murray and Evans looked startled. They had not known all this personal stuff.

Billy said: "I have one more point to make. The German kaiser stands accused of war crimes. It is argued that he declared war, with the encouragement of his generals, against the will of the German people, as clearly expressed by their representatives in the Reichstag, the German parliament. By contrast, it is argued, Britain declared war on Germany only after a debate in the House of Commons."

Fitz pretended to be bored, but Murray and Evans were attentive.

Billy went on: "Now consider this war in Russia. It has never been debated in the British Parliament. The facts are hidden from the British people on the pretense of operational security—always the excuse for the army's guilty secrets. We are fighting, but war has never been declared. The British prime minister and his colleagues are in exactly the same position as the kaiser and his generals. They are the ones acting illegally—not me." Billy sat down.

The two captains went into a huddle with Fitz. Billy wondered if he had gone too far. He had felt the need to be trenchant, but he might have offended the captains instead of winning their support.

However, there seemed to be dissent among the judges. Fitz was speaking emphatically and Evans was shaking his head in negation. Murray looked awkward. That was probably a good sign, Billy thought. All the same he was as scared as he had ever been. When he had faced machine guns at the Somme and experienced an explosion down the pit, he had not been as frightened as he was now, with his life in the hands of malevolent officers.

At last they seemed to reach agreement. Fitz looked at Billy and said: "Stand up."

Billy stood.

"Sergeant William Williams, this court finds you guilty as charged." Fitz stared at Billy, as if hoping to see on his face the mortification of defeat. But Billy had been expecting a guilty verdict. It was the sentence he feared.

Fitz said: "You are sentenced to ten years' penal servitude."

Billy could no longer keep his face expressionless. It was not the death penalty—but ten years! When he came out he would be thirty. It would be 1929. Mildred would be thirty-five. Half their lives would be over. His façade of defiance crumbled, and tears came to his eyes.

A look of profound satisfaction came over Fitz's face. "Dismissed," he said.

Billy was marched away to begin his prison sentence.

CHAPTER THIRTY-SEVEN

May and June 1919

On the first day of May, Walter von Ulrich wrote a letter to Maud and posted it in the town of Versailles.

He did not know whether she was dead or alive. He had heard no news of her since Stockholm. There was still no postal service between Germany and Britain, so this was his first chance of writing to her in two years.

Walter and his father had traveled to France the day before, with 180 politicians, diplomats, and foreign ministry officials, as part of the German delegation to the peace conference. The French railway had slowed their special train to walking pace as they crossed the devastated landscape of northeastern France. "As if we were the only ones who fired shells here," Otto said angrily. From Paris they had been bused to the small town of Versailles and dropped off at the Hotel des Réservoirs. Their luggage was unloaded in the courtyard and they were rudely told to carry it themselves. Clearly, Walter thought, the French were not going to be magnanimous in victory.

"They didn't win, that's their trouble," said Otto. "They may not have actually lost, not quite, because they were saved by the British and Americans—but that's not much to boast about. We beat them, and they know it, and it hurts their pumped-up pride."

The hotel was cold and gloomy, but magnolias and apple trees were in blossom outside. The Germans were allowed to walk in the grounds of the great château and visit the shops. There was always a small crowd outside the hotel. The ordinary people were not as malign as the officials. Sometimes they booed, but mostly they were just curious to look at the enemy.

Walter wrote to Maud on the first day. He did not mention their marriage—he was not yet sure it was safe, and anyway the habit of secrecy was hard to break. He told her where he was, described the hotel and its surroundings, and asked her to write to him by return. He walked into the town, bought a stamp, and posted his letter.

He waited in anxious hope for the reply. If she were alive, did she still love him? He felt almost sure she would. But two years had passed since she had eagerly embraced him in a Stockholm hotel room. The world was full of men who had returned from the war to find that their girlfriends and wives had fallen in love with someone else during the long years of separation.

A few days later the leaders of the delegations were summoned to the Hotel Trianon Palace, across the park, and ceremonially handed printed copies of the peace treaty drafted by the victorious allies. It was in French. Back at the Hotel des Réservoirs, the copies were given to teams of translators. Walter was head of one such team. He divided his part into sections, passed them out, and sat down to read.

It was even worse than he expected.

The French army would occupy the border region of Rhineland for fifteen years. The Saar region of Germany was to become a League of Nations protectorate with the French controlling the coal mines. Alsace and Lorraine were returned to France without a plebiscite: the French government was afraid the population would vote to stay German. The new state of Poland was so large it took in the homes of three million Germans and the coalfields of Silesia. Germany was to lose all her colonies: the Allies had shared them out like thieves dividing the swag. And the Germans had to agree to pay reparations of an unspecified amount—in other words, to sign a blank check.

Walter wondered what kind of country they wanted Germany to be. Did they have in mind a giant slave camp where everyone lived on iron rations and toiled only so that the overlords could take the produce? If Walter was to be one such slave, how could he contemplate setting up home with Maud and having children?

But worst of all was the war guilt clause.

Article 231 of the treaty said: "The Allied and Associated Governments affirm, and Germany accepts, the responsibility of Germany and her allies for causing all the loss and damage to which the Allied and Associated Governments and their nationals have been subjected as a consequence of the war imposed upon them by the aggression of Germany and her allies."

"It's a lie," Walter said angrily. "A stupid, ignorant, wicked, vicious, damned lie." Germany was not innocent, he knew, and he had argued as much with his father, time and time again. But he had lived through the diplomatic crises of the summer of 1914; he had known about every small step on the road to war, and no single nation was guilty. Leaders on both sides had been mainly concerned to defend their own countries, and none of them had intended to plunge the world into the greatest war in history: not Asquith, nor Poincaré, nor the kaiser, nor the tsar, nor the Austrian emperor. Even Gavrilo Princip, the assassin of Sarajevo, had apparently been aghast when he understood what he had started. But even he was not responsible for "all the loss and damage."

Walter ran into his father shortly after midnight, when they were both taking a break, drinking coffee to stay awake and continue working. "This is outrageous!" Otto stormed. "We agreed to an armistice based on Wilson's Fourteen Points—but the treaty has nothing to do with the Fourteen Points!"

For once Walter agreed with his father.

By morning the translation had been printed and copies had been dispatched by special messenger to Berlin—a classic exercise in German efficiency, Walter thought, seeing his country's virtues more clearly when it was being denigrated. Too exhausted to sleep, he decided to walk until he felt relaxed enough to go to bed.

He left the hotel and went into the park. The rhododendrons were in bud. It was a fine morning for France, a grim one for Germany. What effect would the proposals have on Germany's struggling social-democratic government? Would the people despair and turn to Bolshevism?

He was alone in the great park except for a young woman in a light spring coat sitting on a bench beneath a chestnut tree. Deep in thought, he touched the brim of his trilby hat politely as he passed her.

"Walter," she said.

His heart stopped. He knew the voice, but it could not be her. He turned and stared.

She stood up. "Oh, Walter," she said. "Did you not know me?"

It was Maud.

His blood sang in his veins. He took two steps toward her and she threw herself into his arms. He hugged her hard. He buried his face in her neck and inhaled her fragrance, still familiar despite the years. He kissed her forehead and her cheek and then her mouth. He was speaking and kissing at the same time, but neither words nor kisses could say all that was in his heart.

At last she spoke. "Do you still love me?" she said.

"More than ever," he answered, and he kissed her again.

{ II }

Maud ran her hands over Walter's bare chest as they lay on the bed after making love. "You're so thin," she said. His belly was concave, and the bones of his hips jutted out. She wanted to fatten him on buttered croissants and foie gras.

They were in a bedroom at an auberge a few miles outside Paris. The window was open, and a mild spring breeze fluttered the primrose-yellow curtains. Maud had found out about this place many years ago when Fitz had been using it for assignations with a married woman, the Comtesse de Cagnes. The establishment, little more than a large house in a small village, did not even have a name. Men made a reservation for lunch and took a room for the afternoon. Perhaps there were such places on the outskirts of London but, somehow, the arrangement seemed very French.

They called themselves Mr. and Mrs. Woolridge, and Maud wore the wedding ring that had been hidden away for almost five years. No doubt the discreet proprietress assumed they were only pretending to be married. That was all right, as long as she did not suspect Walter was German, which would have caused trouble.

Maud could not keep her hands off him. She was so grateful that he had come back to her with his body intact. She touched the long scar on his shin with her fingertips.

"I got that at Château-Thierry," he said.

"Gus Dewar was in that battle. I hope it wasn't he who shot you."

"I was lucky that it healed well. A lot of men died of gangrene."

It was three weeks since they had been reunited. During that time Walter had been working around the clock on the German response to the draft treaty, only getting away for half an hour or so each day to walk with her in the park or sit in the back of Fitz's blue Cadillac while the chauffeur drove them around.

Maud had been as shocked as Walter by the harsh terms offered to the Germans. The object of the Paris conference was to create a just and peaceful new world—not to enable the winners to take revenge on the losers. The new Germany should be democratic and prosperous. She wanted to have children with Walter, and their children would be German. She often thought of the passage in the Book of Ruth that began "Whither thou goest, I will go." Sooner or later she would have to say that to Walter.

However, she had been comforted to learn that she was not the only person who disapproved of the treaty proposals. Others on the Allied side thought peace was more important than revenge. Twelve members of the American delegation had resigned in protest. In a British by-election, the candidate advocating a nonvengeful peace had won. The Archbishop of Canterbury had said publicly that he was "very uncomfortable" and claimed to speak for a silent body of opinion that was not represented in the Hun-hating newspapers.

Yesterday the Germans had submitted their counter-proposal—more than a hundred closely argued pages based on Wilson's Fourteen Points. This morning the French press was apoplectic. Bursting with indignation, they called the document a monument of impudence and an odious piece of buffoonery. "They accuse us of arrogance—the French!" said Walter. "What is that phrase about a saucepan?"

"The pot calling the kettle black," said Maud.

He rolled onto his side and toyed with her pubic hair. It was dark and curly and luxuriant. She had offered to trim it, but he said he liked it the way it was. "What are we going to do?" he said. "It's romantic to meet in a hotel and go to bed in the afternoon, like illicit lovers, but we cannot do this forever. We have to tell the world we are man and wife."

Maud agreed. She was also impatient for the time when she could sleep with him every night, though she did not say so: she was a bit embarrassed by how much she liked sex with him. "We could just set up home, and let them draw their own conclusions."

"I'm not comfortable with that," he said. "It makes us look ashamed."

She felt the same. She wanted to trumpet her happiness, not hide it away. She was proud of Walter: he was handsome and brave and extraordinarily clever. "We could have another wedding," she said. "Get engaged, announce it, have a ceremony, and never tell anyone we've been married almost five years. It's not illegal to marry the same person twice."

He looked thoughtful. "My father and your brother would fight us. They could not stop us, but they could make things unpleasant—which would spoil the happiness of the event."

"You're right," she said reluctantly. "Fitz would say that some Germans may be jolly good chaps, but all the same you don't want your sister to marry one."

"So we must present them with a fait accompli."

"Let's tell them, then announce the news in the press," she said. "We'll say it's a symbol of the new world order. An Anglo-German marriage, at the same time as the peace treaty."

He looked dubious. "How would we manage that?"

"I'll speak to the editor of the *Tatler* magazine. They like me—I've provided them with lots of material."

Walter smiled and said: "Lady Maud Fitzherbert is always dressed in the latest fashion."

"What are you talking about?"

He reached for his billfold on the bedside table and extracted a magazine clipping. "My only picture of you," he said.

She took it from him. It was soft with age and faded to the color of sand. She studied the photo. "This was taken before the war."

"And it has been with me ever since. Like me, it survived."

Tears came to her eyes, blurring the faded image even more.

"Don't cry," he said, hugging her.

She pressed her face to his bare chest and wept. Some women cried at the drop of a hat, but she had never been that sort. Now she sobbed helplessly. She was crying for the lost years, and the millions of boys lying dead, and the pointless, stupid waste of it all. She was shedding all the tears stored up in five years of self-control.

When it was over, and her tears were dry, she kissed him hungrily, and they made love again.

{ III }

Fitz's blue Cadillac picked Walter up at the hotel on June 16 and drove him into Paris. Maud had decided that the *Tatler* magazine would want a photograph of the two of them. Walter wore a tweed suit made in London before the war. It was too wide at the waist, but every German man was walking around in clothes too big for him.

Walter had set up a small intelligence bureau at the Hotel des Réservoirs, monitoring the French, British, American, and Italian newspapers and collating gossip picked up by the German delegation. He knew that there were bad-tempered arguments among the Allies about the German counterproposals. Lloyd George, a politician who was flexible to a fault, was willing to reconsider the draft treaty. But the French prime minister, Clemenceau, said he had already been generous and fumed with outrage at any suggestion of amendments. Surprisingly, Woodrow Wilson was also obdurate. He believed the draft was a just settlement, and whenever he had made up his mind he became deaf to criticism.

The Allies were also negotiating peace treaties to cover Germany's partners: Austria, Hungary, Bulgaria, and the

Ottoman Empire. They were creating new countries such as Yugoslavia and Czechoslovakia, and carving up the Middle East into British and French zones. And they were arguing about whether to make peace with Lenin. In every country the people were tired of war, but a few powerful men were still keen to fight against the Bolsheviks. The British *Daily Mail* had discovered a conspiracy of international Jewish financiers supporting the Moscow regime—one of that newspaper's more implausible fantasies.

On the German treaty Wilson and Clemenceau over-ruled Lloyd George, and earlier that day the German team at the Hotel des Réservoirs had received an impatient note giving them three days to accept.

Walter thought gloomily about his country's future as he sat in the back of Fitz's car. It would be like an African colony, he thought, the primitive inhabitants working only to enrich their foreign masters. He would not want to raise children in such a place.

Maud was waiting in the photographer's studio, looking wonderful in a filmy summer dress that, she said, was by Paul Poiret, her favorite couturier.

The photographer had a painted backdrop that showed a garden in full flower, which Maud decided was in bad taste, so they posed in front of his dining room curtains, which were mercifully plain. At first they stood side by side, not touching, like strangers. The photographer proposed that Walter should kneel in front of Maud, but that was too sentimental. In the end they found a position they all liked, with the two of them holding hands and looking at each other rather than the camera.

Copies of the picture would be ready tomorrow, the photographer promised.

They went to their auberge for lunch. "The Allies can't just order Germany to sign," Maud said. "That's not negotiation."

"It is what they have done."

"What happens if you refuse?"

"They don't say."

"What are you going to do?"

"Some of the delegation are returning to Berlin tonight for consultations with our government." He sighed. "I'm afraid I have been chosen to go with them."

"Then this is the time to make our announcement. I'll go to London tomorrow after I've picked up the photographs."

"All right," he said. "I'll tell my mother as soon as I get to Berlin. She'll be nice about it. Then I'll tell Father. He won't."

"I'll speak to Aunt Herm and Princess Bea, and write to Fitz in Russia."

"So this will be the last time we meet for a while."

"Eat up, then, and let's go to bed."

{ IV }

Gus and Rosa met in the Tuileries Gardens. Paris was beginning to get back to normal, Gus thought happily. The sun was shining, the trees were in leaf, and men with carnations in their buttonholes sat smoking cigars and watching the best-dressed women in the world walk by. On one side of the park, the rue de Rivoli was busy with cars, trucks, and horse-drawn carts; on the other, freight barges plied the river Seine. Perhaps the world would recover, after all.

Rosa was ravishing in a red dress of light cotton and a wide-brimmed hat. If I could paint, Gus thought when he saw her, I'd paint her like this.

He had a blue blazer and a fashionable straw boater. When she saw him, she laughed.

"What is it?" he said.

"Nothing. You look nice."

"It's the hat, isn't it?"

She suppressed another giggle. "You're adorable."

"It looks stupid. I can't help it. Hats do that to me. It's because I'm shaped like a ball-peen hammer."

She kissed him lightly on the lips. "You're the most attractive man in Paris."

The amazing thing was that she meant it. Gus thought: How did I get so lucky?

He took her arm. "Let's walk." They strolled toward the Louvre.

She said: "Have you seen the *Tatler*?"

"The London magazine? No, why?"

"It seems that your intimate friend Lady Maud is married to a German."

"Oh!" he said. "How did they find out?"

"You mean you knew about this?"

"I guessed. I saw Walter in Berlin in 1916 and he asked me to carry a letter to Maud. I figured that meant they were either engaged or married."

"How discreet you are! You never said a word."

"It was a dangerous secret."

"It may still be dangerous. The *Tatler* is nice about them, but other papers may take a different line."

"Maud has been attacked by the press before now. She's pretty tough."

Rosa looked abashed. "I suppose this is what you were talking about that night I saw you tête-à-tête with her."

"Exactly. She was asking me if I had heard any news about Walter."

"I feel foolish for suspecting you of flirting."

"I forgive you, but reserve the right to recall the matter next time you criticize me unreasonably. Can I ask you something?"

"Anything you like, Gus."

"Three questions, in fact."

"How ominous. Like a folktale. If I get the answers wrong, will I be banished?"

"Are you still an anarchist?"

"Would it bother you?"

"I guess I'm asking myself if politics might divide us."

"Anarchism is the belief that no one has the right to rule. All political philosophies, from the divine right of kings to Rousseau's social contract, try to justify authority. Anarchists believe that all those theories fail, therefore no form of authority is legitimate."

"Irrefutable, in theory. Impossible to put into practice."

"You're quick on the uptake. In effect, all anarchists are antiestablishment, but they differ widely in their vision of how society should work."

"And what is your vision?"

"I don't see it as clearly as I used to. Covering the White House has given me a different slant on politics. But I still believe that authority needs to justify itself."

"I don't think we'll ever quarrel about that."

"Good. Next question?"

"Tell me about your eye."

"I was born like this. I could have an operation to open it. Behind my eyelid is nothing but a mass of useless tissue, but I could wear a glass eye. However, it would never shut. I figure this is the lesser evil. Does it bother you?"

He stopped walking and turned to face her directly. "May I kiss it?"

She hesitated. "All right."

He bent down and kissed her closed eyelid. There was nothing unusual about how it felt to his lips. It was just like kissing her cheek. "Thank you," he said.

She said quietly: "No one has ever done that before."

He nodded. He had guessed it might be some kind of taboo.

She said: "Why did you want to do it?"

"Because I love everything about you, and I want to make sure you know it."

"Oh." She was silent for a minute, in the grip of emotion; but then she grinned and reverted to the flip tone she preferred. "Well, if there's anything else weird you want to kiss, just let me know."

He was not sure how to respond to that vaguely exciting offer, so he filed it away for future consideration. "I have one more question."

"Shoot."

"Four months ago, I told you that I love you."

"I haven't forgotten."

"But you haven't said how you feel about me."

"Isn't it obvious?"

"Perhaps, but I'd like you to tell me. Do you love me?"

"Oh, Gus, don't you understand?" Her face changed and she looked anguished. "I'm not good enough for you. You were the most eligible bachelor in Buffalo, and I was the one-eyed anarchist. You're supposed to love someone elegant and beautiful and rich. I'm a doctor's daughter—my mother was a housemaid. I'm not the right person for you to love."

"Do you love me?" he said with quiet persistence.

She began to cry. "Of course I do, you dope. I love you with all my heart."

He put his arms around her. "Then that's all that matters," he said.

{ V }

Aunt Herm put down the *Tatler*. "It was very bad of you to get married secretly," she said to Maud. Then she smiled conspiratorially. "But so romantic!"

They were in the drawing room of Fitz's Mayfair house. Bea had redecorated after the end of the war, in the new art deco style, with utilitarian-looking chairs and modernistic silver gewgaws from Asprey. With Maud and Herm were Fitz's roguish friend Bing Westhampton and Bing's wife. The London season was in full swing, and they were going to the opera as soon as Bea was ready. She was saying good night to Boy, now three and a half, and Andrew, eighteen months.

Maud picked up the magazine and looked again at the article. The picture did not greatly please her. She had imagined that it would show two people in love. Unfortunately it looked like a scene from a moving picture show. Walter appeared predatory, holding her hand and gazing into her eyes like a wicked Lothario, and she seemed like the ingénue about to fall for his wiles.

However, the text was just what she had hoped for. The writer reminded readers that Lady Maud had been "the fashionable suffragette" before the war, she had started *The Soldier's Wife* newspaper to campaign for the rights of the women left at home, and she had gone to jail for her protest on behalf of Jayne McCulley. It said that she and Walter had intended to announce their engagement in the normal way, and had been prevented by the outbreak of war. Their hasty secret marriage was portrayed as a desperate attempt to do the right thing in abnormal circumstances.

Maud had insisted on being quoted exactly, and the magazine had kept its promise. "I know that some British people hate the Germans," she had said. "But I also know that Walter and many other Germans did all they could to prevent the war. Now that it is over, we must create peace and friendship between the former enemies, and I truly hope people will see our union as a symbol of the new world."

Maud had learned, in her years of political campaigning, that you could sometimes win support from a publication by giving it a good story exclusively.

Walter had returned to Berlin as planned. The Germans

had been jeered by crowds as they drove to the railway station on their way home. A female secretary had been knocked out by a thrown rock. The French comment had been: "Remember what they did to Belgium." The secretary was still in the hospital. Meanwhile, the German people were angrily against signing the treaty.

Bing sat next to Maud on the sofa. For once he was not flirtatious. "I wish your brother were here to advise you about this," he said with a nod at the magazine.

Maud had written to Fitz to break the news of her marriage, and had enclosed the clipping from the *Tatler,* to show him that what she had done was being accepted by London society. She had no idea how long it would take for her letter to get to wherever Fitz was, and she did not expect a reply for months. By then it would be too late for Fitz to protest. He would just have to smile and congratulate her.

Now Maud bristled at the implication that she needed a man to tell her what to do. "What could Fitz possibly say?"

"For the foreseeable future, the life of a German wife is going to be hard."

"I don't need a man to tell me that."

"In Fitz's absence I feel a degree of responsibility."

"Please don't." Maud tried not to be offended. What advice could Bing possibly offer anyone, other than how to gamble and drink in the world's nightspots?

He lowered his voice. "I hesitate to say this, but . . ." He glanced at Aunt Herm, who took the hint and went to pour herself a little more coffee. "If you were able to say that the marriage had never been consummated, then there might be an annulment."

Maud thought of the room with the primrose-yellow curtains, and had to suppress a happy smile. "But I cannot—"

"Please don't tell me anything about it. I only want to make sure you understand your options."

Maud suppressed a growing indignation. "I know this is kindly meant, Bing—"

"There is also the possibility of divorce. There is always a way, you know, for a man to provide a wife with grounds."

Maud could no longer contain her outrage. "Please drop the subject instantly," she said in a raised voice. "I have not the slightest wish for either an annulment or a divorce. I love Walter."

Bing looked sulky. "I was just trying to say what I think Fitz, as the head of your family, might tell you if he were here." He stood up and spoke to his wife. "We'll go on, shall we? No need for all of us to be late."

A few minutes later, Bea came in wearing a new dress of pink silk. "I'm ready," she said, as if she had been waiting for them rather than the other way around. Her glance went to Maud's left hand and registered the wedding ring, but she did not comment. When Maud had told her the news her response had been carefully neutral. "I hope you will be happy," she had said without warmth. "And I hope Fitz will be able to accept the fact that you did not get his permission."

They went out and got into the car. It was the black Cadillac Fitz had bought after his blue one got stranded in France. Everything was provided by Fitz, Maud reflected: the house the three women lived in, the fabulously expensive gowns they were wearing, the car, and the box at the opera. Her bills at the Ritz in Paris had been sent to Albert Solman, Fitz's man of business here in London, and paid without question. Fitz never complained. Walter would never be able to keep her in such style, she knew. Perhaps Bing was right, and she would find it hard to do without her accustomed luxury. But she would be with the man she loved.

They reached Covent Garden at the last minute, because of Bea's tardiness. The audience had already taken their seats. The three women hurried up the red-carpeted staircase and made their way to the box. Maud suddenly remembered what she had done to Walter in this box during *Don Giovanni*. She felt embarrassed: what had possessed her to take such a risk?

Bing Westhampton was already there with his wife, and he stood up and held a chair for Bea. The auditorium was silent: the show was about to begin. People-watching was one of the attractions of the opera, and many heads turned to look as the princess took her seat. Aunt Herm sat in the second row, but Bing held a front-row seat for Maud. A murmur of comment rose from the stalls: most of the crowd would have seen the photograph and read the article in the *Tatler*. Many of them knew Maud personally: this was London society, the aristocrats and the politicians, the judges and the bishops, the successful artists and the wealthy businessmen—and their wives. Maud stood for a moment to let them get a good look at her, and see how pleased and proud she was.

That was a mistake.

The sound from the audience changed. The murmur became louder. No words could be made out, but all the same the voices took on a note of disapproval, like the change in the buzz of a fly when it encounters a closed window. Maud was taken aback. Then she heard another noise, and it sounded dreadfully like a hiss. Confused and dismayed, she sat down.

That made no difference. Everyone was staring at her now. The hissing spread through the stalls in seconds, then began in the circle, too. "I say," said Bing in feeble protest.

Maud had never encountered such hatred, even at the height of the suffragette demonstrations. There was a pain in her stomach like a cramp. She wished the music would start, but the conductor, too, was staring at her, his baton held at his side.

She tried to stare proudly back at them all, but tears came to her eyes and blurred her vision. This nightmare would not end of its own accord. She had to do something.

She stood up, and the hissing grew louder.

Tears ran down her face. Almost blind, she turned around. Knocking her chair over, she stumbled toward the door at the back of the box. Aunt Herm got up, saying: "Oh, dear, dear, dear."

Bing leaped up and opened the door. Maud went out, with Aunt Herm close behind. Bing followed them out. Behind her, Maud heard the hissing die away amid a few ripples of laughter; then, to her horror, the audience began to clap, congratulating themselves on having got rid of her; and their jeering applause followed her along the corridor, down the stairs, and out of the theater.

{ VI }

The drive from the park gate to the Palace of Versailles was a mile long. Today it was lined with hundreds of mounted French cavalrymen in blue uniforms. The summer sun glinted off their steel helmets. They held lances with red and white pennants that rippled in the warm breeze.

Johnny Remarc had been able to get Maud an invitation to the signing of the peace treaty, despite her disgrace at the opera; but she had to travel on the back of an open lorry, packed in with all the female secretaries from the British delegation, like sheep going to market.

At one moment it had looked as if the Germans would refuse to sign. The war hero Field Marshal von Hindenburg had said he would prefer honorable defeat to a disgraceful peace. The entire German cabinet had resigned rather than agree to the treaty. So had the head of their delegation to Paris. At last the National Assembly had voted for signing everything except the notorious war guilt clause. Even that was unacceptable, the Allies had said immediately.

"What will the Allies do if the Germans refuse?" Maud had said to Walter in their auberge, where they were now discreetly living together.

"They say they will invade Germany."

Maud shook her head. "Our soldiers would not fight."

"Nor would ours."

"So it would be a stalemate."

"Except that the British navy has not lifted the blockade, so Germany still cannot get supplies. The Allies would just wait until food riots broke out in every German city. Then they would walk in unopposed."

"So you have to sign."

"Sign or starve," said Walter bitterly.

Today was June 28, five years to the day since the archduke had been killed in Sarajevo.

The lorry took the secretaries into the courtyard, and they got down as gracefully as they could. Maud entered the palace and went up the grand staircase, flanked by more overdressed French soldiers, this time the Garde Républicaine in silver helmets with horsehair plumes.

Finally she entered the Hall of Mirrors. This was one of the most grandiose rooms in the world. It was the size of three tennis courts in a line. Along one side, seventeen long windows overlooked the garden; on the opposite wall, the windows were reflected by seventeen mirrored arches. More important, this was the room where in 1871, at the end of the Franco-Prussian War, the victorious Germans had crowned their first emperor and forced the French to sign away Alsace and Lorraine. Now the Germans were to be humiliated under the same barrel-vaulted ceiling. And no doubt some among them would be dreaming of the time in the future when they in turn would take their revenge. The degradation to which you subject others comes back, sooner or later, to haunt you, Maud thought. Would that reflection occur to men on either side at today's ceremony? Probably not.

She found her place on one of the red plush benches. There were dozens of reporters and photographers, and a film crew with huge movie cameras to record the event. The bigwigs entered in ones and twos and sat at a long table: Clemenceau relaxed and irreverent, Wilson stiffly formal, Lloyd George like an aging bantam cock. Gus Dewar appeared and spoke in Wilson's ear, then went over to the press section and spoke to a pretty young reporter with one eye. Maud remembered seeing her before. Gus was in love with her, Maud could tell.

At three o'clock someone called for silence, and a reverent hush fell. Clemenceau said something, a door opened, and the two German signatories came in. Maud knew from Walter that no one in Berlin had wanted to put his name to the treaty, and in the end they had sent the foreign minister and the postal minister. The two men looked pale and ashamed.

Clemenceau made a short speech, then beckoned the Germans forward. Both men took fountain pens from their pockets and signed the paper on the table. A moment later, at a hidden signal, guns boomed outside, telling the world that the peace treaty had been signed.

The other delegates came up to sign, not just from the major powers but from all the countries who were party to the treaty. It took a long time, and conversation broke out among the spectators. The Germans sat stiffly frozen until at last it was over and they were escorted out.

Maud was sick with disgust. We preached a sermon of peace, she thought, but all the time we were plotting revenge. She left the palace. Outside, Wilson and Lloyd George were being mobbed by rejoicing spectators. She skirted the crowd, made her way into the town, and went to the Germans' hotel.

She hoped Walter was not too cast down: it had been a dreadful day for him.

She found him packing. "We're going home tonight," he said. "The whole delegation."

"So soon!" She had hardly thought about what would happen after the signing. It was an event of such huge dramatic significance that she had been unable to look beyond it.

By contrast, Walter had thought about it, and he had a plan. "Come with me," he said simply.

"I can't get permission to go to Germany."

"Whose permission do you need? I've got you a German passport in the name of Frau Maud von Ulrich."

She felt bewildered. "How did you manage that?" she said, though that was hardly the most important question in her mind.

"It was not difficult. You are the wife of a German citizen. You are entitled to a passport. I used my special influence only to shorten the process to a matter of hours."

She stared at him. It was so sudden.

"Will you come?" he said.

She saw in his eyes a terrible fear. He thought she might back out at the last minute. His terror of losing her made her want to cry. She felt very fortunate to be loved so passionately. "Yes," she said. "Yes, I will come. Of course I will come."

He was not convinced. "Are you sure this is what you want?"

She nodded. "Do you remember the story of Ruth, in the Bible?"

"Of course. Why . . . ?"

Maud had read it several times in the last few weeks, and now she quoted the words that had so moved her. "'Whither thou goest I will go, and where thou lodgest I will lodge; thy people shall be my people, and thy God my God; where thou diest . . .'" She stopped, unable to speak for the constriction in her throat; then, after a moment, she swallowed hard and resumed. "'Where thou diest will I die, and there will I be buried.'"

He smiled, but there were tears in his eyes. "Thank you," he said.

"I love you," she said. "What time is the train?"

CHAPTER THIRTY-EIGHT

August to October 1919

Gus and Rosa returned to Washington at the same time as the president. In August they contrived to get simultaneous leave and went home to Buffalo. The day after they arrived, Gus brought Rosa to meet his parents.

He was nervous. He desperately wanted his mother to like Rosa. But Mother had an inflated opinion of how attractive her son was to women. She had found fault with every girl he had ever mentioned. No one was good enough, especially socially. If he wanted to marry the daughter of the king of England, she would probably say: "Can't you find a nice well-bred American girl?"

"The first thing you'll notice about her, Mother, is that she's very pretty," Gus said at breakfast that morning. "Second, you'll see that she has only one eye. After a few minutes, you'll realize that she's very smart. And when you get to know her well, you'll understand that she's the most wonderful young woman in the world."

"I'm sure I shall," said his mother with her accustomed breathtaking insincerity. "Who are her parents?"

Rosa arrived at midafternoon, when Mother was taking her nap and Father was still downtown. Gus showed her around the house and grounds. She said nervously: "You do know that I come from a more modest background?"

"You'll get used to it soon enough," he said. "Anyway, you and I won't be living in this kind of splendor. But we might buy an elegant small house in Washington."

They played tennis. It was an uneven match: Gus with his long arms and legs was too good for her, and her judgment of distance was erratic. But she fought back determinedly, going for every ball, and won a few games. And in a white tennis dress with the fashionable midcalf hemline she looked so sexy that Gus had to make a major effort of will to concentrate on his shots.

They went in for tea in a glow of perspiration. "Summon up your reserves of tolerance and goodwill," Gus said outside the drawing room. "Mother can be an awful snob."

But Mother was on her best behavior. She kissed Rosa on both cheeks and said: "How wonderfully healthy you both look, all flushed with exercise. Miss Hellman, I'm so glad to meet you, and I hope we're going to become friends."

"You're very kind," said Rosa. "It would be a privilege to be your friend."

Mother was pleased by the compliment. She knew she was a grand dame of Buffalo society, and she felt it was appropriate that young women should show her deference. Rosa had divined that in an instant. Clever girl, Gus thought. And generous, too, given that in her heart she hated all authority.

"I know Fritz Hellman, your brother," Mother said. Fritz played violin in the Buffalo Symphony Orchestra. Mother was on the board. "He has a wonderful talent."

"Thank you. We are very proud of him."

Mother made small talk, and Rosa let her take the lead. Gus could not help remembering that once before he had brought home a girl he planned to marry: Olga Vyalov. Mother's reaction then had been different: she had been courteous and welcoming, but Gus had known her heart was not in it. Today she seemed genuine.

He had asked his mother about the Vyalov family yesterday. Lev Peshkov had been sent to Siberia as an army interpreter. Olga did not go to many social events, and seemed taken up with raising their child. Josef had lobbied Gus's father, the senator, for more military aid to the Whites. "He seems to think the Bolsheviks will be bad for the Vyalov family business in Petrograd," Mother had said.

"That's the best thing I've heard about the Bolsheviks," Gus had replied.

After tea they went off to change. Gus was disturbed by the thought of Rosa showering in the next room. He had never seen her naked. They had spent passionate hours together in her Paris hotel room, but they had not gone as far as sexual intercourse. "I hate to be old-fashioned," she had said apologetically, "but somehow I feel we should wait." She was not much of an anarchist really.

Her parents were coming for dinner. Gus put on a short tuxedo jacket and went downstairs. He mixed a Scotch for his father but did not have one himself. He felt he might need his wits about him.

Rosa came down in a black dress and looked stunning. Her parents appeared on the dot of six o'clock. Norman Hellman was wearing white tie and tails, not quite right for a family dinner, but perhaps he did not own a tuxedo. He was an elf of a man with a charming grin, and Gus saw immediately that Rosa took after him. He drank two martinis rather quickly, the only sign that he might be tense, but then he refused any more alcohol. Rosa's mother, Hilda, was a slender beauty with lovely long-fingered hands. It was hard to imagine her as a housemaid. Gus's father took to her immediately.

As they sat down to eat, Dr. Hellman said: "What are your career plans, Gus?"

He was entitled to ask this, as the father of the woman Gus loved, but Gus did not have much of an answer. "I'll work for the president as long as he needs me," he said.

"He's got a tough job on his hands right now."

"That's true. The Senate is making trouble about approving the Versailles peace treaty." Gus tried not to sound too bitter. "After all Wilson did to persuade the Europeans to set up the League of Nations, I can hardly believe that Americans are turning up their noses at the whole idea."

"Senator Lodge is a formidable troublemaker."

Gus thought Senator Lodge was an egocentric son of a bitch. "The president decided not to take Lodge with him to Paris, and now Lodge is getting his revenge."

Gus's father, who was an old friend of the president as well as a senator, said: "Woodrow made the League of Nations part of the peace treaty, thinking we could not possibly reject the treaty, therefore we would have to accept the league." He shrugged. "Lodge told him to go to blazes."

Dr. Hellman said: "In fairness to Lodge, I think the American people are right to be concerned about article ten. If we join a league that guarantees to protect its members from aggression, we're committing American forces to unknown conflicts in the future."

Gus's reply was quick. "If the league is strong, no one will dare to defy it."

"I'm not as confident as you about that."

Gus did not want to have an argument with Rosa's father, but he felt passionately about the League of Nations. "I don't say there would never be another war," he said in a conciliatory tone. "I do think that wars would be fewer and shorter, and aggressors would gain little reward."

"And I believe you may be right. But many voters say: 'Never mind the world—I'm interested only in America. Are we in danger of becoming the world's policeman?' It's a reasonable question."

Gus struggled to hide his anger. The league was the greatest hope for peace that had ever been offered to humankind, and it was in danger of being stillborn because of this kind of narrow-minded quibble. He said: "The council of the league has to make unanimous decisions, so the United States would never find itself fighting a war against its will."

"Nevertheless, there's no point in having the league unless it is prepared to fight."

The enemies of the league were like this: first they complained that it would fight; then they complained it would not. Gus said: "These problems are minor by comparison with the deaths of millions!"

Dr. Hellman shrugged, too polite to press his point against such a passionate opponent. "In any case," he said, "I believe a foreign treaty requires the support of two-thirds of the Senate."

"And right now we don't even have half," said Gus gloomily.

Rosa, who was reporting on this issue, said: "I count forty in favor, including you, Senator Dewar. Forty-three have reservations, eight are implacably against, and five undecided."

Her father said to Gus: "So what will the president do?"

"He's going to reach out to the people over the heads of the politicians. He's planning a ten-thousand-mile tour of the entire country. He'll make more than fifty speeches in four weeks."

"A punishing schedule. He's sixty-two and has high blood pressure."

There was a touch of mischief in Dr. Hellman. Everything he said was challenging. Obviously he felt the need to test the mettle of a suitor for his daughter. Gus replied: "But at the end of it, the president will have explained to the people of America that the world needs the League of Nations to make sure we never fight another war like the one just ended."

"I pray you're right."

"If political complexities need to be explained to ordinary people, Wilson is the best."

Champagne was served with dessert. "Before we begin, I'd like to say something," Gus said. His parents looked startled: he never made speeches. "Dr. and Mrs. Hellman, you know that I love your daughter, who is the most wonderful girl in the world. It's old-fashioned, but I want to ask your permission"—he took from his pocket a small red leather box—"your permission to offer her this engagement ring." He opened the box. It contained a gold ring with a single one-carat diamond. It was not ostentatious, but the diamond was pure white, the most desirable color, in a round brilliant cut, and it looked fabulous.

Rosa gasped.

Dr. Hellman looked at his wife, and they both smiled. "You most certainly have our permission," he said.

Gus walked around the table and knelt beside Rosa's chair. "Will you marry me, dear Rosa?" he said.

"Oh, yes, my beloved Gus—tomorrow, if you like!"

He took the ring from the box and slid it onto her finger. "Thank you," he said.

His mother began to cry.

{ II }

Gus was aboard the president's train as it steamed out of Union Station in Washington, D.C., at seven o'clock in the evening on Wednesday, September 3. Wilson was dressed in a blue blazer, white pants, and a straw boater. His wife, Edith, went with him, as did Cary Travers Grayson, his personal physician. Also aboard were twenty-one newspaper reporters including Rosa Hellman.

Gus was confident Wilson could win this battle. He had always enjoyed the direct connection with voters. And he had won the war, hadn't he?

The train traveled overnight to Columbus, Ohio, where the president made his first speech of the tour. From there he went on—making whistle-stop appearances along the way—to Indianapolis, where he spoke to a crowd of twenty thousand people that evening.

But Gus was disheartened at the end of the first day. Wilson had spoken poorly. His voice was husky. He used notes—he was always better when he managed without them—and, as he got into the technicalities of the treaty that had so absorbed everyone in Paris, he seemed to ramble and lose the audience's attention. He had a bad headache, Gus knew, so bad that sometimes his vision blurred.

Gus was sick with worry. It was not just that his friend and mentor was ill. There was more at stake. America's future and the world's hung on what happened in the next few weeks. Only Wilson's personal commitment could save the League of Nations from its small-minded opponents.

After dinner Gus went to Rosa's sleeping compartment. She was the only female reporter on the trip, so she had a room to herself. She was almost as keen on the league as Gus, but she said: "It's hard to find much positive to say about today." They lay on her bunk, kissing and cuddling; then they said good night and parted. Their wedding was set for October, after the president's trip. Gus would have liked it to be even sooner, but the parents wanted time to prepare, and Gus's mother had muttered darkly about indecent haste, so he had given in.

Wilson worked on improvements to his speech, tapping on his old Underwood typewriter as the endless open plains of the Midwest sped by the windows. His performances got better over the next few days. Gus suggested he try to make the treaty relevant to each city. Wilson told business leaders in St. Louis that the treaty was needed to build up world trade. In Omaha he said the world without the treaty would be like a community with unsettled land titles, all the farmers sitting on fences with shotguns. Instead of long explanations, he rammed home the main points in short statements.

Gus also suggested that Wilson appeal to people's emotions. This was not just about policy, he said; it touched on their feelings about their country. At Columbus, Wilson spoke of the boys in khaki. In Sioux Falls, he said he wanted to redeem the sacrifices of mothers who had lost their sons on the battlefield. He rarely descended to scurrility, but in Kansas City, home of the vitriolic Senator Reed, he compared his opponents to the Bolsheviks. And he thundered out the message, again and again, that if the League of Nations failed there would be another war.

Gus smoothed relations with the reporters on board and the local men wherever the train stopped. When Wilson spoke without a prepared speech, his stenographer would produce an immediate transcript, which Gus distributed. He also persuaded Wilson to come forward to the club car now and again to chat informally with the press.

It worked. Audiences responded better and better. The press coverage continued mixed, but Wilson's message was repeated constantly even in papers that opposed him. And reports from Washington suggested that opposition was weakening.

But Gus could see how much the campaign was costing the president. His headaches became almost continuous. He slept badly. He could not digest normal food, and Dr. Grayson fed him liquids. He got a throat infection that developed into something like asthma, and he began to have trouble breathing. He tried to sleep sitting upright.

All of this was kept from the press, even Rosa. Wilson continued to give speeches, although his voice was weak. Thousands cheered him in Salt Lake City, but he looked drawn, and he clenched his hands repeatedly, in an odd gesture that made Gus think of a dying man.

Then, on the night of September 25, there was a commotion. Gus heard Edith calling for Dr. Grayson. He put on a dressing gown and went to the president's car.

What he saw there horrified and saddened him. Wilson looked dreadful. He could hardly breathe and had developed a facial twitch. Even so, he wanted to carry on; but Grayson was adamant that he call off the remainder of the tour, and in the end Wilson gave in.

Next morning Gus, with a heavy heart, told the press that the president had suffered a severe nervous attack, and the tracks were cleared to speed the 1,700-mile journey back to Washington. All presidential engagements were canceled for two weeks, notably a meeting with pro-treaty senators to plan the fight for confirmation.

That evening, Gus and Rosa sat in her compartment, disconsolately looking out of the window. People gathered at every station to watch the president go by. The sun went down, but still the crowds stood and stared in the twilight. Gus was reminded of the train from Brest to Paris, and the silent multitude that had stood beside the tracks in the middle of the night. It was less than a year ago, but already their hopes had been dashed. "We did our best," Gus said. "But we failed."

"Are you sure?"

"When the president was campaigning full-time, it was touch and go. With Wilson sick, the chance of the treaty being ratified by the Senate is zero."

Rosa took his hand. "I'm sorry," she said. "For you, for me, for the world." She paused, then said: "What will you do?"

"I'd like to join a Washington law firm specializing in international law. I've got some relevant experience, after all."

"I should think they'll be lining up to offer you a job. And perhaps some future president will want your help."

He smiled. Sometimes she had an unrealistically high opinion of him. "And what about you?"

"I love what I'm doing. I hope I can carry on covering the White House."

"Would you like to have children?"

"Yes!"

"So would I." Gus stared meditatively out of the window. "I just hope Wilson is wrong about them."

"About our children?" She heard the note of solemnity in his tone, and she asked in a frightened voice: "What do you mean?"

"He says they will have to fight another world war."

"God forbid," Rosa said fervently.

Outside, night was falling.

CHAPTER THIRTY-NINE

January 1920

Daisy sat at the table in the dining room of the Vyalov family's prairie house in Buffalo. She wore a pink dress. The large linen napkin tied around her neck swamped her. She was almost four years old, and Lev adored her.

"I'm going to make the world's biggest sandwich," he said, and she giggled. He cut two pieces of toast half an inch square, buttered them carefully, added a tiny portion of the scrambled eggs Daisy did not want to eat, and put the slices together. "It has to have one grain of salt," he said. He poured salt from the cellar onto his plate, then delicately picked up a single grain on the tip of his finger and put it on the sandwich. "Now I can eat it!" he said.

"I want it," said Daisy.

"Really? But isn't it a Daddy-size sandwich?"

"No!" she said, laughing. "It's a girl-size sandwich!"

"Oh, all right," he said, and popped it into her mouth. "You don't want another one, do you?"

"Yes."

"But that one was so big."

"No, it wasn't!"

"Okay, I guess I have to make another one."

Lev was riding high. Things were even better than he had told Grigori ten months ago when they had sat in Trotsky's train. He was living in great comfort in his father-in-law's house. He managed three Vyalov nightclubs, getting a good salary plus extras such as kickbacks from suppliers. He had installed Marga in a fancy apartment and he saw her most days. She had got pregnant within a week of his return, and she had just given birth to a boy, whom they had named Gregory. Lev had succeeded in keeping the whole thing secret.

Olga came into the dining room, kissed Daisy, and sat down. Lev loved Daisy, but he had no feelings for Olga. Marga was sexier and more fun. And there were plenty more girls, as he had found out when Marga was heavily pregnant.

"Good morning, Mommy!" Lev said gaily.

Daisy took her cue and repeated his words.

Olga said: "Is Daddy feeding you?"

These days they talked like this, mainly through the child. They had had sex a few times when Lev got back from the war, but they had soon reverted to their normal indifference, and now they had separate bedrooms, telling Olga's parents it was because of Daisy waking at night, though she rarely did. Olga wore the look of a disappointed woman, and Lev hardly cared.

Josef came in. "Here's Grandpa!" Lev said.

"Morning," Josef said curtly.

Daisy said: "Grandpa wants a sandwich."

"No," said Lev. "They're too big for him."

Daisy was delighted when Lev said things that were obviously wrong. "No, they're not," she said. "They're too small!"

Josef sat down. He had changed a lot, Lev had found on returning from the war. Josef was overweight, and his striped suit was tight. He panted just from the exertion of walking downstairs. Muscle had turned to fat, black hair had gone gray, a pink complexion had become an unhealthy flush.

Polina came in from the kitchen with a pot of coffee and poured a cup for Josef. He opened the *Buffalo Advertiser*.

Lev said: "How's business?" It was not an idle question. The Volstead Act had come into force at midnight on January 16, making it illegal to manufacture, transport, or sell intoxicating liquor. The Vyalov empire was based on bars, hotels, and liquor wholesaling. Prohibition was the serpent in Lev's paradise.

"We're dying," said Josef with unusual frankness. "I've closed five bars in a week, and there's worse to come."

Lev nodded. "I'm selling near-beer in the clubs, but nobody wants it." The act permitted beer that was less than half of one percent alcohol. "You have to drink a gallon to get a buzz."

"We can sell a little hooch under the counter, but we can't get enough, and anyway people are scared to buy."

Olga was shocked. She knew little about the business. "But, Daddy, what are you going to do?"

"I don't know," said Josef.

This was another change. In the old days, Josef would have planned ahead for such a crisis. Yet it was three months since the act had been passed, and in that time Josef had done nothing to prepare for the new situation. Lev had been waiting for him to pull a rabbit out of a hat. Now he began to see, with dismay, that it was not going to happen.

That was worrying. Lev had a wife, a mistress, and two children, all living off the proceeds of the Vyalov businesses. If the empire was going to collapse, Lev would need to make plans.

Polina called Olga to the phone and she went into the hallway. Lev could hear her speaking. "Hello, Ruby," she said. "You're up early." There was a pause. "What? I don't believe it." A long silence followed; then Olga began to cry.

Josef looked up from the newspaper and said: "What the hell . . . ?"

Olga hung up with a crash and came back into the dining room. With her eyes full of tears she pointed at Lev and said: "You bastard."

"What did I do?" he said, although he feared he knew.

"You—you—*fucking* bastard."

Daisy began to bawl.

Josef said: "Olga, honey, what is the matter?"

Olga answered: "She's had a baby!"

Under his breath, Lev said: "Oh, shit."

Josef said: "Who's had a baby?"

"Lev's whore. The one we saw in the park. Marga."

Josef reddened. "The singer from the Monte Carlo? She's had *Lev's* baby?"

Olga nodded, sobbing.

Josef turned to Lev. "You son of a bitch."

Lev said: "Let's all try to stay calm."

Josef stood up. "My God, I thought I'd taught you a damned lesson."

Lev pushed back his chair and got to his feet. He backed away from Josef, holding his arms out defensively. "Just calm the fuck down, Josef," he said.

"Don't you dare tell me to calm down," Josef said. With surprising agility he stepped forward and lashed out with a meaty fist. Lev was not quick enough to dodge the blow and it struck him high on his left cheekbone. It hurt like hell and he staggered back.

Olga snatched up the howling Daisy and retreated to the doorway. "Stop it!" she yelled.

Josef lashed out with his left.

It was a long time since Lev had been in a fistfight, but he had grown up in the slums of Petrograd, and the reflexes still operated. He blocked Josef's swing, moved in close, and punched his father-in-law's belly with both fists in turn. The breath whooshed out of Josef's chest. Then Lev struck at Josef's face with short jabs, hitting the nose and mouth and eyes.

Josef was a strong man and a bully, but people were too scared of him to fight back, and for a long time he had had no practice at defending himself. He staggered back, holding up his arms in a feeble attempt to protect himself from Lev's blows.

Lev's street-fighting instincts would not let him stop while his assailant was upright, and he kept after Josef, punching his body and head, until the older man fell backward over a dining chair and hit the carpet.

Olga's mother, Lena, came rushing into the room, screamed, and knelt beside her husband. Polina and the cook came to the doorway to the kitchen, looking scared. Josef's face was battered and bleeding, but he raised himself on his elbow and pushed Lena aside. Then, when he tried to get up, he cried out and fell back.

His skin turned gray and he stopped breathing.

Lev said: "Jesus Christ."

Lena started to wail: "Josef, oh, my Joe, open your eyes!"

Lev felt Josef's chest. There was no heartbeat. He picked up the wrist and could not find a pulse.

I'm in trouble now, he thought.

He stood up. "Polina, call an ambulance."

She went into the hall and picked up the phone.

Lev stared at the body. He had to make a big decision fast. Stay here, protest innocence, pretend grief, try to wriggle out of it? No. The chances were too slim.

He had to go.

He ran upstairs and stripped off his shirt. He had come home from the war with a lot of gold, accumulated by selling Scotch to the Cossacks. He had converted it to just more than five thousand U.S. dollars, stuffed the bills into his money belt, and taped the belt to the back of a drawer. Now he fastened the belt around his waist and put his shirt and jacket back on.

He put on his overcoat. On top of his wardrobe was an old duffel containing his U.S. Army officer's-issue Colt .45 model 1911 semiautomatic pistol. He stuffed the pistol into his coat pocket. He threw a box of ammunition and some underwear into the duffel; then he went downstairs.

In the dining room, Lena had put a cushion under Josef's head, but Josef looked deader than ever. Olga was on the phone in the hallway, saying: "Be quick, please! I think he may die!" Too late, baby, Lev thought.

He said: "The ambulance will take too long. I'm going to fetch Dr. Schwarz." No one asked why he was carrying a bag.

He went to the garage and started Josef's Packard Twin Six. He drove out of the property and turned north.

He was not going to fetch Dr. Schwarz.

He headed for Canada.

{ II }

Lev drove fast. As he left Buffalo's northern suburbs behind, he tried to figure out how much time he had. The ambulance crew would undoubtedly call the police. As soon as the cops arrived they would find out that Josef had died in a fistfight. Olga would not hesitate to tell them who had knocked her father down: if she had not hated Lev before, she would now. At that point, Lev would be wanted for murder.

There were normally three cars in the Vyalov garage:

the Packard, Lev's Ford Model T, and a blue Hudson used by Josef's goons. It would not take the flatfoots very long to deduce that Lev had left in the Packard. In an hour, Lev calculated, the police would be looking for the car.

By then, with luck, he would be out of the country.

He had driven to Canada with Marga several times. It was only a hundred miles to Toronto, three hours in a fast car. They liked to check into a hotel as Mr. and Mrs. Peters and go out on the town, dressed to the nines, without having to worry about being spotted by someone who might tell Josef Vyalov. Lev did not have an American passport, but he knew several crossings where there were no border posts.

He reached Toronto at midday and checked into a quiet hotel.

He ordered a sandwich in the coffee shop and sat for a while contemplating his situation. He was wanted for murder. He had no home and he could not visit either of his two families without risking arrest. He might never see his children again. He had five thousand dollars in a money belt and a stolen car.

He thought back to the boasts he had made to his brother only ten months ago. What would Grigori think now?

He ate his sandwich, then wandered aimlessly around the center of town feeling depressed. He went into a liquor store and bought a bottle of vodka to take back to his room. Maybe he would just get drunk tonight. He noticed that rye whisky was four bucks a bottle. In Buffalo it cost ten, if you could get it at all; in New York City, fifteen or twenty. He knew because he had been trying to buy illicit liquor for the nightclubs.

He returned to the hotel and got some ice. His room was dusty, with faded furniture and a view of the backyards behind a row of cheap stores. As the early northern night fell outside, he felt more depressed than ever in his whole life. He thought of going out and picking up a girl, but he did not have the heart for it. Was he going to flee from every place he ever lived? He had quit Petrograd because of a dead policeman, and he had left Aberowen literally one step ahead of people he had cheated at cards; now he had fled Buffalo a fugitive.

He needed to do something about the Packard. The Buffalo police might cable a description to Toronto. He should either change the plates or change the car. But he could not summon the energy.

Olga was probably glad to get rid of him. She would have her inheritance all to herself. However, the Vyalov empire was worth less and less every day.

He wondered if he could bring Marga and baby Gregory to Canada. Would Marga even want to come? America was her dream, as it had been Lev's. Canada was not the fantasy destination of nightclub singers. She might follow Lev to New York or California, but not to Toronto.

He was going to miss his children. Tears came to his eyes as he thought of Daisy growing up without him. She was not quite four: she might forget him altogether. At best she would have a vague recollection. She would not remember the largest sandwich in the world.

After the third drink it struck him that he was a pitiable victim of injustice. He had not meant to kill his father-in-law. Josef had struck first. Anyway, Lev had not actually killed him: he had died of some kind of seizure or heart attack. It was really just bad luck. But no one was going to believe that. Olga was the only witness and she would want revenge.

He poured another vodka and lay on the bed. To hell with them all, he thought.

As he drifted into a restless alcoholic sleep, he thought of the bottles in the shop window. "Canadian Club, $4.00," read the sign. There was something important about that, he knew, but for the moment he could not put his finger on it.

When he woke up next morning his mouth was dry and his head ached, but he knew that Canadian Club at four bucks a bottle could be his salvation.

He rinsed his whisky glass and drank the melted ice at the bottom of the pail. By his third glassful he had a plan.

Orange juice, coffee, and aspirins made him feel better. He thought about the dangers ahead. But he had never allowed himself to be deterred by risks. If I did that, he thought, I'd be my brother.

There was one great drawback to his scheme. It depended on reconciliation with Olga.

He drove to a low-rent neighborhood and went into a cheap restaurant that was serving breakfast to workingmen. He sat at a table with a group of what looked like housepainters and said: "I need to trade my car for a truck. Do you know anyone who might be interested?"

One of the men said: "Is it legitimate?"

Lev gave his charming grin. "Give me a break, buddy," he said. "If it was legit, would I be selling it here?"

He found no takers there or at the next few places he tried, but eventually he ended up at an automobile repair shop run by a father and son. He exchanged the Packard for a two-ton Mack Junior van with two spare wheels in a no-cash, no-papers deal. He knew he was being robbed, but the garageman knew he was desperate.

Late that afternoon he went to a liquor wholesaler whose address he had found in the city directory. "I want a hundred cases of Canadian Club," he said. "What's your price?"

"For that quantity, thirty-six bucks a case."

"It's a deal." Lev took out his money. "I'm opening a tavern outside of town, and—"

"No need to explain, pal," said the wholesaler. He pointed out of the window. On the neighboring vacant lot, a team of building laborers were breaking ground. "My new warehouse, five times the size of this one. Thank God for Prohibition."

Lev realized he was not the first person to have this bright idea.

He paid the man and they loaded the whisky into the Mack van.

Next day Lev drove back to Buffalo.

{ III }

Lev parked the van full of whisky on the street outside the Vyalov house. The winter afternoon was turning to dusk. There were no cars on the driveway. He waited a while, tense, expectant, ready to flee, but he saw no activity.

His nerves stretched taut, he got out of the van, walked up to the front door, and let himself in with his own key.

The place was hushed. From upstairs he could hear Daisy's voice, and the murmured replies of Polina. There was no other sound.

Moving quietly on the thick carpet, he crossed the hall and looked into the drawing room. All the chairs had been pushed to the sides of the room. In the middle was a stand draped in black silk bearing a polished mahogany coffin with gleaming brass handles. In the casket was the corpse of Josef Vyalov. Death had softened the pugnacious lines of the face, and he looked harmless.

Olga sat alone beside the body. She wore a black dress. Her back was to the door.

Lev stepped into the room. "Hello, Olga," he said quietly.

She opened her mouth to scream, but he put his hand over her face and stopped her.

"Nothing to worry about," Lev said. "I just want to talk." Slowly, he eased his grip.

She did not scream.

He relaxed a little. He was over the first hurdle.

"You killed my father!" she said angrily. "What could there be to talk about?"

He took a deep breath. He had to handle this exactly right. Mere charm would not be enough. It would take brains, too. "The future," he said. He spoke in a low, intimate tone. "Yours, mine, and little Daisy's. I'm in trouble, I know—but so are you."

She did not want to listen. "I'm not in any trouble." She turned away and looked at the body.

Lev pulled up a chair and sat close to her. "The business you've inherited is shot. It's falling apart, almost worthless."

"My father was very wealthy!" she said indignantly.

"He owned bars, hotels, and a liquor wholesaling business. They're all losing money, and Prohibition has been in force only two weeks. He's already closed five bars. Soon there will be nothing left." Lev hesitated, then used the strongest argument he had. "You can't just consider yourself. You have to think about how you're going to raise Daisy."

She looked shaken. "Is the business really going bust?"

"You heard what your father said to me at breakfast the day before yesterday."

"I don't really remember."

"Well, don't take my word for anything, please. Check it out. Ask Norman Niall, the accountant. Ask anyone."

She gave him a hard look and decided to take him seriously. "Why have you come to tell me this?"

"Because I've figured out how to save the business."

"How?"

"By importing liquor from Canada."

"It's against the law."

"Yes. But it's your only hope. Without booze, you have no business."

She tossed her head. "I can look after myself."

"Sure," he said. "You can sell this house for a good sum, invest the proceeds, and move into a little apartment with your mother. Probably you could salvage enough from the estate to keep yourself and Daisy alive for a few years, though you should consider going out to work—"

"I can't work!" she said. "I've never trained for anything. What would I do?"

"Oh, listen, you could be a salesgirl in a department store. You could work in a factory—"

He was not serious and she knew it. "Don't be ridiculous," she snapped.

"Then there's only one option." He reached out to touch her.

She flinched away. "Why do you care what happens to me?"

"You're my wife."

She gave him a strange look.

He put on his most sincere face. "I know I've mistreated you, but we loved each other once."

She made a scornful noise in her throat.

"And we have a daughter to worry about."

"But you're going to jail."

"Unless you tell the truth."

"What do you mean?"

"Olga, you saw what happened. Your father attacked me. Look at my face—I have a black eye to prove it. I had to fight back. He must have had a weak heart. He may have been ill for some time—it would explain why he failed to prepare the business for Prohibition. Anyway, he was killed by the effort of attacking me, not by the few blows I struck in self-defense. All you have to do is tell the police the truth."

"I've already told them you killed him."

Lev was heartened: he was making progress. "That's all right," he reassured her. "You made a statement in the heat of the moment when you were stricken with grief. Now that you're calmer, you realize that your father's death was a terrible accident, brought on by his bad health and his angry tantrum."

"Will they believe me?"

"A jury will. But if I hire a good lawyer there won't even be a trial. How could there be, if the only witness swears it wasn't murder?"

"I don't know." She changed tack. "How are you going to get the liquor?"

"Easy. Don't worry about it."

She turned in her chair to face him directly. "I don't believe you. You're saying all this just to make me change my story."

"Put your coat on and I'll show you something."

It was a tense moment. If she went with him, she was his.

After a pause, she stood up.

Lev hid a triumphant smile.

They left the room. Outside on the street, he opened the rear doors of the van.

She was silent for a long moment. Then she said: "Canadian Club?" Her tone had changed, he noted. It was practical. The emotion had faded into the background.

"A hundred cases," he said. "I bought it for three bucks a bottle. I can get ten here—more if we sell it by the shot."

"I have to think about this."

That was a good sign. She was ready to agree, but did not want to rush into anything. "I understand, but there's no time," he said. "I'm a wanted man with a truckload of illegal whisky and I have to have your decision right away. I'm sorry to hustle you, but you can see I have no choice."

She nodded thoughtfully, but did not say anything.

Lev went on: "If you turn me down I'll sell my booze, take a profit, and disappear. You'll be on your own, then. I'll wish you luck and say good-bye forever, with no hard feelings. I would understand."

"And if I say yes?"

"We'll go to the police right away."

There was a long silence.

At last she nodded. "All right."

Lev looked away to hide his face. You did it, he said to himself. You sat with her in the same room as her father's dead body, and you won her back.

You dog.

{ IV }

"I have to put on a hat," said Olga. "And you need a clean shirt. We want to make a favorable impression."

That was good. She was really on his side.

They went back into the house and got ready. While he was waiting for her he called the *Buffalo Advertiser* and asked for Peter Hoyle, the editor. A secretary asked him his business. "Tell him I'm the man who's wanted for the murder of Josef Vyalov."

A moment later a voice barked. "Hoyle here. Who are you?"

"Lev Peshkov, Vyalov's son-in-law."

"Where are you?"

Lev ignored the question. "If you can have a reporter on the steps of police headquarters in half an hour, I'll have a statement for you."

"We'll be there."

"Mr. Hoyle?"

"Yes?"

"Send a photographer, too." Lev hung up.

With Olga beside him in the open front of the van, he drove first to Josef's waterfront warehouse. Boxes of stolen cigarettes were stacked around the walls. In the office at the back they found Vyalov's accountant, Norman Niall, plus the usual group of thugs. Norman was crooked but persnickety, Lev knew. He was sitting in Josef's chair, behind Josef's desk.

They were all astonished to see Lev and Olga.

Lev said: "Olga has inherited the business. I'll be running things from now on."

Norman did not get up out of his chair. "We'll see about that," he said.

Lev gave him a hard stare and said nothing.

Norman spoke again with less assurance. "The will has to be proved, and so on."

Lev shook his head. "If we wait for the formalities there will be no business left." He pointed at one of the goons. "Ilya, go out in the yard, look in the van, come back here, and tell Norm what you see."

Ilya went out. Lev moved around the desk to stand next to Norman. They waited in silence until Ilya came back.

"A hundred cases of Canadian Club." He put a bottle on the table. "We can try it, see if it's the real thing."

Lev said: "I'm going to run the business with booze imported from Canada. Prohibition is the greatest business opportunity ever. People will pay anything for liquor. We're going to make a fortune. Get out of that chair, Norm."

"I don't think so, kid," said Norman.

Lev pulled his gun fast and pistol-whipped Norman on both sides of the face. Norman cried out. Lev held the Colt casually pointed in the direction of the thugs.

To her credit, Olga did not scream.

"You asshole," Lev said to Norman. "I killed Josef Vyalov—do you think I'm scared of a fucking accountant?"

Norman got up and scurried out of the room, holding a hand to his bleeding mouth.

Lev turned to the other men, still holding the pistol pointing in their general direction, and said: "Anyone else who doesn't want to work for me can leave now, and no hard feelings."

No one moved.

"Good," said Lev. "Because I was lying about no hard feelings." He pointed at Ilya. "You come with me and Mrs. Peshkov. You can drive. The rest of you, unload the van."

Ilya drove them downtown in the blue Hudson.

Lev felt he might have made a mistake back there. He should not have said *I killed Josef Vyalov* in front of Olga. She could yet change her mind. If she mentioned it, he decided he would say he didn't mean it, but just said it to scare Norm. However, Olga did not raise the matter.

Outside police headquarters, two men in overcoats and hats were waiting beside a big camera on a tripod.

Lev and Olga got out of the car.

Lev said to the reporter: "The death of Josef Vyalov is a tragedy for us, his family, and for this city." The man scribbled shorthand in a notebook. "I have come to give the police my account of what happened. My wife, Olga, the only other person present when he collapsed, is here to testify that I am innocent. The postmortem will show that my father-in-law died of a heart attack. My wife and I plan to continue to expand the great business Josef Vyalov started here in Buffalo. Thank you."

"Look at the camera, please?" said the photographer.

Lev put his arm around Olga, pulled her close, and looked at the camera.

The reporter said: "How did you get the shiner, Lev?"

"This?" he said, and pointed to his eye. "Oh, hell, that's another story." He smiled his most charming grin, and the photographer's magnesium flare went off with a blinding flash.

CHAPTER FORTY

February to December 1920

The Aldershot Military Detention Barracks was a grim place, Billy thought, but it was better than Siberia. Aldershot was an army town thirty-five miles southwest of London. The prison was a modern building with galleries of cells on three floors around an atrium. It was brightly lit by a glazed roof that gave the place its nickname of "the Glasshouse." With heat pipes and gas lighting, it was more comfortable than most of the places where Billy had slept during the past four years.

All the same, he was miserable. The war had been over for more than a year, yet he was still in the army. Most of his friends were out, earning good wages and taking girls to the pictures. He still wore the uniform and saluted, he slept in an army bed, and he ate army food. He worked all day at weaving mats, which was the prison industry. Worst of all, he never saw a woman. Somewhere out there, Mildred was waiting for him—probably. Everyone had a tale to tell of a soldier who had come home to find that his wife or girlfriend had gone off with another man.

He had no communication with Mildred or anyone else outside. Prisoners—or "soldiers under sentence" as they were officially called—could normally send and receive letters, but Billy was a special case. Because he had been convicted of betraying army secrets in letters, his mail was confiscated by the authorities. This was part of the army's revenge. He no longer had any secrets to betray, of course.

What was he going to tell his sister? "The boiled potatoes are always undercooked."

Did Mam and Da and Gramper even know about the court-martial? The soldier's next of kin had to be informed, he thought, but he was not sure and no one would answer his questions. Anyway, Tommy Griffiths would almost certainly have told them. He hoped Ethel had explained what he had really been doing.

He received no visitors. He suspected his family did not even know that he was back from Russia. He would have liked to challenge the ban on his receiving mail, but he had no way of contacting a lawyer—and no money to pay one. His only consolation was a vague feeling that this could not go on indefinitely.

His news of the outside world came from the papers. Fitz was back in London, making speeches urging more military aid for the Whites in Russia. Billy wondered if that meant the Aberowen Pals had come home.

Fitz's speeches were doing no good. Ethel's "Hands Off Russia" campaign had won support and been endorsed by the Labour Party. Despite colorful anti-Bolshevik speeches by the minister for war, Winston Churchill, Britain had withdrawn its troops from Arctic Russia. In mid-November the Reds had driven Admiral Kolchak out of Omsk. Everything Billy had said about the Whites, and Ethel had repeated in her campaign, turned out to be correct; everything Fitz and Churchill said was wrong. Yet Billy was in jail and Fitz was in the House of Lords.

He had little in common with his fellow inmates. They were not political prisoners. Most had committed real crimes, theft and assault and murder. They were hard men, but so was Billy and he was not afraid of them. They treated him with wary deference, apparently feeling that his offense was a cut above theirs. He talked to them amiably enough but none of them had any interest in politics. They saw nothing wrong with the society that had imprisoned them; they were just determined to beat the system next time.

During the half-hour lunch break he read the newspaper. Most of the others could not read. One day he opened the *Daily Herald* to see a photograph of a familiar face. After a moment of bewilderment he realized the picture was of him.

He recalled when it had been taken. Mildred had dragged him to a photographer in Aldgate and had him snapped in his uniform. "Every night I'll touch it to my lips," she had said. He had often thought of that ambiguous promise while he was away from her.

The headline said: WHY IS SERGEANT WILLIAMS IN JAIL? Billy read on with mounting excitement.

> William Williams of the Welsh Rifles (the "Aberowen Pals") 8th Battalion is serving ten years in a military prison, convicted of treason. Is this man a traitor? Did he betray his country, desert to the enemy, or run from battle? On the contrary. He fought bravely at the Somme and continued to serve in France for the next two years, winning promotion to sergeant.

Billy was excited. That's me, he thought, in the papers, and they say I fought bravely!

> Then he was sent to Russia. We are not at war with Russia. The British people do not necessarily approve of the Bolshevik regime, but we do not attack every regime of which we disapprove. The Bolsheviks present no threat to our country or our allies. Parliament has never agreed to military action against the government in Moscow. There is a serious question as to whether our mission there is not a breach of international law.
>
> Indeed, for some months the British people were not told that their army was fighting in Russia. The government made misleading statements to the effect that troops there were only protecting our property, organizing orderly withdrawal, or on standby. The clear implication was that they were not in action against Red forces.
>
> That this was exposed as a lie is in no small measure thanks to William Williams.

"Hey," he said to no one in particular. "Look at that. Thanks to William Williams."

The men at his table crowded around to look over his shoulder. His cellmate, a brute called Cyril Parks, said: "That's a picture of you! What are you doing in the paper?"

Billy read the rest of it aloud.

His crime was to tell the truth, in letters to his sister that were written in a simple code to evade censorship. The British people owe him a debt of gratitude.

But his action displeased those in the army and in government who were responsible for secretly using British soldiers for their own political ends. Williams was court-martialed and sentenced to ten years.

He is not unique. A large number of servicemen who objected to being made part of the attempted counterrevolution were subjected to highly dubious trials in Russia and given scandalously long sentences.

William Williams and others have been victimized by vengeful men in positions of power. This must be put right. Britain is a country of justice. That, after all, is what we fought for.

"How about that?" said Billy. "They say I've been victimized by powerful men."

"So have I," said Cyril Parks, who had raped a fourteen-year-old Belgian girl in a barn.

Suddenly the newspaper was snatched out of Billy's hands. He looked up to see the stupid face of Andrew Jenkins, one of the more unpleasant warders. "You may have friends in high fucking places, Williams," the man said. "But in here you're just another fucking con, so get back to fucking work."

"Right away, Mr. Jenkins," said Billy.

{ II }

Fitz was outraged, that summer of 1920, when a Russian trade delegation came to London and was welcomed by the prime minister, David Lloyd George, at number 10 Downing Street. The Bolsheviks were still at war with the newly reconstituted country of Poland, and Fitz thought Britain should be siding with the Poles, but he found little support. London dockers went on strike rather than load ships with rifles for the Polish army, and the Trades Union Congress threatened a general strike if the British army intervened.

Fitz reconciled himself to never taking possession of the late Prince Andrei's estates. His sons, Boy and Andrew, had lost their Russian birthright, and he had to accept that.

However, he could not keep quiet when he learned what the Russians Kamenev and Krassin were up to as they went around Britain. Room 40 still existed, albeit in a different form, and British intelligence was intercepting and deciphering the telegrams the Russians were sending home. Lev Kamenev, the chairman of the Moscow soviet, was shamelessly putting out revolutionary propaganda.

Fitz was so incensed that he berated Lloyd George, early in August, at one of the last dinner parties of the London season.

It was at Lord Silverman's house in Belgrave Square. The dinner was not as lavish as those Silverman had thrown before the war. There were fewer courses, with less food sent untasted back to the kitchen, and the table decoration was simpler. The food was served by maids instead of footmen: no one wanted to be a footman these days. Fitz guessed those extravagant Edwardian parties were gone for good. However, Silverman was still able to attract the most powerful men in the land to his house.

Lloyd George asked Fitz about his sister, Maud.

That was another topic that enraged Fitz. "I'm sorry to say that she has married a German and gone to live in Berlin," he said. He did not say that she had already given birth to her first child, a boy called Eric.

"I heard that," said Lloyd George. "I just wondered how she was getting on. Delightful young woman."

The prime minister's liking for delightful young women was well-known, not to say notorious.

"I'm afraid life in Germany is hard," said Fitz. Maud had written to him pleading for an allowance, but he had refused point-blank. She had not asked his permission for the marriage, so how could she expect his support?

"Hard?" said Lloyd George. "So it should be, after what they've done. All the same, I'm sorry for her."

"On another subject, Prime Minister," said Fitz, "this fellow Kamenev is a Jew Bolshevik—you ought to deport him."

The prime minister was in a mellow mood, with a glass of champagne in his hand. "My dear Fitz," he said amiably, "the government is not very worried about Russian misinformation, which is crude and violent. Please don't underestimate the British working class: they know claptrap when they hear it. Believe me, Kamenev's speeches are doing more to discredit Bolshevism than anything you or I could say."

Fitz thought this was complacent rubbish. "He's even given money to the *Daily Herald*!"

"It is discourteous, I agree, for a foreign government to subsidize one of our newspapers—but, really, are we frightened of the *Daily Herald*? It's not as if we Liberals and Conservatives don't have papers of our own."

"But he is contacting the most hard-line revolutionary groups in this country—maniacs dedicated to the overthrow of our entire way of life!"

"The more the British get to know about Bolshevism, the less they will like it, you mark my words. It is formidable only when seen at a distance, through impenetrable mists. Bolshevism is almost a safeguard to British society, for it infects all classes with a horror of what may happen if the present organization of society is overturned."

"I just don't like it."

"Besides," Lloyd George went on, "if we throw them out we may have to explain how we know what they're up to; and the news that we're spying on them may inflame working-class opinion against us more effectively than all their turgid speeches."

Fitz did not like being lectured on political realities, even by the prime minister, but he persisted with his argument because he felt so angry. "But surely we don't have to trade with the Bolsheviks!"

"If we refused to do business with all those who use their embassies here for propaganda, we wouldn't have many trading partners left. Come, come, Fitz, we trade with cannibals in the Solomon Islands!"

Fitz was not sure that was true—the cannibals of the Solomon Islands did not have much to offer, after all—but he let it pass. "Are we so badly off that we have to sell to these murderers?"

"I fear we are. I have talked to a good many businessmen, and they have rather frightened me about the next eighteen months. There are no orders coming in. Customers won't buy. We may be in for the worst period of unemployment that any of us have ever known. But the Russians want to buy—and they pay in gold."

"I would not take their gold!"

"Ah, but Fitz," said Lloyd George, "you have so much of your own."

{ III }

There was a party in Wellington Row when Billy took his bride home to Aberowen.

It was a summer Saturday, and for once there was no rain. At three o'clock in the afternoon Billy and Mildred arrived at the station with Mildred's children, Billy's new stepdaughters, Enid and Lillian, aged eight and seven. By then the miners had come up from the pit, taken their weekly baths, and put on their Sunday suits.

Billy's parents were waiting at the station. They were older and seemed diminished, no longer dominating those around them. Da shook Billy's hand and said: "I'm proud of you, son. You stood up to them, just like I taught you to." Billy was glad, although he did not see himself as just another of Da's achievements in life.

They had met Mildred once before, at Ethel's wedding. Da shook Mildred's hand and Mam kissed her.

Mildred said: "It's lovely to see you again, Mrs. Williams. Should I call you Mam now?"

It was the best thing she could have said, and Mam was delighted. Billy felt sure Da would come to love her, provided she could keep from swearing.

Persistent questions by M.P.s in the House of Commons—fed with information by Ethel—had forced the government to announce reduced sentences for a number of soldiers and sailors court-martialed in Russia for mutiny and other offenses. Billy's prison term had been reduced to a year and he had been released and demobilized. He had married Mildred as quickly as possible after that.

Aberowen seemed strange to him. The place had not changed much, but his feelings were different. It was small and drab, and the mountains all around seemed like walls to keep the people in. He was no longer sure this was his home. As when he had put on his prewar suit, he found that, even though it still fit, he no longer felt right in it. Nothing that happened here would change the world, he thought.

They walked up the hill to Wellington Row to find the houses decorated with bunting: the Union Jack, the Welsh dragon, and the red flag. A banner across the street said WELCOME HOME, BILLY TWICE. All the neighbors were out in the street. There were tables with jugs of beer and urns of tea, and plates loaded with pies, cakes, and sandwiches. When they saw Billy they sang "We'll Keep a Welcome in the Hillsides."

It made Billy cry.

He was handed a pint of beer. A crowd of admiring young men gathered around Mildred. To them she was an exotic creature, with her London clothes and her Cockney accent and a hat with a huge brim that she had trimmed herself with silk flowers. Even when she was on her best behavior she could not help saying risqué things like "I had to get it off my chest, if you'll pardon the expression."

Gramper looked older, and could hardly stand up straight, but mentally he was still all right. He took charge of Enid and Lillian, producing sweets out of his waistcoat pockets and showing them how he could make a penny disappear.

Billy had to talk to all the bereaved families about his dead comrades: Joey Ponti, Prophet Jones, Spotty Llewellyn, and the others. He was reunited with Tommy Griffiths, whom he had last seen in Ufa, Russia. Tommy's father, Len, the atheist, was gaunt with cancer.

Billy was going to start down the pit again on Monday, and the miners all wanted to explain to him the changes underground since he had left: new roads driven deeper into the workings, more electric lights, better safety precautions.

Tommy stood on a chair and made a speech of welcome; then Billy had to respond. "The war has changed us all," he said. "I remember when people used to say the rich were put on this earth by God to rule over us lesser people." That was greeted by scornful laughs. "Many men were cured of that delusion by fighting under the command of upper-class officers who should not have been put in charge of a Sunday school outing." The other veterans nodded knowingly. "The war was won by men like us, ordinary men, uneducated but not stupid." They agreed, saying "Aye" and "Hear, hear."

"We've got the vote now—and so have our women, though not all of them yet, as my sister, Eth, will tell you quick enough." There was a little cheer from the women at that. "This is our country, and we must take control of it, just as the Bolsheviks have taken over in Russia and the Social Democrats in Germany." The men cheered. "We've got a working-class party, the Labour Party, and we've got the numbers to put our party in government. Lloyd George pulled a fast one at the last election, but he won't get away with that again."

Someone shouted: "No!"

"So here's what I've come home for. Perceval Jones's days as M.P. for Aberowen are almost over." There was a cheer. "I want to see a Labour man representing us in the House of Commons!" Billy caught his father's eye: Da's face was aglow. "Thank you for your wonderful welcome." He got down from the chair, and they clapped enthusiastically.

"Nice speech, Billy," said Tommy Griffiths. "But who's going to be that Labour M.P.?"

"I tell you what, Tommy boy," said Billy. "I'll give you three guesses."

{ IV }

The philosopher Bertrand Russell visited Russia that year and wrote a short book called *The Practice and Theory of Bolshevism.* In the Leckwith family it almost caused a divorce.

Russell came out strongly against the Bolsheviks. Worse, he did so from a left-wing perspective. Unlike Conservative critics, he did not argue that the Russian people had no right to depose the tsar, share out the lands of the nobility among the peasants, and run their own factories. On the contrary, he approved of all that. He attacked the Bolsheviks not for having the wrong ideals, but for having the right ideals and failing to live up to them. So his conclusions could not be dismissed out of hand as propaganda.

Bernie read it first. He had a librarian's horror of marking books, but in this case he made an exception, defacing the pages with angry comments, underlining sentences and writing "Rubbish!" or "Invalid argument!" with a pencil in the margins.

Ethel read it while nursing the baby, now just more than a year old. She was named Mildred, but they always shortened it to Millie. The older Mildred had moved to Aberowen with Billy and was already pregnant with their first child. Ethel missed her, even though she was glad to have the use of the upstairs rooms in the house. Little Millie had curly hair and, already, a flirtatious twinkle in her eye that reminded everyone of Ethel.

Ethel enjoyed the book. Russell was a witty writer. With aristocratic insouciance, he had asked for an interview with Lenin, and had spent an hour with the great man. They had spoken English. Lenin had said that Lord Northcliffe was his best propagandist: the *Daily Mail*'s horror stories about Russians despoiling the aristocracy might terrify the bourgeoisie but they would have the opposite effect on the British working class, he thought.

But Russell made it clear that the Bolsheviks were completely undemocratic. The dictatorship of the proletariat was a real dictatorship, he said, but the rulers were middle-class intellectuals such as Lenin and Trotsky, assisted by only such proletarians who agreed with their views. "I think this is very worrying," said Ethel when she put the book down.

"Bertrand Russell is an aristocrat!" Bernie said angrily. "He's the third earl!"

"That doesn't make him wrong." Millie stopped sucking and went to sleep. Ethel stroked her soft cheek with a fingertip. "Russell is a socialist. His complaint is that the Bolsheviks are not implementing socialism."

"How can he say such a thing? The nobility has been crushed."

"But so has the opposition press."

"A temporary necessity—"

"How temporary? The Russian revolution is three years old!"

"You can't make an omelette without breaking eggs."

"He says there are arbitrary arrests and executions, and the secret police are more powerful now than they were under the tsar."

"But they act against counterrevolutionaries, not against socialists."

"Socialism means freedom, even for counterrevolutionaries."

"No, it doesn't!"

"It does to me."

Their raised voices woke Millie. Sensing the anger in the room, she started to cry.

"There," said Ethel resentfully. "Now look what you've done."

{ V }

When Grigori returned home from the civil war he joined Katerina, Vladimir, and Anna in their comfortable apartment within the government enclave in the old fort of the Kremlin. For his taste, it was too comfortable. The entire country was suffering shortages of food and fuel, but in the shops of the Kremlin there was plenty. The compound had three restaurants with French-trained chefs and, to Grigori's dismay, the waiters clicked their heels to the Bolsheviks as they had to the old nobility. Katerina put the children in the nursery while she visited the hairdresser. In the evening, members of the Central Committee went to the opera in chauffeur-driven cars.

"I hope we are not becoming the new nobility," he said to Katerina in bed one night.

She laughed scornfully. "If we are, where are my diamonds?"

"But, you know, we do have banquets, and travel first-class on the railway, and so on."

"The aristocrats never did anything useful. You all work twelve, fifteen, eighteen hours a day. You can't be expected to scavenge on rubbish tips for bits of wood to burn for warmth, as the poor do."

"But then, there's always an excuse for the elite to have their special privileges."

"Come here," she said. "I'll give you a special privilege."

After they had made love, Grigori lay awake. Despite his misgivings, he could not help feeling a secret satisfaction at seeing his family so well-off. Katerina had put on weight. When he first met her, she had been a voluptuous twenty-year-old girl; now she was a plump mother at twenty-six. Vladimir was five and learning to read and write in school with the other children of Russia's new rulers; Anna, usually called Anya, was a mischievous curly-headed three-year-old. Their home had formerly belonged to one of the tsaritsa's ladies-in-waiting. It was warm, dry, and spacious, with a second bedroom for the children and a kitchen and living room, too—enough accommodation for twenty people in Grigori's old lodgings in Petrograd. There were curtains at the windows, china cups for tea, a rug in front of the fire, and an oil painting of Lake Baikal over the fireplace.

Grigori eventually fell asleep, to be wakened at six in the morning by a banging on the door. He opened it to a poorly dressed, skeletally thin woman who looked familiar. "I am sorry to bother you so early, Excellency," she said, using the old style of respectful address.

He recognized her as the wife of Konstantin. "Magda!" he said in astonishment. "You look so different—come in! What's the matter? Are you living in Moscow now?"

"Yes, we moved here, Excellency."

"Don't call me that, for God's sake. Where is Konstantin?"

"In prison."

"What? Why?"

"As a counterrevolutionary."

"Impossible!" said Grigori. "There must have been a terrible mistake."

"Yes, sir."

"Who arrested him?"

"The Cheka."

"The secret police. Well, they work for us. I'll find out about this. I'll make inquiries immediately after breakfast."

"Please, Excellency, I beg you, do something now—they are going to shoot him in one hour."

"Hell," said Grigori. "Wait while I get dressed."

He put on his uniform. Although it had no badges of rank, it was of a much better quality than that of an ordinary soldier, and marked him clearly as a commander.

A few minutes later he and Magda left the Kremlin compound. It was snowing. They walked the short distance to Lubyanka Square. The Cheka headquarters was a huge baroque building of yellow brick, formerly the office of an insurance company. The guard at the door saluted Grigori.

He began shouting as soon as he entered the building. "Who is in charge here? Bring me the duty officer this instant! I am Comrade Grigori Peshkov, member of the Bolshevik Central Committee. I wish to see the prisoner Konstantin Vorotsyntsev immediately. What are you waiting for? Get on with it!" He had discovered that this was the quickest way to get things done, even though it reminded him horribly of the petulant behavior of a spoiled nobleman.

The guards ran around in panic for a few minutes; then Grigori suffered a shock. The duty officer was brought to the entrance hall. Grigori knew him. It was Mikhail Pinsky.

Grigori was horrified. Pinsky had been a bully and a brute in the tsarist police: was he now a bully and a brute for the revolution?

Pinsky gave an oily smile. "Comrade Peshkov," he said. "What an honor."

"You didn't say that when I knocked you down for pestering a poor peasant girl," Grigori said.

"How things have changed, comrade—for all of us."

"Why have you arrested Konstantin Vorotsyntsev?"

"Counterrevolutionary activities."

"That's ridiculous. He was chair of the Bolshevik discussion group at the Putilov works in 1914. He was one of the first deputies to the Petrograd soviet. He's more Bolshevik than I am!"

"Is that so?" said Pinsky, and there was the hint of a threat in his voice.

Grigori ignored it. "Bring him to me."

"Right away, comrade."

A few minutes later Konstantin appeared. He was dirty and unshaven, and he smelled like a pigsty. Magda burst into tears and threw her arms around him.

"I need to talk to the prisoner privately," Grigori said to Pinsky. "Take us to your office."

Pinsky shook his head. "My humble room—"

"Don't argue," Grigori said. "Your office." It was a way of emphasizing his power. He needed to keep Pinsky under his thumb.

Pinsky led them to an upstairs room overlooking the inner courtyard. He hastily swept a knuckle-duster off the desk into a drawer.

Looking out of the window, Grigori saw that it was daybreak. "Wait outside," he said to Pinsky.

They sat down and Grigori said to Konstantin: "What the hell is going on?"

"We came to Moscow when the government moved," Konstantin explained. "I thought I would become a commissar. But it was a mistake. I have no political support here."

"So what have you been doing?"

"I've gone back to ordinary work. I'm at the Tod factory, making engine parts, cogs and pistons and ball races."

"But why do the police imagine you're a counterrevolutionary?"

"The factory elects a deputy to the Moscow soviet. One of the engineers announced he would be a Menshevik candidate. He held a meeting, and I went to listen. There were only a dozen people there. I didn't speak, I left halfway through, and I didn't vote for him. The Bolshevik candidate won, of course. But, after the election, everyone who attended that Menshevik meeting was fired. Then, last week, we were all arrested."

"We can't do this," Grigori said in despair. "Not even in the name of the revolution. We can't arrest workers for listening to a different point of view."

Konstantin looked at him strangely. "Have you been away somewhere?"

"Of course," said Grigori. "Fighting the counterrevolutionary armies."

"Then that's why you don't know what's going on."

"You mean this has happened before?"

"Grishka, it happens every day."

"I can't believe it."

Magda said: "And last night I received a message—from a friend who is married to a policeman—saying Konstantin and the others were all to be shot at eight o'clock this morning."

Grigori looked at his army-issue wristwatch. It was almost eight. "Pinsky!" he shouted.

The policeman came in.

"Stop this execution."

"I fear it is too late, comrade."

"You mean these men have already been shot?"

"Not quite." Pinsky went to the window.

Grigori did the same. Konstantin and Magda stood beside him.

Down in the snow-covered courtyard, a firing squad had assembled in the clear early light. Opposite the soldiers, a dozen blindfolded men stood shivering in thin indoor clothes. A red flag flew above their heads.

As Grigori looked, the soldiers raised their rifles.

Grigori yelled: "Stop at once! Do not shoot!" But his voice was muffled by the window, and no one heard.

A moment later there was a crash of gunfire.

The condemned men fell to the ground. Grigori stared, aghast.

Around the slumped bodies, bloodstains appeared on the snow, bright red to match the flag flying above.

CHAPTER FORTY-ONE

November 11–12, 1923

Maud slept in the day and got up in the middle of the afternoon, when Walter brought the children home from Sunday school. Eric was three and Heike was two, and they looked so sweet in their best clothes that Maud thought her heart would burst with love.

She had never known an emotion like this. Even her mad passion for Walter had not been so overwhelming. The children also made her feel desperately anxious. Would she be able to feed them and keep them warm, and protect them from riot and revolution?

She gave them hot bread-and-milk to warm them; then she began to prepare for the evening. She and Walter were throwing a small family party to celebrate the thirty-eighth birthday of Walter's cousin Robert von Ulrich.

Robert had not been killed in the war, contrary to Walter's parents' fears—or were they hopes? Either way, Walter had not become the Graf von Ulrich. Robert had been held in a prisoner-of-war camp in Siberia. When the Bolsheviks had made peace with Austria, Robert and his wartime comrade, Jörg, had set out to walk, hitchhike, and ride freight trains home. It had taken them a year, but they had made it, and when they returned Walter had found them an apartment in Berlin.

Maud put on her apron. In the tiny kitchen of her little house she made a soup out of cabbage, stale bread, and turnips. She also baked a small cake, although she had to eke out her ingredients with more turnips.

She had learned to cook and much else besides. A kindly neighbor, an older woman, had taken pity on the bewildered aristocrat and taught her how to make a bed, iron a shirt, and clean a bathtub. It had all come as something of a shock.

They lived in a middle-class town house. They had not been able to spend any money on it, nor could they afford the servants Maud had always been used to, and they had a lot of secondhand furniture that Maud secretly thought was dreadfully suburban.

They had looked forward to better times, but in fact things had got worse: Walter's career in the foreign ministry had been dead-ended by his marriage to an English-woman, and he would have moved on to something else, but in the economic chaos he was lucky to have any job at all. And Maud's early dissatisfactions seemed petty now, four years of poverty later. There was patched upholstery where the children had torn it, broken windows covered with cardboard, and paintwork peeling everywhere.

But Maud had no regrets. Anytime she liked she could kiss Walter, slide her tongue into his mouth, unbutton his trousers, and lie with him on the bed or the couch or even the floor, and that made up for everything else.

Walter's parents came to the party bringing half a ham and two bottles of wine. Otto had lost his family estate, Zumwald, which was now in Poland. His savings had been reduced to nothing by inflation. However, the large garden of his Berlin house produced potatoes, and he still had a lot of prewar wine.

"How did you manage to find ham?" Walter said incredulously. Such things could normally be bought only with American dollars.

"I traded a bottle of vintage champagne for it," said Otto.

The grandparents put the children to bed. Otto told them a folktale. From what Maud could hear, it was about a queen who had her brother beheaded. She shuddered, but did not interfere. Afterward Susanne sang lullabies in a reedy voice and the children went to sleep, apparently none the worse for their grandfather's bloodthirsty story.

Robert and Jörg arrived, wearing identical red ties. Otto

greeted them warmly. He seemed to have no idea of their relationship, apparently accepting that Jörg was simply Robert's flatmate. Indeed, that was how the men behaved when they were with older folk. Maud thought that Susanne probably guessed the truth. Women were harder to fool. Fortunately they were more accepting.

Robert and Jörg could be very different in liberal company. At parties in their own home they made no secret of their romantic love. Many of their friends were the same. Maud had been startled at first: she had never seen men kissing, admiring one another's outfits, and flirting like schoolgirls. But such behavior was no longer taboo, at least in Berlin. And Maud had read Proust's *Sodome et Gomorrhe*, which seemed to suggest that this kind of thing had always gone on.

Tonight, however, Robert and Jörg were on their best behavior. Over dinner everyone talked about what was happening in Bavaria. On Thursday an association of paramilitary groups called the Kampfbund had declared a national revolution in a beer hall in Munich.

Maud could hardly bear to read the news these days. Workers went on strike, so right-wing bullyboys beat up the strikers. Housewives marched to protest against the shortage of provisions, and their protests turned into food riots. Everyone in Germany was angry about the Versailles Treaty, yet the Social Democratic government had accepted it in full. People believed reparations were crippling the economy, even though Germany had paid only a fraction of the amount and obviously had no intention of trying to clear the total.

The Munich beer hall putsch had everyone worked up. The war hero Erich Ludendorff was its most prominent supporter. So-called storm troopers in their brown shirts and students from the Officers Infantry School had seized control of key buildings. City councilors had been taken hostage and prominent Jews arrested.

On Friday the legitimate government had counterattacked. Four policemen and sixteen paramilitaries had been killed. Maud was not able to judge, from the news that had reached Berlin so far, whether the insurrection was over or not. If the extremists took control of Bavaria, would the whole country fall to them?

It made Walter angry. "We have a democratically elected

government," he said. "Why can't people let them get on with the job?"

"Our government has betrayed us," said his father.

"In your opinion. So what? In America, when the Republicans won the last election, the Democrats didn't riot!"

"The United States is not being subverted by Bolsheviks and Jews."

"If you're worried about the Bolsheviks, tell people not to vote for them. And what is this obsession with Jews?"

"They are a pernicious influence."

"There are Jews in Britain. Father, don't you remember how Lord Rothschild in London tried his best to prevent the war? There are Jews in France, in Russia, in America. They're not conspiring to betray their governments. What makes you think ours are peculiarly evil? Most of them only want to earn enough to feed their families and send their children to school—just the same as everyone else."

Robert surprised Maud by speaking up. "I agree with Uncle Otto," he said. "Democracy is enfeebling. Germany needs strong leadership. Jörg and I have joined the National Socialists."

"Oh, Robert, for God's sake!" said Walter disgustedly. "How could you?"

Maud stood up. "Would anyone like a piece of birthday cake?" she said brightly.

{ II }

Maud left the party at nine to go to work. "Where's your uniform?" said her mother-in-law as she said good-bye. Susanne thought Maud was a night nurse for a wealthy old gentleman.

"I keep it there and change when I arrive," Maud said. In fact she played the piano in a nightclub called Nachtleben. However, it was true that she kept her uniform at work.

She had to earn money, and she had never been taught to do much except dress up and go to parties. She had had a small inheritance from her father, but she had converted it to marks when she moved to Germany, and now it was worthless. Fitz refused to give her money because he was still angry with her for marrying without his permission. Walter's salary at the Foreign Office was raised every month, but it never kept pace with inflation. In partial compensation, the rent they paid for their house was now negligible, and the landlord no longer bothered to collect it. But they had to buy food.

Maud got to the club at nine thirty. The place was newly furnished and decorated, and looked good even with the lights up. Waiters were polishing glasses, the barman was chipping ice, and a blind man was tuning the piano. Maud changed into a low-cut evening dress and fake jewelry, and made up her face heavily with powder, eyeliner, and lipstick. She was at the piano when the place opened at ten.

It rapidly filled up with men and women in evening clothes, dancing and smoking. They bought champagne cocktails and discreetly sniffed cocaine. Despite poverty and inflation, Berlin's nightlife was hot. Money was no problem to these people. Either they had income from abroad, or they had something better than money: stocks of coal, a slaughterhouse, a tobacco warehouse, or, best of all, gold.

Maud was part of an all-female band playing the new music called jazz. Fitz would have been horrified to see it, but she liked the job. She had always rebelled against the restrictions of her upbringing. Doing the same tunes every night could be tedious, but despite that it released something repressed within her. She wiggled on her piano stool and batted her eyelashes at the customers.

At midnight she had a spot of her own, singing and playing songs made popular by Negro singers such as Alberta Hunter, which she learned from American discs played on a gramophone that belonged to Nachtleben's owner. She was billed as Mississippi Maud.

Between numbers a customer staggered up to the piano and said: "Play 'Downhearted Blues,' will you?"

She knew the song, a big hit for Bessie Smith. She started to play blues chords in E flat. "I might," she said. "What's it worth?"

He held out a billion-mark note.

Maud laughed. "That won't buy you the first bar," she said. "Haven't you got any foreign currency?"

He handed her a dollar bill.

She took the money, stuffed it into her sleeve, and played "Downhearted Blues."

Maud was overjoyed to have a dollar, which was worth about a trillion marks. Nevertheless she felt a little down, and her heart was really in the blues. It was quite an achievement for a woman of her background to have learned to hustle tips, but the process was demeaning.

After her spot, the same customer accosted her on her way back to her dressing room. He put his hand on her hip and said: "Would you like to have breakfast with me, sweetheart?"

Most nights she was pawed, although at thirty-three she was one of the oldest women there: many were girls of nineteen and twenty. When this happened the girls were not allowed to make a fuss. They were supposed to smile sweetly, remove the man's hand gently, and say: "Not tonight, sir." But this was not always sufficiently discouraging, and the other girls had taught Maud a more effective line. "I've got these tiny insects in my cunt hair," she said. "Do you think it's anything to worry about?" The man disappeared.

Maud spoke German effortlessly after four years there, and working at the club she had learned all the vulgar words, too.

The club closed at four in the morning. Maud took off her makeup and changed back into her street clothes. She went to the kitchen and begged some coffee beans. A cook who liked her gave her a few in a twist of paper.

The musicians were paid in cash every night. All the girls brought large bags in which to carry the bundles of banknotes.

On the way out, Maud picked up a newspaper left behind by a customer. Walter would read it. They could not afford to buy papers.

She left the club and went straight to the bakery. It was dangerous to hold on to money: by evening your wages might not buy a loaf. Several women were already waiting outside the shop in the cold. At half past five the baker opened the door and chalked up his prices on a board. Today a loaf of black bread was 127 billion marks.

Maud bought four loaves. They would not eat it all today, but that did not matter. Stale bread could be used to thicken soup: banknotes could not.

She got home at six. Later she would dress the children and take them to their grandparents' house for the day, so that she could sleep. Right now she had an hour or so with Walter. It was the best part of the day.

She prepared breakfast and took a tray into the bedroom. "Look," she said. "New bread, coffee . . . and a dollar!"

"Clever girl!" He kissed her. "What shall we buy?" He shivered in his pajamas. "We need coal."

"No rush. We can keep it, if you want. It will be worth just as much next week. If you're cold, I'll warm you."

He grinned. "Come on, then."

She took off her clothes and got into bed.

They ate the bread, drank the coffee, and made love. Sex was still exciting, even though it did not take as long as it had when first they were together.

Afterward, Walter read the newspaper she had brought home. "The revolution in Munich is over," he said.

"For good?"

Walter shrugged. "They've caught the leader. It's Adolf Hitler."

"The head of the party Robert joined?"

"Yes. He's been charged with high treason. He's in jail."

"Good," said Maud with relief. "Thank God that's over."

CHAPTER FORTY-TWO

December 1923 to January 1924

Earl Fitzherbert got up on a platform outside Aberowen town hall at three o'clock in the afternoon on the day before the general election. He wore formal morning dress and a top hat. There was a burst of cheering from the Conservatives at the front, but most of the crowd booed. Someone threw a crumpled newspaper, and Billy said: "None of that, now, boys. Let him speak."

Low clouds darkened the winter afternoon, and the streetlights were already lit. It was raining, but there was a big crowd, two or three hundred people, mostly miners in their caps, with a few bowler hats at the front and a scatter of women under umbrellas. At the edges of the crowd, children played on the wet cobblestones.

Fitz was campaigning in support of the sitting M.P., Perceval Jones. He began to talk about tariffs. This was fine with Billy. Fitz could speak on this subject all day without touching the hearts of Aberowen people. In theory, it was the big election issue. The Conservatives proposed to end unemployment by raising the duty on imports to protect British manufactures. This had united the Liberals in opposition, for their oldest ideology was free trade. Labour agreed that tariffs were not the answer, and proposed a program of national work to employ the idle, together with extended years of education to prevent ever more youngsters coming into the overcrowded job market.

But the real issue was who was to rule.

"In order to encourage agricultural employment, the Conservative government will give a bounty of one pound per acre to every farmer—provided he is paying his laborers thirty shillings a week or more," said Fitz.

Billy shook his head, amused and disgusted at the same time. Why give money to farmers? They were not starving. Unemployed factory workers were.

Beside Billy, Da said: "This sort of talk isn't going to win votes in Aberowen."

Billy agreed. The constituency had once been dominated by hill farmers, but those days were over. Now that the working class had the vote, the miners would outnumber the farmers. Perceval Jones had held on to his seat, in the confused election of 1922, by a few votes. Surely this time he would be thrown out?

Fitz was winding up. "If you vote Labour, you will be voting for a man whose army record is stained," he said. The audience did not much like that: they knew Billy's story, and regarded him as a hero. There was a mutter of dissent, and Da shouted: "Shame on you!"

Fitz plowed on. "A man who betrayed his comrades-in-arms and his officers, a man who was court-martialed for disloyalty and sent to jail. I say to you: do not bring disgrace on Aberowen by electing to Parliament a man such as that."

Fitz got down to ragged applause and boos. Billy stared at him, but Fitz did not meet his eye.

Billy climbed onto the platform in his turn. "You're probably expecting me to insult Lord Fitzherbert the way he insulted me," he said.

In the crowd, Tommy Griffiths shouted: "Give him hell, Billy!"

Billy said: "But this isn't a pithead punch-up. This election is too important to be decided by cheap jibes." They became subdued. Billy knew they would not much like this reasonable approach. They enjoyed cheap jibes. But he saw his father nodding approval. Da understood what Billy was trying to do. Of course he understood. He had taught Billy.

"The earl has shown courage, coming here and stating his views to a crowd of coal miners," Billy went on. "He may be wrong—he is wrong—but he's no coward. He was like that in the war. Many of our officers were. They were brave, but wrongheaded. They had the wrong strategy and the wrong tactics, their communications were poor, and their thinking was out-of-date. But they wouldn't change their ideas until millions of men had been killed."

The audience had gone quiet. They were interested now. Billy saw Mildred, looking proud, with a baby in each arm—Billy's two sons, David and Keir, aged one and two. Mildred was not passionate about politics, but she wanted Billy to become an M.P. so that they could go back to London and she could restart her business.

"In the war, no working-class man was ever promoted above the rank of sergeant. And all public schoolboys entered the army as second lieutenants. Every veteran here today had his life needlessly put at risk by half-witted officers, and many of us had our lives saved by an intelligent sergeant."

There was a loud murmur of agreement.

"I'm here to say those days are over. In the army and in other walks of life, men should be promoted for brains, not birth." He raised his voice, and heard in his tone the thrill of passion that he knew from his father's sermons. "This election is about the future, and the kind of country our children will grow up in. We must make sure it's different from the one we grew up in. The Labour Party doesn't call for revolution—we've seen that in other countries, and it doesn't work. But we do call for change—serious change, major change, radical change."

He paused, then raised his voice again for his peroration. "No, I don't insult Lord Fitzherbert, nor Mr. Perceval Jones," he said, pointing at the two top hats in the front row. "I simply say to them: gentlemen, you are history." There was a cheer. Billy looked over the front row to the crowd of miners—strong, brave men who had been born with nothing but had nevertheless made lives for themselves and their families. "Fellow workers," he said. "We are the future!"

He got down from the platform.

When the votes were counted, he won by a landslide.

{ II }

So did Ethel.

The Conservatives formed the largest party in the new Parliament, but they did not have an overall majority. Labour came second, with 191 M.P.s, including Eth Leckwith from Aldgate and Billy Williams from Aberowen. The Liberals were third. The Scottish Prohibitionists won one seat. The Communist Party none.

When the new Parliament assembled, Labour and Liberal members combined to vote the Conservative government out, and the king was obliged to ask the leader of the Labour Party, Ramsay MacDonald, to become prime minister. For the first time, Britain had a Labour government.

Ethel had not been inside the Palace of Westminster since the day in 1916 when she got thrown out for shouting at Lloyd George. Now she sat on the green leather bench in a new coat and hat, listening to the speeches, occasionally glancing up to the public gallery from which she had been ejected more than seven years ago. She went into the lobby and voted with the members of the cabinet, famous socialists she had admired from a distance: Arthur Henderson, Philip Snowden, Sidney Webb, and the prime minister himself. She had her own desk in a little office shared with another female Labour M.P. She browsed in the library, ate buttered toast in the tearoom, and picked up sacks of mail addressed to her. She walked around the vast building, learning its geography, trying to feel she was entitled to be there.

One day at the end of January she took Lloyd with her and showed him around. He was almost nine years old, and he had never been inside a building so large or so luxurious. She tried to explain the principles of democracy to him, but he was a little young.

On a narrow red-carpeted staircase on the border between the Commons and the Lords areas, they ran into Fitz. He, too, had a young guest—his son George, called Boy.

Ethel and Lloyd were going up, Fitz and Boy coming down, and they met on a half landing.

Fitz stared at her as if he expected her to give way.

Fitz's two sons, Boy and Lloyd, the heir to the title and the unacknowledged bastard, were the same age. They looked at each other with frank interest.

At Tŷ Gwyn, Ethel remembered, whenever she encountered Fitz in the corridor, she had had to stand aside, up against the wall, with her eyes cast down as he passed by.

Now she stood in the middle of the landing, holding Lloyd's hand firmly, and stared at Fitz. "Good morning, Lord Fitzherbert," she said, and she tilted her chin up defiantly.

He stared back. His face showed angry resentment. At last he said: "Good morning, Mrs. Leckwith."

She looked at his son. "You must be Viscount Aberowen," she said. "How do you do?"

"How do you do, ma'am," the child said politely.

She said to Fitz: "And this is my son, Lloyd."

Fitz refused to look at him.

Ethel was not going to let Fitz off lightly. She said: "Shake hands with the earl, Lloyd."

Lloyd stuck out his hand and said: "Pleased to meet you, Earl."

It would have been undignified to snub a nine-year-old. Fitz was forced to shake.

For the first time, he had touched his son Lloyd.

"And now we'll bid you good day," Ethel said dismissively, and she took a step forward.

Fitz's expression was thunderous. Reluctantly he stood aside, with his son, and they waited, backs to the wall, as Ethel and Lloyd walked past them and on up the stairs.

Historical Characters

Several real historical characters appear in these pages, and readers sometimes ask how I draw the line between history and fiction. It's a fair question, and here's the answer.

In some cases, for example when Sir Edward Grey addresses the House of Commons, my fictional characters are witnessing an event that really happened. What Sir Edward says in this novel corresponds to the parliamentary record, except that I have shortened his speech, without, I hope, losing anything important.

Sometimes a real person goes to a fictional location, as when Winston Churchill visits Tŷ Gwyn. In that case, I have made sure that it was not unusual for him to visit country houses, and that he could well have done so at around that date.

When real people have conversations with my fictional characters, they are usually saying things they really did say at some point. Lloyd George's explanation to Fitz of why he does not want to deport Lev Kamenev is based on what Lloyd George wrote, in a memo quoted in Peter Rowland's biography.

My rule is: either the scene did happen, or it might have; either these words were used, or they might have been. And if I find some reason why the scene could not have taken place in real life, or the words would not really have been said—if, for example, the character was in another country at the time—I leave it out.

Acknowledgments

My principal historical consultant for this book has been Richard Overy. Other historians who read drafts and made corrections, saving me from many errors, were: John M. Cooper, Mark Goldman, Holger Herwig, John Keiger, Evan Mawdsley, Richard Toye, and Christopher Williams. Susan Pedersen helped with the subject of soldiers' wives' separation allowances.

As always, many of these advisers were found for me by Dan Starer of Research for Writers in New York City.

Friends who helped include Tim Blythe, who gave me some essential books; Adam Brett-Smith, who advised on champagne; the sharp-eyed Nigel Dean; Tony McWalter and Chris Manners, two wise and perceptive critics; trainspotter Geoff Mann, who advised on locomotive wheels; and Angela Spizig, who read the first draft and commented from a German perspective.

Editors and agents who read and advised were Amy Berkower, Leslie Gelbman, Phyllis Grann, Neil Nyren, Imogen Taylor, and, as ever, Al Zuckerman.

Finally I thank family members who read the draft and gave me advice, especially Barbara Follett, Emanuele Follett, Marie-Claire Follett, Jann Turner, and Kim Turner.

About the Author

Ken Follett was twenty-seven when he wrote *Eye of the Needle*, an award-winning thriller that became an international bestseller. After several more successful thrillers, he surprised everyone with *The Pillars of the Earth*, about the building of a cathedral in the Middle Ages. *The Pillars of the Earth* continues to captivate readers all over the world. His last book was the long-awaited sequel, *World Without End*, a number one bestseller in the United States, Great Britain, Germany, Italy, Spain, and France. He lives in England with his wife, Barbara Follett. Visit Ken Follett's official Web site at www.ken-follett.com.